COSMIC FORCES:

THE PANDORANS

THE PANDORANS:

BOOK ONE

THE PANDORA SEQUENCE

THE
PANDORA
SEQUENCE

ALEX JAMES

Also by Alex James:
Check www.GalexyTales.com for Pre-orders
(titles, title order and suggested release schedule subject to change)

COSMIC FORCES

THE PANDORANS

Book One: The Pandora Sequence
Book Two: The Pandora Inheritance
Book Three: The Omega Sequence
Book Four: The Pandora Arcana
Book Five: The Sirens Sequence
Book Six: The Daughters of Pandora
Book Seven: The Lucifer Sequence

AMAZON SEVEN

Book One: Mission Queen
Book Two: Queen Renegade
Book Three: Intergalactic Ingenue
Book Four: Princess Executor

THE CHRONICLES OF THE TERRAGUARD

Book One: Maker of Rules

SAGA OF THE URBAN SORCERERS

Book One: The Summoning of Barker Moon
Book Two: The Reckoning of Emerald Tarragon
Book Three: The Shaping of Cheryl Equinox

DARK STREETS

Book One: Agents of Fear
Book Two: Avatars of Wrath

Author's Note

While *The Pandora Sequence* has now become the first novel in a larger series, it is essentially a stand-alone novel than can be read and enjoyed with great satisfaction and no further obligation. So I am told.

Alex James
June 2018

The Pandorans
Book One:
The Pandora Sequence

Printed by Galexy Tales with kind permission of Gary Turner.

Cover Design and Illustration by David G. Williams.

Book production by Ingram Spark.

First Paperback Edition 1.2
May 2019

This book is dedicated to the memory and works of

Robert Anton Wilson

"I don't believe anything, but I have many suspicions."

FOREWORD

Although the following tale is presented as allegorical fiction, many of the events contained within are based either on personal experience, stories told to me firsthand or researched testimony of second or third hand accounts.

Furthermore, the pantheon of otherworldly beings contained herein are based on what many in the increasingly large, worldwide metaphysical community believe to be fact: that such worlds and beings truly exist, and are encroaching further and further every day into our own sphere of influence.

Look it up for yourself.

See what happens.

I dare you.

Alex James
2013

PROLOGUE

The white American sedan on its way to Jorge Chávez International Airport carried a man whose mind held the secrets to the existence of life on Earth. The information his research had unlocked over the past year offered nothing short of a radically altered perspective, perhaps even a new beginning for the human race. It would allow them to fully comprehend their past, to understand their present, and if all went well, place them among the stars.

The man's name was Holland Pankhurst and despite all that knowledge, or perhaps because of it, he was hanging out for a cigarette.

'Can you open the window again, please?' Pan asked the driver, shaking a packet of cigarettes from the back seat.

'Sure thing, Mister – Pan.'

Everyone called him Pan.

The driver spoke in an incongruous accent that made Pan feel as though he was not being chauffeured away from a Peruvian rainforest in a glistening corporate car but was, in fact, in the back of a New York cab. The passenger window slid down three quarters and a gush of warm air roared in, hitting Pan full in the face. He had to cup his hands and repeatedly click the lighter from various angles before the tip of the cigarette finally ignited.

'Thanks!' Pan exhaled over the roar, his smoky breath instantly vacuumed out of the window.

The driver waved loosely and nodded.

When the journey had started some three hours ago, Pan had made a deal with the driver that allowed him to light up in the designated smoke-free car so long as the window was down. Pan possessed the kind of charm that made those kinds of arrangements easy; people simply liked him without him even trying. He had tried and generally succeeded all his adult life not to take this for granted.

Pan assessed the passing landscape again; it was hot and the sun was directly above the car. He didn't know where in Peru they were now, not exactly. The road was asphalt but outside all he could see were the colorful but poor homes of the Peruvian working class, a patchwork of cracked rainbow colors flashing past. They were at least an hour out of the jungle now, on the edge of outer suburbia, but by his reckoning still somewhere outside of Lima itself, maybe an hour from the airport.

'An hour?' Pan yelled forward.

'Give or take!'

Pan had accepted the offer his boss had made to fly him home in a private jet, although he had come to learn in the past few days that there were faster methods of travel. Much faster.

But he had dared not risk any such method.

He had enemies now.

The kind of enemies that he'd never truly believed existed.

Waiting for him.

He knew they would act to prevent his passage, sooner or later. One way or another. Even so, the safest course home was via private jet.

And then…

Well, he would see what he would see.

His phone vibrated on his lap and, far from the first time in his life, he realized that his earphones were still in his ears even though his playlist had long ago expired. He knew the number and answered, surprised at the coverage.

'Boss?'

'Where are you son?'

He angled his head away from the open window.

'On my way. Maybe an hour from Chávez.'

'Listen, Pan, as soon as you were gone, the research base was gutted. Your people have vanished. Are you on your own?'

Pan grimaced at the news. There was silence for a second. Pan guided the tip of his cigarette to the edge of the window. He watched its glow increase in the hot wind, whisking the ash away like an ejecting booster rocket.

'I'm alone.'

'Pan, I should have had the jet pick you up in Iquitos. It's been a long day. I dropped the ball.'

'It's okay, I –'

'No. It's not okay. I've sent Harding with another car. He's tracking your phone. You can trust the driver you have, but he's not trained security. Harding will be with you in twenty, with his team.'

Pan gulped. Harding's team.

'Thanks.'

'Pan, are you going to tell me what this is all about?'

'Not like this. It's too important.'

Another pause.

'You know what this means? Someone, one of your team, is a double agent. You understand?'

Pan closed his eyes, tight, and tried to keep his voice steady.

'I understand.'

The notion that one of his team might betray him was knowledge that Pan had lived with for a year. Everyone had their price and it must have occurred to each of them as their research had proceeded that they could cut and run. They were working for a billionaire, sure, but he, in turn, competed with others on his level. There were deals to be made, the potential to have it all.

On the other hand, confirmation of this fear, that one of his team had betrayed him, was another matter. Potential had become reality. That reality would have to sink in, but for now he was freshly wounded by the news. It already stung.

'Pan, what did your people know? Do they have this new information?'

'No, they don't have it…' Pan considered again for a second.

'But our early breakthroughs, the commercial implications alone could make anyone rich. Richer than even you, boss.'

He heard his boss grumble.

'Pan, you have to tell me. What is this new information? I don't want to be alarmist, but…'

'I know. If I don't make it back, it all dies with me, right?'

'That's not going to happen Pan. But I have to know. *Would it* die with you?'

Pan ground his teeth then drew very heavily on his cigarette.

'No,' Pan exhaled. 'No, it wouldn't. I split the information and sent it out.'

'Split it? Split it how?'

'Into six; there are six pieces.'

'Pieces?'

'Each piece is invaluable on its own, but together they form a critical mass. That's the real thing. That's when the secret catches fire.'

'Pan, I don't understand. You're speaking in riddles. Is it *that* important?'

'It's a Rosetta Stone, a Dead Sea Scroll.'

'Dammit, you have to make yourself clearer, son.'

Pan sighed. 'Last night was a long dark night of the soul. I think I sensed this coming. I had to decide. The six people I trust most in the world. I sent it to them, one piece each.'

'You *what?*'

'It was the only way.'

'Pan, this doesn't make sense! Are you sure the drugs you've taken haven't – '

'Affected me? You know they have. You did the ceremony too. They affect everyone. I've become my own experiment, that's half the problem. But it's also the solution.'

His boss sighed, heavily. There was deep concern in the sigh, beneath the general frustration. 'Pan, son, I need information. I need to know, so I can protect you. Can you at least tell me the nature of the discovery?'

Pan took another drag.

'This is a secure connection?'

'Of course. Hinch is bouncing the signal.'

Pan nodded to himself.

'Boss, what if it were all real?'

'What if *what* were real?'

'I mean, what if Earth has been visited? Is still being visited?'

'Pan, if that were true, we would have evidence.'

'You know as well as I do, there's anecdotal evidence everywhere. You just have to spend five minutes online, you just have to listen to one of those podcasts I used to do – but that's not what I'm talking about. Not really. What I'm talking about is – what if they're here, but we've *forgotten how to see them?*'

'Forgotten?'

Pan muttered absently. 'Sometimes I think we've forgotten almost everything…'

'Pan, focus.'

Pan sighed. 'All those crazy stories from all our sacred books. Not just the Judeo-Christian stuff, I mean everything, from the Mahabharata to Madame Blavatsky. Atlantis through to Area 51. What if all our myths and fantasies, our fringe sciences and metaphysical concepts, our darkest fears and spiritual truths have at least *some* basis in reality?'

'But –'

'But what if we could prove it?'

His boss went silent for a few seconds.

'Pan, I went through that ayahuasca ceremony. I know what these drugs can do.'

'And you know what Yelina can do. She's there with you, isn't she?'

'Yes, she's here, but… Pan, it's just storytelling, archetypal myth. Regardless of who Yelina is.'

There was silence again.

'Boss! *What – if – ?*'

There was another pause. Pan very rarely raised his voice.

'I don't know Pan. I really don't. It would…'

Pan could hear the frustration rising as his boss entertained the notion.

'…I suppose, it would change everything. Everything we know about the very nature of our existence.'

Pan sighed. 'I know how crazy this all sounds. But you'll see.'

'I'll be honest. I'm very worried about you, Pan.'

'Me too. But you were down here. The ceremony changed you.'

'That's different Pan. Whatever happened during that ceremony, it was localized. It happened inside my mind. There's no way I can connect that with… whatever it is you're talking about.'

'What if I told you that there is a way to connect it? What if I had proof that *consciousness itself* is not what we think it is?'

'Pan, shall I tell you what I really think?'

'Sure, boss. Always.'

'I think you've had some sort of psychological break. I think you've been experimenting too long with hallucinogenic drugs, and that you need to come home and detox.'

'Is that really what you think?'

'How could I think anything else?'

'You really need proof?'

'How can there be proof, Pan?'

'Okay. Wait.'

'For what?'

'Just wait.'

Pan thrust his hand outside the car, extinguished the cigarette, then reclined and closed his eyes. He sat for a few seconds before his body slumped and fell against the inside car door. The driver saw this and would have assumed that Pan had simply fallen asleep, if his body had not fallen at an odd angle, forcing his neck out over the open window and his head to loll out of the car.

'Sir!'

The driver veered sharply into a wide track of white dirt that ran parallel with the road, unbuckled and spun out of the car toward the passenger door, leaving the engine running.

As he cracked the door handle open, he saw that Pan was awake again, sitting up inside the car, rubbing his throat and coughing in a plume of white dust. The driver stood on the roadside, holding the open passenger door, confused.

'You – are you okay sir – Pan?'

Pan smiled up reassuringly. He grabbed a bottle of water from the seat beside him, got out and stood beside the driver. He took a long swig.

'I need to stretch my legs,' he gasped.

'I don't know this area sir. I wouldn't want to stay long.'

Pan summoned a charming smile, the one that made people feel as though nothing could possibly go wrong.

'Just a minute?'

Reluctantly, the driver nodded. Pan took a few steps away from him.

'You still there boss?'

'I'm here.'

'Give me a second.'

Pan glanced back at the driver and they assessed their surroundings together.

The long asphalt stretch divided a wide, shallow valley. Dust swirled up from the dirt tracks, one on each side of the road. A thin but regular stream of traffic flashed beside them, mostly small trucks and old cars. Just ahead was a group of shops: a general store, a hotel and a tourist station. Immediately behind that was a poor suburb, thousands of wood and mud brick houses all jammed in together, the plaster façade of each painted in a bright color so that together they resembled a mighty patchwork quilt that stretched to the top of the hill.

'I suppose this qualifies as a highway,' the driver sighed. 'No idea what town that is.'

It was hot. High noon. Hotter than Pan had realized from within the air-conditioned car.

The driver nodded sharply at Pan.

'You mind?'

Pan took out his cigarettes and lit one for the driver, then another for himself.

The voice in Pan's headphones spoke softly.

'Pan?'

'Still here, boss. So, what do you say?'

'Okay. Okay. You… you've definitely impressed me. But that's not proof of everything you've said.'

'But it's a start, right?'

His boss was silent for a few seconds.

'Pan… what have you done?'

'What you asked me to do. I found a way.'

Down the road, Pan watched as one of the old cars turned off the main road and parked at the front of the general store. He thought it looked familiar.

'Pan, I don't understand this, but…'

'Hang on a sec.'

'What is it?'

Someone had gotten out of the car and was staring along the road at him.

'I'll call you back.'

'Pan – ?'

Pan ended the call.

The driver was staring at the man also. 'You know that guy?'

'Yeah, yeah, I do.'

'We'd better get back in. Get going.'

'I need to talk to him.'

The driver looked horrified.

'This is a bad area. I wouldn't – '

Three gunshots sounded off from somewhere in the dusty suburb. Pan appeared not to have heard them.

'I need to talk to him,' Pan repeated, and started walking down the road toward the general store.

'Sir, I – '

'Five minutes!' Pan called over his shoulder, seemingly

transfixed by the man.

The driver watched as Pan walked about thirty yards down the dusty highway and approached the man. At the last moment, the man turned away and led Pan down a side street between the general store and the tourist stand. The driver watched for a minute or so, then returned to the car and sat waiting with the windows up.

There were several more gunshots at irregular intervals and then a startling burst of fire from an automatic weapon that echoed up through the suburb. The driver tried to relax, told himself that someone was having target practice. With the echo factor there was no telling from which direction or from how far away the shots were being fired. Besides, there was no screaming. He knew murderous gunshots were always followed by the sounds of human terror.

The driver sighed.

He had waited longer, in worse places.

He got out of the car, lit one of his own cigarettes and paced in the white dust while he smoked. Then he smoked another inside the car with the windows down, but raised the windows again when another series of gunshots resounded.

Fifteen minutes went by before an old woman approached the car. She walked up from the general store, faster than her apparent age would suggest she was capable. As she drew nearer, the driver knew that her grim expression was a harbinger.

He wound down his window.

Dust blew in as she held open a small leather-bound passport.

It had Pan's picture in it.

'Australian.'

The old woman spoke with a thick Peruvian accent.

'Dead.'

THE PANDORA SEQUENCE

PART ONE

DRINK

CHAPTER ONE

In the dream, Mitch Pyne was running through bedlam.

There was a deafening roar all around.

The ground was shaking and he could barely keep his footfalls steady.

He was sprinting down the pavement of a city street, somewhere outside the central business district. Not far in the distance he could see a huge crop of skyscrapers trembling, parts of their facades crumbling and falling away.

Parked car alarms and security sirens were wailing.

Moving cars were skidding to a halt.

Hydrants were spraying water, mains pipes were bursting.

Power lines were sparking, he could smell gas in the air.

It was an earthquake.

People were fleeing clumsily out of the buildings along the street. He could hear a woman screaming. He ran past the people on the street, bumping and colliding through them, desperate to get somewhere.

There was an all-encompassing crack, like thunder, from below the ground.

Up ahead the ground split and half the intersection rose up like a drawbridge. Water burst from beneath it like a city square fountain. All the vehicles there were tipped or thrown over. The gigantic rumble of the quake was drowning out all other sound now and Mitch was terrified; from somewhere deep and primal inside him a pure fear like he'd never experienced rose up and claimed him; but he kept running, out onto the street, even though he knew he would fall, knew it was impossible to keep his balance, knew that he was on auto-pilot now and had forgotten to where and to whom he was running before the quake had started. Flight instinct had claimed him and he was just pounding his feet forward, one after the other after the other, fueled by pure adrenalin.

A building gave way and collapsed in on itself just behind him.

Then another down the block, the front wall just dropping all at once into a mighty pile.

He didn't hear them, he felt and saw them.

Then he remembered.

He was trying to save someone.

Someone he loved.

But he couldn't remember *who*.

He just kept running.

The first of the skyscrapers fell.

Then another, taking out a third.

He watched, his personal passage of time so acute they seemed to fall in slow motion. They were closer than he'd first thought: the nearest glass titan fell sideways and for a second he thought the tip of it would fall onto him. Instead, it fell perhaps half a block away, but the consequent domino effect on the smaller surrounding buildings blasted a shockwave that knocked him flat on his back.

For a second he saw a clear blue sky before a plume of dust and smoke billowed in at volcanic speed and he felt debris rain down on him.

Then he was up again, running down the middle of the street, through the dust, toward the forty-five degree plateau that had once been a city intersection.

He had to save her because –

That's right! She was at the intersection!

He had been at one intersection, she had been at the other.

Intersection.

Why did that word seem like…

…seem like it meant *something else*?

The cars there were all overturned, or halfway into the sewer system. He watched as one slid into the crack and vanished completely.

There was another underground thunderclap, the earth shook again and didn't stop. As he fell, flat on his face this time, he saw more skyscrapers fall. From beneath the intersection a subway train exploded into daylight with an almighty smash, flinging up cars and earth, concrete and asphalt, metal and pipes. The airborne train was going to land directly on him; time slowed down again as it careened unnaturally upwards then began to descend upon him. He could not move, could not do anything but lay on his stomach and crane his neck up and know that the last thing he would ever see, the thing that killed him, his last vision, was at least totally spectacular.

'Mitch!'

She was running toward him.

The woman he loved, the woman he had been rushing to save, had given his life to try to save. There was horror on her face. She had seen that he was about to die, that nothing could prevent it.

Then a gas main exploded beneath her, claiming her in a massive orange plume.

A plume that… paused.

The train above him had paused too, frozen in mid-flight.

Time had stopped.

Pause had been hit on reality itself.

A voice whispered in his ear.

'Answer the phone.'

He turned sharply to his left and saw a face staring down at him, a woman. He couldn't make her out but she was crouching beside him, smiling serenely.

He felt a vibration in his pocket.

What was that?

He reached in.

It was a phone, a new one.

Why did he have that?

He hated them; he had had sworn never to own one.

That seemed stupid now, now that he knew he was going to die in three months time, on the outskirt streets of a huge American city, half a world away from his home, failing to save the life of the woman he loved.

What difference had his pathetic stand made, not to own a mobile phone, here at the end?

Time remained frozen.

He rolled onto his side and got to his feet beneath the subway train.

He didn't even know how to answer one of these things.

The woman was standing beside him now.

She was stunningly beautiful, but at the same time plain and asexual.

'Answer the phone,' she smiled, again.

Mitch saw a huge icon on the phone.

Accept call.

He pressed it then held the phone to his ear.

'Hello?'

'You cannot save her.'

The male voice was oddly familiar.

'Who is this?'

'Foolish even to try.'

Ahead, denying the paused reality of the scene around him, someone was walking toward him, right out of the frozen orange core of the gas explosion.

A man, carrying something in his arms.

It was then that Mitch made the full realization.

This wasn't a dream.

It was real.

It was *his future*.

'You can't save any of them, Mitch.'

'Where am I? What's happened to me?'

'Mitch.'

'Yes?'

'Answer the phone.'

Someone pressed play.
Reality resumed.
The train fell and was claimed by the orange plume.
Nothing remained.

CHAPTER TWO

Mitch woke on the couch and cried out in terror.

The phone was ringing.

He was home. *Home.*

At least, the closest thing he had to a home; a borrowed apartment just outside of Sydney Harbor.

He almost reached into his pocket but then remembered that had been the dream. In real life, in the here and now, he had a landline, and a landline only. It was ringing behind him, in the kitchen, on the wall.

What the hell had happened?

How had he been *dreaming*?

He quickly surmised, as he stood from his couch chair and walked groggily past the open dining area to the kitchen bar, that he had again downed a few too many beers and fallen asleep watching a DVD. Evening had fallen in the interim, the apartment was suddenly dim and unlit.

Answer the phone.

He was unsteady on his feet but not from the beer. He was still shaking, still pumped with adrenalin from being in the earthquake.

He fumbled as he snatched the cordless phone from the wall cradle.

'Hello?'

'I'm looking for Holland Pankhurst?'

A woman. American accent.

Mitch's head remained very unclear. 'Holland…?'

'Holland Pankhurst. This is the number I have for him. Is he there?'

'Is he…?' Mitch was still groggy. 'You mean *Pan?*'

'Yeah. Is Pan there?'

'No, he's…'

Why the hell had he answered the phone? He always screened his calls.

There was an answering machine here for that express purpose, a good old fashioned dedicated answering machine.

But he knew.

He'd answered because of the dream.

And yet… *had it* been a dream?

Or a premonition?

No. It had been one of those weird dreams, the ones where you think what's happening is real, until you wake up and cry out in relief.

Thank God! It was just a dream!

It was already fading. In half an hour, he'd have forgotten it.

That was the way with dreams.

'Yeah…' Mitch muttered wryly to himself, still half-awake. 'Answer the phone, Mitch…'

'Pardon?'

'Sorry,' Mitch laughed, his mind beginning to clear. 'I fell asleep on the couch. I had some kind of apocalyptic dream. A voice kept saying, answer the phone, answer the phone…'

'Oh!'

The woman responded with surprise, but nicely, in the sort of tone that suggested she was okay with the conversation suddenly becoming less formal than she'd bargained.

'Long day?' she asked in a friendlier tone.

'No, I…' Mitch shrugged to himself. 'I just had to watch a whole bunch of movies in a row. Most of them weren't very good; a few drinks can help with that sometimes, but I think I just had one too many and crashed.'

Why was he telling her this? He was still half-awake, more talking to himself than her, really. But he was being over-familiar; he had to pull himself together.

'Right…' she half-laughed. 'I used to do that. Hire more

movies than I have time to watch. We always think we have more time.'

'No, I…' Mitch grumbled and rubbed his eyes. Did he really need to explain? 'I get paid to watch movies.'

'Lucky for some!'

'Yeah, everyone says that. But think of the ratio of all the great films you've seen compared to all the lousy ones.'

It was something he said to everyone, an auto-pilot response.

'Hmm,' she said, and considered that for a few seconds.

Her accent was fairly neutral; he couldn't pick where in the States she was from. Pan traveled a lot, so she was probably a friend, maybe just arrived here in Sydney, looking him up. She was out of luck; Mitch had been house-sitting Pan's apartment for almost a year now.

A year, Mitch suddenly thought.

Had Pan been gone that long?

It felt like…

'To tell you the truth,' she decided, 'most movies are just kind of average. You forget them almost as soon as you see them. Like dreams.'

'Like… dreams. Yeah. Exactly.'

'So you're a film critic?'

Mitch paused for a second.

Why had he even started down this rabbit hole?

Was he looking for pain?

Why was he even still talking to her?

'I was,' he uttered. 'But now I just write the blurbs for DTV jackets.'

'DTV?'

'Direct To Video; movies that don't get a cinema release. I write the description on the back cover that makes the movie you've never heard of, and probably don't actually want to rent, sound much better than it is. You've probably read a million of them.'

'Someone really writes those things?'

'Yeah.' He sounded almost ashamed. 'Me.'

'I never thought that someone actually *writes* those.'

'Yep.'

'I mean; they can't all be good, can they?'

'Sometimes I think it's entirely possible that *none* of them are any good.'

She laughed again, politely. 'I know the ones you mean. The ones with aging action stars, or TV stars from the 'eighties – or just people you've flat out never heard of.'

'Yeah.'

'And it says, like, starring Joe Schmo, then in brackets the other two movies he's been in, that you've never heard of either.'

Mitch laughed darkly. 'Exactly. But they send me the actor bios. I just have to write all the actual lies.'

'Wow.'

Suddenly, Mitch didn't like her tone. She sounded almost disappointed with him. He was feeling pretty crappy about himself already, he didn't need some anonymous American to reinforce that.

'Look, Pan's not here, so –'

'So what did you fall asleep watching?' she asked, suddenly perky.

'A thriller.'

'Oh… I kind of like thrillers.'

'Me too. But Hollywood hardly makes them any more. Procedural cop shows tell the same stories for free, with decent budgets and name actors.'

'Yeah, I don't really watch those shows.'

'Me neither.'

'But I don't really watch television. What's your excuse?'

Mitch sighed. 'Don't get me started.'

'No really, I'm interested. Give me your professional opinion.'

Mitch wondered who the hell she was. Still, he hadn't left the apartment for days, and this was the first time the phone had rung in recent memory that hadn't been a cold caller or a bill threat.

He wondered. Was he still talking for the sake of it, to clear his head of the dream, or was he entertaining some barely tangible fantasy that the American girl with the cute voice might be all alone in Sydney, with nowhere to stay? Maybe it wasn't just her voice that was cute? Maybe he could offer her the spare room and… well, take it from there? See how it went?

He shrugged to himself.

'Okay. Those forensic shows are mean-spirited; all those shredding bullets and puncture wounds, and gruesome autopsies in graphic detail, they just play upon people's fear of injury and mortality.'

'Huh. I guess they do, don't they?'

'And, the cops are always squeaky clean and cool. But the civilians are all portrayed as either suspects, victims, murderers, or simply a corpse waiting to happen; it's dehumanizing.'

'Dehumanizing?'

'They implant and reinforce the idea that anyone you know could be a killer, that you could be a killer, given the right circumstances, and that only law enforcement can be trusted. That deliberate murder isn't just a rare evil but an everyday event, to be digested and processed weekly, or even several times a week, as freely as sitcom. These DTV movies are pretty much the same. Just mean-spirited trash.'

'Wow. You sound like you've given this a lot of thought.'

'It's – it *was* my job. And you did ask.' He was genuinely apologetic. This wasn't exactly small-talk. 'By the way, who is this?'

The woman laughed.

'Why are you laughing?' he asked.

'It's obvious you hate this stuff, but here you are watching it for a living!'

Mitch sighed.

'Look, it's not only that. Most of these cheapie flicks are just lazy. This last movie had a funeral scene, in a cemetery. Gloomy day, heavy rain and the black umbrellas clustered around the open grave, the black casket lowered to its final destination, a crowd of black-clad mourners gathered around, ashes to ashes, dust to dust. I think there was even a crow on a church steeple. You know the scene.'

'Sure. Everyone does.'

'Exactly. It's a lazy cliché. That *never* happens. I mean, people die in summer too, right? Why is it always raining?'

'Been to a lot of funerals, have you?'

'I'm a year off forty; my friends are all too young to be dead.'

'That's not always true.'

'I know – I guess I've been lucky.'

'Older people still have graveside ceremonies. Religious people.'

'The only funerals I've been to were for my grandparents, and they were indoors. Two in crematoriums, and two in little funeral parlor chapels.'

Mitch cradled the phone on his shoulder, went to the fridge and opened the last bottle in the current six-pack.

'I heard that. Are you opening another beer?'

He took a swig. 'It's bad luck not to finish the six-pack.'

'Wow.'

'Wow what?'

He could practically hear her smirk.

'Nothing,' she lied.

He let it go.

'So this handsome but emotionally stunted cop shows up at the funeral to question the bereaved female protagonist, and of course she went ballistic, like, *how dare you interrogate me here at the funeral!* But you know they're going to team up, right? And about an hour into it, they're going to sleep together.'

'Did they?'

'Then, one or the other will get captured by the killer, and one or the other will come to the rescue.'

He took another gulp but somehow the beer fizzed up and spilled all over his chest. Suddenly he was annoyed; at the beer, at his shitty job, at the clichés, at the woman.

'Are you okay?'

Mitch juggled the phone, cradling it again as he reached for a dishcloth.

'Yeah –'

'It sounded like you fell over!'

'I'm okay – look, you haven't said who you are yet.'

'So did they?'

'Did who?'

'Did they sleep together?'

'Yeah. But it was one of those ridiculous sex scenes where they do it under the sheets with their underwear on. I hit fast forward after that.'

The woman giggled.

'I just needed to find out who the killer was, how he was dispatched and whether one or more of the hero couple were killed at the end.'

'But that never happens.'

'Almost never. If they are, I'm required to include the phrase "shocking conclusion" or something like that.'

'And did it happen?'

'No. The cop and the woman rode off in the modern equivalent of the cowboy riding off into the sunset.'

'What's that?'

'An ambulance driving off in the middle of the night.' Mitch threw the dishcloth onto the counter as he returned to the couch. 'Their final dialogue was atrocious, I'm glad I didn't sit though the whole thing.'

'Sounds like you need to get out more often.'

'Why?' Mitch demanded, knowing that he did.

'Well, it sounds like all you do is sit around watching bad movies, hoping the actresses get naked. That's bound to get frustrating.'

Was there a hint of suggestion there?

Should he ask her now?

Listen, do you have anywhere to stay?

There's a spare room, we can open a bottle of wine and watch terrible movies togeth –

Mitch's attention was suddenly caught by the notepad he kept by the couch. The notes he'd scribbled down, a few choice phrases, were terrible clichés in themselves.

Sexually charged thrill-ride.

Hi-octane action.

Heart-pounding suspense.

'Christ,' he muttered. 'I could write down twenty phrases on separate bits of paper, throw them up in the air and just randomly string a few together. I'd be right more often than not and tehn I'd never have to watch a single frame of this shit ever again!'

She was laughing again. 'Like David Bowie!'

'Wow.' Now Mitch was saying it. 'That's an archaic reference.'

'I like the old stuff.'

'Sure, sure.' Who the hell *was* this woman? 'Do I get a name yet?'

'Do I? You're not Pan, but this is Pan's number.'

'How do you know I'm not Pan?'

'Oh, I know Pan when I hear him, and *you're not Pan.*'

Mitch became annoyed again. A cute voice was one thing, but this was getting weird.

'Look, either tell me who you are or don't. I have to get back to cobbling together a bunch of crappy clichés to form a series of paragraphs that will persuade a potential rental customer that this movie is indeed worth taking home for the night, and not just another piece of recycled trash they've seen a million times before.'

The woman became more assertive, almost accusatory.

'But isn't recycled trash exactly what people want? We all know what those bottom shelf movies are. We just don't want to be *told that.* I mean there are *a lot* of these movies, right? Even cheap movies cost millions to make; it follows that someone must be watching them, someone must have been making a profit. Millions of someones, worldwide, right? Repeat business?'

'Sure… I mean… everybody knows…'

'But how much of that do *you* see? I bet you don't get paid much. Not as much as you did when you wrote for the paper, not as much as when you were on TV, interviewing celebrities.'

Mitch suddenly felt as though his life was on trial. He heard himself reply reflexively, with total honesty, in the quiet tone of a guilty child's confession.

'It's… it's enough. It covers bills, food and booze.'

'Bills, food and booze.' It sounded very grim the way she said it. 'What about rent? Pan doesn't charge you?'

The mention of Pan snapped Mitch out of his defensive trance.

'Look, who the hell are you? I – I never told you I used to be on TV. I never told you anything about –'

'After the divorce went through, you couldn't afford to buy another house. You rented for a while, but the work dried up. Really dried up. And you don't know how to do anything else; that's why you always screen your calls, because the only people who call you any more are cold callers, from call centers, and that's the next logical step; that's where you think you'll end up, or at least, *that's what you fear.*'

Mitch could hear the quake again, echoing in his mind.

'Who are you?' he repeated weakly.

'You knew Pan's apartment had been sitting empty, even before he was away. You knew that Pan never used it, that he didn't like to stay there. He just used it to store all his anthropological junk.'

Mitch looked around the dim room.

The apartment block was old, a converted 'fifties office building: high ceilings, deep spaces and wide walls. It had been bequeathed to Pan ten years ago, in some distant relative's will, a black sheep only Pan could tolerate. He had lived in and out of the place periodically but this woman was right. For some reason he didn't like to stay long and it had gradually become a storage flat.

Most of the belongings stored here were old books, or anthropological souvenirs from Pan's travels. The four high bookshelves that were stacked tightly, at one end of the large open living space, were surrounded with things like African masks, Chinese statues, Japanese art and Aboriginal bark shields. Mitch had kept away from that end of the room. He preferred to remain on the other side, near the open kitchen and dining, the leather couch set and flat-screen. Just walking past all that weirdness to get to his bedroom every night gave him the creeps.

Mitch stared at it. 'How do you…?'

'You'd never have asked Pan yourself, you're too proud. But Pan heard about your predicament, as friends do, and offered you this house-sitting gig; an apartment like Pan's, so close to the city, with security and working amenities, you jumped at the chance. And who knows when Pan will be back? He could be away for years still… and in the meantime, you get to clear your head and get your life back on track.'

'What are you? Some kind of stalker?'

'The reality has been quite different though, hasn't it Mitch? You hate your job but it earns you just enough to *coast*, to do essentially *nothing* other than *get by*, and remain fairly consistently *intoxicated*. Funny, isn't it, how easy it is to drink? And you've been drinking a lot lately. A lot this year, and the year's flown by, hasn't it? Watching all those bad movies, day in, day out. And still, your daughters have grown up without you in their life, half way across the world. But you won't contact them; you won't buy a phone, you won't go online, you don't even own a computer, even though they asked you to, so they could keep in touch. Do you know the apartment block has wi-fi, high-speed broadband? Do you even know what that is, Mitch?'

Mitch was standing, frozen.

'Who – *are* – you?'

There was fear in his voice.

Was he really being stalked?

This was all just too bizarre.

Could he still be dreaming?
She spoke again.
'Answer the door, Mitch.'
'What?'
'I said, answer the door.'
The security buzzer sounded.
The woman hung up and the line went dead.

CHAPTER THREE

Mitch put the phone down.

His hands were shaking.

Would it be her?

The American woman?

Who else could it be? Nobody dropped in any more. Hardly anyone knew where he was. He crossed to the door and pressed the intercom.

'Hello?'

'Mitch Pyne?'

It was a different accent this time, a London accent, like someone from *EastEnders*.

'Yeah.'

'Got a parcel. Was told to get it to you.'

'What parcel?'

'Told to get it to you tonight.'

'Who are you?'

'I'm a friend of Holland Pankhurst.'

Again, Pan's full name.

The man spoke again. 'I mean Pan – I'm a friend of Pan's.'

Mitch grumbled. 'I know who Holland Pankhurst is. Do you know the woman on the phone? Did she send you?'

'What?'

'The woman who just called me. Did she send you?'

There was a short pause.

'I… I don't know, mate. What are you talking about? No – Pan sent me.'

The guy had a particular kind of clueless tone that was very difficult to fake. He spoke again, sounding a bit nervous.

'It's apartment twenty-three, right? Can I come up, or shall I leave it at the door?'

Mitch pressed the button.

'Come up.'

Through the intercom he heard the front doors clunk and knew the guy was through.

Holland Pankhurst.

He hadn't actually heard anyone say that name aloud for more than a decade, until tonight.

They'd called him Pan for short at university because even in his early twenties he'd still collected the toys, games and action figures from many of his favorite childhood television series. This had been back before the geeks had inherited the Earth, before comics had become respectable, and it had been much less socially acceptable to collect almost anything.

Holland had not initially enjoyed the reference to Peter Pan, the boy who never grew up. As he'd grown into his looks, however, he'd discovered an easy charm and along with that, he'd cultivated the distinctly dandy-bohemian fashion sense that had corresponded to the counter-culture of the late nineteen eighties. With these elements in place, the name Pan had likewise refashioned itself and metamorphosed into something more desirable. Somehow Holland Pankhurst, the classic arrested adolescent, had repurposed his nickname so that it reflected his interest in the pantheons of ancient mythology, and the anthropological fascination that he'd parlayed into a masters degree.

Somewhere amidst those early days at university, Pan the nerd had regenerated himself into Pan the wild child, the epicenter of the best parties, the object of desire of any number of cute college girls, secret lover of beautiful women (including several lecturers) and covert purveyor of the latest 'in' psychedelics and party drugs.

They had been inseparable: Mitch and Pan, and their clique.

Mitch had been Pan's loyal right hand man, his best friend. And usually, because Mitch had quickly realized he had very little tolerance for drugs, he'd also been Pan's slightly less intoxicated minder, driver and sometimes even cleaner, when things got messy.

At least, he had been, before the whole Saph thing had kicked off.

Five years that had lasted. Then, during that first post-grad year of the real world, their tight-knit clique of friends had slowly and amicably unraveled, to become absorbed into the respective worlds of their chosen fields.

It happened to everyone, he knew.

Since then, Mitch had been married, had a career as a minor television celebrity, started a business, lost it, lost his wife; and then lost everything.

Christ, it seemed like an aeon had passed since then.

He saw Pan maybe once a year now.

He knew that Pan was in South America, and had been for some time, but he had no idea what he was doing there.

Or if he was still with Saph.

Research or something.

Whenever he came back for a quick holiday, they always got so drunk that the next day Mitch could hardly remember what they'd talked about. And besides, Pan had never seemed to want to talk much about his work.

The strongest genuine connection they had these days was this apartment, a loose-lease agreement. Free rent for minding the store.

Mitch stood by the front door and waited. The elevator was fast and he counted the floors in his mind: six… seven… eight.

Through the door he heard the 'ding' from down the end of the hall, the elevator doors open and the soft footsteps as the man approached the apartment along the carpeted corridor.

Then, there was a knock at the door.

CHAPTER FOUR

Mitch waited a few seconds before answering the knock.

When he did, he found himself faced with what he immediately identified as one of Pan's People.

The man was in his mid twenties, thin, with pale skin that had recently been exposed to the sun but would not take a tan. He was dressed in baggy but totally coordinated earth-toned clothes, and was unshaven with shoulder length hair and slightly bloodshot eyes. Back at university, Pan had collected these types like the *Star Trek* figurines he kept in a glass case in the living room of his university share-house.

Pan had naturally grown older since then but his followers, it seemed, had not.

'Hi…' The man was grinning, a little wary, and spoke again in his Albert Square accent. 'Mind if I come in?'

He looked friendly enough though, so Mitch stepped aside and allowed him to enter. He checked the corridor outside.

Empty.

He'd half expected to see the American woman from the phone dash behind the corner at the end of the corridor.

'Thanks mate.'

The scent Mitch caught as the man passed indicated that this neo-hippy had recently been smoking dope and had likely just stubbed out a cigarette on the footpath outside the apartment building.

He was carrying a small wooden box under his left arm and, as Mitch closed the door, the man turned and extended his right hand, shaking with a deceptively firm and wiry grip.

'I'm Tim.'

'Tim,' Mitch repeated.

'You're Mitch Pyne, right?'

'Well…' Mitch shrugged. 'Yes.'

Or else someone else claiming to be him has just let you into this apartment.

'Pan told me about you. You used to be a film critic, huh? Used to be on the telly? I used to read that magazine you wrote for, my old comics store used to import it; way cool mate.'

'I owned the magazine, actually.'

'Really? What happened to it? Haven't seen one in years.'

'It went under.'

'Went under?'

'It went broke.'

'Really? How's that?'

'The internet killed it.'

Tim nodded slowly and made a serious hum to indicate he understood.

'So…?' Mitch indicated the box under Tim's arm, clearly a container for some kind of bottle.

Tim jolted. 'Oh right.' He extended the box with a light bow and Mitch accepted, feeling the bottle shift within.

'Thanks. So, what is this? Late birthday present? He doesn't usually send anything. It's been more than a year since I last saw him –'

'Don't ask me mate. Pan made me bring it all the way back and swear to give it to you tonight.'

'All the way back? You were in South America with him?'

'Yeah. He hired me when he first got the research grant. Been down there a year.'

'And he said to give this to me tonight, specifically?'

'Yeah. I left a week ago but I took in a few sights on the way back. Finally got in last night but I slept for, like, a whole day. We were nearly done with the current research phase, he just had a few loose ends to deal with. I'm surprised he's not back here himself by now. We've got meetings all next week. Haven't heard anything, have you?'

It all sounded pretty odd.

'No,' Mitch frowned. 'I haven't. But surely if he was going to be back by now, he wouldn't have given you this to give to me tonight, would he…?'

Tim looked at him blankly. 'Suppose not.'

'…never mind.' Mitch smiled. 'Beer?'

It was the question Tim had been waiting for and he smiled broadly.

'Cheers mate.'

Mitch spoke as he went to the fridge and opened another six-pack.

'I was pretty plastered last time I saw Pan but I think he did tell me he was off on some kind of anthropological mission. Something about the hallucinogenic drugs the natives found in the rainforest plants, right?'

He handed Tim his beer.

'Yeah, that's right. Thanks.'

Mitch smiled. 'Typical Pan. Any excuse to trip out. So what do you do?'

Tim opened the beer with a fizz. 'Gene sequencing.'

'*Gene sequencing?*'

'Yeah.' He swigged the beer. 'Bioinformatics. Got some kick-ass processing power down there. Big money.'

Mitch smiled. 'I don't really know what any of that means.'

Tim shrugged. 'We use supercomputers to map gene sequences.' Tim gazed around the apartment. 'So this is Pan's place, huh?'

He noticed that Tim was assessing the apartment with a keen eye: left, right, up, down, all around. As though he were taking inventory.

'Yeah…' Mitch nodded. 'Although he never uses it. It's like his garden shed. But he's letting me stay a while, get my life together.'

Tim looked around and smiled.

'How much longer's that going to take?'

'Sorry?'

Tim gave Mitch an enormous grin.

'No-one ever gets it together, mate. That's the point, you know? The journey, not the destination?'

Mitch frowned. He supposed that Tim might have been right but for some reason resented what felt like a criticism.

'Smoke?' Tim asked suddenly, pulling a pack of rolling tobacco from his jacket pocket.

'Err, okay. Out on the balcony though. It's about the only rule Pan gave me.'

Tim shrugged in agreement.

Mitch was uncomfortable but curious. Like most of Pan's friends, this fellow was quite amicable but also a little unsettling.

As he put the boxed bottle on the kitchen bench, he caught sight of what lay behind it.

It was as though he were seeing it for the first time.

He knew what Tim, what anyone, would make of it: the scene of the crime, the evidence he'd missed that was right under his nose.

Cardboard cartons filled with empty beer bottles, lined up beside empty wine bottles and empty wine boxes that he couldn't be bothered putting out, hadn't bothered to put out for weeks; way too many. A dozen empty pizza boxes, a kitchen bin overflowing with take-out containers. Gleaming, un-used cooking surfaces. More empty beer bottles lined up on the coffee table in front of the television; hell, the whole apartment probably stank like an old bar.

And the fridge, when he'd opened it; just half-empty take-out containers and more beer.

Mitch was suddenly uneasy.

When had this happened?

When the hell had his life begun to stagnate like this?

He hadn't even noticed it happening… the rot setting in.

There came a sudden shrieking from the balcony door and

something wide and black flapped into the room.

With another shriek and a fluttering of massive black wings, a huge raven soared into the apartment and settled on one of Pan's bookcases.

CHAPTER FIVE

Tim stood at the balcony doors, eyes wide and mouth agape.

'Bloody hell mate!'

Mitch froze.

'That's not your *pet* or something is it? Is it *Pan's*?'

'No…' Mitch uttered, his heart pounding.

'It just bloody flew in – like it lives here!'

The huge black raven was perched on a high bookshelf, looking right at home amongst all the creepy anthropological keepsakes, staring down at Mitch with its cold, piercing white eyes as though it was Mitch who somehow didn't belong.

'Come out here, man!' Tim urged. 'We'll leave the door open and it'll just fly back out!'

Mitch edged around the couch and crossed to the balcony doors. Tim slid them open full-length and a blast of freezing winter air rushed in.

The raven shrieked again but didn't move.

It just watched them through the open balcony door.

Out on the balcony there were two empty wine bottles, an ashtray overflowing with dead cigarette butts and four screwed up cigarette packets, along with a single chair and one empty glass, stained with the dregs of a cheap merlot.

Again, Mitch saw this through Tim's eyes.

How it would look to him.

How it *was*.

Tim instantly lit a pre-rolled cigarette. Mitch reached for his own packet, waiting on the table as Tim looked back at the raven.

'That, is *wild*.'

'Yeah,' Mitch grimaced, not so excited.

Was it a bad omen or something?

Ravens weren't good were they?

All that tap-tap-tapping Edgar Allan Poe stuff?

'Classic Pan,' Tim smiled. 'Shit like this happens to him all the time.'

'I remember,' Mitch uttered.

'How long you known him anyway?'

Mitch kept staring at the raven and shrugged. 'Since university. More than twenty years now.' The raven seemed to be assessing the apartment in the same way Tim had, taking inventory. 'How about you?'

'A few years now. We both work for Bo Everett.'

Mitch looked sharply back at Tim.

'Bo Everett?'

'Yeah,' Tim shrugged. 'He's pretty cool actually.'

Mitch rarely watched the news channels any more but he'd seen Bo Everett on television recently, perhaps two or three news cycles back. He'd been making a bold claim about the future of his private space-shuttle service and how he was going to put America back into contention for the Second Space Race by beating the Chinese, or Indians, or Russians, to put the first manned mission on Mars. The whole thing had seemed ludicrous, like Donald Trump announcing an underground expedition to find the center of the Earth.

'So that's the big money you mentioned before? Bo Everett?'

'We're just a hobby for him really.'

'I guess he can fund whatever hobbies he likes. What is he now? Third, fourth richest American?'

'Something like that.'

'And he's funding this *gene crunching* thing you're doing? Down there in the Amazon?'

Mitch realized he'd said *Amazon* as though it were a single place, a town or something; the river itself was immensely long and being 'down in the Amazon' could conceivably mean just about anything.

'He's interested in biochemistry mainly. Like Pan. Bo hired

Pan and Pan hired me to run the processing. There are millions of plants down there that nobody's ever really sorted. Nobody from our side of things, anyway. I think Everett wants to catalog them before they're all wiped out by deforestation.'

'You mean, like, in case there are any natural cures we didn't know were there?'

'Kind of.'

'Is that your area too? Drugs?'

Tim grinned. 'Lots of ways I could answer that question, hey?'

Mitch smirked. 'Pan was always interested in going there. But he never had the money.'

Tim grinned again. 'Bo Everett.'

Mitch nodded knowingly, lit his cigarette and exhaled slowly. 'The first I heard of Pan going anywhere was when he called me up and offered me this place. Said he wouldn't be around for a while and needed someone to look after all his old crap.'

He shivered suddenly. It really did spook him, all that stuff, especially with that goddamned raven sitting there, like a dark angel sitting atop some black magician's Christmas tree.

Tim nodded. 'That's about when he called me.'

'And he was supposed to follow you back here?'

'That's what he said. About a week ago. Wonder what's held him up?'

Shit, Mitch thought.

What did that mean?

Find another place to live?

That was not good.

Mitch sighed.

Truth be told, he didn't much care what Pan was doing with his life. If he found the cure for cancer, terrific. But in the cold light of day, on a personal level, their friendship had burned brightly at university but was ultimately rooted in the past. It was now one of those things men nearing forty wrapped up with every other carefree memory that they soon came to associate with The Best Days. His contact with Pan since, a string of fleeting alcohol binges, had been a mere reflection of that time; the house-sitting really could have been for anyone.

In fact, if Pan moved back and settled down again, would they still be friends?

Would Pan even *let him* stay?

Could he *live* with Pan, even if he did let him stay?

Honestly, Mitch couldn't say for sure.

Coldly, probably not.

Mitch wasn't any good at the friends thing any more. He didn't think he could live with anyone again; not even someone who'd once, quite earnestly, been like a brother to him.

He realized that Tim was watching him think this through.

Tim grimaced. 'Time catching up?'

'Yeah.' Mitch moved to the edge of the balcony. 'So why'd he send me a bottle?'

'He didn't say. I thought you might know.'

Mitch stared out.

It was an odd thing to do.

It would be more like Pan to send dope cookies, even Peruvian cigars.

Peru.

That's right – that's where he was – *Peru*.

He saw that Tim was taking in the view as well.

It was a decent enough view of the Sydney Harbor Bridge, not picture postcard stuff but an odd and seldom photographed angle, still grand enough to sit and watch for hours over two bottles of red.

God, had he really done that?

Two bottles on his own?

Not the first time either.

Far from it.

And it hadn't started just with moving in here, nor with those piles of trash movies he had to watch. It had started when the magazine had begun to fold, when long nights of coffee followed by a glass of red had slowly shifted into long nights or red followed by a cup of coffee.

Slowly, over a few years, until…

He looked at the ashtray. It might have been a sculpture commissioned by the Quit Foundation.

When had that started?

He used to carefully limit the amount he smoked…

Mitch saw that Tim had noticed him, staring at the ashtray abomination.

'Pan could never quit either. He was buying cartons of duty-free smokes to take with him – down to Peru. Cigarettes in the rainforest. Believe that? Always said that when he figured out time travel, the first thing he'd do was go back and tell himself not to start.'

'I only smoke a lot when I drink,' Mitch heard himself say, like a litany.

'So, a lot lately?'

Tim's smile suggested he knew exactly whereof he spoke.

'I guess so,' Mitch sighed.

The woman on the phone had said as much.

Who the hell had she been?

She had seemed to know everything about him.

Everything.

And she had *let him know* that she did.

Why?

To what end?

'Are you sure you don't know the woman who called me?'

Tim frowned. 'Not a clue, man. What's it all about? Got you all freaked out, huh?'

'It was just before you turned up. I thought she was looking for Pan. We chatted for a while, but then she kind of… opened up, and revealed that she knew all this stuff about me. Then she told me to answer the door – *before* you rang the buzzer.'

Tim looked highly concerned.

'That's not good man. That's surveillance. And when they rub it in your face like that, that's harassment. What kind of shit are you into, mate?'

'Nothing; I write the crappy blurbs on the backs of DVD jackets!'

'Really? I always wondered who wrote them.'

'Well, not all of them. Just one company.'

Tim smiled. 'Mate, there's only *one* company.'

'What?'

'There is only one company. It's all the subverted Hegelian dialect. Thesis, antithesis, synthesis. An endless fractal loop of news and current affairs and moral panic. Mass media cycles, mass distraction cues.'

Mitch nodded and grinned, unconvinced.

'Conspiracy theories. Pan and I used to go over all this stuff twenty years ago. I didn't buy it then and I'm not buying it now.'

Tim smiled. 'You don't believe in conspiracies?'

Mitch shrugged. 'It's too difficult to keep secrets these days.'

'Then, who's watching your door, mate? Who's calling you late in the evening, making a show of what they know about you?'

Mitch held his breath.

He didn't know.

'I don't know,' he muttered. 'But there must be plenty of expl –'

The raven shrieked and flew out over his head, making him duck instinctively and freak out.

'Far out!' Tim watched it fly away through the city, then vanish into the black sky. He looked up. 'Can't see many stars from out here.'

'The city lights…' Mitch told him, straightening up.

'Wonder where it came from?'

Tim extinguished his cigarette and Mitch felt more uneasiness creep in, as he also placed his spent cigarette into the pile of butts. There were so many butts, and so much ash, that it slid into the ghastly sculpture like a spoon into a sugar bowl.

This isn't right, Mitch heard himself think.

'Well, I'd better be going.'

'Okay,' Mitch shrugged.

He'd been hoping for that.

'Look, I tried to call but I think your phone's out.'

Mitch was stunned.

'Do you have a mobile, in case Pan wants to get in touch?'

'I don't have one.'

'Oh. Sure. Email, then?'

'I don't have a computer.'

Tim looked at him as though he were an alien. 'Well, I guess…?'

Mitch croaked something out. He barely knew he was saying it.

'The internet destroyed my life.'

Tim gave him a look, brief but unmistakable: something close to pity.

'I'm sorry mate,' Tim said quietly.

Tim found his own way to the door as Mitch trailed behind, eying the gift on the edge of the kitchen bench, half hoping Tim would just scoop it up and leave with it, saying nothing, just steal it back and leave like he'd never been.

He smiled brightly but, with an edge of concern, as he exited, turned to Mitch.

'Just one more thing mate.'

'Yeah?'

'I couldn't get through on the landline number Pan gave me, right? I got a disconnection message.'

'So you said.'

'So how did this woman call you?'

'Maybe you had the wrong number?'

Tim smiled. 'Pan's got everyone's number mate. Be seeing you.'

Mitch returned the cheeky British smile as best he could and closed the door.

CHAPTER SIX

The next film on the pile was a horror movie of the Seven Teens Too Dumb To Live genre.

Mitch loaded the disc, drained his now-warm sixth beer, then went to the fridge as the movie started up automatically; these were bare bones pre-releases, no trailers, no menus. Creepy intro music kicked in as he stared inside the fridge, half-drunk now.

Only half-drunk after a whole six pack?

When had his tolerance…?

Screw it, he thought, and removed another beer.

He was one of those people now, he realized.

He drank alone.

His mood shifted abruptly.

He picked up the phone and tried to call for pizza delivery.

Please press one to contact your service provider.

Damn.

And yet… how *had* the American woman's call come through?

Frustrated, he called his service provider and, after ten minutes patiently deciphering an accent he could barely understand and with the first act of the teenie horror playing out in the background, he managed to pay the bill and the late fee with his credit card.

The customer service agent had assured him that it had not been possible for any calls to come through in the past seven days, given that the line had been disconnected since then.

Seven days?

Mitch was astounded.

He'd been drunk, watching movies, surviving on leftovers and snacks from the local store, on his own for… weeks.

Months maybe?

Time had ceased to have any meaning for him. He wasn't even sure he knew what day it was any more. It didn't matter; he just did his job, day after day, alone in the apartment.

Had it been the American woman or Tim that had snapped him out of the trance? A combination of both?

Still, he'd be reconnected by morning.

No wonder nobody had called lately.

An hour later, by the time the teens had whittled down to three, screaming, bloodied and running for their lives, he was another four beers down. One beer for each death. He didn't really understand what the creature was, why it was chasing them, or who the hero was supposed to be. What little plot there was, he had lost.

His focus was on the teens themselves, again on how cheaply and easily their screen deaths were meant to be taken, at how slowly but surely modern audiences had been taught to casually accept the brutality and torture and murder that was basically all these films had on offer.

They could be his daughters, these girls.

His daughters were that age.

Sixteen, eighteen.

The woman on the phone had been right.

He'd lost touch with them because he'd refused to adapt to the new technology. He hadn't spoken to either of them since he'd moved in here; and only three times a year before that, birthdays and Christmas.

On a landline.

Jesus, they really could be dead for all he knew.

He felt the tears coming; and through the haze of alcohol he recognized that this was something that had happened before, many times; and that tomorrow, when he woke, he would barely remember it, and what he did remember he could easily ignore.

He would drink it away again, tomorrow night.

He cried, then wept to himself.

Deep, bitter sobs of regret and self-pity.

Tomorrow he would relent. He would get a mobile, so his daughters could text him, he would get a computer so they could talk to him via web cam, he would do all that, he would relent, as they'd been begging him to do for years.

Beer wasn't enough now.

He staggered through tears to the kitchen bench and opened the wood box. The tiny nails came away easily with one wrench. The third to last teen victim was screaming as the creature tore her to bits. It was gross, extremely bloody and over-the-top. Was it meant to be funny? Ironic? Post-modern? Meta?

It was awful.

The bottle looked ordinary: classic Southern Comfort, his drink of choice at university.

There was a small card attached.

Drink Me.

He screwed off the lid, the plastic seal cracking like the bones of a screaming teen in the creature's jaws, took the bottle back to the couch, flopped back and swigged.

Spirits now.

He was drinking spirits out of the bottle.

So. It had come to this.

How? How had he gotten here?

Three years ago he'd been an entertainment reporter on the number one television breakfast show. His column had been syndicated in papers across four capital cities. He'd been a regular on the number one drive-time radio show. Flown to premieres to interview stars in penthouse suites.

For ten years, he'd been there, done that.

Then the magazine.

The first few issues had done well; then circulation had fallen; then plummeted.

It's a great magazine; but no-one reads magazines any more.

It's all online.

You need a website.

Not just a website, a web portal.

And you need web content, now.

He'd barely known how to use the internet, his wife had done all that.

He'd ignored terms like webmaster, podcast, RSS feed, iPod and broadband revolution.

He'd ignored all the advice because he'd been too afraid to admit: he didn't understand it. Somehow, he'd let it slip. He'd missed the boat and now he was drowning. Then suddenly people were talking about MySpace, Facebook, then Twitter. He hadn't known what those things were either; but by then it had been too late. He'd managed to get a site up and running but it had just vanished into the blur of the web. He'd needed a small fortune for web marketing but all his money was gone with his folded magazine.

Bad luck, they said.

Nobody could have foreseen it.

Worst time in history to start a print magazine.

Magazines are dead.

Then, almost three years ago, his wife had taken his daughters to London for a holiday.

He'd let them go without him; he'd stayed to try and make the magazine work.

No mention that she had a job with an online publishing company until she called two weeks later to say she wasn't coming back. No money for lawyers; he let her divorce him. She let him keep the bankruptcy.

It all made the papers and, so he was told, the internet.

Then, one fatal night.

Out on the town.

Drowning his sorrows.

Caught on camera.

Drunk.

Abusive.

Naming names.

It went viral.

He hadn't known what that meant either.

Mitch swigged at the bottle again.

Sacked by the television network, by the radio, his newspaper column 'on leave'.

He'd tried to get work, go back to his roots; but paid reviewing was dead.

Hundreds of reviews online, all free, all saying the same thing about the same movies.

Who's going to pay to read reviews?

Who's going to pay anyone to write them?

No-one cares about that shit any more.

It's the democracy of the internet.

The paid critic is dead.

Newspapers are dead.

Print, finally, was dead.

His daughters could be dead for all he knew.

He took another swig and sobbed himself to sleep on the couch with the whole sorry story of his life splayed out in his mind before him, like some terrible movie he was forcing himself to endure, with the final victim screaming right up to the bitter end.

CHAPTER SEVEN

'Mitch?'

Mitch woke, squinting. He still felt drunk.

Maybe he was about to be sick?

No. He felt okay. Just, still drunk.

The room was bright though. Morning?

Crap. He'd slept on the couch all night again.

But he must have put a lot away, to still be drunk…

What time had he fallen asleep?

Had he wept again?

His eyes were puffy.

He supposed he had.

Jesus.

Pull yourself together. It's morning.

Someone was standing across the other side of the coffee table, looking down at him. Someone familiar…

'Pan?'

'Hey Mitch.'

'What the…?'

Pan smiled, assessing him.

Mitch was groggy. He could barely move.

'What the hell are you doing here?'

Pan frowned. 'How much of that stuff did you drink?'

Mitch looked down – in his hand, the tell-tale bottle of Southern Comfort was resting against his chest, the lid screwed on.

'A few swigs…'

'I don't think you should drink that any more, Mitch. Not for a while, okay?'

'Jesus no.'

With a Herculean effort, Mitch sat up and leaned forward, staring up at Pan in amazement.

Even at thirty-nine, Pan was still a beautiful human specimen. With his tousled black hair, piercing green eyes, striking bone structure and wry, hypnotic smile, he could conceivably stand beside any famous silver-screen icon and not look out of place.

'Sorry mate,' Mitch leaned forward and planted the bottle solidly on the coffee table. 'Shouldn't have opened it until you got here.'

'You're in a bad way, Mitch.'

Mitch nodded. 'Can't seem to pull out of it. I think it's been going on for months and I didn't even realize it.'

'That's okay. We all have our low points. Do you mind if I hang around?'

Mitch was confused. 'Why are you asking me? This is your place, Pan.'

'Not really, not any more. You've spent more time here than I ever did. Don't mind if I stay a while, do you?'

'No… no, of course not, I don't even know why you're asking…'

'Thanks mate.' Pan frowned. 'You look like you could use a bit more sleep.'

'Yeah, I… usually sleep through the morning.'

'It's not morning.'

'What?'

Mitch turned to the balcony. The sunlight was blinding. What the hell was Pan talking about?

'Listen, Mitch, there's something I want you to do for me, okay?'

'Now?'

'I want you to find Suzie Saturn, okay?'

'Suzie…?'

'Write it down, on your pad.'

'Okay.'

Mitch obeyed.

The name seemed oddly familiar yet he was sure he'd never heard of her.

'And tomorrow, I want you to tell Saph, *there's no place like gnome*, okay?'

'Saph? Is she with you?'

'You'll see her tomorrow.'

'Tomorrow? What is tomorrow anyway?'

'Just another day. But tell her, okay? Remember. I won't be there.'

'Look, Pan, I feel like shit. I gotta sleep. Do you mind sleeping in the spare room? I'm all set up in the main. If you want food, you'll have to order in. We'll catch up in the morning, okay?'

Pan smiled. 'But you sleep through mornings, Mitch.'

Mitch stood, slow but steady. Pan watched him.

'Pan, this is too weird. First that phone call, then that guy Tim… and now you're here. What's this all about? It doesn't seem real.'

'It's what you drank.'

'You sent it. Drink me, it said.'

'That's why it seems like a dream. It isn't though. I am really here.'

'Yeah, well, I can see that.'

Mitch staggered past Pan's weird corner of anthropological keepsakes and down the hall to the spare room. It was hotel-level immaculate and probably hadn't been slept in for years.

'Here you go.'

He pulled the sheets and blankets across, because it seemed like the welcoming thing to do.

Mitch shuffled back past him and went across the corridor to the door of what he now considered his own bedroom. When he turned, Pan was staring at him, framed within the doorway of the spare room, smiling with a strange affection.

'Thanks mate. This really is your place now. I don't want it. You need it more than I do.'

Mitch was speechless. It almost brought a tear to his eye.

'Talk in the morning, hey mate?'

Pan smiled affectionately.

Mitch nodded back.

'It's good to see you Mitch.'

'You too, mate. To be honest I could use a friend. I think I just about hit rock bottom last night.'

'We can do something about that.'

'We? Oh, Saph's here too, huh?'

'I know how you feel about her, Mitch. I think I always did, but I never really understood 'til now.'

'Go to bed, Pan. That's ancient history.'

Pan laughed, lightly, as Mitch closed his bedroom door.

The phone was ringing.

The second landline cradle, on the bedside table.

Why was that happening?

It made his head hurt.

The phone.

The phone hadn't rung in ages.

Mitch recollected, vaguely, last night's events.

He wondered what time it was, as he snatched up the phone and spoke tersely.

'Yes?'

'Mitch?'

'Yes?'

The woman sounded relieved. 'Mitch, it's Saph.'

'Saph. Wow...' He felt dizzy. 'How's it going?'

'Not that great actually Mitch. That's why I'm calling.'

'Oh. Okay. Look, he's here but… he said he'd be out today.'

'What are you talking about?'

'He gave me some weird message for you. I can go see if he's still asleep. What time is it anyway?'

'It's quarter to eleven.'

'In the morning?'

'Yes, in the morning. Bloody hell Mitch, what's wrong with

you? I've been trying to get through to you for days. Your phone's been disconnected and you never answer the door buzzer; there's a new security man but Pan didn't leave my name and the bloody idiot won't let me up!'

'Look, you sound kind of distraught. I'll go get him.'

'Get who? Look, Mitch, listen – I have some bad news.'

'Bad?'

'It's about Pan.'

'Pan?'

'Mitch, he's dead. I'm sorry to break it to you like that but it's kind of urgent. The funeral is this afternoon at three o'clock. I know he would want you to be there. Can you make it?'

'Pan's not dead, Saph. He's here. He's sleeping in the spare room.'

'What?'

'He turned up out of the blue last night.'

'Mitch, this is not funny.'

'I'm not joking.'

'Then you must have been dreaming. Pan is dead. His body's been identified. He was murdered in Peru, a week ago today. Now are you coming to the funeral or not?'

INTERLUDE

'We can do anything with this,' the scientist stated to his benefactor, with supreme confidence. 'Anything.'

The two men watched the boy through the one-way glass, as he scribbled down notes on large sheets of white A2 paper.

The scientist had only met his benefactor in person for the first time that day, although they had corresponded frequently via his many representatives. Oliver Hines was an important man and, upon finally meeting him in person, the scientist felt almost as important by proxy. Then again, he was important too. In fact, at this juncture, he was probably one of the most important people on Earth.

Oliver Hines nodded.

He seemed quite calm, considering the implications of what he was witnessing. The sheer scale of it…

Hines did not seem at all like he did on television.

On television, he was always quietly composed, if not humble.

In person, he seemed almost completely blank, as though there were some aspect of his personality missing; he seemed to have no ego at all.

Perhaps he was, quite simply, genuinely odd.

The boy in the bland room behind the glass had been writing for weeks now, staring ahead into space at something only he could see, yet producing copious handwritten notes as though by divine guidance. He only stopped for meals, three times a day, and to sleep for exactly eight hours a night on a comfortable bed in the next room. He spoke very little and, when he did, it was usually a friendly request for a glass of water or to use the bathroom and, occasionally, for some freshly brewed organic coffee.

The sheer scale of it… yet from such an unassuming resource.

'Has any of this been transferred?' Oliver Hines asked quietly.

'No,' the scientist shook his head. 'In accordance with your wishes, it's all on paper. Nothing digital. It's clearly discernible. He has very neat handwriting, especially considering the speed he writes.'

'When will he be finished?'

'Who can say? Weeks? We don't know how much he plans to write.'

'But, what have we got so far?'

The scientist raised his eyebrows. 'What we have so far, well, it's enough to change the world as we know it. Every aspect of the world as we know it.'

Hines seemed to consider this. He stroked his chin a while, then placed his hands in his trouser pockets.

'What have your people come up with, in practical terms?'

'Well, not a lot. Not a lot practically. I've assessed what he's written so far, and there is certainly potential for some early applications. But, for the true worth of this information to be distilled, it will need to be digitally transferred and processed. It's remarkably dense but surprisingly uncomplicated. It shouldn't take long to create some initial byproducts. It will just be a matter of which, for what, and for whom, I suppose.'

'Yes.'

'And there's something else,' the scientist added. 'It's not all code.'

'What do you mean?'

'The junk information I told you about. We don't think it's junk at all. It seems to be a mathematical language, one we don't understand. Nothing we can decipher from just looking at it. We'll need to bring in –'

'No,' his benefactor grunted.

'No?'

'I don't care about the language. Create something for me from the other information. Anything. But it must have demonstrable properties.'

'I'm not sure…'

'Work from the papers. It doesn't have to be earth-shattering.'

'Anything that comes from this will be –'

'Am I not making myself clear?'

'To be honest sir, no.'

'I need something that I can employ to prove I have the ability to do what I say I can do. I need –'

'Oh, I see sir,' the scientist relaxed, 'you need authentication? A… proof of concept? Something applicable, perhaps even public, but easily disguised.'

'Indeed. Can you handle that?'

'Nothing we haven't handled before, sir. When do you want it?'

Hines seemed to shift slightly, then he blinked as though he'd been briefly blinded by a bright light.

'Well, golly,' Hines shrugged. He seemed more animated now, less internal. His voice was like it was on television, friendly and Midwestern. 'I guess we'd better have it all done and ready as soon as you can?' Hines touched him on the shoulder. 'How's that sound?'

The scientist was honored.

'Of course, Mister Hines!'

As far as he was concerned, it was the green light from God himself.

The man kept writing.

He knew that the old scientist thought of him as a boy.

But he was no longer a boy. He was a man now; he'd done things only a man could do, and for which only a man could atone.

He'd maintained the charade of benign receptor for weeks now, writing down the information as it came to him, going with the flow as the flow, in turn, seemed to take charge of his body, regulating him with perfectly timed meals and sleep periods.

However, what the old scientist didn't know was that he could stop any time he liked.

But then there would be questions.

And, in reality, he didn't know whether or not, if he were to stop, he could reconnect with the flow again. It had been going for weeks and he had the feeling that, should he stop, he would have to restart, right at the beginning and all over again.

And that would surely drive him mad.

Because, what they also didn't realize, those three wise monkeys outside the room who were dancing blindly to the tune of their obscenely wealthy organ grinder, was that he could read the strange language and he was following the story.

If he stopped now, and ceased his connection with the flow, he might never find out how the story ended.

And it was truly the greatest story ever told.

He suspected that when the story ended, the information would be complete.

Then, and only then, might he be redeemed.

The hominid subject has responded well to the first experiment. There is little sign of psychological trauma and every indication that he will assimilate well with his brothers and sisters within the species. It is interesting to note that after a prolonged period of isolation, the hominid's mood becomes downcast, if not emotionally depressed, and this must be carefully monitored. Efforts must be employed to ensure that it does not spread to the species at large, nor effect their capacity to work.

Tomorrow the hominid will be released back into his community.

It will be of great interest to note how he acquits himself when dealing in the customs of his clan and species in general.

He knew that the organ grinder had a dread fear of storing his secrets digitally. He had listened to the old scientists speak with his minions, heard the story. Right back at the start of the digital revolution, the grinder's company search engine had been the best on the market. Yet his competitors had hacked their way into his programming files and stolen the templates for his next upgrade, then tweaked it and released their own version. The organ grinder's search engine, which had once supported sixty-three percent of internet traffic, and been a byword for user-friendliness, had been stunningly superseded. His once-lauded search engine was now virtually unheard of by anyone who'd come to the net later than the turn of the millennium. The organ grinder had never forgotten that. So now that he'd stumbled across the greatest discovery known to mankind, he was obsessed with it being kept in one secure research station, on paper.

The scribe's magic marker was running out. He tossed it into the trash basket with the others, uncapped a fresh one from the full pen jar on the table before him, and kept writing.

He did feel a little like a boy, the scribe confessed to himself, drawing pictures on butcher's paper with crayon.

And according to the information he was receiving, mankind's highest achievements so far pretty much equated to just that.

Mere childish scribblings.

He had to get the information out.

It had to be made public.

Or this one organ grinder would have total power over a planet full of monkeys. And the scribe was only just starting to guess the end of the story; and how badly that had turned out, the last time it had happened.

THE PANDORA SEQUENCE

PART TWO

WAKE

CHAPTER EIGHT

Mitch listened to the mid-morning radio playing from the stereo in the living room as he dug out the black suit he'd used for business meetings, back when he'd been seeking investors for the magazine. The clothes he'd worn on television had been somewhat more casual, and his own choice, but his wife had been present to help purchase the suit, to ensure it was a sufficiently serious brand and a good fit.

It was his only suit.

As he dressed, the song that played was one by Mistress, the single-monikered pop sensation who had swept the globe, and several Grammy ceremonies, over the last four or five years.

He had to confess, it was catchy.

It was a vengeful breakup song, called *Take Your Place*, as in, 'anyone could take your place'; but also 'take your place in the annals of my past'.

Amazing, he thought, how the top-tier stars always managed to reinvent themselves, to change their look, their tempo, to seek out the best songwriters for their material and flashiest directors for their music videos.

He was surprised when he heard the radio presenter announce that it was, in fact, an old Mistress track, one of her first. Although he knew he must have heard it before, he could have sworn he was hearing it for the first time.

As he mused upon this, he had one of those strange moments where his brain got a little discombobulated; he kept repeating the word, Mistress, in his mind. Over and over...

Mistress. Mis-tress. *Mistress*. Me – *stress*...

...until it seemed to detach itself from the singer, then

language itself.

To lose all meaning and become completely abstract.

He did this as he dressed, noticing that while he had let himself go over the past few years, he still looked as though he were okay.

He had several un-ironed black cotton shirts to choose from and sorted through the fresh laundry pile quickly to find the one that was least wrinkled. The suit jacket still sat well over his shoulders and the trousers still did up. He could even close the jacket buttons without the bulge of his slight but larger-than-recalled beer paunch poking out.

Again he asked himself: when did that happen?

What would his ex-wife think of him now?

The man who used to swim laps and eat organic?

What would the magazine investors think of a man in a too-tight suit, sucking in his guts to hide his beer paunch?

He caught his own thoughts again and realized briefly how he had come to edit them.

His ex-wife. The magazine.

They had names but he'd mentally cut and pasted them into harmless nouns.

Janine.

Cinema Now.

Now.

How ironic. A magazine with *Now* in the title that had turned out to be a dinosaur.

Still, the name of the singer echoed in his mind.

Mistress.

He couldn't get a fix on her, what her current look was, what her current anything was.

Did she even really exist?

How funny that he should hear that song, one he must have heard at a hundred parties back when it was a new release, when it was hot, and yet still fail to recognize it.

And yet he knew that he *had* heard it.

Many times.

He even knew some of the lyrics, the chorus.

He shook it off; it was the mind playing tricks, a hangover side-effect.

He dug out an old pair of Doc Martens. The heavy shoes were so scuffed on the toes as to be almost gray, but they were the only shoes he had that were not some variety of sneakers. Or runners, trainers… whatever the term was now.

Now.

He was deliberately out of touch, he knew that. And he'd wept himself to sleep over the reasons for that last night, again. Yet once again he was willfully ignoring that fact in order to get on with the day.

To take his mind off it, he wondered deliberately as to what Pan's funeral would be like; but figured he'd know soon enough.

Mitch had showered quickly after Saph's call, which had terminated abruptly after she'd made him write down the address of the church. This struck him as odd, as Pan had never been conventionally religious. The church was halfway across town and he knew that with school traffic it would take half an hour. As there would no doubt be a wake, and drinking, there was no question as to taking a cab. He booked for two fifteen then showered for the first time in days, shaved for the first time in weeks, and cleaned his teeth thoroughly for the first time in – he didn't want to know how long.

The toothpaste made his gums sore and his tongue sting.

He needed a haircut but it sat okay dry.

He realized he was thinking about what kind of impression he would make on Saph. What would she make of him now?

Assessing himself in the mirror, he thought he'd cleaned up alright. He didn't look old, or ill, but at the same time he looked a bit pale and out of shape.

Nothing he could do about that today, he shrugged at his reflection.

The radio was now playing a short interview with Derek Nurding, the latest in the recent line of celebrity atheists. Nurding was promoting his new book, *No Reason For God*, subtitled, he heard, *A Modern Rationalization For The Abolition of Spiritual Thought*.

"That a mouthful!" The interviewer slash breakfast-announcer, kept it simple. Nurding was addressing a crowd of like-minded followers tonight at a major lecture, to open a Science Center at one of Oliver Hines' Olivera Technology Parks.

Atheism for breakfast.

The world was just so used to it now; sugar-coated, lo-fat nihilism. Mitch started to wonder, given that he was about to attend a funeral, whether or not he would count himself an atheist. Maybe he was an agnostic? He stared at Pan's bizarre collection and shrugged to himself. He really didn't care.

The cab driver buzzed up a few minutes early. He buzzed back down and told the driver two minutes.

He'd written down the address on his blurb pad. He went to the couch and pulled the top sheet off. Underneath, on the previous sheet, he'd written *Suzie Saturn*.

He stared at the words.

Pan had told him to do that in the dream.

He'd actually done it.

He went to the spare room. When Saph had told him of Pan's death, he'd almost robotically gotten out of bed and gone to the spare room. It had of course been empty. But he'd been half awake then; checking again he saw that the sheets had been pulled back.

Had he sleepwalked through the dream?

He must have.

He didn't know what to think of that.

The cab was waiting.

He couldn't find his black winter coat but it was badly in need of a dry-clean and was probably too scraggy to wear to a formal occasion anyway. As an afterthought he grabbed the bottle of Southern Comfort and, when he did, a black feather fluttered across the kitchen bench and onto the floor.

As it did, he noticed that someone had slid a white A-4 envelope under the door.

He stared at it a second, then at the feather.

He opened the front door and picked them both up.

Then he left.

When he got into the cab, the radio was playing another Mistress track, this time an angry love song about lack of empowerment in a relationship called *Cat Collar*. The song had been well received at the time of release for avoiding the obvious analogy to 'pussy', especially when one line ended with 'tushie', but the next rhymed it with 'pushy'. It was nothing much, everyone knew, but in these times of overtly sexualized lyrics in even tweenie-oriented love songs, it had passed for wit, and had been celebrated for that small mercy.

Yet again, he had the weird feeling; even though he'd heard the song many times before, and knew the notorious lyrical twist, he could not shake the odd feeling that this was the first time he had actually heard the famous pop song.

It was creepy and he asked the driver to change the station.

Instead, the driver misunderstood and turned it off completely.

The cab ride was slower than he expected. Mitch tried to start a conversation with the driver but his English was too poor. Both he and the driver gave up and, after a polite enough pause, he opened the envelope that had been pushed under the door.

It was a printed email.

The addresses and domain names had been blacked out but the body of the email remained. It read:

H FIELD REPORT - 005 - 019

Hi U,

This is an informal report – For Your Eyes Only – to accompany the hard data and other information, such as press clippings, media, medical and surveillance reports in the larger file.

It's the first of the three high profile cases you wanted me to look into; this one is in regard to the American actress Gabrielle Fenwick. In Hollywood terms, U, this is your coverage – although I would strongly suggest you at least look through the accompanying material to get a good sense of the visuals.

First, that's her real name. Gabrielle Gwendolyn Fenwick (her friends still call her 'GG') first emerged in the early eighties as a Hollywood starlet; it's almost certain that she had some naked, perhaps borderline pornographic photo shoots taken when she first came to LA but they are long scooped up by her first major studio and probably reside in a vault somewhere along with similar material from all the other Hollywood actresses who are now stars.

This is par for the course, and it was pre-internet; a simpler time when uncompromising material could still be sourced and destroyed, with the mission controllers being almost certain that they still had the only copy of the material in existence.

I mention this because it's a matter of record that she came to LA in the summer of 1980 – on a Greyhound bus no less, from a small town in Michigan, where she had indeed, as her press bio states, come third in a state beauty pageant, and where she had told the judges in all earnestness that she wanted to be an Oscar-winning actress. General consensus is that the answer cost her the crown; the runner up wanted to save homeless animals and the winner wanted world peace.

Good luck, hope she got there in the end.

The photographer in question, Todd Mendoza, was a known quantity at the time; he would hang around the various travel terminals and select the prettiest girls right off the bus, convince them that they would need an updated portfolio and pretty much have them naked, shot (photographed, that is) and more often than not in his bed within three days.

Mendoza was quite an operator, clearly a Heffner wanna-be with a little more Larry Flynt in him than he wanted to recognize. At times he was juggling up to five different 'starlets' at once.

GG isn't the only actress you've heard of that got caught up with Mendoza; his strike rate was actually pretty high. She actually lived with him, in his loft in the San Fernando Valley, for the best part of five months in 1980–81 and when he died earlier this year (heart attack, undiagnosed congenital) GG quietly attended his funeral.

It sounds as though, back in the early eighties, Mendoza had some sort of deal with the studios; not a low-life exactly but certainly some kind of lower-mid level procurer. He certainly had strong lower level contacts in the studio system, as it was back then. His deal seemed to be that if the studios wanted to test any of the girls he discovered, they would pay Mendoza for the compromising photo shoots and from there take over 'management'. Most of Mendoza's girls ended up as high-end escorts, fewer than you'd imagine ended up in the porn market, and the vast majority are now married and living happily somewhere outside of LA with their prior lives safely erased.

From what I can gauge, at least four Hollywood actresses, whose names you'd recognize, followed the same path as Gabrielle Fenwick to where they are today; spotted as talent by Mendoza, procured to a studio, groomed as starlets through the eighties to become major stars through the nineties, only then to take a career dive through the new millennium as their youth and broad-range sex appeal diminished. It's the Hollywood career path, right?

The main reason to mention Mendoza is that this seems to be the only blemish, if you can even call it that, on Fenwick's unofficial resume. From there her reality follows her bio and studio press releases exactly, right up to the present day. The studios tested her and discovered she had the 'it' factor; she radiated a cool, on-screen beauty. Her early party-girl roles didn't resonate with audiences or critics, and it wasn't until they tried her in 'ice-queen' roles that the accolades came a'calling and in the nineties she was nominated for no less than four leading actress Oscars (no wins).

But 'blemish' is a funny word, isn't it U? And the beautiful will go to extreme lengths to remove what they perceive as 'blemish' from their features.

In common terms there are three readily accepted terms for blemish (read: age) removal for the beautiful: an old-fashioned, scar-behind-the-ears face-lift; needle injected botox treatment; and skin peel. It seems our girl GG fell pretty heavily for the latter to the point that even her most defensive critics and adoring fans seemed to take exception to her 'look' in her last few roles of the nineties.

I'm sure you are aware that Hollywood sticks to a fairly limited range of iconic 'looks' and the ice-queen must be porcelain and fragile; by 1999 GG was pushing forty and to maintain those porcelain good-looks the skin peels had to come thick and fast (or, thin and fast, as the case may be). The trouble with these kinds of extreme beauty maintenance regimes is that they decrease exponentially; the more you have the more you need, the more you need, the less effective they are.

By all accounts, by the end of 2000, GG's facial dermis was so damaged by chemical peeling that she was put on a course of industrial grade antibiotics to prevent infection on the only remaining layer of skin on her face. This culminated in a quiet semi-retirement during which GG allowed her skin to heal naturally; essentially for her face to grow back.

Trouble was, as you might gave guessed, by the time she was once more ready for her close up, the phone had stopped ringing. After she'd taken a few meetings, it started again, but the offers were all for roles that she still considered outside of her age range – older mothers, mentors, Mrs Robinsons. Still, she took a few of these, and although critically praised they went nowhere; male admirers were not yet ready to let go of the thirtysomething ice queen of the nineties, and female fans certainly did not want to see GG as an 'older woman', lest *they admit the same to themselves; that they too had gotten older.*

So, now we come to the third act; it should be that Gabrielle Fenwick gracefully semi-retires once more, then returns to the screen in about five to ten years time when she is actually ready for the maternal role of a lifetime, and wins her Oscar (or at least, receives one of those honorary ones for the big stars with unlucky streaks).

But instead what we now have, as of about six months ago, is a totally rejuvenated Gabrielle Fenwick.

U, I can't understate how strange this is.

It's been staged very well over the past few months; she announced starring roles in three new films for the new Olivera Studios, all three roles ticking her ice-queen, femme fatale boxes. The initial cry from the online fan community was that she was too old; one of the roles is in the adaptation of a much-loved best seller that focuses on a mother-daughter relationship, the mother in her early fifties, the daughter in her mid-thirties, a kind of modern revamping of Terms of Endearment. It was assumed she would be playing the fiftysomething (Shirley McLain) mother, however it soon became clear that Fenwick had been cast as the thirtysomething (Debra Winger) daughter. When a new spate of photoshoots hit the magazine racks, blogs and internet celebrity sites, there was further criticism that the images had been massively photoshopped, to an embarrassing extent, to make her seem ridiculously younger than her true age.

(Sidebar: her studio bio has her as born in 1962, but a bit of digging suggests she may in fact be two years younger than that, born in '64 – certainly an oddity for a studio to raise the age of a starlet, however it's possible that this might have something to do with Mendoza's potentially illicit photography sessions, which would mean that she was only sixteen, perhaps seventeen, when the nude photos were taken. It's hard to believe the studios would have done this to protect a character like Mendoza, particularly as those photos have never and will never see the light of day, but stranger things have happened. Maybe Mendoza had more pull, or better friends, than we can discover? I'll keep looking. Regardless, our girl GG is clearly now past her half century.)

So anyway, the bashers on the internet were quite surprised when it became apparent, under professional analysis, that these new images had not been altered. In fact, quite the reverse; when GG once again began appearing in public, and the paparazzi had their turn, it became very much apparent that she was not 'digitally enhanced'. With the current so-called Ultra High Quality standard of digital imaging, you can zoom into a paparazzi shot, taken with a telephoto lens, so intensely that it's possible to see the skin pores on someone's face better than you can see them on the back of your own hand; once you're out in public, there are no more secrets.

DPI's tell no lies.

A few months ago GG started giving interviews again (that is to say, the media suddenly wanted to talk to her again) and at first she denied anything other than 'a good diet, exercise, healthy living and keeping out of the sun' (this has been her standard response, repeated like a mantra). Occasionally she smiles beautifully and adds 'oh, and a good sex life', although publicly she has not been romantically connected with anyone since her quiet separation from her music composer boyfriend three years ago.

Little do they know...

So, okay U, here's the thing.

I've investigated extensively. I've spoken to all the right people and rubbed all the right palms. She has not had a skin peel, face-lift or botox treatment. She has attended several health spas, including Olivera's Regime Spa out in the Mojave, but nothing out of the ordinary, and nobody else who has attended these 'spas' or 'retreats' (often fronts for the above-mentioned treatments, or celebrity rehab outfits) has benefited with the kind of rejuvenation as seen with our girl GG.

We activated alpha-plus satellite surveillance two weeks ago, crossed it with ground surveillance reports, and compared it all to her pysch profile built up as far back as we could go; in other words, the Full Monty. By all accounts she is reliving the life she lived in her mid-thirties. Her previously carefully managed macro-diet diet has gone to hell, but her exercise regime is heavier, her social calendar is full again, and her sex life is on fire – three young actor-models for three days each in those two weeks alone.

U, the bottom line is that Gabrielle Fenwick is almost exactly who she claims to be. A country girl who came to the big city looking for stardom and got all the right breaks. But below the bottom line… to all intents and purposes, to all available evidence, Gabrielle Fenwick has discovered the fountain of youth; she has reversed her physical body by fifteen, possibly twenty years.

And no-one knows how.

Report ends

H

***

Hello H,

Thank you for the report. For the record, I am a fan of GG and enjoy her performances.
Please pursue the Mendoza connection.
I think there is something there.

U.

CHAPTER NINE

Mitch arrived at the church a few minutes before three but there was nobody outside. It was a large suburban construction built with huge bluestone blocks, clearly dating back to the early days of the city. He had no idea if it were Catholic or Anglican or whatever.

Pan had certainly never been either of those things.

Mitch folded the printed email and put it in his pocket.

He wondered who U was, who H was, and why someone would send him such a document.

He'd met Gabrielle Fenwick and interviewed her twice. She had always been polite and professional and yes, she'd always looked ten years younger than she ought have.

But why send him this?

Why now?

To what end?

Was someone trying to give him a scoop? A new angle on an old star, to get him back into the game?

Such a strange report and such an odd conclusion.

Did he even want to go back to entertainment reporting?

He pushed it from his mind and assessed the church from the pavement.

There must have been hundreds of churches all over the city but he couldn't remember the last time he'd actually stopped to look at one.

This church was pretty much as he remembered his own from childhood and Sunday School, cold and austere but also somehow solid and reliable; and in its own way very beautiful. As a child Mitch's maternal grandparents had insisted he attend but when they had both died within six months of each other, his grandfather passing in his sleep just before Mitch's twelfth birthday, and with high school on the way, it had been deemed a waste of time to have him go on and become confirmed. He'd barely set foot inside one since.

This one was located in the middle of an upper-middle class suburban sidestreet, bordered on the left by a car park and on the right by a beautifully renovated but equally austere sandstone house. The churchyard proper was bordered by a lush, well-tended privet hedge that came up to Mitch's shoulder.

As Mitch stepped from the pavement toward the central, gateless gap in the hedge that afforded entrance to the church grounds, he realized he was holding the bottle, as though approaching a party. What had he been thinking? He assessed the street. The cab was long gone and a couple of cars were approaching from either direction; they passed and he stepped to the side and shoved the bottle into the middle of the hedge. The bottle sat there, suspended securely within the dense but tiny, spindly branches and held steady. He covered the slight gap he'd made and let it be.

To all intents and purposes, it was completely invisible.

Stupid thing to do, bringing it.

Mitch sighed and made his way up the gravel path, gazing up. The imposing stained glass windows on the church were covered in bars, as all church windows had been since the late eighties, to prevent vandalism.

We're all just used to that now, he thought as he approached the tall, arched doorway.

There was an usher at the end of the entrance alcove. It might have been Pan's brother, or cousin, but he wasn't sure. It had been too long. The man, handsome and perhaps thirty-five, stood to one side at the entrance to the main… what did you call it? Not just a 'room', surely.

Chamber? Cathedral?

Too small for such a large word. Just church, he supposed.

Those in the faith probably had a proper name for it. The man handed him a fold of photocopied paper, which Mitch unconsciously rolled into a tube.

'Sorry for your loss,' Mitch muttered, to which the man nodded once and briefly closed his eyes.

Dismal organ music played softly as he took a few steps down the central aisle. The church interior was deceptively large, even though the building from outside had not seemed exactly small. He realized that it was essentially one room, floor to pointed ceiling, and that gave the sense of immense scale.

To make you feel tiny in the presence of the Lord, he supposed.

A mindfuck, Pan would have said.

It was certainly practical: you enter, go straight down the middle to the altar, aesthetically pleasing along the way. Totally functional.

And cold. A heating nightmare, he supposed.

Then he remembered how the church of his childhood had heated up, with all the human bodies packed together. But that would not happen today.

The turnout was disappointing, to say the least.

There were perhaps a dozen attendees clustered in the first few rows. The other pews were empty apart from a few of Pan's People further to the back; two to the left and three to the right.

No sign of Tim.

He wondered if Tim even knew.

He certainly hadn't acted like it last night.

To the right at the front he saw a woman that must have been Pan's mother, sitting beside Saph on the aisle, and three girls to her other side. Pan's three sisters. They hadn't seen him come in.

To the left at the front were a group of older people he didn't recognize, probably Pan's uncles and aunts, then across the aisle behind them were a group of people Mitch hadn't seen gathered all in one place since university.

It was the old gang.

Christ, he thought, this is like *The Big Chill*.

If the organist started playing *You Can't Always Get What You Want* he was going to completely freak out.

But the organist, hidden away somewhere, was playing some hymn Mitch had no hope of identifying.

He suddenly felt angry.

What the hell was going on?

Pan would hate this!

He stopped at the third pew from the back and looked across at the cluster of three of Pan's People to his right, aware that he was frowning deeply. They frowned back and he realized that they thought he was somehow disapproving of *them*. To counter this he ceased frowning and shrugged at them. Now *they* looked confused.

Mitch looked towards the front again, to his old friends. Their proximity to the altar somehow reflected their approval. He stared at the backs of their heads, stared at the back of Saph's head, and realized that he did not approve. He was angry with them. What the hell were they all doing here, in a Christian Church for Chrissakes?

The man's name had been Pan!

He had been a pagan, if anything!

He blinked heavily for a second.

That meant something.

The Greek Pan – was the old Christ.

Or, something?

Pan, his friend, had told him that. Many times. That the 'Christ Myth', as Pan had called it, incorporated many of the old gods, including the Greek Pan. Or, wait. Maybe the 'real' Pan had been the prototype for the Devil?

Mitch sighed. Clearly he couldn't remember who the Greek Pan had been any more. They'd always been so bloody out of it whenever Pan had ranted about his namesake.

The high, post-noon sun was coming in through the barred stained glass. A cold winter breeze blew through the back of the church. Mitch knew that everyone down the front would turn, as people did, when the breeze hit them. They would see him. Call him down to sit with them.

Mitch's knees jerked, just a bit.

Move.

He stepped to his right, sat on the closest pew and slid quickly down to the cold stone wall. The slide was fast and clean; the bench was well-polished by decades of parishioners' bottoms.

They turned as one and looked toward the back of the church.

If they saw him, none of them recognized him.

None, except Saph.

Saph saw him.

She had felt the chill wind, looked back to the open doors, and then looked straight at him for a second. Then she'd turned back.

Expressionless.

Mitch heard a boom echo from behind him as someone closed the heavy church doors.

He gulped.

Was she that pissed with him?

Their phone conversation this morning had certainly ended abruptly.

A guy whispered behind him.

'When's it gonna start?'

A woman responded.

'When's it gonna end?'

Neither laughed.

Mitch turned and gave them a look, like, *yeah*.

They were classic Pan's People, good-looking and bright-eyed, neat but eclectic dress, but almost too earthy-looking, with that wan look vegetarians often had.

Organic people.

The surfer-looking guy sat in the middle of the two women, all three probably in their late twenties. One of the women was sour-looking, with sharp features beneath a long pageboy cut that was dyed jet black. The other was more conventionally attractive, despite her natural brown dreadlocks, with bright eyes and a devilish smirk on her full lips. He would have slept with either of them in a heartbeat.

The two Pan's People across the aisle were probably a couple; they were each as catwalk model gorgeous as the other. Both had long blonde hair, both were dressed in dark 'fifties suits with black shirts and white neckties as though, Mitch frowned, the funeral were some kind of opportunity to express their taste in retro-fashion.

Mitch caught this thought and was surprised at himself; it made him feel old, thinking that.

He tried to switch tacks.

In truth, if the funeral had been for another of the old gang and Pan himself had been here, he might have struck just the same kind of pose; and from what he understood of his old friend he had never been deliberately pretentious.

Stop being so goddamned judgmental, he scolded himself.

They're just fucking people.

Who cares what they're wearing?

They were here for Pan and that was what counted.

The organ changed tune and became louder.

Perhaps it was about to start.

Suddenly he was afraid.

It had all happened so suddenly.

He was at a funeral.

A *fucking funeral*.

For *Pan*.

Pan, his best mate who he hadn't seen for a year.

Pan, who'd been murdered somewhere in *Peru*.

Whose *ghost* had visited him last night.

It didn't make sense.

The sun came out from behind the clouds again and shone through the stained glass. He blinked in the momentary brightness. It seemed like his hung-over eyes could not absorb the light. He couldn't see anything.

The priest was approaching the altar.
A messy-haired man in a giant frock.
It was too much.
The sun was in his eyes.
In his eyes.

CHAPTER TEN

'Get in!'

Mitch blinked.

'Jesus Mitch, get in!'

He was standing in the churchyard, on the gravel path, in the rain.

The sun had vanished behind an expanse of dark clouds that now filled the entire horizon. He wasn't wet, not yet. The rain had just started, the sun had only then been obscured.

'Mitch for Christ's sake!'

Saph was in a car, on the side of the road, on the other side of the privet hedge entrance. The passenger door was open and she was waving frantically from the driver's seat for him to get in. Other cars were departing and from the back seat of a large black sedan one of Pan's sisters threw him a filthy look before the car accelerated away.

On auto-pilot Mitch obeyed, walking down the front path and through the hedge gate. He sat in the car, closed the door, and was immediately warmed by the heating. He wished briefly that he had been able to find his old coat.

Saph started at him, daggers.

'Are you high?' she demanded.

'No,' he heard himself say. 'Not that I know of.'

'Can't you save that shit for the wake? Pan's mother thinks he's gone to Heaven, she doesn't want to be reminded that her eldest son was a drugged out pagan! What's wrong with you?'

'I don't – I don't know. Last night I think I reached rock bottom.'

'What?'

'The closest I wanna get, anyway.'

Saph blinked, turned to the road, released the handbrake and slowly accelerated. They were last in the procession. She was silent for half a minute before picking up.

'You were outside staring at the sun for the best part of an hour and you're not tripping?'

'No, I – I was *what*?'

'People tried to snap you out of it. You were like a statue! Did the funeral freak you out or something?'

'An hour?'

'Probably!'

Like waking from a dream, Mitch searched his mind for his last conscious memory.

It was true.

He had absolutely no memory of the funeral service.

Saph stared at him intensely. 'They said that when the ceremony started, you just got up and left.'

'They?'

'The three sitting behind you! Why didn't you come and sit down the front with the rest of us? Actually scratch that, if I were you I probably would have done the same thing. Pan would have hated that medieval shit. It's all just for his mother, and two of the sisters. His mother's been religious all her life and the sisters are both born again. Only Trudy's in our camp and she took more persuading to come here today than I did.'

'Trudy. I remember her.'

'Yeah, well, she's okay. The other two are unbearable. We never really got along, then they found God and it was all over, believe me. Jesus, if we open that casket Pan will be spinning like a rotisserie chicken.'

'That's not true Saph. He loved his mother. She's just from another paradigm. You can't expect two thousand years of spiritual conditioning to change in one generation.'

'Jesus Mitch, you sound just like him.'

As they pulled up at some lights, he noticed her hands were tremoring against the wheel.

Mitch sighed. 'How did it happen, Saph? Do they know who did it?'

'Just gangs, they think. Shot him in the chest. He died instantly. Stupid thing is, he was on his way home. The driver said he saw someone he knew on the way to the airport. The driver warned him it was a bad area, but he got out anyway.'

'Why?'

'No-one knows. A few minutes later an old woman showed up and told him there was a dead Australian lying on the street outside some seedy bar.'

'Jesus.'

The lights changed and the procession restarted.

'Fucking Bo Everett and his hobbies. Pan had no business down there. He fancied himself a psychonaut wild child but he was a bloody private school neo-hippie poser with no street smarts beyond how to score a bag of weed in a suburban bar. He had no business being down there, none at all.'

'I know he was in Peru, but where exactly was *there*?'

'It's a long story. I was with him for a while but I've barely seen him these past two years.'

'You split up?'

'God yes, we were all but split last time the three of us got together.'

'That was three years ago! I mean; I saw him about a year ago but he told me you were just busy and sorry you couldn't make it.'

'Well, I'm sorry it's been three years Mitch, I really am. And I'm sorry it's taken something so goddamned awful to catch up with you again. But that last time, we all got so drunk, and it was such a happy night, that we just never told you. Don't take this the wrong way but it was a bit too much like mummy and daddy telling the kids.'

Mitch couldn't help but laugh.

'Yeah. I guess it would have brought things down.'

'To be honest, I kind of thought you'd worked it out for yourself.'

'Well, I hadn't.'

Saph took her eyes off the road and looked at him for a second; for some reason she didn't believe him.

'God, Mitch. I mean, we were never really together in that sense, we always had separate places. I hated that spooky old apartment he's lending *you*. I couldn't sleep with all those ancient artifacts in the next room.'

'I try to ignore them.'

'I mean, they're beautiful on their own terms, don't get me wrong. But who wants to sleep in a museum?'

'Well, needs must.'

Saph chuckled.

Mitch sighed. 'I can't believe you two split. You were… like Brad Pitt and Jennifer Aniston.'

Saph was silent for a few seconds and then threw him a look.

Mitch's brain caught up with him.

'Oh yeah,' he hissed. 'But… after all that time, he still never told me…'

Saph shrugged. 'I think he thought it would all just somehow… work itself out, down the track. But it was almost three years. I'm not stupid; a man like Pan, single. I know he must have seen other women since then. And you know he had that thing for strippers.'

Mitch smiled. 'Yeah. Remember that club in Adelaide? When we all went down there for – what was that?'

'Roland's thirtieth.'

'That was a hell of a night.'

'He used to think striptease was *sacred*,' Saph groaned. 'And I *really believed him*. He always wanted me to come with him; he was like a stripper critic. This one's got it, this one understands…' She shook her head. 'They were just girls, lost girls, and he thought they were channeling the goddess.'

Mitch smiled. 'He was a cool guy. You have to give him that.'

They were silent a while, and then Saph started talking, as though suddenly vocalizing a hitherto silent train of thought.

'I mean, half the time we weren't even living together. Then he took me down there and wanted us to live there, in Peru. In the fucking jungle, Mitch! Rainforests look beautiful on a plasma screen in high def but the truth is they're humid and oppressive and filled with insects and poisons and predators and you *never stop sweating* and you can *never wash it off*.'

Mitch watched her. She was starting to lose it.

He wondered if he should offer to drive.

She sighed, changing track again.

'Eventually it just died a natural death. Thank God we never had children.'

Her hands were still shaking.

She started to cry.

'I'm so sorry Saph.'

'Yeah, well…' she sniffed. 'What are we gonna do about it, huh?'

They drove on, silent for a minute, then Mitch spoke.

'Look, I'm sorry about the whole – leaving the church thing. I really don't know what happened. I don't remember anything.'

Saph shrugged. 'Grief does weird things to people. Look at you last night. Seeing his ghost and all that.'

Mitch considered her comment a second.

'That wasn't grief, Saph. I didn't know he was dead when I saw him. I don't know what that was.'

'You just happened to dream about him, Mitch. That's all. It's coincidence.'

'I suppose. I mean, it *was* a weird night. A raven got into the apartment –'

'Sure you didn't dream that too?'

'Oh yeah. I had a witness. Some British guy named Tim. I suppose that put Pan in my mind…'

'Tim?'

'Yeah. He delivered a bottle of Southern to me, from Pan, all the way from Peru. Classic Pan's Person.'

To his annoyance, Mitch realised he had left the bottle behind, for some lucky hedge-trimmer to find.

'Tim was at your apartment last night?'

'Yeah.' Still, he consoled himself, there would be plenty there to drink. It was a wake, after all. 'Why?'

'Nothing.'

Clearly it was something, but Mitch decided not to push it.

'Are you going to the wake?' she asked.

'Sure. Where is it?'

Saph sighed. 'I don't know yet. I was hoping you did. Pan's People won't tell me.'

'Won't tell you? What do you mean?'

'They don't trust me. You know about Pan, right? What he's become?'

'What he's become?'

'He has a podcast. Thousands of downloads per day.'

'Okay.'

'You haven't heard it?'

'No.'

He barely knew what a podcast was.

'You should. I can give you a list of the best ones – they'll bring you up to speed.'

'What's it about? Like, Roswell aliens and the JFK assassination? Atlantis and Bigfoot? Conspiracy theory?'

'It started out like that. But it went beyond: way, way beyond. More into psychonautics and the nature of reality. Theoretical physics and metaphysics. Consciousness expansion. That kind of thing.'

'So he's like a cult leader now?'

'Pan's People started as a joke. Like his name. I mean, Pan's People? They used to be cheesy dancers on some old British variety show...'

'*Top of the Pops*,' Mitch responded. 'Big in the 'seventies. But these kids aren't going to know that.'

Saph growled. 'These kids don't trust anyone born before nineteen eighty.'

'Do you blame them? If we think they're from another planet, they must think the same of us. Or worse. We're the generation who sold the environment down the toxic river.'

'Yes, yes. I know all that. It's just... I always thought that when I got to this age I'd be one of those cool, older people that got along with them. They don't like me.'

'Are you sure?'

'They like you though.'

'They do?'

'The ones from the funeral do.' The rain was getting heavier now; Saph shifted the wipers up a gear and they started squeaking. 'They were laughing at you, said you were getting a *solar download.*'

'A what?'

'Pan used to do that sometimes. Stand with his eyes closed, directly facing the sun. That's what he used to call it. You really don't remember standing there?'

'No. I remember the funeral was freaking me out; but nothing after that.'

'That's strange, Mitch. That's Pan strange.'

'I thought you and Pan were simpatico with all that mystical shit.'

She stared at him a second. 'I see you made your mind up.'

'Sorry. Look I'm probably no different than I ever was. I just don't get any of that stuff. I don't see the point.'

She fell silent again.

'I was on board with it all for a long time,' she eventually replied. 'When it was positive, when it was still about self-development. But Pan took it further. He started to think he could change things.'

'That's never a good sign.'

They turned off the main road and into a cemetery. The rain was pouring down hard now and he couldn't clearly make out the road ahead, just that gravestones and tombs surrounded them. Saph parked in a bay near the center of the cemetery along with the rest of the procession, about six cars that he could see, then cut the engine.

'Do you want to be a pallbearer?'

'A what? Carry the coffin?'

'That's what a pallbearer does. Do you want to?'

'I don't think so.'

She nodded to herself. 'Good for you. Wait here.' She leaned back and grabbed a small, black rolled umbrella from the back seat. 'I'll see if anyone's got a spare.'

She opened the door. There was a roar of rain, then she flicked the umbrella open and was gone, slamming the door behind her.

He watched her run through the downpour. She was wearing a black suit with a long tailored jacket. Her thick but fine blonde hair, halfway down her back as it had always been, blew about with the wind, then the rain obscured her.

The sound of the heavy downpour was a constant roar. He sat there watching it pelt upon and flow down the windscreen.

'Shit,' he said to himself.

This was awful.

He hadn't eaten, needed a hair-of-the-dog drink to kill his hangover, and now he might not even be allowed into the secret wake.

He could half see in the mid-distance that the coffin was already being taken out of the hearse. He couldn't make out who was carrying it, whether it was Pan's People or his old university buddies. He felt embarrassed to see them now, after the 'solar download' incident. Yet, like an alcohol blackout, it was difficult to feel ashamed of something he couldn't remember.

He watched as they carried the coffin away, past the hearse and deeper into the cemetery.

What now?

The door beside him opened. Saph leaned in, her face close to him, her long hair a little damp now. She looked radiant, almost angelic with it, as she shouted over the rain.

'Come on! We'll have to share! If anyone's got a spare umbrella they don't want to give it to you!'

He grunted and rolled his eyes.

Saph shrugged. This or nothing.

He stepped out as she stepped back, then quickly closed in again, shifting the umbrella to cover them both as she placed a hand in the center of his back, then they hurried after the coffin.

It was slow going over the gravel path.

'Bad choice of footwear,' Saph grunted. 'I nearly went A over T before.'

By the time they reached the graveside, the coffin had already been lowered and everyone was standing in a large circle around the open grave. Everyone had an umbrella. At first nobody paid him any attention. The priest, or father, or whatever he was, was being sheltered by an umbrella, held by a middle-aged woman, so that he could hold his Bible. She in turn held an umbrella of her own. When the priest noticed him, he took one of the umbrellas from the assistant, then nodded toward Mitch.

The assistant fished into a large plastic bag on the ground beside her, filled with small rolled up black umbrellas. She darted around the mourners and handed the umbrella over to Mitch with a polite smile, then returned to her duties. Mitch smiled tightly in thanks and immediately opened it, moving away from Saph. The man standing beside him, the organic surfer who'd been behind him at the funeral, moved closer so that their umbrellas touched sides, and Mitch noticed that in fact all the mourners had done the same, creating a contained black semi-circle of shelter around the graveside.

The priest's voice, prayers, service or whatever, started. His volume reached over the rain, and the clattering of the rain on Mitch's umbrella, but the words were essentially intelligible. Everyone stared down at the wet hardwood coffin and the raindrops scattering off the dark, polished surface.

Nobody made eye contact.

Mitch suddenly realized that he had no desire whatsoever to rekindle anything with any of the old gang; they were all dead to him.

They had died with Pan.

He kept staring at the coffin.

It seemed surreal, especially when Mitch also realized that this wasn't just cinematic convention.

It actually *did* happen in real life.

Standing by the grave, black umbrellas, miserable weather…

How strange that just the night before…

One of Pan's sisters threw some dirt onto the coffin.

Had the priest decided to wrap this up quickly?

Or were graveside services just fast?

The second born-again sister followed suit, then both walked away.

Pan's mother remained still, staring down. The priest remained beside her with her third daughter, Trudy, at her back.

One by one, everyone shuffled to the pile of dirt, bent over and repeated the ritual. Still nobody made eye contact but everyone moved slowly and carefully; it was all too macabre that they all seemed to have processed the very real potential of slipping on the muddy ground and toppling into the grave.

Finally, it was Mitch's turn.

Pan's mother met his eye. Emotionless. She turned her gaze back to the coffin. He wanted to say something; he might not get another chance.

He bent over and tossed the dirt onto the coffin.

Could he?

Suddenly he found himself turning to her, bending down to speak loudly over the rain.

'I'm sorry!'

She stared at him. Again, emotionless.

'I'm not on drugs!'

He sounded like a lunatic but he wanted to make sure.

'Something really happened to me!'

He squinted in at her, their umbrellas bumping, his face earnest, looking for some sign of forgiveness.

She didn't look at him but reached up and laid her hand firmly for a second on the wet forearm of his black jacket. She nodded to herself, then took her hand away.

'Pan was my best friend!'

This time, he shouted. And this time she turned up and met his gaze.

He felt tears forming.

'Mitchell,' she said, somehow confirming that.

'Yes!'

She nodded again, then returned her gaze to the coffin.

He moved away.

That would do.

As he moved away the rain began to thin, then within a few seconds it had stopped. Everyone lowered their umbrellas and looked up, palms to the sky.

Across the cemetery, the two Christian sisters were standing in the middle of the gravel path back to the cars, staring at him as though he had urinated on the coffin in front of everyone. Saph caught up with him as they drew closer. The sisters weren't budging.

They were waiting for him.

'Bloody hell,' Saph hissed in his ear. 'I've never seen them so angry!'

Mitch watched as they slid their umbrellas closed with distinct clicks, reminding him of cinematic gunmen, pulling back the loading mechanism on a pistol in preparation for a shootout.

As he drew closer, he saw that they had inherited scarcely any of same mix of physical characteristics from their parents that Pan had. Although the older sister had his flared nostrils and thick lips, and the other, the middle sister, had his blazing green eyes, they were both fair-haired. They were both very beautiful, however, and even through their plain, neck-to-knee funereal black he could see they had full but slender figures.

Come to think of it, he thought now that he remembered having a one night stand with the younger sister in the first weeks of university, before he knew Pan well enough to know better. She sure as hell hadn't been into chastity back then.

What happened to people, he wondered?

Saph hissed in his ear again. 'Jillian on the left, Rebecca on the right.'

Jillian, his past indiscretion, started in.

'What are you doing here? You're not wanted!'

Rebecca was silent, but her look of righteous indignation backed Jillian to the hilt.

'I'm sorry, I just wanted to pay my –'

'This is a Christian ceremony!'

'I know! I didn't mean to –'

'You're not welcome at the house!'

'I didn't even –'

'Don't think I don't remember you!' Mitch didn't know what to make of that. She seemed to be implying that he had somehow corrupted her.

'What you did to me!'

Something in her eyes made Mitch realize that she didn't truly believe a word of what she was saying. She was unhappy, that was all. Still, he couldn't help himself. He leaned right into her.

'Don't think I don't remember what you did to me!'

She took a sharp, deep intake of breath, then paused before slapping him hard across the face.

The sound ricocheted – everyone looked.

'Jillian!'

It was Pan's mother, passing by. Her voice carried serious weight as she proceeded without stopping.

'Leave Mitchell to get to the wake!'

Trudy was at her mother's side; she looked directly at Mitch.

It was startling.

Trudy had indeed inherited Pan's genetic mix; she might have been his twin sister with her beautiful features and jet hair. She was smiling, as Pan might have, in wry approval. Somehow Mitch knew it was the only thing that had made her smile all day.

Trudy waved a hand at him briefly. At first he thought it was the devil sign, the heavy metal salute, and he was shocked. Then he realized it was the phone sign; a quick 'call me' signal. Then she was lost to the throng as the rain showered down again with a hissing roar, and a swarm of sympathetic umbrellas moved in to protect her mother.

Saph pulled him away and he found himself being hurried on, shepherded toward the car. If Saph's shoes were still giving her trouble, there was no indication. Before long they were safe, the double door slam sealing them back in the air-conditioned warmth. Saph threw her wet umbrella behind her seat, so Mitch did the same.

'I'll see it gets back to the church,' Saph nodded. Then she let out a short laugh. 'My God, I don't think anyone's ever spoken to Jillian like that. Not even before she was a Christian. Did you really sleep with her?'

'She was my first girl at college.'

'What was she like?'

'Drunk!'

They both laughed.

It suddenly occurred to Mitch that despite spending the last hour or so in close proximity to Saph, this was the longest he'd ever gone in her company without the thought of sleeping with her.

He wasn't sure that he was even truly thinking about the possibility now; Saph had always been more of a symbol for him, he'd eventually realized, after years of unrequited love and, he had to face it, deep lust. A symbol of something he would never have, the kind of unattainable beauty only men like Pan could possess. The two of them, together, had been an almost supernaturally attractive couple.

Even now, at – what must she be? Thirty-eight? She had retained that beauty; bone structure, you couldn't beat it. That, and the symmetry of her gaze, the fullness of her lips and the angle of her smile against her cheekbones. The bronze-brown eyes, with flecks of gold, shone at him as they laughed together for the first time in years. He remembered her mother had named her because her eyes had been sapphire at birth. A few days later they'd changed, but the name had stuck. She'd taken good care of herself; he saw health in her porcelain skin, and of course the developing lines on her brow, and at the sides of her eyes, about the only sign of age he could see on her, had emerged in exact and aesthetically pleasing patterns.

As the laughter died and they maintained eye contact, he thought it would be, under any other circumstances, the ideal opportunity to try and kiss her, and see how it went.

He suddenly remembered, years ago, seeing her emerge from a swimming pool, in a tight one-piece that because of the water and the way the sun had hit her, had been virtually transparent. It had been a seminal moment for him; other men his age had seen Bo Derek in *10*, or Phoebe Cates in *Fast Times*, but he had seen it for real. A real Ten. She had been totally within herself, unaware of the reaction she had caused in the men around her, and someone beside him had whispered:

'Whoever ends up with her...'

Mitch had expected them to say '...will be the luckiest man alive.'

That, or something the like. Instead, the other person had said:

'...will have a total nightmare keeping her.'

He realized, then.

That had been the moment he'd decided, unconsciously perhaps, to maintain that image of her in his mind, to give it iconic status, and to set her on a pedestal labeled 'unattainable'.

A knock on his car window startled him.

Saph hit a button on the central console and it rolled down one third.

Outside in the rain, umbrella-less, an older man who looked like a former rugby player stared through the gap. He had a serene poker face as his thick, dry lips moved to speak in a solid South African accent and his giant hand extended a small white card into the car.

'Mister Everett would like to see you.'

Mitch accepted the card. It was blank, other than a neatly handwritten mobile phone number.

'Mister Everett?' Mitch asked.

'Mister. Everett.'

Mitch didn't know how to respond.

The rugby player continued. 'At your convenience. But as soon as possible. He's been made aware of your availability.'

Then he was gone.

Had that been a slight?

His availability?

He was always available.

He basically had no life.

Saph closed the window.

'I have no life,' he told himself, and Saph in the process.

Saph stared at him. 'Are you going to call?'

'I suppose.'

He placed the card in his shirt pocket. If he were any kind of normal person, with any kind of life, he would pull out his mobile phone and call Everett then and there.

'What do we do now?' he asked Saph.

Saph stared out through the rain.

An old green Mercedes was moving off.

'We follow that car. We're going to crash the secret wake.'

'You really want to go?'

'I want to know who killed Pan – and I'm betting whoever did is going to be there.'

CHAPTER ELEVEN

The old green Mercedes made no attempt to lose them as they followed it though the suburbs. The rain hadn't ceased and the clouds didn't part.

'I feel bad for not talking to the others,' Mitch confessed.

Saph spoke quickly but her tone was deliberately neutral.

'Curtis is obsessed with some new online share trading software, I think he's chasing a lot of money he's sunk into it already. I got the feeling he's lost all his savings. Imelda's a soccer mom with four kids, all boys. She's so tired all the time she can hardly string a sentence. She's going from the church straight to a concerned parent meeting. Something about new research showing that sugar is as destructive as alcohol and whether they should ban it from the school entirely. I got the feeling Pan's funeral was just another dutiful appointment. Peter's okay, he owns a few restaurants, at least he can still tell a story, but he's flat out too; you know how he was, always micro-managing. His phone never stopped and you could see whenever he turned it off he was really uncomfortable. And Craig owns the funeral chain that's taking care of all this – that's why Pan had such a nice coffin.'

'Didn't know there was such a thing.'

'Pan's mum does, and that's what's important. But you haven't missed anything. Maybe some other time we can get them all together again, get them all drinking. Then maybe we'd hear some stories. For real.'

'God. Imelda, she was the most promiscuous of all of us!'

'Maybe that's why she has four kids.'

'What about the others? What about Frieda and Michelle?'

'Didn't show. The others are all overseas.' She looked across at him. 'Janine of course, she called. She thought Pan and me were still together too. We had a chat. A short chat. And Pan's mum says that Dieter called but he's in the middle of a film shoot somewhere in South Africa.'

So, she knew he was divorced. Knew everything, probably.

Mitch nodded. 'What about you? What have you being doing?'

'Same old.' Saph shrugged. To be honest, Mitch couldn't remember what her 'same old' was.

'How about you?' she asked.

Mitch decided not to go there. 'Yeah, same old. Just for less money and less self-esteem.'

'That bad, huh?'

He didn't respond.

'I can tell you've been drinking. You smell like a brewery.'

'Really?'

'Oh yeah.'

'Jesus.'

She let out a laugh. 'That's what you get.'

She'd never been judgmental, Saph.

He guessed that was one of the things they'd all liked about her.

Right from the start their clique of a solid dozen, with fluidly exchangeable satellites of half a dozen more, had formed around the most stable trio; Pan, Saph and Mitch. Whatever signals their combined concoction of personalities gave off, it had attracted a certain kind of 'other'. Most of them had been art students but a few had been from the sciences, or business faculties. All of them had been natural conversationalists and critically sharp. Together they'd been the smart-asses, the cool intellectuals, the pop culture kids. There had been relationships within the group, virtually all of them had cross-pollinated at one time or other during their five years together. Some had lasted and some had not; but it never came between the group. Like the cast of some idyllic ensemble sitcom, they were all just too together to allow a break up to break up the group.

Mitch though, had never slept with Saph.

The core dozen had been a stable gestalt three years before Saph's inevitable pairing with Pan; but once they started it had seemed as though things had always been that way.

Seemed as though they always would.

Always.

Huh.

Mitch wondered whether he had genuinely begun to process Pan's death.

If he ever would.

'When did you find out?' he asked.

'This time last week. He still had me registered as emergency contact. They took his money but not his wallet – otherwise we might not have known for weeks, or months. If ever. Christ, can you imagine?'

'They got his body out pretty quick.'

'He had friends.'

'Bo Everett for one.'

'Apparently.'

'I wonder what he wants with me.'

'Call him and find out.'

Ahead, the Mercedes slowed and pulled into a drive-through liquor store attached to the side of a suburban bar. Saph pulled into the car park and took position at the drive-through exit. Mitch saw the same surfer-type guy he'd seen twice at the funeral get out and enter the liquor store, then the dreadlocked woman got out of the passenger side and came directly toward them.

'Here we go,' Saph warned, winding down her window.

Dreadlocks ran through the rain and leaned directly in, her arms folded tightly across her chest as though that would help keep her dry.

She was pretty, Mitch saw.

Not genuinely beautiful, like Saph, but certainly attractive.

If only she hadn't gone with the dreadlocks.

'Listen, just keep following okay?'

Mitch was surprised. She spoke with an American accent. Not the same as the woman on the phone last night, not as neutral. This was a huskier voice, and the accent sounded educated, refined.

Saph was taken aback. 'Okay…'

'It's stupid, you not being told. He loved you. I know he did.'

'Thank you.'

'I'm Heather. Jimmy's driving; he won't try and lose you or anything. But he told me to make sure you bring *him*.' She nodded past Saph at Mitch.

'I'm in,' Mitch told her.

Definitely attractive, pretty, but with a hard edge.

'Good. It probably won't be your scene but it's at least right that you should be there.'

She nodded to herself, walked backwards for a few steps, then turned and ran back to the old Mercedes. As Jimmy exited the liquor store, he saw Heather running back and stared at them for a second or two. Then he made a broad, waving gesture at Saph that said 'follow'.

Saph seemed suspicious. 'That was easier than I thought.'

'Why do you think they want me there?'

The Mercedes exited the drive through. Saph restarted her car and again began to follow. 'You had a solar download, remember? You're one of them now.'

Mitch smirked. 'Yeah. I'm in.'

They'd been traveling for about ten minutes after that when Mitch first saw the thing in the sky.

CHAPTER TWELVE

The thing in the sky was difficult to notice at first, being white against the clouds, but after a while it seemed to gel in Mitch's vision and remain within his line of sight. Almost as though, he thought creepily, it was moving with the car to deliberately remain within his eye-line.

'Can you see that?' Mitch asked.

'I wasn't going to say anything,' Saph responded.

'What do you think it is?'

They turned a corner and for a while the light was gone. Then it returned, seeming to glide effortlessly though the air, and resumed its position in the sky high above them, yet immediately within their view.

Saph's car was traveling fairly constantly just below the speed limit; it followed that the light was moving much faster.

'It changed position,' Saph uttered. 'It's not a star, or a planet.'

'It's still daylight.'

'The stars are there in daylight and so are satellites. We just can't see them. Sometimes there's an anomaly though. People report Venus and Jupiter as UFOs all the time.'

'Well,' Mitch shifted uncomfortably in his seat. 'At least one of us said it.'

'Said what?'

'UFO.'

Another brief silence descended.

'See that?' Saph asked suddenly.

Indeed, Mitch had. Two other lights had swept in to join the first. They were smaller but just as bright, except these seemed to hover more erratically, perhaps in orbit around the first.

'Jesus,' Mitch muttered. 'What are they?'

'Could be anything,' Saph responded, keeping her vision one third on the road, one third on the old green Mercedes ahead, and one third up to the sky.

Without warning, the green Mercedes pulled over.

'You think we're here?' Mitch asked as Saph pulled up behind.

They were on a fairly average street in an upper-middle class suburb; neat front lawns and well-washed cars in straight driveways that led to renovated three-bedroom 'fifties houses.

'Nice place to live, no doubt,' Mitch aired.

'Not as nice as you'd think.'

'Huh?'

'I grew up around here.'

'You're kidding?'

'Nope.'

'Huh.'

In front of them, Heather and Jimmy got out of the car. Both were staring into the sky, at the lights. Jimmy turned back briefly and glanced at them, as though inviting them to get out.

Mitch and Saph exchanged glances, then simultaneously opened their doors.

It was cold outside the car but the rain had stopped.

The winter sun was approaching on the western horizon but to the east, where the lights were hovering, the grey and white patterned rain clouds remained fully illuminated. The main light seemed still now, with the two others buzzing on either side.

Mitch and Saph approached Heather and Jimmy and they stood together in the middle of the rain-soaked street, their necks craned up as though watching fireworks.

'We thought you'd see them,' Jimmy spoke. His voice was deep, chesty.

'What do you think they are?' Mitch asked.

He saw Saph assess the pair carefully, as though their answer would somehow count toward something.

'Classic orbs,' Jimmy shrugged. 'There's thousands reported every year. Different colors, sizes. They clearly want us to know they're there, they've been hovering in our line of sight since we left the graveyard.'

Graveyard, thought Mitch. Not cemetery.

For a few seconds the largest one pulsed more brightly.

Mitch didn't know what to say.

Classic orbs?

As opposed to what?

Cherry orbs?

'Mitch is new to all this,' Saph offered. 'I don't think he knows what an orb is.'

Mitch glanced at her. Thanks a lot.

Saph shrugged at him, like 'don't ask, don't get.'

'Does anyone really know what they are?' Heather said quietly.

'I don't know,' Mitch responded. '*Does* anyone?'

Jimmy turned and smiled at him. He seemed to find that witty. Then he turned back and spoke.

'Everyone's got their own theory. Apparently if you signal them they'll come closer and sometimes bring more. But like most sky-based unexplained phenomena, they're easier to see at night. There may be just as many around during the day; and they might come closer if you find a way to signal them.'

'How do we know they're not just helicopters or something?'

'Why would helicopters follow us – and deliberately remain in our line of sight?'

'Why would a UFO do that?'

'I don't think they're trying to intimidate us,' Heather spoke. 'Just letting us know.'

'Pan was being watched,' Saph said abruptly.

Mitch stared at her, incredulous. 'Pan? Why?'

Jimmy looked at him again. 'Are you serious? He was doing research on mind expansion for Bo Everett down in Peru.'

'He was?'

'Yeah,' Saph muttered. 'He was.'

'*That's* what he was doing there? Mind expansion? What, like, taking acid in the jungle? Like the soldiers in 'Nam?'

'Not really, Mitch,' Saph offered. 'I'll tell you about it some time.'

In other words, shut up.

Jesus, how was he supposed to know the right questions? He'd never been any good at the whole counter-culture secret code bullshit.

He sighed.

'Well, they're there,' he stated. 'I guess I can say I've seen my first UFO, for what that's worth. At least, until they explain it on the news tonight.'

Jimmy guffawed, incredulous.

'Man, you won't see this on the news.'

Conspiracy talk; again, Mitch had heard this before. He frowned.

'Seriously? You think all the networks could conspire not to show it? There must be hundreds of people, minimum, filming it on their phones.'

Even he knew that.

Heather turned to him and for the second time in two days one of Pan's People regarded him with something close to pity.

'I don't think you can even call it conspiracy any more. The divide's too big. If you're still watching the network news, there's no way you'd even see something like this. Your brain would just filter it out, or make you forget it, or rationalize it away, or something.' She turned back to the orb. 'If you really feel the need to record this experience and re-watch it, like it's more television, it'll probably be on YouTube.'

'It's probably already on YouTube,' Jimmy shrugged.

Suddenly Mitch felt angry again.

That was his world they were dismissing so flippantly.

The old world.

The world of dead print.

These were the people responsible for making his skills irrelevant.

He had been on television, he had been a celebrity.

And when that had ended, when that had been stolen from him, by YouTube and the thousands of little shits like these two who'd destroyed his life, so too had his marriage ended; and his family; and his income and his fucking whole identity!

He reached into his coat pocket and whipped out his cigarettes. He had one in his mouth, alight, in record time. It was the first one he'd smoked all afternoon; it was probably nicotine withdrawal that was making his feel so pissy right now, making him think – he knew – so irrationally.

Jimmy turned to him.

'Mind if I steal one?'

Mitch wanted to tell him to go fuck himself.

Instead, he let Jimmy take one, even lit it for him.

'You think those things are alive then?' Mitch demanded.

'Huh?'

'Those orbs. You think they're some form of… higher consciousness or something do you?'

'Sure. Why not? When we start moving again, I bet they keep following.'

'Let's do better than that,' Mitch smiled.

He turned and went to the driver's side of Saph's car, opened the door and leaned in.

'What are you doing Mitch?' Saph sighed.

Mitch fumbled around and found the control for the headlights. He started flicking them on and off. Ahead, he saw the sour-faced young woman with the jet-black hair, who had remained in the back seat of Jimmy's car all this time, turn and stare out at him.

'Come on!' Mitch shouted up at the orbs. 'Flash back if you're there!'

It was ridiculous, he knew. They must have been at least ten to twenty kilometers away, whatever they were, and a mile high. But it was just starting to occur to him that if he were indeed losing his mind, as he was beginning to suspect, after seeing a ghost, blacking out at a funeral, then chasing UFOs with a bunch of

Pan's People, he might as well go down screaming.

'Come on ya fuckers!' Mitch cried out. 'Anyone at home!'

He honked the horn three times, then three times again in quick succession. Jimmy was grinning at him but Heather seemed concerned. Saph just kept staring up at them.

Mitch honked again, keeping it up in rapid succession.

Saph turned back now but said nothing. Her face was all-but blank, as though she were only mildly curious as to whether this might actually work.

In the green Mercedes, the other girl started to honk the horn as well. Mitch laughed, like a triumphant pirate. He heard the girl laugh back from inside the Mercedes. The others stood on the street, staring back and forth from the orbs to Mitch, helpless. They both kept it up for a good thirty seconds until, without warning, the orbs jumped.

They had been high in the sky, miles away, then in the blink of an eye they were right above the tree line, three houses down.

They were bright but not blinding, sizzling and electric, but not hot.

But what they were, what was abundantly clear to all, was that they were very *angry*.

CHAPTER THIRTEEN

There were people on the street now, residents annoyed by the car horns.

Mitch and the girl in the Mercedes had stopped honking.

The orbs remained above them, sizzling and huge.

'Ball lightning,' he heard a man say; and was surprised when he realized it was Jimmy. 'It's just ball lightning.'

There was an edge of fear in his voice.

Mitch, however, was unafraid.

It had worked. Whatever these things were, he had their attention.

The street residents were almost all thirtysomething women, all well dressed, but there was a teenage boy, perhaps sixteen, one house down, pointing his phone camera up and walking slowly in an arc around the orbs. Mitch thought, he's not looking at them, he's looking at them through something else.

The young woman with the dreadlocks, Heather, was right.

He's just making them into another digital image – just more television.

Regardless, all of the street residents were looking up: there could be no doubt that they were all seeing the same thing – whatever that thing was.

Mitch was not only unafraid, he was no longer angry.

Perhaps it had been the shock of it but somehow his frustration had simply evaporated. He stared at the orbs, trying to get a beat on what they were. He could see nothing within or behind the light, although he could not see through them. They looked natural, organic, like sunlight, not like a special effect or a projected light show. They were intense but there was no need to squint, or to protect his eyes. He found himself thinking, twenty seconds. Then thirty. Just hovering.

As he realized he was no longer angry, the orbs seemed to sizzle down and simply glow. As though they were contemplating him, as much as the reverse. Then it dawned on him: they were probes. They were reading him. The whole point of their existence was to exist, so they could record his reaction. They had become angry because he had been angry. Now he was regarding them with interest, almost calm; and they were reflecting that back. They had reached a mutual recognition; he was as interested in them as they were in him.

And with that realization, the orbs faded and were gone.

Immediately chatter began on the street. Neighbors gathered first in pairs, then in clusters. Perhaps a dozen women had come out onto the street and within a minute they had made three groups of four, then two of six, then one large group in the middle of the street.

Mitch watched this happen as he returned to his own group and debriefed.

'They were on to you,' Saph said first. 'You were the focus.'

Jimmy seemed edgy, part unnerved and part disappointed.

'They weren't anything,' he muttered. 'It was ball lightning.'

'Ball lightning?' Mitch asked. 'I don't know what they were but it wasn't –'

'You're just projecting,' Jimmy said glumly. 'That's all it was. All this stuff has ever been.'

As Jimmy took a last drag of his cigarette, Mitch saw that his hand was trembling.

'You okay Jimmy?' Mitch asked.

Jimmy said nothing, dropped the cigarette butt on the street and went to his car. Mitch looked to Saph.

'I've seen this before,' Saph smirked unhappily. 'He's gone.'

'Gone?' Heather asked.

Jimmy got into the driver's seat, closed the door and they watched as he turned and spoke to the girl in the back. The talk seemed a little heated. On the footpath nearby, a woman in a bottle-green pantsuit was taking down their license plates on a small white pad.

The Mercedes engine started. The girl in the back got out and slammed the car door hard. Jimmy immediately drove off, the car vanishing around the first corner he came to, and was gone.

'What the hell?' Heather immediately lifted her phone to her ear, thumbing keys she did. 'Jimmy?' There was a pause. 'Where are you going?' Another pause. 'Jimmy, you can't just – ' Heather seemed entirely thrown. 'But what about us?'

Mitch wasn't sure if that referred to a relationship, being stranded, or both.

'Jimmy, just turn around and come back,' Heather ordered. 'I don't even know what-the-fuck suburb we're in!'

The sour-faced goth girl was listening to Heather keenly. Now Mitch was seeing her up close, outside of the funeral, he saw that she was not exactly sour-faced. Her features were angular, with high cheekbones with a sharp nose and chin, but it was her large brown eyes, the wide lids slightly contoured, that lent her a natural expression of dissatisfaction. But as she smiled, clearly somewhat amused by Jimmy's behavior, Mitch saw something less pouting, a kind of wry self-awareness.

'Wanker,' she uttered under her breath, very Australian.

Heather disengaged the call.

'He hung up.' She seemed mystified. 'Said he remembered he had something else to do. A family barbeque or something…'

The goth girl just shook her head, then ran her hand through her jet-black hair, pushing back the long fringe. 'He just got in the car and told me he couldn't take me to the wake; he had something else to do. I tried to argue but he wasn't having any of it. He'd made his decision, nothing would have stopped him.'

'But,' Mitch began, trying to process the event, which in its way was even stranger than the one preceding it, 'surely he's used to this kind of thing?'

'Let me guess,' Saph offered, 'he's only *heard* about orbs

and suchlike, *read* about them, seen badly shot shaky-cams on YouTube, never actually seen one for himself, with his own eyes?'

Heather shrugged. 'He always wanted to. You think…' She struggled with her thoughts for a second. 'You think he ran? It scared him?'

Saph shrugged. 'I've seen it happen. People see things – for real – and their minds refuse to process it. My guess is that he rationalized whatever those things were as ball lightning, decided the whole paranormal underground was a load of crap and went back to live his life. You probably won't hear from him again.'

'Jesus,' Heather hissed. 'Just like Doug.' She turned to the goth girl. 'That's exactly what happened to Doug!'

'And Doug was a posing wanker as well. Jimmy was only ever doing this to piss off his parents.'

Heather frowned deeply. 'He was, wasn't he?'

Suddenly she was off in her own world and wandered a few steps away.

'Can we get a ride with you guys?' the goth girl asked.

Saph smiled. 'Did you actually know Pan?'

'Yeah, I knew Pan,' she smirked again, 'I got him online.'

Great, thought Mitch. Another one.

'You're Servalan?' Saph suddenly demanded. 'The webmaster?'

'My real name's Cricket.'

'Servalan?' asked Mitch.

'Yeah, Server – LAN. Get it?'

He didn't.

'You know who Servalan was?' Mitch asked.

'Yeah,' she looked him straight in the eye. 'I like the old stuff.'

Mitch nodded, unsettled. He felt old and he was pretty sure she didn't like *him*. But it was not only that; she'd used the same expression as the American woman last night, when he'd mentioned Bowie.

I like the old stuff.

He frowned. It was a common enough expression, he supposed.

A brunette woman in immaculate makeup, dressed like a real

estate agent in a tight, sleeveless deep blue dress came up to them.

'Were they chasing you?' She spoke lightly but it was a deeply inquisitional tone. 'Why did that other car leave so quickly?'

'He got spooked,' Cricket replied. 'You don't see that every day.'

'The consensus seems to be that they were police helicopters.' The blue woman seemed unsure. 'Were they chasing you?'

'No,' Saph responded. 'We don't know what they were.'

The blue woman looked back at the others, clustered now on the front lawn of one house, then back to them. 'I know they weren't police helicopters.'

'No, they weren't,' Saph spoke definitively.

The blue woman ground her teeth.

'I think you'd better get going. Daphne called the police. I don't think they'll be here for a while; but if they turn up they won't be happy. They don't like nonsense calls.'

'I think she's right,' Cricket nodded. She turned to Saph. 'We can get a ride, right?'

'Looks like you have to.'

'Old Mrs Galloway says they were angels,' the blue woman muttered. 'But all I saw was light. Just – living, physical light.' She looked at Mitch. 'How does something physical move that fast?'

Mitch shrugged and mumbled through a dumb smile. 'Light moves at the speed of light I suppose.'

Saph smiled warmly at the blue woman. 'Some people can turn that question into their whole lives.'

The blue woman seemed none the wiser. 'Is that what you people have done?'

'I did for a long time. Now we're going to a party for a man who lost his life because of it.'

It was like a slap in the face to the blue woman. 'They kill people?'

'No. But the people who know what they are can make life difficult. Sometimes that kills people. When I realized that, I got out.'

The blue woman frowned. 'I'll have to talk to my brother,' she said as she turned away. 'He knows about these things.'

Mitch stared at Saph as though she were mad; but before he could say anything Heather walked back up to them.

'What did you say to that woman? She looks like she's seen a ghost.'

'They kill people?' Mitch asked.

'Let's go,' Saph spoke grimly. 'If past experience is anything to go by, there are at least three people in that baker's dozen over there who are going to turn very nasty very quickly.'

They collectively assessed the gathered suburbanites; Mitch spotted at least two pairs of eyes looking back that were angrier than he, or the orbs, had ever been. Together, they moved away.

There was silence in the car as they departed the street. Mitch received daggers again as they passed the gathered women, who began to separate almost as soon as Saph had started the car. The blue woman, however, was talking with excited, animated gestures to two others further down the street; they seemed the only three who'd been invigorated by the event and were still focused upon it, rather than the perceived trespass of strangers.

Mitch suddenly realized the neighborhood women had focused their anger on him and his companions to avoid addressing the reality of the strange orbs. There was a psychological term for it, he was sure… was it *transference*?

The blue estate agent smiled tightly, almost conspiratorially at Mitch as the car moved by. Finally they passed the teenaged boy, who didn't look up from his phone.

'It's not far from here,' Heather said. 'I'll direct you.'

They drove out of the suburban block and onto a busy arterial thoroughfare, where Saph merged with the stream of eastbound traffic.

'Keep going down this road until you get to the end,' Heather told her.

'I think I know where we're going,' Saph uttered.

Beside her, Mitch shrugged.

'Don't you?' Saph asked.

He didn't. He angled his head back to speak to Heather and Cricket.

'So was that your first time?'

'No,' Heather answered. 'We've both seem orbs before – but they've never come down like that.'

'I've seen more than that,' Cricket offered. 'I've seen ships, or craft, lots of different ones. My father was in the air force, that's how I got interested. They stopped chasing them in the 'eighties because it was costing too much – you know how much it costs every time they launch a jet fighter? And they never caught up with any of them, they'd just come back with nothing to show for it.'

'Are you serious? The air force knows about this?'

'About what?' Cricket shrugged. 'What were those things? Light, that's what I saw. Light bodies that move at the speed of light. How do you catch that? How do you even measure it? If you catch them on film, if they let you, most of the time they show up as tiny lights, like satellites – or a lens flare or something.'

'But you said you'd seen spaceships? Craft?'

'I've seen all sorts.'

Mitch couldn't believe he was going to ask this.

'Have you ever been abducted?'

Nobody laughed, as he'd expected.

'No,' Cricket answered. 'That's something different.'

'That one there,' Heather announced. 'The middle hotel.'

They had arrived at a beachfront suburb, a shorefront tourist destination for the wealthy that featured several high-end fashion stores, a surf shop and a gourmet pizza and burger bar. The road terminated at a roundabout before a wide esplanade and long wooden jetty. Saph clicked the car windows down and they were all hit with a burst of cold ocean air. Mitch took a deep breath and gazed out as Saph slowly circled the roundabout. The winter sea was gray and turbulent, though the incoming waves weren't particularly high. The chilly beach was populated by the usual suspects, brave surfers in wetsuits, a few people in sweaters walking their dogs and rugged-up fishermen casting off the jetty.

Then, the car was facing back up the main road and Saph pulled over.

The town was quiet.

Above the shop fronts, Mitch noticed that there were several high-rise apartment blocks down the southern esplanade, and three major hotels along the northern. The central hotel, the tallest and oldest of the three, had kept its historical eighteen-fifties veneer.

Saph pointed at it. 'The Vantage Hotel.'

'How did you know?' Heather asked.

'Far out,' Mitch exclaimed, gazing. 'When did they do that?'

Behind the five original balconies, the Vantage had been recently modernized with a tower of hotel rooms rising behind it, each with many balconied rooms. Although great pains had been taken to ensure the augmentation was architecturally aesthetic, there was no doubt that its function, to house as many ocean-view rooms as possible, had won over.

'Ten years ago,' Saph informed him. 'You haven't been here since?'

'Since what?'

'This is where we had graduation drinks. Don't you remember?'

So long ago.

'No,' Mitch said. 'I haven't been here since.'

Saph drove to a bunker-like underground car park entrance, above which they had easily spied the Vantage logo. The car descended and she found a park quite easily, although the hundred-plus capacity was near full. They got out and stretched their legs, looking about under the fluorescent lights for the exit. As they moved toward an elevator, Heather spoke to Saph.

'It's the top two floors, the penthouse and the rooms underneath. Your name should be on the guest list.'

'What about me?' Mitch asked.

'Tell them you're Jimmy. No-one will care.' She huffed. 'I still can't believe he just left like that!'

'What are you so upset for?' Cricket demanded. 'You weren't even long term. He was Transition Guy; you know that. There's no way a girl like you could end up with a guy like *that*.'

Heather turned to Mitch. 'You just pretend to be him, okay?'

The idea filled Mitch with dread; he hated crashing parties. He'd done it before, used a false name, back when he'd been an entertainment reporter. But he'd never been able to unwind once he'd gotten in; the fear of being caught was not one that Mitch had ever found arousing.

The lurch of the elevator made him realize that he had a knot in his guts and he felt irrationally uncomfortable being in a confined space with three attractive women. Nobody was talking.

'What should we expect?' Mitch asked, weakly clearing a frog in his throat as he did. He felt ashamed; the frog made him sound scared.

'It's just a party,' Heather smiled. 'You've been to a party before, right?'

'I thought it was a wake?'

'Pan didn't want a wake,' Cricket shrugged. 'He wanted a party.'

Saph snapped suddenly at Heather. 'You should know; Mitch was throwing the best parties in town while you were home watching *Spongebob*.'

'Raaaawl,' Cricket laughed.

Heather seemed stunned.

'Sorry,' Saph sighed. 'I guess going to a twentysomething party is a bit daunting.'

Heather groaned. 'Is that what you're so uptight about?'

Saph blanched.

'There's going to be all sorts. Pan's vibe attracted people across the board. Besides, we're all looking sharp.'

Mitch looked over his shoulder into the hotel mirror.

For a second he didn't recognize himself.

Immediately the women all did the same. Saph smoothed down the front of the black figure-hugging sweater she wore under the long tailored jacket, and flicked her long straight hair back over her shoulders. Heather ruffled her dreadlocks with a near-snarl that suggested ever so briefly that she didn't really like them, while Cricket simply eyed her black and charcoal ensemble up and down and smiled tightly, satisfied. Mitch hadn't realized until now that Heather was tall, almost Saph's height.

The elevator stopped and the doors opened.

Mitch allowed the ladies to exit first and they all followed Saph to the penthouse entrance. The thin, frosted glass doors were closed but they could see the movements of a crowded room, hear the music and chatter of a large gathering on the other side. Two bouncers, a male and a female security guard, barred their way. Beside them, a well-groomed woman in a formal hotel uniform stood behind a small card table covered in nametags. It was like a prom.

Heather stepped forward.

'Heather Everett.'

The woman smiled. 'Hi Heather, I'm Chasey.' She scanned her list. 'Heather Everett. Of course – please take a name tag if you like.'

'No thanks.'

She stood aside.

'Sapphire Edge.'

Chasey gave her a look, as though she had heard quite enough unusual names for one day. Saph met her gaze and she scanned the list. Once, then again. Then she blinked heavily. 'Oh yes, *Saph Edge*. On the special guest list.'

'Special guest?'

'Did they give you your key?'

'Key?'

'When you came through reception?'

'We came straight up. From the car park.'

'You did?'

'Just then.'

'The elevator doesn't do that without special code authorization.'

'Well, it did.'

Chasey paused. 'How strange.' Saph didn't know what to say, then Chasey spoke again under her breath. 'What a strange day it's been with you people.'

Saph wasn't going to let that go. 'We people?'

Chasey snapped back to her formal manner. 'Please, don't get me wrong. It's just that some groups seem to…'

'Seem to what?' Cricket asked.

'Seem to…' Chasey's shoulders sagged slightly. It was as though she were in it now and might as well take it to the end. 'Some groups just seem to bring an… *energy* with them. Things behave oddly, like the elevators. This morning the booking system went haywire, this afternoon half the televisions in the suites aren't working properly; and now the wireless broadband is acting up… room keys aren't working, or the air conditioning's not right…'

Cricket frowned. 'And this all started today?'

'As soon as guests from your party began to arrive. And it will stop as soon as you're all gone. I've seen it before. As I said, some groups simply bring an odd energy with them.'

The four of them just stared at her.

'Surely, as a paranormal study group, you of all people would understand that? I've been booking groups into this hotel for a decade; I know it happens. There are patterns. Some people just have an energy that interferes with electronics. When you gather a bunch of them together in a hotel, things happen. It's part of the trade.'

Cricket seemed intensely interested. 'Would you meet me for a coffee tomorrow and talk about this on the record for my podcast?'

'Your podcast?'

'You don't have to use your real name. I have an audience of three hundred thousand people worldwide. They'd love to hear your stories.'

'Well, I… three hundred?'

'That we know of. Just a chat, we record it, bang it goes up. Easy.'

'Well, if you think they'd be interested…'

Cricket extended her hand. 'Cricket Wilde.'

Chasey accepted and shook.

Finally, Mitch stepped forward.

'Mitchell Pyne.'

He heard Heather groan; he'd forgotten to use the fake name.

Pathetically, he tried to correct himself. 'Sorry, that's – '

'You'll be needing to get your key from reception, as will Mister Pyne.'

'I will?'

Chasey grinned. 'Provided the elevator decides to take you there, of course.'

Mitch smiled. 'Of course.'

'Enjoy your evening.'

Mitch nodded to himself, chuffed. Someone had remembered him; someone had bothered to check out who Pan's friends really were. He sighed in relief. Maybe he could relax here, seeing as he'd been officially designated as 'belonging'.

They parted the sliding frosted-glass doors. The music was much louder as they entered the party, where there were perhaps a hundred people gathered across the spacious suite. Mitch didn't recognize any of them.

He stood as one does at the entrance to a party, scanning.

'So Heather,' Mitch asked over the music, 'any relation?'

'Everyone asks that.'

'And?'

'He's my uncle.'

'Bo Everett is your *uncle*?'

'Uncle Bo, yeah.'

'Do you know what relationship he had with Pan?'

'They were friends.'

Saph chimed in. 'And what about you? What was your relationship with Pan?'

Heather smiled. 'I hooked him up with my uncle. But other than that, the same as you.'

'The same as me?'

'Yeah. We were lovers.'

Saph went pale; Mitch had never actually seen that before, someone actually going pale.

This was going to be a hell of a night.

CHAPTER FOURTEEN

'How long?' Saph demanded.

'Oh, ages after you two split up,' Heather shrugged. 'At least a month after that.'

'*And how long after that?*'

'Eighteen months. Whenever he was in town. But he was spending way too much time in the jungle. Long distance stuff never works. We split up six months ago. I think he started seeing one of his fellow researchers. Must get lonely down there, just the few of them. Things happen. If it's the one I'm thinking, she was… well, she was his type.'

The lights flickered all across the penthouse. The crowd made spooky noises and laughed.

Heather nodded into the distance. 'There's Mags. I'll catch you guys later.'

With that, she walked off into the crowd.

'I can't see anyone I know,' Cricket shrugged. 'You guys wanna head to the bar?'

'Yes,' Mitch and Saph said simultaneously.

The crowd was large but easily negotiable, and Mitch made uneasy eye contact with several people as they crossed the room. It seemed a fairly ordinary cross-section, perhaps a larger percentage than usual of counter-culture types.

Then again, was that so unusual?

Mitch hadn't been to a proper party in years.

How would he know what was usual?

He caught the edge of a few conversations.

'*…can't believe they had him killed…*'

Mitch gulped. Really?

'*…who's going to take over the movement now? They've killed it stone dead…*'

'*No, you're forgetting, there's someone else, we just have to…*'

He missed the rest.

Cricket reached the bar first. Mitch looked around from his new perspective. There were people crying, he saw now; people distraught. A few to his left, another, alone, to his right, and more across the other side of the room.

Two girls walked away from the bar.

They, too, were weeping.

'Who's going to save us now?' asked one girl.

He didn't hear the response; he was fully creeped out.

Pan: the Messiah?

He couldn't believe it.

Cricket turned to him. 'Open bar. Three beers?'

'Fine,' Saph answered. In her bag, her phone rang and she fished it out. Assessing the screen, she passed it to Mitch.

'Maybe you should take this?'

'Why?'

'It's the same number as the one on the card – the one Everett's goon gave you.'

Mitch gulped. 'I don't know…'

Saph, clearly in a foul mood, answered the call.

'Yes?' She stared Mitch right in the eyes as she held the phone to her ear. 'Yes Mister Everett. He's standing right here. We thought it might be you.'

Mitch's eyes bulged. Saph passed the phone to him. He gulped but accepted.

'Mitch Pyne,' he uttered weakly.

'I understand you've met my niece Mister Pyne.'

It was a very strong, very American voice.

'Yes. Although she only just told us a minute ago.'

'Well, when you're ready to meet with me, you tell her.'

'Why do you want to meet with me?'

'Well now, Mister Pyne. That would spoil things, wouldn't it?

I understand you're pretty big on spoiler alerts. Do you want a spoiler now Mister Pyne? Or would you rather have our story play out as it's meant to?'

'Does that mean you don't want to tell me over the phone?'

'Why don't you just come and talk to me when you're ready Mister Pyne?'

'Through Heather.'

'Heather knows what she's doing. You can trust that anything she tells you is alright by me.'

'Okay.'

'Don't leave it too long now Mister Pyne.'

'I won't.'

The call ended.

Cricket was handing him a bottle of premium lager. He accepted it, gave the phone back to Saph, and swigged.

'Some people wait their whole lives for that call,' Cricket grinned.

'I don't know what he wants with me.'

'Information,' Saph answered. 'That's all people like that ever want.'

'You have currency,' Cricket shrugged. 'You should ask him for something.'

'Like what?'

'What do you want?'

'I want to get drunk, have a cigarette and get laid.'

Saph grimaced. 'Jesus, Mitch.'

'Okay. So, I want to stop drinking, stop smoking and get a girlfriend. But none of those things are going to happen here tonight are they?'

'I think she meant, big picture. Like – something he could give you in return for the information he wants. Something a man like Everett could give you that nobody else could.'

'What, like money?'

'Why not?' Saph shrugged. 'You're broke.'

'How do you know?'

'I've seen you broke before Mitch. This is what it looks like.'

'Wow.' Cricket swigged her beer. 'How long have you two known each other? The way you talk!'

They couldn't help laughing as the music lowered for a second, before another track started. It was a Mistress song.

'Wow,' Mitch guffawed. 'Third time today!'

'What's that?' Cricket asked.

'Mistress, this is the third time today I've heard one of her songs!'

Cricket smiled, then listened for a second. 'It's funny,' she stated. 'How they always sound so fresh, her songs, don't you think?'

Mitch looked at her, curious. 'That's just what I was thinking this afternoon.'

'Yeah,' Cricket nodded. 'I only just realized that! It just – came to me!'

Mitch smiled at her; Cricket smiled back and shrugged.

'So do you guys know anyone?'

Saph nodded. 'A few faces. None I want to talk to.'

Mitch scanned. He was pretty sure he wouldn't –

Through the crowd Mitch saw something that sent a chill down his spine. Standing across the room was a man; at least he assumed it was a man, who had the face of a lizard.

Mitch blinked sharply, then again; the man was still a lizard.

He was talking to a couple of people who didn't seem to notice.

The lizard man had huge black eyes, dark olive scaly skin and clawed reptilian hands extending from the cuffs of his black suit. In one scaled hand he held a long-stemmed glass of champagne.

'I think I'm hal…'

The reptilian turned to look at him; as he did, his face morphed and changed into that of a middle-aged man. It was a hard face with narrow eyes that bored into him, as though somehow sensing that his disguise had been breached. The reptilian man excused himself from his conversation, turned away and walked away through the crowd. Mitch couldn't be sure but he thought he'd gone into another section of the penthouse, behind a pillar support. But he might as well have vanished into another dimension.

'Are you okay?' Saph asked.

'Did you see…?'

'That guy?' she asked. 'He turned and looked at you for no reason, like you were his mother's killer out on parole.'

'I actually do know that guy,' Cricket offered. 'I've never been introduced formally but he was always having meetings with Pan, always asking Pan to come work for him. Silly money. Wanted to buy the website, fund the whole thing. Pan wouldn't have a bar of it.'

Saph frowned. 'What's he doing here then?'

'Pan never accepted the offer, but they were always talking. I guess they were friends, if you can call it that. He was more like a kind of business stalker. I think Pan kept the relationship going in case things ever soured with Everett.'

'So he's big money?'

'Don Eissley? Big money, yeah. I think he's been tapped to run Oliver Hines' new movie studio. Olivera Pictures or something. You know how these big execs go from business to business. Eissley's in chemicals: additives, sweeteners – high fructose corn syrup and aspartame and all that shit. Guess we'll be seeing a lot of product placement and cross-promotion for Eissley's diet drinks in Hines' new movies.'

'You believe all that stuff about aspartame?'

'I believe it tastes like poison; whether it is or not, who knows? It's definitely addictive for some people. Pan always suspected Eissley wanted to use his influence with his podcast to quash all the bad press the Big Pharma's are always getting.'

'Big Pharma? Is that his company?'

Saph smiled, somewhat condescendingly. 'Big Pharma's counter-culture shorthand for the pharmaceutical industry, and the clout their lobbies have in world governments.'

'Oh.'

Cricket continued. 'I mean; Pan had a worldwide audience.'

'Three hundred thousand.'

'That's just my podcast. Pan's website had ten times the traffic.'

'You do your own?'

'Pan and I didn't always agree. But he supported me when I said I wanted to cover some stuff he didn't.'

'Like what?'

'Like ghosts, the occult. Hauntings and stuff. Alien abductions; I like the dark stuff. Pan didn't like that, at least, not in the end. He said it was too low-end. Too *lower astral.* That it was more about scaring people than enlightening them.'

'And you don't agree?'

'I think if it's out there, and people are seeing it, then it should be addressed. But I knew what he meant.'

Mitch scanned the room again.

Things seemed wrong.

It was as though as soon as he'd noticed the reptilian disappear behind the pillar...

'Excuse me a second.'

Mitch stepped away from the bar and walked a few steps into the room so he could see what lay beyond the pillar. There was another section behind it; a raised dining section that was filled with people standing around a long table, lined with water jugs and trays of finger foods.

The man wasn't there.

Mitch stepped back and assessed the pillar again.

That was weird.

From where he'd been standing, Mitch should have seen Eissley walk past the pillar, *before* ascending the stairs. As he recalled it, Eissley had just – vanished, like he'd walked behind something. But there was nothing there for him to have walked behind...

'That's not possible,' he uttered.

He kept looking around the room. Something really wasn't

right. He could see patches of space that seemed askew. As though there were slits, here and there, where space didn't join up properly. It was like an Escher illustration. The spacious penthouse, with its open planned areas, divided by pillars and railings and short stairways, didn't fit together properly.

And nobody but him seemed to notice.

Except – again, there were people looking at him.

A very tall, pale blonde couple, who stood at the edge of a large chatting group across the room, were both staring at him. As he stared back, Mitch had the oddest sensation. He thought for a second that he felt them, in his mind. They kept staring at him, blank yet somehow expectant.

Mitch focused his thoughts.

Can you hear me?

Strangely, he felt another odd sensation, as though someone was breathing down his neck. Maybe this Nordic-looking couple hadn't heard him project a concentrated thought across the room but someone else had!

The Nordics kept staring at him.

If you can hear me, do something.

He had no idea why he thought they could; the idea had just popped into his mind the minute he'd made eye contact with them, as though it was quite natural, the normal thing to do when you ran across…

An unsettling thought hit him.

He ignored it.

He repeated. *If you can hear me…*

Simultaneously, the pair angled their heads to the side slightly, like two domestic animals transfixed by the same insect.

You can hear me?

Maintaining eye contact, they angled their heads slightly more.

Can you reply?

He did not hear their response as words exactly, more as part of his own thoughts, but more pronounced than usual.

Something that was not part of his own series of everyday loops, observations, recognitions, mantras and background chatter.

We do not know you.

This was real. This was real and he knew it.

Who are you? he asked.

They straightened their heads and looked at him squarely once more.

We do not know you.

He thought a second.

Are you hiding? Can other people see you? Why just me?

We don't know. We do not know you.

Are you from another dimension? Is that what I'm seeing?

Just as suddenly as they'd recognized him, they ignored him. Turning away, they rejoined their circle and once more focused their attention on the conversation there. As they did, Mitch was stuck by another unusual feeling. To keep watching them, or to even approach them, would have been making the most awful faux pas imaginable. Somehow, he had stumbled upon yet more alien imposters at Pan's party…

Holy crap.

Had he really just thought that?

Aliens?

Was he now seeing… *aliens?*

Aliens at Pan's wake?

'They hate that,' a man spoke from behind him.

Saph and Cricket seemed equally startled by the man's approach. Mitch didn't know what they'd been thinking as he'd looked around the room, then stared at the Nordic couple but clearly they'd not suspected that anything too unusual was afoot.

Mitch turned to the man.

'They hate being called out. It offends their sense of order. We're like children to them; what you did was precocious. They only like us when we're being cute; unless of course they speak to us on their own terms, then they're fine.'

'Who – ?'

'Hello Saph darling.' The man smiled. 'Just as gorgeous.'

Saph narrowed her eyes. 'Do I – ?'

The man was tall and lean, with short dark hair and a white goatee beard. He was perhaps mid-forties, dressed in a black suit with a black silk shirt and a thin grey tie.

'Imagine me fifteen years younger, with more of a bushranger look, and much, much heavier around the waistline.'

Mitch and Saph exchanged looks. They hadn't a clue.

'*Hell is empty!*' the man suddenly bellowed, spreading his arms. '*And all the devils are here!*'

This garnered them quite a lot of attention but only briefly.

'That's from *The Tempest*,' Saph frowned. 'That's the play we did in third year – oh my God!'

Saph launched forward and gave the thin theatrical man a huge hug.

'Vance! Vance McLeod!'

'Vance?'

Saph let him go and Mitch shook his hand.

'The very same!'

'Okay,' Cricket sighed. 'Who the hell is he?'

'He's the Dean of Drama!' Saph exclaimed. 'From our university!'

'I can't believe it!' Mitch's jaw dropped. 'You look terrific!'

Back then Vance had been enormous and had sported a full, unkempt beard.

'Thank you my good man, thank you.'

'What are you doing here?'

'Oh, Pan and I maintained contact. It was me who started all this. I was the one who first introduced him to ayahuasca…' Vance turned to Mitch with a knowing look, almost a wink and a nod. '*As well you might know.*'

Mitch didn't. 'Aya - what?' Mitch asked.

'Ayahuasca. The South American shaman's drug of choice. Our Lady of the Vine; dimethyltryptamine!'

'Die - ?'

Vance stared at him, puzzled. 'Not DMT? Then, some other variety of pineal modification? Perhaps so; you seem to be quite lucid and yet… you can see things that others cannot.'

'Mitch, what's he talking about?'

Mitch didn't answer.

Vance frowned at him, leaning down to stare into his eyes.

'If you are truly not making the connection, then I have some news for you. If you can see and speak telepathically to Pleiadeans, if you can percieve the spacial dimensions beyond our three, and you are not currently riding the wave of some powerful pineal-altering hallucinagen, then you my dear boy have been spiked, spiked hard, and I suspect, spiked for good.'

Mitch was amazed – and a fear began to grow within him.

'Spiked?' Saph was aghast. 'By who?'

'Who can say, dear girl? But I can tell you this; your consciousness has had an upgrade. You are a walking talking searchlight in a cave of sleeping monsters.'

'Monsters?'

Mitch thought immediately of the lizard man he'd seen.

'That's right. And if you don't find some way of switching yourself off, one of those monsters is going to do it for you – premanently, and forever!'

CHAPTER FIFTEEN

'You still smoke, I take it?'

Mitch nodded.

'Then come with me; hardly anyone does any more, and *they* all hate it. It will be the safest place to talk.'

'*They?*'

'Of course dear boy. *They.*'

Mitch followed Vance across the room, trailed by Saph and Cricket. Saph gave her a look, as though she might not actually have the right to be in on this conversation.

'Don't think I'm going to miss this, do you? Not after this afternoon.'

They exited the penthouse onto the southern-facing balcony, which was wide enough to afford a view of both the sunset in the west, and the ocean in the east, without being too badly obscured by the hotel itself.

The winter sun was setting behind a thick bank of brilliant apricot and bruised purple ocean clouds, rippled in layers across the horizon like marble, right over the top of the hotel and across the ocean.

Vance led them to the eastern corner, away from the sunset where the majority of people were gathered. Mitch lit a cigarette, offered one to Vance, then the women. Cricket accepted.

From below, the sound of the increasingly rough waves, crashing in pulses, filled the balcony and obscured the music from inside.

'So you've taken no drugs?'

'No.'

'None at all?'

He indicated the beer in his hand. 'It's my first drink for the day. But I don't understand – you were the other presence, right? You could hear me talking to that Nordic couple.'

'Nordics?' Cricket asked. 'You mean like, alien Nordics?'

'They're Pleiadeans. Although they're not from the Pleiades cluster, not any more, they're… look, it's a long story. Very, very few people can tell the difference between them and humans. Usually it's someone of a highly refined mentality, or people whom for whatever reason they want to be seen by. In my case, it's something I was born with. In your case, it's clearly none of the above. So why is it that you can see them? And what are these dimensional anomalies you're seeing?'

With that, Mitch told him everything, from Pan's ghost right up to their meeting.

When Mitch had finished giving as short a version of his story as he possibly could, Vance nodded.

'I see. That's very interesting.'

'What does it mean? What's happening to me?'

'I don't know, not exactly. But if you have the ability to see these entities, past their disguises, that places you in – well, perhaps not grave danger, but danger nonetheless.'

'Why?'

'Because they only want to be seen by those they choose to see them. These beings, these races, have been with us for hundreds of years, some of them thousands, perhaps even longer. There are rules to this sort of thing. Rules of nature, physics, politics and etiquette; a serious breach of which you just made in there. There are even rules for what we would call spirituality. It's like that ridiculous *Star Trek* business with its Prime Directive – these matters are extremely delicate.'

'How the hell do you know all this?'

'Oh, dear boy, the information is out there for anyone to read, particularly since the birth of the internet. Even Carl Sagan speculated on the possibilities that we are already being visited, and watched, although his rationality would never allow him to fully believe it.'

'I'm not sure I believe it.'

'Belief makes no difference, dear boy. Something either is or it isn't. Personally, I'm as interested in this as other people are interested in music or sports or cinema or Lord help them even politics. And I did enjoy your magazine by the way, terrible pity about all that. I would have sent you a condolence email but nobody knew your address.'

'Thank you,' Mitch responded bluntly.

'But what I don't understand is *how*. How has this happened to you?'

'Listen, the only thing you've said that really makes sense to me is that someone's drugged me. That's the obvious explanation. It's the only rational –'

'Rational, eh? Very well, how's this then? Even if you have been drugged, and I'm sure you have been, even if that is the only explanation, there are people who do not see that as the only rational explanation. They will act as though what I've said is true. Now, from their rational point of view, given the facts they have at hand, you are a walking decipher code for who is and who isn't; and who is what and who is not. Do you follow? There are people in this world who will now view you as both an extremely valuable commodity *and* as a huge security risk.'

'I can't believe all this, surely? I mean, tomorrow the drug will wear off and I'll be back to –'

'Tomorrow? I wouldn't say this drug you've taken shows any signs of wearing off, would you? Ayahuasca lasts anywhere from thirty minutes to eight hours, depending on the dosage and the individual – although the ramifications of the realizations, the epiphanies people gain from it last a lifetime. Other similar drugs, like psilocybin, the sacred mushroom, typically last as long; but none of them are particularly known for endowing genuine mental *gifts* on people. At least, not gifts that permanently alter perception.'

'I don't know anything about that…'

'But you, my dear boy, have been experiencing extra-dimensional visions since your dream last night – let's say a good sixteen to eighteen hours? On top of that, you are still able to easily navigate and function normally within the ordinary world, your so-called solar download notwithstanding.'

'So what was that?' Saph asked. 'What happened to him then?'

Vance nodded thoughtfully.

'Let me see. Let me put it this way. You must think of the universe as a giant machine, designed for the propagation of DNA. The function of DNA is to create vessels through which consciousness can perceive the universe; in our little corner of the cosmos, the highest form of evolution, at least presently, is designed to perceive three dimensions of space and one dimension of time. That is our lot. But DNA has evolved other vessels, on other planets, in other parts of the galaxy, who perceive differently to us. They understand the balance of nature better, or at least *differently* than we do, and they come here to secretly observe us, and to ensure that we do not upset that balance.'

'Are you serious?' Mitch guffawed.

Vance ignored the interruption and proceeded.

'Their aim, as I understand it, is to see whether or not we might begin to understand and perceive reality as they do, or at least on a level of our own that corresponds to their own perceptions. Some of them are benign, like teachers, while others are exploitative, like corporations. Others still are somewhere in between: pure science, pure research. Some just come for fun even. But the point is that our level of consciousness must evolve out of the three to one paradigm it's currently in as a natural consequence of evolution. It cannot be forced. If the existence of those other races were to be revealed, along with their *secrets*, humanity might jump the queue, so to speak.'

'Secrets?'

'Technological, biological, astronomical…'

'But, so what?' Cricket shrugged. 'If we do, we do. We evolve.

It's nature. I mean, if we evolve as a consequence of absorbing the knowledge of a superior biological force, or by reacting to its presence, then that's still evolution, isn't it? Isn't that what evolution is, in a way?'

'Indeed, you may be right; but it may not be in the vested interests of some of those fourth party aliens for us to do so. Look, this is going to get very complicated very quickly and it is a long and detailed story; the upshot is that there are some who like us the way we are for their own reasons.'

'Reasons?' Saph interjected. 'What reasons?'

'I'm afraid I don't know, I'm only going by what I've read. Occasionally I see one, and they see me; but whenever that occurs I'm snubbed like poor Mitch in there.'

'They snubbed you?' Cricket asked, stunned.

'I think so,' Mitch shrugged. 'They certainly didn't seem keen on me.'

'But still,' Vance sighed, 'there seem also to be those who like us the way we are because they think it's for our own good. I think those Pleiadeans in there are typical of that. Likewise, there are some who seem to think we *should* evolve and are nudging us that way, but for their own reasons. Others believe we should evolve because we're ready, and for our own good; but my readings suggest that they are few and far between. Surely, you all know this already?'

'How would I?' Mitch frowned.

'Well, this is all in Pan's research. On his podcasts, in his essays and YouTube documentaries.'

Vance assessed them all.

'I guess I know some of it,' Cricket confessed. 'I'm more of a ghost hunter really.'

Saph sighed. 'I have heard all this before. Of course I have. But I left this world behind years ago.'

Vance seemed disappointed. 'I see. And you, Mitchell?'

Mitch smiled apologetically. 'It's all new to me. Sorry, Vance.'

Vance took a long drag of his cigarette and exhaled slowly.

'The main thing to understand...' Vance resumed slowly, thoughtfully. '...is that none of these beings are any better or worse than us, from any rational perspective. They are simply *differently evolved*. They are all part of the machine that exists to spread DNA as a vehicle for consciousness; cosmic, perhaps universal consciousness.'

Mitch frowned. 'You sound like you're saying that DNA is a vehicle for...'

'You didn't answer my question,' Saph snapped.

'I was getting to it.' Vance took another heavy drag, then exhaled a plume high into the cold night air, waving the cigarette like a magician's wand. 'Part of the machine is the solar system. The sun is the hub, the information center. When it senses that an individual consciousness is evolving, it will send information to the consciousness to help it understand what it's going through, so as to evolve more efficiently. Essentially, it's no different to understanding that the sun means warmth, that the sun feeds growth, that the sun is what the sun is. Everything is information; this is just more information, another level of it.'

Mitch shook his head. 'Look, I can't get a grip on this...'

'Can't you? You said that young man you were with saw one group of orbs this afternoon; and despite all the reading and preparation he'd done in readiness of seeing something extra-dimensional, he still turned tail and fled, bee-lined back to his life prior to all this – to a family barbeque? To the safety of the family, the hive. And yet you Mitch have not. You have not simply blundered forward but actively pursued more involvement by coming here tonight. At any time you could have returned home. Yet you did not.'

Mitch was silent.

Cricket lit another cigarette.

'Mitch,' Saph spoke softly. 'I know that what he's saying sounds crazy – but Pan believed all this.'

'But... the sun?' Mitch pressed. 'The sun is an *intelligence*?'

Vance sighed. 'Not as you and I can comprehend it. That's the crux of the matter. Consciousness exists in many different forms, and it will move to protect itself. If you are a new kind of vessel, at this stage of conscious evolution, your life will begin to offer you choices. There will be synchronicities; signs for you to follow. This is what the machine does. Think of it as an intelligence test the universe is giving you to see whether you are a path of evolution worth following. You must survive, you must show the universe that you are worthy of existing. And it will let you, if you let yourself. There should be several paths open to you; you must chose the one that leads to safety. Is there somewhere you can go? Somewhere you can be safe from those who would prey upon you?'

'But who would prey upon me?' Mitch protested. 'I haven't done anything!'

Several of the doors leading out to the balcony opened simultaneously. There were raised voices from within, a mix of protest, indignation and fear. Two pairs of men emerged from either side, in black suits, buzz-cuts and sunglasses. They were all well over six feet tall, wide shouldered and highly intimidating. From their corner of the balcony, they watched as the men turned, virtually as one, and eyeballed their group.

'Holy fuck,' muttered Cricket.

'And so it begins,' said Vance.

CHAPTER SIXTEEN

Mitch's first instinct was to freeze.

Fight or flight, he realized.

Saph grabbed his arm; this didn't help. It anchored him. The weakness of family, he thought. The impulse of the family, to cling and be protected. Family pinned you down when morals and ethics failed, neutralized flight. You would be forced by the female to protect her. He saw Vance stand straight, firm. He saw Cricket clench her fists. The flipside, Mitch realized, strength of the group. One need not fight alone. A middle-aged man and a girl, though. No match for these goons.

And flight – really?

In his condition he'd last a block before stitching up and vomiting his lunch. And given he'd had no lunch, and half a beer on an empty stomach, it would be more like half a block before dry retching.

He was pathetic.

Suddenly he heard himself saying something.

'We need to find Heather.'

Nobody responded as the men came forward and blocked their exit. The people watching the sunset muttered behind them, alarmed, but none of them moved to help.

'Can we help you?' Vance asked calmly.

'We're investigating a disturbance,' the first man said. He spoke deeply, slowly and clearly. 'We need to ask you some questions.'

Mitch was amazed at the man's tone. It made him feel immediately as though he had done something wrong. He was guilty; and he was in danger of being punished. Although he could not put his finger on exactly what he had done. Suddenly things came rushing to the front of his mind; dodgy items he'd claimed on tax, pirated movies he'd downloaded, ignored parking tickets, illegal drugs he'd bought, and Jesus yeah, that car he and Pan had 'borrowed' on a lost weekend twenty years ago, fingerprints all over it – he'd never quite managed to shed the feeling that some day that would catch up with him. And that time, smashed out of his mind, when he'd ordered a hooker, and the next day a cop car had been parked, all day, at the end of the street – like these men *knew all that*.

'We'll help in any way we can,' Vance responded smoothly.

Mitch started to sweat. Could they see that? Of course they could, it was coming out in beads all over his beetroot red face! What would they think? He was acting guilty – because he *was guilty*. How was Vance remaining so calm?

'You didn't see anything,' the man said.

Was it a question or a statement?

The man's tone – it was such that one could project anything onto it.

'Anything,' the man added.

Again, was it a question or a statement?

'No,' Cricket croaked. 'We didn't see anything.'

'You didn't talk to anyone.'

Again – it might have been a question, might have been a statement.

'No,' Cricket continued. 'We didn't talk to anyone.'

The men stood there. Moving only his neck, one man turned and looked at the sunset, then turned back. When his gaze returned, Mitch realized; he could have been looking at any of them. Looking straight at him, or at Vance, or Saph, or Cricket. It was impossible to tell. The sunglasses were impenetrable. Best to assume they were all looking directly at him.

'The human body can only survive a fall from three floors,' the man stated. 'This penthouse is eleven floors high.'

What the hell did that mean?

'And to survive,' the second of the men added, 'would not be pleasant.'

'Best to stay on the ground,' the first man continued. 'Best to stay with both feet planted. There's nothing to see – above the ground. Nothing you would ever talk about.'

'Nothing of interest,' the second said, 'nothing to tell.'

'Nothing to tell anyone.'

Mitch gulped. 'No.'

The first man seemed to take offense, just a small rearing back of his head.

'No?' he asked.

Mitch stammered. 'I – I mean, yes. Yes. You're right. There's nothing.'

'Nothing,' the first man nodded. 'You're sure of that?'

'I'm sure,' Mitch rasped, his throat suddenly dry, 'there's nothing.'

'Absolutely nothing.'

'Absolutely.'

The first man looked at the second, who nodded almost imperceptibly. Then he looked back to Mitch.

'We appreciate your cooperation. Have a nice night.'

Then he pointed to the bottle in Mitch's hand.

'Drink aware,' he said. 'Don't drink and drive.'

Mitch spoke before he realized he was speaking. It was as though he were completing a litany, a movie cliché from one of his D-Grade assignments, speaking a line of badly scripted, predictable dialogue before the actor did.

'We don't want any accidents,' he said.

Instantly, the temperature on the balcony seemed to drop. All conversation around them stopped. If there had been any question before, it was now as clear to Mitch as anything he'd ever known that behind the sunglasses, the man's eyes were boring into him like diamond tipped drills.

The stare seemed to last forever. Mitch believed for a second, perhaps for a minute, that the stare, the moment, would never end. That this was it, he was dead and this was hell; this feeling of total and unrelenting intimidation.

'There are no accidents,' the man spoke finally. 'Only careless choices.'

He held the stare another few seconds, then as one they turned and departed.

Only when the balcony doors had closed behind them did Mitch let out a long breath. He heard Saph do likewise, then some mild chatter began around them on the balcony once more.

'Well,' Vance uttered. 'You seem to have gained someone's attention.'

Mitch gulped, his throat like sandpaper, and raised his beer to his lips. Despite the chill weather the lager was warm and flat, killed by the heat of his sweaty grip. He drank deeply anyway and finished the bottle.

A man separated from the crowd who had been watching the sunset and approached them. He wore a plain white shirt and blue jeans and seemed excited, freaked out. His wide eyes were bloodshot, stoned, but his speech was quick and clear.

'Man, what did you do?' he asked Mitch keenly. 'What did they say to you?'

Mitch couldn't quite remember. It all seemed dark and hazy.

'You got a visit from The Men, man,' the stoner added, amazed. 'You must have seen something!'

'No, I…' Mitch stammered. 'I didn't see anything.'

'Yeah,' the stoner nodded, smiling. 'I get it man. No sweat. You didn't see nothin'. Yeah, that's cool, that's cool.' He slapped Mitch softly on the shoulder. 'Just make sure when you call it in on the podcast you use a prepaid, untraceable. Make sure you toss it, man.'

The stoner nodded to make sure Mitch understood, which he didn't, then wandered back to his group.

'The Men?' Saph asked. 'Were they *The Men in Black*?'

Vance sighed. 'They were indeed. Is it any wonder nobody shares their experiences?'

'They're not like they are in the movies!' Cricket cried.

'Of course not,' Vance smiled at Mitch. 'You'll find that very little in their world actually is.'

'They made me feel…' Mitch searched. 'Guilty…?'

'That's exactly their purpose,' Vance scowled. 'Fear and submission. You'll be pleased to know that that's mostly all they do. They're bound by certain regulations; they cannot truly harm us. Not for just *seeing*. Their main purpose is to be archetypically intimidating. Very effective wouldn't you say?'

Nobody disagreed.

'Listen,' Mitch grumbled. 'I need another drink. What's going to happen if I go back to the bar? What if I see something else?'

'I suggest you both check in, and stay in your rooms until you can think of somewhere safer. His line about driving might have been intimidation, but wherever you go from now on I would assume you're being followed. You are now officially a person of interest.'

'Why go to our rooms?'

'Because at least there you can think, it's what they'll expect you to do – run somewhere and hide. At least if you do so here, they'll believe you to be so scared that you ran to your first available bolt hole and assumed the embryo position. But you're not going to do that, are you Mitch? You're not going to simply curl up into a ball?'

'No,' Mitch frowned. 'If anything they've made me madder.'

'But the important thing is this; at the moment they believe you to have been an anomaly. You just had a moment, a glitch, and you saw them. The men arrived so quickly because at a gathering such as this they will have been poised somewhere in the hotel for just such an occurrence. You must do nothing further to draw attention to yourselves, or the consequences may be dire.'

'How so?'

'I've no idea. I say *may be* dire. I've never met anyone like you, so who can say how they'll respond? Remember, the *others* are essentially people, like us. They're simply differently evolved. But as I said, life has an uncanny ability to move to protect itself against threat – wherever it's emerged from.'

Mitch told Vance that he had left his mobile at home, so the thespian swapped numbers with Saph instead as they all exchanged hasty goodbyes with him. Mitch and Saph walked directly to the elevator, not making eye contact with anyone, although Mitch sensed that their exit was for its brief duration the center of the room's collective attention.

It was only when the elevator arrived, and Mitch entered, that he realized they had been followed by Cricket. She looked at him, then Saph, and shrugged. He didn't mind but Saph seemed a little put out. Nevertheless, it seemed that the sour but attractive little goth chick was along for the ride, at least for now.

They disembarked at the lobby and went quietly across the plush but bland surroundings to the main desk, where the attendants were more than pleased to hand over swipe keys for two opposing rooms on the tenth floor. The hotel was busy, Mitch thought, for a beachside destination in mid-winter, but he supposed that, like Pan's wake upstairs, business of all kinds continued all months of the year in what was essentially a conference center. They made their way back through the lobby and up to the tenth floor without speaking to anyone, avoiding eye contact and, as far as they could tell, without being overtly observed.

The tenth floor was eerily noiseless and when Mitch checked his watch he realized that it was nearing seven o'clock in the evening; probably everyone was out to dinner at any of the many beachside cafes along the promenade.

His room was halfway down a tight, low corridor off to the left of the elevator exit, with Saph's door opposite his; rooms 1010 and 1011. They were definitely now in the newer section of the hotel; no attempt had been made here to mimic the historical facade.

Mitch watched as Saph swiped her key, turned the handle and entered. He watched her hold the door open and slot the key into the security cradle, then saw the lights come on. Before he opened his own room, he paused.

Under the door was another of the white A-4 envelopes.

'What's that?' Cricket asked.

Saph turned from the doorway and saw the envelope.

'Let's see,' Mitch shrugged.

They followed Saph into her room and found themselves in a suite that was essentially like any other hotel room, as bland and inoffensive as any hotel in existence, albeit spacious and with a very large and very clean bathroom. The décor was modern, with blends of steel blue, gray and cream. The suite had two bedrooms, which Mitch immediately checked. He did so with a confidence that came from being almost totally sure that there would be nobody waiting inside.

When they'd made sure that they were alone, Saph filled the kettle while Mitch and Cricket sat in the two single chairs of the three-piece lounge suite that faced the huge plasma screen.

Mitch sighed as he opened the envelope. '*Think*, Vance said. Think about what? I mean, Vance was barking mad when he was teaching us drama, it doesn't look like the passing years have exactly made him any less eccentric does it?'

'It's no surprise I suppose,' Saph shrugged. 'He definitely used to talk about some weird stuff; I know he genuinely thought the muses were real. And his stories about haunted theaters – remember them?'

'I could never sleep after a session of him going on like that,' Mitch smiled at Cricket. 'Perhaps you should interview him as well?'

Cricket grinned weakly back at him. Mitch suspected this was all becoming a bit much for her.

'You okay?' he asked. 'You can go if you like – you don't have to get yourself tangled up in all this.'

'Are you kidding?' Cricket seemed deadly serious. 'This is a hell of a story. I'm not leaving you guys 'til we get to the end. I mean, I've seen some stuff, don't get me wrong. That's not the first time I've seen the Men – they came to my door after I saw some other stuff, aliens and stuff in the forest when I was out camping. And the things Vance was telling you – it's not my area but I've heard Pan's podcasts; that's the sort of material I hear every day. And I know enough about it all to know that you are the mother load – you're the Rosetta Stone that can translate what it all means, put it all in one context and give it meaning – you know?'

Mitch just stared at her.

He was?

When the hell had he become that?

He turned his attention back to the envelope and slid the contents out.

It was another email, the same as the first, but titled: REPORT TWO.

'What is it?' Saph asked.

Mitch stood and fished the earlier delivery from his pocket.

He handed it to Saph.

'I got this on my way out this morning. Looks like this new one is a follow-up. Have a read, while I read this one.'

Saph looked at him, tired and doubtful.

'Really?'

Mitch smiled. 'You'll like it. It's interesting.'

Saph huffed, but sat at the kitchen bench and unfolded the A4 papers. Mitch returned to his chair to read the second report. It read:

H FIELD REPORT - 005 - 024

This is an informal report – For Your Eyes Only – to accompany the hard data and other information, such as press clippings, media, medical and surveillance reports in the larger file.

It's the second of the three high profile cases you wanted me to look into; this one is in regard to Ben Corner, son of US Republican Senator Kenneth Corner. Again, U, this is your coverage – and I would strongly suggest you at least look through the accompanying material.

Okay, so we all know the story. To ensure his support at the recent republican Nation Convention, North Carolina Senator Kenneth Corner had to court the Christian Right and disavow his gay son Ben. As it happened, this backfired in a way that it didn't when, say, Dick Cheney disavowed his lesbian daughter several years earlier under the Bush–Cheney partnership.

There is something about the father/son bond that resonates with North Carolina – they saw right through Senator Corner. The general view is that he was doomed from the start – that he should simply not have run for office. While the majority of Republican voting North Carolinians certainly did not approve of Ben Corner's sexual orientation, neither did they approve of a father who would turn his back on his son – especially not when Ben was revealed to the press as a classic 'Gay Republican', looking more like the love child of Sarah Palin and Steven Colbert, rather than the kind of colorful Mardi Gras stereotype that the God fearing NC's find easy to hate. The (albeit fairly moderate) backlash lost Senator Corner the nomination; and, word has it, conservative advisers ensured that the public gap between father and son remained completely severed.

The general consensus in the aftermath was that the North Carolinians were somewhat torn over this; their conservative instincts said that this was one of their own – a straight-talking conservative, a Constitutional purist who decried Big Government and backed Big Business, all the while somehow 'loving the little guy'. On top of this, at thirty-five he was very good-looking, the camera loved him, and he had been in a monogamous relationship with a life-partner for almost five years; hardly the kind of promiscuous, serial-sodomizing heathen a good father would have every right to turn his back on.

If only he wasn't gay, came the buzz-phrase.

If only he could 'get religion' and 'get straight'.

Flash forward to a few months ago; in what most liberals now claim is a cynical political stunt, Kenneth and Ben Corner met with the American media machine to announce that Ben was no longer gay; he had found God and God had straightened him right out. He had separated from his 'long-term partner' and was engaged to a beautiful woman who was newly pregnant with twin sons.

The new family was filmed and photographed going to church; the new couple were snapped kissing and cuddling over ice cream in the park, or a walk down the block for coffee; the newly bonded father and son were repeatedly seen deep in what was clearly very serious conversation (Political? Religious? Both?); and before long their new plans were announced; Kenneth was once again vying for Republican nomination, and once in the White House, his son would run to take over Senatorial duties in North Carolina.

It's still quite a way and several election results off yet, as you know U, but it seems an 'everybody wins' situation: a win for Kenneth, for Ben, for North Carolinians, for God.

'God turned the Corner!' was the catch cry.

The only thing that might have gotten in the way was Ben's long-term partner, Max Gould, but he killed himself a few days after the new family's press launch. Ben was suitably saddened; they had remained friends, and he had urged his old friend to come to Jesus, just as he had.

But Max had resisted. And now he was dead.

Plus, and here's the kicker, Ben told the press that Max had always suffered depression. It had been very difficult for Max and, it was implied, for Ben. The message was that those who have friends or loved ones with depression should always be vigilant. A genuine tragedy.

I don't know about you U, but watching this footage I get the impression that Ben Corner is indeed Born Again – as a Politician, that is. He somehow manages to suggest through all this that Max was depressed because he knew that being gay was wrong, and that somehow he'd always known this, and that this was what caused his depression, and his ultimate demise.

Now, we've all heard the stories of politicians, on both sides, who are still in the closet but ultimately get caught out in some embarrassing variation of male bondage, rent boy hi-jinks or glory hole scenarios. On the Republican side, it's usually the ones who are the most God-fearing and fag-hating. I don't think there is one liberal in the world who doesn't automatically assume that this is something of that sort; an opportunistic power grab from a charismatic right-wing family who value power over… well, just about everything it seems. Bush III if you will. So I was surprised when you asked me to look into it – like there was something more to it.

Then, I was surprised again.

(Sidebar: the access you've given me to the satellite tracking is creepy to say the least, U. I don't know how people can sleep at night a) if they use this technology all the time and b) if they even know it exists. I am watching people go about their business from the sky, very clearly – even at night (the heat-detection is eerily clear) and certainly craps on Google Earth from, you guessed it, a great height. This is voyeur heaven, and should never be released to the public – it's not just a game-changer, it's an all new game).

Back to the story.

To begin with, you don't have to go very far to learn that Ben Corner was definitely gay. For a time in his twenties he was indeed one of those Mardi Gras stereotypes and was very lucky to come out of the eighties unscathed and healthy. But he settled down and by all accounts; friends, friends of family, even family members themselves, he and Max were very much in love and very faithful. In fact it seems that if either were to go astray, it would have been Max, who was the more free-spirited of the two.

Friends noticed that Ben had 'turned off' Max about six months ago — he became quite hostile (openly passive-aggressive was a term used by several interviewees) to his long-term partner and began to express his dissatisfaction with the relationship at any given opportunity. This was described, also by several interviewees, as occurring 'practically overnight'.

Friends go on to say that it became apparent that Ben was having an affair soon after that, the realization of which was the major cause of Max's renewed bout of depression, a condition which had apparently been under control for the duration of their five year relationship — Ben's spiel at the press conference about him being depressed at home for years, and difficult to live with, is complete bullshit. But it was the revelation that the affair was with a <u>woman</u> that pushed Max over the edge, and when Ben moved out, Max stopped communicating and became a recluse.

Now, here's the flip side. By all other accounts, i.e. — the straight world Ben entered, he and his new wife were also very much in love. Of course, all the country club types Ben had despised, but now embraced, were as suspicious as anyone — but all the people I spoke to claim that the kind of passion they exhibited 'could not be faked'. That phrase came up again and again — these are conservative people who, while staunch in their ideology, are not easily fooled. There are numerous stories of how they couldn't keep their hands off each other, how when separated they'd be caught out with loving gazes across the room, how they'd vanish together and return flushed, like they'd just had a quickie. These are multiple accounts, multiple occasions.

Now, all of this could have been staged (after all, it's been done before) and without a leaked sex tape to prove the relationship was actually consummated, who's to say? But the thing is (and here come the heat-detection satellites) I have been watching these two on and off for three weeks; they are still shagging all night, every night. Ben and the new love are clearly two people who are very much into each other in a very hetero way, and still very much in the first stages of a very passionate relationship. I've seen it for myself (God help me) and it's as real as it gets.

Which reminds me; the God thing.

Ben makes it seem in interviews that he started going to church and had some kind of Road to Damascus moment where Jesus appeared and took away his gayness. But we can find no accounts at all of him attending a church, or a Christian support group, nor taking spiritual guidance of any kind – until well after his sexual conversion, and even then it's very much Obama-style press opportunities and token appearances, all well staged and well covered.

So that's all complete lies as well, and well documented in the liberal press.

Of course, you don't need a church for a religious conversion, or to have a spiritual revelation; I had my own personal epiphany one afternoon while I was walking home with the groceries, and I have never been to church, as you know U. And also as we both well know, these conversions do not necessarily lead to Christianity; in fact it's usually the last thing you want.

We'll never know for sure, but my money is on 'there was no religious conversion'.

Take that out of the equation, and what are we left with?

Going by the evidence – Ben Corner is now totally straight.

So the thing is – what makes a demonstrably gay man turn straight?

(I have looked, for the sake of it, and there are none of the usual circumstances that might lead to sudden personality transformation; no head trauma, no drug use, no hypnotherapy – he's never even seen an analyst.)

Because that's what's happened here – this is not a bisexual man having a mid-life crisis and opting to return to the straight world for a change of lifestyle. This is a total, and apparently spontaneous, one-eighty turn in sexual orientation, which is now being exploited for political gain.

But how does someone do that, U?

I don't know if that is what you were after when you asked me to look into this guy – but that's what you got. Straight conversion, no tricks.

H

***

Hello H,
Thanks for the report.
I will not be voting for the father, or the son.
Nor the holy ghost, for that matter.
I am looking forward to your third and final report.
Can you see where this is going?

U

PS – keep digging on the Mendoza matter. Seek and ye shall find.

U

CHAPTER SEVENTEEN

Mitch sat thinking as Saph and Cricket read the two reports.

He couldn't help but wonder what his mind had been doing while he'd been staring at the sun, getting the 'solar download'.

His memory of that hour was blank. Had his mind been blank for that whole hour? If not, what could possibly take a whole hour?

Surely, if information was being transmitted – God knows how – from something as powerful as The Sun, it would only take… what? A millisecond?

But then again, how would he know?

Then a thought struck him, from back in the days when he did have a computer, when he had tried too little and too late to make a website. When the techs had installed a new program on his computer, hadn't they needed to turn it off and turn it on again, to make it work?

And didn't new programs take time to be put on the computer? To be *installed*? Installed, and then… what was the word?

Rebooted.

That was it.

Rebooted.

'Wow,' Cricket put the paper down.

Mitch looked up; Saph appeared to have finished reading some time ago. She'd been watching Cricket, examining her as she had been reading.

'What do you think it all means?' Mitch asked.

Saph stood and began to make herself a second cup of tea.

It was interesting, Mitch thought, that she had not offered one to either of them.

'Who can say?' Saph shrugged. 'It's strange stuff, but where does the information come from? Who wrote it?'

'And to whom?' asked Cricket.

Mitch watched Saph. She looked tired, maybe even pissed off. He stood.

'Listen, I think I'm just going to check my room.'

'Do you want me to come with you?' Saph asked airily.

'To be honest I just want five minutes to have a smoke on the balcony and a think.'

Cricket stood. 'Maybe I should go too – but is it okay if I come back?'

'With a recorder?' Mitch smirked.

'Would that be okay?'

Mitch was a little surprised. 'I suppose. I guess someone should make a record of this in case something happens to –'

He stopped himself.

Saph glared at him. 'Don't be ridiculous. You've been spiked. That's all. Vance is as mad as a bag of snakes. Even Pan didn't really take all of this seriously.'

Strange, thought Mitch. Ten minutes ago she'd been all about how Pan *had* taken this seriously.

Mitch shrugged. 'Sure. Look, I'll come back after I've had a think. Come and get me in an hour, just in case I fall asleep. I'm suddenly feeling very tired.'

Saph nodded and sipped tightly on her hot tea.

'Bye Saph,' Cricket smiled. 'Thanks for letting me tag along.'

'That's okay. Maybe I'll see you tomorrow?'

'Sure.'

Mitch gave Saph a wide smile, his best attempt at reassurance, as he exited with Cricket behind him. Right now he was dying for a cigarette, to sit and put all this weirdness in perspective. He was sure that when he did that, the situation would seem perfectly rational. He just needed a quiet five minutes and some perspective.

He turned to Cricket as he slotted his key and pushed the

handle down, opening the dark room.

'I guess I'll see you later then, huh?' he smiled.

She came at him quickly, pushing him inside the room with a force he'd never expected from her stature.

CHAPTER EIGHTEEN

She was perhaps five feet five and so, when she launched her mouth up at his, she had to wrap her arms around his shoulders and pull his head down. The kiss was ferociously passionate, wide and with an aggressive tongue. He heard the door slam automatically and suddenly they were kissing in the dark, his back against the wall in the short corridor that led to the room. She had not paused, or spoken, or asked permission; she had simply made her move. He responded openly but in complete shock. For the first few minutes he was totally going through the motions; he'd not had sex sober for years and, in fact, his last two one-night stands had occurred during alcohol blackouts, so he'd simply woken beside a stranger with a vague memory of fumbling intercourse, got up and left as quickly as possible. This attack was so startling that he was not even sure that he would get it up, until he did, or that he could maintain his stamina without gallons of alcohol numbing his senses, until he did that as well.

It was a classic quickie, Mitch realized, the kind they like to portray in films because they contain so much visual momentum. They were kissing all the way to the bed, but undressing at the same time. Then, when that became impractical, they simply parted for half a minute and disrobed as quickly as possible. Then they were on the bed. There was a brief concession to the notion of touching and caressing but this was not about that.

There were several things Mitch had forgotten; the first was the fumbling of it all, the elbows and knees, bending limbs and clicking teeth; the second was the heat of penetration, the actual sense of high body temperature when inside someone else; the third was the oddness of it all. He was actually having sex with a cute girl – she was actually attracted to him and here they were, here he was, actually doing it. It seemed impossible. Like George Costanza, he had at least on some level given up on the idea of ever having sex again; he could simply not conceive in his mind of any realistic circumstance that could ever lead to it happening. And yet, here he was.

It was energetic and he quickly realized exactly how out of shape he was; and that she was, indeed, ten years younger than him, and that she needed to be on top. At one point his leg almost cramped, and he was forced to shift position very quickly. She misread this as enthusiasm and seemed to enter into things with even greater gusto.

They paused only for a few seconds, just once. He thought he'd been about to pop, when she suddenly stopped, got off him and went to the end of the bed where her coat was lying on the floor. From her coat pocket she produced a wide purse, and from the purse she produced a condom, which she ripped open with her teeth. Then she had it on him and they were back at it.

The pause gave him fresh momentum and, when they started again, things seemed just slightly calmer and less desperate. Friendlier and more human. Then, after a short while, the pace returned and they were animals again.

It was about hammering, he realized. Just keep going, don't stop.

'Don't stop!' she would hiss, even at his slightest pause.

He kept going, and going, until he didn't.

He warned her, and this seemed to excite her to the extreme; she tightened her legs around him and grabbed his face, watching his expression with mild amazement, as though it never failed to surprise her. When it was done, they kissed some more and he rolled off her, panting.

He'd done it.

He'd done it again.

She pecked him on the lips and seamlessly slipped off the used condom, then laughed as she walked across the room with it and picked up Mitch's key from where he'd dropped it, halfway to the bed. She vanished down the short corridor, Mitch heard a click and the lights came on, then Cricket turned them off again. Then she reappeared, the condom still held high and away from her, dangling between her fingers, and went to the bathroom.

'Me first,' she told him. Then the bathroom light came on, and Mitch blinked to adjust his eyes. The room that was an exact duplicate of the one Saph had been designated. Cricket closed the door, then he heard the toilet flush and the shower start to run as he lay back with his hands behind his head, feeling pretty good about himself for the first time in a long while.

A pretty girl. It never fails.

The bedside phone rang.

He wondered for a second, then picked it up.

'It's me,' said Saph. 'Hope I'm not interrupting anything?'

'No, that's okay.'

For some reason he felt incredibly guilty all of a sudden.

'Is she gone?'

'Who?'

'That girl. Cricket.'

'Yes,' he lied.

'Good. I just couldn't shake her, but I didn't want to make it obvious.'

'Make what obvious?'

'I'm not sure I should say this over the phone.'

'Say what?'

'Look, I'm going to come over.'

'I'm just about to shower. Can you wait ten minutes?'

There was a pause. 'Look, I think I should tell you in case she comes back. She's definitely coming back, you know.'

'Why do you say that?'

Another pause.

'Look, Mitch, I did speak to a few people after Pan died. People on his team. Not Pan's People as such, people he actually worked with and trusted. Pan believed in keeping his enemies

166

closer, you know? And the word was that Pan's webmaster wasn't to be trusted.'

'Cricket?'

'Exactly. Pan kept her close to keep an eye on her, to control the flow of information, but he knew.'

'Knew what?'

'Cricket, Mitch. She's CIA.'

CHAPTER NINETEEN

'You're sure?'

'That was the word – Servalan, Pan's webmaster, was CIA. Whatever you do, don't tell her anything, and you sure as hell can't let her interview you.'

Mitch tensed. The shower was still running.

'Saph, I'm going to get some sleep. I'm exhausted.'

'I understand. That's probably a good idea.'

'I'll call you when I'm awake, okay?'

'Okay. But don't hesitate. Two AM, three AM, I don't care. I won't be sleeping tonight.'

Mitch saw the beside clock. 8.08.

'Thanks. I appreciate that.'

'Do you want me to come in? Maybe you should have someone looking out for you?'

Jesus, how could he end this call quickly without seeming suspicious?

'I'm just so tired.'

'Okay. I'll let you go. You sure you're okay?'

'Yeah. I'll sleep like a baby.'

'Okay then.'

'Okay.'

'Night.'

'Night. And thanks.'

Click.

Mitch dressed in his pants and shirt and was heading for the door in record time. It was easier when you weren't hung-over. The hardest part was closing the heavy hotel door without making a clunk, but he managed that and was grateful for the sound proofing in the hotel corridor. His bare footfalls were fairylike, silent.

He pressed the elevator button to go up one floor, to the penthouse, and waited for it to arrive as he put on his jacket, shoes and socks. He only managed one shoe before the doors opened and quickly embarked. A couple of young kids dressed in neo-punk outfits watched, knowingly amused, as he fixed his second shoe and tightened the laces.

The walk of shame.

Then he was back at the penthouse.

Chasey smiled politely as he re-entered the party. He assessed the crowd, which was much larger now, perhaps doubled, but still nowhere near the enormous suite's full capacity.

When 'The Men' had arrived, he'd heard himself say it. From somewhere in his subconscious, he knew it.

Then he saw her; Heather.

She was dancing in a corner of the suite near where a DJ had set up. There were only a few men making a go of it, some of them acquitting themselves admirably, but at least three quarters of the twenty or so dancers were female. He wasn't sure how to do what he needed to do without making a scene. Should he simply go out there and dance?

He'd had proper sex tonight for the first time in years; would it be the first time he tried sober dancing at a party as well? In nearly a decade, or more?

It was a modern track playing. He had no idea what it was, and unlike the structure of the music he'd grown up with, there seemed no easily identifiable progression in this music that identified which section of the track you were hearing. Based on what little he knew of dance music, it might go on for another twenty minutes or so.

He ambled to the bar, trying not to make eye contact with anyone, but quickly realized that whatever this 'new perception' of his had been, that had switched on before, it was not switched on now. The room seemed stable, without any dimensional anomalies. In fact, the atmosphere seemed fine. Welcoming even. People had stopped crying, at least openly.

It was a good room, he decided.

Maybe he should just stay and unwind?

Even dance?

He ordered a beer and the barmaid handed him the same premium brand he'd drunk before. On the dance floor, Heather was dancing hard and showed no indication of ever letting up. Her hands were raised high above her head, punching the air. Beneath her loose earthy garments he could see her boobs bouncing; her ass was jiggling and her dreadlocks were whipping. Her eyes were closed and she was smiling a big wide toothy smile to herself. She looked amazing, almost a modern icon of sexual independence. Mitch assumed she was on ecstasy, or something. Whatever the kids were taking these days. He didn't care – he just needed to speak to her, right now.

Mitch walked up to the edge of the impromptu dance floor and stood behind a bunch of much younger guys who were watching, but were presumably not yet high and/or drunk enough to make the move to the floor.

He knew he couldn't dance.

He assessed the men. Some of them were not so young, maybe in their thirties.

He had to think; what would get Heather's attention very quickly?

The men were in their thirties…

An idea was forming.

What did they like? What had they grown up with?

He moved a little closer to a thirtysomething dude. He knew these types. These were unlike the well manicured, hard-bodied, fashion-coiffed men who were already on dance floor; these men lacked their confidence. But then again, why shouldn't the men on the floor feel confident? They were fit, good-looking, well-dressed weekenders. They had devoted their lives to scoring on the dance floor. But these other men were ordinary men. Men who didn't dance.

He caught the eye of one of the watchers and nudged his head towards one of the girls dancing near Heather. She was totally gorgeous and deep into the music. He made a face as if to say 'eh?' and the man responded with a cheeky smile, then nodded. They had made a connection.

'Shit music,' Mitch blurted.

The other guy made a face like he'd bitten into a lemon.

'Wish they'd play something decent!' Mitch added.

'Aw yeah!' the guy replied.

'Some Floyd or something!'

'Floyd!' the man responded.

It felt a bit too much like a caveman ritual, but Mitch knew this type.

'Or some Zepp!'

'Yeah, some Zepp!'

'Or Hendrix! Some Jimi yeah!'

The man howled. 'Jim-aaaaaay! Woooooh! Jim-aaaaaay!'

Mitch watched Heather's eyes snap open.

She zeroed in on the drunken man beside him, then saw Mitch.

Mitch already had his hand at his face – he made a quick gesture that said 'come here', over a facial expression that said, 'now!'

Heather immediately understood.

Her arms came down and she let out a huge breath, as though she were suddenly exhausted. She bent over with her hands on her knees, then stood straight again. Looking around the room, she feigned suddenly seeing Mitch. Her eyes popped, pleased to see him, and she pointed with enthusiasm and a huge smile as she crossed the floor to him.

'Lucky prick,' the man beside him muttered.

'Mitchie!' Heather cried. She threw her arms around his shoulders and kissed him on the cheek. 'I thought you'd ditched me!' The she whispered in his ear, deep and angry. '*Where the fuck have you been?'*

Mitch was taken aback at the tone.

She released him, maintaining the façade of girlish glee, and immediately dragged him back to the bar.

'Mitchell Bitchell! Buy me a drink, buy me a drink!'

She practically wrenched his arm from its socket and when they reached the bar she slammed her hand down on it and shrieked.

'Beer me!'

'Erm, okay…'

She leaned in and whispered in his ear. 'If people think I'm into you, they might just buy that there's nothing fishy going on. Now laugh like I just said something filthy.'

Mitch was stunned, so leaned back and grinned, shaking his head.

'Now that I can do! Beer, please! Make it two!'

With that he swilled down what remained of his first drink.

'Now listen,' Heather began, her hitherto leveled American accent suddenly very clandestine and sinister, 'whatever you did before to draw all that goddamned attention to yourself has made this a hell of a lot more dangerous. I understand why you made contact with me; there was no other way… where were you by the way? Don't answer that – just follow my lead. If you left with me before, you were a nobody, just some weird old guy I was picking up. Now you're a hot commodity, and my uncle being who he is, no one's going to misinterpret me making a move to get away with the merchandise. The only hope we have is that because we came in together, people will assume we already knew each other. I'm going to kiss you, but I'm not going to like it.'

She kissed him, hard. No tongue.

When she released him, the look she gave him made him believe that he was more than ready to go again, despite the fact that it could not have been more than half an hour since his last effort.

'I'm looking at you this way because people need to believe

we're hot for each other. If we make it to the lift, I can get us to the ground floor but then we have to run. You know which way the pier is?'

'The jetty? Yep.'

'Don't wait for me; don't look back. Get to the end of the *jetty*, and jump. Okay? Just – jump.'

'Are you fucking serious with all this?'

She kissed him again, longer.

When they parted, she was staring at him like she was jealous of something.

'Are *you* fucking serious with all this?' she demanded, then pulled out a phone and started texting at a speed Mitch thought was one of the most supernatural things he'd seen all night.

'What?'

'Listen – we go together, straight for the door.' She shoved the phone back in her pocket. 'Put your hand on my ass and act like you're onto a sure thing. Can you do that?'

'Of course.'

'Jesus. How can you have seen so many films and be such a piss-poor actor?'

Mitch had had about enough of this. How had the sweet girl in the green Mercedes become this sex-kitten uber-bitch?

'Woah, yeah!' he cried out, and slapped her hard on the rear. 'I got a room on the next floor!'

She let out a wailing, drunken party girl laugh and the two of them stormed toward the exit. She immediately had a hand tight about his waist and he, as per instructions, placed his hand firmly on her bum. She squealed raucously as they scampered across the room. The crowd parted for them, grinning and laughing, and their exit was in sight.

They passed the security guards and Chasey, then Heather hit the down button and they waited.

The elevator hummed.

Three men emerged from the party behind them. Mitch looked over his shoulder and saw them. They were not 'The Men' but Mitch found that he could not quite meet their eyes, nor get a fix on whom, exactly, they were. He immediately looked forward to the lift again.

'I told you not to look,' Heather hissed.

'Who are they?' Mitch hissed back.

One of them cleared his throat – the message that they were being overheard was unmistakable.

'They're not with us,' was all Heather offered.

One of the men stepped forward and stood just behind Heather. He leaned in and pressed the down button again. The message was once more unmistakable; they were captives.

'What do we do?' Mitch asked.

'I don't know.'

The elevator dinged and the doors opened.

There, standing before them, were the two Nordics.

Pleiadeans, Vance had called them.

It was the weirdest feeling Mitch had ever had. As though he were trapped between two worlds, neither of them real so far as he'd had any experience with. The Pleiadeans assessed and immediately took in the situation. He felt an immense pressure on the back of his head, although he was sure nobody and nothing had touched him there. Yet he felt an odd, if not pleasant sensation in his chest, as though compelling him to move forward. It was as though he had been chained by a collar, rooting him to the spot from behind, yet was strapped with a child harness and lead, extending from his chest, pulling him forward.

He looked at the Pleiadeans; their expression was that of pet owners discovering their dog had gotten loose. Here he was, having soiled the floor and ripped up the furnishings at an expensive party, for which they were ashamed. Yet, for some reason, they still wanted him back and were making the effort to take him home. The problem was – the pound had him on a leash and wanted to take him off somewhere to be put down.

With a look of mixed disgust and sympathy, the Pleiadeans parted and exited the elevator on either side of them, making way for them to enter. As soon as they did this, Mitch found that his feet were moving. Forward. Into the elevator, Heather at his side. They heard the doors close and the elevator started to descend. Only then did they release a breath and separate.

'What was *that?*'

Heather shook her head. 'I've researched the Pleiadeans. That's the first time I've seen them; but that was them. On the other hand, whatever was behind us… what did they look like?'

'I couldn't really see.'

'What do you mean? I saw you look!'

'I mean – I couldn't actually *see* them. It was like, they were shaped like men, but my eyes just couldn't take in anything about them, like my mind just couldn't accept what I was seeing. I couldn't *process* them.'

'That's not good.'

'Why? Why are they any worse than any other weird people I've met today?'

'Because…' Heather considered heavily for a second. '…I've heard rumors. Of shapeless…' Her eyes were far away, focused on a memory. 'Look, if they are who I think they are, and they even partially manifested in front of us, and ordinary people, in public, then they just broke about a thousand rules in one go, just to get a chance at you.'

The elevator was approaching the lobby.

'Remember – straight to the door, then run to the end of the jetty. Don't stop. I mean it. This is worse than I thought.'

'I don't see why I should trust you.'

'Because I'm the only person you've met all day who isn't outright lying to you. And because your instincts were correct; my uncle is the only man on this planet who has the slightest hope of protecting you.'

Mitch looked at her.

He had no choice.

'Okay.'

'Good.'

The elevator dinged and the doors opened to the lobby.

Two uniformed police officers stood before them. Upon seeing them they seemed shocked and immediately drew their guns.

The first one immediately yelled.

'Hands behind your heads!'

Followed by the second; 'On your knees, now!'

CHAPTER TWENTY

Mitch obeyed, dropped to his knees, slapped his hands behind his head and clasped them tightly.

Heather followed.

'Fuck,' she uttered.

'Shut-up!' yelled the first cop.

Mitch could see behind the cops, into the lobby. There were at least thirty people either at the desk, at the bar, or at the café, staring across the lobby floor at them.

The cops seemed hesitant, shaky.

Mitch was on his knees. So far as he knew, the next step was the cuffing. Sure enough, one of the cops fumbled on their belt for the plastic cuffs. They seemed incredibly nervous and it took more than a few seconds for the cop to get them off his belt and into his hand. When he had them, he seemed thoroughly reluctant to take his aim away from them and almost too frightened to step toward them. It was his hesitancy that cost them the arrest.

The doors dinged and started to close.

Mitch thought that this was it, he was going to die; in a split second he saw the look in his cop's eyes, the one that had his gun trained on him and saw his thoughts. It was nothing to do with Mitch's spiking; anyone would have seen the cop's reaction, his mental processes, move across his face as his thoughts moved through his mind.

Mitch thought; this is what they mean.

In crisis, time slows down.

You can read micro-expressions on a person's face.

Read a language from them that only exists in a slowed temporal state of perception.

It went like this.

The cop had frozen, not wanting to take his gun off Mitch.

The doors were closing. To stop that, he had to reach over and hit either the closing doors themselves, or hit the open button, thus losing his aim. It would be easier, Mitch saw the cop think in a microsecond, to shoot him. In another microsecond Mitch must have reacted, because something in the cop's face made Mitch realize that the cop saw something in his face that said:

I am a human being.

Primal, faster than light, the cop recognized a moral imperative and the doors closed.

The elevator rose.

Heather immediately hit every floor on the panel.

'What are you doing?' Mitch shrieked.

The elevator dinged; first floor. The doors re-opened.

'Run,' she stated, and bolted off to the right, down the corridor. Mitch had no choice but to follow.

He ran a short distance; the corridor turned right again.

When he turned the corner, he saw a young couple exiting their room. Heather was running full-pelt toward them. The couple froze at the sight. When it became apparent that Heather was running *at them*, the woman screamed.

'Hey!' the young man yelled.

But Heather simply pushed past them, all but ignoring their presence, and vanished into their room. Mitch followed but made quick eye contact.

'I'm sorry! I'm sorry!'

'Hey!' the man yelled again.

Mitch suspected that the guy had taken a few steps after them, into the room, but didn't turn to see. Heather had gone immediately to the bay window, unlocked it, crashed outside to the tiny balcony, and had started to climb over the railing. She looked straight at Mitch as he staggered up to her.

'Ten foot jump, max. Roll when you land, then run like fuck. Adrenalin will do the rest.'

With that she turned and jumped into the night. She landed below on a stretch of well-lit lawn with a thump, tried to roll but kind of didn't, but got up and moved immediately across the lawn to a gate; the gate led out into a side alley lined with industrial bins, dividing the Vantage and another shorefront hotel. She didn't pause to look back, and was gone, running down the alley toward the beach.

'Pan, you bastard,' Mitch uttered; and climbed over the rail.

Without thinking, he jumped.

The impact through his legs was jarring but not hideous; he tried to roll but his left leg, the weaker, just gave out and he fell to the side. He thought that something had happened to his ankle, but when he stood he was okay. There was pain there, but nothing he couldn't walk on. He got across the lawn and to the gate, then out to the alley.

The alley was dim but he could see straight down between the two hotels, through to the foreshore with its brilliantly lit park and walkways, and the darkness of the ocean behind that. Heather was still running, some way ahead. He started after her. Now his ankle hurt; and hurt the more he ran. He ignored it and tried to increase his pace. He could; he could feel his heart pounding, and was aware that he was running faster, much faster, than he had ever run in his entire pathetically non-athletic thirties. In fact, he estimated that he would catch up with Heather before she reached the end of the alley, and he did, just as she halted abruptly pressed herself back against the alley wall to their right.

Mitch did the same.

The alley ended between two high walls that elevated the front section of the Vantage café-restaurant, to their left, and dedicated open-frontage café, to their right. With his back pressed hard against the cold concrete surface, Mitch could hear the loud chatter of the patrons above them and smell the strong coffee aroma that shrouded the café drifting down. Immediately above them, they could see the many diners in the well-lit Vantage restaurant, in the middle of their evening meals, but the inner light reflected on the glass within meant they couldn't see out.

Mitch checked the foreshore, panting. The jetty was out there, a decent run to the edge of the beach. He re-checked windows of the Vantage café. Somehow, the couple at the table closest to the window had seen them; refugees from the law who moments ago had escaped arrest in the elevator. The man had already signal a waiter and was pointing out at Mitch and Heather, agitated. His female partner was looking down at them, her nose close to the glass, cross. He saw the waiter call out across the café at the two cops, who were just now re-entering the café from the elevator.

'Heather, move, now!'

Without asking why, she bolted. The two of them dashed across the wide sidewalk that ran before the Vantage, across the grass and between the palm trees of the carefully landscaped foreshore, and toward the jetty. They heard someone shout out, behind them. It seemed like a dreamy hallucination as Mitch kept running, the darkness and black clouds above, the neon lights along the jetty standing out like computer graphics against the stark and gloomy reality of everything else that surrounded him, passing a blur of startled faces amid the street-lit green and brown of the night beach-garden, then suddenly they were off the grass and onto hard bitumen again, then they were on the jetty, the boom-boom-boom-boom of their running steps on the old hard wood echoing underneath, people screaming, grabbing their children out of the way, balloons let go, ice creams dropped, and someone shouting behind them, a threat, a gunshot, then another gunshot, the end of the jetty so close now.

He didn't know how he vaulted the railing at the end of the jetty but he did. Somehow, faultlessly, smooth as an athlete, he just ran up to the rail, planted both his hands on it and without losing momentum allowed his last two running steps to propel him up rather than forward. The momentum carried him over and for a second he was upside down, then free falling. He felt his feet clip something and realized it was Heather's feet; she too was free falling. They must have jumped in unison. In the darkness as he descended toward the freezing ocean – he could feel the temperature drop dramatically the instant he had passed the edge of the jetty – he heard a shot and saw a spark as the bullet hit the jetty rail, then heard the bullet ricochet and whiz past his ear.

Time seemed to slow down again and he realized that any second now he would hit the mid-winter water that was cold enough to bring him to hypothermia in under three minutes and wondered with a hit of panic whether it had really been so wise to trust Heather in the first place.

CHAPTER TWENTY-ONE

He hit something hard, yet soft.

Not water.

Something else hit the same surface, simultaneously beside him, and he bounced.

Like a balloon castle.

There was a roar of an engine and momentum; he was looking up at the end of the jetty from what should have been water but was not. The two cops aimed their weapons down at him, then there was a loud clunk from behind and above him and the cops were suddenly hit with an incredibly bright light; they threw their arms up to protect their eyes. Then he heard a powerful motor kick in, and saw the cops, and the jetty, recede at high speed.

Mitch was amazed. Had a UFO beamed down a light to protect him? Was he on a spaceship, being spirited away?

No, he was moving across the water.

The light above him went out.

He looked beside him.

Heather, in the dark, her round pretty face and sweaty deadlocks very close to him.

'Are you okay?' she asked, grimacing, panting.

He could feel her hot breath on his face.

It smelled like beer.

'Yeah. I think I sprained my ankle.'

She looked down at his feet.

'I think I sprained my wrist. Tried to roll.'

'Doesn't work so good, does it?'

'I need more training. Holy shit. That was fucking intense.'

'That was very fucking intense.'

They laughed.

Mitch looked up and back and it became suddenly apparent where they were, and what had happened. They had jumped onto a large dinghy raft that was attached to a modern fishing boat. At the back of the boat was a wide arc light, the light that had blinded the cops.

'Your uncle sent this?'

'Standard procedure.'

'You've done this before?'

'I've had to jump off the back of a jetty into a rubber dinghy before. Not exactly the way that just happened though.'

'Really?'

She shrugged. 'It's different every time.'

'I hope I never have to find out.'

'That's the trouble with this kind of thing. Once you're in, you tend to get used to it. In fact,' she knelt up and waved at the back of the boat, a kind of *we're okay* wave, 'you kind of get to like it.'

Mitch nodded to himself, then fell on his back, still panting.

'Worst thing is, I kind of get that.'

'You do?'

'Yeah. I kind of do.'

He waited until the boat slowed and the dinghy came to rest before he decided to get to his feet again. The dinghy's surface was wobbly and he figured probably the worst kind of surface for anything sore but his ankle handled it okay. He suspected it would be much worse in the morning; assuming he could ever sleep again.

Someone pulled the dinghy closer and a rope ladder was thrown down. Heather went first and he tried not to stare at her bottom as he followed. When they embarked onto the boat, he discovered that it had parked beside some kind of yacht, or ocean cruiser, and then had to climb another rope ladder, this one much longer, up onto that.

The cruiser was enormous; when Mitch came aboard he could

easily have been back on the balcony of the penthouse suite, given that the central area of the top deck was all glass and within it was what seemed to be a… well, a penthouse suite.

They were met by a Latina woman who resembled what at Mitch's best guess Sofia Vergara would look like in her early forties if she took extremely good care of herself. Despite the chill she wore only a dark blue one-piece bathing suit and a sheer white sleeveless gown; he assumed the cruiser had spent most of the day somewhere much warmer along the coast. She carried and immediately offered him a premium beer of a brand more exclusive than that on offer at Pan's wake, which he gladly accepted. When she spoke, because of the resemblance, he expected to hear an outrageous Latina accent but her English was clear and pronounced with only a small trace of something European.

'That must have been quite a ride, Mister Pyne?'

'Yes. Thank you.'

He swigged the beer. It was cold and crisp and tasted magnificent. She offered one to Heather, who also accepted.

'Thanks Yelina.'

Yelina hummed, as though assessing. 'I will get you some bandages, to keep your wrist warm. Bo will meet you in the bar, in just a minute. You know the way.'

'Okay. Thanks.' Heather turned to Mitch. 'This way.'

Mitch winced on his ankle as he moved; Yelina noticed and gave him a tight smile as she moved away in the opposite direction.

Heather went directly to a glass door and ushered Mitch through, into what appeared to be an entertainment suite, complete with its own cinema screen, spa, dining setting and bar. The entire suite was surrounded with glass windows but felt enclosed and secure. Perhaps it was just the night; once inside, with the internal lighting, every windowed surface acted like a mirror. If not for the slight bobbing of the boat on the ocean, he could indeed have been in a penthouse suite just about anywhere.

Heather moved to the bar and sat on a high stool. Mitch sat beside her and sighed heavily. Heather smiled at him reassuringly, as though to indicate they were safe now.

'Who was that?' Mitch asked.

'That was Yelina.'

She didn't add to that.

'Okay,' Mitch nodded, swigging his beer. 'So how much do you know about all of this – really?'

Heather smiled and reached into her loose jacket. She pulled out a folded A-4 envelope, just like the ones that had been slipped under his door.

'You?'

'Uncle Bo thought it would be good if you were brought up to speed. He asked me to deliver these to you. I do lots of these for him but he wanted you to read these three specifically.'

Mitch accepted the envelope. 'You want me to read it now?'

'Uncle Bo wants you to read them before you meet. But there's been so much rushing around, it's been hard to drip-feed them to you. I figured if you got all three, you wouldn't read them; one at a time and you did.'

Mitch smirked, opening the envelope. 'Clever girl.'

Heather smirked back. 'No shit.'

Mitch slid the third and final report from the envelope.

'I'm way too tired to read this, y'know?'

'It's not long, and it will perk you up. It's about sex.'

Mitch shrugged. 'Okay then. If you insist.'

The third report read:

This is an informal report – For Your Eyes Only – to accompany the hard data and other information, such as press clippings, media, medical and surveillance reports in the larger file.

It's the third of the three high-profile cases you wanted me to look into, this one is in regard to Kashmira Khan, the former Bollywood actress – and I would strongly suggest you at least look through the accompanying material, although it's definitely NSFW.

Okay, U. This third one really took me by surprise – mostly because Kashmira Khan must be the most famous celebrity in the world that no-one's ever heard of – or at least, that no-one will admit.

Khan's 'Quantum Faith' website has had more than five billion hits and a billion downloads – I can't imagine they are all from India, although one assumes the majority are men.

So, Kashmira Khan was the third highest grossing Bollywood star for a ten-year period, throughout the late nineties and into the first half of the new millennium. Being a highly conservative country, with a strong Muslim presence (although they represent less than fourteen percent of the population) the Bollywood film industry is extremely vibrant but features virtually no strong representations of sexuality or nudity. Overt expressions of sexuality are generally thought to be taboo, and shameful. Khan not only toed this line for a decade, but also actively supported it, as do all of the major actresses; even a kiss is a big deal in a Bollywood film. (Remember the Hayes Code? It's pretty much like that.)

In answer to one of your earlier questions U, yes, I'm starting to see where this is going because what we have again here is another high profile, radical change that occurs virtually overnight.

According to sources, about six months ago (again, like the others, six months ago) she walked off the set of her latest musical (they are almost all musicals) after a rant that condemned the entire Bollywood industry as being massively hypocritical and sexually repressive. She almost immediately caught a plane to LA and took interviews with several major magazines, in which she essentially repeated the same rant. She posed topless for the cover of Rolling Stone (but with her arms covering her boobs, ala Jennifer Aniston, Janet Jackson et al) and proceeded to pose semi-nude for several of the racy men's magazines, then in lingerie and plunging necklines for most of the major fashion mags.

The interviews – and accompanying pictorials – were instantly published; Cosmo bumped Natalie Portman off their cover, Esquire bumped Kate Beckinsale.

The fury this caused back home was immense; in the west she was treated as a cheeky vixen, breaking loose from her conservative restraints, but over there she was a pariah; there were personal death threats, threats to her family (many of whom were forced to disown her, some of whom now live under tight security protection) – but none of this was reported in the mainstream western media, at least, not for long.

Khan then vanished again, but re-emerged online only a few weeks later. Startlingly, she had renamed herself Quantum Faith and began to post high quality pictures of herself in various states of striptease and undress. Her site is subscriber based, and took about a month to catch on – then it exploded. I suspect at least half the hits and downloads are from India, but a fair portion is also from 'the west'. Over the past five months, Faith's website has gradually become more and more explicit, with posts in the last two months featuring the ex-Miss Khan in lengthy vignettes that are fully pornographic.

Faith does not address her past other than to post on her blog that she now feels totally free to express her sexuality, and encourages other mainstream actresses both in Bolly and Hollywood to follow her path and end the hypocrisy of sexual repression as supported by the mainstream media. She talks a lot about world consciousness being held back by sexual repression and seems to be connected to something called Conscious World Wellness, which is run by an Indian guru who talks pretty much the same line as Faith does. He is immensely wealthy.

In essence, she is one of the growing legion of pornographic super-starlets who believe that it is healthier to show real sex in movies than it is to show constant fake but extreme violence. Her basic request is that all of Bolly and Hollywood start to include pornographic scenes in mainstream movies.

Good luck – let us know how you go with that!

The bottom line is that although a lot of her material is pirated within the sharing software community, she too is clearly extremely wealthy and is happy to tell her fans as much. This is part of how she hopes to encourage other famous actresses to follow her career path.

Like I said, five billion hits in five months, one billion downloads, subscriber based.

The girl's got a point, I suppose.

Satellite tracking suggests pornography's very own Salman Rushdie avoids assassination via fatwa (although none have been officially decreed, several extremist groups have declared they are actively hunting her) by commuting between three large properties in the Southern hemisphere; one south of Launceston in Tasmania, one north of Alice Springs, the other south of Wellington, the local scenery from all of which have featured heavily in her productions.

Credit where credit's due, they're beautifully photographed, genuinely erotic; and she must be one of the most naturally gorgeous women to ever have graced the planet. But it is what it is, and what is it is hardcore porn.

So, U, three for three.

An actress regenerated by twenty years, a gay man tuned straight, and a virgin turned whore. All three massively profitable to various degrees and by various definitions. I mean, Brittany Spears shaved her head, but she's still Brittany Spears; these people are truly <u>no longer who they once were</u>.

Is someone sending a message?

I will send one more report in this series; have been digging into Mendoza. Odd, very odd.

H

***

Hello H,

> *Yes, someone is sending a message.*
> *The message is — look what we can do.*
> *Let me know about Mendoza, then come home.*
> *I have someone for you.*

U

CHAPTER TWENTY-TWO

'I have someone for you?' Mitch frowned. 'What does that mean?'

Heather shrugged as she swigged her beer. 'Another assignment.'

'And who was that?'

'I don't know. That was right before Pan died. He never got around to telling me.' Heather grinned. 'Maybe it was going to be you, huh?'

Mitch sighed.

Was she lying?

She was surveillance for a billionaire.

Had she been the voice, the mysterious call?

Mitch moaned and leaned heavily on the bar.

'Jesus, what a day.'

Heather nodded. 'That awful funeral.'

'Seems like days ago.'

A voice bellowed from behind him.

'Time, perspective, the mind!'

Bo Everett had arrived.

'There are two UFO researchers sitting at a bar. One of them says, *hey, did you hear about our fellow UFO researcher, Bob?* No, says the other, what about Bob? *Well, Bob had a sighting, a big one – a whole fleet of flying saucers off the coast. He watched them for hours, and there were multiple witnesses who all support his story.* No, says the other, I didn't hear about that. *Well*, says the first UFO researcher, *all the witnesses went on record, and Bob's latest YouTube post had more than a five million views.* No, says the other, I didn't hear about that. *And*, says the first, *that got him a book deal with a big publisher. Big money.* I didn't hear about that either, says the second. *So, says the first, then the aliens got in touch with him – and Bob started channeling messages from them. Thousands of followers waiting on his every word of ancient wisdom.* The second guy shakes his head, really frustrated now – I haven't heard about any of this! *Then one of the messages was a prediction that the UFOs were going to show themselves above the White House last week. It didn't happen, and now Bob looks like an idiot.'*

Bo Everett grinned, big and wide and impossible not to like.

'Now *that*, says the second researcher, I *did* hear about.'

Mitch laughed.

Bo Everett clearly liked that Mitch was laughing.

'It's an old Jewish gag,' Everett nodded. 'Still good. And it works for just about any profession.'

He kissed Heather on the cheek as he moved behind the bar and proceeded to splash himself a neat glass of timeless scotch.

Bo Everett was a tall man, maybe six three, with a bearded face of thick auburn hair that for some reason made Mitch think of a Canadian lumberjack. He was fit and lean, but wide-shouldered and barrel-chested. It was impossible not to be impressed by a man in this shape who by all accounts was somewhere in his early sixties. Despite his obvious health he was pale, as though he'd not seen a day's sun in years, and his blue eyes had a clarity that was at once young and terribly ancient. Seeing him in person though, not on the television as he had many times, Mitch was struck by the sheer Irishness of the man, as though someone had reached back through both myth and time and plucked a stereotypical Celtic chieftain from the mists of yore.

The auburn beard was not short, though carefully groomed to appear un-groomed at first glance. His hair was swept back over a large forehead, with only the thinnest streak of white starting to show. His ego clearly did not extend to hair color; the man had to be working out every day though.

'I'm real Mitch,' Everett smiled. 'The very man.'

Mitch smiled again, realizing that he'd been staring.

'I'm sorry. You must get that a lot.'

'Don't meet that many ordinary people Mitch. Then again, after last night, you're hardly ordinary any more are you?'

'I don't know how to answer that.'

'Fair dues.'

Yelina entered with some bandages, which Everett immediately noticed.

'You're not hurt are you? Heather?'

'Sprains,' Yelina said, handing one roll of cotton bandages to Heather, placing the other on the bar. She then leaned down and raised Mitch's left leg with a steady hand. Mitch reclined slightly as Yelina undid his laces, pulled off his old black Doc and gently examined his ankle.

'Does this hurt?'

'No.'

'This?'

'Ow. A bit.'

'You're okay. Not a bad sprain. No running tomorrow, you will feel okay in the morning.'

She proceeded to remove his sock, then started wrapping the bandage around his ankle. It made him feel sleepy.

'Your toenails need a trim.'

'I know.'

'Nobody to sleep with, to tell you this? A man like you?'

'I –'

Heather laughed, softly, and shook her head.

'I can't believe you fell for her.'

'For who?' Mitch asked, prickly.

Heather turned to Everett. 'Cricket seduced him.'

'Is that right?' Everett smiled. 'She's fast that girl.'

'How do you know?' Mitch demanded.

'I smelt her perfume all over you when we kissed at the bar.'

'Oh.'

Yelina finished her wrapping and began to replace his sock. 'Seems you have had a good day,' she smiled. It was more maternal than anything.

'Define good.'

'To feel the kiss of two young women in one day,' Yelina smiled, less maternal.

Heather groaned. 'It was a fake kiss Yelina. I had to do the whole party girl thing to get us out of that fucking awful party. Even then we nearly got shot.'

'But you didn't,' Everett grumbled.

'No, we didn't. But I've never had anything on me like those three *things* at the elevator. They were definitely not from here.'

Yelina handed Mitch his shoe. 'Business talk. You can manage this yourself.'

She nodded at Everett and departed.

They were silent until they heard a sliding door clunk shut at the other end of the deck.

'She totally jumped me,' Mitch muttered. 'And it's been a while.'

'If I said "*men*" now, would you blame me?'

'No.'

'Look, that's her M.O.' Heather shrugged. 'Cricket thinks that men will like her if she sleeps with them.'

'But I do like her.'

'Because she screwed you.'

'No,' Mitch frowned. 'I liked her when she honked the car horn. I thought that took spirit.'

'She knew that.'

'She knew?'

'Look, she did her research. She probably knows more about you than you do. She had you pegged as a guy with not much going for him who'd be grateful for any action going. She knows she's good-looking and she knows she's ten years younger than you. She knows that you think that she's out of your league – although you're wrong about that.'

'Do I thank you here?'

'Look, it's not *all* you. She just did the math. Your self-esteem is at an all-time low. Like I said, she's one of those girls. If she sleeps with someone, they like her. If they like her, they let her hang around, and that's how she gets her intel. Oldest infiltration method in the book. She's used it a million times.'

'So you've always known she's CIA?'

'Oh yeah.'

'And, Pan knew she was CIA?'

'Totally.'

'And you really are Pan's ex?'

'Going back a while now.'

'And you hooked him up with your uncle, who then sent him on covert missions to South America, to research mind expanding drugs?'

'That's about the sum of it.'

'Where he was killed; but not before – presumably – somehow spiking me with one of those drugs?'

Heather fell silent.

Everett hummed. 'That, we don't know. But it seems probable.'

Mitch nodded. That, he was fairly sure, he did know. But he was not going to let that one out. That one stayed hidden.

'So what do you know?' Mitch asked. 'And what do you want from me?'

Exchange of information, in other words.

Mitch was pretty sure Everett would understand things in those terms.

'I'm a self-made man, Mitch. I don't come from any of the traditional colleges or networks; I made myself from the ground up. I don't belong to any societies, or organizations to which I owe my allegiance. I don't know, or should I say, I don't use any of the secret handshakes or known phrases that open doors or court special favors. Because of that, the establishment doesn't know what to make of me. I'm hardly the only one but I am the most powerful of a very small minority. But I have integrated myself, and my money, into the world, the business and financial world, in such a way that to remove me would upset the balance of things. The position allows me special privileges of a very unique variety; I have my own perspective, my own view of things, I can explore areas that others deem irrelevant, irrational, even irreverent or sacrilegious. I can see other futures, different paths for humanity.'

'Different to what?'

'Different to what they have planned. Don't think there is no plan for humanity Mitch. And I don't mean God's plan, or anything like that – although some who have a plan believe it to be God's plan. There are several plans for humanity; some are opposed, some are aligned, some run parallel but ignore each other. All of them, the Americans, the British, the Russians, the Europeans, the Chinese, the Indians, the Jews, the Muslims, the Christians, even the Buddhists have a plan for humanity. Whether they admit to it or not. Whether they know it or not. But they all have one thing in common.'

'What's that?'

'They all need lots and lots and lots and lots of money to make their plans happen. And that's where people like me, the point zero-zero percent who control all the money, come into things.'

'All the money? I thought the super-wealthy controlled more like eighty percent?'

'Is that not enough Mitch?'

'Point taken.'

'So,' Everett narrowed his eyes. 'What do I want with you then?'

Mitch stared back. At that moment, Everett's eyes seemed pitiless.

Then he smiled. 'I want you to do something for me.'

'I figured. You want some of my blood, right?'

'Absolutely. You won't object?'

'I figure someone like you has the resources to analyze blood and figure out what's in mine. Right?'

'That's not all I want Mitch.'

'Okay.' He was getting nervous now.

'But to tell you the rest, I have to tell you about Pan. And if I tell you about Pan, the real Pan, the Pan I knew, the Pan who came to work for me, and I am sad to say I called a friend, because coming to work for me got him killed, then I have to tell you, knowing about the real Pan means that the minute you step back on shore, there will be people willing to kill you. Not aliens, not misguided cops, but real people in the real world. So, Mitch Pyne, tell me now, or forever hold your tongue…'

Everett leaned forward so that Mitch could stare right into his pitiless blue eyes.

'…are you ready to know about the real Pan?'

CHAPTER TWENTY-THREE

'The real Pan was an intuitive genius. Aside from all the mystic and metaphysical material he propagated about the internet, he had a mind for chemical biology and its sister discipline, biochemistry, like nothing I or any of my people have ever seen. He was completely untrained, yet he took to it like a savant. I won't go into details but he made certain discoveries, certain advances, into the nature of consciousness as applied to chemical biology that others had sought to prove, or disprove, for centuries.'

Mitch frowned.

'Look, Mister Everett...'

'Bo.'

'I know you're into telecommunications. You have your own satellites. I know you have an airline as well. I assume that's just what the general public knows about; but I also know that your big thing is space travel. It's your passion. I saw you on TV, maybe only yesterday...'

Mitch's thoughts paused and suddenly stopped in their tracks.

Yesterday?

Mind, time and perspective, Everett had cried out.

It truly seemed a lifetime away.

'Are you okay Mitch?' Heather asked.

Mitch nodded slowly. 'I'm fine.' He met Everett's gaze again. 'But I've never heard anything about you being interested in... well, I don't know... whatever this is I'm involved in.'

Everett nodded. 'That's okay. That's as it should be. Can I go on?'

Mitch shrugged and Everett nodded.

'The long and short of it was that in studying the human

genome sequence, Pan was looking for a particular sequence, a genetic formula if you will, that would determine which genes related to the forming of human consciousness. To do this, he was using a combination of mind-expanding drugs, principally DMT, that occur naturally in some of the plants in the jungles of Peru. His proposition was this: that by studying human DNA, by using supercomputers to crunch sequences out of the human genome map, that he could manipulate human biochemistry and genetically expand human consciousness. It was Pan's belief that by essentially accelerating the evolution of human consciousness, through genetic manipulation, it would be possible for mankind to perceive outside of our mundane three dimensions of space and one of time.'

'But isn't that just tripping?' Mitch shrugged.

'No. What Pan proposed was that we could do this – yet remain fixed within an ordinary human perspective.'

Mitch sighed. 'The next step in the evolution of consciousness. That's what Vance was talking about.'

'No doubt.'

'Well, where is it? What did he do with the results?'

'The problem is – we don't know. I like to give my researchers free reign, free will. Pan worked very hard, and he and I discussed his early genetic discoveries at length. The last time I spoke to him, he told me he had discovered something that would change everything: presumably this gene sequence and the *formula* to crack it. He suggested it was like a Rosetta Stone for the evolution of human consciousness. He did not want to tell me very much via phone, he wanted to come home and see me in person. And he was on his way to do that when he was killed.'

'But, surely he stored all his research?'

'It's all gone. Hardware, drives, security footage, even the note pads, gone – along with every last byte of online backup. As for his fellow researchers, there were three. They all vanished without trace.'

Mitch gulped.

He wondered if he should say something.

One of them is in town… one of them paid me a visit.

And one sinister, anonymous American woman knows all about it…

He looked at Heather. Her expression gave him nothing.

So instead of confessing, he asked Everett a question.

'You think aliens did it?'

'I doubt it. They're real but they're mostly observers. We have treaties with them going back to the dawn of the Industrial Age, maybe earlier. And besides that, there seems to be something, some kind of agreement between them that somehow designates that they cannot interfere with this planet's evolution. Of that much, we're almost certain.'

'Vance said something similar.'

'Vance knows a lot; we don't really know how much, or where his knowledge comes from. We know he kept in touch with Pan, suggested topics and guests for his podcast interviews. But he remained outside of the greater organization that formed around Pan. You might say he was Pan's guide, his mentor – his guru, even.'

'They kept that quiet.'

'Indeed.'

'So are you in touch with any of them? These aliens?'

'They won't speak to the likes of me,' Everett grumbled. 'I'm part of the problem.'

Heather leaned forward and placed her hand on his.

'But you're trying to fix that, aren't you?'

Everett grasped her relatively tiny fingers in his giant pale orange-freckled maw. He nodded, almost imperceptibly. It seemed to mean a lot to him.

'There's more to this than the pure evolution of human consciousness, Mitch. Much more. But this is where it begins. This is where all the secrets begin to unravel. This is where humanity enters a new age.'

New age was right, Mitch thought. If he hadn't been through

all he'd been through today, if he'd been himself, yesterday, then that's what he'd be saying right now.

New Age Bullshit Billionaire.

But he *had* been through it.

And he needed to know.

'So – where do I fit in?'

'We think Pan spiked you with something that opened up your consciousness. Perhaps from some part of the formula he spoke of. Perhaps the very formula itself. Before he ended his call, just before his fatal shooting, he told me something unusual.'

'More unusual than telepathic aliens…?'

'Or should I say cryptic?'

'Okay.'

'He told me that he had six gifts. That he had prepared them before his departure, and that he had sent one each to each of the six people he trusted most. He said that when the gifts were opened, I would know. That I would see that what he said was true.'

'Jesus. That sounds a bit… well, Biblical doesn't it?'

'He was an eccentric.'

'Still. Given what he was doing, that's *pretty eccentric.*'

'I know. But do you see what that means?'

'That – I got one of the gifts?'

'It would seem that way. You are able to perceive, at least to an extent, an expanded reality. Alternate, parallel dimensions. And yet you are clearly lucid, clearly functioning normally and rationally. I would guess, given Pan's research, that your genetic codes, perhaps to do with the excretions of DMT from the pineal gland, have been rewritten so that you have, in essence, expanded your consciousness in a completely natural way. No side effects, no psychological trauma, no psychedelic noise. Simply cogent perception of an expanded reality.'

Mitch nodded.

Great. Vance was right again.

Spiked.

'And that makes me dangerous?'

'It makes you a commodity. A very rare commodity.'

Mitch suddenly frowned. 'But why do that? Spike me? Send out these six – *gifts*? It sounds like… like he was almost expecting to be killed? That he might not make it back home…?'

'My thoughts exactly.'

There was silence for a second, before Everett picked up.

'So, Mitch, that's what I want you to do. I want you to go looking for the others. The *other* five people he trusted most in the world. You were his good friend. His oldest friend by all accounts. If anyone will be able to get to the truth, it's you.'

Mitch sipped his beer.

How the hell?

Just last night he'd been thinking that they were no longer truly friends, not in the long years since college.

And yet, he'd come to him, in a dream.

In a dream.

'I think I know who one of them might be. I think I have a name to go on.'

'Well, that's a start. May I ask who that might be?'

'Someone called Suzie Saturn.'

Everett frowned. 'I'm sure I'd remember someone by that name – and I don't. But – why does it ring a bell?'

Heather frowned. 'I know what you mean. It's like… a name I've never heard before, but somehow… I *should* have.'

'That's odd,' Mitch looked from Everett to Heather. 'I had exactly the same reaction.'

An eerie silence descended, then Everett shook it off.

'I'll get my people on it. I want you to use anyone you think can help. Put a team together. I'll want some of my people with you but they won't get in your way. Just for your protection. You let me know who you want, I will run a security clearance; and you will be free to tell them what you like.'

'Anything?'

'Like I said, I like my operatives to have free will.'

'Enough free will to get them killed.'

'Indeed. Though hopefully, the people I employ make more intelligent choices than that.'

'Pan wasn't intelligent? I thought you said he was an intuitive genius?'

'He was. But, somewhere down the line, he *somehow* trusted the wrong person. Whoever he saw on the side of the road that day, whoever it was he trusted enough to get out of the car, is someone I would almost certainly state as being the person who either killed Pan, or got him killed, and therefore, someone most categorically not to be trusted.'

'And you have no idea who that was?'

'Not as yet. I have a list of names, but so far none of them have shown up. Like his three researchers, they've just vanished.'

Mitch gulped again.

Should he confess?

That he'd met one of them?

That he'd delivered a parcel?

'Can I get that list? The people who worked with him; and the suspects?'

'If you agree, then yes. But I can tell you; the two lists are not very different. I will have a dossier sent to your room at your new hotel.'

'My new hotel?'

'One I own. One where nobody will disturb you.'

'Okay. If I agree, I want to be able to tell Saph. I don't know if she'll want to be involved, but I need to tell her.'

'Security's already cleared her. Tell her what you like.'

'Vance seems to know a lot about all this. I'd want to confide in him, see what else he knows.'

'Already cleared. Next.'

Jesus, Mitch thought, how long had this been going on?

'I can't think of anyone else. Unless you can get those Pleiadeans on board?' Mitch turned to Heather. 'The ones who protected us in the lift?'

Heather sighed, unsure. Everett responded.

'Chances are they were just enforcing the rules. It's my understanding they have already expressed a disinterest in you. But those other things – they're new. I'll have to see about them.'

'That's not reassuring.'

'No,' Everett stated firmly. 'It is not.'

'Okay. If you can protect me, I'm in.'

'I'm pleased to hear that Mitch.'

'I'll need to contact the old gang. Half of them didn't show, but –'

Everett reached under the bar and produced what was unmistakably a legal contract.

'Sign here. Look at it if you like, but there's no tricks. Just everything we discussed plus standard non-disclosure.'

Mitch was surprised. He had assumed Everett would want none of this on paper. Yet as he flicked through the contract, a mere seven pages, it outlined almost everything Mitch had agreed to as though Everett had been reading from a script. Everett offered him a pen, and he signed.

What the hell.

'And sign again on the last page,' Everett nodded. 'This time in blood.'

Mitch freaked, quickly flipping to the last page on the contact.

Everett laughed. 'The sooner we get you to your hotel the better. I'll arrange to have your friends sent there. Heather will go with you. She'll be part of the team. And for reasons of my own I want the government in on this one; you'll keep Miss Cricket around, because you like her. Agreed?'

Mitch shrugged.

'I've been through more with these people in the past day than I've been through with anyone in years. Why the hell not?'

Everett nodded, took the signed contract away, replaced it under the bar, then came up with three white A-4 envelopes. He placed them on the table like a Three-Card Monte dealer, then tapped the first.

'Hotel swipe key, a copy of the contract you just signed, and a credit card. My airline. There's a cash limit, but call me on the number I gave you and I can extend it. But frankly, if you go over *that* limit, you had better have a damned good reason for extending it. Understood?'

Mitch gulped. 'Completely.'

He raised the second, much thicker with content.

'Heather has been collecting information for me; in here are copies of the coverage. It will tell you everything you need to know about what and who we might be dealing with, once you leave this boat.'

Everett tapped the third envelope, a white A-4.

It was thick.

'A copy of Smart Tech For Dummies, latest update; and a hardcopy instruction manual.'

'For what?'

Everett removed a new phone from his jacket pocket and handed it to Mitch.

'It has a tracer so don't lose it. Welcome to the firm. Any more questions?'

Mitch considered.

It was all a bit overwhelming.

He gulped his beer.

Clearly, Everett expected him to say 'no, no! thank you so much!' and depart.

What Mitch really felt like saying was 'thank you so much for letting me run out and risk getting killed for you, for taking part in a world I had no hand in creating and no intention of ever knowing about or becoming involved with!'

But he also remembered some advice, spoken earlier that night.

It was like the genie's wishes.

Careful what you wish for – there's always a catch.

Everett watched him.

Everett knew that he was thinking it through.

Everett had seen this before, and was pleased that he had hired someone who at least was willing to ask.

At least, that's what Mitch thought he saw.

Really, Everett could have been thinking about anything.

He was probably thinking about how many minutes longer this would take before he could get back to Yelina and her giant bosom.

'You are a billionaire. Multi, right?'

'Yes.'

'And, solving this problem means a lot to you. Right?'

'I could say that.'

Heather leaned forward. It was as though she couldn't quite believe what she was seeing; like she had always wanted to see this.

'I am so very tired Mister Everett.'

'Yes. I know.'

'I want ten million bucks for each of the other five gifts I locate.'

'Ten?'

'Is that too much or too little? Am I weak because I ask for too little, or strong because I dare to ask in the first place?'

'Pan cut a deal. Everyone cuts a deal. I have money. That's what I have to offer.'

Mitch shrugged. 'It seems like it would be okay to ask that.'

'I tell you what, Mister Pyne. If you bring back all five, whatever form they take, I'll double it.'

It seemed very surreal to Mitch. All that money.

'Okay,' he said.

'I'll have the extended contract to you by morning. But what about the sixth, Mister Pyne? What do you want for your blood?'

'You could just take it. You haven't. You've asked.'

'I have. And you agreed.'

'Then, in that case, what I want is a favor. In the bank. A solid. It may take the form of parts; but it will be one favor. Agreed?'

Everett looked at him curiously, as though a household cat

had just done something very clever and unexpected, like using cutlery, right before his very eyes. Bo Everett extended his giant hand and they shook.

'Mister Pyne,' he smiled. 'That is without a doubt the wisest choice you have made all day.

CHAPTER TWENTY-FOUR

Alone with the ocean and facing into a mild breeze, Mitch stared out at the vast moonlit body of water before him, leaning on the railing as he chomped through a club sandwich that had been specially prepared by Everett's personal chef. The accompanying fries were very salty, which kind of went with the general aroma of being several miles offshore, and he was glad of the fresh beer that had been served alongside them. He could see Heather and Everett inside the boat's massive glass-walled penthouse, having a private discussion at the bar.

He doubted they were catching up on family gossip.

For the first ten minutes veils of cloud obscured the stars. However, as he munched down the last of the fries, the wind came up and, of the two banks of overlapping clouds, the higher was traveling much faster than the lower, allowing a gap through to the night sky.

Mitch was shocked at the sheer volume of stars he saw.

At home, the oddly angled harbor view from his balcony contained a lot of ambient city light, with the Sydney skyline almost completely blocking out the night sky anyway. Somehow, moving through various suburban flats and houses, then apartment to apartment over the span of his adult life, he'd almost forgotten what an awe-inspiring spectacle the Milky Way actually was.

Virtually incomprehensible.

A vast machine for replicating DNA…?

He tried to remember how long it had been since he'd ventured out of the city, or even the suburbs, and gotten away from the fake lighting; and taken the opportunity to remind himself of what the cosmos, the cosmos he lived in, really looked like.

Many years, he suspected.

He looked back down and out at the ocean horizon, as the clouds closed in again. Shit, he could barely get a grip on how many thousands, or tens of thousands, or millions of other people lived in the city with him. And there were thousands of other cities, just like it, all over the world. Not to mention that there was a whole other different global ecosystem, larger again, right under him, right now…

…let alone that there were thousands of *other* planets, all presumably with the *same deal running.*

Multiple planets, multiple deals, apparently.

How much could the mind deal with, on that scale?

Really deal with, truly process?

His mind broke away from the idea.

Incomprehensible.

He shrugged to himself and laughed a bit.

It was just more stuff, he supposed.

More information.

The sound of a heavy sliding glass door broke his reverie, as the clinking of the ice in his glass signaled that Everett was approaching.

Mitch turned from the horizon and there he was again, in the flesh. The big man himself.

'We're just past the point on the horizon where you could see the lights on the coast. I like it just here, just out of sight.'

Mitch shrugged. 'Yeah. The dinghy ride wasn't long, I figured we couldn't be too far out.'

'Do you need to sleep, Mitch? I told them to take you back whenever you like.'

'What time is it? I left my watch in my hotel room.'

'It's around ten thirty. You can sleep here a while, if you like.'

'I am tired. But I feel I should go back and let Saph know.'

'Why don't you call her? Her number is in your new phone.'

Mitch looked back into the suite, at the bar. The envelopes

were still there.

'I wouldn't know how to make a call on one of those things.'

Everett smiled. 'I think I'd be more impressed if you'd resisted technology out of some moral or ethical stance; like people who still listen to vinyl records.'

'How do you know I didn't?'

'Because I know about you.'

'More than I know about myself? Like Cricket?'

Everett smiled. '*Oh would some Power the gift give us, To see ourselves as others see us.*'

Mitch nodded. 'Robert Burns. My grandfather used to quote that. I guess I knew I was on a long sulk. It was just easier to give up.'

'The world is in flux. Technology is moving too fast for the systems we have in place to keep up. You're not the only person to fall through the gap.'

'I know.'

'You should sleep, if you can. It's my understanding that people who've been through a major epiphany can remain sleepless for days; and you've had several. Sleep will help you process your experience, and integrate it within your psyche, better than staying awake and turning it over and over.'

'Is that right?' Mitch sounded dubious. He felt he'd heard enough wisdom for one day.

'Then again, with sleep there is loss; staying awake keeps the experience fresh – and alive.'

'Look, my epiphany, if you want to call it that, was artificial. It didn't come from decades of sitting in a cave contemplating "the gap", or whatever the monks call it; and it didn't come from lying for three years on a bed of nails. It came from a drug, not from scripture or discipline. I didn't ask for it; and I'm not sure I even want it.'

'That's how epiphanies work. The universe, the conscious universe, doesn't see a difference between a meditation and a dosage. That's all baloney. It wants us to evolve, to seek new perspectives. And it doesn't particularly care how we do it. An epiphany is always an epiphany.'

'You've had one?'

'Several. Don't invest in dot com was one of my most enlightening.'

'A financial epiphany?'

'Money is a mechanism, an energy, and right now my money is protecting you. You are unique; maybe in the grand scheme of things I made all my money so that when the time was right, I was here to point you in the right direction?'

Heather returned to the deck, the glass doors again hissing heavily.

Mitch was shocked at her appearance; the heavy brown dreadlocks were gone, cut away, down to an all-over number three cut, and the heavy earthen hippy-wear had been replaced by a simple dark brown bikini, revealing broad but elegant shoulders and a solid, curvaceous figure that her previous costume had all but obscured, even when he'd admired her on the dance floor. Mitch gulped; now she looked like a dryad, a tree spirit of some kind, natural and vibrant with a dark-brown crown of bark.

'Thank God,' she smiled at Mitch, rubbing her hand over her new hair with a beaming smile. 'That was not easy to live with. The things we do for credibility.'

'Then you're not… actually one of them?'

'One of who?'

'The UFO people? Pan's People?'

'I had to grow those so they'd take me seriously, as Uncle Bo's niece. Now I don't care what they think of me. But I am still one of them, as it happens. I'm not some three-timing proto-spy like Cricket, who doesn't know who the fuck she is half the time. And when she does, she hates herself.'

Everett threw Mitch a look that all men knew; there was more going on between the two women than either of them knew and it was better to keep out of it.

Heather cast her eye back into the suite.

'I'm going to sit in the spa for an hour then get some sleep. You don't care if we wait 'til morning to get back to the mainland, do you Mitch?'

It was difficult to say no to a woman in a bikini.

'Of course not. I'm exhausted.'

Heather turned and walked back. 'You won't want to join me then. Can't have you falling asleep in the spa.'

The thought crossed Mitch's mind; could he?

He thought.

He decided not.

Everett read the decision on his features.

'Dear me, Mitch,' Everett smiled. 'You *must be* tired.'

CHAPTER TWENTY-FIVE

Mitch watched the ocean and the sky a while longer with Everett, who casually named a few of the stars and constellations they were able to spot between the passing cloudbanks. Mitch was interested, but weary.

After some silence, Everett turned to him.

'There are a lot of Heather's reports in the file I prepared for you. She's very good at what she does.'

'Did you get her to watch me?'

Everett smiled. 'I give my people free reign. Maybe she did, maybe she didn't.'

Mitch sighed and looked up at the stars.

'You really think…?' Mitch pondered, almost rhetorically.

Everett reached into his back pocket and pulled out a thin selection of perhaps six folded sheets of A-4 paper.

'There are some things I keep with me, Mitch. Things I look at when I want reinforcement, to keep me going.'

Mitch watched him unfold and sort through the sheets, then select one. He handed it to Mitch. The paper was rough, and had clearly been kept long and been assessed many times. Mitch gulped.

What the hell did a billionaire keep in his back pocket to read every day?

He looked at the paper and could just read the print by moonlight. It was the last thing he felt like doing, reading text, but how did he say no to a man with tremendous power and who may very well have been revealing one of his secrets?

So, despite his gathering fatigue, Mitch read:

Theoretical physicist, co-founder of string theory and science 'popularizer' Michio Kaku is well-known to many mainstream thinkers, seen by some as the successor to Carl Sagan when it comes to popularizing science for the masses.

In Kaku's 1994 book ***Hyperspace: A Scientific Odyssey Through Parallel Universes, Time Warps, and the Tenth Dimension*** he popularized the Kardashev Scale, a speculative method first proposed by Soviet astronomer Nikolai Kardashev in 1964, used to determine the technological level, and later the corresponding size (and in an addendum by Sagan himself, the information level) of four types of civilizations he believes might exist out there: Types 0, 1, 2, & 3.

We are a Type 0 civilization, stuck on one planet, dependent on dead plants, still using giant contained explosions just to break orbit.

Type 1 civilizations harness the energy output of the whole planet. They manipulate planetary energies, like hurricanes, volcanoes and earthquakes, altering, controlling and harnessing the power of planetary phenomena. An advanced Type 1 would colonize its solar system and be looking outward to others.

Type 2 civilizations harness the energy output of a star. They generate approximately 10 billion times the energy output of Type 1. Kaku likens an advanced Type 2 civilization to the Federation on *Star Trek*, exploring the galaxy and seeking out new life forms and... well, you know the drill.

Type 3 civilizations harness the energy output of a galaxy – 10 billion times the energy output of Type 2. Type 3 civilizations are like the Empire from *Star Wars*; they own the galaxy.

Kaku's best estimate is that we will reach Type 1 status in a couple of hundred years, with Earth currently approaching 0.8 on the Kardashev Scale, Type 2 in a few thousand, and Type 3 status in anywhere from 100,000 to one million years hence.

But he stresses, somewhat glibly, that these time scales are insignificant when compared with the age of the universe itself.

Furthermore, in a later book, ***Parallel Worlds: A Journey Through Creation, Higher Dimensions, and the Future of the Cosmos*** (2005) Kaku also suggests that there may even be a Type 4 civilization that harnesses as yet unknown extragalactic energies, such as those that might be associated with dark matter. Others have suggested that a Type 4 civilization would harness the gravitational power of super clusters, or even some vast, undiscovered universal energy that would render them completely undetectable to us, their very existence indivisible from the workings of the greater cosmos itself.

For us though, the problem with comparing these advanced civilizations to *Star Trek*, and *Star Wars*, is that it leaves out what we understand as consciousness expansion; *Star Trek* and *Star Wars* are all very well but they are essentially morality plays, inhabited by beings of Type 0 and Type 1 'human' consciousness, played out on a canvas of Type 2 and Type 3 civilizations.

Probably closer to what we'll see (and fans of both of the above franchises will loathe this analogy) are the likes of the Shadows and Vorlons from the lesser known but still cult-popular series *Babylon 5* – or those in Arthur C. Clarke's *2001: A Space Odyssey*.

Still, that aside, within their human-consciousness-bound limitations, Kardashev and Kaku's Civilization Types correspond pretty much exactly to the greater portion of contemporary metaphysical beliefs, as to what is out there, or what may already be here.

'Far out,' Mitch muttered, weary but genuinely intrigued. 'Who wrote that?'

He handed it back to Everett, who placed it back on the top of his papers, refolded them and returned them to his back pocket.

'Just something to ponder when you star gaze, Mitch.'

'Okay.'

'As for the other reading material, the one on the top of the pile, you should read that as soon as possible. Tonight if you can.'

Mitch nodded and stared into the black of the ocean.

'I'll try.'

Everett patted him on the shoulder. 'Good man.'

Yelina arrived and offered to show him to his room. It was one flight down and along a short corridor, a guest room already made up, the bed the same king-size as the one in his room back at the Vantage.

'The mattress is new,' she said. 'You will sleep very well.'

'Do you know how to use this phone Yelina?'

'Who do you want to call?'

'I thought I should call my friend Saph.'

'Give it to me.'

He'd taken the envelopes from the bar on the way down; they were still in his hand and he gave her the one in which he'd placed the phone. She fished it out and examined it for all of a second, then waved her fingers over it like a magician, or someone out of *Star Trek*.

He suddenly thought of the quote he'd always heard attributed to Arthur C. Clarke that any sufficiently advanced technology would appear like magic to a less-advanced civilization.

Well, in this case, *he* was the less advanced, he was Type Zero-Zero.

But tied to the information Everett had made him read, the thought stuck: shape-shifters who walked through pillars, men who were there but you couldn't see… even the sun transmitting information.

A giant machine for DNA.

Machines were technology…

Before he could think any further, Yelina handed the phone back.

'It's ringing.'

'Jesus!'

He'd only considered calling, he'd not yet decided!

He put the phone to his ear and heard, 'Hello? Is anybody there?'

'Saph?'

'Mitch?'

'It's me! You won't believe where I am!'

'Where the hell are you!'

'Saph – *I'm using a phone! A new phone!*'

'Good night,' Yelina uttered, leaving him to it.

'Who was that?' asked Saph.

The cabin door clicked shut.

'That was Yelina,' Mitch smiled.

'Who's Yelina? Mitch; where are you?'

'I think Yelina is Bo Everett's girlfriend.'

'Bo Everett?'

There was a pause.

'Mitch, are you with Bo Everett?'

'Not right now. But he's here.'

'Here? Where?'

'I can't say. At least, I don't know if I can say. He said I could tell you anything I want, but…'

'He's dictating to you?'

'Dictating?'

'Telling you what you can and cannot do?'

'No, He's – '

'Mitch, where are you exactly? I'm coming to get you.'

'You can't, I'm not in the city any more.'

'You're not in the… Mitch *what the hell is going on?*'

'Look, he gave me this phone, so I'm assuming it's somehow

secure. Are you sitting down?'

He told her everything, all except the bit about having sex with Cricket, hoping that if she were still there, still in his room, at the wake or at the hotel, she would not say anything.

Saph didn't sound happy, exactly, and ended the call quite abruptly, only saying that she needed time to think.

Mitch sat on the bed in his cabin, feeling as though he had somehow betrayed her.

But he had acted in their best interests, hadn't he?

Acted to protect them all?

He lay back and stared at the white ceiling.

Hadn't he?

He hadn't realized that he'd fallen asleep until he woke; he didn't know how much later it was but it felt like a full cycle, perhaps ninety minutes. His body felt like lead and his mind was barely functional. He only half-remembered where he was and when he stood to remove his shoes and jacket, and trousers, it seemed to take an eternity. He hadn't expected to sleep but desperately wanted more; he moved with as much clear purpose as he could muster, to disrobe with smooth practicality, in the hope that the activity would not wake him any further. He saw two light switches above the bed and climbed in, naked, and hit the top switch. Annoyingly, it turned on the bedside light; the second killed the room light and as soon as he put out the bedside light and his head hit the pillow, he was gone.

He was in a strip club.

The woman on stage was young, nineteen maybe, and was performing her act. She was very good, a slender brunette with a natural body, dressed in a tight white lab coat with bright blue lingerie underneath.

To his left, there was a small film crew, shooting a couple having sex on a bed. He looked from the stage to the bed… it seemed very much like the same woman, in two places at once.

The men, the crew, the audience, even the man having sex, were all faceless.

Because it was a dream, Mitch took all this in his stride.

A woman sat beside him at his table.

It was the same woman again, almost regal in a formal red cocktail dress and jewelry.

The same woman, thrice.

A photographer moved to the stage and, as the stripper began to disrobe, started taking pictures. The dance changed; now it was more stilted, less fluid, breaking up unnaturally into a series of staged poses.

'I'm all that's left,' said the woman on stage.

The woman on the bed wailed in orgasm, perhaps even a real one, and Mitch looked over. She looked at him, just a little sad.

'They took all of me,' said the woman in the porno shoot.

Mitch heard this. He looked to the woman, the same woman, who was sitting beside him. He had paid a high price, he knew, just to have her at his side, just for one night. She was incredibly beautiful, a rare beauty, the kind that could be exploited for millions.

'I've been everywhere,' she smiled.

CHAPTER TWENTY-SIX

Mitch woke.

Light was coming through a cabin window that last night he hadn't realized was there. Somehow he knew Yelina had been in and opened it.

The dream stayed in his mind and he felt sexually charged because of that. He stretched and lay for a while. There was a bathroom; he got up and took a shower. It wasn't until he began to soap himself down that he realized there was a small, round band-aid in the crook of his elbow.

Blood had been taken during the night.

He almost shuddered; it was practically vampiric.

But he didn't shudder.

A deal was a deal.

Quick and painless.

Assessing himself in the bathroom mirror, he looked bleary eyed but his pale face seemed to shine. He shaved and brushed his teeth with the new, unwrapped items supplied, then dried himself and quickly redressed.

On the cabin dresser was another contract and a pen.

The contract outlined the rewards deal Mitch had negotiated, if he could call it that, last night.

He signed it and left it on the dresser.

Mitch had no idea what time it was but, as he recalled his way back up to the penthouse deck, he saw that the sun was still very low in the sky and that the thick morning clouds were once again looking like rain.

It was still winter and he had not slept, as he'd suspected, for months. He'd merely had a good night's rest after a long day.

Heather was on deck, outside the glass walls, and she smiled as she saw him approach. She was still dressed in shades of brown, but the outfit was more conventional: a tight chocolate sweater, dark brown jeans, a thick black coat and deep crimson scarf, with the same heavy hiking shoes she'd worn last night, the same as those favored by her uncle. She looked warm and when Mitch opened the door he realized why. A cold wind blasted through his black funeral suit like a band saw.

'Jesus!' he exclaimed; but still moved toward her.

Out to sea, the storm clouds were moving in. They were almost black and he saw three wide strikes of lightning before he reached her at the railing.

She laughed sympathetically as he shivered beside her.

'I think Uncle Bo has a wardrobe on board. I don't think he'd mind if I borrowed something warmer for you.'

'Where is he? I have a few more questions.'

'Gone. But you can ask me.'

'Gone?'

'You didn't hear the helicopter?'

'No. I slept like a baby.'

'It woke me.'

'Where'd he go?'

'Who knows? We're just his pet project. He's got real business in the real world.'

'Like revamping the space program?'

'I think that's just a hobby too.'

'So who's minding the boat?'

'The crew. Who else?'

'Where are they?'

'Below.' She turned back to the seaboard penthouse. 'There's one.'

A man was bringing a large tray to the bar; two others followed. Heather ushered Mitch back inside, to find that a breakfast smorgasbord had been prepared and left for them; Mitch chomped immediately into a hot ham and cheese croissant while Heather chowed into a plate of fruit. The coffee was the best Mitch had tasted in a long time.

They spoke while they ate.

'How was Saph?'

'Angry.'

'Cricket?'

'Don't know.'

'Uncle Bo will have programmed her number. Have you read the manual yet?'

'I was out as soon as I hit the pillow. Before, actually.'

'What's it like? To have all that in your head?'

Mitch wondered. 'Right now, it's not like anything. It just hits. I suppose, thinking back on yesterday… whatever it is doesn't activate unless there's something to see.' He nodded to himself. 'Yeah. That… that seems apparent now.' He nodded again. 'I think the sleep helped.'

'Well, you see anything, you tell me. Okay?'

'What are you Heather? You said last night you needed more training. I thought you were an agent or something.'

'I'm just adventurous. My uncle couldn't stop me, so he brought me in. Works well for both of us. I think I'm the most like him, in the family. He likes me. Better than he likes my dad, or my brothers anyway.'

Mitch nodded.

'So you really missed the whole tech revolution thing huh?'

'Seems so.'

'I think that's amazing. I don't know how you could.'

'It's amazing alright. Amazing what defeat can do to you.'

Heather nodded and hummed thoughtfully.

'Hope I never get to find out.'

Mitch huffed.

'He asked me to ask you if you read the report; the one on ayahuasca?'

'Aya-what?'

'Obviously not.'

'I think Vance mentioned something about it last night.'

'You'd better go get it. He didn't want us leaving here 'til you'd read it.'

I don't know exactly what you'll experience when you head down south, U, but here's what I've been able to find.

You can wiki the drug ayahuasca and get a fairly decent run down of what it means so far as the meanstream beliefs are. In short, it's a ceremonial drug used by various South American tribes, the active ingedient being the hallucinagen dimethyltryptamine (DMT).

DMT has been known about for a while, since the fifties at least. Its reputation is for being a quick, powerful drug of mind expanding qualities; the reasons for it being not as widespread as LSD are probably to do with its intensity – this is not a leisure drug (although there are currently several knock-offs doing the counter-culture rounds that claim to be).

Its use has even been covered formally by National Geographic, and you can find several such scientifically-based reports online.

If you're still game after you read those…

There are several unsual facts and qualities ascribed to ayahuasca.

Firstly, DMT has no psychotropic effects in its pure form, it must be mixed with a ingredient that counters the human digestive system's tendency to neutralize it.

The amazing thing is, despite the millions, maybe billions of plant variations in the jungles of South America, somehow these tribes managed to 'trip' upon a combination that allows this. The odds of the natives making this discovery are astonomical, and some of the shamans claim that their ancestors were shown the combo in dreams.

The second thing is that ayahuasca trips often have common qualities; people see the same creatures, spirits, or beings, who seem to inhabit some common ground in the collective consciousness that ayahuasca allows us access to. But these are not 'shared hallucinations' as such, as shared hallucinations happen simultaneously in time. These common experiences occur at different times, days, months, years and decades apart; not unlike the tiny bubble creatures that notorious psychonaut Terrence McKenna, and many others, reported seeing under influence of the drug cylicybin.

People under the influence of ayahuasca see the same, or very similar beings; common hallucinations include talking serpents, entities that seem to embody biological abstracts, and blue 'repair men'. It's all anecdotal, and could be down to the power of suggestion, but the list goes on. These entities, if we can call them that, address the trippers individually, and offer a wide and varied range of 'advice'.

The current metaphyscial thinking goes that there are other dimensional realities, and beings that exist within them – and that ayahuasca changes our perception so that we can experience them.

Now here's the kicker: recent research suggests that the pineal gland, the little pine-cone shaped gland that exists at the front of our temporal lobe, in exactly the place the mystics claim to be the location of our third eye (and therefore the seat of all metaphysical experience) actually secretes very small levels of DMT that is created within the body.

And, at the present time, nobody knows why.

At least, nobody is willing to really commit to a scientific definition of what function this might serve.

Current metaphysical thought, and fringe science research, suggests that the pineal gland is a kind of 'reality thermostat' for our conscious perception of concensus reality, ie, the world. That it regulates, by creating and excreting into our brain chemistry small doses of drugs like DMT, and a few other similar chemicals, the way we process and perceive reality. What's certainly true is that by altering the amounts of DMT in the brain, we seem to expand our perceptions of reality beyond what we've evolved to experience.

In other words, the pineal gland might possibly be the thing that allows us to interpret what we call reality through all the masses of waves and signals and energies we receive; we don't see all of the electromagnetic spectrum for instance, just a portion of it, and our whole concept of the everyday is based around that. The same with sound; we only hear certain wavelengths, and our world is essentially based around these. In effect, we all co-create our reality around these limitations, and we have come to do this, we've evolved to do this, and therefore evolved our own reality, over millions of years.

You can imagine the abstract speculation that has gone on in metaphysics as to the so-called ethereal world. Like, if our perceptions were permanently expanded, what would it be like if we could sense and interpret another person's mental energy, or chemical excretions, like pheromones? If we could somehow read a complicated mood as easily as we read a series of expressions, or understand a complex sentence? Would this be something like telepathy? Or a new common sense, like the five others, but empathic somehow?

If you think about this long enough, your brain starts to hurt, but greater minds than mine have tried to imgine such things and the best of them is reportedly a book called A Voyage To Arcturus, *by David Lindsay.*

In the book Lindsay imagines what new organs would be like, organs that would allow us to perceive these 'new senses'. He even invents new colors. It's always been a cult classic, but is now considered one of the most important science fiction books of the twentieth century, and is, I must confess, pretty far out for a book written in 1920, and well worth a read.

But the implications raised by the existence of DMT also give rise to certain important philosophical questions: why have humans evolved as such? Wouldn't it be useful for us, on an evolutionary scale, to evolve a brain that clearly understood the emotions of others? Why don't we have a genuinely 'empathic sense'? Is that what psychics are? The start of that? Or are they just a remnant of something we've lost? Or just a freak mutation, an evolutionary dead end?

Is that why they're so hit and miss, why those who at times seem genuine are then seen resorting to fraud?

Furthermore, some go on to suggest something altogether more sinister. It's one thing to say that the pineal gland may be what allows us human perception within three dimensions of space and one of time, to narrow our reality down to a definitive focus within wider spectrums and wavelengths and all that good stuff, and perhaps even helps to form consciousness itself.

However, it's alternately suggested, given the possibility that we somehow co-create physical realty through our shared perceptions, that the pineal gland could also be viewed as the thing that has slowly, as we have evolved, limited *us to this reality, in essence encasing our consciousness in a kind of material straight-jacket that evolution has for some reason dictated to us.*

Aside from Lindsay, there's almost no end of popular literature that incorporates, usually within analogous sci-fi, this kind of thought; anything from the larger analogy in The Matrix *movies, to graphic novel series like Alan Moore's* Promethea, *or Grant Morrisson's* The Invisibles. *Metaphysical researcher Lynne McTaggart has long written about something she calls* The Field; *admittedly, most rational materialists would tell you it's fantasy and pseudoscience, but I'm not so sure she isn't on to something. Her book is one of the primary gateways to current New Age and metaphysical thought.*

Regardless, this is really complicated stuff, perhaps better branded philosophy rather than pseudoscience, as the basis of it is very real, if not reality itself.

On the pro side, many biologists, psychologists and philosophers now believe that DMT research is the key to proving that consciousness exists at least to some extent outside of the body; that it extends into reality and essentially shapes it according to the way our brains have evolved.

But putting that aside, there's still the issue of ayahuasca itself, and the ceremonies that take place in South America (one of the only counties where it is not considered a major narcotic) where it is beginning to support a thriving 'hippie trail' tourist trade.

One of the main things about the creatures people see in the visions (given the above speculation, let's maybe not call them hallucinations for now) is that they seem to induce not only terrifying awe, but genuine inspiration – one of the main consequenes of having taken the drug is that people leave the ceremony with a renewed verve for life, and a restored or reinforced sense of purpose.

In short, more often than not, the visions inspire a deep personal epiphany, thus its general designation as 'non-recreational'. It's not just pretty colors that make vinyl albums seem more profound.

Anecdotally at least, and with great regularity, people claim to feel cleared out of their old emotional and psychological baggage. They claim to be inspired to reset their life path, or life mission, back from the negative, distracting and in some cases outright destructive life paths down which they've strayed. These things are almost impossible to measure, and no studies have been undertaken to follow up on those who've had the experience, but anecdotal evidence seems to indicate that there is about a fifty-fifty recidivism rate once people get back from Peru and re-enter Western Culture. About half shrug their personal revelations off, like a New Year's resolution, a holiday affair or a midlife crisis, and go back to their normal lives.

But the other half have a complete spiritual and psychological spring clean, and reboot their life patterns totally. Anecdotal evidence also suggests that again, about half of those for whom it doesn't take seem to return to try again, usually within six months.

Compared to just about any other self-help method, that's at least worthy of remark.

Anyway, one thing seems sure – the effect is rejuvenating, even for those who don't incorporate the messages from their vision quest into their ordinary lives. For those who do walk out of the jungle and back into their lives to make changes, almost all of them find some kind of massive creative outlet, almost all of them drop all ties with conventional religion, and almost all of them drop all interest in conventional science.

It must be quite a trip, U.

Let me know how you go.

H

CHAPTER TWENTY-SEVEN

The dinghy took them back, slowly this time, to a private mainland pier. Before they'd disembarked the yacht, Heather had found a long black coat that was at least a size too large for Mitch, went down to his ankles and an inch over his wrists and shoulders, but was tailored from a high quality wool blend that protected him extremely well from the ocean chill and the high, strong winds that were constantly at their back all the way to shore.

They disembarked onto the pier, which led to a long, high hedge that was clearly created to protect whatever lay beyond it from the ocean winds. Given that they had been essentially unable to converse over the outboard dinghy motor, Mitch immediately started up.

'So have you ever tried ayahuasca?'

Heather grinned. 'No. Uncle Bo has though. Pan made him go down there.'

'No shit?'

'I thought about it, but I don't think I'm ready for Mother Nature to slam me with the granddaddy of all passive-aggressive assaults. I like my life the way it is, just fine.'

Mitch hummed thoughtfully.

Heather smirked. '*You* might want to give it a go though?'

She walked on before he had a chance to respond.

But even if he had, what would he say?

That he agreed? That he liked his life just fine?

The wind carried away her next remark, as they moved on up the beach, but he thought he heard part of it.

'*...can't believe you slept with...*'

He let it go.

When they reached a small gate in the hedge, Mitch saw that beyond it was an old rose garden, surrounding a central lawn upon which there were several garden settings.

Beyond that was a mansion.

The building was huge: five floors and, by window count, at least twelve rooms wide. It had been recently restored, with great care and attention to detail, Mitch saw as they strolled in. No, not so much a mansion, he corrected his initial thoughts, more like a *manor*.

There can't have been many like it in Australia, he realized, with its circular driveway and vast grounds extending in every direction away from the beach. But as their feet crunched on the gravel driveway that encircled the manor, he got a closer look and saw a few telltale signs that the manor had been converted into an exclusive hotel.

'This is what he meant by a hotel he owns?' Mitch asked.

'Don't complain Mitch. It starts at two grand per night and there doesn't seem to be anyone else here.'

'He's evacuated the hotel for us?'

'He means business.'

Mitch supposed that he did.

'Hey before we go in, I wanna ask you something.'

'Okay?'

'You know Suzie Saturn?'

'Yeah.'

Mitch smiled. 'Go on…'

Heather hesitated. '…Suzie Saturn, yeah.'

'Yeah.'

'She's… you mentioned her last night.'

'But you thought you knew who she was, right?'

'Because you mentioned her last night.'

'No, I mean, a split second before that. The millisecond after I asked you, you were about to respond like you knew who she was.'

Heather went quiet.

'Maybe… I suppose. Who is she anyway? Why are you so interested?'

'Like I said, she's someone I have to find. But I'm starting to wonder… if she can be found at all.'

Heather gave him a weird look and they proceeded into the manor hotel.

Two black-suited security guards nodded them through to the entrance hall and immediately they heard voices from a parlor to their right. Before they could investigate, however, a skinny white-haired man dressed in a long leather coat stormed across the first floor landing and came stomping down the grand staircase, the whole time swearing in a thick Geordie accent.

'Fucking gas leak, my arse!' he snarled at them as he passed; and continued storming and swearing all the way outside.

Mitch knew the man on sight; almost anyone over twenty would. Mitch had several of the rocker's albums in his collection, at home, on vinyl. He had even interviewed the man once, when he had taken his one and only disastrous shot at being a film star.

Mitch and Heather exchanged glances. There was nothing much to say; the man was a walking definition of the word famous, he'd been right there in front of them, and now he was climbing into a white limousine that had pulled up instantly on the gravel driveway.

The limmo stereo was playing a Mistress song.

Again, Mitch knew it, but creepily felt as though it were new.

'Turn that crap off!' the rock star shouted. The music died and the limmo spirited him immediately away, tires skidding on the gravel.

'Mistress *again*,' Mitch muttered.

'Huh?'

'I keep hearing Mistress songs; and they all sound like I'm hearing them for the first time.'

'Weird.'

'Yeah.'

'Maybe the universe is trying to tell you something?'

Mitch considered a second. 'I'd better check my messages. I think they're starting to pile up.'

Heather smiled and they followed the voices into the parlor.

Once there, Mitch had fully expected to see Saph, Cricket and Vance but was surprised to see three total strangers. More surprising was that they seemed to have been waiting for him.

'Hello Miss Everett. You must be Mister Pyne?'

The first man was middle-aged but looked hard as nails with short, dark-blonde hair, a leathery life-long tan and a tough, wiry physique, dressed in plain khaki fatigues.

'My name's Harding,' he spoke in a clipped South African accent, extending a handshake that caused Mitch no little pain. 'I'll be leading the security on your team.'

Mitch suddenly realized. 'We've met before – you gave me Everett's card, at Pan's funeral.'

Harding smiled. 'Good memory. This is Jo Sara; she'll run what we call the sentries, the people you can see, like the fellows at the door there. You might have seen a few more in the gardens as you came in.'

'I didn't.'

'That's alright. And this is Bill Hinchcliffe, he runs perimeter – the people you can't, and won't see.'

Hinchcliffe shook his hand also; he was younger, taller and slimmer with a neat geek beard and silver-rimmed glasses, dressed in old jeans with a checked shirt over a tee-shirt featuring a design from a demonic superhero character Mitch didn't recognize. He was the tech guy though; at least Mitch recognized that.

'Sara, Hinch and I will be with you the whole time. We all know what to expect; they answer to me, I answer to Mister Everett. Any questions? Have you had breakfast? Coffee's over there.'

The parlor was decorated with a colonial theme; most of the furniture looked like almost-new replicas, apart from a few genuine antiques positioned strategically away from the center of the room to avoid contact with the public. There was a central serving table, solid oak, on which sat an espresso machine and the leftovers of a hotel breakfast smorgasbord, surrounded by six clutches of deep leather chairs, four per setting, arranged like a gentleman's club. At least three of the clutches had been commandeered and were now place-held by laptops and backpacks; he suspected one each for the three security heads. At a guess they had arrived not long ago and immediately set up in the parlor as a temporary base of operations.

Harding saw him scan the room, nodded and smiled tightly.

'Haven't been here long, seemed as good a place as any for a command center. Doesn't look like much but you'd be surprised the size of an operation that can be coordinated with three Macs – ten years ago we'd have needed half the building. That's progress.'

They all had earpieces, Mitch saw.

Bluebeards? Was that what they were called?

They seemed to realize that Mitch wasn't saying anything.

Sara stepped forward and shook his hand.

'The espresso machine's pretty straightforward,' she spoke clearly but in a friendly cadence, with an undertone of posh British. She was around Mitch's age, sporting long blonde hair in a tight ponytail, with severe features that were undercut by huge, soft blue eyes and a wry smile.

Mitch smiled tightly in return and shrugged to Harding.

'Look, what have you been told to expect?' he asked. 'I mean, I don't really know what to expect myself.'

'That's why we're here,' Harding said, narrowing his eyes condescendingly as though to say, *you let the grown-ups take care of that.*

Beside each other, Harding and Sara seemed very uptight, a matching pair, only just 'at ease' in the military sense. Hinchcliffe though seemed tense in a different way, over-caffeinated as he gulped at a huge white hotel mug. Mitch didn't know which of them he would have less in common with, the ex-military mercenaries or the epic tech geek.

Heather had said nothing but as she headed to the espresso machine she chirped, 'Good to see you all again.'

Mitch nodded to himself.

'The rest of your team will be along shortly,' Sara stated evenly. 'There was some trouble with Miss Edge but we understand that's all been sorted now. Their car is en route.'

So Saph was acting up. Protesting, no doubt.

'You all work for Everett?' Mitch asked.

'We do,' Harding nodded.

'You think he knows what he's doing?'

There was silence.

'Did your briefing include the bit about the Reptilians? Or the Pleiadeans? Or that whoever wants to get me might just appear out of nowhere through a crack in dimensions – or that you might be able to look at them but not see them?'

Harding nodded. 'It did.'

'And what do you make of that?'

He heard Heather laugh as she made coffee, as the machine began to hiss steam.

'We make of that as we would make of any other brief Mister Everett has given us. We make analysis and take all steps to prevent incursion. That is what we do Mister Pyne. You need not worry.'

'Jesus, call me Mitch.'

'Mitch.'

Mitch huffed. He was being a dick because it had just dawned on him; he didn't know what to do. He hadn't a clue, really, where to go or who to see.

'I'm sorry,' Mitch sighed. 'I think I will have that coffee. I take it we can smoke somewhere?'

'I'll show you,' said Harding, as Heather handed Mitch a decent sized mug of flat white.

He thanked Heather, only slightly resenting the feeling of once again being anticipated in his helplessness, and followed Harding to the steps outside. The security men were gone; Mitch assumed they were somewhere near. Harding took out a packet of Marlboros and offered Mitch one; they were harsher than the brand he preferred but he accepted because he didn't want to look weak.

Mitch put it in his mouth and Harding was instantly there with a lighter. Harding saw that the cigarette was trembling a little. There was no hiding it but Harding simply said, 'Cold out here,' and left it at that.

They stood smoking on the wide concrete steps, together in silence for a few seconds, gazing out at the wet table settings in the rose garden by the long hedge.

'Long time to grow something like that,' Mitch stated absent-mindedly.

'Nightmare to maintain,' Harding nodded.

Mitch wasn't sure if he meant as a gardener or as a security expert.

'Sea air,' Harding added. 'Salt. Needs to be hardy.'

Another pause, and another few drags went by.

'So how does this work?' Mitch asked.

Harding nodded, just once.

'You stay here until you're ready to go somewhere. Tell us who you want to see, we'll get you there unharmed.'

'Right.'

'Or, if you prefer, we can have people brought here. We can route calls so they can't be traced, but we can't make sure you're not followed once you get back to the city. Your friend Pan was well known, so if there's anyone else out there who has the same information we do – that he sent packages to his closest friends – there's no guarantee they won't be watching those people. No guarantee they haven't taken them already.'

'Taken them?'

'It's a consideration. So the sooner you figure out who has these packages, the safer it will be for them, once we get them back here.'

'You mean the packages. Get the packages back here?'

'It's my understanding that the packages may take the form of the people themselves – such as yourself. If that's the case it's better for them that we ensure their safety until the mission is over.'

'And what makes this place so secure?' Mitch asked.

'We do.'

'I mean – I know you do. But how?'

Harding turned and looked at him, a short but deep assessment.

'You're scared,' Harding said. 'That's okay. You should be. I've worked with intuitives before, remote viewers and such. I know how it works. How it works sometimes, doesn't sometimes, and sometimes it's difficult to interpret. Not many times before, but enough. So if you get anything, let me know, okay?'

'Get anything?'

'A feeling. A sense. If you have a strange thought that won't go away. Or a repeating idea, or a vision. Particularly a repeating vision – or a synchronicity. Coincidences are key. But most important – if you suddenly feel more frightened, very frightened, for no particular reason. Pay attention to the spikes. That's one thing I've taken from intuitives. The spikes are important.'

Harding exhaled heavily.

It was odd, hearing someone so totally grounded in reality, in physicality, talk like that. But again, he realized, it was just more information. More data that experience had somehow taught Harding to incorporate as useful.

'I'll try,' Mitch said softly. 'I'll let you know.'

'Good man.'

Mitch nodded to himself, then Harding suddenly answered his previous question.

'We have satellite tracking and surveillance on a five k radius, all roads out of the city are monitored, four men under me who are paid to take a bullet for you, and probably would, two dozen under Sara and another three dozen under Hinchcliffe on the perimeter. We're getting constant updates from Mister Everett's people and we have people twenty four seven on the people we suspect most likely to be interested in you, and what you're going to do. As yet, we don't believe they have a clue about Pan's packages, but they do know that you escaped police last night with Mister Everett's niece. So that narrows the time frame a little. You do have the benefit of being protected by the largest private security force of all the parties involved in this mission, so there's that.'

'*Have* you ever had to deal with aliens who walk through walls?'

'Even if that is what happened, that's not who we're dealing with.'

'It's not?'

'No. We'll be dealing with the people who deal with them. Real people, who can't walk through walls. Men who have to be careful. Who can't send men out to shoot guns in public. And who can still be prosecuted for conspiracy to abduction, or kidnapping, or murder.'

'Well, that's reassuring.'

Harding laughed, just a bit. Mitch sipped his coffee.

'There's not a lot I find reassuring any more,' Harding grimaced, just a little. 'So I take satisfaction in professionalism. If anything happens, don't leave my side. You'll get through.'

'Okay.'

Harding planted his cigarette in a marble birdbath at the edge of the stairs that was filled with tan sand, along with many other butts, and went back inside.

'Think clearly, pay attention to the spikes,' he said over his shoulder as he re-entered.

'Will do,' Mitch answered, not in his most reassuring tone.

Sara exited as Harding entered and smiled tightly again at Mitch as he extinguished his cigarette.

'I have some questions,' Sara stated squarely.

'About aliens?'

'About accommodation.'

Mitch sighed.

It seemed outright *odd* that no-one was asking him about aliens.

'You'll be stationed in the rooms on the second floor. The hotel will function as normal, albeit with a skeleton staff of trained operatives. Will you be requiring a double or single room?'

A car was approaching; they could hear it clearly, a short distance away, over the sea breezes.

'Double?'

'The CIA operative, are you intending to share a room?'

'I don't –'

'Or Miss Edge. We can arrange that if you prefer?'

The car drew nearer.

'Share a room with Saph?'

'We can use any pretext. I've found over the years that sexual comfort is conducive to a smooth operation. If we put you in a room with whomever you'd prefer, things will go more smoothly.'

'You mean, which ever woman you put in my room, we're likely to sleep together because we're frightened, and that will make me more relaxed and easier to deal with?'

'Something along those lines.'

She was pragmatic, you had to give her that.

The car pulled up in front of them; a long black car. Saph was in the front passenger seat. She immediately looked out at him, murderous as she fumbled in her anger to open the door. Cricket was in the rear passenger seat, also looking out at him. Her sour expression had returned and her look suggested that he had really screwed things up. There would be words.

'Single room,' Mitch croaked. 'Definitely single.'

CHAPTER TWENTY-EIGHT

It went better than he'd hoped.

Cricket said nothing, just walked past him.

Saph, although angry, was more pleased to see him alive and well than anything. She gave him a look that could kill but countered it with a tight hug.

They gathered with Vance, more theatrical than ever, pronouncing and enunciating as though cast in the role of a lifetime, in the parlor where a short debriefing took place, introductions to the security staff were reiterated, and the espresso machine was steamed into overdrive.

Saph had already contacted several of their old university gang, both those who had and had not made it to the funeral, and had no leads. They had none of them received any unusual parcels, witnessed any strange occurrences, nor felt any strange feelings.

'We can't assume it will be the same,' Heather offered. 'We don't really know if Mitch was spiked with the whole of Pan's genetic formula, or just part of it. And we don't know how different people with a different genetic makeup and-or biochemical physiology will respond, even if it was the whole formula. Maybe your old friends have been spiked, but for some reason it didn't work, or hasn't kicked in yet.'

There was something odd about the way Heather suggested this, almost as though she really wanted it to be true. Mitch wondered why.

'They've been observed for that since yesterday,' Harding told them.

None of them found that surprising.

Mitch sat back.

'Everett said that Pan's formula was a kind of Rosetta Stone, a decoder for human consciousness. And we're assuming that it's somehow been split up into six parts, these *gifts* Pan told Everett about. Now Vance, if what you told me about the solar consciousness is correct, and that just somehow, because of the way the solar machine works, I would be getting these – serendipities?'

'Synchronicities,' Vance corrected.

'Pay attention to the synchronicities,' Harding uttered.

'…that would lead me to where I should be, at least, where I can make choices to prove that I'm a viable evolutionary path?'

'Correct.'

'Well, it seems to me that you and Saph know more about Pan than I did, knew him better than I did, kept in touch better than I did; and that I was, in some shape or form, connected to you pretty damn sharpish as soon as all this started. So, while Harding is right that we should monitor the old circle of friends to see if they start acting strangely, Heather is equally right; who's to say how someone is spiked, or when it will kick in? I can't imagine Saph, that you were not one of his six closest friends. And Vance – you say you were born with this ability, the same as mine?'

'Not the same – my gift is purely intuitive, whereas yours seems very clearly rooted in with the rest of your normal brain function.'

' – but you kept in touch with Pan? All these years?'

'Something of a mentor, I might say. A mentor surpassed, but a mentor nevertheless.'

'So the only reason I can think of for him not to send a gift to you is that if you have one already, he might not want one person to have two parts of the same puzzle.'

'I see… that's probably what I would do, what I would think. Yes, yes you might have it there my boy.'

'Saph?' Heather pressed. 'Are you sure? You didn't receive

anything?'

'Mitch didn't receive anything,' Saph shrugged. 'Who knows how he got spiked?'

'It's easily done,' Sara chimed in. 'Distraction. Misdirection. You bump into someone on the street, or someone asks the time while you're having coffee. You don't even feel the scrape on your skin, or see the passerby drip something in your cup. It's just like pickpocketing, you see? And even that's old fashioned.' She turned to Mitch. 'I thought you were a film critic. If those idiot Hollywood scriptwriters can work it out, surely your friend Pan could have found the right people to spike his targets without them knowing about it?'

Mitch hummed insecurely and there was silence for a few seconds. Suddenly the world seemed a much, much less safe place.

As though to reinforce this, Mitch's phone buzzed in his jacket pocket. He hadn't even remembered he'd put it there and it made him jump in his chair.

'Dear me,' Saph groaned.

Mitch pulled it out and stared at it.

Saph just took it from him, answered for him, and handed it back.

'Hello?' said Mitch.

He was expecting to hear Everett's deep tones but instead it was a slow and steady voice with an upper class British accent.

'Hello Mitchell. It's very important that you listen to me but say nothing. If you understand, say 'Hello' again.'

'Hello?' Mitch repeated.

All eyes in the room were on him.

'Do you recognize my voice? It's alright if you don't, I'm not important. What is important is what I have to say to you. Mitch, this is Professor Derrick Nurding, do you know who I am? If you do, say out loud that you can't hear me. That reception isn't good.'

'Can you talk a bit louder?' Mitch asked. 'The reception's terrible.'

'Good, Mitchell. That's very good. Mitchell, I am patched into your phone but I'm not sure how long this can go undetected. Everett is tracing your every move, watching you, listening. The drug you've been spiked with is a very powerful hallucinogen; these people are playing a very dangerous game, and they are using your sanity as a chess pawn. The things you've seen, reptilian men, men who seemed blurred, they are all classic symptoms of hallucinogens. They are archetypal forms, from deep in the recesses of the human mind. But they are not real, Mitchell. The so-called Men in Black you saw were actors, paid performers designed to reinforce your sense of belief in the hallucinations. The orbs you saw, they were light projections, clever illusions that trick the brain. Everything you've been told is a lie, a fantasy that you are being coerced into believing. You must break ranks with these people at the first opportunity and come to see me. I am at the hotel where the wake took place. You must get here as soon as you can. Believe me, they will continue to feed you the hallucinogen, they will keep you on the psychotropic drug until they have you where they want you – which is most likely dead, but only after you've performed some sinister task for them. You've seen those kinds of movies Mitchell, haven't you? *Arlington Road*, *The Parallax View*. And I'm sure we've all heard of *The Manchurian Candidate*. You know what I'm talking about. You know who I am, Mitchell. You know that I am a highly rational man, and only want the best for you. Trust your doubts, Mitchell. Ask yourself; can this really be happening to me? If you hear what I'm saying, and understand, I want you to complain about reception again and end the call. Mitchell – have I made myself well understood?'

Mitchell realized that he was holding his breath.

He let out a sigh.

'Look, I can hear you, but I can't understand you. The reception's terrible. Try calling back.'

Mitchell took the phone from his ear and stared at the interface. There was a red symbol, beneath it the words 'end call'.

He pressed it. The screen changed. The call ended. He handed the phone back to Saph.

'It's yours,' she reminded him.

Hinchcliffe looked up from his laptop. 'No tracing that one – it was bouncing around like a lotto ball. Did you hear anything?'

'Just the odd word; sounded like a sales pitch – it didn't make any sense.'

None of the three security heads seemed pleased about that one.

They were wary now, suspicious.

The siren had sounded; their game had begun.

Which would make it all the more difficult, Mitch realized, when it came time to give them the slip.

CHAPTER TWENTY-NINE

Mitch entered what was essentially his third hotel room within twenty-four hours and found it easily the most impressive. It was, as he had suspected, a room fit for a rock star, movie star, elite CEO or billionaire on retreat; a large, high-ceilinged suite as plush, comfortable and well-appointed as two grand per night would suggest. The wide balcony window looked out over the ocean, opposite the widest flat-screen television he'd ever seen. The screen moved casually through intensely vivid wallpapers of modern and classical art, of beautiful anonymous landscapes and undersea vistas. The bed was enormous, orgy-sized. He would have been happy to curl up and sleep for days in one of the massive pillows alone. He thought of Jack, climbing the beanstalk and stumbling in the giant's bedroom.

Still, he reminded himself, that was all false comfort.

He was wanted, if not hunted, in a game whose rules he still did not totally comprehend.

There was a knock at the door. He did not particularly want to see anyone of those few it might be, but when he called out for whomever it was to enter, and saw that it was Vance, he was relieved. Vance brought with him a glass of straight scotch, poured no doubt from his room's mini bar. Given the short time since each of them had located their rooms, Mitch knew that it must have been the first thing Vance had done immediately upon entering.

'It seems we're metaphysical celebrities,' Vance smiled.

Mitch smiled back.

'It's a very dangerous game you're playing,' Vance continued to smile.

Mitch's smile dropped and Vance proceeded.

'These are trained security operatives. They see everything. And I knew from my training as an actor. Through observation.'

'Knew what?'

'That the connection on your call was fine. That you were listening to someone speak on the other end. Your features, small responses, betrayed you. Harding, Sara, Hinchcliffe, they could all see quite clearly that someone was speaking to you, and that you were listening. They knew that you were lying when you told them the connection was bad.'

Mitch said nothing.

'No doubt you have your reasons, and no doubt you have not responded to me because you suspect, as do I, that our every word is being recorded, if not directly monitored by Hinchcliffe at this very moment. But as I said, I am not telling them anything they do not already know.'

Mitch still said nothing.

Vance nodded, as though this was to be expected.

'I'd like to ask you a question, Mitch. Bearing in mind what I told you before, that the universe will respond to your actions, as a gaming program would respond to your commands. If you make wise moves, by its own predefined version of wisdom, which is at your level the urge to seek protection, or at least, protect the new path of evolution you represent, it will open to you. Make foolish moves, it will contract around you. The question is: do you trust Bo Everett?'

Mitch frowned curiously but remained silent.

'You made a move. You sought his protection. By all accounts, this has been rewarded, and we are all, relatively speaking, safe.'

'But safe from who?' Mitch asked.

'I see,' Vance nodded. 'You want clearly defined roles, good and evil. Are you working for the good guys? Or, are you working for people who tell you they are the good guys, but are really the bad guys?'

'I suppose.'

'But you made your choice on instinct, you chose the path of protection offered.'

'I suppose.'

'And that phone call; it offered you another path?'

Mitch frowned again. He suddenly felt completely dwarfed in the enormous room. Was this the giant coming home?

'Mitchell, I want you to answer my question: do you trust Everett?'

Mitch scowled to himself. There was no getting around this. What was he supposed to do? Never have another open conversation? Never speak honestly to anyone ever again in the fear it might get back to Everett and upset him? Why would that matter? He had money to lose now, a lot of money, but he had lived for years without wealth, and he could keep going. Something would come along…

And yet, on a deeper level, offending Everett meant more than that. It meant… losing Everett's protection. The security the man offered was real.

But what if Nurding had been right?

What if he were just being drugged and set up?

He had seen those movies, those paranoid thrillers, and this was exactly how they worked.

Suddenly he had his answer.

'I trust Everett to protect me. Until he gets what he wants. Given that he already has my blood, my DNA, I'm not exactly sure what more that could be. I mean, he's set me these tasks, to find the other five ingredients in Pan's Potion, because I am his best lead, but given that he has the technology to spy on anyone, anywhere and any time, that seems a little flimsy to me. I mean, he could employ a small army of people to watch everyone Pan ever knew, every minute of the day. Sneak into their rooms while they're sleeping, like he did with me, and take their blood. If they have powers like mine, they're bound to show up, or give themselves away eventually, right? So why doesn't he do that?'

Vance nodded.

'I want to bring Mister Harding into this. Is that alright with you?'

'Okay.'

He wasn't really sure that it was but he equally wanted to see where Vance was going with this.

Vance cocked his head up to the ceiling. 'Mister Hinchcliffe, would you please ask Mister Harding to come up here as soon as he can please?'

Mitch stared at him. Did he really think they'd give themselves away like that? Then again, they had been told they were being monitored, that the hotel was totally secure. What did he suppose that meant? Why not take the shortcut?

There was a knock at the door and Harding entered.

'You asked for me?'

He did not seem phased at all by either his summons or the nature of it.

'Mister Harding,' Vance nodded. 'Please dispel my friend here of the notion that satellite tracking can find anyone anywhere at any time.'

'That's true.'

'What is?' asked Mitch.

'Mister Everett owns several geostationary satellites for his telecommunications interests. As do his competitors. Most of them are equipped with high definition long-range GPS surveillance cameras that can monitor the activity of a city, or suburb, or even a home. This is not public knowledge. So far as the public is concerned, geostationary satellites are too far out in orbit to get a clear picture. Mister Everett's people perfected long-range geostationary photography eleven months ago. If that were public knowledge, there would be hell to pay.'

'But one still has to be outdoors, correct?'

'No. Mister Everett also has one such satellite that is equipped with thermal imaging, which is able to detect anything alive, at night, larger than a mouse. With intuitive real-time graphic enhancements, it can essentially see through walls, or more to the point, roofs and ceilings. People can be watched almost anywhere, anytime, doing anything. But these new surveillance satellites do still have some of the regular satellite problems; they still require a clear line of sight. They clearly can't penetrate water, or earth, or, say, a concrete bunker. But we can track a target if they're tagged; a cell-phone, or a purpose-specific tracking device via GPS. There's also the Pinscan. That's the real trick.'

'Pinscan?'

'The Pinhole Security Camera Network. Most governments have them covertly installed. They can remotely activate web-cams, phone-cams; pretty much tap into any camera anywhere. CCTV used to be too difficult because it relied on videotape; most of those cameras you hear about in London aren't even activated, they're just a deterrent. But now, with increased bandwidth and storage compression, every moment of your life can be recorded – should you become a 'person of interest', it's all stored away. It's enough to make you lose sleep.'

'But for a person on the move – say, if Mitchell and I were to for whatever reason flee this place?'

Mitch was shocked at that. Harding registered this, that the idea of flight was something new to Mitch, but still did not look pleased.

'We would track you using your phones. If you left the phones behind, we'd try and pick you up using EverSky 3, the geostationary satellite that is currently trained on a five k radius around this hotel. Failing that, we'd hack Pinscan.'

'But if we got the jump on you, left our phones behind and managed to get outside of the five kilometer radius before you realized, how would you track us then?'

'We'd calculate time verses thoroughfare, extrapolate all possible trajectories of flight and take it from there. In a car at top speed, if you exceeded satellite radius before we knew you were gone, we'd probably have you pegged in under three minutes, tops.'

'And if we were, say, to just vanish from here, through a

crack in the dimensional fabric of the universe, and reappear somewhere else? Like one of our alien friends? How would you track us then?' Vance was grinning now. Harding didn't like it. 'Assuming of course, we leave our phones behind.'

Harding scowled. 'You're safe here.'

'You would assess our psych profiles as to the most likely places we would hide, is that not correct?'

'Yes.'

'An educated guess?'

'I suppose,' Harding growled.

Mitch piped up. 'Why are you asking him all this?'

'Mister Harding, as you know, your job is to protect us. Mitch and I are about to leave, and you will not be able to track us. But we would like you to come with us.'

'What are you talking about?' Harding was outright grumpy now.

'We require your protection,' Vance smiled. 'Given that we are about to walk into the lion's den.'

'Lion's den?'

Vance turned to Mitch. 'You require another perspective? Perhaps that of the enemy? Then we require Harding.'

'I don't understand,' Mitch stated angrily.

'Neither do I,' Harding grumbled. 'There's no way either of you are leaving this hotel without a full security and surveillance detail.'

'Yes,' Vance smiled. 'There is.'

Vance turned and gestured to the massive flat screen television.

Harding reached for the pistol on his belt but paused at the sight before him.

The television was mounted and covered the entire length of the wall. Beside it was an alcove, which led to the bedroom suite, and the bathroom. Within the alcove, however, they could all see that something was odd. Something about the space itself: on the surface, it was a small square room, the only function of which was to provide a space for two doors that led to other rooms. Yet the alcove, or at least the space where the alcove was located, did not lead to those two doors.

It was the oddest feeling Harding had perceived outside of combat.

'I can't actually see it...' Harding uttered. 'But, I know it's there...'

Mitch shivered, then turned to Harding.

'You said pay attention to the spikes,' Mitch gasped. 'I'm spiking.'

CHAPTER THIRTY

Mitch, Vance and Harding walked out of the alley beside the Vantage Hotel and merged with the morning crowd along the shorefront gardens.

'That isn't as weird as it should be,' Mitch uttered.

'That's because it's perfectly natural,' Vance shrugged. 'But can you imagine what it would be like, if Pan's formula gave us all the ability to walk through the cracks in dimensions? Where would your growing security state be then, eh Harding?'

'It's not mine. But it would be chaos,' Harding said. 'Total anarchy.'

They were walking aimlessly, Bo Everett's giant black coat billowing at Harding's legs. He'd snatched it from Mitch's bed before they'd departed; it actually looked a little too small for the mighty mercenary, but nicely concealed the various weapons that decorated his belt.

'I don't understand why you want to talk to this man,' Harding grumbled, eyes darting about the seafront crowd, perhaps as informal as they'd heard him so far. Then his tone changed as he gave them a brief instruction. 'Go to the start of the jetty. Lean against the south-facing rail.'

They obeyed, then stood and leaned back for a few seconds with Harding facing them, his narrow gaze sweeping over their heads.

'There are three security agents on the promenade. One is having coffee in the Vantage Hotel café, in the seat closest to the entrance, looking out through the glass. When you go in, do not meet his eye. Try to look at the girls passing by. He will know who you are, but if he knows you can identify him, he will know that you have been briefed. Did this man say where he wanted to meet exactly?'

'He just said he'd be at the hotel where the wake was, and to come as soon as possible.'

'He's here on a book tour,' Vance said. 'But he's not speaking today. Maybe he's down this way for the day, or maybe someone persuaded him to come here specifically to see you Mitch. Who knows?'

'I need to tell you something,' Harding mumbled over the wind. 'I have a GPS chip implanted in my rib bone. Technically I'm supposed to be on a sleep shift, so they won't notice I'm gone for another thirty minutes; I'm supposed to be on duty at eleven thirty. When I don't show, and they can't contact me, they'll GPS me. I'd say we have ten minutes after that, at most, before they realize you've gone, that we've not taken any communication, and send people after me. They will assume the worst; that I have either betrayed Everett and kidnapped you, or that we have all been kidnapped. My people will be here by helicopter within fifteen minutes after that. That gives us fifty-five minutes before they send in the troops, so to speak.'

'There might be a problem with that,' Vance uttered, checking his wrist-watch, then gazing up to an old but well-restored clock tower that rose above the local town hall.

The clock-tower read eleven thirty.

All three checked their wrist watches; all three synchronized at one minute to eleven.

The town hall clock chimed to signify the half hour, as though to make matters more ominous.

'I thought as much,' Vance grimaced. 'It's happened before; a few times when I was practicing.'

'How long have you been able to do this?' asked Mitch.

'Since Tuesday night,' Vance answered. 'One of the first things I noticed was that you tend to lose time. Ten minutes, half an hour. I believe it's a side-effect of being new to the game. Whatever causes it, our little dimensional trip appears to have moved us half an hour into the future.'

'Not good,' Harding growled, his South African accent very pronounced. 'Not bloody good.'

'Do we get it back when we return?' asked Mitch.

'Not that I've noticed,' Vance shrugged. 'But I haven't been at it long. Look at it this way; you're half an hour younger than you were, and you'll live half an hour longer than you were going to.'

Mitch shrugged. He supposed that was *something*.

'On the other hand,' Harding gazed back at the hotel, 'we may have just set the entire space-time continuum completely balls up. Did you think of that on your travels – Magician?'

Vance folded his arms and looked entirely indignant. 'Impossible!'

Harding just nodded to himself. 'We now have only twenty-five minutes,' he stated sourly.

'Besides,' Vance mumbled. 'There are other… side-effects. But there will be time for that later.'

'I don't even want to know what that means,' Mitch sighed.

Harding mumbled again. 'They will have located my implant by now.'

Mitch turned to Harding. 'I can't believe you let them implant you!'

Harding stared him down like a father would stare down his tiny little daughter.

'I want you in and out of there in fifteen minutes. Then the Magician here takes us directly back to the hotel.'

'Okay.'

'Make the conversation short.'

'Okay.'

'Fifteen minutes, no more.'

'Okay.'

'Reset your watch. It's eleven thirty-one.'

'Okay.'

'Now you need to go.'

Mitch gulped.

'Now.'

'Okay, okay!'

Mitch started off toward the hotel, then quickly turned back to them.

'If I'm not back in twenty minutes, come and get me.'

Harding sighed. 'If you're not back in fifteen, I'm coming to get you. What part of fifteen did you not understand?'

Mitch walked away.

This time he didn't turn back.

'You're sure you can get us back through one of those dimensional doors, Magician?'

Vance nodded. 'So long as the first one through has a very clear image of where they want to go.'

They watched Mitch as he approached the hotel. A brunette woman in a tight skirt walked out as he entered.

'The universe provides,' Vance muttered.

'Why didn't you say you were one of the packages?' Harding asked.

'Because you call us packages.'

When Vance had asked Mitch to focus on the clearest memory of the place he intended to travel to, the first image that came to mind had been the alley. Somehow, after his escape from the cops with Heather, and the jump from the window, it had been reaching the end of the alley that had crystallized events in his mind; the thought of 'now or never', the moment just before he and Heather had made a break for it across the shorefront.

And that was exactly where they'd come through.

Exactly where his strongest visualization had been.

Mitch marveled at that briefly.

For the first time he thought, really thought, that he could get used to this.

The Vantage lobby, bar and café were exactly as they had been yesterday. Nobody could imagine that last night, a few steps from where he was walking now, he'd been on his knees and under arrest.

Mitch knew what Nurding looked like from his many television appearances; he didn't see him anywhere so approached the lobby desk.

'Hi, my name is Mitch. Professor Nurding asked me to come and see him.'

He could practically feel the laser-like eye-line of the security agent at the window as it seared into the back of his head.

'Professor Nurding?' the clerk repeated. 'I don't think we…'

Mitch heard the elevator ding and reflectively turned to look.

Exiting the elevator was Professor Derrick Nurding.

Before Mitch could even begin to offer a polite smile of recognition, the face of the famous man began to change.

Mitch gulped.

Derrick Nurding was a Reptilian.

CHAPTER THIRTY-ONE

'It's alright Mitch,' Nurding held up his hands. 'I can see you are distressed.'

Mitch took a few steps back.

'Is everything alright, professor?' the clerk asked.

'Yes, thank you,' Nurding responded calmly, warmly, 'my friend here has had a very trying time. He's just a little shaken. Please, will you show him your name tag?'

'The one you asked me to wear, Professor?'

'Indeed.'

The clerk removed his name-tag and handed it to Mitch.

Mitch was rooted to the spot, frozen in terror. He could hardly move, let alone reach out for something. Nurding took the name-tag instead and held it up so Mitch could clearly read it.

It read: Vantage Hotel – Don.

In much smaller letters below the conventional label, the tag also read: "Nurding = Reptilian."

Mitch was stunned.

Nurding, his reptilian features still very much real before Mitch's eyes, turned to the hotel door. The brunette woman in the tight skirt he had passed as he'd entered, who had conveniently drawn his eyes from the security agent, had re-entered and was heading toward them.

'This is Katie, one of my researchers.'

Katie smiled. The tight black skirt was matched with an equally tight, plunging black top that revealed a small bosom pushed into a tight bra for maximum cleavage. Around her neck she wore a long red ribbon that was attached to a plastic name-tag, the kind people wear to conventions. It sat right between her breasts.

'I asked Katie to dress for attention; Katie, would you please show Mister Pyne the name-tag you're wearing?'

Katie smiled; she was wearing lots of mascara, long false eyelashes and bright red lipstick. On the name-tag were two pictures and a symbol. One was a publicity head-shot of Nurding, the other a pencil sketch of a humanoid-reptilian alien that looked as though it had been printed directly from an alien conspiracy website. Between them was the symbol "=".

'If you look across to the bar, you'll see I placed a stuffed toy dragon there that I purchased down the shore at a children's gift shop. And just over there, by the elevator, the staff kindly allowed me to place a poster on the wall; I believe that character's name is G'kar. He is a lizard-man alien, from a 'nineties science fiction television series. A dragon statue on the table there, and over there, again, on the security monitor, Nurding is a Reptilian.'

Mitch saw all these things, then turned back to Nurding.

He was no longer reptilian.

He was a man, a human.

'Thank you Katie.'

'My pleasure professor.' Katie smiled at Mitch. 'I'm sure it will all make sense very soon Mister Pyne.'

Then she was gone.

Nurding began to walk to the café bar, nudging Mitch lightly to accompany him. Mitch fell in step.

'So you see Mister Pyne, how convincing the power of suggestion can be. You've been heavily dosed with an hallucinogen that allows this process to become very powerful. The human mind takes in all sorts of cues and triggers without even being aware. It is a powerful sponge, but you see evolution has not deemed it necessary that we process absolutely everything we see. Only the things that are most essential to our survival. But because of this evolutionary dead-end, it makes us very susceptible to all sorts of trickery, and hoaxes. It makes us very vulnerable, when used in the wrong hands.'

Mitch's mind was reeling.

'Hallucinogen?'

'Some sort of psychotropic drug no doubt. They're feeding you, one assumes.'

'I… I suppose they are.'

Mitch thought immediately of all the beer he'd been offered.

Of the specially prepared sandwich.

Heather handing him the coffee; and that feeling of having been anticipated.

'The initial dose must have been put in something you consumed Tuesday evening some time. Do you remember feeling strange, perhaps soon after consuming something you otherwise might not have? A gift, perhaps?'

Mitch was struggling to keep his head together. 'No,' he stated squarely. 'I was very drunk Tuesday night.'

'I see,' Nurding nodded sympathetically. 'So it could have been anything.'

'I – I suppose. Yes.'

'Mitch, I have been briefed on your situation. Some friends of mine are very concerned for your welfare. They know the people you've fallen in with, these people who are brainwashing you, and they want to help you escape them. They thought that if I could make you see reason, that if someone like me, well known and reputable, I suppose they thought, could show you a path back to a reasonable state of mind, that you might become open to an offer of help.'

'Help?'

'Two strong espressos please,' Nurding acknowledged the barista, whom Mitch hadn't even seen. 'Think about it, Mitch. Can this be real? This story they're spinning you? Is it rational to suppose that aliens, from across the vast distances of space, have come to Earth, to somehow interfere with our politics? With our culture? Why would they do such a thing? These creatures Mitch, these Nordics, these Reptilians, these Grey abductors, these are all very strong archetypal images, icons that are stored in the human unconscious, that sometimes emerge under times of great stress or mental, emotional trauma. These people you're with, they could have you seeing elves, or ghosts, or even vampires if they so desired. These myths are all around us, every day. Even the names of sports teams: Dragons, Demons, Devils, Angels… the mythology and iconography is weaved into they very fabric of our culture. The brain absorbs it; the senses make no independent judgment, Mitch. Everything we see is processed on the same basic level. It's our higher brain function: reason, logic and intellect, that make the distinction between what is real, what is plausible, and what is not. Reason based on centuries of accumulated science and study, based upon tested theory and established fact. We know Mitch, beyond a reasonable doubt, that Earth has never been visited by aliens. We are almost completely sure that to survive long enough to have the technology to reach us, any alien society, should they exist, will have died out long ago. The odds of life existing elsewhere in a galaxy, a universe, this size, simply does not allow for the possibility of alien intervention.'

'I came here…' Mitch croaked. 'Through a gap in dimensions. We were in the hotel, then we stepped into the alcove – out onto the street, right outside. We even lost time, half an hour…'

Nurding shook his head.

'I'm sorry Mitch. That's the oldest trick in the book. I understand you have a man with you named Vance. Vance is an actor, he's being paid to perform a role, a role you play into. Several years ago, he was also a stage magician, and a hypnotist. It's very easy for a hypnotist to persuade someone under the spell of hallucinogens, or psychotropic drugs, that almost anything is happening to them. You did not step into a crack in space-time and lose half an hour Mitch. I would warrant that you were acting under post-hypnotic suggestion. Your companion Vance spoke a pre-established word and you lost consciousness. He drove you here, then reawakened you; no doubt he even drew attention to the fact that you had lost time?'

'He… he did.'

'It's an old con man's trick, Mitch. You have to understand that.'

The espressos arrived on the bar before them. Mitch took a sip, then gulped the whole thing. It scalded his tongue and throat, but shook him out of the shock of what Nurding was telling him.

'Take the other Mitch. They're both for you. Drink it more slowly.'

Mitch nodded.

The world simply didn't make sense to him any more.

There were too many choices.

Too many realities, possibilities.

Or were there?

Were there too many, or was there really just one?

Less than forty-eight hours ago, he had been a rational man.

He had not been a man of harsh reason, a man like Nurding.

But he had been… normal.

Aliens were nonsense.

Everyone knew that.

There was no collective consciousness; the sun was not a machine for transferring information to those approaching some sort of new-age enlightenment.

They'd poisoned him Tuesday night, and they'd been poisoning him ever since.

'I understand,' Mitch nodded. 'What do you want me to do?'

'I want you to come with me Mitch. I have a car waiting for us at the back of the hotel. I'll take you to some people who can help you.'

'They'll help me detox?'

'They'll help you see reason again Mitch. It might take while, it's a long path to recovery after what they've put you through, but at the end of it you'll be a rational human being once again, with all this put behind you.'

'I'd like that.'

'Finish your coffee Mitch. Then we can go.'

CHAPTER THIRTY-TWO

Mitch sipped at the espresso.

He felt sad.

It might have been a delusion, it might have been confusing, but it had been exciting. Sex, chases, bullets, exotic yachts… mysterious alien beings. It had been like being in a movie, a cool movie. One he would have given a decent review. He wondered how it would have turned out, then realized.

It turned out like this: like *Shutter Island*.

This was the end of the movie.

His '*Total Recall* moment', as film buffs had come to call the great reveal in any movie with a mind-bending plot, was a bummer. But that was real life, he supposed. Real life was a bummer.

And yet there had been that sense, that he had belonged somewhere, possessed a purpose.

He'd forgotten about this real life: his deadline, his bankruptcy, his distant daughters and his divorce.

He'd have to go back to that now, back to that reality.

No, not *that* reality.

Just *reality*.

Maybe he'd make a decent go of it this time.

He wondered why those cops had tried to arrest him last night.

He didn't care.

He'd probably done something psycho at the party without realizing; he knew from his heavy drinking that it was possible to think you were behaving well, when the whole room thought you were a complete idiot.

He just didn't care any more.

Nurding took out his phone and spoke.

'It's me. He's seen reason. We'll be out in the car in a few minutes.'

Nurding listened a second, then disengaged the call.

'Can I use that for second?' Mitch asked.

'Are you sure that's a good idea, Mitch?'

'I want to say goodbye to someone. Not one of them. She's caught up in it all, but I don't think she really believes any of it. She's a skeptic, like you. I just… I don't want to leave her behind without letting her know I'm safe.'

Nurding smiled and handed him the phone.

'Of course.'

'Can you just do it for me? I'm no good with phones.'

Nurding slid his fingers over the interface.

Mitch felt like a caveman. Why had he resisted all this? Now he looked like even more of a moron, sitting here before the world's most respected intelligence, unable to use something as commonplace as a smart phone.

Nurding handed the phone back.

'Just enter the numbers, and press the green button.'

'Thanks.'

Strangely, he remembered Saph's number. It was odd. Now he'd been dispelled of his delusions, he was thinking more clearly than he remembered thinking for years. He smiled. Of course. It all made sense.

He would stop drinking now, stop smoking.

He'd simply rest.

They had drugs for that.

To help people rest.

Didn't they?

Somewhere in the back of his mind, he realized where he was going, where Nurding was taking him.

And, somewhere in the back of his mind, from far, far away, he heard a terrible, gut wrenching scream.

He ignored it.

He didn't care any more.

The ten digit number came to him like an eidetic memory; there on the screen of the phone Everett had given him, in his cabin on the boat, when Yelina had handed it to him.

'Hello?' She sounded frantic.

'It's me.'

He smiled tightly at Nurding, who smiled back with understanding.

'Mitch where the hell are you? You have to stop doing this! You can't just keep disappearing! Where's Vance? Are you with Harding? They're sending in the troops – he has some sort of a chip in him, it says he's back at the Vantage Hotel!'

'Listen, I'm okay. But I'm not coming back. I'm with someone who's explained to me what's been happening. How I've been drugged and hypnotized. I… I just don't believe it any more.'

'What? Mitch, what are you talking about? Who are you with?'

'It doesn't matter. You wouldn't believe me anyway. But listen, there's just one thing that I need to tell you before I go.'

'Go? Go where?'

'The last night I saw Pan, or at least, I dreamed I saw Pan, he made me promise to tell you something…'

At this, Nurding frowned. He could see that the professor was considering a move to take the phone back. But Mitch held up his hand and smiled weakly. The smile said; this is not what you think.

This is sentimental pity.

Nurding seemed to understand, and relaxed.

'…and, I think this might be the last opportunity I get to speak to anyone for a while.'

'Mitch, listen to me. I don't care about that. Who are you with, and where are they taking you? Where's Harding? Why isn't he stopping you?'

'In the dream, Pan said to tell you, *there's no place like gnome.*'

Saph fell silent for a second. He heard her gulp, heard dry lips smack.

'Mitch, there's no way you could know that.'

'That's all there is. That, and…'

'Mitch, there is *no way you could know that.*'

'…and, I think I loved you once. Before Pan. I thought maybe I still did, but I know now that's just sentiment, just nostalgia. But I think you were the one person in this whole scheme that never lied to me. And I want you to know that I appreciate that.'

Nurding nodded to him and smiled tightly.

Enough now.

Time to go.

'I'm going now. But I want you to get out of there. If you can, I want you to find Derrick Nurding, okay? You know who he is. Find him and he'll take you to me.'

Nurding seemed uncomfortable with this, but nodded tightly in agreement.

He reached out for the phone.

'Oh, shit Mitch. Oh, Jesus. Mitch, are you with him now?'

'Yes. And I'm so glad he talked me out of all this nonsense, I really –'

'Mitch, Nurding is on the level. You have to understand that. He's not lying to you; he believes every word he says. He's a scholar and a gentleman and one of the most intelligent people on the planet, but Mitch, you have to get up from wherever you are, you have to get out of wherever he has you, and you have to run. Mitch, if you really believe that I am the one person who never lied to you, if you ever trusted me, then trust me now. Get up and run, Mitch, run, *right fucking now.*'

CHAPTER THIRTY-THREE

Despite himself, Mitch found that he was edging off the bar stool.

'Are you moving Mitch?' Saph demanded.

'It's okay Saph, really.'

Nurding's eyes bulged. 'Are you talking to Sapphire Edge?'

Mitch's eyes betrayed him.

'Mitchell, hang up the phone. Now.'

Anger grew within Nurding's hitherto passive eyes.

'Now Mitchell!'

It was a British schoolmaster tone, virtually impossible to disobey.

Saph sounded as though she were on the verge of tears. 'Mitch, do not hang up the phone! Oh Jesus, Mitch, do not hang up the phone, Mitch, please!'

'Saph, I…'

Mitch was on his feet now. Nurding extended his hand further.

'My phone Mitchell. Now, please.'

Mitch's feet were moving.

He was backing away.

'Now Mitchell!'

'Mitch,' Saph spluttered. 'Listen, Pan and I once had a shared dream. It was a happy, silly dream. We were dancing. And I know, I know this is absolutely the last thing you want to hear right now, the most ridiculous and stupid and worst of all things to tell you right now, but we were dancing with elves, Mitch. In the dream we were dancing with goblins, and faeries and sprites…'

Saph was full-on weeping now, crying between the words.

Mitch continued to back off.

'And we were singing a stupid song, a stupid, stupid, silly song. And the song was called There's No Place Like Gnome.'

Mitch shuddered.

'When we woke up Mitch, we knew we'd had a shared dream. It was so bizarre, but it happened. We talked about it; we finished each other's sentences of descriptions of what happened in the dream. It was like talking about a movie together in the car on the way home. I admit, we'd been high as kites the night before on God knows what Mitch, but it happened, it really happened!'

Mitch had backed out of the café now, into the edge of the lobby, and Nurding was following him, hand still extended. Nurding turned to Don, the concierge.

'Excuse me Don, I wonder if you could give me a hand again?'

Mitch eyed Don. Don didn't like him; didn't like crazies who bothered celebrities.

'This man is psychotic. I have called the authorities, and they are coming. But I fear he may escape, and he has stolen my phone.'

Don reached for the desk phone and spoke quietly but urgently. 'Security to the lobby please.'

Already the security agent at the window was creeping out of his chair and placing himself between Mitch and the hotel exit.

'Mitch, we never spoke the name of the song out loud. *We never spoke it.* After the dream, Pan said to me, *do you remember the silly song?* And I said *yes, I remember the silly song.* But for some reason he stopped me saying the name out loud. He said, let's make it a thing between us that we both *just know.* It was strange Mitch, I know, but it was so mystical, such a romantic idea! Mitch, I had completely forgotten it until now, I'd completely forgotten it the next fucking day! I had never thought of it again until this very minute!'

'You wouldn't lie to me?'

'I… I *couldn't* Mitch, not about this! On my life Mitch, I have never spoken those words out loud until today! *There's No Place Like Gnome.* It's real Mitch, the dream you had about Pan, it was *real!*'

'Saph, I'm surrounded.'

Three hotel security guards had appeared from behind the desk and were emerging to take position.

'Mitch,' Nurding urged him, hand still extended. 'I really, really don't want to cause a scene.' He looked around the lobby. Other people had their phones out, and were filming.

It was only a matter of seconds before security mobbed him.

Saph had never sounded more desperate. 'Mitch, whatever you do, don't get taken by Nurding. He means well, but he is going to have you sectioned. He'll take you straight to a mental hospital, he'll have you interviewed, the doctors will sign the papers, and you won't see the light of day for God knows how long.'

'How do you know?'

'Because he did it to me, Mitch. *He did it to me!*'

The security guards now surrounded him.

'Careful gentlemen,' Nurding warned, 'he's potentially very dangerous.'

The sound of Saph's weeping, which had broken such that she could no longer speak, shifted something in Mitch.

'No - I'm - not!'

He surprised even himself with the authority of tone that emerged from his own larynx; strong enough that everyone seemed to relax and back off, if only just an inch or two.

He extended the phone to Nurding.

'Jesus, Nurding, calm down you bloody idiot, here's your stupid phone back!'

He tossed it casually back across the lobby to the professor, who caught it neatly with both hands. Mitch turned to Don.

'Don isn't it? Look Don, you can see what's going on. The professor here tried a practical joke and it backfired. He got you to wear that stupid name-tag, didn't he? And you agreed, because he's a celebrity, right? He got a pretty girl to dress up and walk in front of me, right over there, remember?'

Don frowned, confused. Clearly he did remember.

'He put a stupid toy dragon on the bar and put up a ridiculous poster from an old sci-fi series – and it's all supposed to make me look like an idiot, right?'

'I –'

'Thing is, I was onto it from the start, and got the better of him. Now he's shitting himself that the whole thing's going to backfire, the media's going to get a hold of it, and he's going to look like an idiot all over the internet. So let's all just calm the hell down, and sit and drink our coffees shall we? What do you say Professor? Is that okay with you?'

Nurding looked at his phone, looked back at the small army of people who were almost certainly podcasting the incident directly to their blogs as they all stood there, and made the intelligent assessment.

'It's okay chaps – just a bit of tomfoolery that got out of hand. I apologize for my behavior... Mitch, perhaps we can sit down again and discuss this like rational people?'

Nurding's security guy was the only one who'd not demonstrably moved back. Mitch was still not getting out of the hotel, not past him anyway, but at least the situation, the tension in the room, had been dispelled.

How long now, Mitch wondered.

A minute, two, before Harding came looking?

He checked his watch: eleven forty-three.

All he had to do was stall for two minutes.

Slowly, he returned to the bar, and sat cautiously with Nurding, who leaned over and hissed.

'You fool, Pyne. *You bloody fool.*'

'You have no idea what I've seen in the past few days. It's true I've been spiked, and it's true I'm more susceptible to illusion than normal. You've proved that, and I thank you for it. I'll be all the more wary because of it. But I'm no danger to anyone. And I certainly don't need to be sectioned. You are way out of line here Professor.'

Nurding stared blankly at him. 'You're surrendering to delusion! There's no way back for you after this! Don't you see, man. *I'm trying to help you!*

'I know. That's the hardest part of all this. I totally respect that. But you're wrong about me.'

Nurding's head sagged and he saw that the phone, which was still in his hand, remained connected.

'May I?' Mitch asked.

'Here,' Nurding handed him the phone. 'Jump down your rabbit hole. Be my guest.'

Mitch put the phone to his ear. 'Saph?'

'I heard most of that. I don't resent him Mitch, tell him that.'

'She doesn't resent you.'

Nurding shook his head. 'She was released too early. It's tragic.'

'This isn't over Mitch. Nurding's work is funded in part by a man who is very dangerous. Nurding knows nothing of it, he's completely innocent; but a corporation that has a strong interest in competing with Everett owns the company that publishes his books. That's all I know, I'm just putting the pieces together now, but I think it goes a lot further than whatever Everett's told you.'

'This call's sure to be monitored, Saph.'

'I don't care any more.'

Vance and Harding walked up behind him. Harding leaned over his shoulder and spoke to Saph.

'Tell Sara to call off the troops, we're coming in.'

There was a pause, then Saph responded.

'Hinch says Sara will meet you at the pier.'

'Done,' said Mitch, and returned the phone to Nurding. As he did, Harding snatched it back and removed a small metal plate from behind a hatch on the back, then tossed the phone back to Nurding. Mitch had to assume that the phone was now somehow disabled.

'I enjoy your work Professor,' Harding smiled grimly. 'I hope one day we meet under less stressful circumstances.'

'You people,' Nurding shook his head. 'You seek to destroy everything I have worked to achieve. By giving magical thinking and hallucinations a basis in the fantasy of pseudo-science, you'll set the cause of rationality back a thousand years. We'll enter a Second Dark Age of superstitious ideology and New Age dogma that will give birth to a thousand new cults, block and distort the minds of the next generation and countless to come, and set the course of science back to a new dawn of medieval hypocrisy. You belong in a mental institution, Mitchell. You are damaged, and you know it. You and all your poor deluded new-age, space-alien occultists. Damn the lot of you.'

There didn't seem to be much else to say.

Mitch turned to go but, just as he did, he had a strange thought.

'Professor Nurding, can I just ask one more thing?'

Nurding looked at him blankly, through tired though still-bright eyes.

'Can I stop you?'

Mitch smiled. '

You've heard of Suzie Saturn, right?'

'Yes of course I…' Nurding's eyes narrowed. 'No… no I haven't. Why? Who is she?'

'That's okay. I hope we never meet again Professor.'

Nurding threw down what remained of Mitch's now-cold second espresso.

'Amen to that.'

INTERLUDE II

The subject has been reintroduced back into general population. Although there has been suspicion from various quarters, and cliques within those quarters, he has re-engaged with his world via his new and primarily physical senses, fulfilling his newly enhanced sensual desires. Several of the group that has accepted him seem keen to follow in his footsteps, especially those of the group he has found who are naturally more inclined toward the physical senses. The process will proceed with other candidates – it certainly seems that after the process has been performed, the newly-enhanced subjects find their new physicality, and the sensual pleasures rooted within it, irresistible.

Miris
MX-ven-66-Leum-23z

THE PANDORA SEQUENCE

PART THREE

WAR

CHAPTER THIRTY-FOUR

After the incident with Nurding, the helicopter returned to the manor hotel where there was a debriefing with Everett, via webcam, during which Harding did most of the talking. Harding told the truth as he saw it, took full responsibility for Mitch's near capture, and Everett seemed satisfied.

Everett told Mitch that he was pleased with his efforts to investigate his situation, and admired his resolve; however, he also requested that Mitch and his fellows now remain at the hotel, at all times, and that they should make formal requests, for their own safety, if they felt the need to leave the hotel grounds.

Apparently Mitch had somehow 'upped the ante', and although matters with the police had been dealt with, things from here on would most likely escalate to the point where it was no longer safe for any of them to be seen out in public.

Mitch agreed to the terms, realizing that there had now been a major and dramatic shift in this strange adventure, to which he now found himself wholly committed. Despite this, he could still not quite shake the feeling that he had somehow chosen insanity over rationality. As though to counter these fears, he spoke up.

'But how did I up the ante?' Mitch asked. 'All I did was prove my sanity to a man who was determined to prove the opposite.'

Everett smiled. 'Nurding has been used before to neutralize people my enemies don't like. People are extremely vulnerable in the first stages of the transition to higher consciousness; all it takes is a nudge from a reputable icon of scientific reason and you fall into the abyss between consensus reality and abstract reality. It's like an artist who is told by the first critic he comes across that his work is worthless, then spends the rest of his life working in misery as a corporate functionary. As I said Mitch, I admire your resolve.'

The conference ended shortly after that, with Everett asking if they would all excuse themselves while he spoke to Heather. She then spent the next two hours speaking privately to her uncle before leaving the hotel without a word as to when she might return.

After that, he suggested to Saph that they talk. She smiled softly and told him that they would do so when the time was right, then retired to her room and did not come out for the rest of the night.

Vance also disappeared, shortly afterwards. Not through a crack in the cosmic fabric but in a long black car that arrived in the afternoon and whisked him quietly away.

Mitch guessed he was being taken to see Everett.

He wondered if Vance would be offered the same deal, and if he too would ask for something only a billionaire could give.

The afternoon passed quietly, with Mitch staring out to sea in Everett's huge black coat, replaying the events of the morning in his mind, wondering how such a great mind had become so entwined within a worldview that allowed him to feel justified in condemning others who did not share that view to a life in a psychiatric hospital.

That evening, with Saph locked in her room, and Vance and Heather both having departed without formal explanation, Mitch had started to feel very much alone.

It was perhaps the peaked adrenalin of the morning's confrontation wearing off, giving way to a low mood swing, but he found that he needed company.

He had not seen Cricket since the debriefing but felt awkward approaching her, given that he now knew that her seduction had been at best an act of pure pragmatism.

To be honest, Mitch wasn't sure that he cared.

To find out whether he did, he went looking.

Instead he found Hinch, alone in the mission control parlor, watching You Tube footage of his minor skirmish in the hotel lobby with Nurding. A press release had explained that it was all due to a Candid Camera style show gone bad, with Nurding claiming that he had been on holiday, had no idea that he had been set up for a prank, and was annoyed by what he assumed to be a loony conspiracy theorist bothering him over mid-morning coffee. Few people asked who Mitch actually was, but there was message board speculation, according to Hinch, that he might have been 'that guy who used to do the entertainment report on morning television'.

Nobody really cared.

Mitch found comfort in the fact that it at least looked as though he might be back in work, in front of the camera, and therefore now considered employable again.

'People just fill in the gaps,' Hinch shrugged. 'They don't even know they're doing it most of the time. And then, you know how it goes, by tomorrow someone else in the world will have done something bizarre. Something else will find itself leaked to the net; a cute animal doing something unexpected to make it seem even more cute, a geek having an epic geek-out, a slacker doing something suicidally stupid, a starlet with a sex tape, or another movie star rant. It'll be something – and all eyes will turn to that. It doesn't matter that it exists online forever – people still have to give a shit in order to go find it, and unless the news cycle points it out, it's as good as gone forever.'

It seemed clear that Hinch was on duty and had work to do, so Mitch made a bit more small-talk about the transitory nature of things while he made more coffee then went off to explore the hotel. He wandered about through the lower level, sipping his latte, found the kitchens where the skeleton staff of four, a maid, a chef and his assistant, and a kind of concierge odd-job man, were playing cards.

He discovered their roles, again through unwanted small-talk, and that they were, in fact, a team who had been together almost a decade, like a sub-culture within the security network, who did this for a living.

Mitch was quite amazed. 'You take on staff duties at hotels commandeered by security teams?'

'Covert staffing, yeah. Good money,' the chef nodded as he played a card. The others all groaned in response. He'd trumped them or something; Mitch didn't play cards. 'A few weeks every two or three months; danger money of course but we've never seen any serious action. First sign of trouble, standing orders are to lock ourselves in the hotel fridge and wait for extraction. Only ever happened twice, and one of those was a false alarm.'

'What was the other one?'

The chef sat back and scowled. 'The other one was messy. Very messy. You don't wanna know. You really don't wanna know.'

After that, Mitch could practically feel their collective wills pushing him to leave. He didn't want to seem like a lonely and pathetic prisoner, so he made a short show of putting together a ham and cheese sandwich by himself, then departed.

He wasn't hungry, so he went back up to his room, left the sandwich on the bedside table for later, and returned downstairs. There were two ground floor sections he'd not explored. One was the second parlor, opposite the operations room, which was the hotel bar. He avoided that and took a look behind the abandoned reception desk, below the grand landing and its accompanying grand staircase, that yesterday one of the world's most famous aging rock stars had stormed down, forced out of his thousands per day hotel room so that Mitch and his companions could set up house.

The memory of that made him feel over-rated.

The door behind the reception desk led to a warren of abandoned offices, like the decks of a modern Marie Celeste; screensavers were still running on still-operating PCs, coffee cups in the staff room lay unwashed in the sink, copies of FHM and Cosmopolitan lay open on desks.

He did not even want to think about the fact that magazines, apparently, *still sold*. But he knew better: brand recognition, market share, blah blah blah… enough already.

The offices exited into a long rear perpendicular corridor, where the back entrance to the kitchens led out to the rear hotel grounds.

Mitch exited the heavy wood-framed doors, feeling pleased with himself for breaking the thought-chain on his usual loop of self-pity, and caught the chill of the evening as he walked out and stood on the wide-stepped landing.

He stared out into a bright, thinly-clouded night. The full moon illuminated tennis courts, an Olympic-sized pool and a huge winter garden. The immaculately maintained landscaping featured paths that led off in all directions, then back into each other again, dissected by a large gazebo, a raised rock garden with a covered picnic bench, a covered section with hanging vines and a central fountain feature, disabled, along the way. The grounds must have covered more than an acre, Mitch guessed, as he gazed out into the semi-darkness, with the gardens somewhat illuminated in the moon's weird grays and blues, as its light reflected off the clouds, until his ears tuned into the sound of repetitive splashing.

Just as he realized there was someone swimming in the pool, something moved beside him and he jumped out of his skin.

'Evening chief.'

The security guard had been standing there the whole time.

'Jesus.'

'Sorry chief. Didn't mean to startle you. Can't sleep?'

Mitch sighed. 'Haven't tried. Is someone really swimming out there?'

'Good for the heart,' said the guard.

Mitch laughed, nodded at the man with a wry smile, and headed off to see who it was.

The path to the pool was directly across the gravel drive, then down a landscaped path to the back of the garden; you could see the edge of the enormous pool from the house, but not the pool itself.

As he approached, he heard the unmistakable sound of someone doing laps, then they stopped. He reached the edge he realized, as he saw her climbing out, that it was Jo Sara. Her hair remained in a tight ponytail, and as she dried herself off, and met his eye with a tight smile, he saw that she was clearly a bodybuilder; she had virtually no bosom and her physique was almost masculine in tone.

'Sorry,' Mitch said, in a mousey tone. 'I was just curious to see who was out here.'

Sara nodded and pulled out a thick robe from a sports bag at the edge of the pool.

'Can't sleep?' she asked.

Her posh British accent was outright bizarre in contrast to her physique; women with voices like that were supposed to be pouting, pale and fragile.

'Haven't tried yet. Bit of a strange day.'

She pulled on the robe, tight, then hugged herself, rubbing her upper arms.

'I won't sleep with you if that's what you're after. Against regs.' She smiled, almost cheekily. 'And besides, you're a bit on the flabby side for my liking.'

Mitch laughed. 'Thanks.'

The thought had occurred to him only for the briefest moment; but even if she'd been game, he'd probably have been far too intimidated to go through with it.

'Why don't you go and find your CIA concubine? Sure she'd be up for it. Probably still on her brief. Probably has orders to take more samples. Lord knows why the boss wants her here, she's essentially working for his competitors.'

'Take samples?'

Sara took out a second towel and began drying her hair.

'Forget I said anything, it's your business.'

'I'm not sure what you...'

'Delicate business with Harding this morning you know. Put

him in a right spot. Shoot us or come along through the wall, wasn't that the gist of it? Have to say it took balls, but Harding's a chancer, good for him for going along I say. None of us really know who's running the show anyway do we? God and all that palaver?'

She grinned, amused.

'About time someone sorted it all out, the old Blighter's been giving us a bloody good run for our money. It's high time someone gave a damned good knocking at old Saint Peter's gate to see if anyone's home, and if there is someone there, let him know that it's jolly poor form that he doesn't make a decent show of it and come on down from the Ivory Tower and give a fair account of himself after all this time, don't you agree?'

Mitch was a bit stunned. She talked about God as though she were talking about the horse trials at Ascot. She seemed surprised that he hadn't responded.

'Isn't that what this whole thing is about in the end? It's all very well that there's boog-a-boo snake men and hippie Norsemen and whoever else bugging their noses into our business, but if you ask me it seems like it's all just another level of good old fashioned bureaucracy leading the way, just another few levels of it from outer space, wouldn't you say?'

'I don't really know *what* they want.'

'But you see what I mean, surely? In the end, where does it all lead? You've read the briefs: the Reptilians have dimensional technology, but they're essentially here for business. The Pleiadeans might very well be some kind of super-psychic mental beings but they're essentially just priests trying to lead us up some ill-defined ethical higher path. Where does it all lead, do you see? Do they really know why we're here? Any more than we do? Or are they simply us in a thousand years time, trying to tame the savages? Wandering through the unexplored Amazon, trading us shiny beads and Bible stories in exchange for our souls?'

Mitch stared at her. He didn't know what to say. She seemed to read his mind as she stuffed her towels back into her bag and threw it over her shoulder.

'You *have* read the briefs old boy, haven't you?'

'Not all of them. I… I haven't had time.'

Her stare was more than mildly chastising.

'Well. From what I understand, your actions today have stepped the game up quite a bit. Two sides, maybe three or four, are preparing to go to war because you refused to submit to control. Now good for you I say, no-one should submit to anything they don't want to, but if we're going to war, and we're going to war for you and your friends, then I would jolly well appreciate it if you weren't completely out of the loop as to why some of us might fight and die for you. Capiche, old boy?'

'Of course, I had no idea –'

'No idea's not good enough I'm afraid. Now I suggest you find the concubine Mister Everett's seen fit to supply you with, even at the risk of a security leak, and give her the jolly good rodgering she's here to provide you with, so that you can have a decent night's sleep and tomorrow do your homework. It's not often you can say to someone "this is not all about you" and be wrong, but in this case, this is indeed all about you, and you are all about what's in that brief. Now I don't like to play Miss Bossy Trousers, but it needed to be said.'

'Of course.'

'No hard feelings then?'

'No, no of course not. It needed to be said.'

'Good chap then.'

She walked off and left him standing there.

He was cold and he felt like crying.

Suddenly she turned back, raising her hand as though in afterthought.

'Look, it's not my job to tell you your business, it's not even my job to ensure your safety. Truth be told, I'm here as last line of defense to take a bullet for Miss Edge, if it comes to it, and it very well might. But I can see you're a bit of a soft sort and not used to any of this, so I'll help you out with that other matter; when you had coitus with Miss CIA was your expulsion internal?'

'*What?*'

'Internal expulsion, or external? On her belly or such like?'

Mitch gulped. He supposed this is what the British meant when they said 'no-nonsense approach'. He thought back.

'It was…' Mitch suddenly frowned. 'I was still inside her. She had her legs wrapped round me like a vice – but we used a condom.'

'And she got up immediately and went to the bathroom?'

'Yeah…'

'Took the soiled prophylactic with her?'

'Yeah, she did… it seemed sort of cute at the time…'

'Well there you have it. CIA sample. Packaged and ready for dispatch.'

'You mean…?'

'The CIA has your DNA, old boy.'

CHAPTER THIRTY FIVE

The dilemma Mitch faced on that night was one of perspective.

It didn't take him long to figure out that Sara could have been lying to suit her own end; to get him to hunt down Cricket, confront her, and in the heat of the moment rekindle their animal passion and resume their sexual liaison for the duration of his stay in a huge hotel where, it had to be said, there was precious little else to do. From Sara's perspective, it would stop him wandering aimlessly about the hotel and gardens, keep him basically in one place, and easily monitored.

But that was another thing; even if he did go to Cricket, he didn't like the idea of Hinch listening in, and possibly watching as well.

Still, if that were true, and Sara was manipulating him, that was her perspective. It was what she thought best. Sectioning was what Nurding had thought best for him; and in a way it was the denial of Nurding's reality that calmed him down when it came to the notion that Cricket had slept with him only to get a semen sample. That was her reality, she was doing what she thought best. But really, if the CIA wanted his DNA, all they had to do was go through his garbage. He could think of a dozen different items he disposed of, on a weekly basis, that would be just as viable. Then again, since Tuesday? And Cricket had acted extremely fast.

Where the hell was she anyway?

He walked back from the pool and headed to the bar.

He'd been trying to keep away from booze; in the last two days, although he'd had a few drinks here and there, he'd abstained from the pattern of heavy drinking he'd fallen into over the past year or so and his mind, despite all that had happened, was clearer for it. He hated to think what might have happened if Nurding had tried to convince him that he was insane if he'd been drunk this whole time. There would have been no hope at all.

He surprised himself when he realized that he had barely thought of Janine, or *Cinema Now*, or his daughters this whole time.

It was like another life, far away, long ago.

He decided that Cricket could come to him.

If she wanted another sample that badly, she could work for it.

He decided that he would use his time in hiding productively.

He would read the tech manual and treat Saph by calling her in her room, using the phone, to say good night. That he understood that she wanted to be alone.

He thought of her tearful reaction to Nurding.

How long had she been locked away, he wondered?

On what grounds?

Association with Pan?

There had to be something more to it.

And had he really told her he loved her, or didn't love her, or something?

He entered his room and spread the contents of Everett's envelopes over the enormous bed, found the manual, put the phone on his lap and leaned back into one of the giant pillows.

He had every intention of opening his first window to the new world of technology in almost a decade, but within thirty seconds, he was asleep.

He was on a huge vessel of some kind, overlooking a rainforest that stretched as far as the eye could see. The vessel seemed to be enormous, and circular, with a curved floor-to-ceiling window that stretched onward around the wide corridor where Mitch was seated. It was like a massive café, with chairs and tables set all the way around at the edge of the ringed observation deck.

Deck.

Was it a ship?

They were high in the sky…

They.

There were other couples, many of them, talking, a few rows along, but he was facing the beautiful woman again. The stripper, the porn star, the high-class call girl. The woman with dark hair, with such lovely, alluring features that it seemed impossible to look away.

'What were we talking about?' he asked.

They had been talking, he realized, as though they were friends.

She was dressed casually now, as one would to meet a friend for coffee.

She smiled, radiant.

'I'm sorry, to me it was just a second ago that I was talking to you in the club. Things are more fluid for me than they are for you.'

'That's okay. I think I understand. So what were you going to tell me?'

'I remember once that I was dancing, in that club, and I overheard a conversation. They were not like most of the other men who watched me dance, they were spiritual men, but they also liked to see women dance. Many spiritual men are like that. One was teaching the other; he was telling him about blackness. Many people, he said, believe that when divided between black and white, men are black and women are white, and that this is how they are divided. The student agreed; that is how it was.'

'I suppose,' Mitch shrugged.

'The teacher went on to say that this assumption was incorrect. He said that the male energy is white; it is the inspirational impulse, the creative, the flash of lightning, of intellect and the conscious mind. It is the rational, and the expansive male urge to explore and conquer, the white explosion of semen, of the atom, the whiteness of Heaven, of the masculine representation of God, of the white void. The female energy is protective, enclosing, it is the black of the womb, of darkness and the safety of sleep, the intuition of dreams and the instinct to remain enclosed and safe. It is the dark comfort of the embrace, and the containment and security of the cave. He said that some of the ancients saw the stars as white semen, splashed through the black womb of the cosmos.'

'But at a wedding, men wear black, and women wear white.'

'Because they are surrendering to each other's energy. The woman is white and virginal, representing the surrender to the male energy, a recognition that she is willing to be a vessel of reproduction.'

Mitch frowned. 'You mean, the white of the wedding dress represents her willingness to become a receptacle for semen?'

'It can, let me put it that way.'

'Oh. And I suppose the black tuxedo symbolizes the male's willingness to be contained – to be faithful.'

'That's right.'

'Okay.'

'The feminine is always underappreciated, the teacher said; we focus upon the stars but never upon the blackness in between, although that is far and away the greater proportion of the night sky. The student then looked around him and asked; then why do serious men wear black? Why do the businessmen who surround us in this club shroud themselves in such dark cloth, if that is not the shade of men? The teacher answered; these are men of business who must contain their secrets, contain their inner thoughts and plans so that they might gain power over others. So they hide themselves in wombs and caves of their own making; they embrace the power of the feminine to masculine ends; the black is containment, and in masculine form it is represented as the god Saturn, he who constricts and brings order, contracts and brings solidity. He brings law and seriousness, and structure. This is what these men in black suits represent. They are cold and joyless, they live to compete, by implied threats and psychological leverage, but within that they bring slow momentum, and consideration. They play it safe, but act quickly when they must, to protect. What is more feminine that that impulse? In their way they hold the world together. The student saw this, and agreed. He nodded.'

The beautiful woman sipped her coffee.

'And I nodded to myself, even as I danced. I had never thought to listen to the conversations of the men; not the older men in black suits, not the younger men in tee-shirts and jeans, and certainly not the artists and holy men that came to the club less frequently. There was a moment then, when I realized that I represented something to them; I was more than just a sex object. I was somehow an externalization of that dark, male-feminine principle. I was an object of desire, something outside of their world that they could watch, yet not touch. I was outside of their zone of comfort; I was a stripper, an erotic dancer. I was sexual abandon, everything spontaneous they desired, yet sacrificed to hold the world together. I was that idea, formalized in a dance routine called the striptease; at least, this is what is sacred about the striptease, when it is well-performed. I saw the teacher look at me when I realized this; he looked at me as though he had not been talking only to the student, but to me also. And at that moment, I became a student also. At that moment, I realized that from then on I would listen. I would listen to the conversations of the men in black, who contained their white male energy, held it at bay within black wombs of their own making, to use only when they deemed best to strike with white lightning. And I would learn the power of the old god, so as best to entertain him, and pacify him so as to gain his confidence, and learn more of the men who held the world together. I would learn that, so as to become a better dancer. A dancer who could mesmerize the men in black, and come to know their secrets. I knew then, that was my purpose. I knew then, that my name was Suzie Saturn.'

Mitch woke with a start, bouncing as though he had fallen

from the window of the massive craft and landed on his bed.

It was morning, and Cricket was sitting cross-legged on the end of his bed.

CHAPTER THIRTY-SIX

'Morning,' Cricket said.

She was examining the contents of Everett's envelopes, laid out across the enormous bed.

Mitch didn't know what to say; she was wearing black thigh-length boots, blue jeans, a white tank top and a navy leather jacket that squeaked as she moved, sorting the files into piles.

'Morning,' he responded croakily.

'Sara said you wanted to see me; thought I'd let you sleep though. She also wanted me to make sure you've done your reading.'

'Did she?' He didn't know what else to say. 'I – should you be reading those?'

Cricket grinned, slightly superior.

'It's nothing I don't already know. Some of it I even put together; the alien agenda files are all sourced from Pan, and Pan's People. His podcast, some others, even some from mine. You know, Everett's actually printed out web pages and transcripts for you; you really don't know how to go online?'

'I could if I had to.'

'Really? How would you start a web browser?'

Mitch thought. He didn't really know. 'In a menu?'

Cricket gave the superior grin again but left him alone.

'I can tell you what's in all these; won't take long. Otherwise it'll take you the whole morning to read it all.'

'How do I know you won't leave something out?'

Or, Mitch wondered suspiciously, that I won't get the amended CIA version…?

Cricket didn't look up as she sorted a few more papers. 'Not in my interest to lie to you. I'm on your side in all this, don't forget.'

'Collecting samples, Sara said.'

Cricket was silent for a few seconds, then shrugged.

'Yes.'

Mitch sat up. The back of his throat was sore; he'd slept on his back and snored. Suddenly he realized he was undressed and under the sheets; he didn't remember doing that.

'Did you undress me?' he asked, almost paranoid.

She met his eyes. 'No. You were in bed when I came in. About an hour ago you rolled onto your back and started snoring like a walrus. I tried to roll you back onto your side but you wouldn't budge.'

'An hour ago? How long have you been here?'

'Since about five. I went to bed early. It's about eight now. I've just been sitting here reading.'

Mitch scratched the hairs on his chest then ran a hand through his hair; it was sticking out at all angles.

'So you did collect a sample?'

'Yes. I told you I did.'

'And you are CIA?'

'Yes. Heather told you that.'

Mitch frowned. 'Everyone knows. Even Pan knew.'

'Yes.'

'Why?'

'Why what?'

'Why collect a sample?'

'It doesn't matter. It didn't match. That's all we needed it for.'

'Match what?'

'The other people we suspect have altered DNA. Their DNA has been altered, but not in the same way yours has.'

'What other people?'

Cricket tapped a small pile of papers. 'These people.'

Mitch leaned forward to take the pile from the bed but could not reach them without completely abandoning his quilt cover. He didn't want her to see that he had awakened aroused. Cricket handed them to him. He flicked through them, reading only the report titles, as Cricket removed her calf-length boots.

He watched her do it but said nothing.

When she'd finished, she threw the boots off the bed, they clunked onto the floor, and she massaged the toes of her left foot, wincing.

Mitch assessed the files again.

They were the ones Heather had delivered to him, one by one.

'Gabrielle Fenwick. Ben Corner. Kashmira Khan. I've read these.'

Cricket nodded. 'They've all received some new sort of gene therapy. We think Fenwick is the only one who actually consented. The coverage is good. Their conclusions are right.'

'Whose conclusions?'

'Heather and Everett. He's got better surveillance tech than we have; sometimes we even hire it from him. That's how all this started, the alliance. He sends her out on spy missions. Mostly corporate surveillance but sometimes infiltration; like with Pan's People.'

'Like you?'

'That's how we became friends, Heather and me. You get to recognize other spies. We realized we were essentially on the same side and agreed to trade information; three years inside an organization like that, you need someone who understands. Trouble was, she fell in love with her target. Then after that, she settled for that Jimmy idiot. Pan extra-lite.'

Mitch stared at her.

'How can you pretend like that? Pretend to be someone else for so long?'

'It's not always pretending. I had an interest in the paranormal so they matched me with the job. And Heather was really in love with Pan. She wasn't supposed to sleep with him. Her uncle didn't like it, didn't like her using her body like that, but she swore to him that it was real.'

'And you and me the other night?'

'I find you attractive if that's what you mean. You like me too, if that boner under the sheets is anything to go by.'

Mitch shifted, embarrassed.

'I had a dream.'

'We all have dreams, Mitch.'

She stared at him, waiting. It seemed that he would have to make the first move this time, if anything were to happen.

'Is Saph awake?' Mitch asked.

'Hasn't left her room according to Hinch. And Heather and Vance haven't come back yet.'

Mitch felt distinctly uncomfortable at the mention of Hinch. Cricket smiled again, perhaps reading his thoughts, and nodded at the papers in his hand.

'Someone else has cracked the genetic code; at least to an extent. Those three cases are demonstrations of their ability to do it. Gabrielle Fenwick had her age reversed by twenty years or so. Ben Corner had his sexuality flipped. And Kashmira Khan had a total moral reconfiguration. These are all high profile cases of how genetic restructuring can be used to acquire wealth and power.'

Mitch scanned the documents.

'Who's done it?'

Cricket handed Mitch another pile, much thicker this time.

'By the time they realized Pan was dead, everything in his research center was gone; has Everett told you that much?'

'Go on.'

'It was a very small-time operation; Pan had three assistants. They've all vanished without trace. What we don't know is which one gave our rivals the information that allowed them to do that,' she pointed to Heather's three reports, 'and which two were killed.'

'Killed?'

'The gist of it is Pan cracked the genetic code to expanding consciousness. As soon as he did this, he contacted Everett, and wanted to see him in person. He must have suspected foul play because he – according to Everett at least – broke the formula into six pieces and sent them out to persons unknown. We don't even know how he did this, or what form they take; whether he snail-mailed them as parcels, had a courier dispatch them, or even sent the information out as emails, in written or digital form. As we're dealing with consciousness, which is a pretty gray area, it's even possible he might have sent the information in a dream, or over some kind of mental or psychic channel.'

'Is that very likely?'

'Who knows? My organization has several covert departments that research this kind of thing; I'm sure you've heard of MK-Ultra? Or the Stargate Project?'

'Only in the movies. The Men Who Stare at Goats, stuff like that.'

'It was real, but it was just the tip of the iceberg. But we can't do this. Whatever gene sequence Pan discovered, it will change everything. Which is why we believe one of his three people killed the other two as soon as Pan left the research station, then arranged to have Pan killed en route to his flight to see Everett, then sold Pan's information to our rivals. It's standard play.'

'Standard?'

'In the spy world. Not difficult to arrange on a project this small, a pet project of a billionaire that wasn't expected to produce anything spectacular. At least, not this spectacular.'

Mitch nodded; if this were true, if there were a genetic formula that could be easily delivered that actually had the power to radically transform the human body, and brain, within such short periods…

Cricket watched his face, then spoke. 'Our rivals have essentially weaponized the human genome. They've hinted at a kind of immortality, shown how it can be used for political gain, and indicated quite strongly that cultural and religious influences can be completely reversed. In essence, the course of humanity is now totally fluid. Anyone can be turned into anything. The main question is: who are these demonstrations intended to impress;

and what do they want in return for the genetic codes?'

Mitch considered this.

There had been enough moral panic at the mere possibility of the notion that parents would be able to choose the sex of their child, or select their skill-sets, when the human genome had first been mapped more than a decade ago. Now the field was wide open.

Cricket stared into his eyes.

There was no hint of seduction; this was an intellectual gaze. She was taking a reading on his internal extrapolations.

'We could...' Mitch muttered. '...do anything with this.'

CHAPTER THIRTY-SEVEN

'So you get the idea; immortality to the highest bidder. Total social manipulation to the highest bidder. Humanity, in essence, to the highest bidder.'

Mitch nodded.

'But… what does this have to do with what's happened to me? And to Vance? What you're talking about is all physical; what we're guarding is metaphysical.'

Cricket nodded, then shrugged. 'There's a lot you haven't figured out. Let's say you manipulate the brain to alter body chemistry; changes occur. Whether they are cosmetic, or personality changes, or changes in perception that allow you access to higher states of consciousness, or to perceive different dimensional states, it's all still genetic manipulation. But there is a big difference between you and Fenwick, and Corner, and Khan.'

'There is?' He caught himself. 'I mean I know there is; they're all famous. But – is there really any difference? Like you say, in the end, it's all just brain chemistry.'

Cricket gazed on sympathetically, as though there was something so big, right in front of his eyes that he still couldn't see.

'The thing no-one seems to understand, or at least confirm yet,' Cricket continued, 'is whether or not our rivals have the complete map, and if they don't, why not? So far there has been no public demonstration of what you call the metaphysical. There's just you.'

Mitch considered a second.

'So – whichever of Pan's three assistants took the formula,

they perhaps only took part of it.'

He thought about Pan; how he might have responded to his discovery. Pan was no fool; he would have seen this coming. He *had* seen this coming and he'd gone to Everett. He'd trusted Everett. But had he trusted his assistants? Had he let them in on the consciousness discovery?

'Listen,' Mitch spoke quickly, 'I think what happened is that Pan contacted Everett as soon as he made this discovery. He didn't tell the others; it must have been fast, a Eureka moment. He realized the potential consequences and ordered the lab shut down, then whoever betrayed him made their move – and took the information they had access to. From that, they extrapolated the formulas that were used to de-age Gabrielle Fenwick, and affect the others. But Pan kept the consciousness stuff close to his chest, with the one insurance policy of sending it out in parts. Whoever's doing the public demonstrations doesn't have access to the consciousness stuff – that part is just me…'

Mitch stared at Cricket, as the penny dropped.

'That's who's after me, isn't it? Whoever's doing the public demonstrations.'

'That's right.' She tossed a folder at him. 'And everything you just said is the conclusion both Heather and her uncle have come to. All in there. And this,' Cricket raised a third folder, 'is the profile of the man who sent Nurding to section you, and who we suspect is behind the genetic manipulations, and public demonstrations. The man who is offering humanity to, presumably, the highest bidder.'

This time she leaned forward and handed the folder to him, her navy leather jacket squeaking as she did. She seemed to find that annoying, and removed the jacket, tossing it to the end of the bed.

Mitch stared at the folder. Did he really want to know?

'His name,' Cricket offered instead, 'is Oliver Hines.'

'Oliver Hines?' Mitch couldn't believe his ears. '*The* Oliver Hines?'

'There's only one Oliver Hines. I'm glad I don't have to explain who he is.'

'Bill Gates is Microsoft, Steve Jobs was Apple, Oliver Hines is Olivera,' said Mitch squarely. 'Even the Kalahari bushmen know that.'

'Well he's the reason you're here in lockdown with only me for company.' She smiled, crawled up the quilt a bit and sat, again cross-legged, closer to him. 'And we think he had Pan killed.'

'We being the CIA?'

'Yes.'

'So you wanted my DNA to cross-check with – presumably Gabrielle Fenwick?'

'Hers was the easiest DNA to sample. But we got Ben Corner's as well. It will take months, they say, to figure out what happened to you – but it's quite easy to see what happened to them. As for genetically reverse-engineering any of it, that's close to impossible. Years, if it is.'

'So Pan really hit the jackpot?'

'Then the jackpot hit Pan.'

Mitch nodded, grim.

'So who were these assistants? Do they have any connection to Oliver Hines?'

'Not that we can tell; in fact, if they weren't all likely dead, they'd be strong candidates for Pan's most trusted people. They all came to him through his organization, and he requested them all personally when Everett offered to set up a research station for him down south.'

She stretched back across the bed and grabbed another folder.

'Here's the details.'

It became apparent to Mitch that she was bra-less beneath the tank top, as she indicated a fifth and final folder at his feet.

'Then it's just the alien agenda folder.'

Mitch ignored that and accepted the fourth folder.

The first profile was of a woman, attractive of course, in her mid-twenties. Her resume was incomprehensible to Mitch, apart from conveying her qualifications to be part of Pan's team. He name was, or had been, Pam Winters.

The second was a Peruvian professor, Adriana Fontana, who'd been researching ayahuasca and similar psychotropic drugs for more than a decade. She, too, was very attractive.

Christ Pan, Mitch wondered, did it never end?

He flipped over to the final profile.

He knew what he was going to see.

It was Tim.

Mitch must have shown at least fleeting recognition because Cricket shifted back.

'What's wrong?'

She snatched the folder from him and examined it.

'You know her?' she asked. 'You recognize her?'

'Her?'

'The woman; Fontana?'

He wondered how to play this. The folder must have flipped back as she'd grabbed it. Had that been fortunate? A synchronicity? He still had that; his last secret, his last card to play if things spiraled out of control.

'Yeah, yeah I think I had a dream about her...'

'Do you think that means anything?'

'I don't know – I just saw her face and...'

Cricket stared at him. 'You're sure?'

'Not entirely... it was a dream...'

'But if she was in your dream... was that why you woke up all horny?'

'No,' Mitch recoiled. 'That was someone else.'

'So Fontana must be important somehow?'

Mitch thought again. Should he keep lying to her?

'Look; I don't know why I should be telling you anything. Everett seems to trust you, but you totally misrepresented yourself to me, and I still don't know what the hell the CIA are doing in the middle of all this anyway.'

'I told you. We're – *I'm* working in liaison with Everett to get to the bottom of all this. The United States government has a vested interest in ensuring that these weaponized genetic codes don't get into the wrong hands.'

'The US being the right hands?'

'You'd prefer some radical nation with a fundamentalist agenda? Don't you understand? The world is made up of the *powers that be*. Not the powers that might be, or the powers that you want there to be, the powers you'd prefer – the powers – that – be. If a weapon exists that has the power to turn the whole of humanity blonde and blue-eyed, or give everyone some manufactured disease that only one corporation has the cure for, or to target one genetic lineage – to be released let's say as a virus, or technologically, as a nano-swarm, or just any way, who would you prefer gets hold of it?'

'I think it should be destroyed.'

'Look, Mitch, I might even agree with you, but that's not going to happen. You can't un-invent things. Someone is going to get it – it's like the bomb, it's nuclear now. Someone will get it first, and someone will use it first – big time. There is no question that someone already has it, has used it, and that things are going to escalate from here.'

'But you haven't explained why they want me? They have what they want – what does consciousness expansion have to do with all this? If anything, advancement to a higher plain of consciousness is the opposite of what's going on; it's revelatory, it makes what they have…'

It suddenly dawned on Mitch.

That's why they wanted him – or, wanted him out of the way.

'…it makes what they have meaningless.'

'Meaningless is probably a bit strong. Less powerful, for sure. But you do get it now?' Cricket urged. 'They're on the verge of total physical control of the human race. You represent a step beyond physical. Just when they have us all finally swallowing their poisoned pill from their toxic paradigm, for which only they have the antidote, along comes *another* paradigm. An alternative agenda, an alternative will, that doesn't need an antidote. In fact, it's potentially the antidote to their whole system. You, and the others who have the pieces of that antidote, that alternative paradigm, are the only things that stand in their way.'

She stared into his eyes, breathless, looking at him as though he were the most valuable, astonishing thing she'd ever seen.

'You. Mitch Pyne, and what you represent, are the only hope for humanity.'

This time he launched himself at her.

He'd never felt so powerful; so self-possessed.

It was so primal, he was barely in control of himself.

Strangely, he heard an echo of Vance's voice, echoing down through time, but he couldn't quite make it out. It was distracting, so he ignored it.

Cricket pushed him back and took charge; she reciprocated his primal energy and became something else also. She was, at once, adoring and ferociously attentive, but at the same time receptive, enveloping. She moved about him, from act to act, position to position, leading him into her, out of her and around her. He was above her, below her, behind her, before her. He lost all sense of time; there was only rolling momentum.

He realized; she was trained, expert.

She was manipulating and coaxing him, professionally; and suddenly, in the middle of it all, he just perceived the edge of it. Her performance was almost invisible but he felt suddenly like a lion, catching a slight edge of fear from his tamer. Sara had been right; Cricket was a courtesan, there was no way he could stop or resist, even if he wanted to. There was only procession and a seemingly relentless energy.

He heard Vance's voice again; this time clearly.

The universe is a machine for replicating DNA…

But when he realized what it meant, what his unconscious, or even the universe, was trying to tell him, draw his attention toward, it was too late.

It will take the course of least resistance according to your choices…

He knew that he was reaching climax; he knew it would be a repeat of before. Her legs were wrapped around him like a vice. This time there was no condom.

He spiked; his new brain chemistry saw something it could penetrate and reveal and was activated.

He saw her body beneath him, felt it against his skin; it appeared suddenly as a black, dark receptacle, as the night sky awaiting a lightning strike. He saw and keenly sensed her biology, her mechanics, knew she was ripe and ovulating, knew that she knew, and then released a savage torrent into her.

His pleasure came with a terrible series of almost unbearable blasts as he impregnated her, knew that he had, and for a flash he was no longer present in his body; he was white, pure white.

He felt her body trembling beneath him, shuddering as her heels dug hard into his lower back. Then her legs dropped from their iron grip and began kicking in spasms. Her eyes seemed blind as her hands went to her confused face. She placed her fingers on her quivering lips, then touched her cheeks as though experiencing a revelation of horror. Her arms shot out above her head as though she could not comprehend what was happening to her, and her whole body began rippling involuntarily.

He withdrew quickly and knelt back, gazing down upon her wide-open form, and saw the electricity that was savaging her body, making her brain spark like a faulty strobe, making her limbs and muscles flinch and arc randomly, until the quilt beneath her was drenched. She was weeping silently, her body was wracking with sobs; her face was wet with tears. Then she started crying out; a bizarre mixture of pleasure and fear. He could tell that she was terrified, at once at the thought that it might not end, and it certainly seemed right then that it might not, that it would go on until she could not contain it and it killed her. Then, paradoxically, she was also terrified that it *would* end, that this feeling of immense and overwhelming power, this acute pleasure, would stop and leave her with only the memory of its primal bliss. In some ways, he perceived, she was begging the universe for it not to end, for it to take and ravish her infinitely.

He looked down at her seizure, inhuman and detached.

He thought: *that's what you get.*

Her cries came more frequently now, shock and awe.

As he came down and the spike left him, his normal thoughts began to return. He started to worry.

This had been going on for minutes now – how many?

Three? Four?

It really did look like it might not end; like continuous electroshock therapy. He leaned down and placed the palm of his hand on her chest, between her breasts, as though that might help to sooth this bizarre sexual epilepsy. Instead, it was like heart resuscitation; she jerked massively, almost launching entirely above the wet quilt, then came down quivering.

She was crying normally now, as though hurt, and saliva drizzled from the corner of her mouth. She stared vacantly into space, moaning little words, a few at first then many in quick succession that he couldn't understand. It was as though she were speaking in tongues.

From the window he heard a car approaching the hotel; far away but moving fast, skidding on the long gravel driveway. He knew that car was bringing bad.

He heard the door open and Saph's voice shouting as she came down the short corridor.

'Mitch it's starting! We have to –'

Then silent shock as she instantly registered the scene before her; what the beast had done to the maiden.

CHAPTER THIRTY-EIGHT

The first thing he noticed as he came back into being 'ordinary Mitch' was that he had the hardest and longest erection he ever remembered having, even right back into his teens, and that Saph was staring at it like he was threatening her with a loaded gun. No; not quite. It was more as though he had just murdered Cricket with a butcher's knife.

Cricket remained prostrate, spread-eagled, whimpering and staring into nothingness.

Saph snapped out of her shock.

'Jesus Mitch, is she alright?'

Saph went to her and Mitch backed away, clambering and bouncing off the soft, giant bed and immediately sourcing the underwear and suit trousers he'd somehow discarded the night before. They sat in a pile on a chair, with his shirt and jacket, freshly washed and pressed. As he dressed, Saph knelt at the end of the bed and stroked Cricket's brow.

'Holy shit, Mitch – are you *that good*?'

'No!'

She stared at him, incredulous. 'What happened?'

'You really want to know?'

Saph stared at him; *don't be an idiot.*

Mitch spoke in a defensive, highly-strung tone. 'It was the stuff; the genes! It overtook everything and just savaged her! They told her to do it!'

'They? The genes?'

'The CIA!'

'The CIA?'

'The CIA wanted her to get pregnant by me – they want a

child with these stupid genes!'

'Are you serious? Did she tell you that?'

'No, I – I had a spike, I just know it. And the worst thing is – the genes wanted it too!'

He calmed down a bit but then couldn't find his shoes. This was immensely irritating. Suddenly his one aim, his total focus, was to get out of the room.

'Mitch, that car that's coming – we have to be ready to get out of here.'

'What car?'

Mitch had forgotten and remained focused on his urge to flee the scene.

The engine roared again, still some distance away, and skidded somewhere along the long gravel drive. It sounded as though a drunk were driving. Mitch found his shoes under the chair, grabbed them, sat on the chair and forgot about the car again.

'I have to get out of here,' Mitch muttered to himself, fumbling with the laces.

Saph stood and left Cricket's side, went immediately to Mitch and slapped him so hard in the face that, despite the suite's plush furnishings, the sound of it echoed throughout the room.

Mitch froze, mid-lace.

Saph stared down at him, ice cold, then spoke in a very low voice.

'Something primal has taken hold of you. You've deposited your evil seed and now it's telling you to get away. You are behaving like a base-male primate. Whatever has happened, Cricket is your lover and you've bonded. Now help me get her dressed and on her feet.'

Mitch obeyed, like a terrified child scalded by his authoritarian mother.

He tied his last lace as Saph watched, then they quickly returned to the bed.

'I'm sorry,' Mitch muttered.

Saph wasn't sure to whom he was apologizing.

Cricket hadn't moved an inch, other than seeming to have fallen asleep. Her head had lolled to the side and her eyes were closed but she continued to murmur what sounded like gibberish.

Saph knelt again and touched Cricket's bare shoulder.

'Cricket?' she muttered. 'Cricket, we have to go.'

Cricket stopped murmuring.

Mitch leaned down. 'Cricket?'

Her eyes snapped open. Immediately the relaxation began to leave her face as she looked above her, left and right, from Saph to Mitch, then scrambled to sit upright. She whimpered like a wounded animal as she realized her body would not respond to her commands.

'What – what happened?'

Saph looked at Mitch, grim.

'What happened to me?' Cricket asked again, her voice light, almost innocent. 'Why won't my legs work properly? What's wrong with my arms?'

Saph put an arm around Cricket's shoulders and helped her sit up. The trembling woman could only just prop herself on her elbows, although the muscles in her arms were still visibly shaking. Cricket examined Saph's face in confusion.

'We need to get you dressed…' Saph spoke softly, looking up at Mitch. 'Your instincts were that of a cave man, but they were on the right track at least…'

Cricket turned and looked up to Mitch. 'Mitch? Oh God, we were…' Cricket gasped. 'What happened? What did we do?'

Saph was already pushing the white tank top over Cricket's head, down over her still sharply erect nipples; she had to move Cricket's arms one at a time, and negotiate her elbows through the loose garment. Again she seemed maternal, this time as a patient mother dressing a tired two-year old. Cricket continued to stare at Mitch.

'I do like you, you know,' Cricket said, maintaining the innocence in her voice. Mitch was pretty sure it was honest. 'It's not all an act.'

Saph was at Cricket's feet now, slipping her underwear over her toes, then awkwardly dragging her panties up her legs.

'I know,' said Mitch.

'It's a job…' Cricket uttered, watching as Saph knelt over her and brought the panties up over her hips and under her bum, snapping the elastic over her hips.

'Now for the jeans,' Saph muttered.

'But it's a nice job,' Cricket continued. 'I know you know it's a job, but we're still friends, aren't we?'

'Of course we are.' Mitch felt sick at what he'd done.

Saph had Cricket's feet in the jeans and was pushing them up each leg. She was dispatching her task with incredible speed, Mitch thought. She had to have done this before, several times; probably at the end of Pan's parties, after she'd assumed his job of 'cleaner' for their drunken comrades.

'We have to go,' Cricket stated absently, 'we have to hurry.'

Mitch assessed Saph, as he moved about the bed and helped her with one of the jean legs.

'What is this; why is everyone in such a hurry to leave all of sudden?'

'Blood,' Saph answered, almost as absently as Cricket. 'I see blood.'

Mitch stared down at Cricket. 'Oh God I didn't hurt her did I?'

'No,' Saph corrected impatiently. 'Blood, coming here. It's all I see!'

Surprisingly, Cricket leaned down and pulled the jeans on the rest of the length herself; almost unconsciously.

The sound of the approaching car was very close now, it could not have been more than a minute away from the hotel. Mitch wondered why security hadn't stopped it. Was that what Saph had been going on about; the car was bringing blood? Violence? Were they being attacked?

As though to confirm this, five gunshots rang out through the hotel in quick succession.

'Holy shit!' Mitch cried out.

They froze a few seconds, then there was a sixth, lone shot.

Saph's head was high, like a dog hearing a distant whistle, then she crawled away from Cricket and off the bed as Cricket tried to get up and do the same. She swung her legs off the side but collapsed instantly down onto the plush carpet when she tried to support her own weight. Mitch rushed to her side and Saph started forcing her calf-length boots on. Mitch propped her up on the floor to a sit again.

'Damn,' Cricket gasped. 'I can feel them coming back, but they won't…'

'What the hell's going on?' Mitch asked Saph desperately. 'Do you know?'

Cricket leaned back into Mitch's arms and he took all her weight. He noticed her lips were still trembling but she had enough strength to push when Saph asked her to; finally both her boots were on.

'I know what's happening,' Saph snapped, standing quickly and grabbing Cricket's navy leather coat from the bed.

'How?' Mitch demanded as he helped Cricket put the jacket on, then slowly they both helped her to stand.

'I can't explain – not now. We have to get downstairs, then get out of here.'

'I can't…' Cricket uttered.

Mitch caught her in his arms before she could fall again; Saph stuffed his phone in his trouser pocket and scrambled to scoop up the loose files from all over the bed and floor. Some of them were damp; Saph winced only once, then ignored it.

'To the lobby,' Saph said. 'Carry her if you have to.'

Cricket looked into Mitch's eyes, giving permission. He reached down and with a loud grunt hefted her up into his arms. He hadn't realized how tiny she actually was; still, she was a human body, and heavy.

They moved as one out of the room; Saph paused only to rush into her own room, which was again opposite Mitch's, and returned stuffing the papers she'd gathered into a heavy shoulder bag. Then they rushed down the long, high manor corridor. Mitch paused at the top of the stairs, steadying himself with Cricket's weight.

Two more gunshots went off; simultaneously from what sounded like the lobby. Mitch fixed upon Saph's gaze, up at him from a few steps down.

'Jesus Saph, we're heading right into it, surely?'

'It's okay,' Saph urged. 'It's over. Come on!'

He held her gaze for a second longer and decided to trust her.

Shifting his weight again as Cricket shifted in his arms, he followed Saph, stomping down the main stairway, finding his balance in his momentum.

Maybe that's what it's all about, Mitch thought. No matter how heavy the load, just keep going, keep balance as best you can and maintain the momentum 'til the end?

They made their way into the lobby as the manic sound of the approaching car finally reached the hotel exterior. They heard it pull up outside as it skidded on the gravel to an insane halt.

Saph stopped near the open manor entrance; they heard all four car doors open, one at a time, and panicked voices.

What appeared before them eerily mirrored their own situation.

Vance stumbled up the stairs of the hotel entrance, carrying Heather in his arms; both were drenched in blood. Behind them, hobbling and supported by Yelina, was Bo Everett, clutching a wound to his guts that was streaming blood.

CHAPTER THIRTY-NINE

'It's all on now folks!' Everett cried out, then winced. 'On for one and all!'

'Jesus…' Mitch uttered.

Vance staggered past them and into the lobby; the sight before them presented only more bloodshed.

Jo Sara and Bill Hinchcliffe both lay sprawled on the floor in the middle of the room, opposite each other, each with a gun in their hand. It looked at first sight as though some kind of stand off between them had ended both their lives.

Vance staggered past them, avoiding the splayed limbs, and placed Heather slowly down in one of the plush armchairs. She was conscious, but looked stunned, and sat back in the chair like an old woman who'd been standing all day and was grateful to finally sit down. Mitch could see no wound on her, yet she and Vance were both at least half coated in crimson.

'Who's blood is that?' Mitch demanded.

Vance turned from her and stared at Mitch, his face grave.

'A little bit of everyone's I'm afraid old chap.'

Mitch grunted with Cricket's weight, deliberated shortly, and put her down in a chair beside Heather.

'Thanks,' Cricket muttered dreamily. 'I'll be okay in a second.'

Still, she barely moved.

'What happened to her?' Vance demanded.

'Primal sex,' Mitch answered absently. 'Some kind of seismic orgasm…'

Vance stared at him, incredulous for a second.

'Well, good for her!'

Then he winced and doubled over. Mitch and Saph both went

immediately to either side of their old teacher, propping him back up. Everett staggered through and collapsed upright into another plush chair, opposite the girls. He looked around, quickly assessing each of Hitch's screens behind him, then stared over at the three laptops that were still active at each of the command stations.

'Where's Harding?' Everett demanded, then winced as his hands closed over the wound in his gut.

'Stop moving around,' Yelina demanded. 'I need to take care of you.'

Mitch saw the wheels spin incredibly fast behind her eyes, then she turned and left the room.

'Where is he?' Everett demanded again.

'What the hell happened?' Mitch counter-demanded. 'Were you shot?'

Everett stared down at Sara and Hinch, in the middle of the floor near his feet. 'These two huh?' Hinch was closest; Everett nudged his hip with his heavy hiking shoe. 'They still with us?' He grinned without mirth. 'Alive, I mean. Clearly they are no longer with *us*.'

'We were ambushed,' Vance grimaced. 'As we were coming off Everett's boat. We moored at the private docks on the south side, they were waiting for us as we got to the car. They took out Everett's three bodyguards; probably snipers, bullets to the head, rapid succession. It seems the rest of us were to be taken alive; Heather was hit with a tranquilizer dart, the rest of us took cover in a cargo shed. When it became obvious it was standoff and that we were unarmed, they moved in for close-quarters.'

'Only four of them,' Everett grunted. 'Plain clothed mercenaries, Oliver's men. Guess they figured two women and two old men, only needed one man for each.'

'Oliver Hines hired mercenaries?' Mitch was dumbfounded. 'To capture you?'

Everett grinned. 'Everything's changed, boy. All out in the open now. Stakes are too high. CIA made their move too, huh?

Too bad for them, way too late. Unless – you in love with her yet?'

'What?' Mitch was shocked. 'Cricket? No!'

'Just what I thought. Way too late to play the long game now. They were banking on the whole primal impulse thing; you'd side with them to protect your unborn child. They'll be coming for her soon enough, what she's carrying is a game changer to them; to everyone pretty much, just like all of you.'

Everett's eyes whipped to Saph; she flinched and looked away.

'Yeah, thought as much. Maybe not such a great plan to have you all in one place but it was worth the risk to flush you all out. But it's gonna make things a hell of a lot more complicated Mitchell, if that's what you want, play daddy to the cosmic child there. Easier to have the CIA just swoop in like Child Services and raise it as their own.'

'What are you saying?' Mitch was appalled.

'You know what he's saying,' Saph scalded. 'He's just baiting you.'

Everett laughed, then winced again.

'Goddamn knife fights; I've been out of the game too long.'

'That's a knife wound?' asked Mitch.

'Morons came at me hand to hand; took the first one out real quick, too slow with his tranquilizer gun, but the second one seemed to forget his 'bring 'em back alive' mission brief when he realized the choke hold I had on him was playing for keeps. Left me this little memento with his last breath, what he thought was his last breath anyway. I ain't no killer but I like to see the fear in their eyes if you know what I mean; like to let 'em know I could if I wanted.'

Vance grunted. 'It was the order to catch us alive that saved us; Yelina and I managed the other two. Led them into the boat shed and came at them from behind. When we got back outside there was another man about to spirit Heather off in a van; we simply mobbed him and got Heather back to the car; but as we left, he let off a few parting shots. Probably aiming for the car tires, but bullets don't work like they do in movies. They don't go exactly where you want them to go and they don't necessarily stop on the first thing they hit. I think I can feel it, here in my flab…' Vance poked his stomach, winced and doubled over once more. Mitch and Saph continued to prop him up but moved him toward another of the plush chairs opposite Everett. 'Yes I rather think I can,' Vance uttered as he sat, again wincing. 'Not very deep it seems but the pain rather affected my driving.'

Having seated Vance, Saph turned to Everett.

'We can't stay here long.'

Everett met her gaze. 'It'll be easier if you just confess. Easier for you to help us all, easier for us all to understand.'

Saph stared at him, cold.

'Time to come clean sweetheart.'

Saph let out a long breath and shook her head.

'It's not like I wanted it to be like this.'

Her confession was interrupted by a solid cough from the far corner of the room by the bay windows. From the floor behind the furthest couches, a figure stirred then sat up shakily. The face was ghastly: a puff of shredded skin decorated the side of his temple and had covered his face totally in blood. As he stood and wobbled on his feet, balancing on the back of a couch chair, they saw that the clothes on his chest were shredded with at least five bullet holes.

Somehow, Harding had been shot six times and survived.

'Bloody bitch,' came the strong South African accent, 'sold us all out!'

CHAPTER FORTY

'She can't have!' Mitch protested. 'I don't believe it!'

Harding's thick neck swiveled toward Mitch, and across the room his eyes focused slowly upon him. The effect of the loss of blood was readily apparent; it was as though Harding were very tired and very drunk.

'Sorry lad, truth's the truth; both of 'em sold us out. Couldn't wait, either of 'em. Thought I was asleep, but I can't sleep these days. That goddamned tracker in me rib.' He tapped his breast and coughed out a bloody laugh. 'It's stopped! Well how's that for a …' He smiled again. 'They didn't know I was in the bar; I heard 'em both squabbling over which one of 'em was going to do it. Both of them got the message at the same time, got the offer from Olivera they couldn't refuse. My guess is that the Olivera team wanted to create maximum chaos.'

Mitch sighed heavily. 'You mean Sara? Sara sold us out?'

'And that scrawny tech fucker. Known them both five, six years. I knew Sara wanted out, knew she wanted out faster than she could get out, but Hinch, I think he was just offered more money for one job than he'd make in God knows how long. Bloody idiots didn't understand, eh boss?' Harding winked a bloody eye at Everett. 'You pay 'em what they think they're worth – that's the deal, huh?'

Everett said nothing.

Harding maneuvered uneasily from behind the couch and headed to the parlor's mini-bar. He took a bottle of scotch and, although Mitch expected him to drink straight from the bottle, splashed a giant amount into a glass and gulped it down thirstily, then waved the glass at his two fallen ex-comrades.

'Everyone's got a price, guess Olivera found out what would satisfy these two to stand down in treachery for the rest of their lives.'

Harding pulled at the khaki fatigues across his chest, ripping them away to reveal a shining silver-blue vest. The five bullets were deeply embedded there.

'When I couldn't talk them out of it, Hinch did this. Little prick. I staggered to the other side of the room; thought faking it was my only hope of staying alive, take a dive behind the furniture and play dead, but as I went down that bitch took a head shot...' Harding touched the open puff of flesh across his temple without flinching, poured another, smaller drink and poured it over the wound. This time he did flinch; but only just. 'How long I been out?'

There was a moment of silence as they all stared at the indestructible mercenary.

'What?' Harding asked.

'*Buy a lotto ticket*,' Vance uttered. 'I believe is the expression.'

'This? Been through worse than this. You should see my skin under the vest. I've seen bark that's smoother.'

'Eww', Vance said.

Harding laughed. 'Listen; Hinch stood security down. They'll be coming, the Olivera clean-up team, and it won't take 'em long to get here. Once you hear the choppers, it's too late.'

'But...' Mitch spread his arms. 'What was Saph about to say?'

'That can wait,' Everett grumbled. 'Now some of us have lost blood, but none of us are about to die of it; so I suggest we start thinking about moving out. Vance, you work for me now, how's the cosmic corridor working?'

'Don't think I didn't think of that back at the ambush; fear and panic doesn't seem conducive to metaphysical prowess. That's a rule that goes as far back as any occult system I can name. I could try but I don't think it's going to work, and if it does I can't guarantee it'll take us where we want, nor how much time will have passed when we get there.' Vance grunted, his body spasmed with pain. 'We might end up in the middle of the Gobi desert, in the middle of next year!'

'Might be worth a shot if we can't find another way; damned if I'm waiting here for Oliver Hines to come get me. It was the smart move though; I was too slow. I underestimated him. His public profile, his money; he has more to lose than me. Though I never thought he'd risk… still, I should have been ready.'

Yelina re-entered the room with an almost toppling armful of bandages and medical supplies. 'The staff have locked themselves in the freezer; I let them out and they helped me find these, then they went back in again.'

As though unfazed by the blood, Yelina went instantly to work, spreading the supplies on the large oak table in the middle of the room, sorting quickly through them, then pointing at Vance.

'You first; lay down here. Harding, help me.'

Harding staggered around the table and began searching through the supplies.

'Medical field kit,' he mumbled. 'Sara always had one stashed somewhere.'

He glanced down at her body, grunted, then found a bottle of pills, flipped the lid and chewed at least six of them like candy. Then he threw pills at Vance. Vance caught them on his bloody lap, then stood, slowly, and examined the bottle.

'Pain killers, rapid agent,' he muttered. He unscrewed the cap and removed three, then ate them as he moved to the table. Harding and Mitch helped him sit on the edge, then he lay back with his lanky, black-suited legs dangling over the side.

'Be gentle with me,' he uttered, setting his thin gray tie back over his shoulder.

Yelina undid his blood-drenched black silk shirt, revealing a pale stomach with a late middle-aged bulge. At the edge of the bulge was an open wound; it was no longer bleeding but looked awful, like a giant open boil that needed to be lanced. Yelina took another bottle from the pile of supplies, screwed the lid open and poured clear liquid liberally over the bullet wound.

Vance screamed out in pain but sounded like a hawk.

'It is a bee sting!' Yelina protested. 'Be a man!'

The minor surgery proceeded quickly; having briefly but expertly examined the wound, Yelina sterilized a scalpel with the liquid, then dug in. Vance screamed out again and fell back, his head hitting the table hard.

'I think he's passed out,' Mitch mumbled.

'No I bloody haven't!' Vance shrieked, then screamed out again, as Yelina withdrew the bullet.

'One inch below,' she frowned down at Vance. 'Embedded in your flab, old man!'

'Nargh!' Vance pronounced.

Yelina reached down and placed the bloody bullet in Vance's outstretched hand.

'Souvenir. Good story to tell. You like telling stories, no?'

While this had been going on, Harding had proceeded to clean and patch up the bullet wound on his head; he had now moved to the parlor mirror and was sewing the wound himself with gritted teeth.

Yelina ripped the packaging off a several needles, injected the contents beside Vance's wound, then she too began to sew. Before long, Vance was bandaged and standing; Mitch guessed the whole process had taken less than five minutes. It was like triage.

Everett was next; he lay down where Vance had been and Yelina went to work. As she did, Everett spoke.

'Anyone left on the grounds?'

Harding snapped the thread from his temple, turned and walked around the table to Hinch's laptop.

'Get those bastards out of the freezer again someone,' he grumbled. 'I need some food.'

Everett winced as Yelina sewed his wound. 'Christ, Harding. Oliver's people will be on us before anyone has time to *cook* anything. The only reason they haven't moved on us is because they haven't heard back from your two friends on the floor.'

Harding spoke into the desktop microphone.

'This is Jimmy Barnes to Cold Chisel. Report.'

Nothing.

'This is Barnes to INXS. Report.'

Nothing.

'Barnes to Midnight Oil. Report.'

Again, nothing.

'Jimmy Barnes to all teams. Mission compromised. Stand down rescinded. All available, report to mission command. Or you bastards won't get paid.'

Nothing.

Then, 'Midnight Oil to Jimmy Barnes.' It was a posh male English voice, very clipped. 'Had to make sure it was you, sah. Most of the men have packed up – we've got about half of INXS here, and four remaining Oils, including myself. What's happened?'

'Hutchence and Garrett were compromised. They're decommissioned. You didn't stand down Midnight Oil?'

'We were going to sah, but the orders came through from Hutchence and Garrett separately. Details didn't match. Thought it odd, sah. Thought, with what the big man's paying us, maybe it's good form to stick around, wait it out.'

'Money talks,' Everett grunted as he sat up, splashing disinfectant across his stomach.

'You're a good man, Byford. Dispatch INXS to their previous positions and bring the Oils back here – stay sharp, hostile forces not far away.'

'I know sir. There's a helicopter just off the horizon and two speedboats coming in. But we should make it back in time. Oils out.'

'Barnes out.' Harding sat back. 'Now. Anyone know how to work this damn satellite surveillance?'

'I do,' Heather rasped from the couch, her dry lips smacking as she spoke. 'Anyone got any water?' She clicked her sandpaper tongue a few times to make her point.

Mitch took a plastic bottle from the pile of medical supplies, clearly labeled, opened the lid and handed it to her. Beside her, Cricket was asleep. Heather gulped greedily, then sighed heavily. 'Damn those tranqs dry you out.'

She stood, slowly at first, then walked around the table to Harding. On the way, she looked at Mitch, then to the slumbering Cricket, then to Mitch again.

There was only one message he could read from her expression: disappointment.

Harding stood and Heather took the chair.

'Can't you just call more people in?' Mitch asked Everett. 'Don't you have more?'

'This *is* my security force, Mitch. I'm not a goddamned super-villain; I hired a few men to protect me, and they're dead. I hired my regular auxiliary crew to protect you, and that's it. I would call the police but there is way too much explanation involved and besides, now Oliver's made his move who knows who he controls, or what forces he's aligned with. He was the one that set the cops on you at the Vantage. I have the money and influence, even the friends I need to mobilize, but I need time to speak to those sympathetic to our cause.'

'Our cause?' Mitch blurted. 'What is that exactly?'

'Don't be a moron, Mitchell,' Everett growled. 'We need to get ourselves out of this mess, somewhere safe and then I can –'

Hinch was off the floor and had his elbow hooked around Yelina's throat, his gun to her head, faster than anyone could comprehend. He didn't say a word as he instantly began backing out of the room, toward the lobby and the main doors.

They could hear the engine of the car still running outside; it became readily apparent that he'd simply been listening, and biding his time.

'You fucking little weasel!' Harding spat.

'Ten million!' Hinch shouted. 'In advance!' There was blood, still pouring from a wound in his chest; more blood dribbled from the sides of his mouth as he grinned. 'It's in my account,

Harding! In my account, right now! I can get out of this! I can get to a hospital; there's one in the town! Just let me go and I'll disappear!'

He coughed blood over Yelina's shoulder; it was the first time she'd flinched.

'You pathetic bastard,' Everett uttered, nodding down at Sara. 'You killed your friend.'

'Her? She's killed more dinners than I've had hot people!' Hinch cackled a bit, then reconsidered. 'People, and dinners – you know what I mean!'

He was almost out of the room and into the lobby now. Yelina was making it hard for him, taking small steps, leaning heavily backwards. It was slow going but Hinch, clearly delirious, wouldn't shut up.

'You pride yourself on choosing your people Harding – good sorts you say. But her, Sara, she's been killing peasants in Africa for decades – you need to hire better hackers to do your background checks – she's as psychopathic as they come!'

The top of his head exploded as a single shot rang out.

His body folded behind Yelina as she ran forward, into Saph. They hugged each other tightly.

Sara's hand quivered and she dropped her gun back to the floor, pretty much exactly from where she'd slowly reached out to grab it. She'd lifted only her head and her arm, and now her head fell back as well, thudding like a punctured basketball.

'Not that that… really… makes up… for anything… old boy…' she gurgled. Harding went to her and stood, staring down like the Grim Reaper, waiting.

She stared up at him.

'Little… creep. Liked to watch… ladies sleep. Sleep Creep, I called him…' She gurgled again. 'I… took money, Harding, old boy. I took from Oliver, from Everett… took from MI6, took from the CIA…' She laughed blood and bile. 'But it was… never enough. Mitch – did he do it? I tried to get him to… do it, last night…'

Mitch looked down on her. She saw him.

'You knew,' Sara smiled crookedly. 'Don't tell me you… didn't. Could have had any of them old chap… but you took… path of least…' She coughed blood again. 'You remember what I said… old chap? I'm going to knock on Saint Peter's gate… demand… answers… and you know who'll be there?' She laughed to herself and rolled her head side to side. 'Won't be reptiles, or lovely blondes…' She giggled. 'You think angels look like that? Like Plei… Pleiadeans?' She laughed again. 'Won't be any of them… won't be… any… one.'

Then she died.

Harding stared down at her a moment longer.

'Huh,' he said.

Yelina moved from Saph's embrace to Everett's.

'Blood,' said Saph, dully. 'That's what I saw. Lots of blood.'

CHAPTER FORTY-ONE

Mitch stared down at the body.

A woman in her mid-forties, perfectly physically fit.

Dead because she hated her life so much she'd do anything to escape it.

'I chose to do it,' Cricket spoke.

She'd woken; and although her skin was pale, her eyes were bright and refreshed, as though she'd slept heavily for a full night. All eyes went to her.

'I knew what I was doing,' she added. 'It was a mission, and I accepted.'

'You didn't ask me,' Mitch countered. 'And how do you know what they're going to do with you – with *it*? Even if you do bring it to term… which, given the situation…' Mitch looked down at Sara again, her dead eyes open and staring up to Saint Peter, then at the mess that was Hinch, then back to Cricket. 'How many more have they impregnated? With that sample you got?'

Cricket stood but didn't answer. She seemed perfectly rested now.

'We need to get out of here. I can't help. I'm deep cover; none of my people are stationed anywhere near here.'

The sound of a distant helicopter reached them.

'That's not good,' Harding stated.

Heather spoke up from reading the satellite display. 'It's two minutes away, and it's heavily armed; either he's seconded it from his friends in the military or he's got his own private air force, because this is not a machine a private citizen should… wait; the two speedboats – four men in each, one minute from shore.'

Everett glared at Vance. 'Vance, are you sure?'

Vance shrugged, helpless. 'I'm desperately sorry to let you all down but it's gone I'm afraid.'

Mitch went up to him. 'Vance, I can see them. The gaps. There's one behind us, under the stairs in the lobby. If you can open it…?'

'I'm sorry Mitchell, desperately sorry. But I have nothing – nothing!'

Everett swung around to Saph.

'Well? What happens? Do we die here?'

Saph shuddered and shrugged. 'I can only see paths, and potential; it's becoming clearer, but I can see… three paths; I see escape, I see capture, and I see death. But I can't see which is the way forward…'

'What's she talking about?' Mitch asked.

'I have one of Pan's gifts,' Saph sighed. 'Ever since the wake I've been able to… see things. In the future – and sometimes in the past. That's why I hid away the last two nights. I meditated; I wanted to make it clearer. I've hardly slept at all! But I think it just gets clearer on its own… I think the neural pathways have to form, it's like any skill, any mental process, you have to use it to get better at it… what I see are like symbols, abstracts, but,' she gulped, 'I think the longer we wait, the worse it gets. And what I see… all I see is…'

Saph frowned. It was as though she didn't want to say it.

'…the path out… to escape… it's like…'

'What?' Everett demanded. 'What do you see?'

'What I see is… it's bizarre I know, but it's a webpage. I see a webpage, from a news site.'

Everett frowned. 'What does it say?'

'I can't read it, I can only *sense* what it says. And it says you're dead Everett. It says you've been dead for a long time…'

Everett frowned more deeply. 'What does that mean? The only way for us to escape is for me to die?'

The helicopter sounded very close now.

Harding moved to Heather and tapped a code into the

computer over her shoulder; within seconds the whole technical suite powered down.

'I don't know what Hinch uploaded, but that reformats the drives. There's nothing left on them. If we're going to make a move, we go now.'

Heather knelt beside Sara, frisked her body and collected a second gun besides the one she scooped from the floor. Everett took Hinch's gun and Harding began arming himself from a gym bag under his now-blank workstation.

Four armed men stormed in, Everett spun about and aimed his pistol.

Harding called out. 'Stand down!'

Everett though had already realized that these were men in his employ; the remaining men of Midnight Oil.

Byford, a short and slim man in his fifties with white hair, stood before three other, younger male mercenaries; all were dressed in self-styled military black.

'Marine contingents seem to be holding back at shore, sah. And the chopper's hovering about half a click down the road.'

'What are they waiting for?' Everett asked.

As though in response, a generic ring tone sounded from Mitch's pocket.

He fished out his phone and shakily handed it to Saph.

Heather groaned. 'You still haven't read the manual?'

Saph answered. 'Yes?'

There was a pause and she held the phone away from her, then entered some commands. A clear voice came through; a polite middle-American accent.

'I'm on speaker now?'

'Yes,' Saph answered, holding the phone out before her in her open palm.

'Very good. I'm sure you all recognize my voice.'

'It's Oliver Hines,' Everett growled.

'Hello, Bo. Look, I… I didn't mean for it to get messy back at the dock. I mean, we're not looking for blood here, are we? Just didn't expect you to go all Rambo on my men. To be honest I'm not really used to all this, I… I hope next time I give out orders to hired security they're a little more clear.'

Mitch remembered seeing Oliver Hines on television; although his voice was mild, and very boy-next-door, it was not difficult to detect the tone of supreme confidence, bordering on arrogance, beneath it. He pictured the man in his mind: the generic baseball cap, always white, the nondescript button-down work-shirts and plain denim jeans. The everyman billionaire; Ron Howard, but with the hometown charisma totally faked.

Saph moved the phone to a table and propped it up; there he was. Exactly as Mitch had imagined him, head and shoulders staring out with a wide, toothy grin.

'I can't see you; the cam function on this phone doesn't seem to be activated. Can you see me? Are you all there?'

Nobody spoke.

'I'll just assume you all are there, okay then? Now you may have heard that I don't like using these things and that's true. No doubt you're recording this; that's one of the reasons I don't like them, but that doesn't matter. I've made sure you can't upload and after we're done you're going to hand the phone over and that will be that.'

Saph looked at Everett and shrugged; Mitch supposed that meant it was being recorded somehow.

'Look, here's the deal. I'm going to talk, then I want you to accept my offer. You'll have one minute after I finish talking to make your choices, and I understand you may not all choose the same way, that's okay, so long as you hear me out, but after one minute, then my men will come and get you. Now like I said, I hope my orders to them are clear, but we all know how things tend to get out of hand where men with guns are concerned, so… well, I guess if it gets to that we just wait and see how things pan out. Bo? You still there?'

'I'm here.'

'Bo, you might not be in my league financially, but it will still take a lot of effort to bring your empire down. If you want to go to war, so be it. In six months, I'll have won. It'll cost me, it'll cost me big, but my best people tell me it can be done. But to avoid a war, a costly war, and I don't just mean for you and me personally, a war that will cost stock and jobs and careers and all that jazz, and no-one wants that, here's what I suggest. Just step aside and let your friends come with me. Heck you've only known them a few days! You do that, and we can come to an arrangement. After all, this is all down to you and your friend Pan; and before you get all het up about that I want you to know, his death had nothing to do with me. I took the information that came to me, sure, I had my feelers out, I'll admit that, but darn it I just wanted to meet the guy! What good is a dead genius? So young, too! Just a darn tragedy! Now I know Sapphire there has some strong feelings about that, heck and darn it, maybe you all do – I don't know you all, other than what I've got on paper. But I just wanted you to know; it wasn't my doing. Okay. That's said. Now, Bo, are you open to an arrangement?'

'Go on.'

'Let me tell you how this is gonna work. Your boy Pan hit the jackpot. We've got product lines ready to roll; gene therapy is the new social revolution. You want your son to turn straight, we got Gay Away. You got a man problem, want to try something new, we got Go Lesbo! Now these brands are still in the testing phase you understand. Personally I prefer Sapphic Sojourn but the marketing people tell me we gotta come on strong. Yeah.. I don't know. Anyway, it's all completely reversible within a six week period, personal gene mapping notwithstanding. Anyway, you get the picture?'

'I think so.'

'And speaking of picture; I got myself my own motion picture arm now. You all probably heard about it by now. That's right! Cinema Olivera, can you believe it? We've got stars in their fifties who look thirty again. Stars in their *sixties* who look thirty again! In three-dee no less! Everett, I tell ya, this is the end of depression, of mental illness, of heart disease, of cancer, haiche-eye-vee, obesity, all that good stuff! Now there's plenty for everyone, let me tell you. I'm not gonna keep all this to myself; hell, it's basically yours anyway!'

Everett growled.

'Oliver, you're sending mankind down a path it's not ready for. There's no projection you can make that doesn't end in the extinction of individuality.'

'Okay, okay – maybe you've got a point. Maybe your projections are a little less optimistic than mine.'

'That is my most optimistic projection!'

Oliver sighed. 'Maybe so, maybe so. But you know I'm a good capitalist at heart, Bo. It's not up to me; we let it out and let the market decide. Gene therapy, it's all about freedom, freedom from the genetic lottery, freedom to make yer own decisions!'

'There's only one way to do what you want to do without market collapse, Oliver, and that way is an abhorrence. The scales are weighted too heavily on one side. The people I have with me represent the other side of the scales; they represent the option for humanity to understand its larger place in the scheme of things, they represent the opportunity to expand humanity's consciousness so that it has the balance, the wisdom to deal with the new responsibilities. Without that you will plunge us all into a world of rampant ego, rampant id, with no hope of escape.'

'Now now Bo, there you go, over-dramatizing the situation again. Listen, I appreciate that with great power comes great responsibility. But in *my* future, it's a level playing field. Everyone's young and beautiful. Everyone's a genius, everyone's an athlete, everyone's sane, everyone's rational, and everyone understands!'

'Everyone who can afford it, you mean. And what do you mean by *understand*? Understand what, Oliver? You're turning physicality into a commodity, on the grossest level! You talk a good game but you and I are businessmen – we know how this will work. Your models will all have to be about repeat business; there is no other model that doesn't lead to the total collapse of the free market. You'll give the people what they want, and in some cases even what they need; so long as they can keep paying for the dosage. You'll create a debt-driven culture of ego-addicts permanently on credit to you and your corporation.'

Oliver threw up his hands and grimaced.

'It's just good business, Bo!'

Everett gritted his teeth. 'I'll tell you what, Oliver. I'll agree. I'll turn over my friends, I'll come in with you and share in your new world, so long as you can guarantee me one thing.'

'Name it Bo.'

'I want your guarantee that your science division hasn't been working overtime, devising a way to ensure that these new gene therapies have built-in obsolescence. You guarantee me that these gene courses are one time only; I don't care how much you charge, just one time only, and I'll come in with you. Right now.'

Oliver nodded to himself.

'You have to hand over your people, Bo,' he said sadly. 'You start dispatching enlightenment in a bottle and you know what happens? People stop caring so much about how they look. They stop caring about what car they drive, how big their house is, and whatever else it is they wanna buy next. They stop caring, Bo, they – stop – *caring*. And we can't have that, Bo. We can't have people looking elsewhere for their self-esteem. That has to come from what we give 'em, Bo. People need that, they need guidance, they need control. Otherwise it's just anarchy. It's the death of western civilization. If people start looking inside themselves to find what they need, then our way of living is gone, Bo. Gone. People are happy now, Bo. Hell, happy *enough*, with what we give 'em. They start looking up, Bo, or sideways, or God help us all, inside themselves, then that's the whole world gone. Gone, Bo.'

'You're wrong.'

'You have to know, Bo, this is the way it's meant to be. It's the way they want it, Bo, it's all set up to be like this!'

'They?'

'It's our place in the scheme of things, Bo, and people like you and me, we're the ones who are meant to do it.' Oliver shook his head. 'I really wish you could see things my way, Bo.'

'I'm sorry Oliver. I can't do business with you.'

Oliver went quiet and looked down, as though terribly sad.

'Last chance, Bo.'

There was no response.

'I haven't got any choice, Bo. I'm sorry.' Oliver turned from the phone camera and gave a command. 'Guys… level the hotel.'

There was the sound of the helicopter drawing closer, and of missiles being discharged from the air, then an almighty explosion, followed by more missiles, and an even larger explosion.

And the nameless manor hotel was no-more.

CHAPTER FORTY-TWO

'I don't know what it was,' Vance shrugged. 'I just heard the man talking and I knew he was speaking evil. Not necessarily his sales pitch. I mean; the two of you were talking in extremes. I'm sure the world would survive this new course of gene therapies and go on just as it has for centuries, it's just that…' Vance looked around him. 'I say, what a beautiful day.'

'Where are we?' Cricket demanded.

The six of them had stepped out of the dimensional crack, one by one, and were all slightly disorientated. Byford and his three men followed, then finally Mitch.

'Everett's boat,' Mitch responded. 'Where Vance said we'd go.'

'It's not where I left it,' Everett responded grumpily. 'We're moving, we're out at sea.'

Sure enough the group had emerged through Vance's dimensional tunnel and into the penthouse deck of Everett's ocean cruiser. But the cruiser was certainly no longer moored at the southern docks.

'It was the certainty, you see,' Vance continued, gazing out at the ocean as it passed by. 'I lost all the fear that was blocking me because I was certain that this man had to be fought. I don't think I've ever felt such certainty.'

'Who the hell's at the helm?' Everett demanded of no-one in particular.

The group had emerged in the middle of the deck, beside the bar. Mitch had been the last one through; and as he'd emerged, the dimensional doorway had closed behind him, blinking out like the end of a sparkler.

Heather went immediately behind the bar and poured herself

a vodka.

'Anyone else? Help yourselves.'

Everett turned to Byford and his three men. They were pale, clearly disoriented, but stood steady.

'You men okay?' Harding asked.

'Might need a belt of Dramamine, sah,' Byford gulped.

'I'll see what I can do. In the meantime, search the ship. Find out who's at the helm and bring anyone on board up here. Understand?'

'Sah.'

The four men departed and Mitch could hear them mutter between themselves; they were not calm mutters, carrying more a tone of bewilderment than anything.

'Well,' Saph sighed. 'What the hell do we do now? How do we defeat the fifth richest man in America?'

'Second,' Everett corrected. 'I'm fifth.'

'Look, whatever,' Saph guffawed. 'Was what he said true? Can he destroy you?'

'Probably. But he'd be some way further down that list too, when we were done. A lot further.'

'That's not the point,' Mitch stated squarely. 'The point is, we either stop him, and I don't see how, or we get our side of the product on the market just as quickly. And I don't see how we can do that either, especially when we don't have it. Not all six ingredients anyway.'

'That's what I don't get,' Heather slammed her empty glass down. 'What are these ingredients, anyway? What are they really? I mean, Mitch can spot aliens disguised as humans, and dimensional anomalies, Vance can open dimensional tunnels, and Sapphire seems to be able to divine the future – in an abstract, not very definite way, it seems to me.'

'I believe it's called remote viewing my dear,' Vance offered.

'I know what it's called, Magician. I hung out with Pan and his people long enough to know that. It's just a fancy name for clairvoyance, anyway. And I'd hazard a guess that the next three abilities Pan's potions provide are along similar lines; probably something to do with energy healing, and something to do with channeling beings from other realms, and something to do with… I don't know, out of body projection or telekinesis or something? They're the usual categories aren't they?'

'That's what you wrote in your report,' Everett mumbled. 'Damn fine guess work, if you ask me.'

'They weren't guesses,' Heather countered testily, 'it was, however, work.'

Everett frowned at her, as though unused to having her anger directed, however mildly, at him.

The glass doors opened and Byford returned, holding a man at gunpoint.

Everett stared at the prisoner. 'Mason?'

Mason, a muscular Greek-looking man in his fifties, with a deep tan, his arms covered in navy tattoos, stared at Everett aghast.

'Mister Everett?'

'We found him at the helm, sah.'

'Mason, why are you stealing my boat?'

'I'm not Mister Everett, I would never…'

'Then what's it doing out here? Where are we by the way?'

'We're in the North Pacific Ocean. Out of Hawaii. Less than one day from Los Angeles.'

'And why are we here, Mason?' Everett frowned and scratched his beard. 'Coming to think of it, Mason, *how* are we here? It must have taken…'

'Almost three weeks Mister Everett. With a few stops. I was ordered to take her back…'

'By whom?'

'By… well, by the handlers of your estate, Mister Everett.'

'The handlers of my…?'

'Oh dear,' Vance winced.

'Mister Everett, sir…' Mason stammered. 'I… I don't understand. How are you here? Where have you…? How did you get here?'

Saph pulled out and assessed her phone, then groaned.

'Holy crap! Three months!' she stated. 'We've been gone for three whole months!'

Everett spun about to Heather. 'Get on –'

'I'm on it!' Heather had pulled a laptop from under the bar, started it up, and was furiously tapping keys.

Mitch, Saph and Cricket gathered behind her.

She had entered a Google search on Bo Everett.

'Bloody hell,' Mitch hissed.

Heather read aloud.

'There's a headline: Bo Everett missing after gas explosion!'

Then she frowned.

'It's from three months ago! That is so – *weird*. That's tomorrow's headline! I mean, tomorrow's, if we hadn't… if today was still today…'

She shook her head as the others around her exchanged audible gulps and inauspicious glances, then she clicked on several tabs and moved through them, quickly scanning the headlines and pertinent details.

Then she lurched to stand bolt upright, her eyes still glued to the screen. She paused and there was a sharp intake of breath.

'Fuck. Your memorial service is in Los Angeles – tomorrow! It says you, me, and guests listed as Sapphire Edge, a design consultant, Vance McLeod, a retired actor, and Mitch Pyne, a former entertainment reporter, were amongst the missing after the gas explosion at the exclusive hotel, and are now all confirmed dead after an extensive inquest and confirmation of dental records! Jesus!' She looked up and locked eyes with her uncle. 'Jesus Christ Bo, they leveled the hotel! They completely wiped it off the fucking map!'

Everett said nothing but his jaw began twitching again.

Heather looked grim, like she knew what it meant when her uncle went this quiet. Her eyes returned to the screen.

'We are now assumed to have been entertained by Everett at

the exclusive guesthouse manor. Also dead, several of Everett's security staff and recent partner...' Heather looked up. 'Sorry Yelina, you too.'

Yelina scowled. 'How is this? How has this happened? How do they even *know me*?'

'I'm so sorry,' Vance spread his arms. 'I have no control over the temporal aspect of the tunnel! Until now it's only been ten minutes, half an hour!'

'Amateur!' Yelina hissed.

Heather kept scanning the reports.

'This is a few days after... six bodies discovered in the remains of a remote, exclusive hotel... after several high profile guests were evacuated due to a gas leak... Everett and several friends and business associates were believed to have stayed at the property, despite the risk of explosion... remains of six people yet to be identified...'

Heather clicked through a few more tabs.

'This one says you've been missing for three weeks...' She clicked forward. 'Lots of speculation as to why you were there in the first place... looks like the conspiracy theorists are having field day...' She clicked again. 'And this is about me – it says we've both been missing, for two months, and that was a month ago!'

Heather scanned, muttering absently. 'Six bodies... they must have found Sara and Hinch – and the remains of the covert staffers in the freezer!'

'Poor bastards...' Mitch aired, grimly.

'And now – ' Her hand moved smoothly, clicking over the mouse pad. 'And now, today, you're dead. We're all dead. It says that we were all officially declared dead three days ago!'

'Three days ago? Why'd it take so long?'

'Says there was a long inquest...' Heather looked up and across the deck to her uncle, 'says people thought you might have vanished again, like that time you went AWOL a year back, when you first went to Peru with Pan.'

Everett stared at her, almost blank.

'I guess for a while they thought it possible that you'd done that again? Anyway; world wide search… Christ, this must have been a big deal at the time… and a long wait for the remains to be identified… dental reports… yeah, right. Read: long wait for Oliver to make his bribes and sew it all up to his advantage!'

'Yes!' Mason cried out, clearly at a loss to understand the situation, close to terrified. 'That is why – I was told to bring your boat to Los Angeles! She stayed where you left her for weeks and weeks but people – crazy people – kept trying to board! In the night! Conspiracy people! I kept them away, I knew you would not like it, but now, all your assets are being returned there – to Los Angeles!'

Everett's face was flushed. His fists were clenched.

'How the hell,' he grunted, the muscles in the sides of his jaw bulging like gills, '…am I going to explain this?'

Nobody spoke.

Finally Mitch offered something. 'Saph's remote vision was right, though… you have to admit? She saw a webpage – and you were dead. Had been dead… it must have been the only way…'

'The only way…' Everett closed his eyes, his shoulders tightening, 'for what?'

Mitch knew the question was rhetorical but somehow couldn't help himself.

'Think about it. We're safe. Oliver thinks we're dead. We're not a threat. But we still have all the cards – three of Pan's packages and…' Mitch turned to Cricket. 'The CIA think their asset is dead too; the embryo.'

Cricket seemed stunned. 'The *asset?*'

'You don't have to give it to them! You don't have to surrender yourself to them any more!'

Cricket recoiled. 'I don't? They're my people! What are you talking about!'

Mitch shook his head. 'Cricket, I –'

'It's nothing to do with you!'

Cricket stormed off, opened the glass door and went onto the deck.

'My mother,' Saph uttered suddenly. 'Oh my God, what she must be going through!'

'What do we do?' Heather looked to her uncle.

Everett's eyes remained closed, his fists still clenched.

Behind him, however, two beings appeared out of nowhere. They were human-sized, but shimmering and translucent.

'I told you sometimes there were *other* side-effects to the dimensional travel,' Vance uttered. 'Well, here they are.'

CHAPTER FORTY-THREE

Everett did not turn to look, did not even open his eyes.

'What are they?' he asked quietly.

'I don't know,' Vance responded. 'They're quite beautiful though, if you want to look.'

He didn't.

'They just appeared,' Vance proceeded. 'The first few times after I used the ability. I think they're just curious. I think they just want to see who's traveling.'

The two beings continued to hover behind Everett as the others looked on.

Saph looked at Mitch.

Mitch had gone pale and was whispering under his breath.

'Mitch?' Saph asked. 'Are you okay?'

'Yeah,' Mitch said absently. 'Sure.'

His focus returned to the beings and he continued to make small mutterings under his breath, as though talking to them.

'Mitch,' Saph urged. 'Are you – *talking to them*?'

Mitch nodded; but not in response to Saph.

Suddenly the beings were gone; they just faded away and vanished.

Mitch stepped back and blinked his eyes, as though waking from a nap.

'Mitch?' asked Saph. 'Are you okay?'

Mitch blinked again, several times, heavily. 'Yeah, yeah, I… where did they go?'

'The beings?' Saph asked.

'Beings?' Mitch asked strangely. 'They were… it was…'

'It was what?'

'I… I knew them,' Mitch responded strangely. 'God, it's like… like I had a dream and it's fading… God, I hate that! I knew who they were!'

'The beings?' Heather pushed.

'They were people!' Mitch expelled. 'People I knew and – dammit, now I can't remember who they were!'

Mitch wandered from behind the bar and sat at the head chair at the top of the dining table, facing away from them.

'Leave me a second, I have to try and remember…'

Saph moved to go to him but Heather grabbed her arm. 'Better leave him; he might remember something useful. You know what it's like; waking from a dream. Can't remember. Very frustrating.'

Saph stared at Heather. There was something more to it than that. Something in her eyes. Saph recognized; it wasn't necessarily that she didn't want Mitch disturbed. It was that she didn't want Saph to do it. Saph backed off. If that meant what she thought it meant… what *did* that mean?

Everett's eyes snapped open and he let out a long snort of frustration.

'Bo?' Yelina asked. 'Have you… processed, Bo?'

'Yes, my dear.'

Yelina smiled sweetly to the others. 'He gets like this.'

'I know,' Heather gulped. 'It's not healthy. I wish he'd fly into a rage or something!'

'Mister Everett?' Mason enquired. He was still shaking from the sight of the light beings. 'Mister Everett, what should I do? Should I call the mainland? Notify…' he thought a second. 'Who should I notify?'

'Notify no-one, Mister Mason. Once I've reclaimed my business, I'll pay you one million dollars to keep quiet about this. You have witnesses. Do we have an understanding?'

'One million?'

'Cash.'

'Of course Mister Everett!' Mason's terror seemed to vanish

instantly. 'Of course, I'll ask no questions, I'll say nothing to no-one! Where do you want us to go? Where should I set course?'

Everett frowned. 'Don't change course, Mister Mason.'

'You wish to go to Los Angeles, Mister Mason?'

'Good lord,' Vance uttered. 'You're not actually going to crash your own funeral, are you?'

Everett smiled keenly. 'Mister Mason, how long until we set down?'

'Approximately twenty-two hours Mister Everett.'

'I'm going to my cabin. I suggest you all find bunks and rest. Those of you who need painkillers and penicillin see Yelina now.'

'I've got some stuff in my kit,' Harding offered. 'Heavy duty antibiotics, painkillers; half a glass of vodka and they'll see you out like a light, solid eight hours.'

'I want you all to think, to sleep on it if you need to. For now we're safe, but once we set down, there will be no time for thinking. Once we set down, we will, God willing, have a plan of action that will stop Oliver in his tracks. There are plenty of computers on board; Heather can show you. If you can't sleep, do some research. In twelve hours time I want us to all meet back here; alive and awake. I want to be debriefed. I want to know how far Oliver's gotten with his plans. I want suggestions. I want solutions; whether or not I get any remains to be seen, but by God we're not going to let Oliver sell the human race up the river. Understood?'

Nobody dared say anything.

Everett's piercing blue eyes were narrow but bright as sapphires. He looked each of them in the eye, quickly, one at a time, to make sure they did understand, then turned to Mason.

'For now, Mister Mason, you just stay the course. And for now, we'll all just stay dead.'

CHAPTER FORTY-FOUR

Nobody seemed to notice when Mitch wandered out onto the deck, found Cricket and stood beside her at the rails.

'I'm sorry.'

Cricket said nothing. The wind blew her long black fringe away from her sharp features.

'I just.. it's hard to take in. I don't really feel connected to…'

'I haven't even done a test yet,' she told him. 'How can you be so sure?'

'I just am.'

Cricket nodded shortly. 'These bloody powers you all have.'

'You make us sound like super heroes. It's not that great you know. It's turned my life upside down.'

'Your life?' she scoffed. Then, after a pause, she asked simply. 'You don't love me or anything, do you?'

Mitch didn't want to lie. 'I like you.'

'Huh.'

'I've only known you a few days.'

'Mmm.'

'You were going to give it to the CIA. Just a job you said.'

'An asset you called it,' Cricket nodded. 'You learn fast, don't you?'

'I just… I watch a lot of movies. It's just a movie term.'

'That's what it is though. You were right.'

'It's not an asset. It's… it's a pregnancy. A conception that's not even a day old, with nine months to go. And your choices as to what to do about it just got a hell of a lot more broad. That's all I meant.'

Cricket turned from the ocean and met his eye.

'I'm still CIA. That's who I am. I'm twenty-seven years old and I've been working for them ten years. They needed people to monitor the counter-culture. That's all it was. I was an air force brat. Home to home, country to country. It gave me purpose. It still does.'

'I understand.'

'So. I'm still CIA. And my brief still remains. I work with Everett to investigate Oliver. And as far as I'm concerned, my choices as to what to do about *that* just got a hell of a load more broad.'

'What do you mean?'

'It means, whatever you're going to do, I want in.'

Mitch nodded.

They stood and watched the ocean a while.

Mitch and Cricket reentered the suite.

Everett and Yelina had gone but Heather, Saph and Harding had gathered at the dining table and were seated glumly together, quiet. Vance was resting, stretched out on a couch in front of the blank wide screen; he might have been asleep.

'Are you two okay?' Saph asked as they approached.

'We're not a two,' Cricket responded sharply. 'Okay? But I want in, whatever you're doing. So far as I'm concerned my mission brief is extended via field agent's discretionary powers in the absence of further orders. Reporting back will give the enemy vital information that could be used against the safety of the free world.' She sat heavily beside Harding. 'Does that sound official enough?'

'Sounds fine to me lady,' Harding nodded.

'Why's everyone so quiet?' Mitch asked.

'We think Uncle Bo's not doing so great. He's past sixty; that knife wound and all the stress – and now he's planning to crash his own memorial service.'

Mitch thought a second. 'We could all do that, if we wanted. Crash our own services.'

'Mitch, don't,' Saph countered. 'It's not funny – imagine what all our friends and family have gone through.'

'Unique opportunity though,' Heather smirked. Then she went quiet as she reconsidered.

'No-one's going to miss me, that's for sure,' Harding said gruffly as he stood. 'I don't know about you lot but I'm going to take the boss' advice and get some kip. But first, I'm going to find the galley and eat like a horse. If I'm needed, that's where I'll be.'

He nodded to them, grunted in satisfaction with his decision, and departed, taking the same flight of stairs down at the end of the suite that Mitch had emerged from when he'd found his way back from his cabin a few days ago.

A few months ago now, he supposed.

He thought he remembered seeing, back then, the entrance to the galley at the end of the cabin corridor.

There was a general sense that they would all like to go with him, to eat, but could not raise the energy.

'I'm not tired,' Heather sighed. 'I couldn't sleep now if I wanted to. I think I'll do a few hours research. Find out what's happened in the world.'

Saph stood, forcing herself up from the table with flat palms, and wearily stretched. She arched her spine and stretched her neck backwards, groaning. Her figure was still amazing, Mitch found himself thinking.

'Well I might follow Mister Harding.' She looked around at them. 'We should all eat. If I can manage it, I'll bring some food up. No point in crowding the galley and someone's got to do it.'

Mitch stared at her. She was still wearing the black suit she'd worn to the funeral; coming to think of it, so was he. In fact, he, Saph and Vance were all still wearing the same clothes they'd worn to the wake, and Heather was still in the brown outfit she'd changed into when they'd last been together on the boat.

Strange, he thought, the things you notice.

Or, didn't.

'I might come down in a minute,' Mitch nodded. 'I'm starving.'

'Don't bother,' Saph smiled and followed Harding's exit path.

Heather, Cricket and Mitch remained sitting at the table.

It was a weird vibe, Mitch recognized; physical trauma, emotional exhaustion and general disorientation. All this would take a while to process. It was, he realized, not unlike the survivors of a wild house party, gathered at the kitchen table the next morning, putting the pieces together and wondering why the hell they had all drank so much.

'Maybe we should go help her?' Mitch wondered aloud.

'Yeah,' Cricket responded.

She got up, but rather than following the path Harding and Saph had taken, she went immediately to the second couch in front of the blank wide screen, lay down and closed her eyes. Mitch and Heather watched her, then exchanged smiles across the table. They held the gaze for a while, then Mitch stood. Mitch guessed, based on the slightly-too-long eye contact, that they were friends again. Again? Had they been friends, or had they somehow just become…?

It didn't matter.

Outside, the sun was setting.

'If you're going to be on that bloody computer all night, do you want me to bring you up some food?'

Heather shrugged. 'If you want – don't worry though, I'll make some myself when I need a break. Uncle Bo's going to want a full report, it might take a while.'

'You're really dedicated to him, aren't you?'

'He's dedicated to me. We're a team. And –' Heather paused for a moment, as though considering something candid. ' – I think I can save him.'

Mitch stared at her a second.

'Save him?'

'You don't get where he's gotten without…' Heather shrugged and stood. 'The money has to come from somewhere, right? Every dollar he has is a dollar someone else could have. And he has a lot of dollars Mitch. A lot.'

Mitch nodded. He thought he understood.

'Night then.'

'Night.'

Heather watched Mitch go. She watched him until he'd walked across the floor, until he'd descended the stairs, and had gone from her sight. Then she returned to the bar, and the laptop.

'Oh dear,' Vance muttered, with one eye open, glaring at her across the suite.

'Shut up,' Heather snapped. 'Magician.'

Mitch made his way down to the second deck.

For a second, the image of Heather's smile lingered.

There was something odd about it, he realized.

Unique somehow, perhaps?

Certainly, he confessed, it was a smile any man could live with.

He thought about returning to his cabin, just sleeping for a while, but he was sure that he should eat, even though he didn't feel hungry, and that he should confer with Saph about the shining beings he'd seen, although he still could not remember anything the beings had spoken to him, despite his attempts to retain them.

He thought about Saph a minute; he had many questions. How had Nurding sectioned her? What had she been doing since she'd broken up with Pan? Design consultant, the reports had said. Was that true? And, most pressingly, how had Pan's gift been delivered to her? Was that why she had reacted when he'd told her that Tim had been to the apartment? Or was that because she knew that Tim had been, as they all were now, missing presumed dead?

Presumed *traitor*.

Yes, it would be a good time now to go over all this with Saph. It seemed like the right time.

He pushed the door to the galley. It was silent, smooth.

Then he stood there, perhaps for ten or fifteen seconds, perhaps for a few more. It didn't matter, no matter how many seconds, it seemed like an eternity; an eternal image that would forever be imprinted on his mind. He remembered thinking; if this were a movie, this would be the point where he would find Harding dead, and Saph missing. That Saph had been the enemy agent all along, killed Harding and made off somehow. Some kind of speedboat noise receding in the distance as she made her evil getaway…

The first thing he saw were her forearms, the muscles tight as they gripped the railing above the cooking surface, clinging neatly between the hanging ladles and spatulas. She gripped the railing as though doing press-ups, and indeed the contorted expression on her exquisite features, across her perfect bone structure, the glare of peaked exertion in her bronze-brown eyes was that of someone reaching for the mythical 'zone' of adrenalin rush.

The next thing he took in, with bitter irony, was the thing he'd been wanting to take in for his entire adult life. Her long black jacket and shirt were wide open; her naked lower half was sitting on the tail of the jacket that she was still wearing. Her bra had been pushed up, above her breasts, revealing them almost totally, all but for the strands of long blonde hair that fell about her chest and shoulders. He saw them both only for a second or two, before a huge scarred hand slapped onto one and grasped it, squeezed it.

She made no sound to accompany the silent scream; they were being quiet.

He could see her shoes, black lace panties and suit trousers on the floor, and realized that he was looking at them because he didn't want to look at Harding; he really liked the guy and wanted to edit him out of the picture, not see him, although as Mitch backed out of the galley doorway he was aware of the man's enormous shape, standing in front of her, mounted on the kitchen bench, repeating the rhythm; a huge thrust, then a pause, then a slow withdraw, then a pause, then repeat; thrust, pause, withdraw, pause; and repeat… repeat, repeat, repeat.

As he backed away, quietly, images flashed before him as his mind tried to comprehend.

Her stomach muscles, tense like an athlete.

The full lips, wide open, gaping.

One of her legs, rising up, stretching out as though pointing toward him, pointing him out.

The flesh of her breasts, rippling with each mighty thrust.

The far away look in her eyes; the total abandon.

And the side-view he'd glimpsed, the edge, just for just a second, of Harding's enormous grin, and the back of his stupid head.

CHAPTER FORTY-FIVE

Mitch woke.

He wasn't happy.

He was hungry and immediately realized he could not ever set foot in the galley again, ever.

He hadn't had any dreams, no revelations or cryptic conversations in the night.

And he was fed up with the whole situation.

He showered and dressed in the same clothes, again; this time they hadn't been magically cleaned in the night.

He decided it was childish to sulk and headed up to the suite.

He had no right to sulk.

No right at all.

The suite was empty, except for Vance and Cricket who were still sleeping on the couches. He looked around, saw no-one else, and headed outside to the deck.

It was warmer than the last time he'd been out there and he tried to calculate. It had been winter in Sydney. Three months had gone by, that made it spring, but now he was half way around the world, so that made it… flip one-eighty… autumn in Los Angeles. Fall, as it was called here.

Here, when they got there, presumably in less than ten or twelve hours.

He looked down the side of the deck and saw Heather.

She was lighting a cigarette when she saw him, so he fished out his own packet from Everett's big black coat and lit one as well. They both walked toward each other and met in the middle.

'Morning,' Heather smiled.

Again, something about her smile…?

'Didn't know you smoked?'

'Just started again, apparently,' she exhaled. 'You okay?'

'Yeah. What do you mean okay?'

There had been something in the way she'd said it.

'I mean… I followed you down to the galley last night. I got hungry a few minutes later. I mean… you weren't there, I assumed you saw…?'

Mitch grunted.

'So… you're okay?'

'Why shouldn't I be?'

Heather studied his face.

'They…' Heather began. 'I mean, they slept in separate cabins. I think it was something in the moment, you know? I think they just both needed it. When I got there they were kind of… it had just finished, I think, but it was obvious what had happened. Do they know you saw them?'

'I don't think so.'

'Okay.'

Mitch took a drag and exhaled very heavily. Heather spoke quietly.

'You're… in love with her? Or something?'

'I don't know. Not really. I just guess I always thought… if Pan hadn't been around, maybe it would have been me? But it was only ever Pan, for her.'

Heather nodded. 'I know. I think he really loved me, for a time. But I don't think he ever got over her. I don't think they ever really…' She took another drag and exhaled slowly. 'I always thought,' she continued, 'that if the first big love doesn't work out, the rest can never be the first, can they? It's not like they can't compare; I'm sure some second big loves and even third big loves are just as nice, if not better… it's just, the idea that you found it again. Not – I've found it, this is what it is; the way it is the first time, the first time you fall in love. The second time it's – I've found it *again*. Do you know what I mean?'

Mitch nodded. 'In theory. I loved my wife for a long time. I haven't fallen in love again since.'

'You will.'

'I'm not so sure. Once we get to LA, I'm not so sure I'll live long enough to meet anyone else.'

Heather exhaled smoke and said nothing for a while.

'I did watch you, you know.'

Mitch was stunned. 'What?'

'After Pan vanished. You were right. I watched you for a whole week, drinking yourself to sleep every night. Made a whole profile on you, a Mitchell Pyne dossier. Looked into your past, psychological profile and everything.'

Mitch leaned against the rail and assessed her squarely, with a sour expression.

'You gave it to Cricket, and she used it to seduce me. Thanks a lot.'

Heather smiled crookedly, as though Mitch were too stupid to live.

'Cricket had her own intel. Any woman with half a brain could have done that just by spending three minutes with you. You think Saph didn't know your story the second she laid eyes on you? Mitch, a woman like that could have anyone she wanted. She could have any man as a friend, she could be one of those women who only have male friends, constantly hanging. We both know the type. But she's not. She likes you, you can see that. She is a woman of discernment; she chooses her friends carefully. That's not so bad you know. You don't only judge a man by the quality of his enemies.'

Mitch huffed. 'Suppose.'

'Mitch, some things are just not meant to be. I've been with Pan, but he didn't stick. He was okay, but Pan was always all about Pan. But the difference with Saph is, when he was with her, he was all about Pan *and* Saph. You know if he hadn't gone and gotten himself killed they would have got back together. Somehow, some way. One day…'

Heather stared out to sea.

'… it seems terribly sad to me now that that won't happen.'

Mitch didn't know what to say.

Heather turned to him suddenly.

'You know your problem?'

Mitch stepped back. 'You're going to tell me, aren't you?'

'You fell in love with Janine when she transferred to that university you all went to, and the universe handed her to you on a plate. She was smart and attractive and a good match for you. She was a good mother to your kids. And you got that job on television; handed to you on a plate. And that was who you thought you were; that was your identity.'

'Are you going to tell me I never worked for anything?'

'No, don't be stupid. I know you worked hard. I know you worked hard as hell to get that kamikaze fucking magazine running. But your television material is still on YouTube. I bet you didn't know that, did you? YouTube; it's a huge website where people can upload videos and look at them for free.'

'I know what YouTube is.'

'Jesus, that's a surprise.'

Mitch grumbled under his breath a bit, then relented.

'My stuff is really on there? On the web?'

'Yeah. It is. Someone actually went to the trouble of keeping it, and putting it up. You're a good interviewer. You know your stuff. People are still watching it, it's a resource for film buffs.'

'They are? It is?'

'But your trouble is, you don't actually know who you are. You were on television Mitch, for ten years. You know what the absolute basic requirement for that is?'

'You have to know what you're talking about.'

'No!' Heather huffed. 'Christ no! That comes about third, or fourth!'

'It does?'

'You're good-looking, Mitch. Has anyone ever told you that before?'

Mitch thought.

'Janine did – I think…?'

'Jesus. You have to look good – not be handsome, necessarily, but you have to look *good*. Then, people have to like you. And people liked you Mitch. They liked seeing you, they liked having you on their television. They invited you into their homes.'

'They did? Shit, every time I went on, I was always terrified that if I didn't do well they'd get rid of me.'

Heather shook her head, slowly in frustration. 'Mitch…'

Mitch didn't know what to say.

'You're kind of expected to know that, Mitch. You're expected to take it as read. The thing is – you were so determined that all you had was in your head, you missed the boat by not putting your face online. You didn't know what your strengths were, you didn't know *yourself*.'

Mitch's heart was beating very fast.

'No-one's ever told me this before. Not even when the magazine was going under.'

'No-one should *have* to tell you this. I don't know what's *wrong* with you!'

'I thought you did know what's wrong with me! I thought you were going to tell me!'

'I'll tell you this. And I swear by this – I know it in my heart of hearts, Mitch. The next woman who takes a fancy to you is going to make you work for it. She's going to make you work hard, Mitch, not just to prove to herself that you really want her, but so you prove to yourself that you really want her!'

'I don't understand… why are you so mad with me?'

Heather stared at him for several long beats.

Finally, she spoke.

'You blind fucking idiot,' she said.

'What – ?'

'And here's another thing; all through this, you've been hanging around, waiting for someone to tell you how to work your phone, that was never going to happen, waiting for a signal from Saph that you could kiss her or fuck her or be together or whatever, that was never going to come, and in the meantime, so fucking passive and pathetic that you *slept with Cricket*, who considering the circumstances was clearly, clearly manipulating you, and then you sit around some more, waiting for a message from beyond to make everything clear, that is *never going to come.* Just like the way you pissed away years, drinking and sitting on your ass, waiting for someone to come and tell you; the internet is dead! The magazine is back! That was never, never going to come! That's not the way it works, Mitch. There are some things you have to work out yourself; but you never seem to. When the magazine was folding, why didn't you take the advice? Why didn't you take what money you had left, and put it all into a website? People still knew who you were, people even cared what you had to say! Everyone was telling you to do it, everyone told you the magazine was going to fail. Why didn't you do it?'

Mitch felt faint.

He needed something to eat.

Heather's looming, angry face seemed distant, surreal.

'I...'

Heather kept staring.

'I... don't know. I just wanted that magazine. I wanted it so bad... even when I knew it was doomed, even when I knew it was never going to happen, that the internet was the way to go... I just had it in my head. I just had the idea in my head, and I couldn't let go! It's what I grew up with; paper and pictures that you can hold in your hand and flip through, glossy paper and big headlines! I used to look forward to getting them, once a month, all the magazines I loved; who was on the cover, who would the big profile be –'

'Bullshit.' Heather huffed again.

Mitch spread his hands. 'What do you want from me? Jesus, I just saw the love of my life being sledge-hammered by a tree-trunk mercenary old enough to be her father – and fucking loving it!'

'Yeah, right. Let's talk about that. Let's... *unpack that* shall we Mitch? When I looked back at your history, when I did my investigation, my profile, I could see, there was a moment, a moment when you could have turned the corner. It's strange, but when you have access to a person's records; where they worked, where they shopped, what they bought, and you cross reference that with the same factors of the people they know, the people in their circle, you can build up a pretty clear picture of who they are, and what influences they have. I did that with you, Mitch. Let me ask you; when you had enough money left to make the change from magazine to website work, before it was too late, almost the very day before it became too late, who came and stayed three nights at your house?'

'I… I don't know…'

'I do.'

'Who was it?'

'Who was it? It was fucking Saph, of course! Pan and Saph – the last time you all got blitzed together if the liquor bill on your credit card is anything to go by! Don't think he didn't tell me all about it. Pan talked about you, you and the old gang. He loved catching up with you; he said you were like his home base – something normal to return to, a 'grounding influence' he called it. Your home was more a home to him than his parent's place, that's for sure.'

'The night Pan and Saph…?'

'They'd broken up, but they didn't tell you. But somehow you knew. You knew that they had broken up, and when they'd gone, that's when you decided that the magazine was going to work, that you were going to back it to the hilt. Despite everyone telling you the contrary. Why, Mitch? Why?'

'I don't know… right now, looking back, I really don't know why I became so pig headed – I don't now why I went on such a self-destructive path…'

'Aha!' Heather held up two fingers, her dead cigarette butt squeezed flat between them.

Mitch frowned very deeply. 'I did, didn't I? I hit self-destruct on my own life… I drove my wife and kids away, I lost my home, I went bankrupt… I lost everything.'

'Why?'

'Because…'

It dawned on Mitch with a horrifying clarity.

The one thing he couldn't have.

The 'unattainable'.

'Because even though they'd broken up, they pretended they hadn't. And… I knew they were pretending. And, I knew that the reason they were pretending was because… Saph didn't want to go through the whole awkward thing of explaining to me… that now she and Pan were broken up… that it wasn't me she wanted. That… I could never have her. So I folded. I thought; if I can't have Saph, I don't want any of this. The wife, the kids, the house… even the magazine. I could have taken it online, but when I realized I couldn't have Saph… I didn't want anything…'

There were tears in his eyes.

'Oh, Jesus… I destroyed my life for something I could never have!'

The sound of Saph's voice behind him hit him like a knife between his shoulder blades.

'I'm so sorry, Mitch…'

He spun about, tears still in his eyes.

There she was. In the same clothes.

The same clothes she'd betrayed him in.

The look in his eyes made her gasp.

'Oh Mitch, no…' Saph moaned.

'How much did you hear?'

He heard Heather speak softly. 'Almost everything.'

'Mitch I'm sorry, I'm so sorry. I knew, I've always known. But, I never gave you any indication. I never gave you any signals or… I just gave you friendship. And love, the love of a dear, dear friend.'

'I know,' Mitch told her, his voice croaky.

'I don't know what else to say…'

She started to cry, tears streaming down her face.

Somehow, this helped Mitch pull himself together.

'It's okay. It's better. It's like… a huge weight has been lifted.'

He turned back to Heather.

'It was you wasn't it? The phone call? Answer the door, Mitch.'

Heather stared at him.

'Of course it was, you idiot. I couldn't stand it any more. Watching you do that to yourself every night. It was… heartbreaking.'

Mitch gulped.

Heather suddenly straightened. 'Let's get back inside.'

'But –'

Heather shook her head. 'That's not the only shock you have in store for you today. I've been doing some reading…' She smiled at Mitch. 'Online.'

'Are you okay Mitch?' Saph asked.

He turned back to her.

'I'm fine. Oddly enough. You look different, Saph.'

'Different? How?'

'You look… human.'

Saph recoiled. 'As opposed to?'

Heather guffawed. 'A goddess on a pedestal, what else? Come on, time to debrief.' She turned to Mitch and grinned massively. 'Flash! Flash! I love you! But we've only got fourteen hours to save the world!'

Holding the grin, she turned and walked up the deck, toward the suite entrance.

CHAPTER FORTY-SIX

They woke and assembled one by one, around the table.

Mason and Byford had cooperated to prepare them all a massive traditional breakfast, served a la carte on the bar, that consisted of fried eggs and bacon, sausages, various heavy canned salads, pancakes, flapjacks and waffles.

'A high carb meal for a high carb day,' Vance aired as he served himself a mountain of waffles.

Everett, looking somewhat refreshed, nudged Mitch as they fought for the four remaining eggs. As though to complete the set, he was dressed in a black business suit; somewhat funereal, Mitch supposed.

'You look different,' Everett stated. 'What happened?' He looked to Heather. 'Did you two – ?'

'Talk? Yes. I explained his profile to him.'

'Ah yes! For me it was Lucy Manchester! Art student from my college. In my early days I almost went bankrupt trying to acquire and maintain the world's finest modern art collection, all the while knowing she was shacked up with another woman, a long time partner is the term now, somewhere in the East Village. It's all primal fear, kid. Fix on the unattainable so we can never succeed! So that we will always settle for less, and never truly fear losing the things we come to possess! Like all these millions of miserable schlubs who will cue up for Oliver's instant nose jobs, or age reversals, or whatever else he has on offer, never realizing that no-one will ever love them as they deserve to be loved until they love themselves. Written in neon above Apollo's Temple in Delphi; 'Know Thyself!' – it's the key to all wisdom and happiness.'

'Is that right?' Mitch couldn't help but raise a skeptical tone.

'It is indeed. The trouble is, to know thyself, you must know thy place in the world, and to the know that, you must come to know the world – and that is no easy assignment. Did your idea of Sapphire, your fantasy of Sapphire, make you any wiser? Any happier? Or did the realization of the truth of Sapphire do that?'

'I don't know yet.'

'Well, let's say it at least cleared a block and allowed for the possibility of true wisdom and happiness? Would you agree with *that*?'

'I'll agree to anything if you leave me just one egg.'

Everett roared with laughter and tipped his entire bounty of eggs onto Mitch's plate.

'You've had a hard morning, you deserve the eggs!'

'We all need the eggs,' Vance muttered.

'And you can keep that coat, too. It was always too tight for me, and it suits you.'

Mitch shrugged. 'Thanks,' he uttered.

'I wish you men wouldn't talk about me as though I'm not here,' Saph told them. 'None of this is actually my fault you know.'

'Nice to know I'm not the only one though,' Vance muttered again.

'Pardon?' Saph turned to him.

'Oh yes, dear Sapphire. Oh the desire I had for you in those early years at the university! Fifteen years your senior, you'd think I'd know better, but I'm afraid you are Merlin, my dear.'

'Merlin?'

Vance suddenly bellowed. 'A dream to some! *A nightmare to others!*'

'Bloody hell, Vance! Not you too!'

Vance grinned. 'Oh, I made my realization long ago. You are, dear Sapphire, one of those women. A truly beautiful woman. And that makes you very dangerous; all men want you and all women want to be you. Imagine the psychological minefield you leave in your wake. Imagine the risks men take to follow in that wake, and the response women have when they witness the destruction.'

'I'm not some evil temptress!' Saph shrieked. 'I was born like this! I'm… I'm metaphysical! I'm deep! I spent years looking into all this stuff with Pan! All I want is to help people!'

'I know my dear. You chose to use your power for good. But the reaction of others cannot be controlled. However, as my own response to my lust for you was a large part of the reason I kept in touch with our dear departed Pan, at least initially, I can't help thinking, my sweet unrequited, that it's all part of the universal plan to see whether humanity is worthy of moving on… wouldn't you say? All seems to have worked out rather well in the end.'

'Holy…' Saph slammed her plate on the table. 'Is there anyone here who doesn't see me as some kind of fantasy sex object?'

'I don't,' Cricket smirked.

Heather shrugged. 'I do. Archetypally.'

Harding leaned across the table to Mitch.

'Sorry mate. Didn't realize you had feelings… but you don't turn that down, do you? Not at my age. Not at any fucking age!'

He laughed uproariously.

'Jesus Christ, Harding!' Saph spat.

Harding grinned. 'Not the first time I've heard 'er cry that out!'

Despite themselves, not one of them could suppress a laugh.

Except Saph.

'You bloody pig, Harding!'

Snorting to hold back giggles, everyone but Saph moved quickly from the bar to the dining table. Saph followed shortly after, sitting on the same side, but other end of the table to Harding so as to totally avoid eye contact.

Heather sat at the top, with Everett at the other end.

For a while they ate as one; silently, greedily and without pause, until Everett leaned back and slapped his stomach.

'So!' he bellowed. 'What have you all got for me?'

Heather leaned back also, using a napkin to wipe her mouth, then cleared her throat.

'It's worse than we thought,' she spoke clearly. 'Much worse.'

CHAPTER FORTY-SEVEN

'The day after we… escaped, let's say, Oliver Hines started moving his operation along full pelt. He is clearly assuming, probably quite accurately, that an enlightened population is no longer an option, and that an ego-driven, materially-based, self-satisfaction-seeking population remains the order of the day. And let's face it, why shouldn't he? But before we go on, let me say this: we are all still alive. We are in possession of at least three of Pan's metaphysical formulas, and – on Mitch's brand spanking, barely used phone, we have a recording of Oliver Hines threatening us all with death, outlining his plan for, if not the enslavement, then certainly the mass exploitation of humanity, in no uncertain terms, and thanks to Mitch staying around until the last minute to receive the signal, his ordering the demolition of the hotel that he knew for a fact we were still inside. Now, given we escaped through a dimensional crack, it might be difficult to prove, in a court of non-meta law, that we were in the building at that point. But certainly, Oliver is talking as though he believes we are, which could make good ground for at least attempted manslaughter. Still, that, and the advantage that everyone believes we are all dead, is what we have to work with.'

'Very good,' Everett nodded.

'Thank you uncle,' Heather smiled, dry but sweet. 'The next part might not please you quite so much. It actually didn't take long to figure out that the first stream of Olivera's gene therapies went public two months ago. It's hard to understate the media frenzy that came with it. When we get to LA we're going to see billboards, television commercials, chat show interviews, the lot. In fact, you can go online right now and it's pretty much all anyone's talking about; every argument for every reason, pro and con, under the sun. And it's never going to end.'

Heather sighed.

'Did you know he owned Regime Cosmetics? Well, it's been re-branded to Re*gene* Cosmetics. It's been launched in Los Angeles and New York; most of the European capitals tomorrow, and worldwide in a month. At this stage it's only cosmetic but it's clear that those with enough cash have been treating their illnesses and diseases. Already there have been reports of spontaneous cancer and HIV remission from private hospitals across the country; very private hospitals, very expensive hospitals.'

'How does it work?' Everett asked. 'This Regene Cosmetics?'

'Regene used to have about a dozen cosmetic beauty clinics across California. Day surgeries mostly; nip-tuck shops, boob jobs and face lifts, skin peels and the like. He's opened about a hundred more in strategic areas. They're basically high-turnover medical clinics. You go in, they take a blood sample, you sit and pretend to read *The New Yorker* for half an hour. Then someone calls you in and they outline all the therapies that are possible for you, based on your gene map; you got your mother's nose, but want your grandmother's nose? They can do it. A-cup to D-cup, or vice versa. A few extra inches where it counts? If it's in your DNA, you can have them. So it's not absolutely anything you want – not yet – but if they start a gene splicing line, as is the speculation, that can't be far off.'

'Gene *splicing*?' Mitch asked.

'Where they start taking other people's DNA and map it onto yours.'

'Oh.'

'Right now, it's being marketed as more a *potential* thing; most of the ad campaigns are based around that message. Make the most of what *nature* gave you, but you didn't know you had. That kind of thing.'

'Jesus,' Mitch muttered.

'Jesus has left the building Mitch. Basically, people are

queuing up to register their DNA samples on a giant database; once you register, you get a personalized catalogue telling you what changes you can make to your physiognomy – and how much the treatment costs to maintain per month. It's personal gene-mapping with a speed and scale that is unprecedented, but so far what they're offering is essentially all cosmetic, and all the courses mirror routine cosmetic procedures that are already widely available. They've been smart here, Uncle. Nothing too radical to begin with. Get people used to it. All in line with current social acceptability; but the rest, we're assured, is yet to come.'

'Hmmm,' Everett grumbled.

'The therapies take less than twenty-four hours to kick in; let's say you take the course in the morning, either a needle at the clinic, or a few pills to take home, take over the day, then you go to bed that night and wake up with… well, the nose you might have had if a different set of chromosomes had activated. As you can imagine it's the under twenty-fives who are going for it in the biggest numbers; although the female demographics are strong across the board. Eye color, skin pigmentation; and before you get upset it seems that in LA there are just as many whites who want to be black – again, mostly young males – as there are blacks who want to be white; mostly young females in that category. Sadly, the overwhelming number of young Asians who line up for treatment want "western eyes", as they're called. It's assumed that the young men all want to be gangstas, and the young women want better jobs, and all the young Asians want to be… well Americans it seems; that's the perception anyway. But there are people across the board augmenting their skin pigmentation; anything from a total overnight tan to the anemic gothic look. Hispanics don't seem to be going for it yet, not in big numbers. Go figure; they think it has something to do with Catholicism. The Catholic Church in particular is not happy and is recommending everyone stays clear. And the conspiracy theorists are having a collective panic attack; it's the government genetic register they've been fearing for years. And let's face it, they're probably right. The Religious Right says it's the mark of the beast, and already there have been several bomb threats to clinics across the state.'

'Nothing anyone couldn't have predicted,' Saph sighed.

'Exactly. Anyway, there are different treatments at different costs; it's just like Oliver said. To unpack what I just said, let's say I'm not happy with the way I look. Let's say I'm fixated on my nose, which is too long or too wide to make my face aesthetically pleasing. And because I'm fixated, I know that I got my father's nose, because my nose looks like my father's nose. But I look at my mother, and I can see how her nose is the nose I was supposed to have; the shape of my mother's nose would fit exactly with the rest of my features; it's the natural aesthetic choice, but because of the genetic lottery, I got the wrong one and now have to live the rest of my life, because of pure back luck, with the wrong nose. Regene can fix that!'

'There's nothing wrong with your nose,' Everett scowled with a paternal tone.

'I know, Uncle. It's just an example. But what I just told you is pretty much straight out of one of their infomercials. Like I said, they're playing on the 'natural' angle. This isn't rhinoplasty, it's not *surgery*; this is simply chopping and changing, cutting and pasting from a catalogue *you already posses*.'

'Doesn't sound so bad,' Vance offered gingerly.

Nobody spoke.

'You can take a twenty-four hour course, to see how it looks,' Heather continued, 'for five hundred bucks. Or three days, to get used to it, for a grand. Two weeks, to show it around; two grand. If I'm super-confident the nose will work for me, I take the one month course for three grand. Those prices line up pretty much across the board, no matter what you want changed. No sign of Gay Away or Go Lesbo yet, thank God, but it can't be far away and is probably, going by at least some blogs and forums, already being privately exploited by the super-wealthy. But back to the more everyday miracles; as I said, the longest dosage is one month. After that, you need a new dosage or the changes revert; again, overnight. You can already see how it's going to play to social status; poor Mary couldn't afford this month's payment for her nose dosage and now she has to go around looking plain again. There's also a fail-safe pill; five hundred bucks, it reverses all changes in under an hour in case you've changed your mind. The most popular Regene courses are… well, can you guess?'

'Weight loss,' Saph guessed.

'Pretty much even first place with boob jobs,' Heather nodded. 'Slightly behind penis enlargement for men. Then nose, eyes, then wrinkles, and then skin products in general, then lips. The wrinkles started slow; older people are more cautious to adopt, but it's the fastest climbing. The interesting thing about the weight loss course is that it doesn't make you lose your weight overnight; the sales pitch is that within a day or two you will simply lose the appetite for the foods that make your particular body type store the kinds of fats that make you overweight. It's by far the most complicated course genetically, and there are far more stringent guidelines as to who can use it, but it's out there. Oliver promises that there's a quit smoking course about a month away; people suspect that there are some legal issues with the tobacco companies. It's quite possible that a lot of good will come out of this; the entire American population could stop smoking, and stop eating deadly fats within a month, if they so choose.'

'It's a sugar-coated poisoned pill,' Everett grumbled.

'At the moment,' Heather continued, clearly not so sure, 'the most conservative figures say that Regene has processed nearly two million appointments in Los Angeles alone, just in the past two months; it's not known how many of those appointments are repeat offenders but it won't be long, they say, before any registered user can buy their instant nose jobs, and whatever else, over the counter. Sales were slow in the first few days but once it took off, it went viral. But that's LA for you.'

Everett nodded. 'That's as I suspected.'

Heather reached to a small pile of paper beside her and started handing them out; there were three sheets each.

'It's a list of what's available, what's next, and what's being worked on.'

Mitch studied the first list. It was the usual suspects; cosmetic surgery that had been at best an out-patient procedure, at worst a few nights in hospital, reduced to a few pills and night's sleep.

'This second list; coming soon?' Vance asked. 'I'm assuming these are overnight procedures?'

'That's right,' Heather nodded. 'Most of them require the administration of heavy-duty painkillers; that seems to be the sticking point. It must be painful to have your spine extended, or your shoulders expanded. Gabrielle Fenwick has come clean; she's confessed that she agreed to take part in the trials, and that she had her body de-aged. 'The Regene Regeneration', it's called, but it's apparently a very long and very painful week in hospital, and it won't be released as a public option for at least a few months. The security risks associated with people being able to change their appearance overnight are giving the government enough headaches as it is; they're insisting access to Olivera's database and you can imagine the civil liberties storm that's caused. Again, the conspiracy blogs believe this is already a done deal and active, and it's clear that hundreds of film and television actors have gone through with it but won't admit it; a least, they refuse to comment.'

'And this third list…'

'That's where Olivera's heading with Regene. Total physical transformation. They say that's a few years away, but if they have Pan's research, they'll be doing it now behind closed doors. One of the articles I read online claims that they're approaching film stars and supermodels to negotiate how much they want for their 'total package'.'

'What does that mean?' Mitch winced.

'It means, at some point in the future, if you want to look like Angelina Jolie or Brad Pitt, you can. And not like they look now – the way they looked back in their absolute prime. For a lot of pain, and a very hefty price tag – licensed by the stars themselves. Christ, they've probably already exhumed the corpses of Clark Gable and Vivien Leigh, and who knows who else.'

'Holy shit…' Mitch uttered.

'And then there's the question of brain function, and personality change; Olivera has officially claimed that that is not possible, that it's way, way over the horizon. They say they're close to gene therapy courses for depression, and other mental illnesses, for dementia and the like, but they are months away from public release. It's a slow burn, but it will burn. And burn big, and bright.'

'They're lying of course.' Everett leaned forward. 'The brain chemistry stuff they're keeping for themselves; to who knows what ends.'

'But Uncle,' Heather shrugged, 'what hope do we have? We're essentially offering them the same coin, just the flipside.'

'We're offering balance,' Everett stated. 'That's why Oliver was so desperate to get rid of us. We're offering something that has been repressed in humanity for thousands of years; he is offering more of the same, more of what they already have had, to an exponential level, that will never be reversed unless we get the thin end of the wedge in, then hammer it down like Thor.'

There was silence again as they all tried to process what Heather had told them.

Mitch stared at the list; the list of Regene options seemed to morph into one meaningless blur. The ramifications were too big, the potential too far ranging for his microscopic perception to take in.

'I see pirates,' Saph stated suddenly.

All eyes turned to her.

'A vision?' Everett asked. 'A premonition?'

Saph nodded. 'For some reason, we're all dressed like pirates, and… we're all fighting other pirates… but Mitch is in the middle, holding a treasure chest. A little treasure chest filled with gold that he'd forgotten he had. It's just been returned to him… and then we all sail off, in different ships… into the solar system… to different planets.'

Nobody quite knew what to say about that.

CHAPTER FORTY-EIGHT

'Look, these visions, I know they're abstract representations and everything,' Cricket spoke, 'but what's the point if we can only tell what they mean *after* something's happened?'

'I suppose it's just to say...' Saph pondered. 'That there's something in control of all this? Or at least, there's a larger perspective? Someone watching or rooting for us? A part of our consciousness that can see ahead? That there is a... plan? Or an idea? Maybe even someone or something looking out for us?'

'I'm not dead again in this one, am I?' Everett asked.

'No, but... we're fighting for our lives.'

'We are on a boat,' Mitch offered. 'Maybe we're about to be attacked? Boarded? By... pirates?'

'I don't think it's meant to be taken that literally,' Saph smirked. 'I think it's more that we're in possession of a treasure – and we're going to have to fight to keep it.'

'That's all very well,' Everett nodded. 'But I'd still like to know where we stand in regard to arms. Harding, where are your men?'

'Two are below decks. The other two are patrolling the deck. They only have the arms and ammo they brought with them. Beside that, there's the four guns we have, and my bag of tricks. Fortunately the guns you took from Sara and Hitch will take the clip rounds I have for mine.'

'There's something else,' Heather stated. 'One final thing that I want to come clean about. Last Tuesday night – that's, last Tuesday night plus three months ago now – I was watching Mitch, as ordered, until he fell asleep.'

Mitch's heart skipped a beat.

Last Tuesday.

He'd fallen asleep *after* the visitation from Pan.

Which meant… she knew about Tim.

He gulped.

Had she told Everett?

She *must have…*

'When I returned home, I had a parcel waiting for me.'

Heather dug into her coat pocket and pulled out what looked like a regular 250 gram bag of ground coffee. They could smell the aroma across the table almost instantly.

'Peruvian coffee, direct from Peru, pre-ground, no return address, with a small card attached. The card said, *Drink Me.*'

CHAPTER FORTY-NINE

'Did you?' asked Everett.

'No,' Heather responded carefully. 'Not then I didn't.'

'For me,' Saph confessed. 'It was a package of Turkish delight. *Eat me*, it said.'

She rose and walked to one of the couches by the cinema screen, found the bag she had been carrying, the bag now filled with Everett's briefs for Mitch, and fished around inside. After a moment she removed a brick-sized parcel, wrapped in bright sapphire gift paper, then put it on the table before her as she sat. It had been opened at one end, but was now taped back down again.

'I think I see where this is going,' Vance nodded. 'I have a box of nougat somewhere, couriered to me from Peru – hidden.'

Mitch nodded. 'I have a bottle. It's hidden too.'

Everett nodded, sitting back and pulling a cigar, and a rattling box of cigar matches, from his inside jacket pocket, then lit it carefully, and slowly, with the two inch match. He puffed a couple of times, then smiled.

'I see.'

'And there's another thing,' Mitch added. 'Saph, you reacted when I mentioned Tim. Did you see him too?'

'No, but I asked the security guy at my building to show me the footage of the guy who left the parcel. It was Tim; I knew him from Peru.'

'So…' Everett hummed. 'One of our chief murder suspects is, or was, wandering about Sydney, delivering parcels of narcotics from a dead man…'

'But you must have known?' Mitch complained. 'If Heather

had me under surveillance? I mean, she tapped into my dead phone line –'

'Hacked, Mitch. Hacked,' Heather sighed.

' – hacked into my dead phone line and *told me* to open the door to him.'

Heather nodded. 'Tim used fake names and passports to go travel wherever he went in the week he went missing. When he turned up at your door, it was the first anyone had seen of him since he left Peru. After that, we pretty much figured he was unlikely to be Pan's betrayer. Chances are, Pan trusted him, and sent him back before the research base was raided. He probably got out just in time.'

'So maybe he has one of the gifts? If Pan trusted him?'

Heather shrugged. 'He's vanished again. Gone to ground – he seems to be very good at that.'

Mitch sighed. 'Which leaves, as the traitor, either… was her name Pam Winters?'

Heather nodded. 'Or the professor, Adriana Fontana. One of them betrayed and killed Pan.'

Everett chuckled lightly.

'In any event, it seems we now know for certain who all but two of Pan's most trusted friend are.'

Mitch, Saph, Vance and Heather exchanged quick glances.

There was something about that fact that made the whole situation seem just a little more tolerable.

'You knew that though, didn't you Everett?' Saph asked slyly. 'You said as much, back at the manor hotel. That it had been a risk to put us all in together, but worth it to flush us out. You suspected all along that we were the ones who had the gifts.'

'A little subterfuge for a great gain, wouldn't you say?' Everett puffed out a huge plume of cigar smoke.

Mitch couldn't help but wonder what that meant as to his contract, his finder's fee; had he *found* Saph and Vance? Technically, by choosing to keep them around, it might be argued that way. But he had certainly not 'found' Heather.

'I'm sorry not to have told you Uncle Bo. It's just… I didn't know if I wanted to or not. It was so personal, I had to make the decision on my own. I really didn't know whether or not I should hand the responsibility over to someone else… but after the research I did last night, I realized that it's possible that it might be in some way genetically bonded to me, that I might be the only person that it *could* have any effect on, so I decided that, if it was mine, then it was only mine – and that, well, Pan seemed to know what he was doing.'

'So you drank it?'

'I brewed up a cup this morning.'

'And anything?'

'No. Nothing yet. But maybe I have to drink it all?'

'You don't,' Mitch offered. 'About three swigs did it for me.'

'But that's just what I mean,' Heather shrugged. 'Your gifts, all of you, the way they've come on, is very mild. I wondered whether or not this is a drip-drip situation? Whether, if we consume the whole of what Pan's given us, over say a day or two, if things might not get a little more interesting? Not to mention what would happen – potentially – if we all shared them?'

'If we were to share each other's gifts?' Vance asked. 'All four of us? Swap, and inherit all four, each of us, simultaneously?'

'It's a thought,' Heather shrugged.

'It certainly is!' Vance scoffed. 'And quite frankly, not one I care to entertain! I'm having enough trouble managing just one, let alone juggling it with the psychic ability I was born with.'

'Surely though,' Saph countered, 'the idea of sending them in such large quantities is to ensure there's enough to be experimented with, reproduced?' She turned to Everett. 'Don't you think?'

Everett took a long, thoughtful pull on his cigar.

'I think… there's ample quantities, it seems, to encourage both. If you're up for it?'

Before anyone could decide, Byford entered through the sliding glass door at the end of the suite. None of them had seen him approach, and it startled them all, especially when he immediately spoke, loudly and clearly.

'Sorry to interrupt sah!'

Harding stood. 'What is it Byford?'

'Several things sah; fancy speedboat approaching from the mainland, chopper from overhead and another two boats from somewhere that way.' Byford indicated the stern of the boat, as though they were coming from somewhere other than the mainland. 'They seem coordinated to arrive all at once. I'd say we have only minutes sah!'

CHAPTER FIFTY

The group immediately followed Byford back outside and went on deck. They could hear the helicopter in the distance, although visually it was not much more than an approaching speck to the cruiser's aft, where the cruiser's helicopter pad was located. The speedboat was also making good time, approaching the starboard side. The other two boats, still in the distance, were approaching from portside; to all appearances, from the open ocean.

'They look like ocean cruisers as well,' Cricket noted.

'Smaller,' Everett told her. 'Two, maybe three decks.'

Byford and his three men stood awaiting orders as Harding assessed the situation.

'No way off this boat I suppose?' Harding spoke sideways to Everett. 'No secret speedboat of your own hidden away below decks?'

'No,' Everett responded. 'A few jet skis, but they won't get us to the mainland, and they certainly won't outrun these people. Here.'

Everett handed Mitch a pistol.

'Ever used one?'

'No.'

'Aim, relax, squeeze. Just like they say. If you can't relax, just do the other two.'

Mitch felt the cold metal of the gun as Everett shoved it into his hand. It was the dead man's gun, Hinchliffe's gun; the one he had used to shoot Harding, kill Sara, and threaten Yelina. He had died with it in his hand, for ten million dollars he would never spend. Mitch felt queasy.

'And be careful. The safety's off.'

Heather and Harding both had their guns out.

Cricket looked displeased not to have one as she folded her arms and stared out.

The two smaller cruisers were approaching with great speed now, rapidly closing with every second. One broke away from the other and assumed a course that would lead it around to circle Everett's cruiser. Perhaps to cut off the speedboat, Mitch thought, perhaps to meet with it.

'Course of action?' Everett asked Harding.

'Take a chance on Vance and his cracks in space and we could all end up in the middle of next year. Stand and fight; we could all end up dead. I suggest we stand down, wait and see, but have Vance ready.'

Vance had heard. 'I really am not feeling particularly certain about all this; he's right, without knowing how to control the temporal aspect…'

Mitch had a sudden inspiration. 'Saph! It's you!'

'What do you mean?' she demanded.

'Saph; you are the temporal aspect – you have to focus *with* Vance, but use your – precognition, or whatever it is, to stabilize the… time stuff!'

'What?!'

'I'm not gambling on that,' Heather scoffed. 'If it doesn't work and we end up even two or three months ahead again, Olivera will be unstoppable – I've read their projections; he'll have Europe, Australia, Japan… the whole world addicted by then!'

'But don't you see what that means?' Mitch urged. 'They are supposed to be taken together; these gifts, they *are* complimentary!'

There was a roar to the aft of the cruiser.

The helicopter had made speed and was coming into land.

Within seconds, the two smaller cruisers, the second of which had now circled to the other side of Everett's cruiser, suddenly slowed and ceased their approach, each still a good few hundred yards distant, as though waiting for the helicopter to touch down. Mitch took a long look but could see no sign of anyone on board.

The group split and moved around the deck; Byford and two of his men led the way down the starboard side, followed by Saph, Vance and Cricket. Harding, Everett and Byford's third man led the way down the aft, followed by Mitch, Heather and Yelina.

Mitch wondered for a second where Mason had gone, until he saw him through the glass, standing in the suite, staring at the helicopter as it came in to land on the helipad. He saw Mitch; they exchanged a glance, in which Mitch clearly saw the terror expressed in Mason's eyes, then the ersatz captain ran for the stairs and vanished below decks.

Mitch wondered if it would not be wise to join him.

The helicopter touched down and they felt the cruiser rocking to restore balance. Mitch no longer felt just queasy, but fully ill. In front of him he saw Harding and Byford's man halt and watch the helicopter; the blades showed no sign of slowing down.

It was an unmarked military helicopter, a troop carrier or something, Mitch saw; one of those with sideways sliding doors that could carry a dozen or more troops. The cruiser was still rocking, fore and aft, as the helicopter sat and spun.

Mitch had known it would happen quickly; when it did, he heard himself say, 'yep'.

The doors slid back and two trios of almost ninja-style troops, armed with what looked to Mitch like rifles, leaped out each side; they instantly started firing. Harding and Byford's man returned fire, but the black armor and dark visors the troops wore seemed to repel their bullets; he heard ricochets off their armor and from the helicopter, then the glass windows around the suite started to crack with bullet holes.

Byford's man fell, then Harding followed; the giant mercenary grabbed at his neck, cried out and toppled backwards. Everett turned and fired two bullets into the glass beside him, grabbed Yelina and smashed himself through it, dragging the screaming woman behind him.

Heather turned as Mitch did. They sprinted back down the side of the cruiser, away from the helicopter.

Objects whistled in the air, zipping past Mitch's head.

One thudded into the side of the deck as he spun about the glass corner of the suite; he grabbed it. It was a dart.

'They're trying to take us alive!' Mitch cried out as he turned the corner, shoving the dart into the pocket of Everett's coat.

'Fuck that!' Heather cried back. She stopped and spun about, then rounded her arm, her upper shoulder and head back around the corner, extended her pistol and let off six shots in rapid succession, each with a sound that made Mitch flinch.

'That'll stop 'em for a second.'

Mitch had frozen with her; he stared out at the cruiser, still circling in the distance like some massive mechanical shark, then he saw a flash just above the top deck. It was immediately followed by a crack, then there was a whistling sound and thud from down around the corner, where the black bullet-proof ninjas had paused after Heather's salvo.

Through the glass he saw one of them topple backward into the suite through the shattered panel Everett had created, and fall in a gush of blood, their head jutting off at a terrible angle, practically separated from their neck.

One of the two remaining ninjas screamed in horror, and he heard a young woman's voice cry out.

'He's dead!'

And another, female voice.

'Get down! It's a sniper! He knows our sweet spot!'

Mitch and Heather had already ducked below the rail and were huddled against the deck's steel, storm-proof panels, below the eye-line of the cruiser. They heard another sniper shot hit the starboard side, behind them on the other side of the cruiser, and another scream.

'Get them in the neck,' he heard Heather mutter to herself.

Now there were four, Mitch assumed grimly.

What the hell was happening?

He heard gasping and realized it was his own breathing; he was close to total panic.

Heather bunched up with him, against the bulkhead and below the rail. Further down, the two ninjas had forgotten their prey and were bunched similarly, out of sight. They heard the cruiser shift a gear, then resume approach.

'*They coming!*' he heard one of the ninjas squeal.

Heather leaned into his ear and hissed.

'Clearly, the cruisers are meaner than the choppers, right?'

'Right.'

'And the cruisers don't want the choppers to take us, right?'

'Seems that way!'

'And if they wanted us dead, we were easy pickings, right?'

'Okay!'

The two ninjas were talking again, fast and panicked; an Australian woman and another woman with a distinctly Hispanic accent, muffled but audible from beneath their masks.

'This is a setup!' stated the Hispanic. 'That guy who smashed through the glass – that was Bo Everett!'

'Don't be fucking stupid – Bo Everett's dead!'

'Who the fuck are those guys! No-one was supposed to get killed!'

'We need to get back to the chopper!'

There was another crack, another sniper bullet, and the side cabin window of the helicopter cracked. Mitch couldn't see clearly what damage it had caused, but one of the ninjas could.

'It didn't break the glass! We have to get back!'

Another crack, and another impact on the helicopter.

'They're going for the tank!'

Heather was suddenly furious. 'Who the *hell are you people!*'

The two ninjas turned to them, as one.

'Isn't that…?' The Hispanic uttered. 'Isn't that *Heather Everett?*'

'Yes it is!' Heather spat. 'Who the hell did you think we were?'

'Pirates!' The Australian woman cried out. 'Stealing Everett's cruiser!'

'What!?'

'Bloody hell,' Mitch uttered.

'*Who the hell are you?*' Heather insisted.

The Australian woman suddenly spoke with a clear voice, surprisingly calm given the situation, conveying great pride.

'We're The Pan! We're the activist arm of Pan's People!'

'The *what*!?'

'The Pan!' she insisted. 'The activist arm of – wait a minute… oh my God! No! No it can't be!'

The woman seemed to freeze for a second; whether it was panic or shock, Mitch couldn't immediately tell. Then she reached up under her chin and with one swift pull removed the helmet and visor. A mop of curly, sweaty blonde hair splayed out around a pretty face, albeit damp with perspiration, with bright, wide blue eyes. She was not a woman though, she was a girl, probably not even twenty.

Mitch stared, goggle-eyed.

At first he thought it was his ex wife; she was the spitting image of Janine. But he quickly processed that this was impossible; Janine would be twenty years senior to –

The girl stared back, with almost the exact same goggle-eyed shock.

Almost a mirror reflection.

The girl spoke.

'*Dad?*'

CHAPTER FIFTY-ONE

Three more sniper bullets cracked; three holes popped loudly into the railing wall between them.

'Amy!'

'Dad!'

'Amethyst Pyne what the hell are you doing here!'

'I'm sorry Daddy!'

Three more bullet holes – crack – crack – crack – much closer to his daughter this time.

Mitch stood, turned and faced the cruiser, extended the gun that Everett had given him and he had almost forgotten he had, with arms tense as steel.

And then he spiked.

In a microsecond he saw that the cruiser was shrouded in a kind of supernatural oil-black fog; it was almost multi-dimensional, as though the very spirit of the boat was mean, amoral and emotionless. Then he realized that it was not the ship itself; it was the occupants of the ship, of whom he sensed there were three, who were dark and pitiless creatures, creatures with absolutely no concept of emotion, creatures whose presence in this human dimension was an abhorrence. They were here on a mission, two of them, and that was all. The third being on the ship was a man; the sniper. Mitch could see the sniper clearly now as he took aim and readied fire, zooming in on, he knew, his daughter.

Then, somehow, he relaxed.

He knew that this man had been sent here to die and that he had ceased to value his own life years ago. He was just a machine now, playing out a hollow program. The sniper had surrendered what he was to these emotionless creatures, just as he had surrendered what he was to a long line of missions and masters, losing whatever identity he'd been born to play out decades ago, and cared as much whether he, himself, lived or died as he did for the many people he had killed.

Mitch pulled the trigger, six times.

The second and fifth bullets took the man's shoulder, then a clean headshot. The others just went on.

Still spiking, Mitch saw something leave him; a white orb, speckled with muddy grains of grey and brown, with a thick black shell. The orb didn't float away, up to the heavens as he might have expected, rather it expanded from him, the black shell splitting like tectonic plates and separating, then like a raindrop hitting a surface, the orb expanded, fractured, burst and was gone.

In his mind, Mitch heard the man's departing energy project something into his mind.

'*There are no accidents… only careless choices.*'

Surely, they were the same words?

And that had been the same soulless voice that the…

No, it *was* The Man who'd threatened him on the balcony, back at the Vantage Hotel. And Mitch had just taken his life. Not some anonymous sniper; a man that he'd stood before and spoken to.

Mitch stood still, with his arms and the gun extended, as the two other beings approached the dead man and gazed across the short ocean distance at Mitch.

'It's okay,' he heard himself tell Heather, still crouched below him. 'There was only the one.'

Heather stood from her protective crouch and looked out as well.

'Amy?' Mitch called. 'They can't hurt us. You'd better stand and take a look at what killed your friends.'

Amy and the other ninja stood.

The two aliens, for that, Mitch knew, is what they were, possessed no actual physical form.

'What do you see?' Mitch asked.

'I'm not really sure,' Heather responded. 'They're the things from the hotel though, aren't they? The things that tried to stop us getting into the lift. When we ran into the Pleiadeans…'

She quickly glanced aside at Amy; Mitch's daughter was astonished at their words.

'That's them,' Mitch scowled. 'I don't think they have any actual form in this dimension; I mean, I don't think they can fully manifest here. I'm feeling from them that they… don't like it here. It's abhorrent for them to even be here, to project themselves here, onto this planet, into these dimensions…'

'That's what I thought…' Heather shivered. 'Pan spoke about them… they're eighth dimensional creatures originally, the dimension where the higher energies come down from the Source; the Collective Consciousness. I know it sounds twee, but the literature suggests that the eighth dimension is kind of an administration dimension, for the architecture of the cosmos… but these beings broke away… they're like… the fundamentalists of genetic order… that's why they can't fully manifest here, the eighth dimension is just too far away, too different. What they are… it just doesn't belong here; doesn't translate into three dimensions of space, and one of time… they have no conception of why life in this dimension matters, or how to… how to behave toward it, I suppose?'

'They look totally evil.'

'What can you see? All I can see are two shadowy figures on an unmarked cruiser. And I can barely see that – it's like my mind can't fix, can't interpret. Like my brain puts them in the image of men because… that's all it has to go on.'

'I see a ghost ship from the Dante's Ninth Circle, crewed by Headless Horsemen.'

'Jesus.'

'They're just staring at me. God, it's such an *evil* stare…'

'They're not – not evil, Mitch. Sure, they'd kill us all in a heartbeat if they could figure out how, but they're actually closer to angels than anything… although the idea that they want to *catch us* first…' She shivered again. 'They probably don't know how to catch us. It's like if we tried to catch a fish in a fast running stream with our hands. They must have contacted someone in the US Black Ops who gave them that sniper just to get rid of them; that guy must have been Black Ops, no-one else could stand to be around them that long. They just don't belong in our paradigm. That's why I was so shocked that they would show themselves –'

Mitch shuddered, so hard he almost fell over, then began to utter.

'They don't want *change* – long ago they shaped things to perfection around the initial building blocks of creation… and they want it to stay that way, in their own version of perfection… they don't want *consciousness* to expand and change – they hate change, because it alters the initial perfection of their design-nn-hhhgh –'

'Mitch?'

You call yourself Mitchell Pyne.

Mitch cried out, an odd kind of squeal. Their projected voice made him feel as though the inner wall of his brain was a chalkboard, and they were scraping their nails down it.

'Yes! Mitch Pyne!' he cried out.

'They're talking to you?' Heather was aghast. 'That's *never* happened.'

Mitch grasped his head in his hands; Heather's hands whipped up and cupped his face.

'Mitch! Snap out of it! Break the connection!'

You see us as an abhorrence Mitch Pyne; you are as much as an abhorrence to us; more so, exponentially so; you represent an abominable mutation, a contamination that must never be allowed to proceed. All that the human Pan has created must be eradicated – you must destroy yourself Mitch Pyne, destroy yourself and all you have come into contact with and contaminated. Come to this vessel, come now so we can take you apart and eradicate you down to your smallest constituent parts, bring them all Mitch Pyne; all must be eradicated.

CHAPTER FIFTY-TWO

'You're supposed to be looking for me.'

It was the beautiful woman again; it was Suzie Saturn.

Mitch looked around him.

'Where are we this time?'

They were in the penthouse suite of the Vantage Hotel; Pan's wake was winding down and now there were more people crying.

'They don't know we're here,' Suzie Saturn said. 'I think we continue the conversation here, because if I didn't pull your focus just then, the Orion Renegades would have burned your mind clean. It's better if you just leave for a while.'

'Orion Renegades? That's what they're called?'

'That's what some call them. It's a good enough name for humans to call them.'

Once again, the penthouse suite looked like an Escher painting; the angles of the walls were impossibly askew, and he seemed to be standing on at least three different levels of the same floor, above a ceiling that at once was dizzyingly high, and at the same time dissected his scalp.

'Why did Pan tell me to find you? He got it the wrong way round. *You* keep finding *me*. And – you're not even in our world, are you?'

'Parts of me are. In the third dimension, the human dimension, things can be messy. The Source may be perfect, but the sum of parts is not. Parts of me remain; they have yet to be cleaned out of your dimension. What happened to me was sudden, and unexpected. The universe cracked, then the crack was filled, but particles lay scattered about. Cracks are not clean; they are brittle, and when they are filled too quickly, they leave debris – debris that can be scattered and recollected.'

'Is that so?' Mitch sounded skeptical.

'It is,' Suzie Saturn grinned. 'And it's good that you still have your doubts. One thing we must always remember Mitch is that whatever we are, until we return to the Source, to the Godhead, the Parabrahma, we are merely aspects of the whole, abstract expressions of perfection; until we do that, until we return, nobody knows anything. Not really. And certainly, nobody knows everything.'

'This is supposed to help me, is it?'

'If you like. Really I am just sparing you the bull elephant migraine the Orion Renegades inflicted upon you when they attempted to communicate. The flipside of that is, when you wake, your vision perspective will be greater; you cannot be exposed to mental energy such as theirs and survive without the brain working overtime to comprehend and heal. They have inadvertently expanded your consciousness once again Mitch. I will be curious to see how that manifests in your personality.'

'Will you really?'

She laughed.

'You see Mitch? You've being very grumpy with me because through there, in the third dimension, you have a headache that would make you scream and weep for death. But here, you can just ride it out.'

'*Through* there?'

'Through there; where you came from.'

'Shouldn't it be… down there? This is… the fourth dimension, right?'

'The lower astral. The lower fourth. Yes. But the numbers… you call them the third and fourth, but that is just from the perspective of the third. There is no higher order or succession, not really; there is just purpose. The job of the Orions, in the eighth dimension, is to maintain the basic order, the basic structure of things; they are science, pure science, but totally abstract, totally disembodied, virtually non-physical as you understand the term.

But they are not your superiors. They just evolved differently, in a different paradigm, with a different set of perspectives, billions of years ago.'

'Right.'

Mitch could not help but feel impatient; he supposed what she was saying might be true, on some level of perception or reality or other, and yet he also felt as though if he didn't have a cigarette right bloody now he was going to punch her.

A cigarette appeared in his hand.

It was lit, and ready to smoke.

He took a drag.

It was fantastic; like the first cigarette he had ever tried.

'Where the hell *are* we?'

'Like I said, we're in the fourth dimension; the astral plane.'

'Is this all it is? Just; our world with crazy angles and magic?'

'No.'

'What is it then?'

'It's mental.'

'It certainly is!'

She laughed. 'It's vast, like an ocean. There are tides of energy, eddies and rifts and waves, rips and tsunamis. Everything that happens here is echoed in the third dimension; and vice versa. It's the dimension of mental energy, of thought and ideas and dreams, of archetypal things; where the best and worst of every dream, hope and desire is real and has consequences.'

'Is there a race that lives here? Like the Orions in the eighth?'

'Many things live here. Everything from stereotypes to archetypes to icons. And… other things…'

She turned and looked at the dining table; where he had seen the businessman, Don Eissley, turn into a Reptilian and vanish into another dimension. Then, as he thought that, a Reptilian appeared; right where Don Eissley had disappeared. The Reptilian turned to them, stared at Mitch, then morphed back into Don Eissley.

'You!' Eissley scowled, striding toward him. 'You saw me, just then! How!'

Mitch was dumbstruck.

'That was… that was three months ago…'

Eissley turned to Suzie Saturn, his gaze searing with distaste.

'And you shouldn't be here either!'

With a grumble that was at once dissatisfaction and acceptance, he turned back to Mitch.

'Haven't you explained to him how things work here?'

'No. He's only been here a few minutes.'

'Who's he going to be? I don't know him from anywhere… he's too old to be a new rock star – what, is he an actor? Going to do the big character actor thing are you chief? Worked for years, no-one's ever heard of you, then you suddenly get a big role in a big film and now everyone knows who you are?' Eissley examined him. 'Yeah, I can see it on you, the glamor. You've been on television, haven't you? Got a nicely symmetrical face… making the leap to features now, eh? Gonna be the new Bill Nighy are you chief? Maybe I should pull you into my new thing; got a whole new dream vortex that's funneling down to Olivera Studios; dream money – mega-budgets.'

'No,' Suzie smiled. 'He's not a actor. He's an agent.'

'An agent? A talent agent? Going to let another human have a try at that are we? Where's that come from? Who's idea was that?'

'No, not that sort of agent. He's an agent of change.'

'Of change?'

'That's right.'

Eissley looked at them both, back and forward.

'Who are you with? What clan? Where's your insignia? Let me see something.'

'We don't have any of those things.'

'Who *are* you? You're not some crazy cult members are you? Look, you'd better get out of here.' It was not a warning as such, more a threat. 'I can make it so you don't remember any of this; I can intervene on the human plane and make sure you never get access here again!'

Eissley looked around him, as though searching for more of his kind, for security, then turned back to Suzie.

'You can't just be here! I don't care what archetypal energy you are; you can't just bring a *human* here and… *hang around.*'

Mitch caught the implication. 'You're not human?' he asked Suzie.

'Of course she's not human!' Eissley spat. 'She's – wait.' Eissley stared at her a second. 'You *are* human!' Then he couldn't look away. 'I know who you are…' Eissley stared slyly. 'You're Saturn. Suzie Saturn; you were wiped!'

'Not completely.'

'Maybe not yet but it won't take us long. We'll leave no fucking trace!'

'As you like.'

'You – you can't be here! You can't… you can't *be!*'

'I'd argue very strenuously to the contrary.'

'We'll find you; we'll wipe you again!'

'I don't think so.'

'Oh, I fucking do! You have no right to be here! You have no right to exist!'

'On the contrary, I have more right than anyone to be here, to exist here – this is *my planet.*'

'Don't be ridiculous! It hasn't belonged to the humans for more than six thousand years!'

'What?' Mitch demanded.

Eissley ignored him.

'Don't think we haven't seen your type before; we've had humans ascend into the astral; there's nothing you can do. We've been here for millions of years – we *own* this planet and we come from this dimension!'

The room around them began to shimmer; first one, then another Reptilian appeared, as though from nowhere. Mitch turned around, sensing something behind him. There were three more Reptilians, then three more. They began to form a circle around them.

'What do they want?' Mitch asked desperately.

'They want to trap me,' Suzie responded.

'How?'

'This is the realm of dream – but it's also the realm of magic, or the occult. They're going to summon something; a nightmare to contain me. Things like that can seem very real here; if they win, I'll be trapped here, I'll forget everything I am, everything I was, and live here forever in the nightmare.'

The Reptilians began to chant; some terrible, discordant verse that instantly made Mitch afraid. The fear seemed to come from his gut, from his bowels; it was ancient and primal. The Vantage penthouse suite around them started to fade; everything was becoming darker.

'What can we do?' Mitch whimpered.

'You can't do anything; I'm sending you back.'

'But they'll kill you!'

Suzie turned and stared Mitch in the eyes.

'They haven't seen anything like me, not in six thousand years.'

She turned back to Eissley and stated clearly, with a confidence Mitch thought was barking mad.

'I can take them.'

Then he was gone.

CHAPTER FIFTY-THREE

Mitch woke again.

The whole world was tumbling; he was rocking and rolling, and for a moment he thought he was still on the astral plane, that he'd somehow been caught up in some crazy nightmare designed by the Reptilians to trap Suzie Saturn.

Then he realized that he was still on board Everett's cruiser; he was on one of the couches, and the cruiser was in the middle of a terrible storm. He raised himself and looked around.

It was black outside; he saw himself, and the interior of the suite reflected in the glass windows, and the fractured patterns about the neat holes where bullets had punctured the glass. The floor was wet; sea water splashed in from where Everett had crashed through the single window frame, and tiny shards, like the remains of a windscreen, tinkled and chinked about the floor as the cruiser rode the storm.

He couldn't hold his vision very long in one place; the boat was rollicking, not only dipping and tipping from front to back, but also swaying sideways, back and forth, and he found that he had to hold onto the back of the couch to stop himself falling off. The couch itself seemed to be bolted to the floor; for that he was grateful, but it didn't stop him feeling as though he were on some mad bronco ride in a western-themed bar.

'Mitch!'

He turned about and saw Heather, her arms braced against either side of the open sliding door frame, staring across the room at him.

'Mitch, are you okay!?'

'What the hell's happening!'

Heather made an attempt to cross the room; the boat pitched and she was thrown into the bar, and almost flipped over it completely. She screamed an obscenity, paused, refocused her sights on Mitch again then stumbled over to him, grasping the end of the couch for dear life to stare him in the face.

'Are you okay!'

'Yes! I think so!'

'The storm just hit! We were helping the guy from the speedboat to come on board and it just – descended!'

'Where are the Orion Renegades!?'

'The who?'

'The Shadow Men – with the snipers!'

'They left! They just turned around and left!'

'Where's Amethyst!?'

'Who?'

'Amy! My daughter!'

'She's helping them secure the helicopter!'

'She's out there!?'

'She's okay! She's tough!'

'*She's my daughter!*'

Mitch tried to get up but a massive wave hit the cruiser's aft, pushing the nose high, sending Mitch directly into Heather; he impacted with her and the pair flew backwards, crashed to the suite's deck and slid together back down into the edge of the bar. Just as they were about to hit, the cruiser nose-dived, and they rocked forward to a halt.

Without knowing it, they had grabbed each other in a tight embrace, and now sat together, huddled on the floor, each looking stunned, glancing left and right, then finally at each other as the cruiser continued to rock.

'Holy crap,' Mitch uttered.

'Holy crap,' echoed Heather.

They stared at each other for a second, their faces close; then Heather laughed nervously.

'If this were a movie Mitch, this is where you'd kiss me!'

Neither of them let go of the embrace.

'If this were a movie Heather, I'd end up with Cricket. Middle-American audiences wouldn't accept anything less!'

Heather stared at him. Her laughter had died but her smile remained, though it was bordered with a frown of concern.

'You're not going to do that, are you Mitch?'

Her expression was seeking reassurance somehow, and suddenly Mitch realized what it was about her smile that he'd seen as odd, those few times before, when she'd allowed him to see it. It was the shape of her mouth; it was strange but her lower lip was much larger than her top lip. Most people, when they smiled, their lower lips formed an even, horizontal crescent. When Heather smiled, her large lower lip descended and formed an entirely different shape altogether; it was almost an inverted triangle, a V-shape, and it was totally unique. He'd never seen a smile like it, never seen lips like that. On another woman it might have looked clownish or even grotesque, but the shape of her unusual smile entirely suited the shape of her face; it formed a perfect diamond with the shape of her nose, and the line of her cheekbones, and those outward angled lines between the edge of the nostrils and the corners of the mouth… did those lines even have a name…?

He just kept staring at her smile, her odd, beautiful, unique smile, that was seeking reassurance, and suddenly he realized.

In the middle of the ocean, in the middle of a terrible storm, in the middle of the night, he realized that Heather was gorgeous.

Gorgeous in a way that was totally unique.

Utterly, totally, drop dead gorgeous.

And he'd never seen it.

'Dad!'

They both looked up.

Amy was staring down at them, alongside her three remaining fellow Pan Ninjas and another young woman who Mitch assumed was the helicopter pilot.

'Dad? Are you okay? Are you frightened? Why are you

holding her like that? Who is she!?'

'It's Heather Everett,' said one of her people.

'I know that!' Amy was furious.

There was a clattering from the suite entrance and Everett stormed in, followed by Vance, Byford and two of Byford's men, Mason, and another man; a squat bald man wearing Bermuda shorts and a green and gold Hawaiian shirt, totally bewildered. All of them were drenched through.

'Heather!' Everett barked. 'What the hell are you doing making out with Mitch in the middle of the floor! I told you to wake him up and get him below decks with the others!'

Heather and Mitch were on their feet, Mitch avoiding the ice-cold, accusatory stare from his daughter, as Vance and the other made their way promptly below decks.

'I wasn't - !'

'We weren't – !'

'Get below!' Everett ordered.

Everybody made a rush for the stairs.

CHAPTER FIFTY-FOUR

Mitch tumbled down the steps into Vance as another wave hit.

'Sorry!'

'Not you fault old chap!'

'Actually it kind of is!'

The group tumbled down the corridor as Everett called out.

'Last door on the left!'

Vance reached it first. The door opened into what Mitch first thought was a cupboard, until he realized it was the entrance to a corridor that ran down the side of the ship, around the galley, then into another room. He was hammered against the wall twice before he staggered out, into an enormous wedge-shaped bedroom suite that occupied the entire front section of the second deck; there were two-thirds windows on all sides and outside all they could see was the black, swirling ocean. In the middle of the room was a bed similar to the giant rock-star beds from the nameless manor, upon which Saph and Cricket sat with the dormant, tranquilized bodies of Harding and Byford's third man.

'What's happening!' Saph demanded.

'Ask Mitch!' Vance offered. 'He says it's his fault!'

As everyone crowded in, the huge bedroom seemed to grow smaller with each additional person. Everett turned to Byford.

'Take your men, find a cabin and sit tight.'

'Sah!'

'You five,' Everett turned to Pan's Ninjas. 'Do the same – try and make us some coffee if you can stand straight long enough.'

Amy turned to her father. 'But – !'

'She can stay,' Mitch countered.

'Oh, can she?' Everett growled. 'Not enough to impregnate

the CIA agent and make moves on my niece, now you're got
another one in your sights have you?'

Mitch growled back, perhaps even more ferociously than
Everett.

'It's Amy. She's my *daughter*.'

Everett was stunned. He suddenly spun about and gave Amy
a slight bow, speaking incredibly fast.

'Well isn't that a delightful surprise, I'm so sorry, darling, but
nobody informed me you'd be coming along for the ride, please
by all means take a seat and join in?'

Amy's goggle-eyed look returned, then Everett turned on her
friends.

'The rest of you, white with two sugars, now!'

The three Ninjas and the pilot, who now with their vizored
helmets removed where clearly not much older than Amy,
turned tail, collided with each other and vanished back down the
corridor.

Byford and his men followed in their wake, two of them
carrying their tranquilized fellow.

'And don't forget the soldiers!'

'Sah!'

'And some sandwiches would be nice!'

Amy just stared at him, agog.

'Amy, what the hell are you *doing here*?' Mitch demanded.

Amy stared at him. 'What am I doing here? What are *you*
doing here? Everyone thinks you're dead! And Aunt Saph! And
him! And her!' She pointed out Everett and Heather. 'And I don't
know who these other people are, but I bet they're all supposed
to be dead as well!'

'I'm afraid she is rather correct on that score,' Vance shrugged.

Amy turned back to her father. 'Your funeral's in two days!'

Another large wave hit and everyone grabbed something for
balance. Cricket and Saph had adopted a cross-legged position
on the bed, one either side of Harding, which seemed to serve
them in good stead, while Yelina was propped up against the

pillows on the bed-head.

'Aren't you a little young to be leading commando missions?' Yelina asked. Somehow, her maternal voice made the condescending tone seem caring.

'It's my first mission; we received a call that EverSky 3 was reading more than one person aboard the cruiser. Our leader said it would be a good training run; get on board, stun the pirates and reclaim the cruiser. We thought they'd probably just make a run for it when they heard the helicopter approach. We've been in training for three months; it should have been a milk run!'

Everyone was stunned.

'Amy,' Saph started. 'How are you sweetie?'

'I'm fine Aunt Saph; apart from seeing my friend's head blown off that is – and my father talking to aliens, and…' Amy looked over to Heather.

Heather was sitting sideways on the floor in the doorway of the walk-in wardrobe, her feet bracing her back solidly against the frame.

'…everything else.'

'Amy, sweetie, how did you get involved with Pan's People? And, what's this you say about someone leading them?'

'You're supposed to be in London!' Mitch exclaimed. 'How did you get to LA?'

'Now listen,' Everett crooned. He was crammed into the suite's entrance, his arms raised and his legs apart, braced into every inch of the frame. 'Why don't we just let the girl tell her story? I'm sure we'll get all the answers we require if we just let her talk. Now sit down Mitch, before you tumble into something and crack your skull.'

Mitch sighed. He sat on the floor against the wall, beside Vance. Amy gave an identical sigh and sat on the floor against the bed, facing him.

'It was about three months ago, in London. I'd just turned eighteen…'

She cast Mitch a quick, hurt glance.

Mitch's heart sank. It hadn't even registered with him. Hadn't shown, hadn't called, hadn't sent her a gift. Maybe it had even been the night Tim had come over, and he'd been wallowing, yet again, in self-misery.

'Mom said you were close to getting the website started... that you had important business meetings, and you couldn't get to London in time. I understood, it's okay...'

'I'm sorry sweetie,' Mitch gulped.

'It's *okay*. It's just that, that's when it all started.'

'When what started?'

'Well, I got a lot of presents. I got the clothes I wanted, I got the new phone, the new... the new everything. Jeremy even bought me a new car.'

'Jeremy?'

Amy paused. 'Mum's boyfriend, Dad. You've spoken to him on the phone.'

'Oh, right. Yeah.'

Mitch had no recollection whatsoever.

'But in the end... I thought, what is a birthday anyway? And – why do I need all this stuff? I think it was because... I'd been listening to Uncle Pan's podcasts.'

'Oh God,' Mitch heard Saph utter.

'I couldn't believe it was Uncle Pan. I mean, I thought he was just this old stoner. I remember when he used to come over, with Aunt Saph, when we all lived in Sydney, when we were kids, and you'd keep us up all night laughing and shouting and singing and playing all your old music, *really loud*. I never thought he... like, *knew anything*. Not like that. Not like, how the world works. How the world really works.'

Mitch spread his arms.

'Am I the only person in the world who hadn't heard these podcasts?'

'You don't need to any more,' Saph grunted. 'You're living them.'

Amy stared strangely at her father, then resumed.

'I think, just getting all these gifts for my birthday just kind of brought it all together; it was just more stuff. And that stuff would soon be superseded by something else, more stuff; even before I got it, there was something else. Some of the people Uncle Pan talks to in the podcasts, they think that somehow the world all went wrong somewhere, and I started to think they were right. I don't know why it happened then, I can't explain it… I didn't want to be ungrateful, but all the gifts just made me feel… empty. The thoughts I had, they just… happened.'

'It's okay,' Mitch smiled. 'There's no need to feel bad about it.'

'I didn't! Dad, you don't have to try and make me feel better, you don't have to tell me how to feel!'

Mitch bit his bottom lip.

Jesus, she was a real person.

And it had all happened without him, on the other side of the world.

'Uncle Pan was my godfather after all. He did his job. At least, in one way or another. When the speakers on his podcasts started saying that they thought there were people, behind the scenes, who want the world the way it is, who have kept it that way, and are keeping it that way, I started to see it. I didn't just *believe* them. I listened to what they had to say and I looked around and I could *see* it.'

'I know exactly what you mean…' Heather mumbled. 'Jesus, she could be me at eighteen.'

Amy ignored her.

'So I started to talk to Mum about it, and she just had a fit, I mean, a blind, raging fit. I mean, I know she used to be with you and everything, I mean, she was up all night with you and Uncle Pan and Aunt Saph, and I thought she was into it all, all the stuff you talked about. But a few years after we got to London, and she met Jeremy, she got really interested in the atheist movement, the Brights and all that. I mean, Jeremy is a television producer, he makes documentaries, he knows Richard Dawkins. He and Mum just love him; him and that other guy, Derrick Nurding. It was like, after 9-11, and 7-7, those guys just became the people everyone turned to when they got angry. They just filled this big *gap* for people who couldn't understand why people would do something like that. I remember being at school after 7-7 and every other kid was walking around calling themselves an atheist; and I was like, *I grew up with this. You don't know what you're talking about… you're just filling the same gap that people fill with…*'

Amy shook her head; she was terribly frustrated.

'They tried to get me on SSRIs, had me go get a prescription for anti-depressants. Thought I was having some sort of nervous breakdown. Didn't even have to tell the doctor what was wrong; he just wrote out the prescription and handed it over. I had to pretend I was taking them – pretend I was 'normal'. I mean, what is normal anyway? Isn't it normal to look around you and go *what the fuck?* What's *happened* here? Who's *running* this show? It shouldn't *be* like this!'

For some reason, Mitch felt extremely proud.

'Good for you Amy…' he whispered.

'I've read a lot about 9-11. I've seen the documentaries that Jeremy says are bullshit; but, it's not like I believed them all. It's not like I saw *Loose Change* or *Zeitgeist* or even some Michael Moore film or something and swallowed it whole. I mean, there's other stuff out there too. I've looked at a lot of it. So have some of my friends; I mean, we're not stupid. We just want to know. But what I came to, what I decided, for myself, was that, well, 9-11, it didn't matter whether it was fanatics, or whether it was a set up from inside the US government, or if it was both, or neither. The main thing was that it was used, it was *exploited*. It was used for the greatest power coup of the century. Never let a good crisis go to waste, isn't that what they say? Not only did it increase corporate control of oil, ensuring that our dependence on it, and their profit from it, was here to stay; I mean, we all know that. The other thing, the thing people didn't notice as much, was that the fear and panic and general unease it instilled led people back, exactly where they'd been trained to go; to material purchase.

What did Bush suggest after it happened? Go shopping! The west went into a decline of… *orgiastic* credit spending, and a few years later, what did we get? The credit crunch, the Wall Street collapse. Because people in the west just went wild with credit, and money they didn't have, because not only was the environment trying to kill them, but the terrorists were too; *religion* was trying to kill them! God himself! The world was falling apart and they needed something to make them *feel better*, and the corporate banks just took and took, and absorbed more and more money… I mean they were throwing around trillions. *Hundreds of trillions.* And printing trillions *more* – based on nothing! And all the while more of the people lost more of their material possessions, lost their jobs and their homes, which in the end, basically all returned to the banking corporations! So who's still standing after all this? The corporations! And why? Because there is a metaphysical vacuum in this world; created by – guess who? The corporations!'

Her shoulders sagged. Nobody said anything.

'But… who else rose to prominence after 9-11? The rational materialists, the so-called "Brights". The atheists were another coup for the corporations. They're just the ideal corporate priests, and half of them don't even know it. They don't *know* they're being used. By corralling all metaphysical knowledge, all spiritual knowledge; the sum total of all the learning of the mystery schools and mystical teachers, the shamans, the druids, the spiritual masters, and the list goes on, into one stable, and labeling that stable 'fanatical extremists', or 'radical fundamentalists' by claiming that all metaphysical knowledge depends on faith, blind faith and delusion, and faith and delusion alone, they have given the well-trained public no alternative to the corruption of the spiritual kindergarten we call organized religion; no alternative – just pejorative terms like 'magical thinking' and 'blind faith' and 'delusion', so that the one option for us, other than a corrupt parody of a metaphysical system we call The Church, is to worship the Gene Machine. A cold void of a machine with no function, no purpose, no meaning, other than to replicate its DNA into infinity. And is it any wonder people despair, as they lose their homes, their jobs, and descend into drinking and drugs to numb the pain, as depression skyrockets in record numbers and doctors hand out SSRI's like aspirin? And what is their solution?'

Amy shook her head.

'The day after my birthday I was walking through London and what did I see? You know what their solution was? To hire ad space on the side of a red London bus, a red London bus no less, the symbol of the London bombings that struck fear and panic and reinforced rampant consumerism into the heart of England, and they had a new slogan on the side; "God Probably Doesn't Exist, So Go Ahead And Enjoy Your Life", it said. There were posters and billboards all over town. Jesus wept; does he realize how truly evil that is, when he's photographed, grinning beside that slogan, having sold millions of copies of his books, stopping off on his world promotional tour? Do they realize how that makes them look?'

'I don't think they do,' Heather muttered. 'I don't think they can...'

Amy huffed. 'Do people ever stop to think that there is a force behind their impulses to buy those books? That they are mass-marketed and promoted? I mean, why *his* books? Why *then*? I mean; hey, I'm mad about fanatical terrorism! I'm pissed about religion! Oh, here's this book that tells me exactly how to think about them, and support the corporate mindset at the same time. What a coincidence! I mean, do they realize that there are forces in motion behind that? To create the campaigns that make people want to buy them? That the publishing company behind the books is at the end of a tentacle that extends back to another company that is owned and operated by a major corporation, whose sole vested interest is to see that people fill the spiritual vacuum within themselves with possessions and products that *they sell*? That they have trained us to buy, for that express purpose? So that we never fill the void, by looking beyond what it is they have to sell us, that will make us *feel better*? Do you think Nurding knows that? Or do you think that he thinks he is just a machine, just a receptacle for selfish DNA?'

Amy huffed a bit.

'I'm sorry…' she uttered, barely audible over the waves. 'I didn't even know I thought that until I started speaking…'

'I've met Nurding,' Mitch smiled. 'He seems like a nice man. I think he believes what he says.'

'I think he's a genius, Dad. The things in his books, his theories… they're genius. But he's a one-eyed genius. He's a genius with no empathy for… ordinary delusions. The delusions that make people's lives worthwhile. Or the peaceful realities that can come from magical thought; even if that's what it is. Sometimes I think that people like him are lacking something; they're a different strand; they haven't had that big experience that – I don't know, *switches them on* or something?'

'Sounds like you had an epiphany,' Everett offered quietly.

'What makes you think that?' Amy smiled, sweetly sarcastic. 'And now this Olivera business?' Amy shuddered. 'It's all wrong; it's got its good side, I know, but it's all going to go wrong, I just *know it*. Because it's the same people, all over again. I had to do something; I just had to. So I became an activist. For Uncle Pan's movement. And now, here I am.'

'There are Pan's People in London now, eh?' Everett asked.

'There are Pan's People everywhere now. But they hate that name. We just call ourselves The Pan. That's it. Just *The Pan*.'

'You mentioned that The Pan has a leader…' Everett aired.

'Pan's sister.'

'Which one?' Mitch asked.

'The good one,' Amy smiled. 'Trudy.'

'Trudy's taken over?' asked Saph. 'Wow.'

'Well, Mister Everett gave the organization a lot of money.' Amy smiled.

'I did?'

'It wasn't you?'

'Yes,' Yelina spoke. 'It was him.' She turned to Everett. 'Darling, you *kind of* got Pan killed; I thought it was the least we could do.'

Everett stared at her.

'How much?'

'Enough,' Yelina shrugged. 'Greenpeace money.'

'Oh,' said Everett. 'That explains the helicopter.'

'So does your mother know you're here?' Mitch asked softly.

'I'm eighteen Dad.'

'Does she know?'

'No.'

'What about Jade? What does Jadey think of all this?'

'She hates me. She thinks I hate Mum and hate Jeremy and I want to ruin the family – again. She doesn't even know what physics means, let alone metaphysics.'

'Right. So she's still at home with your mother?'

'Yes.'

'Good.'

There was silence in the room for a second.

'I'm very proud of you, Amethyst Pyne. Very proud.'

Father and daughter shared a long look, then Amy leaped forward and buried herself in Mitch's chest and started weeping uncontrollably. One by one everybody left the room and left them there on their own.

Outside, the storm raged on.

CHAPTER FIFTY-FIVE

After Mitch and Amy had finished their first step toward re-bonding, Amy slept on Everett's enormous bed. Her tears had left her drowsy and disorientated, so she didn't seem to mind the hulking figure of Harding beside her; there was plenty of room and she was asleep as soon as her head hit the pillow. It reminded Mitch of one of those cute animal pictures; a kitten sleeping peacefully beside an old Rottweiler.

Mitch left the room and went directly to find Everett. The boat was still rocking, albeit slightly less, but Mitch quickly got his sea-legs and was able to, most of the time anyway, anticipate the rolls and ride with them. The Pans were still making espresso; they had figured out that if they made it in small batches and put it in a large vessel, like an urn, it could probably be served with minimum accident. Mitch came upon, then left them, as they triumphantly discovered half a dozen plastic travel mugs in a cupboard.

Byford and his men were sleeping in his old cabin, but the other three cabins were empty.

Mitch figured there must have been a third level, and a fourth, maybe even a fifth and sixth, but took the stairs to see if anyone had decided to risk the damaged penthouse suite; it turned out that everyone had.

Everett and Heather had just finished bolting a metal sheet across the window Everett had demolished; Saph and Cricket had found some super glue and were sticking anything from compact discs to coasters over the eleven bullet holes they're found in the glass; while Vance and Yelina had managed to collect most of the broken glass and had almost finished mopping up the blood. The bodies of the two Pan Ninjas had gone; Mitch was told that they had been carried below decks to the walk-in freezer, after which they could be processed at the appropriate time.

Whenever the hell that was, Mitch thought.

Poor kids.

Including them, the covert staffers, and the bodyguards from the ambush, at least nine relatively innocent people had died in this fight so far, eleven if he counted Sara and Hinch. He wondered what the number would be when another twenty-four hours had transpired.

Mason was steering them out of the storm as best he could, and it seemed Mitch had arrived on deck just as all the work had been done. Heather stood back from the metal sheet and admired her handiwork, reached into her pocket, took out a packet of cigarettes and lit one. Everett threw her a scathing look.

'Well I'm not going outside!' Heather complained.

Everett grumbled something unintelligible, in a tone that amounted to acquiescence and, behind him, Mitch heard another lighter click. Spinning about he saw the man in the Hawaiian shirt from the speedboat.

'Sorry,' the man said, 'didn't see you there.'

Mitch was stunned; while he'd spoken to the others, to assess what was happening, this man might as well have been invisible. He was standing behind the bar and had already helped himself to a beer.

'Todd Mendoza, pleased to meet you.'

Heather approached them. 'He's supposed to be dead too.'

Mendoza grinned; it was a Mafiosi grin, superficially friendly, almost impish, with a concrete mixer's worth of malice just under the surface.

'Nobody stays dead for long,' he opined, with a diluted Boston accent.

'What does that mean?' Mitch asked, immediately not wanting to know the answer.

'You know what that means,' Mendoza responded slyly. 'Even

if you haven't figured it out yet.'

'Wait a minute…' Mitch had almost remembered something. 'Mendoza…?'

The fumes of Mendoza's cigarette wafted closer; it was a joint. Mitch stepped back, figuring it was the last thing he needed. As he did, his pocket began to vibrate. His phone was ringing. He fished it out and stared at it. It was the same number Oliver Hines had used.

'Don't answer!' Heather cried out.

'I don't know how!' Mitch retorted.

Everyone stopped what they were doing and came to the bar, staring at the phone in Mitch's hand.

'See,' Mendoza smiled.

'Why would Oliver Hines be ringing me? He thinks I'm…'

Mendoza nodded. 'The dead phone, in the dead man's hand – still ringing.'

Heather grimaced. 'The phone should have been destroyed in the explosion. He knows we got away; at least he knows you did Mitch. And he knows we still have his message.'

'We're only a few hours from the coast,' Everett spoke. 'If we divert…' he trailed off as Heather shook her head.

'He'll be tracking the boat. If your satellites registered extra crew aboard, so did his. And he probably saw the helicopter and the cruisers approach. He's just been waiting for us to start clearing the storm. He'll be sending a team to intercept us; they're probably on their way now.'

There were footsteps up the stairs as Amy approached. She was carrying an urn and was followed by her four companions, who were carrying the mugs, milk and sugar.

'Just what I need,' Everett growled. Mitch at first thought he was annoyed by the intrusion but as the Pan Ninjas placed their offerings on the bar, Everett moved quickly to help them so as to pour himself a strong coffee with utmost dispatch. He gave an almighty sigh at the first gulp and grasped the shoulder of the closest Pan; a young man, perhaps twenty, with fair hair and elfin features, who could not hide the fear in his eyes.

'I like it when my people pitch in,' Everett grinned. 'What's your name, man?'

'Terry,' he said. 'This is Lorena, and Capri, and April.'

Lorena and Capri were Hispanic; both medium height, Lorena was broad shouldered and owlish, Capri slimmer but more wiry. April, the pilot, looked tougher; bustier and broad-shouldered with long unkempt hair.

'Pleased to meet ya Mister Everett,' she spoke in a broad Northern Australian accent, extending her hand.

Everett shook. 'Indeed.'

Lorena gave them a scowl. 'Franco and DJ are dead, aren't they?'

'I'm afraid so,' Everett nodded. 'There's nothing we can do about that, but in a while I want you to brief me about your organization, how it's evolved in the past three months. I might be able to help you – and in some small way help avenge your friends' deaths.'

Amy brought her father a hot travel mug. He sipped; milk and no sugar. She remembered.

'So what happened, Dad? For a while everyone thought you'd been killed at the Vantage Hotel, the night of the storm. People saw you there, with her.' Amy again indicated Heather with some disdain. 'And Aunt Saph. But they say you disappeared after some men threatened you.'

'The night of the storm?' Mitch asked. 'There was no storm…'

'Yeah there was; weren't you there? A massive storm came in off the coast, after midnight. The Vantage Hotel was hammered; people said it was Uncle Pan's spirit having one last party.' She shrugged. 'Some corporate guy was struck by lightning.'

'Corporate guy?'

'Yeah, some movie producer who works for Oliver Hines…'

'Not Eissley? Don Eissley?'

Everett growled. 'What do you know about Don Eissley, Mitch?'

Mitch shot Everett a look; he'd tell him later.

'Yeah –' Amy nodded. 'That was him.'

'Is he dead?'

'No, he survived.' Amy shrugged again. 'Some people do.'

'Yes. Yes, they do, don't they?' Mitch suspected that Don Eissley would survive almost anything. 'But that storm wasn't your Uncle Pan, sweetie. That was someone else. And that storm, believe it or not, was the other end of this storm here; and it's all connected with you and me and Aunt Saph and Uncle Pan – and someone named Suzie Saturn.'

'You've heard of Suzie Saturn?'

'*You've* heard of Suzie Saturn?'

'Everyone who was there when the storm hit, and the lightning stuck, has heard of Suzie Saturn. Afterwards, that name; it was in everyone's heads. It was like someone shouted out her name when the lighting stuck. I know it sounds bizarre but it was all anyone could talk about. It's like, she's someone we should have known, but no-one's, like, *ever heard of her*. And she didn't Google. Do you know who she is?'

'No... I don't think anyone does. But I know her... we've talked. She's in the astral dimension... but I don't think she was always there. I think she's the first human being to fully manifest – as a human being – in the astral plane for a very long time. I just don't know why, or why that's so important...'

'Mitch...' said Saph. 'The astral plane? Surely that's... that's just a metaphor. For the unconscious? For dreams...?'

'No, it's a real place. I'm beginning to get a grip on all this now; how it all works. But what I can't understand is – why doesn't anyone remember Suzie Saturn?'

'I do.' Mendoza smiled again. 'I remember her. And I'll tell you who she is – who she *was*. I'll tell you everything you want to know... but first, I want your help.'

CHAPTER FIFTY-SIX

'You're the photographer, right?' Mitch asked. 'I read about you in Heather's report; you discovered Gabrielle Fenwick. You blackmail film studios. What are you doing here?'

'Suzie sent me,' Mendoza narrowed his eyes. 'At least, she let me know that now was the right time to approach you. Came right into my dream. Wouldn't let it go; said to go, go now. Right in the middle of the goddamn storm. Wouldn't let up – so I went. Figured, I've known her since she and Gabrielle Fenwick got off the bus together from Michigan; she's been looking out for me all that time, why would she stop now?'

'Gabrielle Fenwick and Suzie Saturn?' Heather asked. 'There's nothing in her records that says she came to LA with anyone else…'

'Haven't you figured it out yet?' Mendoza smirked.

'They wiped her,' Mitch said softly.

'Who did?' asked Heather.

'The…' Mitch gulped.

He realized how ridiculous this was going to sound.

'The Reptilians,' he said.

'*Reptilians?*' Amy exploded. 'You mean like, *David Icke* Reptilians?'

'Who's David Icke?' Mitch asked.

'I'll tell you later,' Heather stepped in quickly. 'Mitch, have you seen them?'

'I saw Don Eissley turn into one, then back again, at the wake. They have the ability to do that; but then after the Orion Renegades zapped me, I went into a dream world. But it was real. They said it was some kind of lower level of the astral dimension, the fourth dimension. Suzie Saturn was there, and so was Don Eissley. She's trapped there I think. Eissley called up more Reptilians and they fought and, somehow, the reflection of that fight turned into a storm – both here and now, and three months ago at the Vantage. That's where I spoke to Suzie, at the Vantage, three months ago, at Pan's wake, *after* we left… I think she sees time differently… I think, in the astral, time has another dimension. It's like, there's still four dimensions, but two of space and two of time. You don't perceive time as a straight line there, it's more… spiral. At least, that's how it *feels*.'

'I've been watching you, you know.' Mendoza exhaled dope in Mitch's face. Mitch held his breath. 'Watching you, since *you* started to spiral.'

'Spiral?' Mitch huffed.

'Drinking, Pyne.' Mendoza stepped forward, close to Mitch. 'Never know which way that's going to go. A blast for some, a bummer to others.'

Suddenly he whipped out his hand and thrust it into the breast pocket of Mitch's jacket. Mitch was so stunned that he barely realized Mendoza had done this, until he was standing before him with a black feather in his hand; the raven feather Mitch had picked up from the floor, the morning of the wake.

'Even paid you a personal visit,' Mendoza grinned.

Everett snatched the joint from Mendoza's other hand and stubbed it out on the bar.

'You said you wanted our help; that you were sent by someone who wanted to help us. If Mitch says this Suzie Saturn woman helped him, that's good enough for me, but you had better explain who you are and why you've come, or God help me, you will walk the plank.'

Mendoza smirked. 'Easy now chief.'

Everett leaned into him. 'You came here to give us an advantage; now tell us what that is.'

Mitch allowed himself a small smile; fairy stories be damned, it was always about the information with Everett. It was the smart way to play.

'Okay,' Mendoza nodded. 'You want to play it that way, fine. Here's how I see it going.' He turned to Saph and smiled. 'You're the precog, right? Pan juiced you up? Switch it on and see if you don't concur…'

Mendoza almost growled with that last word.

'Conan O'Branson here,' Mendoza nodded at Everett, 'is going to take the whirly gig, and the kiddies, and the soldiers, back to La-La Land and hook up with The Pan. You're going to offer the kid sister what you have to offer: money. You're going to offer to fund her whole operation on the proviso that they run the drugs for you – the *real deal* drugs – am I right?'

Everett narrowed his eyes.

'Thought as much.' Mendoza tapped his third eye. 'Up here, it's already happening.'

'You mean,' Mitch began, 'you're going to mass produce Pan's gifts? And use Pan's People – The Pan – to circulate them?'

Everett rolled his tongue a second. 'The thought *had occurred*.'

'But – aside from any other concerns that arise,' Saph guffawed, 'you don't have all six; there's just me, Mitch and Vance. We don't even know if Heather's coffee is worth anything; if it is, she hadn't manifested anything yet!'

'Yeah he does,' Mendoza smiled again, creepily. 'At least, when he gets back to LA he will.'

'Is that true?' Saph demanded. 'You have all six?'

Everett's eyes narrowed even more; he did not take them off Mendoza.

'It's possible.'

'Uncle,' Heather huffed. 'Why didn't you tell us?'

'Because until this moment, I wasn't sure.'

He was still staring at Mendoza.

Mendoza nodded smugly to himself. 'I've been plugged into all this, all my life. There are thousands like me, all around the world. The only advantage I have is that I'm plugged in via the LA energy; and that's what this is all about. That's why you're on a boat, three months later, heading full speed into the gaping maw of Leo.'

'What the hell is he talking about?' Cricket demanded.

Mendoza turned to her, smirked, but spoke to the others.

'Next, you ditch the Incubator.'

Cricket was stunned. '*I beg your pardon?*'

'You all know it,' Mendoza continued to smirk. 'Listen, sweetheart.' He addressed Cricket now, looking directly into her eyes. 'You know it too. I read women, that's what I do. I read their energy; I've done it for decades, I made a living out of it. We're all born with an energy; first thing you do when you realize that is figure out where that energy came from, and where it's best employed here in this plane. You got lucky, kid. You found your base real early in life; now it's time to go back. You don't belong with these people; you got what you came for, so say your goodbyes. It won't be long now before they reign you in.'

'Fuck you!' Cricket spat.

'Now we all know that's not going to happen,' Mendoza nodded, grinning. He turned back to Mitch.

'Now, you, Hugh Jackman – and Geoffrey Rush and Naomi Watts here – I want your help to break into Don Eissley's mansion in Beverly Hills; I wanna break open his safe. There's something there for me, sure, but there's a hell of a lot more for you. And then I'll show you – everything. Everything about how this world works – and why.'

INTERLUDE III

The subject has become integrated into a solid social group formed of various complimentary personality archetypes who are also affected to varying degrees by the genetic restructuring.

There seems an even greater emphasis now on separation of the dimensional scale; a greater reliance on the physical sensations, and the navigation of the three dimensions of space to which they are now limited.

Conflict between sub-groups, even within the same broader cultural arenas, has bloomed and we can perhaps make use of this in maintaining focus on the grosser physical structure to which their new genetic code forces them to adhere.

The original specimen, while at first disorientated, seems to have reoriented himself once confirming his new social status with those likewise altered into the new physicality.

It would seem that with the changes we have made though, self-identification for the primitives will become increasingly internalized, leading to a lack of, or perhaps even complete ignorance of, consciousness external to the new limitations.

Should the project proceed on a global scale, conflict on a global scale is inevitable. This should be long-range projected and assessed on multiple tiers so as to ensure maximum exploitation of the primitive energies associated with such activities.

Miris
MX-ven-67-Leuk-29w

THE PANDORA SEQUENCE

PART FOUR

CHASM

CHAPTER FIFTY-SEVEN

Mitch watched the helicopter take off.

Saph watched it with him, speaking loudly over the helicopter blades.

'Pan used to say that at some point in our lives we all make a choice…'

Yelina was waving down from the co-pilot's window, receding upwards from their perspective.

'…between art and science. Between yin and yang, between the masculine principle and the feminine principle as the dominant force in our lives. We make the choice at least once, and most people stick to it. But some people choose again, and shift polarities.'

'I don't remember ever doing that,' Mitch told her, still waving at Yelina. 'Choosing, way back when.'

'Most people don't. Most people don't even want to know, it's totally unconscious. For most people it's something they just manifest in themselves; like whether men like blondes or brunettes, whether women like bad boys or nice guys. And before you ask, don't ask.'

'I wasn't going to.'

'But the real trick, Pan said, once you realize that it's there, the choice, is to open yourself to them both, and balance them.'

As the helicopter accelerated they lowered their voices, with only the rough seas to compete.

'That's a bit simplistic don't you think?'

'It's just a notion; a chess board for a thought experiment.'

'Okay.'

Mitch turned away from the helicopter and looked over the

edge of the cruiser. The sun was rising, bathing everything in pinkish apricot. Beside them, Mendoza's speedboat floated in the ocean, tied to the edge of the cruiser. The boat had taken six men to secure during the storm, but only two to lower it again. Its black hull was battered on the side that faced the cruiser, where it had smashed during the storm, streaked with silver cracks in the matte finish, but it was there, and it would take them where they needed to go.

Mendoza came up behind them.

'It'll be crammed but it will take us all; should get us to the mainland in an hour, Mason says. Then the storm really kicks in.'

Mendoza removed his Hawaiian shirt and Bermuda shorts, dived naked into the ocean and swam around to the boat, where he loosened the ropes and started the engine, bringing it around to the ladder that Mitch and Heather had climbed after their rescue. One by one they climbed aboard, as Mendoza helped them down, and Saph returned his clothes, clutching the bag that contained Mitch's documents and their collected gifts. Above, Mason came around to check that they were all secure, shouted them good luck, then vanished back into the cruiser.

There were only four seats; if Mendoza stood at the wheel, he told them, it was possible for two people to cram in beside him.

Cricket grimaced.

'I'm not sitting up there with you unless you put your clothes back on!'

Heather made a face at Cricket. 'I've seen domestic animals run from lizards smaller than that thing!'

'Woman,' Mendoza muttered, stumbling to pull his shorts back on. 'Is she never satisfied?'

Even so, Cricket went to the back of the boat and sat in one of the two front-facing chairs there. Saph did the same, while Heather sat on the floor between them. Mitch and Vance crammed side by side into the front seats, Mitch in the middle beside the redressed Mendoza.

When the engine started it made a noise such that group

conversation was immediately impossible, then the speedboat accelerated shockingly and they were all thrown back into their seats. Jets of water shot up either side of them. Suddenly the sea was passing beside them like a highway and Everett's cruiser seemed to grow more and more tiny with each second. Mitch faintly heard Saph and Cricket shouting the odd exchange behind them, then became aware, as their speed leveled, that Heather was standing directly at his shoulder, between him and Vance. Weirdly, he felt safer. She leaned down and spoke loudly to him. He could feel the hot breath of her words on his ear.

'Might as well get the view!'

Mitch could hear her quite well.

They were heading east, to California, the west coast of the United States, with the sunrise before them. The sun itself had not yet crested the horizon, but it was almost fully daylight. Mason had estimated the trip would take perhaps half an hour if Mendoza maintained full speed, which he assured them was upward of one hundred and twenty knots.

'So you drank potions that allowed you access to the fourth dimension!'

Mendoza seemed unfazed at the notion of having a metaphysical conversation at the top of his lungs.

'I suppose!' Mitch shouted back. 'I never really thought of it like that before!'

'Sure you did! One of you sees it, one of you feels it, one of you can use it as a shortcut!'

'I guess that's true!'

'You tried it all together yet?'

'No!'

'Uh huh.'

'We only just figured out…'

'Yeah, yeah, I know the drill!'

'What do you mean?' Heather shouted, apparently following their conversation over the engine noise.

'I was into the occult, heavily into it! Crowley, Chaos Magic, the lot!'

'What is that?' Mitch asked.

'It's the long way round to getting a fraction of what you all have!'

'How so?'

'It uses ritual and symbols to focus the will! To try and shape the fourth dimension so that it affects the third!'

'It sounds complicated!'

'It's not complicated; you just have to know what you're doing; it used to be a big secret, but now, all the secret books, you can get them on the internet. There's a lot of rigmarole around it; a lot of ritual. Some of the people who wrote the books wrote them in code, but once you get around that, there's not a lot to it. You just have to know the symbols.'

'Symbols?'

'The occult symbols! They represent things; big emotions, impulses, ideas, situations, even reinforced social rules and commands; they represent in the abstract the primitive impulses that are hardwired in our minds, deep and primal, that go way back. They're all over the tarot cards; worst kept secret in the whole of metaphysics! Once you know how to manipulate them, you can start getting things to happen, happen to things, happen to people, make things happen. They're in all the big advertising and marketing campaigns, all the logos and famous slogans, and all the movies. There used to be people in charge of all that, years ago, but now it runs on auto-pilot. That's why you can never find anyone in Hollywood who knows what works and what doesn't, or anyone in advertising who knows more than even basic psychology; they all just go on instinct now, the symbols are so imbedded, they've been used so many times that they just get repeated and repeated. Advertising, marketing; nobody really knows anything, and nobody knows exactly what small fraction of the art they do know – they just know a few tricks that work!'

'Who *was* in charge?'

'What!?'

Heather leaned over. 'You said there used to be people in charge!'

Mendoza laughed heartily. 'Jesus, I tell you, if you got a few of the old turn-of-the- twentieth century magicians back into Hollywood nowadays, the *real* magicians who knew the symbols, knew the occult systems, none of those corporate studios would ever lose a buck! But there you go – systems decay, that's what they do! Look at who Olivera hired: a money man from a pharmaceutical company! Even if he is really a goddamn Reptilian; what does he know about superheroes and why people want to see them! All he cares about is alchemy!'

'Alchemy?'

'Chemicals! For him, chemical addiction! That is his stock and trade! You say Suzie gave him an ass-kicking! Good for her!'

'What if he kicked her ass too!?'

Mendoza either didn't hear, or ignored him.

'And some of these screen writers today; Lord Almighty; they're not even connected to the astral – not even channeling the great stories any more. Just copying what they've seen, just second-rate pastiche after second-rate pastiche. No magic at all; just screen writing programs and a loosely connected series of set-pieces we've seen time and again; or third-tier stereotypes standing in for genuine archetypes or icons, lifeless characters going through soulless journeys having meaningless deaths in routine order!'

Mitch wanted to say something but couldn't.

He felt like, if he did say something, if he acknowledged his old life, he would suddenly wake up on his couch and realize that this had all been a dream, a dream that would slip through his mind like sand in an hourglass, and by the afternoon become merely a collection of loose, grainy images and potent feelings of something he might once have had; something more.

'Still; they could fix it if they wanted!'

'Who could!?'

'Any of the clans of what you call Reptilians!'

'Clans!?'

'This isn't science fiction my friend! Alien races aren't just one thing! They're not some simple analogy for some larger aspect of humanity! If the current version of recorded human history can be said to be a description of hundreds of different cults and clans and bloodlines and organizations, secret or otherwise, utilizing different control systems to compete for dominance of human hearts and minds, then so can be described the history of the Reptilians in the astral! As above, so below! Although they're not really above, or below – they're more *around*!'

'How could they *fix it* then?'

'They could open up the channels and send it all down; real dreams again, real stories that fully resonate from the astral into the Earth! Characters we truly respond to! Stories that feel real! That have impact and meaning on our lives! But they don't want it; the longer they control us, the emptier they want us! You ask me, I think they're bored with us. Lost interest! Too much control! I mean, what happens in the astral is supposed to echo what happens on Earth, and vice versa. It's supposed to be balanced. But when they totally control the astral, when they harvest fourth dimensional energy and keep it all to themselves, then that's the end of it; that's why nothing ever changes down here. Everything is out of balance, and they control everything. I guess it just must be the way they want it…!'

Mitch turned to Vance. Vance had his arms folded and was frowning.

'Geoffrey Rush indeed…'

The rest of the trip went quietly, until they saw the shore in the distance. They realized how fast they were traveling as it came upon them very quickly. Mendoza steered the boat toward a small bay, an inlet of dense foliage and thick trees that receded inland for a short distance, then steeply uphill to a palm-lined ridge. Five isolated beach houses evenly divided the inlet, all of them three floors high, five or six rooms wide, with broad-stilted landings. The first two were close to the shore but widely spaced, each extending with their own private pier from each side of the inlet. The second two had been raised further back, and higher into the rise, but were closer together, with the last one extending from the center of the ridge, just below the palms, like a bejeweled crown.

Within minutes they'd reached a small and presumably communal pier that extended from the beach at the center of the inlet. Mendoza tied the boat to the end of the pier and the others began to disembark, up an old steel ladder to the seemingly ancient but still solid wooden decking. As they did, Mendoza resumed his lecture.

'So anyway, a century or so back, one of the Rep clans, the Xyntyx, arranged to have Los Angeles built on an energy center that in the astral acts like a massive power line; the San Andreas Fault. The energy from the second density, the planetary interior, gets channeled up into what we call Hollywood; it's literally a dream factory powered by the energy from core of the planet, at first density. Because of what they built on it, the studios and their corresponding temples, that energy attracts people with the right DNA to channel the astral archetypes.'

'What do you mean, studios and temples?' Mitch asked.

'Well, the studios are temples; or *were* before they were broken down and disseminated; too many different corporate Reptilians clans wanted a piece of the astral power the studios offered, and now they're sliced up into bits and spread all over the planet. The Draco control most of them now. Cinema magic is nowhere near as potent as it once was; but still very effective at sending big messages. One idea, writ large.'

Mitch thought of the great old cinemas; how people had once compared them to churches and even cathedrals. Now, with the cineplexes, they were more like processing booths. Mendoza caught his eye.

'Figuring it out, huh?'

'Theaters of worship.'

'Oh yeah; the human race is brilliant at it. Acting, performance, no-one does it like us. Storytelling like we do it, it's something that makes us unique. People used to come from all over the galaxy to see our stories, and to tell stories to us, so they'd be recorded and acted out. We did it better than anyone.'

'So Hollywood itself… is a factory for channeling the astral?'

'Used to be.'

'I remember this,' Saph agreed. 'It was another of Pan's things; like, Columbia is actually another name for Isis, and the Sumerian and Babylonian Goddesses that preceded her. The Statue of Liberty is another manifestation of the same goddess principle, the feminine torch-bearer. She recurs throughout history; a lot of American history specifically. Who – notionally – discovered America? Christopher Columbus. Then the Paramount mountain is Mount Olympus, but also stands in for the Illuminati pyramid – and it's surrounded by pentagrams. Ever noticed that? Leo the MGM lion, 'king of the beasts', is symbol of primal power, royal power, it's even a Christ symbol. Some say that's why the studio was allowed to fall. Universal; the world globe, obviously, but if you look at it when it stops over the American continent some have said it resembles a yin-yang symbol. I mean, that's all pretty basic, and there are many other theories.'

'But movies are a positive force… aren't they? They're an art, they're… the best kind of magic, surely? When they're done right?'

Mendoza shrugged. 'Sure. Haven't you figured this all out yet? Nothing's ever just one thing. It ain't all good, but it's not all bad either; sure, a good movie can change your life. For the better, even. And they used to, but then the other clans got involved. Then we discovered television.'

'They didn't *give us* this technology?'

'No, nothing like that. We do what we do, we invent what we invent. It's our behavior they modify, our dreams and desires. That's astral energy. Look at it this way; if we invent something that has a use for us in our reality, say pop-up toasters, they're marketed, real strong. Everyone wants one; I mean, no-one wants to keep watch and flip handles on their toasters so their bread don't burn any more, right? Makes sense down here in reality. So the Reps, they brand the pop-up toasters. They put a symbol on them; say, a red diamond. Sure there are blue circle toasters, and yellow square toasters, but these red diamond toasters, they're the best; the marketing engine creates a real demand for them, right? By putting that logo on them, they become a totemic item. Whether you know it consciously, or unconsciously, you have just paid tribute to the cult of the red diamond. Maybe your red diamond pop-up toaster works so well, you decide you want a red diamond coffee machine to go with it. Another tribute to the cult of the red diamond. Meanwhile, in the astral, there's a temple. The Temple of the Red Diamond. One of the Rep clans owns that temple; they built it using what they know of sacred geometry, of archetypal forces – and all that energy powers that clan's empire, their power and existence in the astral.'

'Just from branding and marketing something?'

'Soon your whole goddamned kitchen is filled with red diamonds, and every second ad break on television is reinforcing it with images of how great it is to be a red diamond consumer; you're young, wealthy and happy, you're a red diamond kind of guy. A red diamond gal. Oh yeah.'

'Self-identifying brand recognition…' Mitch remembered from somewhere, probably an early morning college class.

'Oh, and don't get me started on television; you want to talk about methods of social control, of psychic reinforcement?'

'But everyone kind of understands that, don't they? You trade the entertainment, the actual programs, for the advertising; it's a kind of… deal. A social contract with the audience – even if it is an unconscious bargain for most people.'

'Of course. But then it becomes imbedded. After a while you're not just taking your purchasing cues from the advertising, you're taking your *social* cues from the way characters behave in the programs. Eventually, you don't consciously agree to consider the products any more, you just unconsciously accept that they are all there is; that *they* are the world, and all there is. We become defined by the narrow choices they offer and don't look outside them for anything else.'

Cricket growled. 'I know people who've gone mad looking into all this; there has to be some structure, and what we have is just what we have. What other symbols are they supposed to use? Not all circles are sun symbols, not all triangles are Illuminati pyramids, not all five sided stars are pentagrams. Sometimes they're just attractive shapes.'

'Spoken like a true company girl,' Mendoza winked at her.

'But she's right Mendoza,' Saph objected. 'I knew people in my time with Pan who went right off the deep end with this stuff; especially when they combined it with drugs. Exposure to the occult, when you first realize that these symbols are there, or can be there, or are potentially there… you see what I mean? Already you're dealing with a paradigm that is totally outside of normal constraints; things that are real on one level, but paranoid fantasy on another. You can't dispute that they are there, and yet why doesn't everyone else notice them? And if they do, why don't they care? Who put them there? Why? Why doesn't this seem to matter to anyone…? It goes deeper and deeper into a descending concentric circle. Eventually you can just crack up. The psych wards of the world are filled with people who think that the television is targeting them with messages designed to control their minds.'

Mendoza nodded. 'That's why you need to be initiated into this kind of stuff; the occult, sacred symbolism, sacred geometry. That's why there are rituals and levels to it. You're exposed slowly, structurally, so your mind has time to process and accommodate.'

Mitch sighed. 'But what you were saying about Hollywood. Why doesn't anyone say anything? Why aren't there whistle-blowers?'

'Because in one way there's nothing to blow the whistle on. It's just there; it's always been there. In one way, Company Girl's right; it's the shape of the world. You don't get a puddle of water looking around and saying; hey, this puddle seems exactly the right shape for me! It's like it was made to control me!'

Mitch laughed. 'I suppose not. It's the same puddle they use to support evolution, isn't it? The puddle that looks around and goes, hey, isn't this great, this space was made exactly for me! And that puddle is a Christian puddle.'

Heather laughed. 'And I suppose the water in the puddle is the water that's also in the famous "half glass". Half-full and you're Christian, half-empty and you're a paranoid.'

'And if you don't give a shit and just drink the water because you're thirsty, you're an atheist!'

For some reason, they all laughed to themselves.

'Anyway,' Mendoza shrugged. 'I was saying about Los Angeles. The Reps can only use very specific people, the people with the precise DNA to channel fourth density, and the astral archetypes that reside there in energy form; the ones they specifically want presented to us so that we worship and admire them, and aspire to be them. People with real 'star power' as we say…'

Mitch followed Mendoza as he led them down the pier.

'…that's why they're called stars, why we use terms like "screen goddesses" and "glamour", because that's the energy they're channeling. The energy of the planets and the stars right in from the astral – it's fucking amazing when you think about it. I mean, think of Tom Cruise. He's had one of the most enduring careers of any film star, essentially channeling the same archetypal force over and over… because it's literally in his genes to do it.'

The list went on, Mitch knew. It was like a pantheon; the gods and goddesses of the silver-screen, the demigods, nymphs and sprites… leads, supports, and character actors… that was what Eissley had mistaken him for a late-blooming actor, searching for a powerful channel.

'I'm getting it now; someone who channels a more off-beat astral energy, perhaps an archetype that gets through despite the Reptilian blocks, or gets through to corral people who are straying from the mainstream; they're called a cult figure, right?'

'Sure. But they're not always sent by the Reptilians. You think the Reptilians wanted Bill Hicks, or Lenny Bruce? No, sometimes the higher forces push down and squeeze someone through like that. But in the mainstream… look, that's what the Oscars are, right? It's not about the acting, it never has been. Everyone knows that. What it is, is their major occult ceremony for the year, in which the most powerfully channeled archetypes are worshipped and honored. Billions of people watch it every year, all channeling their attention into those astral archetypes; my favorite part is when they drag out the old, waning gods and goddesses and give them one last burst of adoring energy.'

When he reached the end of the pier, Mendoza seemed to be searching for something along the shore, his eyes sharply scanning the sand. Mitch was about to ask but Mendoza suddenly bent down and fished a long damp stick from beneath the soggy edge of the sea.

'It's quite a scam,' Mendoza went on, as he began to draw a series of geometric patterns in the sand.

They looked like crop circles, Mitch thought… or, something like that?

He drew a big circle in the sand. 'Archetypal power from the fourth density.' He drew another circle beside it, so they made a figure eight. 'Powered by the planetary fury of the second density in the subterranean, and the iron core of first density – the most ancient solid of the cosmos itself.' He slammed the stick into the sand, upright where the circles met. 'Centered here in the third.' He took the stick out again and drew a line down each side. 'Exploited by our biology, a race that only experiences one dimension of…'

He looked at Mitch.

Mendoza had drawn a sideways hourglass.

'Time,' Mitch nodded.

Mendoza nodded back. 'It's all abstract of course, but Einstein drew a picture something like this once.'

Mendoza slammed the stick in the middle again.

'He said this was us, our experience of time. Our limited perception is stuck in the middle here, in the middle of a funnel, while time flows through us. We perceive it as moving forward, but who knows what it's doing really, outside of that perception? What we do know is that our atoms vibrate at a frequency that makes us perceive things that way, creating what metaphysicists call density – and so the use of symbols, embedded in that perception, in our reality of material solids, tends to have a powerful effect on our perception. They can change the things we desire; the things we dream about. And what we dream about affects the astral; that's where our emotional energy rises to. In a perfect world, we would know that; we would draw on the astral just as we draw on the second density, on nature and the planet. But we don't because the Reps are more advanced than us, they have better science, better technology. And for six thousand years, they have been using it to ensure that everything we do feeds them the energy, without us knowing about it.'

'Lava powered mass hypnotism,' Mitch muttered.

Mendoza laughed as he traced out another pattern in the sand; the other patterns he was drawing looked too arty to be mathematical, Mitch thought. But then again, what did he know about math? Nothing truly beyond a decades-old and very rudimentary processing from high school.

What exactly was Mendoza doing?

'But how do they do it?' Mitch enquired. 'I mean, are there machines in the fourth dimension? Like astral transformers or something?'

'Not quite. There are… cities. Like ours. Filled with temples that draw on the symbols we worship. But the Reps are older than us; when they were third density beings, like us, they got further, they harnessed planetary energy, harnessed material energy, and then harnessed astral energy. They ran rampant through the galaxy, terrorizing and colonizing planets, powering their society with fear and exploitation. They live principally in the astral now;

think of it like the holodeck in *Star Trek*, but controlled by will. The Reps with the strongest will rule; they literally shape the world.'

'So they actually channel energy from the planet?' Heather asked. 'What, like, ley lines and energy grids and things like that?'

'All bullshit,' Cricket muttered.

Heather ignored her. 'And this second density energy draws people to it?'

'Yep.'

'And if you build on top of it, depending on what geometrical and architectural patterns you employ, what symbols you use...'

'Yeah...'

'...you can harness the energy and use it like a beacon, to attract people with certain types of biology, of DNA, and channel down astral energy from the fourth density to empower them?'

'That's about right. That's how life has evolved to exploit those energies. Unfortunately, the Los Angeles energy chasm is so powerful that is also attracts just about anyone with the slightest lineal trace of that DNA program – the DNA that channels astral energy.'

'So how do you know all this?' Mitch asked. 'Where do you fit into it all?'

'He's a sorcerer,' Vance said quietly. 'Aren't you Mendoza? You're like me; some of it is in your DNA, you're born with it. It all comes naturally.'

'Yeah. That's right. I was eight years old and I could see through it all; astral energy, archetypal symbolism, occult systems. I couldn't figure out why they weren't teaching us this in school. I thought; right, we'll get it when we get to high school. Then nothing. College looked like it was going to be more of the same, or at least rationalizing it all out of existence, so I skipped it. Pity; turns out that's where people like me get recruited. Might have risen through the conventional ranks, made corporate money. But nah; in the end, I preferred it my way.'

'And what was your way?'

'I was born in nineteen fifty. Seventeen years old in the summer of love. There were still bookstores back then, little ones. Specialist stores. That was my way in; self-taught. I ended up in Los Angeles after Altamont; I could see things weren't going to end well for the flower children. But it was free love and the sexual revolution, and pretty girls were heading to Hollywood. Girls who'd do anything to make it. Anyway, by then I knew enough to know what Los Angeles was. I could tell, right off the bus I could tell, which ones were right for what; go-go dancing, stripping, hooking, porn, modeling, acting, music – cult stardom, semi-stardom, real stardom and superstardom. I knew what their bodies were made for, saw right through to their cellular level, and what their minds could receive and channel.'

Mendoza's symbols were spreading now, covering the sand from one side of the pier to the other. They were so complex, so beautifully intertwined that Mitch thought it sad that they were inevitably impermanent; that in the afternoon they would surely be washed away with the tide.

'Yeah, they came straight to LA, moths to the flame, and straight to me. At least, I was there to sort them. Me, and some others. I wasn't the only one; but I was the best. I had my photography studio built at the right time, when the stars aligned, right on one of the strongest ley lines in the LA energy grid. I pulled in Venus, Aphrodite, Bacchus and even Pan. Zeus turned up a few times, just to see what I had. Randy old bastard. After a while the Xyntyx clan figured out what I was doing – but they figured – it works, hell, why not let him do it? Save them the work. And even the Draco think twice before messing with the old archetypal gods.'

Mendoza paused for a second then admired his handiwork, spread in a long sandy arc around the top of the pier. He looked at Mitch and smiled.

'Sacred geometry,' Mendoza nodded. 'To summon who we want to talk to, you have to show them you know what you're doing, and respect their science. Like I said, this is all on the internet now; just takes a bit of effort, a bit of study and concentration. But nobody can be bothered these days. They'd rather go ghost hunting; the lower astral can be very addictive. Fear and adrenalin can be very addictive, even without the lower astral.'

'Who do we want to talk to?' Mitch asked.

Behind him, the others were gathered but silent. No-one could move any further away from the end of the pier for fear of obscuring Mendoza's artwork.

Mendoza smiled and ignored the question.

'I became sort of unofficially endorsed; a star-finder with a genuine star-map. Of course I took out insurance; got 'em to do whatever it was they were willing to do straight off the bus; got film and photos in the 'seventies, then videotape in the 'eighties – eventually hi-def DVD. It wasn't sleazy though… well, okay, some of it was – but it wasn't anything they weren't born to do, nothing outside of their karma. A lot of them I just frightened and sent straight home; or they ran straight home of their own accord. Karma's like what they say about hypnotism; you can't make anyone do anything that's outside of their karma. It's not strictly true about either; you can hypnotize anyone to do just about anything, it turns out. Ain't that right, Magician?'

Vance said nothing.

'And if you couldn't create new karma, well, this third density would just stop running. And they can't have that.'

Mendoza suddenly turned and looked Mitch dead in the eye.

His eyes were black, and ice cold.

'Oh no, Mitch Pyne. They can't have that.'

Then he broke the gaze, turned up and stared at the highest beach house, the one on the palm-lined rise.

'So I stored it all away, all the compromising material, then sold it back to the Reps when they saw someone they wanted. Had a nice little thing going for a long while there.'

Mitch started to wonder to which beach house they were supposedly headed, or whom, and from which of the five beach houses, these symbols were supposed to impress. Mendoza just stood and looked up at the rise, and kept talking.

'Then, the internet. No more secrets, no more shame. Only the most obscene practices reserved for censorship. And my time was over.'

Mendoza kept staring.

'I had that too,' Mitch said softly. 'But… now I know you have to move on. Or you become consumed by regret.'

He thought of Amy, who'd chosen to go back to her people and speak for Everett and his truth.

'Oh, I know,' Mendoza nodded. 'I did move on. I cut a deal.'

'A deal?' asked Vance worriedly.

'See, they run parallel, the other systems, the other dimensions, or densities, but they are all reflections of each other, and the one we inhabit is no different. We're in the third density; very solid. Not as solid as the first, or second; but they're all reflected.'

'Where's this going?' Heather suddenly asked. 'Where have you brought us?'

Mendoza kept staring up; suddenly Mitch realized that he was not standing and admiring nature and waiting for someone to exit one of the beach houses and come down to them. He was waiting for something *else*.

'The fourth is the astral, and that's been controlled for six thousand years by a race who see us as nothing more than slaves; and the fifth, well, they won't speak to the likes of me. And I resent that; my whole life was about finding beauty, capturing it and channeling it though the only system I had to channel it though, the only one at my disposal. I did what I was born to do. I found my stage and played my part. Nothing more.'

'You entrapped women and exploited them,' Cricket snapped.

Mendoza laughed. 'We're all exploited in some shape or form. The thing to do is find your place, being exploited for something you can live with, or even love. Ask Gabrielle Fenwick, ask if she feels exploited. She came to my funeral for Chrissake. Ask Suzie Saturn if she minded being "discovered".'

'Suzie Saturn,' Mitch snapped. 'I need to find her!'

Mendoza ignored him and continued with Cricket.

'Ask a thousand, two thousand others. Hell I saved more of them than I used. Frightened the shit out of them and sent them packing back to Peoria. I just did my thing, I read their energy and guided them to the place they could best utilize what they had. Let karma do the rest… mostly just let beauty find its way to the beast. But the Pleiadeans, they wouldn't take me; said I was too tainted by the astral, too tainted by the occult magics, and that I needed to… well, they wouldn't take me.'

'Mendoza,' Saph insisted. 'Why are we here?'

'Well ain't that the sixty-four thousand dollar question?' Mendoza smiled.

Mitch, however, had been following.

'You cut a deal with the sixth dimension,' Mitch said. 'That's where you were leading, wasn't it? Around us there's the astral, and around that – some purer version… where the Pleiadeans reside…'

'Love, light, harmony… and beauty,' Mendoza seemed to scoff.

'And what's around that?' Mitch asked. 'What is the sixth?'

'Well let me tell you sunshine,' Mendoza turned to him and grinned. 'Ain't you about to find out?'

There was a terrible rumbling.

Sunrise broke over the top of the ridge and suddenly blinded them with fractured light.

Then the earthquake began.

CHAPTER FIFTY-EIGHT

Mitch fell to his knees, then his hands.

He was staring at the sand, watching it jump and wobble and pop.

The others had all done the same and suddenly, he realized, they were in some strange position of worship, of prayer. Except; they weren't.

Mitch looked up, and spiked.

The beach houses were reflecting the sunrise and issuing lines of light from their architectural plains and angles; shining white, but flashing sparks of the full spectrum as they grew and conjoined, in strange but beautiful and ornate geometric patterns. From one to the other, in flat horizontal spirals and perfectly aligned angles of illuminated structure, the beams and swirls of light began to form between the beach houses, until Mitch realized that the houses themselves were only physical cornerstones, a foundation of sorts over and through which this new, sixth density structure could appear.

In under a minute, a massive crystalline step-pyramid had formed, glistening with the sunrise, absorbing its light, capturing it and somehow incorporating the light itself into its very form, its manufactured solidity in this dimension.

The earth tremor stopped and they each raised their eyes to the most beautiful and bewildering sight any of them had ever laid eyes on. Mitch didn't know if the spike had allowed him to see it form, or whether the others had seen it form as he had; but now, he knew, they could all see it.

Suddenly Mitch realized; this is why we kneel. This is why we supplicate ourselves to the ground, to the Gods. In some lost, primitive way we are trying to conjure the beings whose arrival is heralded by earth tremors that make it impossible for us to maintain balance, that send us instantly to our hands and knees. Somewhere along the line, it had all become confused; it had become superstition, like a sports fan who has to sit in the same seat and wear the same hat every game, thinking that this will somehow affect the result of the game.

The entrance to the crystal step pyramid was just before them, a few steps onto the beach from the end of the pier; a long corridor that extended deep within the illuminated pyramid, into the bright sunlight inside.

And *crystals*, Mitch thought. This is why New Agers clutch at crystals, try to channel energies through them; it was all so mixed up, it was all so *lost*.

'How could we get it *so wrong?*' Mitch gasped under his breath.

As they gradually stood, Mendoza turned to look at him. His wicked grin seemed wiser now, almost *knowing*. So that was why he seemed hostile, beneath the eccentric exterior, Mitch supposed. How could you know about this and not carry an air of disdain, or even contempt, for those around you, whose whole existence was based around only a fraction of the larger reality?

'They are very, very old,' Mendoza told them. 'This seems like a lot to us, but to them it's… pulling their car up in front of your house.'

'That's one hell of a perspective,' Heather gaped, looking up.

'Perspective is the key; this is a big universe and we're one little planet. But it's like binary code; take one tiny planet out before its natural time, and the whole thing's useless.'

There was something moving in the light at the end of the tunnel.

'They have physical form, but not like we do; they have to… you know what I said about pulling their car up? It's not quite like that; it's more like, they've come to the bottom of the ocean, put on their high-pressure hydraulic diving suit, and are now coming out to speak to the bottom dwellers.'

'We're bottom dwellers?' Heather winced.

'Maybe that's a bit much. Let's say, bottom dwelling *dolphins*; bottom dwellers who the higher species think are kind of cute, and have a rudimentary culture and intellect that we can interact with. Imagine if we discovered dolphins had built basic cave-cities at the bottom of the Mariana Trench –'

'Enough!' Heather cried. 'We're dolphins, I get it!'

'Indeed.'

The voice had come from the tunnel. A figure was emerging.

The shape looked feminine.

Although she was walking, Mitch somehow saw it as the illusion of walking; she was certainly traveling somehow toward the group, but the notion that she was humanoid, that she had legs to walk with, was being translated to his brain simply so he could process the intelligence that was now fully manifesting in the physical world before him.

In that regard, he told himself to be careful; however, she had chosen to present herself, this entity, so she would appear as she wanted to be seen, not as she actually was.

Sure enough, she appeared as royalty.

The woman was perhaps seven feet tall with a slender and, most would have to accept, perfect hourglass figure. She looked vaguely Egyptian, and at first seemed to be wearing makeup; false extended lashes, dark mascara and eye-liner, with deep blue eye-shadow. But when Mitch looked closer he saw that this was not the case. On second inspection, this seemed to be her natural pigmentation: she had a faint deep-blue tinge over the light bronze of her skin. It covered her entire body, but was only apparent when the angle of sunlight, refracted off the construction behind her, somehow hit her square on. Her irises were the same shade of deep, dark blue, but crystal clear, and the whites were large and sunlight-white. Her slim but curvaceous figure was draped in transparent cloth robes of yellow and orange, tones calculated exactly to set off the glowing natural tan of her skin, tied with light gold chains about her waist and wrists, obscuring but at the same time drawing absolute focus to her nudity beneath. Her only body hair was on her head; it was dark, almost black, in long ringlets, tied this time with a more ornate gold chain into a high coiffure that exactly mirrored the perfectly aligned, perfectly complimentary angles of her exquisite bone structure, her sensually swollen lips and narrow, gently aquiline nose. Again, Mitch thought that she must have had the hair arranged, it must have taken hours; but again, upon closer inspection, he saw that it was totally natural. Apart from the gold chains, this was how her race's hair grew, back when they had physical form.

The final thing Mitch noted was her feet. For the third time he mistook a natural physical attribute for a feminine adornment; then he realized that she was not walking in stilettos. Like her hands, her feet were extremely slender, extending almost to points, with only the thinnest of nails ringing their pointed edges. But the realization as to her feet was the most startling. She seemed to have natural stilettos; a strong and pointed sixth toe that extended backwards and carried the weight of her step, almost and quite bizarrely like a permanently extended thumb that extended from the backs of her heels. It was striking, and totally alien, yet gave the same grace to her stride as high heels gave to a human woman.

The realization Mitch made, as did the others, surely, was nothing short of shocking. They could immediately see how the features of this creature had affected human womankind. Mitch was aware that definitions of beauty had changed throughout the centuries, from culture to culture, but nobody could deny that this woman exhibited an archetypal, if not extreme classic beauty: women painted their eyes, and glued on lashes to look like she did, they starved themselves and implanted themselves, tortured their feet and spines, spent hours and hours in preparation; all for a distant race memory.

Mitch could not help but think: we are always looking to something else, and this is a big part of it.

Never within, always to some outer ideal of perfection.

This perfection.

If these creatures had visited mankind at the start of their cultural evolution, they had never had a hope: men would want them, women would want to be them. Men would never be satisfied with anything less until they possessed her, women would never settle for anything less until they were adored as she was.

'We never had a hope,' Mitch uttered.

The woman, who was a clear foot taller than Mitch, smiled down at him sympathetically.

'Oh, Mitch.'

CHAPTER FIFTY-NINE

'Meet the Sirians,' Mendoza intoned. 'As we call them. Like the Pleiadeans, they haven't lived exclusively in those star systems for thousands of years, but that's what we call them.'

'Thank you,' the woman intoned. Her voice was low, and so sultry that Mitch suspected she could even seduce someone by reading them the Old Testament.

Misha laughed, catching the thought.

'Yes, my name is Misha, if you like.'

Mitch blushed. 'She was a woman, in a magazine, when I was a teenager. I thought she was the most beautiful thing I'd ever seen...'

'Until you met Sapphire,' Misha nodded. 'Because you adored Misha, before that; Sapphire was Misha in the flesh. And Misha was an adult reflection of the girl who sat next to you in third grade, whom you were too shy to even look at. And the girl who sat next to you in third grade resembled your wife, three lifetimes ago, who was much of what Sapphire is now. The chain is unbroken; the universe never allows us to forget whom we know, why we come together and why we come apart. It always recycles the energy, no matter what form it takes. You and I were friends once Mitch, much of what is you now, and much of what I am. In my last incarnation here in the third density.'

'You're human?' Heather asked.

'No Heather,' Misha smiled. In fact, she never stopped smiling. 'I had made a disservice in my existence as I am now, an error. So I incarnated on Earth, as penance to restore my karmic balance. That is what this planet, in this third density, is for.'

'Is *for*?' Cricket asked. 'Who decided that?'

Of them all, Cricket seemed the least impressed.

'It came to be,' Misha intoned. She turned to Mendoza. 'Mendoza, you have done as we asked. We shall aide you in your quest.' Mendoza seemed pleased, then Misha turned back to Cricket. 'She is of Orion,' Misha said to Mendoza. Then she spoke directly to Cricket. 'Your people are coming for you. You cannot follow where your friends go.'

'What?'

'What do you mean, Orion?' Saph asked.

'Like those awful creatures we saw?' Heather demanded. 'And what do you mean, she can't follow? Where the hell are we going, anyway?'

Misha stared absently at them, musing. 'The new humans…' she hummed. 'I am truly interested in this planet again for the first time in…' She turned back to Mendoza. 'They will not prevent the chasm opening. The balance is already tipped.'

'I am − *was* a chaos magician. I understand that. But they might at least try. Their leader is already proliferating the genetic code throughout the city; at least, he will be trying. That is his aim.'

'Is it really?' Misha raised her eyebrow. Even that was not as it seemed; a perfectly angled, pigmented ridge, Mitch realized. Such a deep blue as to be almost black.

'Were there blondes?' Mitch blurted.

Misha turned to him and held his gaze for a second, as though scanning his mind to more satisfactorily respond to the needs of his query.

'We were like this; just as we had once been as you are − or very close. We too had many pigmentations, and we too reached a phase where that was at our command. There were blondes Mitch. And blues, and greens and reds.' She smiled. 'When we met here on Earth, I was a redhead. You were much as you are now. We followed a man who sought to end war, and I was killed for it. By a man who you then killed; you lived out the rest of that life in sorrow, having children you did not care for, with a women you did not love. But you are learning to make better choices now, attainable choices; you love your children now, at least.'

They heard the distant sound of engines along the beach.

Misha turned to Cricket. 'They come for you.'

'No!' Cricket shouted.

'Who are they?' Saph demanded. Then her face soured. 'Don't worry, I know.'

They could see the cars racing up the beach: two black four-wheel drives, unmarked, with tinted windows. With a whine, a black, unmarked helicopter arose over the ridge, out of the sun, over the crystalline step pyramid, and hovered shakily but almost noiselessly in the sky above them, its instrumentation clearly disturbed by the presence of the great pyramid structure.

'The CIA.'

CHAPTER SIXTY

The four-wheel drives stopped just short of the pier and within seconds two men climbed out of the closest one. They were not Men in Black, so to speak; they were not imposing or intimidating, other than the bulges under their conventional black suits that indicated the possession of firearms. Rather, they seemed to Mitch like regular people, ordinary government operatives.

The two men held back at their car, leaning back on the bonnet in their black suits, gazing around behind their standard issue sunglasses as though the scene on the beach before them was not occurring. The two others came forward from the second car, a man and a woman, both in their thirties, both offering plain but borderline expressionless smiles. The man was wearing tight blue jeans, black lace-less leather shoes and a loose black tee shirt. The woman was also wearing blue jeans, with a white tank top, white bra straps showing beneath, and sensible black shoes. They might, just, have been offering copies of *The Watchtower*.

'Cricket,' the man smiled.

'Young,' Cricket responded neutrally, stepping back a little so she was clearly bordered by Heather and Saph. 'Campbell.'

Campbell smiled. 'How are you Cricket?'

'I'm fine.'

'You know them?' Saph asked.

'We know all of you,' Young offered, grinning a grin he clearly thought made him seem like a top gun. It didn't.

'You have the advantage then,' Vance uttered. 'But I'm afraid you've made a wasted journey.'

'We'll see,' Young grinned again.

Campbell eyed Cricket almost pitifully. 'Cricket, you know

how this ends. We don't want to abort it, we don't want to transfer it. We just want to observe it as it comes to term.' She turned to Mitch. 'You're more than welcome to come with us, make sure she's treated well. It would be better to have the father there.'

'Where?' Mitch asked. 'In a medical *cell* somewhere?'

'In a secure facility,' Campbell nodded. 'Very comfortable. Would you expect anything less for a child that could change the course of human history?'

'And how's it going to do that exactly?' Mitch demanded.

'She said *could*,' Young chimed in. 'It's the *could* part we want to observe.'

'And if it does? If it *could*? What then? Breed an army? Weaponize the child somehow?'

'No!' Cricket cried.

Saph moved forward and placed an arm around her shoulder. 'You're not taking her.'

'And,' Vance added, 'are you really going to stand there and make kidnapping threats, pretending all the while that there isn't a seven foot goddess standing right behind us in front of a giant crystal pyramid?'

Young grit and bared his teeth, making clicking noises in his cheeks.

Campbell smiled at Cricket, condescending, as though what Vance had suggested was somehow very silly and childish.

'Apparently, they are,' Misha smiled. She seemed to find it amusing.

The back door of Young and Campbell's four-wheel drive cracked open. It seemed for a second like a chill and rapid wind ripped down the beach, and it drew everyone's attention. The men leaning on the bonnet of the other car reacted as though startled, then one of them walked instantly to the open door and leaned in. There was a brief exchange, then the agent turned and approached Young as the car door snapped shut again behind him. The agent muttered something low and not a little lengthy in Young's ear, to which Young nodded bluntly three times and raised an eyebrow once. The suited agent turned and went back to the bonnet as Young appeared to mull things over.

'I'm authorized to make you a deal,' Young stated, as though this were a profound pronouncement.

'I'm not interested,' Cricket stated, clearly more than a little untruthfully.

'They do not offer deals often,' Misha stated from behind them. 'They will take you regardless, they are being very reasonable.'

'Who don't?' Saph asked.

'Orion,' Misha stated simply. 'That is who you're dealing with. These operatives have the energy all through them, as do you Cricket. You belong to them because you are part of them.'

'I'm nothing like those things who were on those boats!' Cricket protested.

Misha zeroed in on her.

Mitch noted that, as she did, Young and Campbell went to great lengths to pretend the conversation wasn't happening; Young scratched the back of his hand as though he'd never seen it before, while Campbell took out a phone and stared at the black screen as though she were taking readings from a Geiger counter.

'Really?' Vance demanded, staring amazedly at Young. '*Really?*'

'I see your misapprehension,' Misha finally stated. 'You were threatened by the Orion Renegades. I understand your fear; those who do not fear them are unbalanced. As were the snipers who killed the comrades of the younger Pyne. But these people before you do not represent the Orion Renegades. This organization you have been raised in has ties to what they call the Second Orion Directorate. Cricket, you are dealing with eighth density beings who have little or no physical presence in this dimension; they are aligned with the strongest physical power on this world to ensure its continued integrity. You cannot imagine the repercussions when nuclear weapons are discharged; these are beings of the highest order and responsibility, and their representatives are to be respected. You are, whether you know it or not, one of those representatives. I would listen to whatever offer they have to make you.'

Cricket had gone pale.

'Okay,' Young grinned his grin again, even more false. 'You ready to listen?'

The car door cracked open again. 'Wait.'

The voice was cold and brittle, but not malevolent. Slowly, a man climbed out of the four-wheel drive, stepped down to the white sand and examined the ocean and the diminishing effects the sunrise had on the clouds above it, with his back to them. They could see gray hair, and a thin, frail body wrapped in a dark grey suit. When he turned, he smiled and walked directly to them.

The smile was skeletal but benign, almost caring. Yet it was distracted; the tiny man seemed to have the weight of the world on his shoulders.

'Greetings, Sirius.'

'Orion.'

They nodded in mutual respect.

'Do you know who this is?' Saph asked, fear in her tone.

Cricket gulped. 'I think so.'

'Is he…?' Vance gulped, but ventured forth. 'The Director? Of Counterintelligence? Or something?'

Cricket gasped as she tried to find the words. 'He doesn't have a rank.'

The old man extended his hand to Vance.

'Obsidian,' he said. 'At your service.'

CHAPTER SIXTY ONE

'You're…' Cricket began. 'Just a rumor.'

'Yes.'

Obsidian withdrew his hand from Vance's direction.

Vance had frozen, staring straight ahead at him.

Obsidian didn't seem to mind.

'It is some time since I have walked in the open air, breathed it. Felt the sun. Almost as long since I have spoken with civilians.'

Again, Young and Campbell had adopted poses of willful denial. It was as though the old man were not there, as though they were simply and patiently awaiting some kind of connecting tourist bus to pick them up, to transport them from the beach.

'These are strange times in the third density,' Misha acknowledged. 'Perhaps it is time we took more of an interest?'

'I take an interest,' Obsidian sighed. 'I have done nothing but, for so long now…'

'Yet we hesitate to intervene in what is about to occur,' Misha responded.

'What will occur, will occur. I am an architect; what has been built can be rebuilt. I know that better than any. There is no danger to loss of integrity; not once the chasm opens.'

'The chasm?' Mitch asked.

Obsidian regarded Mitch strangely, then cast his eye toward Saph, then Heather. As he did, each of them couldn't help but shudder.

'What did you just do?' Saph demanded.

Obsidian smiled sweetly. 'Dissembled and reassembled you. No change to the order, merely… professional curiosity.'

'They are new?' Misha asked. 'As the sorcerer claims?'

Obsidian regarded Mendoza shortly, then nodded.

'They are new, and old; there is nothing truly new.'

Misha smiled; but there was a new edge to her smile that suggested cunning.

Obsidian turned to Cricket, and spoke with a soft but professional tone. Mitch felt sadly as though he were watching a rich uncle from a wealthy family come to take the wild child, the free spirit, quite unjustifiably to rehab.

'I will offer you this, Cricket. I will offer you continuity. Lineage. Return to the fold, raise the child within the family, and I will ensure that you, and it, and its progeny, remain and advance within the company. I will offer you three generations as a start, if your energy remains in this form at that point, we can renegotiate then. But you will have continuity; I will return your energy with best integrity into the fourth generation. You will inherit whatever power in this density you and your progeny have amassed in three generations, and you will be reborn into the fourth to reclaim and pursue that power further. Do you understand me child?'

'I accept,' Cricket stated, without reservation.

'*What?*' Mitch demanded.

Cricket spun about to him. 'It's the same deal he offered Bush.'

'*Bush?*'

Cricket nodded. 'Bush.'

Saph was aghast. 'Cricket what the hell are you doing?'

'The smart play,' Heather smirked. 'They want in on ground level, and she has the first existing key to the basement.'

Obsidian turned to Mitch. 'You are the father.'

'I… yes, I am!'

'We will talk; when the time comes.'

Obsidian smiled at Misha.

'Sirius.'

'Orion,' Misha smiled politely. Mitch couldn't help but see a trace of regret at the edge; as though she had been outplayed, or denied something.

'Come along then Cricket,' Obsidian called over his shoulder as he withdrew slowly, back across the sand to the car. 'We must find you a home.'

As Young and Campbell suddenly stood bolt upright and returned to their car, Cricket embraced Mitch tightly.

'I know you don't love me,' Cricket hissed in his ear. 'But we still like each other okay, don't we?'

'Yeah,' Mitch stammered. 'Yeah, sure we do...'

It was the truth after all.

'Come find me,' she added quickly, quietly. 'When it all blows over!'

She released him and kissed him hard on the cheek.

She quickly hugged each of her friends; Saph, then Heather, then Vance. 'Girl are you sure you know what you're doing?' Vance implored.

'I know what I'm doing,' Cricket smiled. 'I'll see you all!'

Then she turned and followed Young and Campbell. As she opened the door and went to climb in, she suddenly turned.

'Say bye to Harding! And tell your uncle I'll be watching him!'

'I will!' Heather cried out as Cricket slammed the door shut. 'Finally got what she wanted...' Heather muttered.

'What's that?' Mitch asked, still stunned.

Heather smiled. 'Total control.'

'Over what?' Mitch asked. 'I'm still not sure I understand!'

'Mitch,' Heather sighed. 'He's going to put her, and her child, on the fast track in the CIA. They're going to be a company family; for three generations. Then when Cricket dies, she's going to be reincarnated back into the family – and know about it. She'll have full memory of her previous life, like those kids who remember being fighter pilots. Cricket is going to be American royalty – she's the start of a new company dynasty.'

'Jesus,' Mitch uttered. 'Maybe I should have gone with her?'

Heather reacted as though Mitch had slapped her. 'Maybe...'

Then she uttered something angrily under her breath.

Mitch looked to her, but could not meet her eyes as they

followed the four-wheel drives away from the beach. The silent helicopter, Mitch realized, had vanished long ago.

'There is wisdom in the dispensing of agents…' Misha muttered. 'It must be reconsidered from the Sirian perspective.' She too watched the cars for second. 'It must be difficult for Obsidian.'

'Difficult?' Mitch asked. 'He's got more power than God!'

Misha looked at him strangely, as though she had never heard the expression before and found it an incredibly bizarre thing to suggest.

'He has sacrificed all that he is, to be here and oversee the power paradigms in this world; to do his best, given the circumstances, to see that you do not destroy yourselves again.'

'Again?'

'To lower his energy vibrations from the eighth to this third density, and remain here so long; generations so far as you are concerned…' Misha's smile dropped for the first time he'd seen, just for a few seconds. 'His every thought must be a despair, his every sight a horror, his every movement an agony. Every moment, an aeon… excruciating.'

Mitch scratched his head and turned back to her.

'So if the original architects are in the eighth density; what's between you and them? What's in the seventh?'

'What else?' Mendoza smiled. 'The Angels.'

Misha smiled benignly. 'Elohim; the architects of the formless things; the engineers of the ethereal; bringers of light and karma. But they will not come; they abandoned their city decades ago.'

'Come where?'

Mendoza laughed.

'Los Angeles, you moron. Haven't you figured it out? Oliver's gene therapy is causing a massive imbalance in this dimension; people are changing their genetic appearance, randomly messing with the form. It's a massive shift in the physicality of this dimension, and to maintain integrity it requires energy from the astral, for the archetypes from the fourth density to correspond.

But the Draco control the astral; and they won't let that kind of energy out of their control. Humanity is finally tipping the scales of the material world over the edge; the only way for the planet to compensate is a massive influx of energy from the earth, the second density. The earth will essentially act to strike at the heart of a new strain of the human virus that it cannot tolerate. Not without the balance of the corresponding genetic codes, the codes you people have. So unless your boss can get his drugs distributed at record speed, it's The Big One.'

CHAPTER SIXTY-TWO

'Let me get his straight,' Mitch frowned angrily. 'Oliver Hines' gene therapy is going to cause an earthquake in Los Angeles?'

'That is so,' Misha smiled benignly.

'I don't understand. Why?'

'In order for a third density sentient biological race to access other dimensions, other densities, two extra genetic sequences must be activated that alter your consciousness, sequences in your DNA that have laid dormant for many thousands of years. One has been discovered and activated by the consciousness cluster that surrounds the man Oliver Hines, the other had been discovered but only partially activated by the Bo Everett cluster.'

'Consciousness cluster?'

'The field of conscious energy, the network of sentience that surrounds each of them.'

'You mean; their *people*?'

'Yes. Their combined conscious energy. The sequence Oliver Hines is distributing is the gross, material side; if you are to fully access fourth density, the astral world of your imaginations, and truly integrate it with third density, then your physical forms must be made more malleable, more able to change and withstand different desires and their corresponding energies – and the clashing wills and desires of others. That is the function of the sequence Oliver Hines has found. The sequence Bo Everett has discovered is the ethereal, non-material side. They are complimentary; the function of the Bo Everett sequence is to allow greater vision, greater insights into the nature of consciousness, so that your wills and desires rise more fully above the primal instincts that heavily influence third density life.

They must be used in balance, but Oliver Hines is suppressing the ethereal strand. The densities, the dimensions; they are held in a delicate balance. As above, so below. Without the ability to channel the corresponding archetypal energy from fourth density to balance the physical changes in the third, humanity will essentially keel over and implode.' Misha shook her head. 'Each time you rise again, you are faster to destroy yourselves. But there is little to be done; too many have a vested interest in things remaining as they are.'

'What do you mean by that?' Mitch demanded. 'I've heard that said before; why is there such as vested interest in humanity remaining as we are?'

Misha narrowed her eyes.

'You have seen many things these past few days Mitchell Pyne. But it is not my place to rescue humanity, and not my place to tell you what all you have seen means.'

Misha narrowed her eyes even further; the cunning there returned.

'Do you understand me Mitchell Pyne?'

'I –'

Misha turned to Mendoza. 'I must go now. There are things to consider.'

'But wait!' Mitch insisted.

Misha turned to him, quickly narrowing her eyes again, clearly completely unaccustomed to his tone. She smiled again, still frowning but absolutely intrigued.

'Mitchell Pyne?'

'I didn't mean to be rude, it's just that; if I live to tell this story, people are going to interpret your words to say that… well, that God is somehow punishing Los Angeles for its sin.'

'Sin?'

'For it's lack of morality and self-obsession.'

'No, that is not the case.' Misha sighed. 'Has understanding of cosmic law been so corrupted here?'

'Some would say so.'

'Clearly. Such a thing *never happens*, Mitchell Pyne. Those who promote such falsities are the true purveyors of this term, *sin*. This is merely an extension of physics, of cosmology, of the laws of energy. And it is those laws under which it must be addressed.'

Misha nodded at Mitch. The nod said; that is the end of the discussion. She turned to Mendoza.

'Now, sorcerer?'

Mendoza smiled. 'You'll honor the agreement? You wanted to meet them, I brought them to you; you said you would aid me in my cause.'

'I will; fear not. We have no agreement with the Draco. Given recent events it is almost appropriate that we act to curb their influence, although I fear it will all come to nothing. Already I feel the harmonic imbalance beginning in the fault line beneath us. I feel the second density structure shifting. It will not be long now. There will be much rebuilding when this is done; we will be needed again, and the Anunnaki will require our assistance to rebuild as they desire. Or...' Misha turned to Mitch, again with the suggestion of cunning, 'not, as the case may be?'

Before Mitch could respond, she turned back to Mendoza.

'You wish to know where the Anunnaki who masquerades as Don Eissley keeps his possessions of power. One of my kind helped him build the cage; it will take one of my kind to open it. Are you willing to make that sacrifice Mendoza?'

'You know I am. You don't need to ask me again.'

'Very well. It is as it should be. Your companions should retreat to the pier. This is done rarely in a century, and it is not done lightly. But they may observe.'

Mitch, Saph, Heather and Vance didn't need telling twice; they immediately backed off one third down the pier.

'What did she mean *masquerades* as Don Eissley?' Mitch pondered aloud. 'Is there a *real* Don Eissley somewhere?'

'I doubt it,' Saph responded sharply. 'Just semantics. You get a lot of it in the metaphysical world.'

They watched from about twenty feet away as Mendoza sat

and adopted the yogic lotus position before Misha.

'Will it hurt?' Mendoza asked, so faintly they almost couldn't hear.

'Very much,' Misha smiled, and placed her hand several inches in the air above his head.

Instantly Mendoza screamed.

There was somehow static electricity in the air; Mitch's hair stood on end and the hair on his arms became prickly. He looked around; the others were the same. He reached out and touched the metal raining on the edge of the pier; there was a spark, and a sting.

Mendoza screamed again, longer and louder.

His clothes vaporized.

He was shaking, vibrating as they all had when Misha and her temple had arrived, but this time it was localized, only for Mendoza. Beneath his flesh there seemed to be seven points of light, burning fiercely down his spine and up to the top of his head, making the surface of his skin glow.

'His chakras,' Vance gaped. 'They're… going nova!'

'What?' Mitch demanded.

'Chakras, the seven points of ethereal energy that run from the brain and down the spine; they're the generators of all spiritual energy in the human body, they connect us with – oh my!'

Mendoza had begun to erupt. The lowest chakra seemed to explode and an awful, toxic smell reached them almost immediately as Mendoza appeared to excrete his lower intestines. He screamed again, agonized, but somehow maintained the lotus position.

Misha remained still, expressionless but for a small smile, her hand remaining extended above his head.

The second chakra exploded and Mendoza's lap seemed to catch fire; his genitals greatly expanded then exploded bloodily across both his belly and the beach, then the third chakra went off. Mendoza projectile vomited as his upper intestines and stomach were excreted, appearing to levitate off the ground momentarily.

A grid of light was appearing around Mendoza; two tetrahedrons had appeared, one upright and one inverted, that seemed to interlock about him. They had the same crystalline form as Misha's temple, the same rainbow reflection, but were not yet as vivid.

Mendoza screamed again as his heart exploded through his chest, exposing bloodied broken ribs and mangled lungs, and now they saw that there were structures of light piercing each chakra, like huge ninja throwing stars, spinning horizontally as each chakra core continued somehow to glow fiercely within the remains of his torso.

The two tetrahedrons began spinning, counter-rotating, glowing brightly.

Mendoza's next scream was cut short as his throat chakra ignited, exposing the ridges of his shoulder blades and the top of his spine. Mitch realized suddenly that his spine was somehow still intact, still holding structural integrity, as though the base was implanted in the sand like a spike, and keeping him upright. Perhaps it was; there was so much blood and guts he couldn't tell.

The next chakra blew out the back of Mendoza's head, then finally the top of his crown exploded in chunks of skull and gray matter.

Horrifically, Mendoza's face remained, his eyes and mouth wide open in a silent, tortured scream.

Now the tetrahedrons were spinning with incredible speed, the shapes blurring into each other and forming a shape like a spinning top; it looked strangely familiar to Mitch and he squinted to make out Mendoza, or what was left of him, inside. The core of the spinning tetrahedrons seemed to create some kind of centrifugal force; what remained of Mendoza's body began to shred and whip in chunks, sucked into the tetrahedral field.

'It's called a merkaba!' Vance gaped. 'It's a kind of vehicle advanced spiritual masters use; the two fields are the natural fields of the masculine and feminine… and when they spin… good gracious!'

The merkaba began to rise above the sand.

Misha withdrew her hand.

They could just see within it; bizarrely, almost comically, all that remained of Mendoza was his spine, and attached to the top of it via the few remaining threads, nerves and tendons, his eyeballs and jawbone. Then they too vanished.

The merkaba shone brightly, became pure white, and then disappeared in a small implosion.

No-one quite knew what to say.

'Is he dead?' Mitch asked.

Before Misha could answer, Mendoza, or something like Mendoza, reappeared.

'Mendoza?' Mitch enquired, calling shakily to him.

'Can you see him?' Vance asked.

'Yeah.'

At least, he thought he could. The being was in Mendoza's general shape; it was definitely his body type, and almost had his face. As Mitch watched, however, the shape seemed to shift into something more generic, more the archetypal silhouette of a man, albeit rendered in brilliant crystalline rainbow energy.

'Can't *you* see him?'

'No.'

'You must have spiked Mitch,' Saph suggested. 'I can't see him either.'

'Me neither,' Heather shrugged. 'Maybe it's time we did share the – '

'He's moving!' Mitch cried out.

The Mendoza form looked up to Misha.

'I'm forgetting…' Mendoza spoke.

'You are in archetypal form,' Misha told him. 'But you have the Mendoza program still; you must re-gather yourself.'

The Mendoza light-being nodded, and looked about him at the blood and human remains in the sand. He stretched out his hand and closed his eyes. A tiny, sandy dust devil funneled up to his open palm.

'What's that?' Heather whispered. 'Is that him doing that?'

'He's making it…' Mitch reported. 'It's coming up into his hand.'

'He still has *hands?*' Heather seemed perplexed.

'I think he's one of them now – a light-being or something.'

Bit by bit the ruined sections of Mendoza's body seemed to gather, then disintegrate and somehow become vacuumed up into the sand devil. Then, almost invisibly, globules of water began to spray up lightly from the sea behind them, as though levitated by an unseen force, or magnetically attracted to the funnel, and meld with the microscopic organic particles that had once been Mendoza's third density human form. The spray continued, heavier and darker, and Mitch now realized that it wasn't just seawater, but some other kind of liquid, perhaps even splices of the primal soup from which life on Earth had first been generated.

The flow from the ocean ceased. First the tips of Mendoza's fingers re-appeared as his genetic material reformed about the light-body, then his whole hand. His right arm reemerged, then his shoulder. The two chakras in his head, at his crown and then where his pineal gland had been, glowed as they began to accrue fleshy matter about them. Something brain-like was reconstructing within the bright rainbow outline of his head. At least, Mitch thought, it resembled a brain, but it was not as he remembered brains to appear. It was whiter, larger, wispier.

Gradually, at least to all outward appearances, Mendoza totally reformed, naked again. He withdrew his hand from before him and sighed heavily.

'By the Gods,' he grimaced. 'You didn't lie about it hurting!'

CHAPTER SIXTY-THREE

'You may go about the world,' Misha spoke with a serious tone. 'Until you are summoned. We will not obstruct your agenda, but do not deviate from the agreed path of momentum.'

Mendoza nodded. 'I agree.'

Misha nodded. 'Very well.' She turned to the others. 'I wish you well.'

Then she and the crystalline temple vanished.

Gone, in a millisecond, without so much as a flourish or a flash of white light, as though they had never been.

Mitch, Saph, Vance and Heather moved slowly down the pier toward Mendoza.

'Are you okay old chap?' Vance enquired nervously, stepping off and moving across what remained of Mendoza's sand symbols. 'I've heard of transmutation before, but I never… never thought it could be *forced*.'

Mendoza eyed them together, but could not stop staring down at the pieces of flesh bone and innards that still remained on the beach.

'Amazing,' he uttered.

'So you…' Heather started in a puzzled voice. 'You… ascended? She *ascended* you?'

Heather moved in closer and stared at the fresh bits and pieces of left-over human remains with Mendoza.

'I suppose I don't need as much now…' Mendoza murmured.

'So now…' Heather surmised, '…you're only – part human?'

'No…' Mendoza spoke quietly. 'I'm still human; just… human six point oh.'

Heather proceeded. 'So… just like the Reptilians and Sirians were once… third density beings, you're now a sixth density being? Like them?'

'Technically,' Mendoza nodded, gingerly feeling out his new body. 'But I'm still human, so… I have to remain here, where the human race currently belongs. And, technically, I should have passed through fifth level density before ascending to sixth. It wouldn't have been that painful, if I had, if I hadn't led such an… *occult* life. Nobody's ever…' He briefly examined his still stud-length penis, as though he'd forgotten what it was for. 'Nobody's ever been through this before. So, basically…' He glanced up at Heather, grinning. There was light in his eyes but edged by a degree of pain on his features. '…I don't know what I am!'

'But *why*?' Mitch asked.

'Don Eissley,' Mendoza answered, finally straightening his posture.

'Why him?'

Mendoza rolled his arms in their sockets. 'It's what he represents.'

'And what's that?' asked Saph.

'He's making the world into a shit hole. Him and his Reptilian clan of alchemic Anunnaki. The fucking Draco – the Draconians; they're the ones behind the chemical addictions in this world, the ones who promote misery so they can dispense anti-depressants like Pez, the ones who promote time as pressure so no-one eats decent food any more, the ones who promote the aspirational lifestyle so everyone's looking over their shoulder, stressed and competing, deadening their hearts; they're destroying the art of everyday life, everyday feeling, everyday contentment. Nobody can feel even melancholy or restlessness, even ordinary dissatisfaction any more, without it being branded a 'mental condition'. And they're the clan who shut me down. Like I explained, they live in the astral and they live by the occult; it's their science. And to be as powerful as they are, they need to possess some powerful totems; physical objects that anchor the power of the astral in the material, a grounding counterpart to their archetypal power, their astral temples. Don Eissley has just been given the golden key; he's got a movie studio that's going to make propaganda that will help narrow humanity's focus down to a keyhole. So that all they'll want are Oliver Hines' genetic makeovers; if I can bust open his treasure chest and break a few of his totems, then maybe that will make a difference. Maybe, I don't know for sure, but I've been working at this for three years, plus a lifetime of occult study. It's what I'm here to do, it's what I was born into this density to achieve. And now I have the backing of the Sirians and the power to go with it; Eissley's security system uses sacred geometry at the Sirian level. I can bust it open and take the fucker down.'

'So why do you need us?' Saph asked.

'That was the deal; I bring you to Misha. She wanted to see you for herself. It must be part of the plan because Suzie Saturn told me to go get you; I don't know what she's got planned but I'm betting that all these plans will come together somehow.'

'Listen,' Mitch growled. 'You talk about Suzie Saturn like you know her. I told you, I have to find her. Where is she?'

'I don't know. She came to me, back in the 'eighties. I read her, and she went.'

'Went where?'

'She became an exotic dancer. Although, to call her a stripper would be too crude; she was the best there was. I don't know why I remember her and no-one else does, but that's all I remember. Now she's in the astral, coming to people in dreams. More powerful than anyone I've ever met who wasn't famous; who isn't a household name.'

'But no-one remembers her other than for a fraction of a second after her name's mentioned.'

Heather shrugged. 'Amy said that all the people at the wake know her name.'

'But not who she is – or was. All I've got to go on is what Don Eissley said…' Mitch frowned deeply, thinking. 'I don't know why I didn't remember this before…'

'The astral's like that; you can't always bring what happens there back here. Like dreams; our brains won't store it, it's not the kind of reality third density beings can process properly.'

'Eissley said, I think, that they would make sure; that it wouldn't be long, and she would be completely wiped.'

'Completely?' Mendoza aired. 'I've never heard of anyone being *completely* wiped…'

'Why would they wipe a stripper?' asked Saph, puzzled. 'If she's as good as you said, surely that works for them? Surely that's part of this whole Hollywood system? The desire for the unattainable beauty? The dream?'

'Maybe,' Mendoza nodded. 'Who knows?'

'So where is this security system?' Mitch asked, suddenly irritated.

'It's in LA.'

'But LA's about to go under!'

'Eissley knows that. I got word yesterday that he'd be moving all his stuff; off to a new home in Beverly Hills. You can bet your bottom dollar that he's moving his totems to somewhere the quake won't damage them. Beverly Hills probably won't suffer a lot of damage. It'll be the plains and the city that take the brunt.'

'But why are the Rep – the Anunnaki going to let this happen?' Heather demanded. 'They built LA for a specific purpose; why are they going to let it just go under? It's more than a century of work for them!'

'The Draco don't give a shit about Hollywood any more. There are better ways of getting their message across now; new technology. A century is nothing to them. They're going to let it crumble, then build it again. Bigger and better – in 3-D; maybe even 4-D now – who knows?'

'But surely… all that money?'

'You know how much Hollywood actually makes?' Mendoza scoffed. 'Compared to almost every other major industry it's nothing; at least, nothing compared to the *attention* it gets, the *focus* we give it. People, rational materialists, scratch their heads and wonder why; why does it get so much focus in our culture?

These vapid celebrities and their meaningless vehicles. And the money that goes into movies; it's almost all lost. *Avatar* happens once a decade, if that! It's the *cultural control* they get from the investment, that's the real trick. It's the basis for everything else that springs from it; the evil of corporate marketing and the manipulation of dreams and desires. That's the only reason Hollywood, as such, exists.'

'Mitch,' Saph began earnestly, 'I'm not so sure this is a good idea. I'm sure Eissley deserves everything he gets, but this isn't our problem; not the big picture anyway. We have to get back to LA and help Everett.'

Mitch wasn't so sure. 'I think we need to get in touch with Everett and tell him to get the hell out – the last thing we should be doing is heading into an active fault line. And we need some way of warning the people – I mean, we have advanced notice of something that could potentially end the lives of millions! You heard Misha; she felt it. The first rumblings have already begun!'

Saph sighed. 'And I heard the *implication* of what she said; we all did. She was suggesting that there *was* some way of stopping it, if only we could figure it out – if only *you* could figure it out.'

'But Suzie Saturn sent Mendoza to us…' Mitch frowned, torn. 'Surely the Anunnaki could stop it if they wanted? Maybe we could speak with them somehow? Get them to release their astral energy…?'

Mendoza shook his head. 'Not even if they wanted; no-one anticipated that humanity would rediscover their lost DNA sequences. Like I said, they can't stop what we invent, they can only manipulate it. At least, if they did stop it, it would have to be… I don't know. The repercussions would be immense. No, we discovered something we can't handle, and they're getting out of the way while the planet recalibrates. That's what happens when you open Pandora's Box: all hell breaks loose, no matter who you are. Everyone has to deal with it. Sometimes it's better to cut your losses.'

Mendoza turned to Saph.

'Look, if we destroy Eissley's totems, at least a part of the Draco clan's control system will slip – I don't know how much but at least some people will get a warning; a precognition. That sort of thing slips through anyway, even with the Anunnaki hoarding all the astral energy. But we could save thousands more, who wouldn't otherwise get a warning, who wouldn't otherwise get out in time.'

Saph frowned. She seemed doubtful.

'Okay,' Mendoza nodded. 'How's this? Eissley was the one who told Hines about your boyfriend's operation down in Peru. Tried to get him to cooperate with Hines. When he didn't, Eissley had him taken out, stole his research and sold it to Hines. That's my theory. At least come for that – for revenge?'

Saph gulped.

'You can't stop an earthquake, sweetie; but if you want to make a difference, Eissley's at his most vulnerable. Believe me, if he's got custody of the Draco totems, and if we destroy them, we'll be striking right at the heart of the bastards who caused all this. Cut the power in their astral temples stone dead.'

'I don't know…'

Heather withdrew her phone and examined it. 'No coverage.' She turned to Mendoza. 'I need to warn my uncle. And we need to contact the news services, and… I don't know? The emergency services?'

'Indeed,' Vance shrugged. 'Who does one call when one has supernaturally-based advanced knowledge of a natural disaster?'

Heather nodded at Mendoza. 'You get me somewhere I can make calls, fast, and I'll help you.'

'Done.'

Mitch turned to Saph, looking for an answer.

Mendoza grinned. 'It's still four hours away yet, sweetie. We'll be done in an hour; plenty of time to make other plans.'

Saph nodded once, silently.

Mendoza turned to where the entrance to the temple had been and raised his hand. A white light appeared, the same long tunnel that had been there before.

'Hey,' Mendoza was impressed with himself. 'I can *do that*.' He clicked his fingers and was dressed again, back in the shirt and shorts that had been burned away in his forced ascension. 'And *that*!' He turned back to the others, grinning again. 'She left the stargate open. Now, my powers are essentially untested but my information says that you can navigate, and that you can hold the temporal feedback steady. That right?'

Vance and Saph both nodded.

'Okay. We only get one shot so you'd better make it work.'

CHAPTER SIXTY-FOUR

Mitch stepped out of the stargate to a spectacular view of the Los Angeles valley through a massive wall entirely made of glass. Around them, the giant slate-tiled living space was empty. Mitch walked across the floor as the others emerged behind him and surveyed their surrounds; there wasn't one piece of furniture on the whole of the open-planned floor. The kitchen and breakfast bar on the other side of the room was gleaming and spotless.

'It looks like he hasn't moved in yet,' Mitch aired worriedly. 'It looks like the house is still up for viewing.'

Behind them, at each corner of the massive room, were two doors separated by a large but tight spiral staircase that dissected the floor and led both up and down.

Vance echoed their collective thoughts.

'Have we come backward in time?'

'No,' Mendoza responded. 'Not at your level. Third density reverse time travel is incredibly problematic and complicated; even for the higher realms. We're on track. Mendoza moved his totems in either last night or this morning. He'll leave the house empty for another week or so, just to let them settle. He and his clan are probably halfway out to the Mojave Desert by now. Plus, if this place is going to shake up a bit, why have all your stuff unpacked?'

'So where's this vault?' Heather demanded as she removed her phone again. 'Coverage!'

'Downstairs,' Mendoza nodded at the spiral stairs. 'Then down again.'

He gave them all an adventurous glance and walked toward the spiral staircase.

'Uncle Bo – thank God!' Heather clutched the phone to the

side of her face. 'You're *where?*'

The next floor down was empty. It was a long rectangular room with a low ceiling set deep into the hill, with a sunken garden at the other end, behind another massive window through which sunlight poured in from above. There was an empty bar in the wall and Mitch could see the dents in the middle of the carpet where the previous owner's pool table had sat. He suspected that the door at the other end would lead through to a spa.

Above, he could hear Heather talking frantically on her phone.

They descended the spiral staircase again; below the empty games room was a huge eight-car garage, its wide doors all closed.

'This is it,' Mendoza stated, as Heather descended behind the others.

'Where now?' Saph asked.

Mendoza grinned. 'It's hidden. But it's here.'

Mitch turned to Heather. 'News?'

'Uncle Bo knows where we are; he's sending someone. Apparently things are pretty bad. Oliver's security force is fighting with The Pan. About ten minutes ago they stopped using tranqs. Three casualties so far, and the LAPD are getting involved.'

'Jesus,' Mitch guffawed in horror. 'My daughter's in that!'

'Uncle Bo said everyone's okay; I think he meant of the people we know. Obviously, not everyone's okay if Olivera are firing real bullets.'

Mitch stared at her aghast.

'He's getting everyone out Mitch,' Heather offered sympathetically. 'It's a dead end. There's no way Uncle Bo can get the formula processed quickly enough; he had some deal with an independent chemical processor in the valley who makes organic supplements. He was going to synthesize the six components, then they were going to grass-roots market the end product. But we lost those three months; when Uncle Bo got there they ran into Draco. The whole organic operation was shut down ten weeks ago. I guess Mendoza's right, they seem to have a hand in controlling every aspect of the chemical industry – New Agers notwithstanding. But even if Uncle Bo could get the formula synthesized and mass produced in such a short time, there's no way to distribute it. I don't know what he was thinking, how he could achieve this…'

'He didn't think he'd have to act so quickly,' Mitch shrugged. 'But I suppose he had to try.'

'He's going to cut his losses and get out I think; I called emergency services but no-one would take me seriously. Uncle Bo's going to try, but…' She looked across at Mendoza. 'Looks like Mendoza was right; this totem deal might be our only chance at genuinely helping anyone.'

Vance had taken a few steps into the empty garage and was looking around thoughtfully, seeming to focus upon several apparently random, empty spaces.

'I can sense them. Yes, they're here alright. Mitch dear boy, can you see them?'

Mitch focused his attention on the empty spaces and immediately realized what Vance meant.

'Apparently I don't need to spike any more…' Mitch realized. 'Suzie hinted that something like this might happen.'

'This is ridiculous!' Saph suddenly turned away from them and put her bag on the spiral steps, then started searching through. 'I can't find that phone – we need to start warning people.' Rummaging frantically around, bent over with her back to them, she suddenly resembled some mad old bag lady.

Mitch ignored her, fascinated with the multi-dimensional security system before him. 'I can see… at least seven dimensional rifts. Doorways. I see what he's done; he's used sacred geometry to create a… I don't know. Trap?'

Mendoza was examining them also. 'As good a word as any. If you came here just using ordinary third density occult practices, you might see one or two of them… you might even see them all, but you wouldn't necessarily know which door to take; or where they lead. You'd have to take a chance.'

'Where do they lead?' Heather asked.

'That one drops you a mile out to sea; this one puts you in the middle of a downtown intersection. This one…' Mendoza turned to his companions and smiled. 'You'll like this one; it'll take you home. To the top of Uluru. The others are all dead ends as well – that one seems to lead to the surface of the moon, and that one to a Swiss bank vault.'

'But which one is the real one?' Vance enquired. 'Or, are none of them the real one?'

'The real *one*,' Mendoza grinned. 'Precisely.'

Mendoza outstretched his hand and concentrated. As Mitch watched, the seven different dimensional rifts began to stretch together. As Mendoza closed his hand, the rifts mirrored the movement; pulling together into one larger rift that was like the center of a seven-sided spider's web.

'There – seven into one. Now…' Mendoza focused. 'Any more surprises?'

They waited.

'No,' he decided, stepping forward.

'And now we shall see.'

CHAPTER SIXTY-FIVE

Mendoza stepped through and was gone.

They waited, staring at the space another few seconds, then he reappeared.

'Are you turkeys coming or not? It's totally cool; there might be other traps when it's fully set up, but he figures he's safe for now, that no-one has the knowledge. Not Sirian knowledge. Come through. It's just a room.'

Mitch held his breath. 'Nothing ventured,' he shrugged.

Mitch stepped through and came out into the middle of a high rectangular room, perhaps two hundred meters by fifty, with no apparent exits. Mendoza followed him back. The walls, floors and ceiling seemed to be made of glass though nothing but a black void could be seen beyond them. Scattered throughout the room was a collection of boxes, widely varied in shape and dimension, perhaps fifty or sixty in all.

Mitch walked over to one of the few items that was not boxed; a purple-hued, head-and-shoulders painted portrait of Eissley himself, sporting his Annunaki game-face, staring out of the frame with an expression that was at once smug and sinister.

'We've come to the right place. That's Eissley.'

'We're somewhere in third density solid space,' Mendoza muttered. He went forward to the glass, pressed his hands up and stared out. 'I think it's desert out there. They love it out here, the Draco. We're probably in the middle of the Mojave somewhere. It's one of the places where the astral world meets the material world naturally. Like a Venn Diagram.'

'One of the places?'

'Wherever people are the least; way out on the ocean, deep in unspoiled forests... the moon.'

Vance and Heather came through in quick succession. Heather whistled.

'So what do we do?' she asked. 'Just open the boxes and smash whatever's in them?'

'Pretty much,' Mendoza shrugged. 'But once we start, it'll raise the alarm, so we'll only have time to do a few. Better check it out – see what looks most important.'

'Raise the alarm?' Vance asked. 'How do we get out then?'

'I can hold them off while you break the glass; then we run through the desert until we find a natural rift. They're all through the Mojave; probably one right outside.'

'They'll hunt us down, surely?'

'Aren't they already?'

'I don't know,' Vance shuddered. 'Are they?'

Mendoza walked up to a series of large black rectangular boxes that stood eight feet tall and looked like sarcophagi. They were stored in a long row, like dominos, down the middle of one side of the room. Mitch followed; he guessed there must have been thirty of them.

'I said I'd show you what it was all about; what this world is all about. That there would be a lot here for you. That was just an educated guess, a hope. That when I got here, I would be able to confirm my suspicions.'

Heather called out from behind them. She had opened a large black chest.

'I think these are the crown jewels of England!' She stared across at Mendoza. 'We can't destroy them – can we?'

'What does it matter?' Mendoza shrugged.

'Not the Crown Jewels! They're priceless!'

'They're symbols. And how do we know they're not fakes? Can you tell?'

'I suppose…' Heather mused doubtfully, rolling the crown itself about in her hands. Then she looked around. 'Where's Saph?'

Vance had wandered over to join Mitch and Mendoza.

'There was always the rumor,' Vance aired, 'that the Anunnaki

could shape shift; Mitch claims he's seen it for himself. But…
these are coffins, are they not? I can't help thinking, intuitively,
that the two might be connected?'

Mitch was suddenly spooked.

'Shall we see?' Mendoza asked.

He ran his hands over the side of the first box, looking for an
opening. There didn't seem to be one. Mitch went to the second
and did the same. The surfaces seemed uniformly smooth. He
shrugged and turned to Vance.

'What do you think these contain? Intuitively?'

Vance hummed. 'The most paranoid and outlandish claim
is that the world's most influential families; political royalty,
Hollywood royalty, European royalty…' Vance tuned and looked
oddly at Heather, who was still examining the box filled with what
certainly very strongly resembled the crown jewels of England.
'…are actually Anunnaki in disguise. That those families, and
their bloodlines, their genetic lineage, are actually interbred with
the corresponding Anunnaki clans. But it got me to wonder; as
above, so below. These other-dimensional beings keep saying
that. What if they are not one or the other, strictly speaking, but
somehow interlinked? If the Anunnaki can somehow… shall we
say, possess these people? These families? When they need to? If
the families and bloodlines are reflections of each other, in the
astral and material?'

Mendoza was paying attention. 'Go on.'

'Well, it just struck me when I saw these coffins; these
sarcophagi. The Sirians seemed linked to the Egyptians
somehow; and the Egyptians created or at least perfected the
sarcophagus, correct? Embalming their dead, as though to be
stored, and resurrected at some later date in the afterlife… in the
astral perhaps?'

Heather dropped the crown back in the box and came to join
them.

'You're spooking me, Magician,' she uttered.

'I'm spooking myself.'

'I think I know what you mean,' Mitch mumbled. 'When Misha arrived, I mean… we all must have felt it, realized. How some of the superstitions of today, echoed back thousands of years, started with the Sirians. You're saying, when the Sirians left, for whatever reason, the Egyptians kept emulating aspects of their technology, ritualizing it until it became religion. Storing their dead in boxes… in the full belief that they would one day be revived…?'

They all stared at the line of black coffins.

'Who the hell are we going to find inside these things?' Mitch uttered.

'Who?' Heather asked. 'I still don't…?'

'What your Magician is suggesting,' Mendoza surmised, 'is that the Anunnaki can shape shift to become whoever they like, so long as the original is stored somewhere. Held in stasis.'

'So inside these coffins… are all the people the Anunnaki control? Or, impersonate?'

'Maybe.' Mitch spoke grimly. 'All the people the Draco Clan control and impersonate, anyway. Presumably there are other Anunnaki clans who control different people?'

'That's right. There are at least one hundred clans present on Earth today, but only about thirteen that have major influence. The Draco and two others; the Gali and the Kova, pretty much have everything divided between them. They're the equivalent of the big three mafia families, or the big three power blocks, like Europe, China and the US. But if the Magician here is right, all thirteen of the upper echelon clans must have a store of sarcophagi like these…'

'So who would be inside them?' Mitch pondered. 'Misha said that the Draco we know as Eissley is masquerading. There was something in the way she said it. What if… in one of these, there's the real Don Eissley?'

They heard a crack from the end of the row.

Everybody froze, exchanging glances of trepidation.

They were all thinking the same thing; was there someone else in here with them?

Slowly Mitch turned and looked down the line. 'Saph?'

There was no response; however, three from the end, the lid of one of the black sarcophagi had opened. It was just a crack, but it looked as though the sarcophagi opened from the left, and that a bright blue light was flooding out from a slight opening all the way down the left side.

'Holy…' Mitch muttered.

The others walked around to see, then as one they approached, down the row to the blue light.

Mitch reached it first and slowly stretched out his hand to touch the surface. It was cold, cold as the others had been. The light from within emanated no warmth. He pulled the door further open; the blue light flooded the room.

Within, floating naked in what looked like a vast sea of crystal blue, was Don Eissley.

CHAPTER SIXTY-SIX

Mitch pushed the door fully open and they stared at the bizarre figure.

Eissley's body was ghostly; glowing from within with a pale grayish light. Edged about his form was a glistening silver aura that seemed to highlight the lines of his face, the tips of his hair and fingernails, the tone of his muscles and flesh, and the general terrain of his skin. He floated like an astronaut in space, his hair, hands and feet waving softly, his head bobbing and rotating slightly on his neck, clearly suspended either in zero-gravity or some kind of liquid; it was difficult to tell. His vision was perhaps active, but he seemed not to be aware of where he was; it was as though he were dreaming with his eyes open.

'He's in astral space, isn't he?' Vance asked softly. 'It's some kind of astral tank, isn't it?'

'It's not him. Not exactly, not entirely. That's his astral body…' Mendoza confirmed. 'Amazing. The dimensional engineering. My mind is new to the Sirian science; I suppose it's like anything. You might be a born engineer but you still need to study the texts. His astral body is somehow… suspended in a part of astral space… contained in this tank. At least, I think that's what we're looking at.'

As they watched, Eissley closed his eyes, folded his arms across his chest, then closed his legs together.

'Like an Egyptian mummy…' Heather uttered. 'He must have woken when the lid cracked.'

'It's like a TARDIS,' Mitch murmured. 'Bigger on the inside.'

From their perspective, Eissley was floating a good ten feet away.

'How they managed to get... astral fluid? And store it in a tank like this...?' It's astounding...' Mendoza touched the surface. 'Glass.' He shook his head, perplexed. 'So much more to learn... the geometry involved, holding the astral and material, the fourth and third, with sixth density physics... it boggles the mind.'

'I'll tell you what else does,' Heather uttered. 'The notion of whoever else we might find in these things. This one opened when Mitch spoke his name, when he said Don Eissley.'

As though to confirm the theory the lid on Eissley's astral sarcophagus swung back automatically and closed with a short hiss, almost a sigh. The room suddenly seemed a lot darker.

'Do we really want to know?' Mitch asked grimly.

'If we're going to destroy these things,' Heather frowned, 'we should probably know who's in them.'

'I wonder what they weigh?' Vance wondered aloud, and pressed his hand against the side of Eissley's tomb. Surprisingly, the sarcophagus shifted gently to its side, balanced on its corner, then returned softly to the ground.

Vance was amazed. 'It's like pushing a blow-up punching bag... weighted at the base but light as air.' He turned to Mendoza. 'Can we move these back, through the rift?'

Mendoza shrugged. 'We can try. I don't see why not...?'

'Then we should. Once they're clear we can cast some kind of spell in here; something that will react with the atmosphere and blow this chamber to oblivion – do you see?'

Mendoza grinned. 'I like your thinking. Who the hell are you really?'

Vance smiled. 'I'm the Magician. Who else?'

Heather was still pondering the line. 'We could stand here and read out names from headlines I suppose?'

'Coming to that,' Mitch shrugged, 'we could read the phone book. I mean, who knows who they have, or why? It doesn't all have to be politicians and celebrities; there could be scientists, writers, military, anyone from media darlings to your local accountant!'

'And my guess,' Vance put a hand on his white-bearded chin, 'given that my intuition seems to be correct, is that the people in these astral cages are interchangeable. When they've finished with one, they return the astral body, which presumably returns control of the physical body to the person in question, and use the empty tank for someone else. It would explain some of the irrational behavior we sometimes see from people in the headlines… of course I'm not suggesting that celebrities aren't capable of outlandish and appalling behavior all on their own, but it's a theory, do you see?'

'I suppose,' Mendoza nodded. 'They could theoretically use drug binges, or alcohol blackouts to explain radical shifts in behavior and personality… even born again conversions?'

'Indeed.'

Heather remained glued to the line of sarcophagi.

'I mean,' she whispered, 'There could be anyone in there. Anyone!'

Mitch suddenly blurted. 'Heather Everett!'

Heather froze. Nothing happened.

'Oh man,' she gasped. 'What of one of them had opened? I mean, maybe the fakes don't know they're fakes? Like – MK-Ultra sleepers?' She turned to Mitch. 'That was a shitty thing to do!'

Mitch grinned.

'Mitchell Edge!' Heather pronounced.

Mitch kept grinning, and turned to the others. 'Vance McLeod! Todd Mendoza!'

Nothing.

'She's right, Mitchell,' Vance scowled. 'That is not a nice feeling.'

Mendoza growled. 'Bo Everett.'

Nothing. Heather stepped forward and punched him on the arm. Then she turned to the sarcophagi.

'Oliver Hines.'

'Derek Nurding,' Mitch enquired, somewhat doubtfully.

'Ermm…' Vance pondered. 'Bill Clinton. George Bush. Barack Obama!'

Nothing, nothing, nothing.

Vance continued. 'Hilary Clinton! Sarah Palin! Oh, I know… *Dick Cheney.*'

Still nothing.

'Oh, come - on,' Vance moaned. '*Richard* Cheney.'

Nothing.

'Hmm,' Vance pondered. 'Doesn't mean they're not kept by some *other* clan though, does it?'

Mendoza chuckled. 'Now you're thinking like they want you to think; keep going along that line and you'll be a full-blown David Icke paranoid within three days.' He scanned the sarcophagi again. 'Not that I can blame him…'

Heather stepped forward and pushed one of the closed sarcophagi.

'Cricket Wilde,' she said softly.

It shifted and bobbed back up, still.

Mendoza shrugged. 'Most of the people you've named are too entrenched in the Orion dimensions to bother much with the Anunnaki. The Reps prefer to influence people on a gut emotion level.' He looked up and down the sarcophagi again. 'Britney Spears. Lindsey Lohan. Lady Gaga.'

All nothing.

'Mel Gibson. Charlie Sheen.'

Mendoza shrugged again. 'We really could be here all fricking day, and we don't have the time. The Mage and I have to rig an explosion – and you two need to start getting these things back into the garage. What we do with them then, God only knows.'

Mitch looked around. 'Where *is* Saph?'

'She was looking for that phone,' Heather reminded them. 'She's probably called half the news networks by now and telling them to evacuate Los Angeles.'

'Should she be using that phone?' Vance asked. 'If Hines had somehow patched into Everett's satellite system it might give away our location!'

'We're going to do a damn fine job of that ourselves very shortly,' Mendoza growled. He turned back to the middle of the room, to where the dimensional rift had opened. 'Yeah… where is she?'

The thought seemed to dawn on them all simultaneously, but Mendoza was the first to speak.

'Saph…?'

'Sapphire,' Mitch said. 'Sapphire Edge.'

There was a crack, and from somewhere near the top of the line, blue light flooded the room.

CHAPTER SIXTY-SEVEN

'You're all very clever aren't you?'

They spun about.

Behind them, holding a pistol in each hand, stood a female Anunnaki, dressed in the black suit Saph had been dressed in all this time, smiling smugly.

It was odd to see a reptilian humanoid smile, and know that the expression was smug. But the emotion could not be misread.

Mitch focused on her features; they were not like Eissley's had been, when he had changed. This Anunnaki had smaller eyes, and a less pronounced snout; her scales were more lime-tinted than olive, and less thick, and there were brighter lime-green scales on the crest of her scalp, giving her the impression of a punk Mohawk hairstyle.

Was she a female Draco, or one of another clan entirely?

'Very, very, clever Hominids.'

Mitch gently broke from the group and began walking to the top of the line, toward the blue glow. The Anunnaki female followed Mitch with one pistol, then waved the second at the others, indicating that they should follow. They obeyed.

'Don't try anything, Mendoza. You're not impervious to bullets; not even after your fancy transformation. At least, not to the amount of bullets I'll put into you.'

'I wasn't going to,' Mendoza growled. 'Why would I run? You have answers, Draco.'

She laughed, as though this were absurd.

Five sarcophagi down from the top of the row stood another that had cracked partially open. Mitch didn't hesitate when he reached it, and swung it wide open.

For the second time in as many days, he was seeing the

woman who had, at least once, not long ago, been the woman of his dreams, his ultimate if unattainable desire, naked in circumstances that were repulsive to him.

Saph's astral body floated just as Eissley's had, with the same half-dreamy expression of bewilderment. Slowly, and to Mitch's relief, she repeated the same gestures, closing her legs, folding her arms to cover her breasts, and went back to sleep. Mitch closed the lid again and turned to the others as they approached with the female Anunnaki.

'It's her,' Mitch confirmed.

There was an audible sigh of great disappointment from Heather.

'No…' she whispered.

'How?' Vance asked, visibly shaking. 'When?'

Mitch turned back to the Anunnaki. 'Are you going to tell us?'

'She hasn't killed us yet,' Mendoza uttered. 'Of course she's going to tell us. How long was she with you?'

'With me?' Mitch stared into the cold, emerald green eyes. 'Since the start of all this.'

The Anunnaki smiled. 'It's not what you think it is.' She took a few steps back and seemed to relax ever so slightly. 'I'm not sure what to do right now; I'm really not. I have a brief, of course, a mission statement. But it never anticipated that you'd get this far. Not really. I'm supposed to kill you all, of course, should my cover be blown, but those orders were given within certain boundaries, within a certain context. And we've all been through so much together. I've even come to like you!'

She seemed to find all this terribly amusing.

'I'm just – torn!'

They all just stared at her. The shock was just settling in.

'Now, Mendoza's clearly wondering just how many bullets his new physiognomy can sustain; and whether he can maintain integrity without at least a partial third density body. Well, let's not put that to the test shall we, Sorcerer? You others are wondering whether you could rush me; that only works in the movies, and not even in them most of the time. So how about I tell you…'

Her eyes narrowed.

'…my name's Xylata by the way, with an 'X' in your alphabet, how about I tell you… how about I tell you the truth? Then we shall see what we can do from here?'

CHAPTER SIXTY-EIGHT

'Take a seat,' Xylata waved her guns toward some boxes. 'All of you. Stay close together, get comfortable, and listen. Your lives and the lives of millions depend on you comprehending what I have to say. Light one of your cigarettes if you like Mitch, I know how much you like them, how you depend on them.'

Mitch, Heather, Vance and Mendoza sat on the chest-like boxes in the section where Heather had discovered the crown jewels. Mitch lit a cigarette and offered Heather one. She accepted. Vance and Mendoza declined.

'There will be some kind of security device on the starcophagi; that's what we call them by the way, in your tongue; star-cophagi. Interesting that the original word was derived from the Greek for 'flesh eaters'. Something to do with limestone. They couldn't have gotten it more wrong of course, but the truth has a way of worming through language; sar, star, astral; language is born from the unconscious you see. It's all over the place, common as the symbols we use to manipulate you. We use language to do that also, of course. Synchronicities even surface in totally different languages, with different root origins; many words end up similar. Sometimes, anyway. Sometimes not. No system is perfect, and all systems decay. And, as Mendoza knows, words and pictures, sound and light at certain frequencies, combined with music and the hypnotic state that rapid editing induces, well; hooray for Hollywood! So anyway, where was I?'

'Security alarms when we opened the starcophagi,' Mitch uttered dryly, exhaling smoke with a dark look in his eyes.

'So we have perhaps only a few minutes before someone – possibly Eissley himself, arrives. He knows that I have you, at least he will assume that. Technically, my mission is over. All I have to do is hand you over, or hand your bodies over. He's probably in the garage now, wondering why his seven-pointed lock won't open; I made a few adjustments but nothing he won't be able to figure out in time. I have a little Sirian knowledge myself, but he will assume Mendoza has done it.'

'Done what?' Mendoza asked.

'I have recalibrated the one exit so it loops back to the garage. It might take him five minutes to reverse it, it might take him twenty; he relies on his Sirian allies, and has little geometric knowledge of his own. They may not come immediately when he calls. If Misha has decided to use her influence, they may not decide to help him at all. But anyway, I will stop rambling, and get on with what I have to tell you.'

'It's not what you think it is, you said,' Mendoza offered, clearly keenly interested. 'What is it then?'

Xylata nodded. 'The starcophagi technology is useful, if unpredictable. Originally it was designed as a kind of prison, or punishment for criminal Anunnaki. To humans it's like sleeping, but to us it's like being in a coma we can't wake from, a living nightmare. But there is an interesting side-effect to the starcophagi. You see, we discovered that when we remove the human astral body, and inhabit the material body with our own astral body, which for us is our *primary* body, something very interesting happens. When we infiltrate other races, on other third density worlds, we of course control the body as though it were our own. But with the human body, even with the astral body removed and in stasis, the original personality remains essentially dominant. The effect is such that we can only take a back seat, so to speak, and leave the humans we inhabit on auto-pilot; we can only emerge to take control in small bursts, when something needs doing. At crucial points, when someone is in indecision and we need them to say no, rather than yes. To throw a punch rather than hold back; those minute fractions where fate hangs in the balance; it's there we can change things.'

'What did you change in Saph?' Mitch asked. 'Did you make her have sex with Harding?'

Heather groaned and slumped. 'God damn it, Mitch.'

'Of course not!' Xylata seemed offended. 'Well, I can't say I stopped her, put it that way. He is a hulking lump of Hominid hotness after all.'

'Ewwww,' Heather cringed.

'Yes, unfortunately our sexual attraction for you is not reciprocated.' Xylata shrugged. 'Oh well.'

'You're disgusting,' Heather moaned.

'Back to the story I think. So even when the astral body is absent, the main personality remains. I say "main personality" but the main drawback is that the whole personality does not. Removing the astral body changes a person in ways we hadn't anticipated. What tends to happen is the person loses interest in their spiritual life, as such. They lose their impulse toward creativity, their imagination, their drive for learning and progression. It's as though their curiosity simply melts away.'

'Those things are all astral traits!' Vance declared. 'What did you expect! What you've done to these people is monstrous!'

Xylata made a face, spread her arms and shrugged. 'It's a necessary evil, from your point of view.'

'From our point of view?' Vance spat. 'What is it, from your point of view?'

'Simply necessary,' Xylata smiled.

'For *what?*'

'To maintain control – what else? Why else would we do this?'

Vance shook his head in disgust, remaining silent.

'The point being, for most of the past three years, Sapphire was herself. At least, she was a large part of herself.'

'Three years?' Mitch exploded.

'Yes. Unfortunately, our intentions rather backfired. The idea was to monitor and influence her boyfriend Pan. But removing her astral body made her lose interest in what it was Pan had to offer; she became more mundane, more interested in "interior design" and raising money to own a home. Not that there is anything intrinsically wrong with these things; they are natural, and we have emphasized that in our control over you. It's just that, for someone as unique as Sapphire, it is perhaps the minimum one would expect.'

'What are you talking about?' Mitch demanded. 'It's all you want from us, the minimum!'

Xylata smiled and shook her head.

'How little you understand. Anyway, not long after we removed her astral body and I began my infiltration operation, she and Pan broke up, and she returned from Peru to Australia. I tried to get her back on track by returning her astral body occasionally, but the truth of the matter was that Sapphire had had enough of her old life anyway; our actions only served as the impetus for her decision. Sapphire wanted Pan to return from Peru. She didn't trust Bo Everett. She wanted them to continue their work but she also wanted to start a family, to raise children. But Pan did not. At least, he saw nothing wrong with starting a family in the jungles of Peru.'

'How do we know this is the truth?' Mitch demanded.

'Hear me out and I'll prove it to you.'

Mitch grumbled but went silent.

'The couple could not see eye to eye on this and it drove a wedge between them that lasted until the day Pan was shot. But, long before that, Sapphire was no longer useful to us. I returned her astral body, and ended my mission – or so I thought – but unfortunately this had catastrophic results for Sapphire. Because of the metaphysical experiences and training she and Pan had undergone, Sapphire had become somewhat sensitive to my comings and goings; even more so when I returned her astral body for what I thought would be the final time, and she came to reflect upon her recent actions. She remembered everything with startling clarity; more than any human agent before her. She became unbalanced, and began claiming to her friends within Pan's circle that she had been possessed by an Anunnaki, that she was no longer in control of her own life. She blamed Pan, and Pan's influence, and ceased communicating with the one person who – perhaps – could have helped her. Instead, she turned to her family. Unfortunately this was not long after her father had died, and bequeathed Sapphire the family home; equally unfortunately, the timing was such that Sapphire walked directly into a karmic situation which was due to play out in her life at this time – that's what families are for, after all.'

'Are they really?' Mitch asked bitterly.

'How can you doubt that Mitch? After all you've been through? Anyway, Sapphire's two sisters never got along with her; there was a large age gap between them and her, and they resented the fact that Sapphire had the advantage of a university education. By the time the two younger sisters arrived in quick succession, Sapphire's parents had lost money in a stock market crash and could not afford to support them through university. Their resentment at this over the years became such that a substantial rift opened between the sisters and parents; the parents decided the two younger daughters were ungrateful, and left the house to Sapphire, exclusively. The mother died, then the father died soon after, as is sometimes the way when two people long in love rely heavily upon each other as a reason for existence; the father's sudden death was Sapphire's reason for her ultimate return from Peru. Pan accompanied her of course, but after the funeral Pan returned to Peru, and Sapphire did not.'

'This matches up,' Heather shrugged with a sigh. 'It's all in the profiles I prepared for Uncle Bo.'

'She could have read them,' Mitch countered.

'Stop bickering,' Xylata snapped. 'Listen. Despite being bequeathed the entire estate, Sapphire always intended to sell her parents' house and split the profits three ways with her sisters, but never got around to it. When she began to claim that she was possessed, and that she no longer had control of her own life, she began to turn to many different sources to find someone who could confirm this to her, or in the event that did not occur, prove to her that she was mentally unbalanced. Unfortunately, as happens in these cases, the paranormal community had no way of dealing with her; although she sought specialist psychiatrists, and while some of them could confirm the story, at least through the gathered anecdotal proof of my race's existence here on Earth, there was nothing they could do to help her.'

'Where were you while she was going through all this hell?' Mitch demanded. 'Why didn't you bloody help her? Appear to her, explain!'

'Wait, Mitchell Pyne.'

There was an irritation in Xylata's tone, accompanied by an expression of hurt that stopped Mitch's anger in its tracks.

'One of the people she turned to,' Xylata held Mitch's gaze a while, 'was the touring professor, professional debunker and media darling Derek Nurding. She accosted him in an extremely unbalanced state, brought on by frustration and fatigue, and begged to tell her story, pleading with him to explain it away for her, to debunk it, *to tell her she was crazy and help her find treatment.*'

The group was quiet.

'Nurding referred her to a decent psychiatrist, but she never attended any sessions. Instead, she confided in her sisters. Really just to make sure they would not stigmatize her for seeking professional help. In short, she was turning to her sisters for support. They supplied the opposite. They played along for a while, but they had a good lawyer who built a strong case that Sapphire was no longer in control of her mental faculties. Poor Sapphire, she had gone about, so very frustrated, telling people as much; shouting it from the rooftops! The sisters had Derek Nurding subpoenaed, and on his word, given what Sapphire had told him, they were able to capitalize on her claims and have her committed. All for one sixth more profit each of a suburban house; a good one, I will admit. In a decent area. We passed it Mitch, that day you saw the orbs. Sapphire was very uncomfortable.'

'I remember; she mentioned something.'

'But essentially they each had their sister committed for the princely sum of one hundred thousand dollars each.'

Mitch felt like crying. 'Everyone has their price,' he spoke. 'Isn't that what your uncle always says?'

'Obviously,' Heather responded bitterly, 'it's true.'

'So where *were you* while all this was going on?' Vance demanded. 'This was you fault!'

'We're not emotionless, as some would have you believe,' Xylata scowled. 'Far from it. We control your race, but we do not despise you. Well, some do. Perhaps the best analogy within your race is that of master and slave; it is a pattern we have recurred throughout your recent history that is very effective. Many of us feel... *sympathy* toward you. Your enslavement is essential to our economy, to the efficient running of this world, but it is not created out of spite. It's simply that if it ended, we would suffer loss. And that is not our way; our culture, in this advanced form, has survived fifty thousand years.'

'Fifty thousand?' Mendoza whistled. 'That's impressive.'

'We began as you did, out of the primordial ooze, we just began sooner. It is the way of the cosmos – you know that now; your connection with the Sirians gives you access to science ten times more advanced than ours. To humans it appears as magic; to us, it is magic also.'

'But what about Saph?' Mitch urged. 'Why have you taken her over again?'

'I have not 'taken her over' Mitchell. I have never until now fully manifested and it is taking an immense amount of energy to do so, so that I can explain myself to you. I am drawing upon astral reserves from natural rifts in the desert outside to do this. If you take a look through the glass you will see a sandstorm severe enough to cut flesh; it is virtually forbidden to do such a thing within the bounds of human habitation, such is the violence of the clash of dimensional energies it requires.'

'Are you going to release her?'

'Let me finish; we do not have much time. I had sympathy

for Sapphire; I went to my clan fathers and requested that we intervene. I told them that her pain was pointless, and that, most pragmatically, she would potentially be more use to us in the future, but no use to us with either her psyche, or her credibility damaged. They agreed.'

'So what happened?' Mitch asked.

'Let me guess,' Mendoza offered dryly. 'Don Eissley.'

Again, the starcophagi cracked open, and blue light flooded the room.

'Yes,' Xylata scowled, her skin now a beautiful shade of turquoise in the bright blue light. 'Don Eissley.'

The starcophagi silently closed again.

'His Anunnaki name is Kyvza. He made a counter plea; he said that this was not the way of the Draco, to display sympathy. He said that leaving Sapphire committed, insane, would serve a dual purpose; it would inspire fear in those who believed her, and prevent them from seeking us out. And it would provoke derision in those who did not believe her, creating an aura of danger, of the occult, around stories of the Reptilians, the Reptoids, whatever alternate names you give to the Anunnaki; that anyone who dared speak as though they were true would be considered insane, even dangerous, as was the path to exploring such lunacy. For my insolence, for my weakness, for my crimes… I was placed in a starcophagi, in a nightmare coma, for two years.'

She paused as though recalling the horror.

'My sentence was longer; one hundred years, by which time I would have been totally insane. As it was, one of the primaries of my clan bloodline bargained for my release; I had taken on the body of Sapphire before. Sapphire was now re-emerging into the metaphysical community at a time of upheaval, with the death of her beloved Pan. They did not know what Pan had discovered; they needed a way in.'

'Why not just possess Bo Everett?' Mitch asked. 'Or Pan himself? Why Saph?'

'Because men like Pan, and particularly men like Bo Everett, cannot be controlled. It is immensely difficult to separate their astral bodies from the material, and even then, virtually impossible to influence them. There are powerful families in this world we can control, dominant families, with dominant personalities, but that is because we have influenced them for generations; even interbred at times. But men, self-made men like Everett, the universe creates them spontaneously; not even we can predict where or how they will appear. We infiltrate their dreams; the dreams are gone when they wake. We send them people we control; their advice is ignored. We even attempt assassination; they survive. From your perspective it may seem that we control much; from ours, we control very little, just as you humans intrinsically control very little of your own world and fates. Higher forces, fate itself it sometimes seems, still intervenes. Races from the higher dimensions, even lower dimensions intervene, the universe itself has other plans; the Pleiadeans, the Sirians, the Orions, even the Elohim, and all will tell you the same. Free will exists; and there is still the Source, from where all of this emerges. It is conscious; beyond what we could conceive mentally as such. Savants like Holland Pankhurst, men like Bo Everett, geniuses like Oliver Hines; they cannot be infiltrated.'

Heather was smiling; not exactly happy as such, but perhaps with pride.

'So when did you begin "infiltrating" Saph again?' Mitch asked.

'When Pan was shot. When it became apparent that she would have to re-enter the world of Pan's People; those who believed her insane. That is why she believed she would be unwelcome. She believed she had disgraced them…'

'And so…' Mitch grappled with the story, 'where did you influence her?'

'Only a few times. I contacted Oliver Hines, gave him the number of the mobile Everett gave you. I suggested he bring Nurding in.'

'Why?'

'My mission was to see how far you could go; to observe, give you free reign, and let you run. But I could see you weren't going to do that; you needed to be forced into a commitment. I saw that as the best way of forcing you, in free will, to make the choice. To give you a radical alternative. Fortunately for me, Vance felt the same and it played out from there.'

'When else?'

'Eissley was aware that Pan had made discoveries; he was sure when he saw you, or should I say, you saw him, at the wake. Pan's People are extremely difficult to infiltrate; like Everett and Hines, they are of such an individual collective mindset that it makes a person without… spirit, shall we say? It makes them stand out as having something wrong with them, something missing. Their intuitives read them as fakes. They are exposed as somehow "inauthentic", and suspected, quite rightly, as spies. Sapphire was such a person; she was tired, she had renounced Pan and all his works. She had gone back to the mundane; the same thing we saw Jimmy do, after witnessing the orbs.'

Xylata paused for a second and smiled to herself, then spoke as though recalling directly.

'Sapphire has a boyfriend; did she tell you that? Six months. They just bought a house together, they have a mortgage. They have two cats, and he plays golf on the weekends. She renovates and tends the garden. All the while, something in the back of her mind is screaming, screaming. And she ignores it. She ignores it until she receives news of Pan's death. Now she wants to return; the news of Pan's death is all she needs…'

'She never told me…'

'The boyfriend believes she is dead, killed in the explosion at the hotel. He has grieved and moved on; as have all of your families. Tomorrow's ceremonies are merely a symbol of that. But Saph was pleased to go back, to see you especially Mitchell Pyne. Your friendship brings her great joy; second only to the love she still feels for Pan. I felt the spike Pan gave her; the precognition, the ability to see through time, or even control the temporal influence in the rifts. And this is the other intervention I made; I withheld it. Sometimes her precognition broke through, but mainly, I withheld it from you.'

'Why?'

'Because she would have found me. Any exposure to the astral, the birth of any higher mental ability, exposes us. In the least it makes humans more sensitive to our existence. If Sapphire's temporal sensitivity or precognitive powers had been allowed to fully bloom, I would have been exposed. So she sat alone, night after night, sleepless, away from you all, searching her mind for me. But I was too strong. I think she knew I was there; but I would not reveal myself. I could not; failure of this mission would mean one hundred years in the starcophagi. That was, and is, unthinkable.'

Mitch stared at her; he didn't know what to think.

'It is my fault you were transported three months into your future; it is my fault that Oliver Hines has the upper hand. I did what I had to do, but it had unforeseen consequences. For that I am regretful.'

Mitch buried his head in his hands. Heather stubbed her spent cigarette under her shoe and let out her last drag with an extreme hiss of disapproval.

Xylata continued. 'The only other time was on the beach. When I tried to persuade you not to come here.'

'Why?'

'Two reasons; exposure to the Sirians expanded your abilities, especially after your encounter with the Orion Renegades. From the moment you saw the security system, you were no longer spiking, you were switching it on and off at will. It was only a matter of time before you looked at me and saw my true face, as you did with Kyvza at the wake. And second, I was sure you would find this place; my mission would be at an end, and I would have to turn you over to Kyvza, or kill you if you tried to put up a fight. I found that my desire not to do that, and my desire to extract vengeance on my clan superior dovetailed. That is why I waited, pretending to find my phone in my bag; I turned my face from you Mitchell, and when you had all come in here, I thought, I thought very quickly, and now I have a plan.'

'And what if we don't like your plan?' Mitch asked.

'You will. But I understand that you do not trust me. I think sometimes trust comes as hard to your race as it does to mine, because your race is more willing to trust; you get broken more often, and it becomes harder with time. Anunnaki almost never trust; when we do, no-one breaks it because no-one would want the shame of knowing they had entered into a trust bargain in the first place. Ironic, but true. So; I will do this. I will release Sapphire Edge.'

There was a click and Saph's starcophagi flooded the room in blue light.

'But you want us to do something first?' Mitch asked.

'I told you; I want you to *trust me*.'

'That's it?'

'Could you take a greater risk?'

'I…' Mitch wasn't sure.

'You won't kill us, or put us in a starcophagi?' Heather asked. 'You're going to help us save Los Angeles?'

'I don't think anyone can do that; but I will ensure that you get out of here with your lives, in short time, and with Sapphire. Do you agree?'

A tiny but intense ball of light appeared in the center of the room; the rift was about to open.

'Do you *agree*?'

'What choice do we have?' Mitch grimaced.

'You have a choice! *Do you agree*?'

'I agree!'

'You all agree?'

They all did.

Xylata turned to Mendoza. 'One last thing.'

'What's that?'
Xylata raised her guns again.
'You have to die.'

CHAPTER SIXTY-NINE

Don Eissley entered the room, instantly withdrawing two pistols from two breast holsters beneath his slick black jacket.

'Thank you Xylata, no starcophagi for you this time!'

'My pleasure clan master, pah!'

'So they managed to get here, huh? All by their little selves? Where's Everett and the gorilla?'

'They're in Los Angeles, pah. The quake will dispense with them; if not we will find some other means.'

'Indeed we will, indeed we will.'

Mitch stared at Eissley; the idiot was acting as though he were a hip gangster in some awful Tarantino knock-off. With his pistols extending sharply before him on overly outstretched arms, Eissley rolled his shoulders and winced.

'Enough of this human shit.'

Kyvza's reptilian body peeled out of Eissley's as though Kyvza was some kind of dated special effect from some ancient British television series; it was obvious how they'd done it, any kid would say today, they've just overlaid one image with another. Two cameras and one monitor; nothing to it. For a brief moment, two realities seemed to exist in the same place. Cheap and crappy; amazing anyone bought it, even back then.

Only this was real; this *was* two realities, overlaid.

Then Don Eissley was lying on the floor and a naked Anunnaki stood before them, with two pistols floating unaided in the air before him. Again, Mitch noticed the difference between the two; Kyvza had enormous and wide almond shaped eyes that covered perhaps a quarter of his face. His snout extended over the whole lower half of his face, and his teeth were exposed and sharp. His scales were much larger, and deep, dark olive in pigment.

But perhaps the starkest difference was his actual physical presence; he seemed to glow, like the prisoners in the starcophagi, with gray and silver astral light.

'So this is what you look like,' Mitch nodded. 'This is your physical-astral body.'

'Nice deduction, ape,' Kyvza grinned, with wide-open incisor teeth, the top of his snout crinkling around his nostrils. 'I'm naked of course, but it's nothing you haven't seen before!'

His hand went between his legs and grasped at a fat, scaly extension there that looked like an olive cobra sitting against his lower belly, then he shook it at them.

'Hominid wankers!'

Mendoza struck out both hands; dust particles suddenly filled the air, whipping up from the boxes and the floor, and the light in the room seemed to bend and be shaped by the particles. Then the dust and the light seemed almost to surround Kyvza and encase him; it all happened in a split second.

Then Xylata opened fire with both pistols.

Mendoza staggered backwards, parallel with the line of starcophagi, bullets ripping into his flesh, tearing his cheek off, his calf, the side of his chest, blasting through his shoulders and ribs.

Xylata stopped.

Mendoza was still standing.

He stared at her with hatred.

'No,' he stated squarely. 'I'm not going to die!'

'Yes you fucking are!' Kyvza spat, and without his touch, the two hovering pistols fired simultaneously, soaring through the air toward Mendoza as they did, blasting his body to pieces for the second time that day.

Mendoza screamed. His body imploded as his flesh ignited and burst into flames. And with that, he was gone.

'Fucker!' Kyvza spat again. 'One hour and he thinks he can hold sixth dimensional physicality?' Kyvza screamed into the ceiling. 'That takes decades you moron!'

'He is human, pah. It might be dangerous to underestimate what he can do on his own planet.'

'It's not their planet it's ours,' Kyvza stated simply. 'Has been for six thousand years. You tell 'em that?'

'We had some time to debrief.'

'What did they say, these jumped up little hominids? Huh?' He turned to them. 'What did you have to say for yourselves? Hominid slaves! Apeys!'

The apeys remained silent.

'Think you can just break your chains do you? Think we didn't know? Been watching you, seeing what you thought you could do. One sequence is exploited, the other sequence hides and complains. Exactly as we've trained you; exactly the kind of Hegelian paradigm we installed in your tiny monkey brains.'

Kyvza laughed, and laughed heartily.

'So *now* what do we do with you? I tell you what; I'll offer you all a deal. After Los Angeles is leveled, you can come and run my new studio; I'll make you all execs! You can write the movie of what's happened to you; no-one will believe it, and when it's a movie, no-one will believe it even more! Beautiful irony, isn't it? The more aliens we put into the movies, the more people believe we're fantasy! Haha! What do you say? Vance, baby? How about you? *You* can be that old character actor! Heather, sweetie, you're hot enough to be anything you want, on screen or off. We'll have 'em eating out of your hand. And Mitch, the dude; you can make good movies, instead of all the cheap, lazy shit you used to pan. Pan! Haha! Get it? Pan the movies! Haha! How come you ain't smilin'?'

Mitch gulped. 'You're really going to let Los Angeles go under aren't you?'

Kyvza shrugged. 'Can't stop it; trouble with you humans is that you never, stop, trying. Even *we* didn't predict the internet, and look at all the trouble that fucking thing caused. Never mind; we adapt. It'll be content controlled within a few years and people will be back to seeing exactly what we want them to see. Around the same time we'll have built the new studios; Olivera of course, erm…Thirtieth Century Fox? Plus all the other oldies, all reborn. Gotta appease Isis, for sure. And Time Warner! Time – Warner! How could they not see through that one! We might as well have called it Armageddon Studios! Ha hah ha!'

He stared at his audience for a reaction; he was dying.

'Right. Okay. Who cares? Once the quake's settled down, Regene will continue regardless; can't slam the lid on the old box once it's opened can we? This quake's just an adjustment; just a recalibration so the physical plane can take the weight. All our people are already out.'

'But there's close to four million people down there – and a whole country that depends on their economy… the United Sates will never cope; you're going to let millions die and destroy a whole country – for what?'

'We're not going to *let it happen*; we can't stop it! It's your fault, fucking apeys! You humans discovered the genetic sequence that made this happen! Don't think we didn't look into it; this ain't part of some grand fuckin' plan chief! Stopping earthquakes is a big goddamn deal! Once the second density decides to move, ain't nothin' anyone can do; not even the Orions have anything to say about this one. Maybe if we'd known, maybe, say, a few years back we could have done something, but this one's off the chart my friend; no-one saw it coming! Like we keep saying; *you weren't supposed to break the genetic codes!*'

'Who says?' Mitch demanded. 'Who hid them in the first place? Why are they…'

The room shook.

'Ooh!' Kyvza grinned. 'There we go! There's a little taster. Now let's watch the panic start; we're estimating about three, four hours tops. It's gonna take out the whole damn valley; with the eight point eight epicenter right smack in the middle of Wiltshire Boulevard. Come upstairs and watch it with me won't ya? Got a beautiful view; we're in prime Mulholland Drive real estate, and our best estimates say the houses up here have a ninety percent chance of staying intact. Shit, half the Draco clan are setting up and having parties tonight, all along this stretch; it's like the Hollywood Ark, we've picked and chosen who lives and dies. Most of the A-List talent in the whole of modern entertainment are somewhere up here this afternoon; at least, those who haven't already felt the call and fled town. Wonderful how these astral channelers seem to sense these things, and in the end ain't that what actors are? At least, the real ones; the ones from the movies? I can take you along to one if you like? Wanna come to a party? Who'd ya like to meet?'

He ended there with a fixed open grin, staring at them with wide-open eyes, and wide- open arms, like some bizarre carnival showman in an alien costume offering a tickets on a spaceship ride.

'No?'

Suddenly the two pistols whizzed through the air and landed with simultaneous slaps back in his hands, pointed straight at them.

'Fuck ya then, ya gonna die!'

CHAPTER SEVENTY

Mendoza reappeared suddenly, behind Kyvza. The whole room shook, throwing everyone to their knees except the Anunnaki leader, whom Mendoza had wrapped his arms around. The pistols fell harmlessly to the ground as Kyvza cried out.

'What the – !'

'That was no taster my friend,' Mendoza hissed. 'That was me!'

Again, the dust in the room gathered, again the light seemed to bend toward Mendoza, toward Kyvza. This time it took on solid form; bars and shards of solid crystal formed from the combining light and dust particles, solidifying into sharply criss-crossing angles around the pair. Mendoza released him and stepped back. Kyvza tried to turn about and face him but the bars had already imprisoned him; the solid crystalline cage had weaved into a funnel and was closing at the top, leaving the Anunnaki caged in a strange, inverted crystalline pine cone, crying out uselessly, barely audible from within.

'Hah!' Mendoza was triumphant.

'Will it keep him?' Xylata asked, clearly excited.

'Unless a Sirian lets him out of it; but even then, the crystal pattern is woven from a distinctly "apey" mental frequency. There's never been one like it, it's formed from an entirely new matrix.'

Xylata reached out and touched the crystal, running a blue tongue across her lips. 'Then we leave him here. We will disable the security when we depart. When I need him again, I will call on you.'

'That was the deal.'

'Good. Now, Magician, Mitchell; will you honor your end of the deal?'

Mitch nodded. 'If you do yours.'

'Very well. Go to the glass; watch.'

Mitch nodded and returned to Saph's starcophagi.

'Sapphire Edge,' he spoke. The door cracked. He opened it fully. Saph's astral body remained there, floating. This time she opened her eyes but did not move, as though only partially waking from deep sleep at some slight disturbance.

'Now,' Xylata grit her teeth.

Just as Kyvza had, Xylata seemed to stretch and for a moment it seemed that two alternate realities, two images, occupied one space. Then Xylata staggered and stepped heavily away from Saph, appearing solidly but with her race's natural astral sheen, beside Saph. Mendoza caught Saph's body as her knees went out and she collapsed upright, back into his arms.

Mitch watched, then returned his attention to the starcophagi; Saph's astral body opened her eyes, suddenly startled. She seemed to see Mitch standing before her. Mitch saw her mouth the word, his name, then the astral body faded and was gone from the starcophagi. Mitch turned to Mendoza.

In his arms, Saph gasped as though surfacing from a deep and long dive underwater. Her eyes snapped open, wide and filled with awe, and she immediately pushed herself out of Mendoza's arms to stand.

'Oh thank God!' she cried out.

Then she spun on Xylata.

The Anunnaki was standing away from them; she would have looked almost vulnerable, with one hand across her chest and another between her legs, if she had not been frowning so deeply at Saph.

'Are you going to kill me Sapphire?' she almost hissed.

Saph stared at her.

'Kill you?' Saph's expression was strange, as though she had not considered that, but was indeed now doing so.

'Saph – how do you feel?' Mitch asked timidly.

'Normal!' Saph exclaimed. 'Whenever she's with me I feel like

I'm on fucking valium!'

Saph spun about to the crystal pinecone that had entrapped Kyvza.

'What are you going to do with *him*?'

'You remember everything?' Vance asked.

'Of course I do, *Magician*. I was here; I just had my… spirit repressed! It's like being *sedated* – and then every now and then you find yourself *sleepwalking*, and doing something without really knowing why you're doing it!'

She was clearly furious.

'I enjoyed it,' Xylata offered. 'If that makes any difference? I liked being you; I like your friends. Your lives here; they are better than mine. There is little joy in a corporate military, unless you advance to Kyvza's domain – or one like it. That is all we have. That is why we strive, to attain his rank.'

Saph regarded Xylata, as though some kind of innocent political prisoner who'd just been released to confront a jailer who'd been sympathetic to her; but a jailor nonetheless.

'Don't you think I know that? This time around I knew what was happening; I couldn't stop it, but there was one thing I could do. I watched you – I *examined* you. You're a functionary with ambition; don't think I don't I know your fear. I wasn't trying to *find* you when I was alone all that time – I was trying to *talk to* you; strike some sort of deal! But you were too afraid, too terrified of revealing yourself!'

'Well that's not a problem now!' Xylata exclaimed. 'Find me some robes! It is the highest shame to be seen naked outside of courtship!'

'Not to us,' Mitch shrugged.

'This is not about you!' Xylata spat. 'For once Mitchell Pyne!'

'Hang on,' Heather uttered, then moved to the black chest that contained the crown jewels. She opened it and fished around, then removed a long fur cloak, purple with thick white trimming, and whipped it before her like a matador's cape, blowing dust up into the air.

'I think Elizabeth wore this on her coronation!'

Xylata, her scaled arms remaining in place to preserve her modesty, scampered across to Heather and snatched the fur from her.

'We shall find out what it is in due course; whatever it is, it will have immense totemic power!'

Xylata threw the cloak around herself, then quickly found a long leather belt in the same box to tie about her slim waist. As she did, Mitch caught a glimpse of the modesty Xylata had almost preserved.

It was color.

Xylata had no breasts.

Cold-blooded, Mitch thought; no mammary glands. Instead there was a vivid diamond-shaped patch of intense color, thin at each corner but increasing in width as the patterns came to the center, like an image from a frozen kaleidoscope across her upper torso. The colors were complimentary to her general lime-green skin pigmentation; deeper limes, then light browns and yellows closer to the middle of her chest, but in the center of the kaleidoscope was a bright diamond outlined in orange, with a striking crimson center. Just the glimpse Mitch caught was truly stunning; not sexually arousing but genuinely beautiful, as were, he recalled suddenly, the colorful skins of many reptiles from Earth.

Xylata scowled at Mitch. 'You looked!'

'I couldn't help it! The colors are so attractive!'

Had Xylata blushed?

'I am considered by my clan as a prime example. My scale shades are the envy of many.'

'Yeah yeah,' Heather guffawed crudely. 'I'm sure you're the "it girl" of the Anunnaki corporate bureaucracy, baby. But right now we have to focus on getting us the hell out of here.'

Saph had returned to Kyvza's crystal cocoon.

'It was his fault; but then if I say Xylata was only obeying orders, or a cultural imperative, I have to say that Kyvza was too.

So who's above him? Where does it end?'

'It does not,' Xylata uttered. 'Where it ends is in death; both backward and forward. Those who initiated the laws and customs of our society are dead. There can be no vengeance. Karma visits vengeance on the dead, if you want solace. And of course, the culture does not end for us, until *we* are dead.'

'Karma is your God?'

'Karma is the machine. You have much to learn human.'

'I thought they only said that kind of thing in the movies,' Vance muttered.

'We make the movies.'

'I see,' he smiled. 'You know, I think I really could make it as a character actor… once all this has blown over.'

'Enough, Magician. This will not "blow over". There is real work to be done if you are to prevent even a small portion of the deaths that approach, on such a massive scale.'

She moved about the boxes, her robe flowing as though now a natural part of her, searching for something.

'What is it?' Vance enquired. 'Maybe we can help?'

Xylata looked up and scanned the room keenly.

'Your plan to destroy the room and all its contents would cause more chaos than you can imagine. Slaves or not, the world around you has structure and stability; mass panic on a global scale would not help anyone.'

Suddenly she saw what she was looking for and headed immediately to a small box near the first of the starcophagi. She bent over and raised it to eye-level, as though examining the contents with x-ray vision. Suddenly Mitch thought of Hamlet, staring into the hollow eyes of Horatio's skull.

Xylata snarled. 'This is the totem you seek.'

'Okay,' Mendoza nodded. 'What is it?'

'We uncovered many seeds in the human psyche, we watered them and they bore a great harvest. Uncertainty, unworthiness, low self-esteem. All these items are blocks to the astral, cages for the third density. There were, once upon a time, a great number of clear channelers and gifted clairvoyants in the City of Angels. Decades ago, most of the channels were blocked by a terrible act of violence that permeated the city with terror, and doubt; then increased exponentially. Many lost faith. Inside this box is a deck of tarot cards, created by a master of the dark energies, many decades old. After his passing, it was purchased by a cult leader who instigated crimes against humanity, but to speak either of their names here in this room would be tantamount to cursing us all. This deck of cards is greatly symbolic of the death of what you would call white magic in Los Angeles. It speaks to the death of hope, of faith, of optimism in the magical arts. Take it outside; do not speak of it or speculate. Do not open it. Destroy it. You must burn it, down to nothing but ash, then Mendoza must use his new skills to dissemble the ashes to the four winds. Once that is done, all true genetic clairvoyants in the city will have clear channels reopened for the first time in half a century. They will feel the echoes through the temporal landscape. They will have a premonition of the coming catastrophe; this was what you hoped to achieve by destroying this chamber, was it not?'

Nobody spoke as Xylata walked forward to Saph, and handed her the box. She accepted; and there seemed to be, at least at that moment, a peace between them.

'Now, that is done. Our bargain has ended; you must leave me the rest of these totems. I shall act quickly to have them moved to a secure location of my own. Then, I shall be the first female in three thousand years to control the Draco. And you have my word that I will not intervene in whatever you do next.'

Mendoza bowed. 'As it was agreed, so shall it be.'

Having restored some of her perceived lost dignity, Xylata bowed in return. 'You should leave now,' Xylata suggested firmly, as she eyed her prizes. 'But there is something else here you should take with you; take the revelations contained within as a sign of thanks if you will, a sign of friendship if you must, for I fear that some strange bond has formed between us all, and this will not be the last of our interactions. But know this also, Hominids;

the revelations contained within will also serve to weaken the reputation of Kyvza, and strengthen my own position. Should you accept these totems, and we meet again, I will be more powerful. Greatly so, I should imagine. Know this and be on your way with no animosity between us.'

She turned and pointed to two more starcophagi on the other side of the rectangular room; they'd not noticed them before, because these were laying down, like conventional coffins. They were also black but had strange ribbing down their sides and over their lids; coils and perhaps pipes. On top of one of the boxes was another, far more conventional box, a generic cardboard storage box from a major office supply chain. Just sitting there, innocently amongst the rest of the black-boxed totems.

'Take them, leave them, the choice is yours.'

CHAPTER SEVENTY-ONE

They left Xylata to her treasure trove as they carried the two strangely decorated starcophagi through the rift and back into the empty garage.

The house remained deserted; the former Don Eissley had come alone.

As for the real Don Eissley, Xylata got to keep him. She gave her word that he would not be killed and they had accepted that.

'What the hell do we do with them?' Vance grunted as he bore the brunt of the starcophagi that he and Saph carried.

'Put them down,' Heather responded huffily, lowering her end to the concrete ground so that Mitch was left balancing the other end until he could lower himself to do likewise.

'They weigh a ton,' Mitch complained. 'If there are people in these, they're not floating astral bodies. They're real corpses.'

'Corpses you think?' Mendoza enquired, returning though the rift with the office supply box under one arm, the evil black box under the other. 'Interesting.'

'Can you do your atomic light thing?' Vance asked. 'See what's in them? Open them perhaps?'

'I couldn't do it with the other starcophagi, but…' Mendoza focused upon the two coffins. 'Apparently not for these either,' he frowned. 'Whatever's in them, they've been sealed by higher sixth density technology than I yet understand. Maybe even beyond sixth?'

'Orions?' Mitch asked.

'Maybe. Elohim? Who knows?'

'Elohim…' Mitch mused. 'Seventh density?'

Mendoza nodded. 'Angels to us. What the Pleiadeans want to

be. But who knows what they are really; like the Orions, no-one can really process them. They may appear in forms we believe we comprehend, but that's not what they truly are. Obsidian is no fragile old man. He's probably the descendent of one of the original races; the races the universe manifested after creating the Source, as a means of expressing self-awareness, understanding itself. Their consciousness evolved when the universe was new, and built a society around basic atomic level structure; learned how to manipulate it as we first learned to use stone tools, or to plough the earth. Who can say what they are now? We call them the original engineers of masculine and feminine principles, the Orions and the Elohim, the arbitrators of the material and ethereal, but at their level it's all incomprehensible to us, really.'

Mitch sighed. 'And not even the Elohim can prevent an earthquake?'

Saph sat on the coffin. 'Mitch; if there's one constant message all the races have given us so far, it's that once Mother Earth gets going, once the chain of energy begins within second density reality, nothing can reverse it. The quake's going to happen; we just have to figure out how to evacuate as many people as we can in three hours.'

'Shit!' Mendoza exclaimed. 'Let's get this damned box outside; burn it back to hell.'

The stench was awful.

Once they had found their way outside, through a locked back door that Mendoza simply made vanish, Mitch and Heather had used their cigarette lighters to each burn an opposite corner of the box's base. Once it had caught, the box and its contents went up extremely quickly, as though dry and brittle matter covered in lighter fuel, leaving precious little ash for Mendoza to disperse.

Then they stood on the lawn, beside a huge swimming pool, and watched the ashes vanish at Mendoza's command.

Mitch thought that the dissembling ashes looked like the so-called 'stars' he sometimes saw when he stood up too quickly.

Mendoza stood bolt upright and frowned deeply.

'What is it?' Heather asked.

'Misha,' Mendoza stated. 'I'm being summoned. If I don't return… good luck. It's been cool hanging with you.'

And with that, he vanished.

'Oh wow,' Saph gaped.

'I'm kind of getting used to it myself…' Mitch shrugged.

'No, not that,' Saph snapped. 'Xylata was right… I'm getting a clear channel for the first time. I can feel – hundreds of others, maybe thousands, getting the same thing. I can see… Los Angeles; the buildings, falling, toppling into each other; houses just giving in, collapsing like tents, right throughout the valley; massive cracks from one end to the other… oh my God, it's… it's beyond words; the death… it's, it's beyond anything I can… we have to get the people out, Mitch!'

There were tears streaming down her cheeks.

'We have to get them out!'

CHAPTER SEVENTY-TWO

The sun was higher in the sky now; it was turning out to be a pleasant fall day in Los Angeles. Autumn leaves in Eissley's expansive back yard were catching the light and glowing with stunning shades of amber, yellow, gold, rose and burgundy.

Five or six dogs were howling across the hillside, from different directions, and maybe dozens more, further away, wailing beneath.

'They know,' Heather muttered.

Her phone rang to announce that Everett was out the front; apparently the 'someone' he'd sent to get them was himself. They found their way around the exterior of the house, jumping a high gate down the side of the property, to the Tuscan-styled entrance that sat at the top of a steep driveway leading back down to Mulholland. Everett still wore his black funeral suit and stood beside his black four-wheel drive with his hands in his pockets, staring up at the wide glass window two floors above. Mitch realized that essentially they were all dressed for mourning, even Heather in her dark browns, and that they had somehow become the metaphysical version of the Reservoir Dogs.

'I think I came to a love-in here once,' Everett stated dreamily as they arrived.

Heather embraced him and he smiled down at her.

'Good to see you all,' he smiled crisply. 'Now, we have a party to attend.'

'A party?' Mitch frowned.

'About ten doors down. I'm reliably informed it's the place to be.'

They piled into the car, Mitch in the front beside Everett, as

Everett took the wheel and engaged the motor.

'The others are meeting us there; Amy's safe, Mitch.'

'Thank God,' Mitch sighed, putting the office supply box on the car floor between his legs.

'What's in that box?' Everett asked.

'So far as I can tell, a bunch of sealed folders and three unmarked video tapes. It's from the Draco clan's totem vault.'

'The *what?*'

'I'll explain later.'

'I say,' Vance asked from the back, sitting between Heather and Saph. 'Are we just going to leave those starcophagi in the garage?'

'Star – *what?*' Everett demanded again.

'Explain that later too,' Mitch sighed. He turned to Vance. 'No-one's going to that house today. Xylata will cover her tracks.' He turned to Everett. 'Can you send some people there? Tell them there are two black coffins in the basement garage that need to be taken somewhere secure?'

Everett frowned, increasingly perplexed. 'You want me to do that?'

'It's probably going to pay off in some massive way we have no idea about.'

'Okay...'

Everett took one hand off the wheel and thumbed his phone.

'Two black coffins in the basement garage of Eissley's Mulholland address. Get them now, make them secure. We might need them in the next few hours.' He hung up. 'Anything else?'

'You sure Amy's okay?'

'You'll see her soon enough. The Pan train their people well, as it turns out.'

'Will she be meeting us at this party?' Vance asked from the back.

Everett didn't answer. 'Where's Mendoza?'

'Ascended to sixth density,' Vance responded again. 'We have allies now; a Sirian goddess and the new clan leader of the Draco. But they claim they can't do anything to prevent the earthquake.'

'Is that so?' Everett hummed.

'Is what so?' Vance enquired. 'That they're allies or that they're impotent to second density forces?'

'Your metaphysical vocabulary has come along, Magician.'

'No it hasn't. I just find it more appropriate to use it now. And you haven't told us whose party it is.'

Everett steered them down Eissley's long driveway and along a short distance on Mulholland; the streets were lined either side with town-cars and limousines. Then he turned into one of the few gaps; another steep driveway, and they suddenly were heading up again.

'And Cricket?' Everett pursued.

'Re-embraced by the CIA,' Mitch grumbled. 'She's now the favored daughter of the Second Orion Directorate.'

'Impressive,' Everett nodded as they reached the top of the drive; the house was similar but it had a distinctly retro, 'seventies stone-wall veneer. 'Have to keep my eye on that girl.'

'Indeed,' Vance uttered. 'She offers the same sentiments in return.'

The circular driveway, surrounding a garish fountain, was packed with expensive new cars. There was nowhere to park so Everett simply stopped the car directly outside front door to the foyer of the house, effectively blocking the main entrance and immediate exit routes of half the other cars parked there.

'Welcome to the lion's den, my friends.'

'Where are we?' Mitch asked.

'A celebrity fundraising benefit for the… well, it doesn't really matter what the benefit's for, does it? That's not the reason it's happening. It's happening to centralize a lot of important people in an area away from the earthquake zone. The main reason we're here is that we have been invited by the fundraiser chairman specifically, and we're here as his honored guests.'

'The fundraiser chairman?' Saph enquired.

Mitch sighed. 'Who else? Oliver Hines.'

'The very man.'

CHAPTER SEVENTY-THREE

In a startling contrast to Eissley house, just down the street and of very similar architectural dimension, this house was filled with people. Everett had paused only to take a small wooden box from under his car seat, then had led them into the party with total confidence. Only the valet had attempted to stop them entering, but he had withered and melted away with one steely stare from Everett.

They walked in together but found, almost immediately, that they had to walk in a line to part and then negotiate the crowd, and had to shout at each other to be heard against the overbearing wave of background music and mass conversation.

There did not appear to be anyone in the house who would have been under the age of forty, and almost everyone seemed to be placed somewhere under thirty.

'They've all had Regene treatment!' Heather turned and shouted at Mitch.

Mitch just shrugged as if to rhetorically ask 'what did you expect?'

He'd been to Hollywood parties, if but a few, years back when he'd been an entertainment reporter. Even so, he'd never seen so many young and aesthetically beautiful people gathered in one place. He wanted to feel disgusted; he wanted them to know that their collective egos were the cause of a critical mass that was about to end life in their country as they knew it. But he could not help but wonder at the sheer accomplishment, the brazenly apparent success of Olivera's product.

Not all the actors had fled town; he saw several male television actors who not days ago, in Mitch's timeline, had been too old to play a lead role on prime time television, but now looked like the nineteen-seventies and eighties images of themselves that ran on *Nick At Night*. He saw actresses, at least he thought he did, who now looked again as they had when he had watched them as a teenager.

A young-looking woman reached out from the crowd ahead of him and lightly grabbed Heather's arm.

'Excuse me darling, aren't you Jacqueline Bisset?'

Heather was taken aback but turned her reaction on a dime.

'Well, can't you tell?'

'Of course I can darling, didn't I say? It's just with all the new flesh in the room –'

'Of course darling, of course, I feel the same!'

'I'm KK Kendrick with Olivera Talent; I have a project which will be fabulous for the new you! You have to do nudity of course, it's all nudity now; it's the new paradigm for the new age, if you've got it, flaunt it darling!'

'Really?' Heather guffawed.

'We're reinventing the sixties darling, putting an end to all that sexual repression! The new Hollywood is all very European don't you know? Gabrielle Fenwick just did full frontal for the first time in her career; a sexual thriller, very exciting! It's all about showing off the new package; we want to show them what they'll get! No point in hiding what's natural! If they can't see the goods they won't buy the product! New paradigm, sweetie: can I see you tomorrow morning?'

'Of course! What's the script?'

'The script?'

'For the project darling!'

'Oh the *script*, oh it's fabulous Jacquie, just made for you!'

'Terrific!'

Heather began to move on.

'Who are you with?' KK called, as she moved away.

Mitch came up behind her. 'She's with me.'

KK made no attempt to hide her expression of shock and

disgust.

'And who are *you* with?'

'I'm with Bo Everett. We came here to kill Oliver Hines.'

KK froze for a second, then burst out in hysterical laughter.

'Priceless darling! Priceless!'

Mitch smiled and moved after Heather.

'Very smart move! Clever niching! The world still needs characters darling!'

KK nodded to herself as Vance passed.

'Better call some of your B-listers before it's too late, my dear,' Vance opined casually. 'Somebody still has to play police chiefs and crusty bartenders!'

KK went pale with realization and reached immediately for her phone.

Everett led them through the party. He, Mitch and Vance weren't the oldest looking people in the room, but they would certainly be counted amongst those who were. Still, people seemed to recognize Bo Everett and whispered as he passed.

'Isn't he dead?' Mitch heard one actor ask another.

'Can Olivera do that now?' The other actor responded, amazed.

Everett found the cue for the bathroom and pushed to the front; the others followed. As one man exited, Everett pushed in front of the next in line.

'Excuse me, fate of the world!'

Saph, then Heather, then Mitch, and finally Vance followed Everett through.

'Hey!' the cheated man cried out, followed by a chorus of complaints from the line.

Vance stared at him. 'I say, aren't you Richard Chamberlain?'

The man rubbed his face gently. 'You think?'

Vance locked the door behind him.

Everett turned to them and raised his phone to his ear.

'We're in,' he said to whomever he'd called. 'Do the knock.'

Then he ended the call and turned his attention to Mitch.

'You have your gift hidden somewhere?'

'Yes.'

Everett turned to Vance. 'And you?'

'Indeed.'

He turned to Saph. 'You have yours, and Heather's coffee in that bag, correct?'

'Yes. Why?'

'Anything goes wrong, anything goes down, we meet back here okay? One of us will stay here with the door locked at all times. I'm not going head to head with Hines without a base of operations in his lair, understood?'

'I suppose,' Mitch shrugged. 'If that's what we're doing. I thought he invited us?'

'It's a trap. Nothing surer. He knows I have nowhere to go. No-one, apart from the morons in this house, knows I'm alive. My business has been taken over by my board members and all my metaphysical contacts have been rounded up and made to vanish. I can get that sorted, but not today. Hines is going to make me the same offer; hand over the goods. If I don't, he's going to have us all killed. He has nothing to lose; we're all dead to the world anyway.'

'Then what are we *doing here*?' Saph gaped.

'The only thing we can do; taking the fight to him. Now Mitch, as you probably heard, our attempts to synthesize yours and Vance's blood samples for the genetic trigger went pear-shaped pretty much the minute the hotel exploded and killed us all. That means the gifts Pan gave us are pretty much all we have.'

'Gave us?' Saph asked.

'You didn't think young Pan would go without leaving me a present did you?'

'You?' Saph was clearly shocked.

'An unmarked box of San Martin Peruvian cigars, sent the day before Pan's death. Everything Pan sent me went to a secure mail address, I had them stored there.'

'You?' Saph was aghast. '*You* were one of the six people he trusted most in the world?'

Everett seemed almost offended. 'I backed him with unlimited funds, believed every word he said to me and never lied to him. He was like a son to me. Well, a favored nephew. Of course he trusted me.'

'I…' Saph's mouth popped open and closed a few times. 'I'm *sorry* I suppose?'

'That will do,' Everett nodded.

There was a knock at the bathroom door. It was the joke-knock; rat tata tat tat, tat tat.

'Open it,' Everett ordered Vance.

They could already hear a commotion outside.

The door opened and Amy entered. Yelina followed, balancing a tray with six steaming mugs on it. Both were dressed in tight-fitting black one-piece outfits, with knee-length boots and high collars, as though prepared for hi-tech cat burglary, and both had lowered the front zip to expose cleavage.

Amy immediately embraced her father, rushing forward in a flurry of long curly blonde locks.

Mitch was stunned on a number of levels; at her overt joy to see him, at the fact that somewhere in the past few years she had inherited and developed a woman's body that was full but slender, and mirrored her mother's in her prime, and finally that she should even be present here in the first place.

'Oy-yoy-yoy,' Yelina exclaimed. She turned and shouted to the line outside. 'This is an impromptu studio meeting that will take the rest of the afternoon; Oliver Hines says use the upstairs bathroom or use the garden!'

There were more complaints and cries of distress but, when Yelina slammed the door hard with a swing of her foot, they could hear the line shuffle quickly away.

Amy released her father from the embrace but stood beside him, holding his hand tightly, like she would never let go.

'Is there an upstairs bathroom?' Heather asked.

'In a house like this, there is always an upstairs bathroom. Probably three.'

Yelina carefully put the tray down on the bathroom surface, beside the basin, as Vance relocked the door. They could all smell the coffee aroma from the six mugs.

Everett sighed heavily. 'Made from the samples you gave me, Heather.'

They all exchanged glances.

'The kitchen is crazy with cocaine,' Yelina scowled. 'It was not easy. There was enough to brew six, but it might be a little weak.'

'So,' Everett shrugged, opening his cigar box. 'You have no doubt guessed what I suggest we do next? I trust you are all in agreement?'

'We each take all six of the gifts?' Mitch asked. 'Is that what you're suggesting?'

'We discussed it before,' Everett nodded. 'Pan gave them to us for a reason. He dispersed the whole formula, but I believe he meant us to share them.'

'But what good will this do?' Saph demanded. 'What purpose is there to this?'

'And aside from that,' Mitch complained, 'we still don't know what Heather's gift is, nor what the sixth is. And what about you, Everett? Have you smoked one of those things yet?'

'Of course.'

'And?'

Everett smiled as the open cigar box floated out of his hands and hovered before Mitch.

'Cigar, Mister Pyne?'

CHAPTER SEVENTY-FOUR

'Telekinesis?' Mitch was amazed.

'If we can see the Anunnaki, as you can Mitch, jump through dimensional rifts, as you do Vance, operate with heightened intuition, as Saph's powers offer, fight them with the mental abilities they use, as I can, then that is a start, you have to admit.'

'A start to what though?' Mitch demanded. 'How does that help us stop the earthquake?'

'It is still two hours and twenty minutes away,' Yelina confirmed.

'How does she know that?' Saph asked.

'Yelina,' Everett nodded. 'Perhaps it is time you removed your glamor?'

'Her glamor?' Vance was surprised.

'What's a glamor?' Mitch asked.

'It's what the Anunnaki use to hide their true selves,' Vance responded, 'from people like you and I, who can see through to the astral body within. Like a spell that's cast to disguise…'

They all turned to Yelina.

'If you have a glamor, why can't I see through it?' Mitch asked.

'Because,' Yelina smiled, 'my magic is older than yours. Older than any magic on this planet. Because my magic is this planet.'

Yelina's features wavered and changed slightly; she was not an Anunnaki, the changes were not that severe; however, her skin and dark hair did gain a natural deep-greenish tinge that somehow projected radiant organic health. Her ears extended up, into points, and her eyes arched upward slightly more than they had. However the main change was how it felt to be in her presence, that her presence seemed somehow sacred now, and yet completely out of place, as though it were wrong for her to be here, like spotting a thriving tree growing in the middle of an enclosed suburban mall. The lacquered wooden door behind her, the gleaming white tiles, the clean lines and polished surfaces of the bathroom that surrounded her suddenly seemed abhorrent, bland and antiseptic, clinical and sterile in contrast to her earthy, natural beauty.

Mitch heard a sniffle and looked beside him to see that both Amy and Heather had spontaneously begun to cry. Mitch didn't feel moved emotionally as such, rather he felt a deep and unbegrudging reverence for her; he wanted to embrace her, to he held by her, and sleep in her arms. He wanted to have more children so that they might meet her, and come to know her. He wanted to eat and talk and walk, and even make love with her, to live with her and spend the rest of his life forever in her presence. He never wanted to be apart from her ever...

Yelina's glamor reappeared.

Mitch snapped out of it; now Yelina was just a woman again, just a very attractive forty-year old woman with giant boobs and an enchanting smile.

Enchanting.

That's what the other Yelina had been; totally enchanting.

Yelina smiled. 'That is why I must wear the glamor. You all come from my world originally; you are all children of the Earth. Although I was once, millennia ago, a mere wood nymph, I am now an elder princess of Gaia, I am dryad royalty. If I were to walk amongst you as you saw me, in my third density form, without the glamor, you would feel the love for me that you once had for nature, for the unbridled elements, and you would do anything for me. But those days have long passed; that is no longer our way, nor our desire. When Bo came to Peru, and underwent the ayahuasca ceremony, it allowed Gaia to fully perceive him. A powerful psyche, a man who had influence but who owed allegiance only to his people in the third density, not to the mystery schools or spiritual cults of the higher realms. Here was such a man, the first for centuries to whom we could speak without fear of reprisal or betrayal or exploitation, who might listen and understand what we wished to convey. We found that we had common purpose, that we could work together. But now this chain of events has begun, I cannot see any way of circumventing it. The Anunnaki's control of fourth density energies is too strong; Gaia will not permit this gross genetic exploitation of her children without the release of the corresponding balancing energies. But she is not acting purposefully to punish, or to remove the genetic progression; this reaction is the closest that the planet can achieve toward restoration of balance, by shifting great levels of energy into the third density world. She is sorry that many of her children will die, but she is old and set in her ways, and this is not only tradition, but planetary – and solar. If there is an imbalance, then what you, Vance, call the 'solar machine' creates restoration of balance. If the imbalance is planetary, so must be the restorative energy. These principles were set in motion at the dawn of the cosmos; they are foundational, immovable, immalleable. They are cosmic law. That is how I know, I come from the earth, from the wood, from the grass, the water and air, where things are more certain than they are here; and one of the things that is certain for we of the wood is that we fear fire. We have had thousands of years to learn it, sense it, know its approach. And it approaches. Two hours and fifteen minutes away. Unstoppable.'

'So what good is taking the gifts, Yelina?' Saph asked. 'How will that help anything?'

'If the machine can register life evolving to the fourth density on Earth, even a mere six of you, that is perhaps enough to register a start; it will not save Los Angeles, but it may make the quake less severe. It *may*. Although, I truly cannot say. But I know this; your city New York, where there is much of this Regene also, that will be next. Then city after city until balance is restored.'

Yelina narrowed her eyes and stared at Saph.

'Use your gift. Focus on what I have told you; what do you see?'

'I see…' Saph seemed to stare into an endless middle-distance.

'I see blame… accusation… awful catastrophes, one after the other. I see… a massive resurgence of End Time religions; scapegoating those they see as sinners; a terrible, terrible resurgence, like a modern day Inquisition; not just burnings but mass executions, rows of electric chairs lined up for the masses to watch live… randomized to go off one at a time for maximum entertainment and tension; television shows like Idol where twelve sinners beg for forgiveness each week and endure trials until only one remains, 'free of sin'… and in the far distance, religious wars… nuclear warfare… and ash. Just ash.'

Saph had gone pale. Now she, too, was crying; but this was no spontaneous response to a spirit that was pure and from the naked earth. Hers were tears of fear and dread, of pity and shame.

'It all begins here,' Saph uttered. 'Oh my God, Yelina, do you think it will make a difference? If we do it?'

Yelina shrugged. 'It surely cannot hurt,' she spoke, with as much optimism as she could gather. 'But you must understand. Your Zen philosopher Alan Watts once said that just as an apple tree apples, a planet peoples; you are not the first third density civilization to emerge from second density. The planetary mind, the core, the first density, is programmed to people the planet, it will keep doing it regardless of what happens to your civilization. Gaia doesn't want you to suffer, but she will take action; she will have no choice. My people can always retreat and wait, as it begins again, as it has before. But Gaia can reset your people back to the stone age, back to primal ooze if she has to, to restore balance.'

'Mitch,' Everett spoke gravely. 'We need what Pan gave you.'

Mitch turned to Vance. 'I can't see anything; no cracks or rifts. Can you see a way out of this bathroom?'

'No. But while our gifts work in conjunction, I believe that each of our individual gifts gain strength over time. Allow me to demonstrate… if I can.'

Vance extended his hand toward the shower cubicle; Everett and Heather shifted slightly aside, one each way to clear his line of sight to the white-tiled space. They heard a hum in the air, and as the lines on Vance's high forehead creased, they saw a bright light form in the center of the cubicle.

'There,' Vance sighed. 'It's all about finding the core of the pre-established dimensional constraints… the center of the rectangular cage. That, and not a little confident focus.'

'I can stabilize the temporal dimensions,' Saph nodded. 'From here, I can do it. Mitch, all you have to do is focus on where you want to go. You won't lose any time. Wherever you hid the gift. Can you do that?'

'Yes. I remember where it is, very well.'

'Better shoot, old man,' Vance smiled. 'Haven't got all day.'

Mitch nodded and turned to the cubicle.

Heather reached out and took his hand. He looked to her expression, and understood that there was nothing that could stop her going with him. He nodded, grimly. She released his hand and they walked into the cubicle.

'Won't be long,' Mitch uttered.

'Don't be,' Saph spoke as he passed through the crack.

As he did, he heard a shuffle behind him, as though someone had moved very quickly. He didn't realize what it was until he stepped out into the churchyard, with Heather close behind him, and turned to see that Amy had followed them.

CHAPTER SEVENTY-FIVE

It was daylight, near sunset. A couple of cars passed on the street behind them but in the distance they could hear rush hour traffic on the main road.

'What are you doing?' Mitch demanded.

Heather turned and saw Amy. 'She doesn't trust me.'

Amy scowled at her. 'Don't be ridiculous. I just want to keep Dad safe.'

Heather scoffed. 'And you don't think I can do that? I've done nothing but, ever since I met him.'

Mitch sighed. 'Ladies!'

They both looked at him; anger stewing in their eyes.

'There is nothing to be kept safe from.'

They had arrived in the partition between the high privet hedge that bordered the churchyard and led up to the church doors; literally at the entrance to the church block. That was interesting, Mitch realized briefly. Was it a coincidence? Or was there actually something to the idea that by building anything, even a gap in a hedge to access a path to a doorway, you were actually creating a dimensional structure, the shape of which actually had some deeper kind of power or symbolic meaning? That somehow resonated throughout other realms of perception, where dimensions were different?

Mitch looked left and right; which side of the hedge had he jammed the bottle into?

'Where is it?' Heather asked. 'What are we looking for?'

Mitch didn't answer. He looked across at the sun, low on the western horizon, sinking behind suburban rooftops.

It had been mid-winter here, just a day ago from his perspective.

Now it was mid-spring.

'Sydney's generally around eighteen hours ahead of LA. That makes it…' Mitch struggled to do the calculation in his head. What time had it been in Los Angeles? Morning when they'd met Misha and then the whole incident with Xylata…

Then, he remembered that his watch remained set to Sydney time.

'Five-fifteen.'

Another few cars passed on the street, using the suburban shortcut to get from one main arterial road to another.

Was that what they'd just done? Taken a dimensional shortcut?

What would happen when this power, this biological technology, Mitch supposed, was revealed? Would there be a need for streets and cars any longer? Probably not, not if everyone could travel instantaneously, at will.

What would happen to the cars and roads? What would happen to the whole transport industry? Car manufacturing would collapse. The oil companies would collapse. No need for trucks, trains, planes…

The stock market would collapse.

Basic social utilities like streets would become redundant. Suburbs and borders would become redundant. If people could just pop in and out wherever they could visualize, security would be a nightmare. Damn the internet, this *really would* be the end of privacy. Christ, *walls* would become redundant!

Just about every aspect of normality that Mitch still felt was stable fell like a house of cards.

Unless… some sort of blocking technology could be devised…?

Surely it would have to be?

Did the Annunaki have that already?

And what about Saph's ability to stabilize time through dimensional travel? What if that wasn't always utilized? If people could jump forward in time, what would that mean? Just – chaos? You could literally open an account with a hundred dollars and keep jumping forward, until you reached a time when the interest had made you wealthy. But then, if everyone could do that, what would money be worth? Surely the whole idea of forward time travel simply neutralized wealth? Wealth would mean nothing if everyone could be as wealthy as they liked. If everyone decided to do it, all jumping and leap-frogging into the future, what would that *mean* for the future? It would change it; change the destiny of mankind irrevocably because the moment we started jumping into the future, then all future generations could presumably do that too, and probably better.

Mitch suddenly visualized the whole human race, all leaping forward, and forward, and forward, all trying to get ahead of each other, get the drop on the future, on and on and on until they were all just swallowed by the end of time, the end of the universe.

Humanity could conceivably just collapse instantaneously into a singularity created out of sheer greed!

Things had been moving so fast that he hadn't considered the ramifications of Pan's gifts, of the urge they all had to get them out into the world, to use them against Olivera's campaign. This was not Pandora's Box; this was not a myth. This was actually about to happen; this was *Pan's* Box.

Pan's Brave New World!

These gifts, once opened, could not be put back in. They would change everything, forever.

He was still staring at the sinking sun.

'What are we doing?' Mitch asked.

'What?' Heather demanded.

'What are we doing?' Mitch repeated.

'Are you having another solar download?' Heather asked.

'Solar download?' Amy asked.

'This is the church where your uncle Pan had his conventional funeral. I met your father here for the first time. But when the funeral started, he got up and left. We all thought he'd just gone until we came outside afterwards and he was staring up at the sun, like he was in some kind of trance. I kind of knew what was happening; I've had something similar myself, but not for as long as that. Vance told me later that he thought your father was being scanned by the consciousness at the center of the solar system, that the sun itself was scanning him, or downloading information into him, because he was a new genetic life form, or at least a new variant of human consciousness. He basically thinks this whole thing is about proving to the Source, through the Sun, that we're an acceptable path for humanity to travel, that it is a viable evolutionary path. Mitch is basically standing in the same place it happened. Only slightly more to the south and facing west this time.'

'That's right,' Mitch nodded. 'I think I just stopped that day, while the genetic changes settled in. Maybe the sun sort of… helped that along. Maybe it gave me information that's taken this long to process. I don't know. But now, I do remember one thing. It gave me a mission, set me a task. It's asking me to answer the questions it gave me to pursue.'

Amy was stunned. 'The sun is *talking to you?*'

'I'm not crazy, sweetheart. It's not *talking* to me. It's more like, something about the *energy* of the sun that's making me pose the questions, internally, and answer them, in my mind. But at the same time, right now, I truly believe that the universe is listening. That somewhere, somehow, the answers I give, the choices I, and we, make right now, are important.'

'So it's a solar *upload?*' Heather surmised.

'I suppose that's as good a way of putting it as any.'

'And what are the questions?' Amy asked.

'What are the *answers?*' Heather added, not a little stressed.

'Can I help you?' asked a quiet voice from the church entrance.

Mitch turned.

The priest was there.

The priest from the funeral.

Mitch wondered.

Could he?

There was a pfft sound from nearby and Mitch was blinded in a splatter of blood.

CHAPTER SEVENTY-SIX

Thoughts raced though Mitch's mind as he frantically wiped the blinding blood from his stinging eyes and heard a woman scream. Had it been Heather or Amy? Which had been shot? Had *he* been shot?

He didn't know which would be worse; losing his daughter or the woman he…

Squinting, his vision returned.

His last thought before reality hit him, through restored sight, was that if he had been shot, if *he* were now lying, dead or dying on the ground, would that have been better? To be relieved of the burden of decision?

Then he saw: it was Heather.

The bullet had gone through her chest, the blood had splattered directly into his face.

She was lying on the ground; her knees had given out and she'd fallen onto her back. He face was expressionless, lifeless, her mouth and eyes open in shock.

He saw the priest rush forward from the open church.

He saw the man, the same kind of man that it had always been, aiming the gun at them from the window of a parked black car down the road. An Orion Renegade agent. A Man in Black. Whatever these soulless parodies of secret agents called themselves.

Amy had screamed.

But she had pulled herself together.

With a strength that belied her frame, Amy squatted, hooked her arms under Heather's body, under her neck and knees, and lifted her. Amy's weight shifted; she had intended to carry her backwards, back through the tiny light of the open dimensional rift to LA, but instead she staggered forwards, with Heather's bulk carrying her, all in one swift movement, into the churchyard.

He felt a weight smash against him, heard another *pfft* in the distance.

Then he was on the ground, the priest on top of him.

'Stay down!' the priest hissed in his ear. 'There's someone shooting at you!'

They were on the ground, protected from the agent's lethal line of sight by the hedge. Amy had dropped to the ground with Heather's body, just up the path. The church doors were open, maybe ten paces ahead. But shock had claimed Amy now, she was limp and crying. She had fallen and she couldn't get up.

Mitch listened and heard the sound of a car door opening then running footsteps; the agent had left the car and was coming to them directly.

'When I say,' the priest hissed again, 'move with me *quickly!*'

The weight of the priest shifted off him, as though readying for something.

'Now!'

The priest leaped to his feet, but remained crouching. Mitch did the same.

'Move!' the priest hissed again.

As one, the two men ran, still crouching behind the cover of the hedge, toward Amy and Heather. The priest almost scooped Amy up; it was practically supernatural, as his daughter seemed simply to accept that she was being taken, moving with the priest's shielding arm as it gestured for her to rise and flee to within the sanctuary of the church. But then she resisted, as she seemed to reregister Heather's lifeless body, her limp form on the ground.

'No!' Amy cried. 'No!'

Mitch tried to lift Heather's body but fumbled and fell to his knees between her and Amy. She was still bleeding but not much; the bullet wound seemed to have cauterized. It had to have pierced her lung, maybe her heart. She had died instantly of physical trauma.

In this realization, Mitch simply collapsed. His body just gave out. His head fell on Heather's chest and, somehow dislocated from himself, he felt intense pain in his jaw as his teeth ground into each other, heard them squeaking inside his skull.

Amy lunged at him, wrapping her arms around his chest.

'No, Daddy I'm sorry! I'm so sorry!'

Mitch stared up at her.

'I wanted her to go! I didn't want her getting in the way! I just found you again! I didn't want her to take you away from me! I didn't want to lose you again!'

Mitch stared at her, trying to comprehend.

Had his daughter betrayed them?

Then he realized; no. She just blamed herself, blamed her own wishing Heather away. In her shock and grief she was making Heather's murder her own fault.

'It's not your fault,' Mitch heard himself say, almost comfortingly. 'I never would have let you go, never again.'

Amy burst into tears, wailing.

Mitch stared into Heather's eyes, open and staring up to the darkening sky, her mouth still ajar.

'No,' he said to himself, 'not now... I just made room. I only just made room...'

He thought about trying to lift her again.

But then a shadow fell over him and there he was.

The agent, standing at the end of the path and pointing his gun between Mitch's eyes.

Then, there they were.

They seemed to step into frame, from either side of the hedge entrance.

Mitch did not know if they were the same Pleiadeans who had refused to acknowledge him, but then rescued him and Heather at the wake, but they looked very much the same.

The female snatched the gun from the man's hand.

The male slapped a hand against the man's chest.

The agent staggered backwards into the street, across the street, and fell on the pavement on the other side.

Still.

The Pleiadeans watched this happen, then turned as one to Mitch.

'Why?' Mitch asked, his voice choking. 'Why now?'

This time, they spoke.

'We recognize you now,' said the female.

'There is so much love in you now,' said the male.

They were smiling, slightly, benevolently.

'But…' Mitch looked from them to Heather and back again. 'Why?'

'Your daughter sees now that you have love in you; you know now the love you have for her, your capability is renewed. You must persevere now. We are all watching.'

'*Watching?*'

'None of us can be seen to interfere. That is universal law. Nothing vulgar. Nothing overt. Only behind the veil, or to preserve the order that protects us all.'

'But you just *saved me!*'

'Yes. To preserve order.'

'*Order?*' Mitch spat. 'But what I bring; what Olivera has brought, what Pan will bring – is *chaos!*'

They both smiled, again benevolently, as though he understood nothing.

'There are two more coming,' the Pleiadean man said. He pointed west, down the street. 'That way.'

'And two more,' the Pleiadean woman pointed east, down the other end of the street, 'from there. You should go inside. If you try to reach the doorway you used to come here, they will shoot you.'

With that, they walked away, out of sight behind the hedge.

CHAPTER SEVENTY-SEVEN

The church was exactly the same.

The priest slammed the heavy wooden doors behind him and fumbled with a heavy iron key. After he locked the door, he raised then slammed down a long wooden board into heavy upward pointing iron hooks across the two doors, barring them.

The priest panted. 'A medieval affectation, I always thought. A decoration, a symbol. But still, no-one's ever broken in.'

Mitch jostled with Heather's body.

'They won't come in here,' Mitch snapped at him. 'They're unholy.'

'I beg your pardon?'

Mitch shocked himself with his answer. 'They have no souls; at least, not located in this dimension. I've seen a lot in the past few days, but those men and the things that control them are the closest thing to true evil I've come across.'

The priest stared at him. He was maybe forty, with deep gray eyes, and a kind face with a scholarly pallor. His scruffy black hair was receding, and his forehead creased with rubbery flexibility as he considered Mitch's comments.

'I'm Father Lance. Lance Shelley.'

'Jesus…' Mitch muttered, looking down at the body in his arms. 'They killed Heather…'

'Maybe not?' Lance placed a hand on Mitch's shoulder, then leaned in to Heather's open mouth. He could barely feel Lance's hand through the padded shoulder of Everett's giant black coat. 'The body sometimes goes into shock, with trauma. She may still have breath, have life, but we cannot see. We need to call an ambulance, and the police.'

Amy was shaking. 'CPR.' Her voice quivered. 'She needs

CPR.'

Mitch nodded and lay Heather's body on the worn scarlet carpet, then stood and stared as Amy tried desperately to resuscitate Heather's dormant form.

'Father,' Mitch muttered, 'there's something going on, something we have to stop, but now I can't get back…'

Lance nodded. 'These people who saved us. I can see there's something… something beyond…'

'It's Regene, Father. It's Olivera.'

Lance frowned again, squinting as he processed. 'Olivera…?'

'It's not evil, father; but it's going to *bring* great evil. Humanity's not ready for it. But there's something I can do – something me and my friends…'

Mitch's heart stung.

Heather was dead.

He knew it; her vacant expression there on the ground. The procedure Amy was performing so desperately; so utterly useless.

'…we can… make a difference.'

'You can?' Lance asked, curious.

'We have the other half of the…' Mitch faltered. 'We have something that could restore the balance that Regene is tipping, but…'

Mitch lifted his tear-filled eyes to meet the cloudy gray of the priest.

'…it will change everything. *Everything.*'

Lance searched his eyes.

'The chaos you spoke of? How so?'

'Father I've seen… I've *met*… beings. Like those you saw outside. Beings who evolved differently from us. On other worlds. And because of that, they occupy different dimensions. They resonate differently with the universe, with the laws of physics and chemistry and time and space… I don't know, I don't fully understand it. But they're here, watching us. They influence us, secretly. It's like we're living in one room of an enormous mansion; only we don't know it's just one room. We think our one room is all there is. We think we're alone but we're locked in one little room when there's a palace around us, filled with… life.'

Lance muttered. *'In my father's house there are many mansions.'* 'At least five that I've come across and I'm told there are many more…'

Jesus, Heather was dead.

Heather.

He had to talk to Father Lance to keep his mind away from that, to keep thinking about something else.

'And father…' His voice broke. 'Fath…'

Lance placed his arm around Mitch's shoulder, then gently guided him past Amy and her continuing efforts, into the church. It was macabre, Mitch realized. Like they both knew that Heather was dead, and gone, but let Amy keep going. For Amy, he supposed.

'Come on,' he heard his daughter utter in desperation. *'Come – on.'*

For some reason, Mitch sat where he had been before; three rows down to the right. It felt familiar. It was here he'd first seen Heather. First seen her, and dismissed her as nothing. Nothing.

'I feel I must make a call to the police,' Lance stared down at him. 'And an ambulance for your friend. Will you wait here while I fetch my mobile phone?'

'Yes.'

Lance nodded. 'You're sure?'

They heard Amy again. 'Come ON!'

'I'm sure,' Mitch nodded.

He hoped he'd been right about the Renegade agents being unable to enter the church.

'Very well.'

Lance moved quickly down the central aisle, turned left and was gone from sight. Mitch heard a door open and close.

Police.

This was it.

Everett and the others would have to go it alone.

When they didn't come back, maybe some of them would come looking.

The agents would shoot them too.

There was nothing he could do about it, other than to give his own life to warn them.

Pointlessly.

Better he live on, with Amy.

It was just them now.

Just the two of them.

They would have to explain Mitch's long absence to the police, probably while Los Angeles was being demolished by Gaia for humanity's rampant vanity. Maybe they would be released in time to see the ghastly footage on CNN later in the evening, and the snippets recorded on phone cameras by the survivors.

He didn't even have a phone to call Everett.

It was still in Saph's bag.

He'd never learned to use it.

Never learned anything.

Didn't even know what Everett's number was.

Behind him in the entrance alcove, Amy was weeping softly now.

He couldn't cry.

He just felt hollow.

He supposed it was shock.

One too many.

He looked around him, at the church, and was shocked again.

The same two people were there.

He hadn't noticed them before.

But he was sure; the beautiful couple, both with long blonde hair, dressed in 'fifties designer suits. He remembered thinking; don't be judgmental. To each their own.

They were still there, staring at the front of the church as though the service was still going. As though nothing had changed.

Then he realized.
He heard himself say it as they turned to gaze upon him.
'Elohim.'

CHAPTER SEVENTY-EIGHT

They didn't say anything.

'You're like Pleiadeans,' Mitch said, almost absently.

The woman smiled.

Mitch suddenly realized that he was looking at Angelina Jolie, and Brad Pitt. Then he was looking at Richard Burton, and Elizabeth Taylor. Grace Kelly and Prince Rainier of Monaco. All at once, in their heyday of adoration. Then he couldn't get a fix on who exactly he was looking at; it was as though his mind were rouletting through a vast series of images, trying to find an accurate descriptor to stay with.

The man nodded and they stopped shifting.

He was looking at Buffy, and Angel.

Two characters from a fictional universe.

Young and beautiful.

Buffy spoke.

'If you think of those you call Pleiadeans as hippy priests, as many do; those who celebrate love and beauty and purity; art and the abstract, romantic love and poetic thought… who feel and channel emotion as a kind of musical energy, and respond to the vibrations they enjoy, then no, we are not as they.'

Mitch stared at Buffy.

She morphed into Elizabeth Bennett, the man shifting simultaneously into Mister D'Arcy.

D'Arcy spoke. 'The more you attempt to ascertain our nature, the less likely it is that you will arrive at any satisfying conclusion.'

Mitch took a guess. 'You're the opposing principle, the opposing force, the opposing ancient species to the Orion beings.'

'That is how you best perceive us,' Elizabeth Bennett smiled.

'Although we do not oppose them. *Complementary*, perhaps would be a better choice of descriptor. We are the feminine principle to their masculine principle.'

'Why did you come to Pan's wake?' Mitch asked.

'Why did *you* come to Pan's wake?' D'Arcy asked.

'He was my friend,' Mitch responded bluntly. 'Saph asked me. It seemed like the right thing to do.'

D'Arcy frowned. 'You are an atheist. You had some time in Sunday School, but nothing of it stayed with you other than a residual fear of punishment from a mean-spirited sky deity, or a sadistic fire-god. You did not even recognize this building as belonging to the church you were half-heartedly raised within.'

Elizabeth spoke a little sternly now. 'If we were to fully reveal ourselves to one who was truly raised in the faith of this church, they would weep for days. Maybe they would go blind for the knowledge they could never see anything such as us, ever again.'

'What are you showing me now?' Mitch asked. 'Or is it like the Anunnaki? To show your full form would summon energies that would level the church?'

Elizabeth spoke very sternly now. 'The Anunnaki create great disturbances when they appear because they do not belong in third density; they are long, long past its inheritance and they disturb the balance greatly. They are unique, as Earthlings are unique. As are all; but they are the cause of great disturbance. As are the Earthlings, by proxy.'

'Disturbance?' Mitch asked. 'You mean the earthquake?'

'Earthquake?'

As she spoke the word, she changed; she was now Ingrid Bergman. The man had become Humphrey Bogart.

'The earthquake, in California. About two hours away. It's going to kill millions of people.'

Bergman looked to Bogart, and Bogart nodded to her.

'You didn't *know*?' Mitch demanded.

'We are very far removed from minor shifts in second density.'

'*Minor*?'

'To us.'

Mitch stared at them, speechless, aghast.

'It is restoration of balance,' Bergman continued calmly. 'It is required. The conscious energy that is released will be recycled; it is the way of third density.'

'The way of all things,' Bogart added.

'The conscious energy that's released? You mean – *the millions of people who are going to die?*'

'Yes. Conscious energy will be recycled. They will be – you would say, reincarnated.'

Mitch leaned angrily toward them. 'Why are you here? Why appear like this? Just to tell me that there's nothing you can do? That this is all nothing to you? I mean, you're *angels*, right? You're messengers of God; or the Godhead, the Source, the Collective – whatever it's called in your system of things? You distribute the energy of the cosmos through the structures that the Orions create. If you don't care about millions of people dying, why do you care about one sad little man like me? Why does my grief count? You don't have to bother with me... why would you?' Mitch narrowed his eyes. 'Or, *do you?*'

They shifted; now they were the two beautiful people again, generic, although this time they had dark hair.

'From our perspective, here is your world, Mitchell Pyne,' the woman began. 'Once, many thousands of years ago, the people of this planet ascended. They were as the Pleiadeans are, as the Sirians are; but different, unique, as is all life, different according to the genetic code of this planet. They reached great heights; they expanded. Into your solar system and beyond. Some ascended even higher over many thousands of years. Some so far that they forgot this world. You branched and diversified, changed and evolved. Part of the being who speaks to you now remembers this world, hundreds and thousands of years ago. But what expands eventually disperses. Every system must face both growth and expansion, and yet entropy and decay. Those of your species remaining here on the planet began to forget their knowledge, experiment and distort the… science? Yes, the science they had come to accept as their nature, their beings. They fell. They fell and rose again, and fell again. Three, four times. Slowly and inexorably becoming lesser, descending in density. Your current species incarnation records these events, as race memories, as the destruction of Mu, of Lemuria, of Atlantis…'

She gestured about the church.

'Your great floods. Until finally, as is her function, Gaia was forced to reset the Earthling race entirely. Back to primordial ooze. She even tried to develop a reptilian race, but that too was reset; at the time, the Anunnaki were growing, as Earthlings once had, and the rate of their advance was seen as premature. The cosmos did not need another reptilian stream. Perhaps that was where things began to go wrong… your residual reptilian cortex, your fear centers…'

She turned and looked at the man, and sighed.

It was a sigh of discontent, of dissatisfaction.

'Perhaps this is another false start,' she uttered sadly.

The man proceeded. 'You were expected to ascend quickly this time; you have the genetic programming, as you might call it, to do so. Where each time you grew, when Earthlings expanded, it was exponential, so, each time you descended, it was exponential. But when this occurs, it recurs again exponentially; the Earthling race by now should be back again amongst the stars, expanding into higher density… but you did not. You *are* not. This is unfortunate. There are reasons, but… they too are unfortunate.'

Mitch stared at them. 'I've heard a lot of stories in the past few days…'

The man shrugged. 'Whether your race was once great or not, it doesn't matter. What matters is that you can, and should be great. But you are not.'

'Why not?' Mitch asked.

'We have explained what we are willing to explain. The story we have told you is true. But if you wish to make a difference here, Mitchell Pyne, the story must be made manifest here in third density. You have seen it made manifest here in third density; you know all you need to know. Several others, of higher density than yourself, have told you this. Now you must prove that you are viable. You must make the decision to act, and act quickly. You must display your intent through action; only then can the energies you require be made to channel through this planet again, only then will this incarnation of Earthling Consciousness proceed.'

'Just so I know,' Mitch grumbled. 'This is what your version of angelic intervention looks like?'

The woman smiled. 'Mitchell, there is an old saying amongst the spiritual people of your current Earthling incarnation. When first entering the mansion, you walk up the front path, to the front door, and knock. You await to be allowed in, and introduced. After that time, you may, if given permission, enter through the side door, or the back door, or just enter and shout a greeting when the front door is left open. But the first time; you must approach via the path displayed, and knock. Mitchell, this is where you are. We are presently outside of the mansion, but we are here, inviting you to the mansion for the first time. You know where the mansion is. You know the path to the mansion. You have been invited. What is it you intend to do with all the information you have Mitchell Pyne? With *all that information*, what is your *intent?*'

Say thank you to the nice angels, Mitch.

Mitch heard her voice behind him.

He turned quickly, stunned, and there she was, sitting in the same place she'd been when he'd first seen her. At least; part of her. It was Heather's astral body.

She spread her astral arms.

Guess I know what Pan's gift was!

She smiled.

Now all I gotta do is get back!

CHAPTER SEVENTY-NINE

The Elohim had vanished, but Mitch didn't care.

'Are you *alive?*'

I think so – I mean, I've been trying to get your attention. I can see my body out there, and I think what Amy is doing is good, but the shock of the bullet just kind of whipped me out. Mitch, I think this is what's supposed to happen when we have body trauma; the astral whips out and the body goes into a deep coma. I mean, my heart's beating about once a minute, I'm breathing so low as you wouldn't notice; but something *is preventing my body from entering into the decay process. I can feel it. Mitch, I think something's been* done *to us. As a* species. *I think that's what the Elohim were saying; somewhere along the line, something went wrong. We* should *have access to the other dimensions. We* should *be out there with the whole galactic rainbow alliance of whatever the fuck they call themselves! But we're* not.'

'Heather,' said Mitch.

Yes?

'Have you been hanging around this whole time?'

Yes – trying to get your attention!

'So you know…?'

She smiled. *Know what?*

'Dad!' Amy cried out. 'I think she still has a heartbeat! I felt it beat! Twice now, about a minute apart!'

Wow. Heather grinned. *So I was right! I'm like some kind of mega-transcendental yogi!*

'Amy!' Mitch cried out. 'Come in here!'

Amy raced out, into the church proper.

'She's alive, Dad! I know it! We just need to get her to a

hospital!'

'Amy, can you see her?'

'She's still in the vestibule!'

'The what?'

'The – ' Amy sighed. 'Out there, she's still on the floor out there!'

'I mean in here Amy, can you see her in here?'

'What?' Amy looked around frantically. 'What are you talking about?'

'Amy, calm down,' Mitch sighed. 'Look there – on the pew behind me. Do you see anything?'

'There's no-one there Dad!'

'There!' Mitch pointed. 'Right there.'

Amy jumped back a bit. 'The air's shimmering.'

'That's her. I can see her because of… because that's what I can do now. She's here, in her astral body. It's kind of a psychic protection mechanism. But you're right, we need to get her body to a hospital.'

'Are you *serious*?'

'I'm afraid he's deadly serious,' spoke a familiar voice from the altar.

They turned to look.

Standing there, with a gun to Father Lance's head, was Don Eissley.

'Pick up her body, or the father gets to meet his maker real quick.'

'Eissley?' Mitch was astounded.

'Come on, move it.'

Mitch stood, moving in front of Amy.

'Who is he Dad?'

'He's either Anunnaki,' Mitch muttered, 'or he's a very ambitious corporate chief. Either way, he's completely insane.'

Eissley laughed. 'Call me Eissley, call me Vgyrl, call me what you like.'

Vgyrl? Heather asked.

Eissley turned to her. 'You think it all just *ends* because your idiot friend traps Kyvza in a sixth density cage? Nice astral body by the way – always suspected you were a prude.'

'What?'

'You're still wearing your clothes, bitch. Ain't no *clothes* in the astral!'

Heather sighed. *Men.*

'Holy Moly, you guys managed a real fuckin' stunt, I'll give you that! I wake up in the vault, totally cleaned out, with my buddy wrapped tight as a virgin in an unbreakable crystal matrix cocoon! I gotta hand it to ya, that was *ballsy*. So I just summoned up another clan! I called in Vgyrl here...'

'Called in?'

'You think they hijacked me? You think I'm some patsy? How do you think anyone gets any power in this crummy world? You have to *align* yourself. Anunnaki's where the money is. It's win-win. Xylata takes control of the Draconians, doesn't need me any more? I go to the Cheneks, make a deal. I've still got a lot of pull with Olivera, a lot, believe me.'

'The Draconians control Olivera.'

'I control Olivera! Took me ten years to get in there! Oliver Hines thinks he's his own man, thinks Bo Everett's gone to war with him! As above, so below – where I go Olivera follows, and I don't care which damn Anunnaki clan gets me the power!'

'The Cheneks, huh?'

'Only Vgyrl's a bit higher up the chain of his clan than Kyvza was; doesn't like to talk as much as Kyvza did; doesn't like to soil himself with your type of apey scum. So he just sits back and let's me do what I have to do to clean up this mess.'

'Where did you *come from*?'

'The *astral* you moron! I can't believe you were so idiotic; you used it to get here! That's like typing Al'Queda catch-phrases into a search engine! *Instant red flag*. You're such rookies I had time to contact the Orion Renegades and have 'em take a pop shot at sweetie here – we knew she probably had one or the other of the six gene sequences bubbling away in her apey blood, turns out we were right. Had to be sure – had to make sure you actually had what we thought you had before we went to the trouble of taking you all out. So, pick her up, we're going outside, and we're going back through your little wormhole to the great big bathroom in the sky.'

Mitch sighed. It didn't seem that they had much choice.

He turned and went to the vestibule while Eissley led Father Lance up the aisle. Amy followed him, backwards, watching Eissley.

Eissley grinned at her. 'Nice kid, Pyne!'

Mitch lifted Heather's body.

Careful, Heather uttered instinctively.

Mitch banged her head on the wall.

I said careful*!*

'Sorry.'

'Okay father, open the gates.'

Mitch looked apologetically at Lance. 'It's okay.'

Lance didn't seem particularly frightened as he moved forward and removed the bar from the doors.

'S'okay father, you're just a pawn. Got nothing' against organized religion; it's a great goddamned racket for us!'

Lance glanced at Mitch as he took out his iron key.

'We were listening. Were they really angels you were talking to?'

'Yes. That's as good a word as any.'

'And there really is a spirit form? Your friend Heather, she's here?'

'Standing right behind you.'

The lock clicked open.

'And they told you to find them; to use your powers to enter God's House?'

'I think so; in your words.'

Eissley sneered. 'That's enough now father.'

'God go with you, my son.'

'Thank you, father.'

Amy squeezed Lance's hand as the doors opened.

They could see the small bright light, still there, still open, just between the hedge entrance and the pavement. Standing there, two on either side, were four agents.

'On we go,' Eissley grinned, still with his gun to Lance's head. 'Straight through.'

'Why are the Orion Renegades working with you?' Mitch asked.

'They're not; not as such. Usually they wouldn't bother with the likes of me, or the Draconians. But politics make strange bedfellows. They've been working to end this planet for six thousand years. Keep getting blocked. But now we're going to make their dreams come true; and all they have to do is stand back and watch.'

Mitch reached the end of the path. 'What do you mean?'

'I mean; Olivera's Regene treatment, triggering global catastrophes on an unprecedented scale in current human history. You know the amount of energy a violent death gives off up in the astral? We haven't had a factory slaughter like this set up since that maniac Hitler sprang out of nowhere; but this is going to make the South American sacrifice cults look like Sunday School. And it's going to last decades. Maybe even a whole *century*. Couldn't have planned it better. But you know what they say; never let a good catastrophe go to waste!'

What does Xylata have to say about this? Heather demanded.

'Not a lot; her coup went extremely well. She doesn't care what happens any more. Which is why Vgyrl here wants to ensure that the Regene disasters go ahead; Xylata thinks you're going to stop it. Vgyrl's clan is betting the other way. If they're right, Xylata's reign is going to last until about… oh, a couple of third density hours from now?'

Eissley shoved Lance aside, training his gun on the others as the agents also raised their weapons.

'Don't try anything Father. Okay, you first Pyne. Then Everett, then the kid. I'm right behind you; any tricks, me and the goon squad start shooting.'

Mitch paused. 'If you're going to kill us, do I get a last request?'

'Now, you think I'm an idiot, Mitch? Don't think I ain't seen as many bad fuckin' movies as you have; that's always the hero's last ditch effort for a surprise escape.'

'It's nothing like that. I'm an alcoholic. I quit drinking two days ago when I came to Pan's funeral with a bottle.'

'No shit Pyne?' Eissley seemed almost genuinely sympathetic. 'Too bad; I bet ya thought ya had plenty of good years left to ride the straight edge too, huh?'

'I just want to get my bottle.'

'Ain't ya heard son? Ya can't take it with ya!'

'No, I mean it. I just want a last drink. Please; the bottle that I stashed? It's in that hedge. Right there. If you're going to kill me, at least let me have a last drink. Jesus, there's not much in this life that I'll miss, but –'

'Sure – I get it,' Eissley shrugged, flicking his pistols. 'If I were in your shoes and someone had a bag of coke stashed on 'em, man, I'd inhale that fucker like a free diver breakin' the surface.'

Eissley went to the hedge.

'Where'd you say?'

'Just in there – about a foot in, chest height.'

Eissley holstered one on his pistols, shoved his hand in and rummaged around. 'Well…' he drawled. 'Whaddaya know?'

He pulled out the bottle of Southern Comfort and stared at it.

'Just like a true alkie; stashes all over town. Whaddaya come here for ya meetings as well?'

Mitch scowled.

Eissley laughed. 'Dirty bum.'

He holstered his second gun, unscrewed the lid and took a swig.

'Ahhh! Sweet as Mother's Milk!'

Eissley paused and stared at Mitch, thinking it over. He could see the mean-spirit in Eissley's eyes. The classic glint of the psychopath. How would he exercise this power? Would it be torture, or mercy? What would this little demi-demon choose?

Mitch's heart skipped a beat as Eissley re-screwed the cap. Then, he extended the bottle. Mitch juggled Heather in his arms, and accepted.

'Don't say we never gave ya nothin, apey.'

Amy came forward, took the bottle from him, and unscrewed the lid. She held it up to his mouth, her hands shaking. He could smell it; beautiful, sweet and intoxicating. He swigged as Amy tipped it, rolled the fluid in his mouth, swallowed and let out a gasp of relief.

He met Amy's eyes; she was terrified. But as she held his gaze, she lifted the bottle to her own lips, trembling, and swigged herself.

Mitch knew; it was her way of showing acceptance. Her way of saying goodbye. It was an act of love.

Then she re-screwed the lid, and placed the bottle back in his hand.

'Enough!' Eissley spat. 'That's all ya get!'

Eissley extended his hand; he wanted the bottle back.

Mitch took a breath.

It was his only choice.

With Heather in his arms and the bottle in his hand, he turned to the portal and stepped through.

CHAPTER EIGHTY

Mitch returned to the bathroom in Oliver Hines' Mulholland home, carrying the apparently dead body of Bo Everett's beloved niece, and a bottle of Southern Comfort, expecting… well, he didn't know what to expect.

'What took you - ?'

'Heather!'

'Jesus Christ!'

'What happened!'

'Trudy!'

There was a bustle as Heather's body was wrenched from his arms and laid down on the bathroom floor. Amy bumped into him from behind and shouted.

'Behind me!'

A shot rang out and Amy fell, just as Vance whipped his arm up and flicked his fingers at the shower cubicle. Mitch saw Amy fall and cried out her name, then heard Eissley shout several obscenities in a row.

What Mitch saw next was a mass of confusion.

A woman with long dark hair was crouching over Heather's body. When she whipped around to see Mitch, she ignored him and went directly to Amy, who'd fallen on the ground beside him, faster than he could himself.

Eissley had shot Amy in the back; the bullet had passed straight through her and embedded in the bathroom wall between Vance and Yelina.

Floating somewhere in the middle of the room was Heather, staring down in horror at Amy, while Eissley pounded on the empty space of the shower cubicle door, screeching obscenities as though it were ten inch reinforced glass.

Mitch was again in shock, again experiencing a mix of emotions containing heavy doses of both panic and grief.

The woman with long dark hair stood, and went back to Heather's body.

'She's alive, barely.'

Mitch half-recognized the voice.

'Trudy?'

Someone had called that name when he'd stepped through, hadn't they?

'Hey Mitch long time,' Trudy snapped without looking.

'What happened?' Saph demanded.

Mitch ignored her and stared at Amy. She was blinking; she looked well.

'Amy?'

'She's fine, Mitch,' Trudy said again, without looking up from Heather's body. She had her hands alternately pressing and hovering over Heather's bullet wound.

'Trudy, what the…?'

Then Mitch realized.

The sixth gift.

That was how Trudy had gained the confidence of the people formerly known as Pan's People. Being Pan's one sympathetic sister wasn't enough. She had healing hands; transferable regenerative energy. She was the living embodiment of whatever it was Pan had symbolized to them; she was, literally, the resurrection.

Maybe they all were, Mitch thought grimly.

'I have to pull her back from the brink…' Trudy muttered. 'There's nothing there!'

Everett turned to Mitch, totally irate, foaming at the mouth.

'Pyne! What the hell – !'

'She's here!' Mitch cried out. 'She's here, in astral form!' Heather was staring at her uncle's rage, totally shocked. Mitch saw this and immediately reported it back to Everett. 'She can see how angry you are! She's very moved!'

Everett stared at him as though he might very well snap

his neck out of sheer frustration. Mitch turned immediately to Heather.

'Heather – get back in your body!'

Heather guffawed. *Are you kidding? You know how much pain I'd be in?*

Mitch sighed. 'She wants to wait until Trudy's finished healing her – she thinks it will be too painful.'

Trudy looked up at Mitch. Her eyes were an intense dark-lime.

'Mitch, you tell her she has to get back in, or this healing is going to take three more of me and three days at that. We don't have the time – or three more people who can heal her like I can!'

Mitch looked to Heather. Her astral face winced and she whimpered.

'You have to,' Mitch urged. 'It'll hurt like a bastard but only for a minute; look at how fast she healed Amy.'

Amy was already on her feet. 'Yeah look!'

Amy wrenched aside the collar of her black cat-suit, which now displayed a neat little bullet hole, to reveal only a slight bullet scar over the top of her right breast, pushing out her chest to show Heather.

'She's over there,' Mitch said, slightly embarrassed.

Amy readjusted the angle.

Ooooh… Heather whined doubtfully.

'Now!' Mitch ordered. 'Be the tough bitch you want everyone to think you are!'

Everett's gaze was flicking intensely between Mitch and the vacant space between them that he accepted as Heather.

Hold my hand? Heather asked.

'Okay.'

Mitch knelt down and took her hand. It was cold.

Fuck, Heather uttered, and jumped back into her body.

Heather's body jolted and her eyes opened wide. She cried out, a weird wail that was part pain, part regret, and part objection. She immediately squeezed and nearly crushed Mitch's hand; he felt weirdly like he had when his wife had given birth. Mitch couldn't see what was happening under Heather's chocolate sweater, but she only screamed once more; then she started panting, then her head dropped back and rolled away from them, and she was breathing normally.

'God,' she moaned. 'That bloody hurt.'

She turned her head back and looked up at her uncle.

He was speechless, but there was a slight glint of moisture under one eye. Then his breathing returned to normal too.

She looked at Mitch, squeezing his hand more gently.

Warmth was returning to her, but she was shivering.

'Thanks,' she uttered.

Mitch stood, and used the grasp to help her to her feet.

They hugged, a gentle hug while Heather regained her balance.

'You almost lost me,' Heather whispered.

'Like that's going to happen,' Mitch whispered back.

They parted, smiling.

'I'm dizzy,' Heather gushed.

'It'll pass,' Trudy smiled.

Heather hugged her, then almost fell into her uncle's arms and squeezed him tightly as he patted her warmly on the back.

Mitch turned back to the shower cubicle. Behind Eissley, four grayish figures were hovering. It didn't make sense, visually or dimensionally, but looked as though they were storm clouds, trapped at the far end of a telescope. Eissley turned to look as well, then swung back.

'You'll never get away with this, you insignificant pricks!'

Vance made a movement with his hand; a snapping grasp. The cubicle instantly and fully crystallized, as though suddenly filled with ice. Eissley was still as a statue, his next impotent threat literally frozen on his lips.

'How are you doing that?' Saph demanded. 'That's more than Mendoza could do!'

Vance grinned, a very dark grin. 'Never you mind about me. We've work to do. I assume you have a plan Mitchell?'

Mitch stared at him.

He had a strange feeling that Vance wasn't Vance any more.

'If you've got anything to tell us, Vance…'

Vance shrugged. The dark grin remained.

'…if you're a Draco agent as well…'

'Don't be absurd!'

'Then what's happened to you? You've been changing since we raided Eissley's stash. Everyone I meet is more than they say they are; Everett's not just a megalomaniac, he's an enlightened megalomaniac. Yelina's a tree. Saph was a Draco, Cricket was CIA, my daughter is a goddamned ninja and Heather's…'

He looked at Heather. She smiled.

'…Heather's alive.'

He turned back to Vance.

'I thought you and me were the only ones who weren't something else?'

Vance nodded, still grinning.

'I'm remembered things, dear boy. Things that are useful to you. Things that are useful to me. To be completely honest with you I have no idea where they're coming from, but…' Vance chuckled. 'I suspect it shan't be very long until we all find out. Until then…' He gazed slowly over at the coffee. 'Might I suggest we simply get on with what we're here to do?' He looked back at Mitch. 'As I said, old chap, I assume that you have some kind of plan?'

Mitch kept Vance's gaze. He was certainly darker; now more devilish than impish. But he had come all this way with them.

'You're still one of us?'

Vance scoffed. 'Always, dear boy! Always!'

Mitch smiled and reached forward, past Vance, and picked up one of the now-cold coffees. 'Bomb's away.'

He swigged down half of it, then offered the other half to Amy.

'You've earned it if you want it, sweetheart.'

Mitch quickly scanned the room for objections; there were

none.

'You sure?' Amy asked.

'Are you?'

Amy considered a second, took the coffee and finished it.

Everett growled some more and followed suit, as did Heather, Vance and Saph. Trudy was last.

'I hope you guys know what we're doing,' she grimaced, then drank the potion. 'This had better not be bloody Cool Aid!'

Everett pulled out a cigar, while Heather climbed onto the bathroom surface, reached up and smashed the smoke alarm. It fell to bits on the floor while Everett lit one stogie, then a second. The room filled with smoke, then light coughing as they passed them around.

'Breathe it in brethren,' Everett growled. 'Good and deep!'

They all took turns taking a light swig from the bottle of Southern Comfort as Saph fished around in her bag and withdrew her parcel of Turkish Delight, pinching off a small portion from one cube for each of them, while Trudy, after watching her, followed suit and broke one piece of thick dark chocolate, taken from a large box, into seven small pieces and dispensed them.

'Sure that's going to be enough?'

Saph nodded. 'It's concentrate; I just had a tiny taste before I went to bed.'

Vance reached under his jacket and pulled out a box of nougat. The box was clearly too big for them not to have noticed it under his jacket before now.

'Any objections?' Vance raised an eyebrow.

Everett stared at him. 'So you really are the Magician?'

Vance smiled. 'If I really did have another agenda, don't you think it would have emerged by now?'

'Maybe,' Everett snarled. 'Maybe not.'

Vance smiled his dark smile again. 'We'll just have to wait and see won't we?'

'For the last time; does anyone not trust Vance?' Saph asked bluntly, then turned immediately to Everett. 'Enough to count him out after coming all this way?'

Everett grunted and took a pull of his giant cigar.

When they'd finished, they all stood in a circle, staring at each other.

Saph extended her hand to Trudy. Trudy handed over the box of chocolates. She did the same to Vance; he didn't hesitate to hand over the nougat. Then Everett. There was hesitation, but he handed over the cigars. Finally, Mitch handed her the liquor bottle. She took a light swig, screwed the cap back, and placed it in her bag with all the other items.

Then she extended the bag to Yelina.

'If we all go mad, I think you're the best person to deal with these.'

Yelina bowed slightly and accepted the bag, putting it over her shoulder.

'So what now?' Heather asked. 'Anyone feel super-different?'

'A little bit high if I'm honest,' Vance shrugged. 'But that could be the sugar rush?'

'And lack of oxygen,' Saph waved her hand across her face, through the haze of cigar smoke.

Mitch cleared his throat. 'I think I know what we need to do. But first, I want a moment with Everett. Heather and Yelina, I'd like you to stay.'

'Stay?' Saph protested. 'You're kicking us out?'

'I want you guys to go see if you can find either Gabrielle Fenwick, or Oliver Hines. They'll both be here somewhere; Fenwick will want protection and Hines is just waiting for us to come see him.'

Everett nodded. 'He'll wait us out a while longer; but it won't be long before he runs out of patience. He won't kill us. He wants to see our faces while we watch Los Angeles crash and burn.'

Vance, Saph, Trudy and Amy exchanged glances.

'Okay,' Amy shrugged. 'It'll give me a chance to try out my new superpowers!'

'No showing off now, sweetie,' Everett warned. 'Oliver's just waiting for that. We don't want to show our hand too early; we don't know what tricks he has in store. He wouldn't have us here without protection.'

Amy sighed and opened the door, holding it ajar for the others.

'Okay then.'

Cigar smoke poured out, almost instantly setting off an alarm in the corridor outside.

'Didn't really think that one through did we?' Vance proclaimed, exiting the bathroom with a flourish of his black, white handled cane.

Which, they were all perfectly aware, three seconds ago had been non-existent.

He used it to smash the alarm.

'Don't be long,' Trudy warned. 'I don't like it here. I need to get back to my people. The fighting might still be going; some of them might be injured.'

Amy followed her, shrugging. She went to close the door behind her, then paused and merely made the gesture with her hand. The door slammed shut without her touching it.

They heard her muffled voice behind it.

'This is gonna be *so cool*!'

CHAPTER EIGHTY-ONE

Everett puffed on his cigar. 'So what's this about Mitch?'

Heather handed him her cigar and grimaced. 'Enough for me. You have it.'

Mitch took a pull and puffed out smoke.

From what he knew, these were very good.

'Everywhere I go, these aliens are telling me stories. And somehow they all fit together. Heather and I met the Elohim while we were at the church; they asked me to come and see them. I reckon I'm gonna do just that.'

'How?' Everett asked.

'We're going to break in – from the bottom up. From third density, right up as high as Pan's gifts will carry us.'

Everett smiled. 'I like the sound of that.'

'But first, I want your story – the real one. What's all this about to you?'

Everett grumbled.

Then the house grumbled.

'That wasn't a Sirian arriving,' Yelina said gravely. 'We have maybe ninety minutes.'

'Then make it quick,' Mitch looked to Everett again.

Everett leaned back against the frozen shower cubicle, blocking out Eissley's frozen ire.

'I told you once Mitch, that the aliens don't speak to the likes of me; the Anunnaki don't like that I have managed somehow without them, the Pleiadeans don't like my energy, and well, the list goes on. But let me take you back from here, here where we know what's going on. Let me take you back a decade ago, when I first read Michio Kaku's work. Remember you read the print out of the Kardashev Scale?'

'Yeah – the different types of potential extraterrestrial societies.'

'Well, as you know, Mitch, I am very interested in the space program, or rather, my own private space program. When I first became aware that there were secret societies within the world governments, and within the global corporations, I did some investigating. I came to realize that there were people in very high places who believe we need to keep the world population below a billion people, some even say half a billion people. Some of those people made their intentions very clear when they created the Georgia Guidestones.'

'The what?'

'A monument erected in Ebert County, Georgia, under the name RC Christian. No-one knows who actually put the Guidestones there, but some believe that the name is a reference to the Rosicrucian movement. But whoever the hell made them, I always keep a copy on me, so I never need reminding of who we're up against.'

Again, Everett removed several pieces of A4 paper, folded together, from his back pocket. Again, he sorted through them and handed one to Mitch.

Mitch wondered what the hell it would be this time; whatever else a man like Everett felt the need to carry around at all times.

'I printed it from Wikipedia, but it's accurate.'

Mitch scanned the paper.

1.   Maintain humanity under 500,000,000 in perpetual balance with nature.

2.   Guide reproduction wisely – improving fitness and diversity.

3.   Unite humanity with a living new language.

4.   Rule passion – faith – tradition – and all things with tempered reason.

5.   Protect people and nations with fair laws and just courts.

6.   Let all nations rule internally, resolving external disputes in a world court.

7.   Avoid petty laws and useless officials.

8.   Balance personal rights with social duties.

9.   Prize truth – beauty – love – seeking harmony with the infinite.

10.   Be not a cancer on the earth – Leave room for nature.

'What do you make of it?' Mitch asked.

'The world needs a new Ten Commandments Mitch, I agree. But this ain't it. Although, I guess, if you're okay with a new global government that eradicates all cultural difference, murders over six billion useless eaters, instigates a healthy program of eugenics and replaces all emotional and spiritual feeling with rational materialism, it's actually pretty good.'

Mitch stopped puffing on the cigar. 'You think that's what it means?'

'I don't know if they're hoping to start that today, if it's all caught up in this business we're all caught up in, or if it's just some private moron's idea of a joke. But at the time, I thought; if this is what they plan, if this is humanity's future at the hands of some anonymous global elite, then there is only one other solution to the over-crowding of Earth; we have to get off this rock.'

'Your private space travel initiative?'

'By Michio Kaku's account it could take centuries before that happens. My ego wouldn't allow that, so I started looking into everything I could, everything and anyone. How could we get it done sooner? How much would it cost? Who was working on new technologies? What were they? That got me into genetics; life extension. I thought; the longer I live the better the chance I have of finding someone who can help me figure this all out. The longer an astronaut can live, the more likely he'll take a trip to Mars, or one of the outer planets with a chance of returning. Maybe even beyond. I thought; the longer everyone lives, the longer they have to think and work something out. That's the cruelest trick the universe played on us, Mitch. In whatever age mankind lives, it gives a man, or a woman, just enough time to figure out one, maybe two, at the outside three things really well. And I'm talking expert level. Then we're gone. Maybe we come back and we get more opportunity to master more things; a guru once told a friend of mine that it takes many lives to learn the violin. Maybe so. But we have no definitive proof of that, and worse, no way to exploit it. Imagine if we all lived two, three hundred years? If your genius-level people could live to be multi-disciplinarian geniuses. That's the key Mitch – connections. Brilliance, wisdom and unexpected connections between different disciplines. And not just the biologically super-intelligent. The longer we all live, the longer we all have for inspiration to strike.'

Everett shrugged and laughed to himself.

'But now Oliver Hines has that ability, and he intends to exploit it in the worst way possible.'

'We're going to stop him,' Heather insisted. 'Somehow!'

Everett smiled warmly at her. 'When Heather introduced me to Pan, and Pan told me his theories, I thought; here's a man who thinks outside the box. I liked him.'

'Everyone liked him. It was impossible not to.'

'Maybe so. Regardless, I thought, if anyone's going to discover the buried secrets in the human genome sequence, it's him. But when Pan took me down to Peru, he did something unexpected. He convinced me to undergo the ayuwashka ceremony; in fact, it was a condition of his coming to work for me. And that gave me an experience that changed the way I perceived my life. I spoke, under what most people would call a hallucination, of course, to beings who seemed to come from another dimension, another level of consciousness. When I say, I spoke; what I mean is, they spoke to me. In no uncertain terms, they made me see what myself and others were doing to the planet; call them nature spirits, nature deities, nature Gods if you will; call it Gaia, call it Pan, even. They ripped my ego apart and showed me how insignificant I was in the whole scheme of the universe, how small and insignificant my plans and me were, to take humanity to the stars. Then they put me back together; and they showed me patterns and schemes and layers, layers of universal or cosmic consciousness, and they made me realize that even though I was infinitesimally small and insignificant, on another level I was everything; that we are all everything, and each one of our tiny identities, no matter how small, is still a reflection of God. Okay, so I said God. That's what it is after all, at the heart of things; one great shining all-knowing entity. God is as good a word as any when we're talking within the paradigm I'm outlining to you now. So when I came out of the hallucination, the experience, I was changed, but I was still me; I still had my ego, I still had my Bo Everett program running in my Bo Everett brain, formed from my Bo Everett DNA. But I realized that; there *are* other entities out there. There *are* other life forms, other civilizations, and that they *do* coexist with us here on the planet. I returned to my dream of exploring space, of taking humanity to the stars, but from an altered perspective. What had become clear to me was that these other beings, these aliens from other planets, traveled here. They traveled. Here.'

Mitch nodded. He was getting the gist now.

'They had to have some kind of technology that allowed them to do that, and my experience of being shown them in an altered state of consciousness told me that that was the key; the key to interstellar travel was somehow linked with altered states of consciousness, and from there, access to other dimensions. So I sent my people out; I sent Heather back into Pan's People and told her to infiltrate them, to learn what she could about these new paradigms in consciousness exploration. There was something about Pan; on his podcast he would interview the people who were trying to get to the bottom of this, and because of who he was, because of his charm or charisma or – maybe because it was his birthright? Who knows? Maybe he was created here, the Holland Pankhurst biological program, to get it all started? Maybe there have been many expressions of the

Holland Pankhurst DNA combination before now, trying to get our human DNA off the planet, manifested to do expressly that, but Pan's was the first combination that *held*, and attracted others of his kind.'

'I can see that,' Heather uttered. 'That seems right to me...'

'No matter. Anyway, because of who he was, Pan would attract these people; scientists, physicists, theoretical physicists, philosophers, artists – and just crazy people. People who caught a glimpse of humanity's full potential, or the dimensions outside of the normal human range, who created the best narrative they could to describe what they'd seen; intuitives who even sometimes seemed to get it right, or at least seemed to balance with grace on the tip of the cosmic iceberg. And as you say, people liked Pan; he was a magnet, a vortex for them; they were all attracted to him. They kept in touch, these mad scientists and cosmic poets, and it became something more than just another counter-culture podcast. The CIA knew it; they sent Cricket to infiltrate the organization, an agent provocateur, but like Heather, and so many others before her, she started to believe. She started to genuinely want to know more, and genuinely become involved. The CIA ordered her to start a rival podcast to Pan's; one that instead of spreading hope and good energy would spread fear and create blocks; dark conspiracy theories, ghosts and demons and the occult. She focused on all the so-called lower astral subjects that are designed to keep people away from the truth, but even then she couldn't really stay away from Pan. Pan knew she was CIA, Cricket knew Pan knew, and the CIA knew they both knew; but sometimes that's how deep cover works. But still, after all this, after all the momentum and energy and the whole group movement that built around Pan, there was still no contact. That was the point you see; that was why I funded Pan to keep going back to Peru, to build his consciousness research station, to keep experimenting. Pan took jungle hallucinogens, took ayahuasca, on a semi-regular basis, and it inspired him.'

'Is that dangerous?'

'It's not something I would do; but I really don't think so. He's not the only one to take it on a regular basis. It's certified non-addictive, but who can say what a person's *personality* will respond to? Something about his own genes; different drugs work for different people. And look where it got us.'

'Yeah,' Heather shrugged cynically. 'Look.'

Everett smiled. 'By this time there was an emerging tourist trade for ayahuasca. Pan was gaining attention down there; people knew him, referred to him. Stories started building. But he would keep turning up, and ask to be given another dose, at another ceremony, for inspiration.'

'What do you think that did to him?'

'He was always lucid. Always sharp, bright. This drug is like nothing else on Earth. It's not fun, not in any sense. But it's transformational. And something transformational happened to Pan after his last ayahuasca ceremony. He seemed to intuit something, something he'd never seen before in the patterns his spirit guides were showing him. He returned to the lab, worked three full nights, then packed up and departed. On the way out, he tried to get to me, but I was busy. When I finally called him back, it was too late. He was on his way and I couldn't get Harding to him fast enough. But he did do one thing, one last thing that convinced me that what he had was real.'

'What was that?'

'During the call, he appeared to me, in his astral body. The driver later told me that he collapsed in the back of the car and that was when he pulled over; the timing corresponds to when he appeared to me. He must have taken the full dose, and had the ability to... well, *astral project* would seem the correct term. And, well, the rest you know.'

'Yeah...' Mitch sighed. 'The rest got him killed.'

Everett sighed. 'Indeed. I have had sleepless nights imagining that somehow my lack of faith in Pan, and his need to make that one gesture of proof to me somehow got him on the radar of these aliens. They were able to locate him because of that one demonstration and, well, we think maybe ten minutes later he was shot. My dream, and my lack of spirit by not fully investing in Pan's abilities, and his claims, cost Pan his life. In a way, I suppose, Pan gave his life so that we could have proof; access to the other dimensions and contact with the aliens. And that was the whole point of this to begin with, Mitch; to find a way of breaking through to them, a point of contact, where we could begin to learn how they do it. Mitch, if they could reveal their science to us, if they can show us the answers to how we get off the planet, how we travel the stars as they do, we could be colonizing other worlds tomorrow afternoon! We know there are Earth-type planets out there; we know that the Milky Way galaxy is so big that to us it might as well be infinite, and that's just one of a trillion galaxies! Every nation could have its own world, its own *series of worlds*. Every religion, every philosophy, each with their own planet! To each their own Eden! All we need Mitch, is for them to tell us how to do it!'

Mitch was grinning like a fool.

'That's some kind of motivation there, Bo.'

Bo slapped him on the shoulder.

'Thanks son.'

'What if I were to tell you that Heather and I just had a conversation with the Elohim that totally backs up what you just said; that angels told us we've already been there, and should still be there?'

'I'd say, that's exactly what I'd expect to hear from an angel.'

Mitch tuned to Yelina.

'Yelina, if this works the way I think it does, I need you to find a sacred natural space, somewhere very close. I think we need you to ground us here, to the second and third densities.'

Yelina nodded. 'Of course.'

She seemed very moved by Everett's speech, so much so that she moved toward him and kissed him tenderly on the lips.

'Okay,' Mitch smiled. 'I'm going to see if the others found Hines. I think it's time we had words.'

Everett and Yelina were embracing. Everett mumbled through her kiss.

'Lock the door behind you. If the world's going to end today, it's not going to end without…'

They kissed again, and Heather locked the door behind her.

CHAPTER EIGHTY-TWO

'So commanding,' Heather smiled cheekily as they made their way toward the party.

'I guess when you get an invitation to storm heaven, it kind of gives you that extra bit of confidence, right?'

Heather laughed. 'Hey, why'd you ask me to stay? I know Uncle Bo's story.'

'I just didn't want you to go.'

'Oh.' She smiled. 'Okay.'

They entered the party from the start of the corridor that led to the bathroom, only to find Vance, Saph, Trudy and Amy huddled together beside a large potted fern, three steps away, staring out at the buzzing throng.

They immediately went to ask why they had not proceeded any further, but the reason became readily apparent.

A terrible stench and a wave of nausea hit Mitch almost as soon as he emerged from the corridor. He grabbed his stomach as he felt bile gurgle up in the back of his throat.

Vance, Saph, Trudy and Amy stepped over to them.

'The sickly feeling goes away after a minute,' Vance muttered.

'I was sick in the pot plant,' Amy confessed.

'What is it?' Heather whined. 'It's…?'

'It's lies,' Mitch realized. 'The whole room is one big lie; don't you recognize the smell? It's feces. Rotting, bovine feces. The whole room literally smells of rancid bullshit!'

Heather smiled, then she started to laugh. The she ran to the pot plant and threw up.

'We can't get past it,' Vance shrugged. 'And if you focus, you can see people's auras; they're not all bad, not all evil by any means, but they're all pushing. Pushing everyone away with their lies. For people like us who are at least one foot in the astral, in fourth density, all their thoughts and emotions are bleeding into our reality. Quite frankly, I don't see how we are going to cross the room without death by toxic personality overload.'

They stood transfixed, staring.

There was nothing they could exactly put their finger on.

It was simply a dark flash of color here, an oily shimmering around someone there; and a very, very bad vibe.

Eventually someone moved through the crowd toward them.

It was a very attractive redhead with a full, busty figure who was, like virtually all the other women present, apparently somewhere in her mid to late twenties. The redhead wore professional-style assistant glasses and a tight auburn business suit that showed off her curves. She looked like a stripper in a sexy secretary costume, but soon turned out to be the real deal.

'Mister Hines will see you now,' the woman smiled as she approached. 'Will Mister Everett be joining us?'

They heard a door open behind them and Everett exited the bathroom, followed by Yelina.

'Very good,' the woman smiled.

'Okay,' Everett growled. 'We're ready. Where's Oliver? And what's that Godawful *smell?*'

'Oliver's upstairs. He was very amused at the practical joke; sending everyone up to his private bathroom.'

'It was unintentional,' Heather shrugged, grinning. 'But who cares.'

'And who are you?' Everett enquired.

'We've met before, Bo.'

'We have?' Everett was blank. 'Oh yes, of course.' He leaned down and examined her features closely. She seemed happy to be scrutinized in this intrusive manner, even proud. Finally Everett straightened and smiled knowingly.

'Very nice to meet you again, Jemima.'

'Thank you, Bo. Now if you will come this way, just down

the wall here; we'll circumvent the party to the other side of the room, then upstairs. Just follow me. Don't want anyone getting lost, do we?'

She smiled tightly, politely, and headed off.

As they followed, not quite in single file down the wall, past the priceless modern art and sculptures hanging there, Mitch turned to Everett.

'You know her?'

'Oliver and I were friends once. A long time ago.'

'Who is she?'

'That's Jemima Hines. She had a singing career once, probably will again. She's Oliver's mother.'

Mitch groaned.

Of course she was.

Jemima led them up several sets of stairs, and past several sets of security men, until they arrived at the end of a short corridor. She opened the wide wooden door and ushered them in.

'Your mortal enemies to see you dear,' Jemima called softly, with a smile. She turned to Everett, concerned. 'Oh dear was that a little too far? It just came into my head and I said it. It was supposed to be funny. Never mind, it's said now.'

'Sure, Jemima,' Everett nodded. 'Great makeover. They say that, amongst your pals, if you don't know which one of your moms is considered "the hot mom", then it's yours. I don't think Oliver ever knew.'

Jemima blushed. 'Oh, Bo. That's why I always knew you'd go far.'

She closed the door behind her.

Oliver was sitting in a wide, single couch chair watching television, with the sound off, on an enormous wall screen. There was a pool table behind him, along with several pinball machines and arcade games. The room was decorated with framed posters from Olivera's various marketing campaigns; new operating systems, new phones, new games' consoles. Olivera's latest games' console was sitting unused on an enormous, low coffee table between Oliver's couch and the television.

Several more couch chairs were scattered about the room.

Everett led the group toward him as he flicked through news channels, then turned to them.

'Ah, terrific! The Magnificent Seven!' He looked more closely. 'Only there seems to be eight of you!' He launched up and stood suddenly, clapping his hands together and rubbing them. 'Now who's this then? The prodigal daughter?'

'My name's Amy.'

'Your name's Amethyst, sweetheart. Why shorten such a beautiful and unique name to something so common? Hah! But you know that don't you? Because in the end, none of us crave difference, do we? We can embrace it, make a… a *good show* of being different, to give us a sense of worth now, can't we? But in the end we all just want to blend in and belong – now why'd ya wanna stop that, Bo?'

'I believe your research is somewhat skewed, Oliver.'

Oliver laughed.

'Yeah, yeah, I suppose you could see it that way, from your perspective. By the way, Bo? What exactly is your perspective these days? Souped up on psychotropic drugs that make y'all feel like Supermen? Superladies? Now what's that all about, Bo?'

Everett was silent.

'Huh,' Oliver's eyes narrowed as he scanned them one by one. 'Now, see, my friend Professor Nurding, he thinks you're all doo-lally. Thinks y're all barking mad on some kind of mass-hallucination, thinks you all wanna start some kind of mind cult; anti-reason, anti-science. But… ah, psychotropic hallucinations don't transport people half a planet and three months away in the blink of an eye now do they?'

'No they don't,' Everett whispered.

'Now, see, when I tried to kill y'all – and you'll have to forgive me for that, I've never had anyone killed before, probably never will again, God willin'; but when I tried to kill y'all, my information was that you were gonna mass-produce some kind of magic hippie drug that had the power to turn the world away from capitalism, from democracy – from the gosh-darn free market! Now don't you tell me that ain't true, Bo.'

'I don't know what it will do,' Everett responded. 'I truly don't.'

'It will,' Mitch interjected.

'Mitch!' Saph gasped.

'It will do exactly that. It will change everything, and everyone. More than your Regene treatments will; there isn't anyone alive who could take even just one component of Pan's genetic sequence without it radically transforming their lives. I'm not saying it would stop Regene; God's honest truth, I don't know what it will do exactly, but it *will* change everything. Nothing will be the same.'

Oliver stared at him.

'That so, huh?'

'That's so,' Mitch nodded.

'Huh,' said Oliver.

Oliver returned to his chair and sat, then reclined.

'I wanna talk to Mitchell. Alone.'

They exchanged glances.

'You others wait outside. I'll have drinks brought up. But don't leave the corridor outside.'

'It's okay,' Mitch assured them.

'Sure you know what you're doing?' Everett asked. 'He's no fool.'

'That's what I'm counting on.'

Everett nodded, then turned to the others. 'Let's go.'

They filed out. Saph, Amy and Heather all gave him reassuring glances; but Vance threw him a look that made him wonder if he were doing the right thing, being alone with Oliver Hines.

'Take a seat.'

Mitch heard the door to the games room click, then lock, and walked over to Hines. He took a seat that was angled for gameplay, where he could see both Hines and the television.

'Drink?'

'How do I know it won't have some kind of Regene spike in it?'

'You want it to? Wanna go back to your twenties?'

'Not particularly.'

'Nor does anyone really. What they want is a chance to be young again, a do-over, in the present day. *If I knew then what I know now.* Who at some point in their lives hasn't said that, Mitch? Is there really anything so wrong with that?'

'Ever heard of the Georgia Guidestones?'

'Sure.'

'What do you think the people who made that are going to do when you start making over all the six or seven billion "useless eaters", so they live forever?'

Oliver nodded.

'I see. You're making a play. Good for you Mitchell, good for you! What's your pitch, huh? Gimme yer best shot!'

'Do you even know what's going on, Oliver? Really?'

'Bo's trying to bring me down. Nothin' wrong with that – it's what we do.'

'But you tried to kill us all over this!'

'I wasn't lying about Pan, Mitch. Oh yeah, one of his assistants sold him out; stole his research, sold it to me. And that assistant is currently away somewhere, spending the… really, I mean *really*, vast amounts of money I gave her. Somewhere on her own little island paradise somewhere I would imagine. I didn't keep track. Kind of the point really. Pam someone… Pam? Pam, Pam…'

He mumbled, trying to remember.

'Pam Winters,' said Mitch.

'That's her! Old Pammie, she wanted out of the human race, wouldn't be sportin' to follow her progress. But Pam didn't kill Pan, Mitch. She didn't and I didn't. Didn't kill any of 'em – not the other researcher who disappeared, and I certainly didn't kill that Timothy fella – as you're well aware, when we last saw him he was alive and at large, and well, doing Pan's bidding. Without even knowing Pan was dead, or so it seems. Last we heard of him he boarded a plane for Central Australia. No, all that nasty business in Peru, that was none of my doing; just the bribe, and the intel.'

Mitch leaned back. 'I think I believe you.'

'As no doubt you are aware, people develop things concurrently. I know you like your movies, Mitch. Think of me as *Deep Impact*, and Everett as *Armageddon*. He's certainly filled with enough doom and gloom, don't you think? No, Mitchell, my own team were one of those teams you may have heard about, several years ago now, who were starting to apply some of the knowledge from the Human Genome Project, and a few other little genetic studies' projects that are happening all over the place. One team that got a lot of the press were the team that managed to create their own life form, and put their signature in its DNA. Do you recall such a thing, Mitch?'

'Yeah. I do. I think it made the news.'

'Well, my team was doing something similar, but they were stopped in their tracks when they made an even more startling discovery. Do you know what that was?'

'No. How could I?'

'Well, gee now Mitch, you're no fun. Take a guess.'

'Kilroy Was Here?'

Oliver laughed. 'Good one, Mitch. Yeah, real good. Huh. And not so far from the truth. You see Mitch, what they found was…'

Oliver paused.

'Y'know, Mitch… ever since that day, ever since they told me what they found… things ain't been the same.'

'What do you mean?'

'Well, to be honest with ya, it feels like I never leave this floor of the house any more. I mean, there's a huge party goin' on down there. Lots of famous people; lots of people who wanna thank me. What am I doin' up here? It was the same at the last party, and the one before that.'

Mitch looked around. The room was almost an apartment.

'Where do you sleep?'

'I have a bedroom and a bathroom down the corridor. My chef brings all my food up to me. I mean, I have bigger houses than this, in nicer places. I've never spent so much time in LA.'

'Where do you usually live?'

'Well… everywhere. My boat, my hotels… what's the use in having money if you can't travel? I can do business from anywhere now. Why do I do it all from here?'

Mitch's heart was beating a little faster.

'Oliver, how long has this been going on?'

'Since they told me.'

'Told you what? Oliver, you still haven't told me what your people found out.'

'Yeah… funny ain't it? I mean, since they told me… I don't think I've ever left this floor. I found out, and I just… set up camp in here and stayed put. What do you make of that Mitch?'

Mitch scanned the room. Everything in the room was, as one would expect, an Olivera product. Television, Blu-Ray, games console; all Olivera brand.

'Oliver?' Mitch began. 'You don't believe in aliens do you? Aliens from other dimensions?'

Oliver laughed. 'No, of course I don't. That's your bag, ain't it? Hippy love and psychotropic drugs? Timothy Leary and Terrence McKenna, talking to plant people in your head? I just wanna make the world a better place Mitch.'

'By blowing us all up in a hotel with a military helicopt…'

Mitch stopped in mid-speech. Something was occurring to him.

'Yeah, I did come on a bit strong there Mitch, didn't I? Real sorry, guess I had a temper I didn't know about. I don't know why all this is so important to me really. So what if Bo Everett has a competing line of gene therapies? That's the free market. That's what I stand for. Competition's healthy. I mean, me and Bo used to be pals, he'll tell you that? Made a pact; we do it on our own. No clubs, no secret handshakes… none of that stuff. Man, did they hate us for it. But we made it, Bo and me. I wonder where it all went wrong between us?'

'Oliver, where did you get a military attack helicopter from?'

'My security force, I guess.'

'What security force? What software billionaire has his own military attack helicopter?'

'Well, I do I suppose. I just called security and…'

'And what?'

'And… I don't really recall much after that.'

'Do you remember talking to us on the phone?'

'The phone?'

'Do you remember giving the order to have us killed?'

'I remember… feeling real bad about it afterwards. That's why I asked Bo here, asked him to bring y'all. Try and make amends. Try and make a deal, like the old days.'

'Oliver, I need to get something. Is that okay? It's just outside.'

'Sure, sure. You wanna drink? I can get you a drink?'

'That's okay.' Mitch stood. 'I'll just be a second.'

Mitch walked to the door. His hands were shaking as he knocked.

'Is this locked?'

There was a click and the door opened. Jemima stood there. The others were gathered in the corridor behind her, leaning against the wall, each with a drink in their hands, all staring in at him with intense concern.

Everett stood bolt upright. 'Everything okay?'

'Sure,' Mitch said, sounding less than reassuring. 'Yelina, my phone's in that bag, can I have it please?'

Yelina nodded. 'Of course.'

'I don't like this,' Everett growled. 'I don't like just standing out here.'

She fished around and dug it out.

'Is this it?'

'Thanks.'

He took it from her.

'Can someone show me how to – ?'

The door slammed before him. He tried to open it but it wouldn't budge. He heard them calling his name, and heard Jemima try the key again.

'Mitch are you okay!' Heather yelled.

'Yeah I'm okay.'

The key, Mitch thought. The conventional key. It was well known that the eccentric irony behind Oliver Hines, the software billionaire, was that he didn't trust software. In the early days of the internet someone had electronically stolen his plans for the Olivera browser; it had set his company back a year and almost pushed them out of the market. Since then, it had been revealed that Oliver Hines wrote everything important on paper, and never used digital technology where secrecy was required. His important notes and memos were all handwritten, hand-delivered. He communicated in person, or through an intermediary, who would also be in person, either delivering a handwritten letter or a memorized verbal message. It worked only because Oliver was wealthy enough to make it work, to have a personal network, a personal postage service. He was like an old-fashioned spymaster, controlling his agents.

And yet, Oliver Hines had called them on a phone that had allowed his death threat to be recorded. He had *made* a death threat and gone through with its execution.

Xylata had told them; people like Everett could not be controlled. The stronger the ego, the cultural awareness, the individuality or, he supposed, the novelty of a personality, the harder it was. Even for someone as fragile as Saph had been, they could only sit back and nudge from the unconscious during moments of indecision. That was, of course, unless you were like Eissley; Eissley who invited them in willingly.

Then Eissley had bragged how it had taken ten years for him to get into Olivera. That he was the one who now had control, not Oliver Hines.

And Oliver Hines, by his own admission, had not been the

same man since being told… what?

Something so shocking that it had opened a door in his mind, and allowed something inhuman a sliver of purchase. The thin end of the wedge had got in. Something that whatever was now possessing Oliver Hines had prevented him from revealing to Mitch three times in the past few minutes.

'Saph!' Mitch called through the door. 'How do I play that video?'

'Use the icons!' Saph called back. 'They're basic, intuitive!'

'Okay!'

He turned and walked back to Oliver. He was just sitting there, flicking through the silent news channels again.

'Why do I get the feeing like something's going to happen? Real soon?'

'Can you use one of these?' Mitch asked, indicating the phone.

'Erm, sure. I think. Don't like 'em though. Not just the brand. Don't like the ones we make either. Don't like my own products, ain't that a kicker? Don't trust 'em one bit. Nice for the kids though, huh? Nice cash cow for us, I gotta say.'

'Here,' Mitch handed it to him. 'There's a video of you on it. I think it's the only one. I want you to watch it.'

'Okay.'

Oliver immediately put the phone down on the arm of the couch chair and ignored it.

'Mitch, I like you. Liked you from the first time I saw your security profile. Nice guy, some tough breaks, now you're just about to bounce back. So I'm gonna tell you something. There's a war in my head Mitch. I can feel it. I feel… kind of distant from my own thoughts.'

Mitch was listening but also thinking, thinking hard.

Eissley also had an alliance with the Orion Renegades.

They had been trying to destroy humanity for six thousands years; and now, with Regene, they thought they had a chance to see it happen.

Why?

Why did they want to end humanity?

'Mitch, you say I gave an order to have you all killed. I kind of remember that; but the way I was talking about it with y'all before… it was kind of a joke to me. Almost, not real. Like a game. But now Mitch, I'm getting the feeling like I should give that order again. I don't know why I want to kill my old friend Bo, or you and your lovely young daughter. She's a credit to you Mitch, I can see that…'

Mitch looked around the room.

There had to be something, some indication of who was controlling Oliver Hines. But there was nothing; it was a games' room, a games' room like any other man-child would have, given the financial freedom.

'But the thing is Mitch, any minute, any second now, I'm gonna give the order for my security force to come in and kill you all. Just a clean head shot, each of you. I wonder Mitch, did I already give that order? Do I even need to? These other thoughts in my head Mitch, they're becoming very clear now, and the clearer they become, the clearer it seems to me that they have been there before. I think I need a holiday Mitch, away from this room. I think he'll let me have a holiday Mitch, if I just give the order.'

'What did they tell you Oliver? What scared you so much they were able to get in?'

'Oh, it's big Mitch. It's a game changer.'

'Bigger than aliens being real?'

'Bigger.'

'Bigger than Anunnaki controlling global corporations? Bigger than Pleiadeans inspiring our art? Bigger than Sirians inspiring our science?'

'Bigger.'

'Bigger than angels being real?'

'Angels are real?'

'In a way.'

'Bigger. It's all that and more; it's what they *all know*.'

'What is it, Oliver?'

'It's who we are Mitch. It's what the Earth has become.'

'*What is it*, Oliver?'

'He doesn't like this Mitch. He's coming, working his way down. It's a long way. He talks to me from afar, but he's coming to see you, Mitch. He's coming to see you in person.'

'Who is?'

'Him… you know.'

'Who Oliver?'

'The man, Mitch. The man himself.'

'Which man?'

'Satan, Mitch. Satan's coming.'

CHAPTER EIGHTY-THREE

'Satan?'

'He's coming Mitch.'

'You mean The Devil, Lucifer? Beelzebub?'

'No Mitch; they're three different things. This is Satan. The ruler of the Void. The Prince of Darkness and Despair.'

Despite the ridiculousness of it, Mitch was frightened.

There had been plenty of things he'd not believed real.

Before.

Satan was not a name you just threw around; not in a situation like this. Not in a situation where angels, or Elohim, were real. Not when he'd seen soulless things like the agents, and the Orion Renegades.

'How do you know all this?'

'When he comes, I know a lot. A lot of things I didn't think were real seem real.'

'Oliver, I want you to play that video on the phone.'

Mitch reached over and snatched it up. Could he even switch it on? How did these things work? The screen was black. Nothing. He had to try and remember; he'd remembered Saph's number when Nurding had been about to claim him. He'd *seen* Saph switch it on. Maybe it was already on? Maybe it was on standby?

Jesus, maybe it needed a recharge?

Suddenly it made a sound and the screen appeared.

How?

Then he realized; he'd been squeezing it, hard. There was a little pressure switch on the top. That had switched it on.

Slide to unlock.

People waved their fingers over these things like magic.

Waved?

Slid.

He slid.

About a dozen icons appeared.

Intuitive, Saph had said.

Mitch felt a sudden jolt.

Like his brain was trying to spike, but couldn't.

Why did it even need to?

Surely, with all the genetically enhancing drugs he'd taken, he should have been able to sense that Oliver was possessed as soon as he set eyes on him; they all should have.

What the hell was happening?

'Oliver, when did this start?'

'He's coming.'

'*When did this start?*'

'Nine months ago – when it *all* started. When we changed the company logo, when we discovered the gene sequence. Just before Regene.'

It was all connected. Mitch had to think.

Fear was grabbing him.

Satan was coming.

Satan.

He was *real.*

And yet; angels weren't angels, were they?

They were Elohim; they were beings that evolved and survived millennia, maybe from the beginning of the cosmos.

Maybe the Prince of Darkness was coming… and maybe he was real… but he was also *real.*

A creature of some reality, somewhere, in some dark and soulless dimension…

Soulless.

Or, the capturer of souls?

Was there such a place?

A *despair* dimension?

Then Mitch clicked.

He realized.

He ran to the door.

'I know what's happening! Try and break the door down!'

'Mitch!' Heather cried out. 'We can't even get near it! There's a shield around the room!'

'What's happening Mitch!' Everett shouted.

'The leader of the Orion Renegades has possession of Oliver! And he's coming!'

There was silence.

'Jesus Christ,' he heard someone mutter.

'Look,' Mitch called through the door. 'There must be some use for our abilities here! Satan is coming from somewhere in eighth density – he doesn't just do that –'

'Satan!' Amy cried out.

'It's just a name, Amy! He's no different to Obsidian, he's just meaner!'

'Who?!'

'Someone explain it to her, for Christ's sake!'

'Mitch!' Vance shouted. 'Obsidian has structure here; he had a body, and an organization. From the black sunglasses to the black cars and the Pentagon Building and all the rest – if Satan is coming through from eighth density he will need structure here too! Orion beings cannot manifest here without a strong web of symbols and structure to focus their energy upon; they have virtually no natural form outside of their basic atomic structure! Find that and destroy it!'

'But you saw it Vance! It's just a games' room! There's nothing in here! There's no alter, no symbols, no – wait!'

Mitch ran back across the room to Oliver.

He was still there, still flicking through the channels.

'Oliver; when did you change the logo? Why?'

'Nine months ago. I just wanted something new. It just came to me; we needed something new for the new era of Olivera and Regene.'

'Did Eissley create it?'

'His marketing team did. I didn't like it, but I was told it tested well.'

Mitch leaned over and picked up the games' console from the coffee table.

'Is this it?'

'Yeah. What do you think?'

Mitch didn't know. It was a stylized olive, for Olivera presumably, the edges of which formed an elliptical pattern. The lines at the top and bottom of the ellipse extended out to create four interlocking circles over the original olive design, creating a further pattern of ellipses.

'What was it before?'

'Just an olive on a branch, and some leaves. It's similar, but far more stylized.'

That had to be it, Mitch thought.

There was nothing else.

'Show me all the Olivera products in the room.'

Oliver smiled. 'All of them? They're everywhere. Why?'

'We have to destroy them.'

'Even that one?'

Oliver looked up.

Above him, painted on the ceiling, directly above where he sat, was an enormous Olivera logo.

'There's one on the roof too. Eissley put it there.'

'Jesus…' Mitch uttered. 'We're gonna have to burn the house down.'

CHAPTER EIGHTY-FOUR

'Guys!' Mitch yelled to the door. 'Think again!'

There was no response.

Mitch stared at the phone.

Icons.

This whole damn thing was about icons.

Was it an illusion, or was the room getting darker?

Whatever it was, none of his abilities worked in here.

Focus on the phone.

There was an icon that seemed to say 'movies.'

He pressed it.

A menu came up.

How did these things work?

Not waving… sliding and tapping.

He read the menu.

Just one item: unknown.

'That has to be it,' Mitch muttered.

He tapped the item on the screen.

Oliver's face appeared.

'Look, here's the deal. I'm going to talk, then I want you to accept my offer. You'll have one minute after I finish talking to make your choices…'

Mitch held it up to him.

'Look; it's you!'

'…but we all know how things tend to get out of hand where men with guns are concerned, so… well I guess if it gets to that we just wait and see how things pan out. Bo? You still there?'

They heard Everett speak.

'I'm here.'

'Bo, you might not be in my league financially…'

'Do you remember this, Oliver?'

'No.'

'You're about to explain why we have to surrender. You're about to give the order that's intended to kill us! You don't remember?'

The video kept playing.

'*…What good is a dead genius? So young, too! Just a darn tragedy!*'

'No, no, I don't Mitch.'

They listened a while longer while Oliver's features began to distort in fear and pain.

'I don't remember at all Mitch!'

'Oliver, you have to fight this; he can't come through if you don't let him!'

They heard Everett growl.

'*You're sending mankind down a path it's not ready for. There's no projection you can make that doesn't end in the extinction of individuality.*'

'*Okay, okay – maybe you've got a point. Maybe your projections are a little less optimistic than mine.*'

'*That is my most optimistic projection!*'

They heard Oliver sigh. '*Maybe so, maybe so. But you know I'm a good capitalist at heart, Bo. It's not up to me; we let it out and let the market decide.*'

Mitch leaned into Oliver.

'Oliver, that's not you. It sounds like you, but that's someone, some *thing*, using your personality to speak through you!'

'I know it is Mitch!'

'You have to fight it! Or it's going to come through, and it's going to trigger the beginning of Armageddon – Bo Everett isn't Armageddon, Oliver. You are!'

'No!'

'Fight him, Oliver!'

'Kill me!'

'What?'

'Kill me Mitch! It's the only way!'

'No!'

'They've taken everything Mitch! Look what they've done to my company!'

'Fight it, Oliver!'

'Kill me!' Oliver was crying now. 'I'm the door he comes through!'

'Oliver, I won't!'

'I can't bear it Mitch, I can't bear him being there, all the time, watching! Listening!'

'You are *Oliver Hines*. You are one of the most revered and respected people on planet Earth; until nine months ago that was *all you* – nothing stopped you, not Microsoft, not Apple, not even Bo Everett!'

'God, Bo! I destroyed him! I've destroyed everything!'

'It can all be rebuilt! You and Bo can rebuild it together! But you must fight the Orion Renegades!'

'I can't, I can't!'

Above them, the ceiling began to shake.

Something was coming through; something powerful, something physical.

The video had stopped.

Mitch looked at it.

Somehow, he'd hit fast forward.

He tapped it and the picture returned to normal.

It was the end of Oliver's speech.

'*Last chance Bo.*'

Silence as he waited.

'*I haven't got any choice Bo. I'm sorry.*' Oliver turned away from the phone camera and gave a command. '*Level the hotel.*'

'I did…' Oliver gasped. 'I did do it!'

'The helicopter was Orion – Black Ops. They have to be the ones controlling you. I know for a fact that Eissley is in league with both the Anunnaki and the Orion Renegades – Oliver, these are *beings*. Very old, but very much people like us, all with different agendas, manipulating each other, manipulating us. *You have to resist.*'

He shoved the phone back in his pocket and the ceiling shook again; this time it might have been a Sirian, or the earthquake starting – but Mitch knew it wasn't. It was something *coming through*.

His hand touched something else in his pocket.

Thin and metal.

He felt something sharp, and pulled it out.

It was the tranquilizer dart from the deck of Everett's boat.

'That's it!' Mitch cried.

He raised it, held it, then jammed it into Oliver's thigh, just as Oliver cried out.

'No!'

Mitch watched his eyes droop. 'He can't come through if you're…'

'Oh Mitch,' Oliver drooled. 'You just made it… sooo… mushhhh… worszzzzz…'

He fell back into the chair, eyes closed, unconscious.

'I did?'

Oliver's eyes snapped back open.

Mitch felt cold.

So very, very cold.

So long as those eyes had him fixed, he would never, never escape.

There was no time; he could not see or feel or think of anything else other than a terrible despair. And he knew he could never escape. He was there forever, not even trapped, just there. There in never-ending, non-specific despair. Nothing outside of that, nothing. Forever.

CHAPTER EIGHTY-FIVE

A voice broke the silence.

Deep and ancient.

'Forever.'

'Yes.'

'Never.'

'I know.'

'Grotesque'

'Yes.'

'So far away.'

'I know.'

'Despair.'

'Yes.'

'Alone.'

'I know.'

Then silence again.

A silence so long and so void that…

Nothing.

Ever.

Again.

Then fire, heat and burning flames.

And Mitch knew he was in hell.

CHAPTER EIGHTY-SIX

The ceiling was on fire.

Huge booted feet were kicking in the Olivera logo, destroying it.

Yet the huge booted feet were standing on – *nothing*.

An invisible ceiling.

The logo was being ripped up, burned, torn away.

Then, crashing; bodies through the ceiling.

The door to the games room opening; his friends rushing in.

Oliver, unconscious on the chair, surrounded by falling embers.

And a face in front of him, huge hands grabbing his shoulders, shaking him.

'Boy!'

A familiar face, shouting right at him.

'Mitchell, you massive dong!'

Who was it!

'Mitchell Pyne, wake up boy!'

Mitch heard himself squeak.

'Harding?'

'There you are!'

Harding's big face grinned in at him, hugely relieved.

'Thought we'd lost you, didn't we lads!'

Byford was standing behind him with a flame-thrower, grinning ear to ear.

'We picked up your phone signal – heard your conversation.' Harding's thick South African accent was the most reassuring voice he'd ever heard. 'Thought, best get to it, eh? Blew the logo on the roof, came in through the ceiling! Figured the supernatural shield around the room would give up the ghost if we burned up the occult symbol, isn't that right Byford?'

'Sah!'

'How you feeling eh?'

'Like hell…' Mitch groaned.

'You should have killed the little bastard when he told you to!' Harding slapped him on the arm. 'Huh! Probably saved his life in the end! Pay attention to the spikes boy, isn't that what I always told you?'

The others were gathered around.

'Is he dead?' Everett asked, genuinely concerned. 'We could hear everything from outside. You did a damn fine job Mitch; held him back well enough!'

'He's tranqed. I thought if I broke the conscious link with the eighth density, he couldn't come through. But I was wrong. Oliver was right. The only way was to kill him.'

'Or destroy the occult logo,' Vance nodded. 'Are you okay Mitch? You looked Satan in the eye. Not many people can walk away from that.'

'It felt like forever,' Mitch grunted. 'My God; if people ever get trapped there…'

Vance nodded. 'Don't think about it.'

'I don't think I'll ever think about anything else, ever again.'

Heather moved forward and embraced him gently.

'Yes you will. I promise. I'll see to that.'

The house shook.

More of the ceiling fell in and nobody kept their balance.

Mitch and Heather held tightly together and didn't let go.

Then it stopped.

After a pause, they heard some screaming but mostly cheering from below.

'A foreshock…' Trudy stated.

Yelina spoke sternly. 'We have less than an hour. If you are going to do something…'

Mitch turned to Vance. 'I don't know if all your knowledge, and your conjuring abilities are something you've been keeping from us, or something –'

'They're something I'm recalling.'

'Well, how reliable is it? Your information?'

'Very.'

'Okay; let me ask you this. That… *thing* just burned a path from an eighth density hell dimension right through to us here in the third. Did it leave a path?'

'Undoubtedly.'

'Is it safe to use – to seventh density at least?'

'He would have come down the levels of density like a hurricane funnel, massed up high, but boring down to a pinpoint here in third. Whatever energetic malignancy he left in his wake, I believe we can avoid, or… or I can handle it.'

'You?' Heather demanded.

Vance nodded. 'Up to seventh. But beyond that, I wouldn't risk it.'

'Then we won't. But it will save us doing rituals, save us time?'

'He will have left a burning trail. It will take time to seal. We'll have to get through some trials, but it's safe to use as a shortcut.'

'Then that's the route we take.'

Heather released Mitch and stared into his eyes.

'We're really doing this?'

Mitch nodded.

'Yelina?'

'Yes Mitch?'

'I kind of planned to do this out in the garden, in a sacred space. We need you to anchor us to the planet, to first and second and third density. Can you do that – right here?'

'All space is sacred, Mitch. But I will need to make some adjustments to the architecture of the house.'

'Will it take long?'

'No.'

Yelina placed the bag on the floor and opened her arms. She dropped her glamor and began muttering in a language they could not literally translate, but because of their gifts, they partially understood.

Yelina seemed to be praying, at least of a kind. She was asking Gaia, her mother, to expand into the space where she stood. She was asking her to be careful, not to harm anyone, and not to destroy anything that would prevent that space they were in from losing integrity. She prayed, she *asked*, for this in such a beautiful language, filled with flourish yet elegantly simple, that Amy and Heather again burst into spontaneous tears.

Yelina spoke further and they began to lose the thread; her words came faster and faster, blending into each other until her mouth ceased to move and she was only changing vowel sounds. Then, almost imperceptibly, the vowels ceased and she was intoning just one long, low note that resonated like a baritone but moved increasingly higher in pitch, until it was so high that it hurt their ears.

Again, the house shook.

It seemed to shake to its very foundations.

Yelina's intonation seemed to cease, but her mouth remained open. They heard dogs barking outside, then there was screaming from downstairs again, accompanied by harsh cracking and splitting. Finally Yelina closed her mouth and huffed as her hands fell back to her sides.

They heard cars start outside as people rushed to depart, and someone cried out in terror.

'The trees are alive!'

Yelina smiled. 'Idiot,' she uttered.

A snake dropped from the hole in the ceiling and slithered around them, then another, then three more.

Yelina reached over and grabbed Amy's shoulder.

'Keep still!'

Vines burst into the room, in through the corridor, then more from above, following the snakes through the ceiling.

'Holy Mother!' Saph exclaimed.

'Indeed,' Yelina smiled.

The floor began to buckle as a stream of rats ran from one side of the room to the other, ignoring them.

'Stand back!' Everett yelled, pulling Saph aside.

The floor exploded, spraying broken wood boards, wooden supports and concrete into the corner of the room furthest from them as a thick, leafy branch sprang up like a serpent, then the floor exploded again on the other side of the room as another branch broke through. The couches and coffee table fell through the crack and smashed on the floor below, then they heard them fall another level and smash again down there; there was more screaming and more cars starting outside. The branches proceeded, smashing the ceiling upward and away, dousing them all in chunks of plaster, dust and debris. Light poured in as the roof tiles broke away, slid and clattered en masse to the ground, revealing the timber beams above, then each of the three external games' room walls fell backwards; first the side facing the valley, revealing through a curtain of vines and branches the panorama of Los Angeles, then the two side walls at once, revealing the naked corridor outside and an adjoining bathroom and kitchen, suddenly bare to the elements as those walls too collapsed. More vines and branches poured in, smashing aside the rest of the ceiling, curling around the roof beams and supports. Behind them the wall facing the side of the hill started to buckle and crack; plaster fell then the drywall burst open, cracking the now-useless timber supports and revealing the dark soil and rocks behind it, which immediately gave and began to pour onto the floor as the quivering mass of a thick root structure became revealed behind it. Bugs poured forth and scattered, then a few more snakes and family of foxes, all so fast that they could barely register it as real. As the root structure shook, almost animate, two damp and muddy tendrils parted and stretched wide, forming a pear shaped aperture that opened into a black tunnel beneath the tree above.

Mitch looked up; he didn't know if the tree had been there, behind the house in the side of the hill, before Yelina had summoned her magic, but it was certainly there now. The massive trunk towered high like the beanstalk of fairy tales, its canopy spread wide over Oliver's ruined house and well beyond.

'What kind of a tree is that?' Mitch heard Heather question with a gasp.

Yelina responded. 'It is not the One Tree, but it is an echo of it.'

'The One Tree?'

'The Asvattha of the Hindus, Yggdrasill of the Norse, the Tree of Knowledge and the Tree of Life; these and many others are but echoes, abstracts; but the One Tree is the tree that links every tree, makes every tree the same tree, the reflection of the one; it is the chain of ecology and life that is the biodiversity of Earth itself, Gaia herself; Jack climbed it to find the Giant, George Washington chopped it down as a child, it is the tree that tested the courage in each of us in childhood, under which we take shelter as adults, admire in retirement and take shade beneath in twilight years; it is the child's Faraway Tree, the Forest of Fangorn, and the Navi's Tree of Souls; the tree that inspired Johnny Appleseed, that dropped the apple on Isaac Newton's head, and from which a thousand outlaws and thieves have hung. It is all trees, but it is One. And it is here, to anchor you in second density and guide you from third.'

Mitch couldn't find words. All that remained of the level around them was the skeleton of the roof, the section of the floor upon which they stood, and the huge gaping entrance of mud and root that had parted before them.

Essentially, they were all now standing in a giant open tree-house.

Yelina's smile was radiant.

'Is that what you desired, Mitchell Pyne?'

Mitch smiled back.

'There's just one thing I should have thought of before I asked you to do that.'

'And what is that, Mitchell Pyne?'

'We need those two caskets we found in Eissley's crypt. I just wonder how we'll get them up here?'

CHAPTER EIGHTY-SEVEN

The rest of Byford's men were still on the ground.

Everett had called Byford to secure the caskets, so they were waiting in a parked van not far down the road.

By the time they arrived with them, the house was all but abandoned, except for Everett's car across the front exit and a few stragglers, whose cars had been damaged when the surrounding garden and forest had come alive to reclaim the house.

Byford's men were sturdy and some of the staircases from the second to the third floor remained intact, so it took them around ten minutes to bring the caskets up to what they were calling 'the canopy'.

'How bad is the damage?' Saph asked.

'Not too bad, considering, marm. What it seems like is that the foliage has all-but replaced many of the walls, with branches replacing the supports. But much of the lower levels are still standing. From the outside it basically resembles a vine-covered coach house. There's still a few actor types wandering around; some of them are clearly inspired by it, some of them simply can't get their cars started. A few of them managed to get the spa started and are making the most of it – very romantic marm, in the classical Greek sense. Recognized a few of them, too.'

'Really?'

'There's that young fellow from that show about the robots, and that rather fetching lass from the police show with the older chap who used to be in the one about the doctor who couldn't quit smoking.'

'I see.'

'Oh, and there's the famous one; the first lady who had the

treatment. Gabby… err, whatsername now?'

Mitch had been staring out at the valley. Hundreds of merkabas had manifested in the sky over Los Angeles and, higher up, he could see shimmering objects that he assumed represented the outline of some kind of cloaking technology. It seemed that everyone had turned up to see the Big One. He wondered if one of the high-hovering merkabas might have been Mendoza, or whether Misha might have been on one of the camouflaged ships.

At the mention of Gabby, however, Mitch's ears had pricked.

'Gabrielle Fenwick?'

'That's right, sah. That's the lass.'

'Byford, could you do me a massive favor?'

'Naturally sah.'

'Could you get her and bring her up here, double time?'

'Right you are, sah!'

They heard her coming, only a few minutes later, as they gathered around the casks.

'Oh, I love it! It's just wonderful!'

She was climbing up a series of easy branches, as her head rose above the edge of what remained of the floor.

'Hello!' Gabrielle Fenwick called as she saw them all. 'Look at you all up here! Were you up here when it happened?'

She really was very beautiful, Mitch thought immediately.

'Oh my God,' Amy muttered. 'It's her!'

'Hello,' Gabrielle smiled at her. 'I'm Gabrielle.'

She extended her hand and Amy shook it, wide-eyed. Mitch couldn't blame her. He couldn't help but think of Mendoza's theory, the one he had, to all intents and purposes, proved over a near-thirty year period. That there was something in the genes of a star, something that made them not simply radiant and charismatic in person, but also translated directly into the illusion of photography.

'Aren't you Bo Everett?'

'Pleased to meet you.'

'Oh, I love your passion, I really do. You must take me into space when you get it done; call my people, I'll do a spot for you at scale. I love the space-race.' She turned to Mitch. 'Hello, I'm Gabrielle.'

'I know you are,' Mitch smiled. 'And this is Saph, and Heather, and Vance, and Trudy…'

'Hello all of you.'

'…and Yelina, and Harding – and Oliver Hines you've no doubt met, he's just taking a nap.'

'Oh, really? Is he alright?'

'He'll be much better when he wakes up. Oh, and this is Byford, and these are Byford's men.'

'Mister Byford, yes we've met.' She turned to his men. 'Hello! I'm Gabrielle.'

'Ma'am!'

'So, what can I do for you all? I really can't tell you what an amazing experience this has been. Do any of you know how this happened? Is it another of Oliver's genetic things? That's what almost everyone thought, until is started getting a bit violent. I don't think anyone was hurt though; not by the trees anyway. There was a bit of a stampede though. A few bruised ankles I'd think. Bruised egos as well, no doubt. Was it an accident? A chemical accident?'

She looked around, searching their faces.

'What are those coffins doing up here?'

Mitch smiled. 'That's what we need you for. We need an identification, and you're the best qualified I think.'

'Identification? Are there bodies in those?'

'I'm not sure, but…' Mitch sighed, and smiled. 'I think we have some mutual acquaintances. I know Todd Mendoza.'

Gabrielle smiled sweetly, sadly, and nodded. 'Tragic.'

Mitch smiled. 'Well, not really.'

'I'm sorry?'

'I think you know, as well as we all do, that he's alive and well. But that's neither here nor there. The real question I have for you is; do you remember Suzie Saturn?'

'Well yes of course, we came in together on the bus from… although she wasn't called Suzie Saturn then…' Gabrielle frowned, although her forehead didn't crease. 'I'm sorry, I was thinking of someone else. Suzie Saturn… Suzie Saturn… now, I wonder who I was thinking of? Because when I first came into LA, I came on my own… I remember, because it wasn't long after that, I met Todd.'

'You and Suzie met Todd. Together. That's what Mendoza told me.'

'Really?'

'Really. And of everyone I've asked about Suzie Saturn, usually they remember her for about one second. But you remembered her for several seconds; before your consciousness filtered her out.'

'It did?' Gabrielle seemed very confused.

'It did.'

Behind her, facing Mitch, two grey shades materialized.

'It's those things!' Heather snapped. 'Those things that appeared on the boat!'

'Right on cue. Two disembodied astral entities, unable to return to third density, two weird caskets.'

'Oh Christ…' Saph gasped. 'I think I know what's going on here…'

'Want to share?' Heather asked smartly.

'Oh no, Mitch,' Saph shook her head. 'It can't be.'

There were tears in her eyes. She was shaking.

'There's only one way to be sure. Vance?'

Vance nodded and approached the caskets.

'Sirian,' he nodded. 'All about the angles.'

He moved his hands along the coil-patterned surface, and pushed several times in what seemed to be strategic locations. 'Like one of those Chinese puzzle boxes.'

The top cracked open, hissing with white gas, revealing a lid that covered the entire surface.

'They're not like the other starcophagi…' Heather observed.

'No,' Vance uttered. 'They're something different. Third density… encased in sixth density technology, but stable. Very crafty. Very crafty indeed. Designed, I would say, to maintain a third density body in stasis, but not allow the astral spirit to return.'

'Oh no…' Saph whispered.

'What is it?' asked Trudy.

Saph fell silent, still shaking as Vance removed the lid.

Everett walked over and helped him, then they both peered in.

'Who is she?' Everett asked.

Mitch and Gabrielle walked to the casket.

Inside lay a woman, a beautiful woman with long black hair, a statuesque figure, and perfect bone structure. She was sleeping, peaceful, eyes closed, naked, and encased in solid crystal.

Gabrielle stared down.

'It's Suzie. Suzie Saturn.'

Vance opened the second casket.

Mitch went to it instantly, as Saph rushed to his side. Instinctively, Trudy followed her.

The handsome, crystal-encased face that stared up at them in a silent scream of agony was instantly recognizable.

'Jesus,' said Mitch.

'It's him,' Trudy gasped. 'It's my brother.'

Sapphire Edge burst into tears. 'Pan!'

CHAPTER EIGHTY-EIGHT

'It can't be!' Heather rushed to the coffin. 'It is!'

Gabrielle Fenwick stared down at her old friend.

'Suzie… it's Suzie… why didn't I remember her?'

'She was taken out of third density reality,' Mitch offered. 'But her astral self is trapped in the fourth. I think she ascended, and the Anunnaki couldn't control her; so they trapped her, took her physical body before she knew what had happened, how to control it. I think it only happened recently, and I think I know who replaced her.'

'What about Pan?' Heather demanded. 'Is he still alive?'

'I think they did the same to Pan; he took all six, he was ready to go, but someone shot him before it happened. The Anunnaki must have been on the scene almost immediately; like what happened to you, Heather. Imagine if your body had been trapped in one of these things, after you were shot. No way back, stuck.'

'But what about Pan's body?' Heather demanded. 'What was in the coffin? His mother identified him!'

'So did I,' Trudy scowled.

'They switched it,' Vance offered. 'Olivera technology can change the way a person looks. It was someone else, but with Pan's physiognomy, genetically altered.'

'So that's why Pan appeared to you as a ghost?' Heather asked.

'Pan died in trauma; I don't think he's pulled himself together enough on the other side yet to communicate properly, just that one time. But Suzie's fully formed in the astral, she's been coming to me in dreams, trying to tell me what's happened. That's why Pan told me to find *her*; she's easier to find than he is.'

Heather looked over to the two ghostly shadow apparitions.

'That's them?'

Mitch nodded. 'That's them. If their physical bodies were freed, if they could re-incorporate, we'd see them as we saw Xylata; as fully manifested fourth density beings. They'd be… well, alive again.'

Saph was kneeling at Pan's coffin, weeping, apparently having taken none of this on board.

'Vance, can you do anything?'

Vance frowned deeply. 'Perhaps – but I dare not risk it. Even if Mendoza were here… the one we really need is Misha.'

Gabrielle remained still, staring down at Suzie Saturn.

'We came in on the bus together; Mendoza was there, waiting for us, but we didn't know that. He just seemed like… a friendly guide. He knew the city, the lay of the land. We posed for him and… he set up screen tests. All over town, at all the studios. They wanted her, but she didn't want to be part of it. She didn't trust it. She started stripping at some of the clubs Mendoza knew; he said she was wasting her talent. But he didn't know. She made some… adult films. She said that she was in control; that this was honest, non-hypocritical. That all the glamor of the real Hollywood was tease, and unhealthy. That she would rather keep it real…'

Gabrielle's face contorted; there were almost creases on her face.

'…that's not how it works Gabrielle, she used to say. People aren't ready for that… and then she started going out with men. She was so beautiful, more than me. She was making thousands every week. But I didn't see it, I didn't understand. She knew things. She had skill; somewhere along the line she started using her dance, using her seduction, to pry the secrets out of men… about their clubs, their… boy's clubs. Their traditions, their secrets, their rituals. Things that no-one else knew; certainly only a handful of women, if that. And she made money, listening to them, seducing them, siphoning the secrets from them. She invested it all; and it grew. And we remained friends, all through this, even as my career took off… and she was still wealthier than me.'

'What happened to her?' Heather asked. 'Why did they do this?'

'She had money; it took her five years…'

Gabrielle tore her eyes from the coffin and stared at them all, horrified.

'Don't you remember?'

'No,' Mitch told her. 'No-one does.'

'She called herself Suzie Saturn; she said that the name meant that she had claimed the secret power of men, the sacred power of men through her sacred feminine power. I thought it was nonsense, I thought it was all talk; the justification for being a high-class hooker. But then she took all that money and…'

She looked at them again.

'You *really* don't remember?'

Nobody responded.

'He knew her from the start. Your friend, Holland. I remember him. He… didn't mind that she called him that, said she was the only one that made it sound okay. He helped her make sense of what she learned from the men. She used to travel, city to city, country to country. Which ever city she was in, they would come and see her dance, and she would "see" her regular clients. Your friend, he used to say that she understood. She understood the sacred feminine, the dance, the parting of the veils, the divinity within the striptease.'

Gabrielle looked over to Saph, who had stopped weeping and was now listening.

'You saw her dance. She said your friend, Pan, he used to bring his sacred spouse with him. They would have been lovers were it not for you; but he would meet her, in whatever city they would find themselves in together, and talk, and he would come to the club. She said there is always one, in whichever city you are in, one club where they understood the sacred dance. You saw her, remember?'

Saph sniffled. 'No.'

'And then she stopped. She took her money and she turned herself into… you really don't remember, do you? Pan helped her write her songs; he wrote the lyrics for her, for half of her biggest hits!'

'Hits?' asked Heather.

'Suzie Saturn was as big as anyone; any of those others. She came from nowhere and dictated her own terms. No corporation, no record label could control her, because she knew how they worked. She knew everything about them, from the inside out. Her songs, they were amazing. And her music videos; she danced like nobody had ever seen. And her message; people listened. She was all about self-empowerment, but also about selflessness. Love yourself, so you can love others. Live an authentic life, on your own terms, so as to be an example to others. It wasn't Christian, it wasn't New Age, it wasn't really Buddhist or even Hindu or Vedic… it was… her. It was the sum of parts that she had learned, becoming greater, *through* her.'

Gabrielle turned to them all again.

'She had eleven number ones on the Billboard charts – that's one more than Janet Jackson and the same as Whitney Houston! Madonna only has twelve! *How could you not remember her!*' They were all taken aback. Gabrielle seemed to be having some kind of psychological break. '*What's she doing in that coffin!?*'

'Do something,' Everett mumbled awkwardly at Heather.

'Me?'

It was Amy who came forward.

'It's okay,' she crooned, putting her arms around the star's shoulders. 'It's going to be okay, we're going to help her.'

'You are?'

'Of course we are.'

'How?' Gabrielle sniffled like a child. 'The man said it was too dangerous…'

'No, no, we just need some help. Isn't that right, Mister Vance?'

Vance was dumbstruck. 'Well, yes, of course, that's right…' He stroked his beard as he stared, clueless, at the imprisoning starcophagi. Then his eyes widened and he clicked his fingers sharply. 'Of course; it must be undone from sixth density. Yelina must remain and guard them, we can free them when we get there.'

'Get where?' Amy asked. 'I still don't really get where we're going!'

'Just follow me, Amy,' Heather smiled. 'We'll stick together, okay?'

For a second Amy regarded her suspiciously, then the expression broke and she nodded. 'Okay.'

'Now,' Mitch huffed. 'How do we actually do this?'

'You must enter the cave, through the root system,' Yelina gestured to the earthen aperture. 'It functions much as the dimensional gaps do, those that Vance generates, but it will make all those you pass through after it linked, and stable.'

'We go in there?' Amy shuddered. 'It looks like a big muddy vagi – '

'*We all know…*' Heather spoke quickly. '…what it looks like Amy. If you can't handle the symbolism, you shouldn't have smoked the cigar.'

'Oh,' Amy blushed. 'So – who's going first?' She looked around the group. 'Where's Mister Everett gone?'

They all looked around.

Bo Everett had vanished.

CHAPTER EIGHTY-NINE

Mitch guessed immediately what had happened.

'Oh God, he isn't really going to do it, is he?'

Yelina shrugged and huffed. 'Yes, he is Mitch. Harding and the men went with him. He asked that you go on without him, said he'll catch up.'

They all exchanged looks.

'But he was just here a second ago,' Amy stammered. 'They all were!'

'I guess his ego couldn't resist it after all,' Heather shrugged.

'Help what?' Amy asked.

'He's going to make an appearance at his own funeral service.'

Mitch started laughing. Then they all started laughing.

Finally, Mitch turned to the root entrance.

'I've been to the astral; it is malleable. But we now have the power to choose its form. I have an idea about that; will you all trust me?'

They agreed.

'Okay,' Mitch nodded. 'Here we go.'

He frowned in concentration and walked to the root aperture. Placing a hand on the muddy edge, he hoisted himself forward and planted a foot inside, over the lower rim of the lowest horizontal root, then bent slightly, grabbed another root at head height, pulled himself forward and placed his other foot inside.

Mitch looked back at them from semi-darkness and gave them a helpless shrug, then Vance suddenly spoke.

'We need to remember, this is dangerous – we're not leaving our physical forms behind, we're taking them with us. This is ascension, our physical forms may seem the same, may even look and feel the same, but each density we cross into, we change our physical forms into another, different form.'

He scanned them all with a grave expression.

'It may seem like a dream, or an abstract, but if we die here, we're gone. For good, most likely.'

Mitch nodded, his grin diminishing. 'Thanks for that.'

Then he plodded forward, slightly stooped, into darkness.

Heather followed, then Amy, Vance, Trudy and finally Saph.

Gabrielle Fenwick stared at them as one by one they all departed and vanished into the darkness.

'Where are they going? Is it a cave or something?'

'It's pitch!' Amy cried out from within.

Yelina looked at Gabrielle, studying her face.

'You had your age reversed by thirty years but still inject botox?'

Gabrielle shrugged. 'Every little bit helps.'

Yelina sighed. 'Maybe primal ooze really is the better option.'

Gabrielle's near-expressionless face reacted, in what Yelina assumed was surprise.

'Primal ooze? Is that a new treatment?'

INTERLUDE IV

A fascinating development; the race memories seem to remain. That is, once altered, the original subject and the subsequent altered specimens seem to maintain a repressed memory of their former conscious status, which seems also to extend to their offspring.

Already systems are evolving within the new culture that reflect, if in an immature and somewhat theatrical style, modes of consciousness that they are now denied.

This also must be observed and exploited, and further alterations will be tested to determine to what lengths this can be made useful.

If nothing else, it possesses the inherent levels of mental imbalance required for low forms of the dramatic and pathetic arts; many of the new specimens have become adept at 'play-acting' through the various conscious states.

It seems there may be potential here for cultural guidance and conditional techniques — however a genuine process of conscious navigation outside of their bondage is unlikely for several millennia, by which time their purpose will be well and truly served.

Miris

MX-ven-68-Kyaer-01z

THE PANDORA SEQUENCE

PART FIVE

ABOVE

CHAPTER NINETY

Mitch walked through the muddy blackness slowly, planting each foot carefully before the other so as to avoid the rocks and roots that he could feel along the path. He figured he was leading the others down a natural tunnel that ran through the hillside, that had perhaps even been traversed quite recently by others, perhaps potholers, that was about as real and solid as things get.

Just up ahead he saw a light; it was the now familiar thin crack of a dimensional gap. He called back.

'There's an opening up here, a gap; I'm going to go through. I want you all to focus on somewhere safe! Nothing specific, just safe!'

There was a general murmur of agreement down the line behind him. As he walked on, nearing the gap, the floor of the tunnel evened out; there were no more rocks or roots, and Mitch felt as though his feet were landing on an extremely tight trampoline surface.

Then he was at the light.

'One small step…'

He went through.

It worked.

Mitch emerged in the top suite on Everett's boat, beside the bar. The others emerged behind him, one by one, staring about them.

'Here again?' Saph asked, the last to emerge, her voice shaky with emotion. 'Is Pan here?'

It was night again, with a full moon high in the sky.

Mitch nodded to himself. 'We were safe here; we were a group. We've slept here, healed here, defended it and bonded here; it's the one place I thought…'

'Good choice,' Vance nodded, looking around. 'Aside from anything else, on an archetypal level, we can use it to travel. It may be all we need to get where we need to go.'

Mitch smiled, a half-grimace. 'Thanks, Vance. So far so good.'

'It's different,' Heather observed.

They were all, at least to some degree, aware that this was not actually Everett's boat; that it was a composite of Everett's boat from their memories and imaginations, made solid in the dimension of fourth density, in the astral. For a start it had suffered no damage; its surfaces were shining and lustrous, as though straight out of the building docks. The windows were not reflective; outside they could see a starscape that was thick and bright, overpowered with stars and constellations. The bar was fully stocked with luminous liquor, and the table was laden with fully prepared hot meals, plates of fruit and bread and pastries, with jugs of milk and wine and juice.

'It's like a Hogwarts' celebration,' Vance mumbled. 'We should eat some of it; if it's here, it's what we need.'

None of them sat but they immediately began picking at the meals and pouring drinks.

'Christ, it's the best chicken I've ever eaten!' Heather stated with a full mouth, half-chewing, having ripped a drumstick from a still-steaming roast. Cheese was stringing from Amy's mouth as she chowed down a slice of pizza, rolling her eyes and groaning in agreement.

The wall screen flickered to life, displaying a television broadcast of a huge church service, held in an enormous cathedral. One by one they picked up their plates, each with an individual meal that seemed to have been plucked directly from their deepest desires for comfort and nutrition, and wandered toward the couches.

The news scroll beneath the images was blurred and incomprehensible, other than a few starkly visible words that punctuated the foggy procession at irregular intervals such as *fear*, *unease*, *concern* and *worry*. They ignored it and stared at the telecast; it was fully rendered in three dimensions with incredible depth of field, and vivid colors that were somehow more than lifelike.

A solo violinist was playing on a balcony behind the mourners, featured amongst them many luminaries of the business world, and a great many grave-looking men in black suits, all of whom Mitch didn't recognize. There were also a smattering of celebrities from the entertainment world, and even a few well-known sportspeople; in all perhaps three thousand people were packed in, standing room only.

'I think this is Everett's memorial service,' Mitch spoke, unable to stop scooping fettuccini carbonara down his throat.

As he did, a man approached the podium.

'That's my father!' Heather announced. 'Oh my God; they *hate* each other!'

As the violinist stopped, Mitch suddenly recognized the music.

'The theme from *Braveheart?*'

'That *was* one of Uncle Bo's favorites…' Heather conceded.

Mitch watched on, curiously viewing Heather's father with suspicion, as though he were some kind of imposter; this man could not be Heather's father, because other than the result of a biological accident, they all *knew*, just as Mitch knew at that moment they were all of one mind, that Bo Everett was Heather's true father.

Images of Bo Everett began to appear on three large screens around the cathedral altar; scenes from childhood and the intervening years through to the Bo Everett they all recognized today.

'Oh God…' Heather groaned. 'What's my father going to say…?'

Heather's father cleared his throat into a microphone and the mourners all settled. Now, as the cameras panned the crowd, they could see the odd Anunnaki, their green reptilian faces showing up clearly on the crystal clear picture. Nobody commented; nobody was surprised.

'Friends, we are gathered here today to celebrate the life of a man…'

Heather gulped.

Suddenly Everett's voice echoed loudly through the cathedral.

'… *whose rumors of death…!*'

Everett himself appeared, out of a bright white light, a dimensional gap, that the cameras were only just now picking up at the back of the cathedral. Although they all knew what it was, and how he'd gotten there, they also recognized that on television it looked staged, as though Everett were back-lit by showbiz lights.

'…*have been greatly exaggerated!*'

There was a great tumult in the cathedral as people began turning and shouting, screaming and gasping, all three thousand of them, beginning as a drop from the back then rippling down the pews, then all at once as a mighty roaring wave of shock and disapproval.

Everett strode down the middle of the cathedral, holding up his hands in a gesture probably meant to ask for quiet while he approached the microphone, but that may also have been read as a hail of the returned messiah.

As he walked he turned and commented at a few faces.

'Do I even know you?'

'You – you Anunnaki bastard! I always knew you were hiding something!'

'Go home you fraud, you hate me and always have!'

As he neared the altar, some of his family at the front got up and moved toward him as though to intercept his path, to check that it was really him. There was a slight pause as Everett negotiated this; smiling and allowing a few brief hugs, sympathetically stepping over a woman who had fainted, pleading briefly for someone to help her, then finally climbing the wide steps and reaching the podium where his brother stared, awestruck and agape, at his resurrected sibling.

'Bo?'

Bo placed huge ginger-freckled hand on his brother's shoulder and, as politely as possible, angled him away from the speaker's dais.

'Thank you Red, I'll take it from here.'

Red stepped backward, still goggle-eyed and open-mouthed, as his brother assumed his customary air of authority and assessed the crowd, who were still chattering loudly. Bo held up his hands for quiet.

The audience hummed down and someone shouted from the audience.

'This had better be good!'

There was a smattering of laughter.

'Cheat!' The call came from near the middle. 'You damned cheat, Everett!'

'Shut up!' someone else responded.

'You'll burn in hell! Burn in hell, you fraud!'

There was a scuffle, which the cameras caught, as several people tried to eject the offending voice.

'Leave him!' Everett spoke, his deep tones now resonating fully through the cathedral's PA system. 'He has a right to be angry!'

The scuffle diminished and the persons responsible returned to their seats. Everett proceeded.

'Friends!' Everett paused and cleared his throat, as though to indicate that many present were anything but. 'I am angry too! I have been hounded, set upon, and harassed. Attempts have been made on my life! I have been taken against my will, and made to flee the business I created, and yes, even the *world* I helped at least partially to create! This has been executed by forces only a few of you here would understand, and even less of you are aware even exist!'

Again, the muttering began. Everett paused expertly to allow them to simmer and die.

'I am here today to tell you that these forces are active in our world! They seek to control every one of us, to manipulate every one of us! To use and abuse every one of us – on every level! From the simple purchasing power of the ordinary consumer, right up to the very nature of our perception, our consciousness, and the basic tenets and principles upon which we live our lives!'

The crowd sparked up again and Everett nodded to them, gravely, as though he knew he were making bold statements, knew their confusion, but was ready to respond.

'I am aware that this is being telecast on several major news stations; and after my appearance it's probably pre-empting a hell of a lot more. But hear this: I am declaring war on those forces! They know who they are, and they know that I know; they know what I have now become; and they know what I am capable of! Listen, and hear me now...'

There was total silence.

'...those forces will topple! They will fall and they will be carried away to the four winds like so much dust! But first, there is something of enormous importance I must tell you all, and then – I must be going!'

A wave of confusion now swept the cathedral.

Everett was grinning from ear to ear.

'Folks, I hate to tell you this. But this city is about to be devastated by an enormous earthquake. I tried to stop it, but the agents of deceit, manipulation, chaos and malevolence blocked me at every turn. God willing, I will stop it ever happening again, but for now, I suggest ladies and gentlemen, *and others*, that you get up out of your seats, and in an orderly fashion, move to the door and go to your vehicles, and make haste to the fastest exit route from this city that you are humanly, or otherwise capable, of taking.'

Everett stared out at the crowd.

As he did, an earth tremor struck Los Angeles.

It lasted about three seconds.

The cathedral remained standing but for a shower of dust

from its aged rafters.

'I don't think you'll get a second warning,' Everett stared them down.

Then the screaming and the panic started.

CHAPTER NINETY-ONE

A few seconds later, Everett appeared on the deck with the others.

'Well, I did what I could!'

They all stared at him, mouths stuffed with food, frozen.

'What?'

A few of them began slowly to chew again.

'I had a platform, I used it; if this little game doesn't play, at least I might have gotten a few people out of Los Angeles who otherwise will perish!'

Everett looked around him at his astral boat.

'Somebody pimped my ride!'

'Good God, uncle,' Heather shook her head, smiling. 'I've never seen you so pleased with yourself!'

'Hah!' Everett grinned.

A grumbling began from outside. Without hesitation the group put down their plates and made for the door; it was Amy who walked right up to the window and walked through it. The others followed suit.

'He said everything was malleable,' Amy shrugged.

The ocean surrounded them, extending to the horizon from every direction; it was silver, gray, glistening and quiet. Although they had gathered toward the aft, on the portside they watched and could see through the glistening glass that a storm was brewing. A dark cloud had stirred in the middle of each of the four central horizon points; fore, aft, port and starboard, like tiny mushroom clouds in each corner of the diamond-patterned distance.

'Can't be good,' Mitch muttered.

Further toward them in the middle-distance, the seas began

to bubble. First to the fore and aft, then to the port and starboard, something was rising in the sea.

'What do we do?' Heather asked. 'We have power here now, don't we?'

Vance cleared his throat. 'But how do we use it? I fear we may be out of our depth, literally.'

The mushroom cloud on the portside flashed; a streak of lightning spat out and in a millisecond struck across the ocean and hit the side of the boat. It rocked savagely and they fell collectively backwards, then another smash of lightning from the starboard side rocked them forward again. The boat wavered uneasily in the silver water as they found their feet again.

Then silence.

'I don't think we're sinking…' Mitch offered gingerly.

'Warning shots?' Everett suggested.

'How *do we* defend ourselves?' Heather demanded, her feet braced tightly apart. 'We *might* be sinking,' she uttered. 'Can we swim in this? How far's the shore?'

'What shore?' Mitch guffawed. 'And where's the next entrance? We have to keep going!'

There was a blast at the front of the ship and they pitched sideways, falling into each other.

'*What do we do?*' Heather demanded again. 'Vance!'

'I don't know!'

Another hit at the fore knocked them just as they were getting to their feet again.

'They're playing with us,' Everett grumbled, gripping the rails tightly.

The mushroom cloud in the distance puffed outwards and seemed to spore. From this distance, it looked to Mitch like dozens of black mosquitoes had hatched; they buzzed about in formation for a second then headed towards the boat. Nobody spoke as fear gripped the group; looking about they saw that whatever these things were, they were approaching on all sides.

'They're coming,' Amy spoke quietly.

Mitch looked to her. She was frightened. Why had he dragged his daughter into this? They were all going to be killed, or taken. Taken, then killed.

There came a sudden voice from inside the suite.

'What are you *doing*!'

Standing there, behind the malleable glass, dressed in deep green combat fatigues patterned in a reptile-skin motif, was Suzie Saturn.

'Suzie?' Mitch was surprised. Then he asked himself; why should he be? This was her domain. And he had seen her at least prepare to fight here; a fight she had survived, if not totally commanded.

She was all but wearing their skin.

'Don't just stand there!' Suzie spread her arms. 'Do something!'

'How?' Mitch pleaded.

'Just do it!' Suzie shouted. 'Like this!'

She closed her eyes and clenched her outstretched fists, tense and still for a second, then she threw her head back and shouted, a short primal scream, and released her fists.

From above the boat, lightning shot down and across the silver ocean, striking several of the mosquitoes at a distance.

'This is our domain; this is the astral space of the planet called Earth. This is space for the human mind, the human spirit and imagination; not theirs. They *cannot* withstand us; even a few of us, that's why they are so desperate to keep us out of here! Now *defend your space* and *find the exit*!'

Amy suddenly perked.

'I get it! It's a first person shoot 'em up!'

'Yes!' Suzie urged. 'If you like! Whatever works!'

Amy nodded. 'Right.'

From her pocket she produced a hand pistol, a tranq gun, and spun about to the incoming mosquitoes. They were closer now and Mitch could see that they were some new winged version of the Anunnaki; soaring like tiny dragons toward them, wearing armor and carrying guns.

'Use the second density connection; use nature!' Suzie urged. '*They* have to work for a connection; sap our energy and channel it, refine it to their ends; we don't! We live here; *we* are a natural part of the planet's energy!'

'Bastards!' Amy screeched, and fired.

The dart spat from the end of the gun and shot across the ocean; in its wake, the sea seemed to respond, to rise and follow it until it had risen to form a mighty fin of water that crested and smashed into the center of the approaching winged Anunnaki and sent them spiraling in all directions. Some fell into the water, some vanished, but the majority managed to get out of the way and keep coming. Amy screamed like a banshee and fired again, and again; there were two more huge fins but the Anunnaki, though delayed, saw them coming. Everett removed his pistol and shot twice. As the bullets seared through the air they became massive fireballs, both of which engulfed a group of Anunnaki who had swerved to avoid Amy's wave. Still, they kept coming, and more shot from the mushroom cloud. To the other three directions, where their flight had not been delayed, the Anunnaki were approaching the patches of ocean where the water was bubbling.

Heather suddenly jolted and ran to the starboard side; as she moved she grasped at one of the windows and seemed to pull the strange, malleable glass with her, then with a grunt and a scream she hurled the glass over the edge at the approaching enemy. The glass fractured and splintered in mid-air, searing like a shrapnel cloud of molten lava shot from a cannon; the Anunnaki immediately weaved to avoid it, but several were too late and fell in fiery balls, as though struck by grenades.

Heather fell to her knees.

'Don't try so hard!' Suzie cried. 'You'll exhaust yourself!'

Mitch ran down the side of the boat to the fore; the Anunnaki approaching there were now over the bubbling section of the ocean.

They would board in seconds.

He thought desperately.

Was it possible to just wish them away? To have a thought so huge and so brave and fearless that they could just reclaim their territory, in one fell swoop, as Suzie seemed to suggest? If so, why hadn't Suzie done it?

Even as he'd paused for the seconds it had taken to process these thoughts, they were closer, closer still.

Anger rose in him as he began to see their outlines more clearly, sense their malevolent confidence; something had to stop them. Something – no, someone, someone here, someone now. Stop them. Stop.

'STOP!'

Mitch's shout was immense; it seemed to carry as a sound wave and scatter the approaching Anunnaki like a brief but powerful hurricane-force wind, sending them soaring in different directions, spiraling out of control; a few even collided and fell to the ocean. Then they evened out, regrouped and proceeded.

He'd done something, but essentially done nothing; he was too new, too afraid to think clearly.

Even as Amy and Everett let off more shots, he could tell that they were all too new at this, that the Anunnaki outnumbered them vastly, and that they simply did not possess the experience required to defend their boat from a limitless supply of enemy warriors.

He needed training, he needed education.

He needed help.

Wait.

He *needed help*.

Now.

Mitch sucked in a lungful of air. He knew sound traveled here; he knew it had a more vital vibration and physical power. But it still carried words, and thoughts, and ideas; that was what the astral was for.

When his lungs were full, Mitch leaned back, and as he shouted, pushed his whole body forward, forcing his diaphragm upward, and cried out for dear life until his throat hurt.

'Heeee - aaaaaalp!'

Then he stood panting.

'Left that a bit short, didn't you?'

The familiar voice came from behind him.

Mitch, however, did not turn to confirm who it was. Immediately the bubbling sections of the ocean erupted with more winged Anunnaki who, much to Mitch's total shock, shot out of the water like bees from a belted hive, and immediately engaged their approaching kin. Mitch turned and looked around. It was happening on all sides; rising from the bubbling waters, Anunnaki were engaging and fighting with other Anunnaki.

Finally Mitch turned behind him.

'You simply had to ask,' Xylata stated squarely. 'It would have been a great dishonor for us to aid one who did not request it; not to mention the shame it would have brought *you*. And I cannot have you shamed, Mitch. You are too important to my cause.'

'Your cause?'

'You are my cause Mitch. You and your cluster.'

Mitch looked out to the astral ocean again. It was a mass of swarming Anunnaki, a sky battle in which thousands, perhaps more were participating. A lightning strike hit the side of the ship again and Mitch toppled into Xylata; she was stronger and more solid than him, caught and steadied him easily. As she did, she stared into his eyes.

'You are going to help exalt my clan.'

There was something sensual in Xylata's eyes that made him uneasy. She released him and he examined her. Her attire was new, Romanesque and resplendent. She still wore the flowing fur cloak of royalty, but a full uniform had been added beneath; shining shoulder and breast pads, several flashy rank insignias on her arms and chest, and glistening high heeled crocodile boots.

'The Draco are helping us?'

Mitch couldn't get his head around it.

'No Mitch. The Draco are in civil war; you see it all around you. I have adopted my maternal clan name, unused for centuries; I am leading the Ymira Clan to victory, its first victory. We shall reclaim the Draco under that name and crush the other clans who seek to defy us. And you Mitchell Pyne, will help us.'

'I will? How? Why?'

'Because this war against humanity is an end unto itself; it must cease. The power we gain from controlling your race is used almost entirely to maintain that control. It is a pointless exercise, an endless wasted cycle we maintain only out of pride of a conquest made six thousand years ago; here our agendas meet. It is wise to ally.'

Another stroke hit the prow; Mitch was again thrown into Xylata's arms.

As she grasped him, Amy ran by, sprinting up the ship's backward sloping deck as though preparing for a high jump, right up to the aft. Mitch's gaze followed her and saw that a group of Anunnaki had broken away from the aerial fighting and were closing in on the boat. As Amy reached the prow, she locked her stride and seemed to defy gravity and skid upwards, one foot in front of the other like a stunt skater. Electrical energy gathered at her feet, sparking and swirling. As the boat tipped back down again, and a dozen Anunnaki were revealed in the sky, hovering and waiting for the boat to stabilize so they could board, the electrical energy seemed to spin out from under Amy's feet and, as though traveling with her continued momentum, spat out of the boat's prow like some kind of freakish ball lightning. The swarming Anunnaki were immediately vaporized in mid-air, to Amy's delighted whooping.

'She is a natural,' Xylata smiled, again releasing Mitch. 'But you must go now. Leave her with me; she will fight for humanity and it will become the stuff of legend. I will protect her; we will win.'

'Leave her?'

'You must leave one of your kind here; otherwise you will lose the sequence. Go now, go on to the fifth; know that you have allies who defend your path, know that your blood fights here for your honor; go, go now.'

CHAPTER NINETY-TWO

Mitch wanted to hesitate but it all seemed right; Amethyst, his daughter, the trained fighter, the independent one. She had been born for this, she had come to this through a chain of realizations and events and even epiphanies that now made her key to the liberation of humanity.

'Yes,' Xylata hissed. 'You *see*.'

'Mitch!' Heather cried out. Behind Xylata, she came storming down the side of the boat toward them. Mitch spun about.

'It's okay! It's Xylata! She's helping us!'

Behind Heather, he could see the others, even Saph, no matter how dazed and confused, using every weapon at their disposal; Everett with his gun, Saph with Amy's gun, Vance with his mysterious cane, Trudy with some kind of pole that she had found at the side of the ship, as tools, as physical symbols that gave them the ability, the shape, to channel their energy, the energy of anger and defense, at the enemy.

Heather reached them.

'You're helping us?'

Xylata regarded her like a python would regard a white mouse.

'Long story,' Mitch stepped between them.

It was impossible for Mitch to tell who was winning and he gazed around at the sky; the main thing was that the Draco did not seem to be gaining ground. And if they did, his daughter would deal with them.

'We need to move on; Xylata and Amy are going to stay and fight, but we have to –'

'*Amy?*'

'Don't argue; it fits, it's right.'

'But if we move on, we take the boat with us, don't we? Isn't that the point?'

'I think that this version of the boat will remain here; the fight will go on. When we travel through to the next level, there will be another version of the boat.'

'And we will become something else? Ascend again, or something?'

'I suppose; we're traveling, at least.'

'And Pan?'

Xylata spoke. 'This was Pan's idea; he suggested that I make a deal with you, with humanity. He is the cause of the civil war. But he is sleeping again now, it takes much for him to manifest. But you will find him. You must.'

Suddenly Xylata's attention was diverted; she had seen something, in the middle of the battle.

'A weakness, they will break through. Good journey, Mitch. We will meet again.'

Xylata stepped up to the rail and sprouted a pair of huge emerald wings like a massive umbrella snapping open, then jumped and was halfway out to sea before anyone could blink.

They watched as she soared in, like a jet fighter, and entered the fray, then was lost amongst the thousands of warring Anunnaki.

Mitch turned back.

'That is one crazy lizard lady,' he muttered.

'Mitch,' Heather scalded. 'Focus.'

'Right. We need to find a way to fifth, quickly; but how do we get from here, from a war zone, to a place of love and light and hippie art?'

'I don't know!'

Suzie appeared behind Heather.

'Tell her,' Suzie urged.

Heather jumped and turned to Suzie. 'Tell who?'

'*Tell her.*'

Mitch looked back to Heather.

He gulped.

'I love you,' he snapped.

'What?' Heather demanded.

'I love you!'

Heather's mouth popped open and closed a few times.

Suzie sighed. 'Not *her*.' She pointed to Amy. 'Her!'

Still on the prow, Amy had dispensed with her gun. She looked like a militarized mermaid, a warrior goddess, standing at the foremost tip of the boat, dispensing lightning bolts with the flicking of her hands and fireballs with the punches of her fists. Mitch suspected that she was actually steering the boat from there, guiding its direction with the shifting weight of her feet, to better take aim with her self-generated battle cannons.

'Amy!' Mitch cried out.

Amy swung around. Her eyes were ablaze.

'Amy you need to stay and defend the ship! You're the only one who can, who really *gets* all this!'

Amy seemed startled. Then she puffed out her chest and smiled.

'*Really?*'

'We're counting on you – and *we'll be back*!'

There was a look of fierce pride in her eyes that Mitch couldn't quite believe; a pride in herself that made her glow like some kind of enlightened mistress.

'Okay Dad! You can count on me!'

Mitch beamed. 'I know!'

The full moon seemed to shine brighter, the stars seemed to sparkle and ignite. Then Mitch realized; it wasn't that they seemed to do those things. They absolutely were doing those things.

The sky was filling with light, the stars were increasing in size and intermingling, and the moon was encompassing it all. Soon the combined moon and starlight were turning the sky to day, and all the light was combining to make a sun, and the sunlight was so overwhelming that Mitch was forced to close his eyes. He felt Heather take his hand as he squeezed his eyes shut; then through his eyelids he felt the light diminish and pale, until he opened his eyes again, a little at first, squinting, then blinking, then fully open.

He was back.

CHAPTER NINETY-THREE

The top deck of Everett's boat remained, but it was no longer attached to the boat as such. Keeping hold of Heather's hand, Mitch looked around. The others were standing, stunned, a little further away, and roughly comparable in distance to where they had been standing before. Except now they were standing in front of a huge curved window, looking down on a massive rainforest.

It was the strange skyborne café where he'd spoken to Suzie in a dream; at least, the penthouse deck of the boat appeared to have become bonded with it. The windows remained ringed with two-seater tables that seemed to curve around forever, and everything remained white, except that now, beside them, as though it had become the centerpiece of this part of the observation deck's curve, was the suite.

'Where are we?' Heather asked.

Suzie responded. 'I've been here a few times. Once I spoke to Mitch here. It's a Pleiadean ship, a floating observation deck and healing center. Humans sometimes come here in dreams, when they need to speak to their guides, or receive messages from the higher realms, or just access somewhere where their spirits can rest a while; it's like a counseling center for understanding the karmic cycle, for the soul. I've met people here I knew in other lives, from other realms or existences. Somehow the Pleiadeans are in charge of all this: healing and mentoring, psychology and self-knowledge. The fifth density is where most of our efforts to express life, the universe and everything emanate, where we get inspired to create. I guess we come here to formulate and discuss, to unblock whatever's blocked and gain a renewed purpose. I was doing that for you Mitch, when we met here. I know you got our conversation in pieces, but for me it was all at once, one long conversation where the dimensions kept changing. I wasn't used to it then. I don't know that I really am now.'

Mitch shrugged. 'It was like a poem you wrote for me, all in one night – but I only read it one stanza at a time, over time, when I had time to absorb it.'

Mitch looked around.

'Why is it deserted? There were people here last time, lots of people.'

Suzie shrugged. 'Who can say? From what I understand, they're a fickle bunch. Maybe they don't like us being here and they removed everyone?'

'Is Pan here?'

Saph asked the question again, like the child of a recent divorce, waiting for her absentee father to come on visiting night.

'I don't know,' Suzie answered squarely. 'I haven't felt his presence since you found the coffins.'

Saph stared at her a few seconds, then turned back to the rainforest below.

'I'm worried about her,' Mitch mumbled. 'I think she's snapped. Seeing Pan like that…'

Suzie nodded. 'Then she's in the right place.'

Everett strolled up to them. 'Quite a sight. How'd you get us here?'

Mitch shrugged. 'I don't really know.'

Heather smiled. 'He released his daughter with love. The emotion was powerful enough to take us through.'

Vance followed Everett up to them.

'I think we should be moving on. I don't like it here.'

There was a sourness in his old teacher that Mitch hadn't seen before.

'It's so peaceful,' Mitch shrugged.

'Too peaceful,' Vance sneered. 'We have a mission to achieve. It would be easy to get stuck here, sleeping on the job.'

Mitch looked up and down the long, curved corridor.

'Doesn't seem to be anyone around.'

'I know,' Vance uttered. 'But they're watching. We came without asking; they don't like that. They want to assess the level of contamination.'

'You sound like Mendoza,' Heather offered.

'Mendoza and I have a lot in common, it seems. Now, how do we move on, and quickly?'

Mitch turned to the suite.

It was just as it had been but seemed brighter and more like an atrium or a greenhouse with all the surrounding light.

'The next level is the sixth. It's all about the angles,' Mitch hummed. 'Remember the beach houses?'

Heather shrugged. 'Well… yeah, I –'

Vance walked over. His feet made no sound, nor was there sound when he slapped a steel support between the suite windows.

'Mendoza said… that it was like she put on a heavy diver's suit, and came down to an ocean trench.' He looked around at the others. 'Does anyone feel any different? Lighter? Less dense?'

'Not particularly,' Everett shrugged. 'But I can't say I don't feel excited at being on a spaceship for the first time…'

Vance muttered on. 'But he also said in the end he didn't know what he was. I think it all works differently for us; we're human, in human dimensions, in human space. This suite is a steel cage, a rectangular block; if I can find the will, the mental key to activate the structure, manipulate it, like Mendoza did with Eissley's safe house…'

'Like you did with the shower?' Heather offered.

'Pulling in the corners, the angles. I'll have to consider it; I don't want to encase us all here in some kind of crystal trap forever…'

Suzie walked up to him.

'If you can do that, but make the sixth density materialize around the structure, we will again take the *idea* of the boat with us.'

Vance pushed at the steel support, a little frustrated.

'We're wasting *time…*'

Everett turned away from Vance and again gazed down at the rainforest, speaking softly to himself.

'Back in the Amazon, eh Pan?'

Then he turned and looked up at the featureless white ceiling.

'I wonder what drives it, how it works?'

A voice echoed around them, apparently from quite close by.

'You see.' The voice was female, soft and deep. 'All he wants is the technology. His yearning for it penetrates his every particle, spreads from him like rot. His greed, his desire.'

Another voice, male and lighter, responded.

'These are human traits. They are essential to their character, but conversely, remarkable in the resultant joy when sated. This is who they are. This is what their most powerful have always been. You must remember that we only observe; you will feel this again in time when they ascend again, and we must trade with them. You will learn it is an acquired harmony.'

'Never,' the woman responded. 'Send them back. We were wrong to even enter into observation of their race; they are unworthy of ascension.'

Heather barked. 'Who the hell do they think they are talking to?'

'They hear us?' The disembodied woman's voice seemed almost fearful.

'Yes; were you not told?'

'How?' The woman was clearly appalled.

'They are genetically enhanced.'

'*How?*'

'They rediscovered the sequence. Now they seek restoration.'

'They seek *revenge*! They must be recycled! Send them to the Source!'

There was a shift in the air; whatever, or whomever had been present were gone.

'What was *that* all about?' Trudy demanded.

'I think we just got judged,' Heather gulped. 'And sentenced.

What the hell does recycle mean? And is the Source what I think it is? *The* Source?'

Vance scowled. 'I warned you; we must get to the sixth density quickly, where we have allies. If the administration side of the Pleiadeans decides we're a contamination, they'll ascend us right up, back to the Source, back to the Godhead, the White Hole from which nothing has ever returned. All the energy that makes us who we are will be reduced to its constituent parts; we won't be reincarnated and all our memories and experiences will remain in the Light, our previous selves superseded, like we never existed. It's like wiping a hard drive, blank, no back-ups; you'll never be able to use that information again.'

Trudy shivered. 'They can do that?'

'It's what the Anunnaki wanted to do to Suzie; only they did the astral variation. They simply wiped all traces of her from our memory, removed every instance of her through her timeline, and trapped her in the astral. All they had to do then was replace her existence in the timeline with another person, another artist, who could refill the empty trench in the timeline that remained; our minds filled in the rest of the smaller gaps, weaved a living lie around this Mistress woman. Isn't that right Mitch? Was that your theory?'

'Yeah,' Mitch nodded. 'That, and it suited their purpose to replace a genuine unique voice, a personality with an agenda, with a cookie cutter pop singer whose music essentially meant nothing; nothing that hadn't been said a thousand times before, and better. Like wiping Bill Hicks from comedy history and replacing him with puns from Christmas crackers.'

'Thank you,' Suzie smiled. 'Although I'm afraid it was Pan's fault. He thought I was the one person he could trust to test the sequence on; thought I could withstand it, channel it into my music and change the world.'

Mitch sighed. 'Never a good thing.'

Saph started to say something, but moved away.

Her face was blank, her expression lost.

Suzie continued to speak, softly and sadly.

'As it happens, he was right. But the Anunnaki made a pre-emptive strike. I was resigned to the astral; sometimes able to come to places like this, but unable to reach anyone other than in dreams.'

Her tone rose, angering now.

'I was left to watch the world move on, as though I had never existed. People, fans, whose lives I had changed, drifting back into the mundane and the melancholy, without knowing why, without being able to understand what was missing in their lives; not just me, or my music, but the gateways to new paths my art had suggested to them, the realizations my work had inspired in them, or simply the support that beloved music brings to those who suffer…'

Suzie was almost enraged now.

'…all that – it was no longer there, and the people who depended on it were left hollow and dry.'

She grit her teeth and squeezed her eyes shut.

It was the first time she had not looked stunningly beautiful.

'I would end them all if I could, these *goddamned Anunnaki*!'

Seven Pleiadeans materialized around them.

It was only then Mitch realized that Saph had vanished.

CHAPTER NINETY-FOUR

'What have you done with her?' Mitch demanded.

'Please, reenter your domicile.'

Mitch recognized the man. He had rescued Mitch twice; he looked around the circle and saw that the woman was there as well. She smiled tightly and nodded.

'Please. Go inside.'

'Come on Mitch,' Everett led the way. 'No point in upsetting our hosts.'

The group re-entered the suite from the sliding glass door. When they arrived inside, the seven Pleiadeans somehow managed to ring them once again, herding them without effort into the lounge area so that they stood around the couches and before the giant screen.

'Where's Saph?' Mitch demanded again.

'Please,' the woman intoned. 'We have met three times but we never introduced ourselves. We have been rude. I am Eya, and this is my partner, Iba, whom you have also met. Your friend Sapphire is damaged; she cannot go on with you. You need one of your party to remain, to anchor your chain of ascent, should you proceed. It seems natural that it be her.'

'We will tend to her,' Iba smiled. 'Then return her to you when she is healed. Things work differently here. We see her as she is, not as she wishes herself to be, nor as you wish her to be. Although, those desires and well-wishes, the projection of how you see her, of your greater expectations, they all work for her when she is here with us. We feel that. She will feel that. And she will become the closest thing to it that present circumstances allow. This is the way of all life energy, of all karma, all dharma, of all will and intent. We only seek to maximize the best of all combinations of those things.'

There was silence as they all registered what had happened. For whatever reason, goodwill or not, one of their number had been taken from them against their will, and maybe against her own.

'We only seek to move through this density,' Mitch spoke quietly. 'Once we figure out the route, we will be on our way.'

'He is dangerous, this one.'

Another of the Pleiadeans had spoken; he recognized the voice as the woman who had spoken in favor of their execution. 'He has the energy of the Dark Orion on him; the nameless one who bored his way down just to see him. He has become a focus for darkness; if the Dark Orion chooses again to descend, he only needs to fix his will on this human. How can this be allowed? Such a thing? The stench he left as he forced his way down, it will always be here on this craft. We must destroy it now, abandon it. Such waste! So brutal!'

Several of the other Pleiadeans nodded.

Eya spoke again. 'Uki is correct; such a thing should never happen, and this ship is now useless to us, but it does. And it will again. And we know why, and we have done nothing to prevent it, nothing while our allies of old are allowed to be trapped in a cycle from which there is little hope of exit or reprieve, on a world we once adored, now turned into a prison, a *factory*, that we exploit, as what passes for humanity today would exploit one of their third world resorts, as a place to admire and to rest and recuperate within, within the protection of restricted zones, while poverty and war shatter the world outside that we ignore.'

'I agree,' Iba whispered.

'We know,' Uki uttered.

Eya proceeded. 'Or worse, a whole world that has become our equivalent of *detox*, we who live longer, and recall more from life to life… it is a disgrace that this has been allowed to continue for so long, to the point where humanity must sink and fall again in order to save themselves. All on the principle that we are some greater society, with greater wisdom; and that it is the fault of their own that this "third world race" has fallen. That the responsibility is their own to raise themselves; when we know very well that the circumstances were long ago dictated, long ago created, that would prevent this. For so long now we have allowed it to proceed, and to cripple the once great race of humanity. We should feel shame for this; nothing but shame.'

The others were silent.

Mitch suspected, from their shifting expressions and occasional flinches, that the fight had become internal, that they were communicating telepathically.

He turned to Everett.

'Remember what we can do; we have to become used to it, make it part of our arsenal.'

'Hmmm.'

'I'm going in. You follow. The rest of you, listen, but just stay quiet. Okay?'

Mitch focused and tried his best to listen; it took a few seconds before he was mentally bowled over by many raging voices, more than the seven who had physically manifested, all speaking at a rapid fire rate, in another language Mitch could not understand but perceived somehow as a passionate debate as to whether he and his friends should be allowed to live and pass through, or die and be forgotten.

His mind reeled with the pace and ferocity of the verbal assaults, until one voice interrupted all the others. There was instant silence as Mitch realized that someone had drawn attention to his mental presence in the psychic cacophony. It was the same feeling he had received at the wake when he had first seen Eya and Iba, but writ large; a social faux pas of monumental weight.

Uki spoke again.

Outrageous!

There was a psychic muttering of agreement, but also something

Mitch had not felt the last time. A mental pattern was weaved, a mix of strong emotion that Mitch had never quite known before; a strong but gentle blend of affection, perhaps stronger than the wave of derision, directed straight at him. It took the form of a pulse, a brief shock of welcoming, of curiosity, and recognition of an engaging diversion having presented itself. He felt like a child who'd wandered into an adult's dinner party, in his pajamas, and said something precocious but unintentionally wise.

Mitch realized what they were picking up on.

His thought, his intention behind all the rest of the concern for his life, and his friends' lives, had been a kind of melancholic desperation.

I just want to stop all the death.

Your activity has ruined my ship, Uki spoke, half in accusation, half in sadness.

There was an edge to it that Mitch recognized. She had been the captain of this vessel, its commander. Her thoughts were at least partially bureaucratic; her mission, her project, had been sabotaged. An unforeseen factor had put an end to her work, a dark force that had broken through and used it as a conduit, in order to get to Mitch, had contaminated her ship. It was his fault her project had been ruined, her good work forestalled.

I'm sorry. It seems like a fine ship to me.

It is useless to me now.

Another voice spoke, near Mitch.

A fine ship like this can be repaired, Everett offered. *Let me repair it for you.*

You? Uki scoffed.

We have our own ways.

Everett's mind seemed to shrug, charmingly.

Just as we are finding our own way. I don't understand exactly what you've spoken, but perhaps you have forgotten after all this time, just as we have forgotten? You say this ship is contaminated, that it is useless to you. Then leave it here. Let me use it. I will bring music, and people, and art, and light. We will use it in your name, for the things we love. Then your project need not have failed. It can become something else. Something different. Differently successful. You must know Pan. He must have come here, seeking restoration. Pan is my son. I will keep him here, and the woman Sapphire. They will begin my project, and I will restore the ship as humans would have it; so that you may allow the others in my party to pass. Bring Pan's casket here. The three of us will remain. The ship is no good to you; but it is everything to us. Allow us this opportunity so that we may again prove to be your allies, your friends. Allow my friends to move through; my beloved daughter and the man she loves; the magician and the healer. They have work to do beyond. I beg of you…

Mitch felt that.

That had been hard, perhaps the hardest words Everett had ever spoken.

He'd begged.

…for humanity.

Mitch opened his eyes.

He hadn't even realized he'd closed them.

The connection had broken, the group had dissembled.

Everett remained across from him but his eyes remained closed.

He nodded.

'Yes,' he spoke.

Then he opened his eyes and turned immediately to Heather.

'You must go on without me.'

'No!'

'You must. My great skill has been to collect information, and my great instinct has been to know when to bargain with that information. I cannot live knowing Pan and Sapphire have been damaged so badly by my dream; and yet here my dream and their healing dovetail in a way I could not have foreseen. Your two Pleiadean friends are going to stay aboard and show me the lay of the land. I will be the new captain. But I must show them that I am as good as my word.'

Heather began to cry.

'I'm… I'm happy for you,' she said, shakily.

'I'm happy for me.'

Heather rushed forward and embraced him. There was no withholding, no masculine embarrassment from Everett this time; he hugged her to him with an unrestricted paternal giving and warmth, tight and unconditional, like a daughter. Then he released her.

'I have to go.'

Vance spoke clearly. 'Sooner, I'd say old chap.'

The Magician was holding his hand up, and each of his fingers seemed to hold a silver thread of light, one each to each corner of the suite's ceiling.

'Will I see you again?' Heather asked, her voice a whimper.

Everett smiled. 'How many times? I'm not dead! You come find me; come find the ship.' He looked to the floor. 'You know where we will be!'

Mitch stepped forward. 'Bo?'

'Mitchell?'

'That favor?'

Everett stared at him a second, then smiled.

'Of course, Pyne. You have my blessing.'

A gap opened around Everett, and he was gone.

His voice echoed throughout the suite.

You always did.

CHAPTER NINETY-FIVE

'And then there were five…' Trudy said.

'This is a healing ship,' Heather stated. 'Are you sure you don't want to stay as well?'

Trudy shook her head. 'I'm going all the way. If Pan's here, if he's healing, I'll find my way back. It seems like we all know where to stop, where to drop anchor. It doesn't feel right to me here.'

Vance began drawing his hand down. The silver threads followed.

'Indeed. Amazing what one can *feel* when one just lets go.'

'Is that what you've been doing lately?' Heather asked. 'Letting go?'

'All of you; place your hands on mine. When you do, I'm going to let go of these threads; the resulting vibrations should propel us through. I hope.'

Mitch placed his hand over Vance's, his fingers between the threads. Heather, Suzie and Trudy did the same.

'Here we go. Three, two –'

Are you ready for another disembodied voice?

Vance gasped. 'Good grief!'

Already, the room around them was changing, becoming more crystalline, and the white Pleiadean light seemed sharper, more defined. From above them, out of a crack in the light, came a hand, as though reaching through a small hatch in the ceiling. It came down and slapped itself over Trudy's hand at the top of the pile.

Here, I'll lend you a… nah, I can't say that.

The disembodied hand wrenched upward.

There was a bright flash and they were back on the boat; the boat proper.

Although this time they were in dock.

The dock seemed to be in mid-air as they looked around them, in the middle of a vast chamber, maybe miles high and miles wide. Docked all about them, across the massive chamber, above them, and presumably below them, were a fleet of spacecraft of all shapes and sizes, crystalline ships that shone from within, with glistening glass walls and indefinable inner dimensions.

'Bloody hell,' Mitch gaped. 'No wonder we can't see them when they visit.'

The boat itself had taken on the character of the other Sirian ships; it was now sleeker and sharper, totally crystalline, a ship of glass.

Mendoza stood in their circle, his hand over theirs, still in his Bermuda shorts and Hawaiian shirt.

'Nice to see you all again.'

Mitch smiled. 'Mendoza. This is Trudy, Pan's sister. Mendoza is a sixth density sorcerer. Who seems to be our friend?'

'Of course he's our friend,' Suzie smiled warmly.

Mendoza stared at her. 'Suzie? Saturn?'

Suzie shrugged. 'Used to be anyway.'

Mendoza cried out and embraced her. 'You made it, baby!'

'Well,' Suzie rolled her eyes as they parted. 'I *had* made it. Then they unmade *me*.'

Mendoza shook his head.

'That fucker Eissley. Took care of him though!'

'No,' Mitch sighed. 'We didn't. He just made a deal with another Anunnaki clan. Turns out the man himself is the cause; he's probably worse than any of them; to use a film quote that seems appropriate, *you don't see them fucking each other over for a goddamn percentage.*'

'Well,' Mendoza sighed, 'actually you do. But they have more class when they do it. So I gather you're trying to prevent the earthquake, huh? Not a lot of time left. You guys are still wearing your human biorhythms; still carrying Earth time all the way through. It's a little skewed; you've kind of forgotten about time every now and then, which, if you see what I mean, actually gives you more time. But I'd say ya don't have long; minutes maybe. Ten? Fifteen? Sure you wanna head on through? It gets a bit tricky from here; there's a big dark void from here to the home of the angels; even some of these guys get lost on the way. Pleiadeans won't even go near it unless it's fate of the universe stuff.'

'I can get us through,' Vance said assuredly.

'You can huh?'

Vance and Mendoza stared each other out for a second, then Mendoza nodded and waved for them to follow him out onto the deck.

'Okay. Whatever it is you're hiding, Vance, I'm kind of glad I'm not going to be there when you let it out.'

Mitch eyed Vance sideways, as they moved to the aft of the boat.

'You've got something to let out?'

Vance smiled; it was not malevolent, but it was truly wicked.

'I'll get us across Mitch. Fear not.'

He heard Heather audibly gulp.

Mendoza pointed out from the boat. The enormous docking chamber of the space station, if that was even what it was, opened out into blackness via a circular gateway.

'Usually,' Mendoza lectured lightly, 'you'd see stars out there. The whole circle opening is just a programmable wormhole, like on television. But that, that's got everyone spooked. They don't see it too often. Misha had it waiting here for you, she opened it a while back, then word got around why. See, no-one knows what to make of you. Everyone's let you pass; Misha said she wouldn't interfere, so she figured she might as well go one step further and make it easy for you. But here's the thing; there's no way back.'

Trudy gaped. 'No way back?'

'No conventional way back.'

'Then, I think this is the end of the line for me.'

Mitch looked at Trudy, astonished. 'Here?'

Trudy nodded. 'I thought I was going all the way, but now I'm here… Mendoza, you saw the coffin my brother is trapped in.'

'Sure did.'

'If I stay, will you help me get him out? And Suzie?'

'Sure. Sure, I can do that.'

'Then that's it; that's why I'm here.' She turned to Suzie. 'What about you? You could stay; work to find your own release?'

Suzie stared at the black gateway.

'No… I need to go on.' She turned back to Trudy. 'But if you can release me, I would appreciate it. I know Pan will too.'

Trudy hummed. 'Okay. Are you sure you can help me, Mendoza?'

Mendoza shrugged. 'Sure. It's just a matter of finding out who did it, what tricks they used. Misha can help us; she probably already knows. But there's probably some very good reason they're still encased in those things.' He looked at Suzie. 'Maybe the world's really not ready for you yet, sweetheart. Not like you are now?'

Suzie didn't say anything, she just kept staring at the gateway. Mendoza shrugged.

'So anyway; Sirians, Pleiadeans, even Anunnaki who've come this far, and go through the void, if we ever see them again, they don't remember how they returned. Maybe they remember the Elohim, or the Orions, but never the path; so maybe this trip ain't about *the journey*, maybe this trip is just about the *information*. Cause that's what's at the other side of the void, brothers and sisters. Pure energy beings, with pure information. Who the hell knows what that looks, or sounds, or feels like? How the brain makes sense of it? I mean; you and me, we can keep our bodies up to here. I can see you're all juiced up with the new gene sequence and all that, but you ain't gotten the wherewithal to use it yet; not even you, babe. That takes weeks, months. But you got enough will, and determination to get this far, dragging what are essentially your third density bodies all the way. They might not say it, but they respect that. And I get word: the big three, up to here, aren't the only races. There are others on the sidelines rooting for ya. They figure this situation with Earth has gone on long enough; too long to let it slide any more.'

'Look,' Mitch snapped suddenly. 'What is this situation with Earth I keep hearing about? What is it that everyone's skirting around telling us? Humans being manipulated for six thousand years; Oliver Hines being told something so shocking it broke his mind; Earth is a factory, a resort, a health spa, a "third world planet". What is it Mendoza? You must know.'

Mendoza slumped a little and leaned on the balcony. Suddenly, he had a bottle of beer and a lit cigarette in his hand.

'Yeah, I know, I know ya wanna know, but any second now...' Mendoza cocked his ear as though catching some distant cry. 'Yeah, there we go. Misha wants me for something. That's her way of telling me, don't tell them. They think if you know, it might stop you going on or something. I dunno.'

'Mendoza, please.'

'Just tell the ship what you want it to do. Keep it real simple. Undock, forward, through. Okay?'

'Please, Mendoza.'

He shrugged, 'Wish I could. Gotta go. Come on, sweetie.'

Trudy hugged Mitch, then Heather.

'I'll see you again.'

Mendoza looked her up and down. 'You ever been photographed, sweetheart?'

Then he and Trudy vanished.

'Damn.'

Suddenly Mitch felt as though a million eyes were watching him.

'You get the feeling...?' Heather uttered.

'Yes,' Vance whispered. 'Millions of them.'

'Billions maybe,' Suzie added.

They stared at the black portal.

'Ship,' Mitch spoke quietly bur clearly. 'Undock.'

CHAPTER NINETY-SIX

It was simply darkness, all around them.

The ship seemed to be moving, but it might have been Mitch's mind projecting that. There was no light by which to navigate, no breeze to suggest momentum, and the ship did not rock or sway.

Their only illumination was the inner light of the ship itself, a soft glow that seeped from its every surface.

'I can't really feel anything,' Heather said. 'I can feel my skin, but it doesn't feel real.'

Suzie was staring over the rail, down into nothing but blackness.

'It's not even black…' she uttered. 'Not when you really look at it. It's… nothing.'

Vance sighed. It was a strange sound; contentment, in such a vast, empty place.

'What is it, Vance?' Mitch asked warily.

'Home,' Vance spoke.

'Home?' asked Heather. 'Here?'

Vance smiled serenely. 'No. But I can get there from here. I can feel it from here.'

He was leaning into the stern railing, his arms extended and feet braced apart, like a captain watching the harbor recede, pleased to be back out at sea.

'And where is that?' Mitch asked. 'Home? Because you haven't been fully human for some time now, have you Vance?'

'I suppose not. It depends how you see it. Was I ever really Vance? Or am I truly the one I am now? You see, old chap, Misha told you something you've not considered. She said that several lifetimes ago, she incarnated on Earth. What do you think she meant by that? What do you think *that means?*'

'I… I don't know.'

'And the Pleiadean; you registered her talk of a "third world resort planet". But there has been a lot of information on your journey. All of you, you need to make the connections. You need to make them now.'

'I know,' Suzie stated, turning from her dark vigil. 'The aliens in the higher realms, they have expanded consciousness. They live longer; they don't need to incarnate like humans do. They're wiser, they've integrated more knowledge, more information into their consciousness. But if they go astray, if they need to be reminded of their purpose, their place, their mission, the reason they exist, they can incarnate on Earth, in human form. It would be like enduring a trial, sharpening the resolve; experiencing the physicality and the hardships, the pain and suffering of third density again.'

'That's right,' Vance nodded. 'Gold record for the pop singer. That is, in essence, what third density existence is for. Crushing the coal of physicality into the diamond of ascension. And it should work, hand in hand with fourth density. But the Anunnaki have put a stop to that. Yet, third density still functions as such; beings from the higher realms still employ its function. They come from all over the cosmos the pay penance to what remains of their guilt and shame and self-pity. And if they want to do that, they come through here; through the void, to where the conscious energy is distributed, where it becomes an over-soul, and from there individual souls, where experience is dictated, and karma, or causality, is weighted and measured, and dharma, the purpose or momentum of consciousness, is debated and decided. On the other side is the great machine that distributes cosmic consciousness from the Source; the Karma and Dharma Police; the Elohim and the Orions. And that is from where I hail.'

'You're an Orion?' Mitch asked.

'I *was…*' Vance smiled. '…an Elohim.'

Mitch gulped. He thought suddenly that he knew where this

was going.

'But you're not any more?'

'Not for an eternity.'

The total quiet seemed even more totally quiet.

Vance proceeded.

'Vance is real. I incarnated partially through him; just a part of me. But as we have drawn closer to my home, I have become more pronounced; I have been able to, well, let's say it, *possess* him more easily. But he knows, and he is accepting that I am and always have been part of him.'

Suzie leaned back on the rail.

'So if you're not Elohim, then you must be…'

'Nephilim is the word you're looking for. The so-called Sons of God who came to Earth, and… intermingled. In reality we are a strand of the beings called Elohim, another culture, millennia old; there were once many of us, many names and races who evolved in the early days on the universe, and came to consciousness on an atomic level. But the Elohim are all that remains now. They have mastered the ancient sciences so well that all of the other initial races have been absorbed into their omniscient culture. All but a few; including us. The Fallen Angels, if you will; those who wished to participate in the universe, explore and come to know the cosmos. We were exiled. But we remain. Here. In the void.'

'How…' Mitch found that his throat had completely dried up. He cleared it, causing Vance to smile knowingly at him. 'How can you live here?'

'It is not what you perceive; there is great peace here. It is the high desert, the open ocean, the cavernous below, the open sky, deep space, cold beyond measure, heat beyond form, all at once, but none of the above. And there are paths out. We have our own science that allows us to move about, incarnate, infiltrate. Essentially nothing more than you would call will, and intent, and the power to manifest.'

'So…' Heather moved almost imperceptibly closer to Mitch. 'Why did you incarnate as Vance? Why him? Why come with us?' She shrugged, shaking a little. 'Are you going to kill us?'

Vance frowned. 'No, dear me no. I saw it happening. I saw Pan, felt him with his Pagan energy, and the energy of the Old Gods, saw him coming. I thought that I would urge him on, encourage him. So I piggybacked on a man who was charming and enjoyable company, but whose desires and love of the arts had the potential to lead him down an occult path. And so, here I am. Vance McLeod. The Magician.'

'Potential?' Mitch enquired. 'What would he have been without your influence?'

Vance grinned, perhaps a little sad. 'Geoffrey Rush,' he shrugged. 'Or, something like him.'

Mitch found himself becoming very angry.

'And so, here we are; ready to change the course of humanity.'

Vance smiled and there was silence for a while.

Suzie turned back and stared into the void, then turned back. 'So who are you? What's your name?'

Heather nodded. 'I feel like I don't even know you any more.'

Vance grinned, the wicked grin again.

He extended his hand to Heather.

'Pleased to... how should I put this? Make your acquaintence? I am assuming that you have managed to, perhaps... guess my name?'

CHAPTER NINETY-SEVEN

Heather elected not to shake Lucifer's hand, just as Vance had elected not to shake the hand of Obsidian.

'The myth states that we are here to lead you astray,' Lucifer shrugged. 'But there is no Hell, not really. Although some consider this place Hell; many do not. Many come here to sleep, perchance…' He smiled serenely. 'There is always an exit, if you want it. No, my cousins, the Orion Renegades; they are true evil. Their prisons, their places or torment…'

'I was there,' Mitch uttered.

'Yes, I believe you were. Where a second feels like a thousand years because hope does not exist, because all identity has become meaningless.'

'That's right.'

'Yes. I would not wish that on you, or anyone, in a thousand years Mitch. No, we exist as an alternative. We deliver options.'

Mitch's mind reeled. 'That's why you were so keen that I was delivered to Nurding!'

'I told you at the time, Mitch. Options. Choice creates momentum. You needed momentum. Xylata's agenda helped me. I offered it and you made your choice. Again, now, here we are.'

'So you're going to offer us something?' Heather demanded. 'An alternative?'

'Indeed, I can offer you something. I can make it Mitch that those contracts you signed with Everett are… slightly different. I can make it so that they say that he signed over full executive power to one Mitchell Pyne. And I can make it so that anyone who decides to contest that falls victim to… an accident. Or a misfortune.'

'You'll kill them?'

'Nothing of the kind, dear boy. Just a… run of bad luck, let's say? Some… major distractions? Then, when you get back, you'll find that Heather has inherited the rest of Everett's interests, and between you, well, let's say you'll be very comfortable. With a lot of influence. More influence than poor Oliver Hines; at the moment he can pull out of it, but a tweak here, a whisper there, and it can be made to seem as though he's mentally incompetent, make his empire just crumble and shrink away. It's not difficult you understand.'

'I'm sure. Nurding was quite convincing and Cricket took no persuading at all.'

'Not my doing,' Vance smiled. 'However, as you know, people can be made to see, to think, to believe just about anything in third density; perspective is so malleable there. Just ask any jury selector in the land, they'll tell you. And then there's the matter of the gene sequence we've all swallowed. When you get back, it's going to take months, maybe years for you both to learn how to deal with all that, to master the new abilities, to use them on command rather than simply when danger strikes, or when you're up against it. It's the human mind you see; there's no real need for these powers once you return. When you get back, all of this, although it seems very real now, although you seem very present here now, is going to fade. There's nothing in third density you can employ to relate all this to, you see? Take me, look how long it took Vance to remember me. And only when he was absolutely desperate, or focused. Nothing to hang on to, you understand? Not even for me. When you return, it will all just melt away like an epic dream, and you'll start to wonder – did it really happen? Or, if it happened, did it really happen in the way you remember it? And your abilities will get lesser and lesser, the less you want to use them, until eventually you'll just rely on them for the everyday things; telekinesis means you won't have to reach for things across the table any more, or get up and walk to the other side of the room for something; reading the thoughts and emotions of others will just become frightening when you meet people; they're so filled with anger and frustration and resentment. It's not nice to be exposed to that every day. You'll stop using it, and eventually you will just not want to leave your house any more. You'll see Anunnaki when they're there, on television, but you won't care; your acceptance of the status quo will return, and you'll become blasé about it, or worse, you'll become embedded in the lunatic fringe and no-one will treat you seriously any more. I mean, look at what happened to poor Sapphire? And she was so beautiful even I could not resist falling in love with her; a beauty of that magnitude, and still she could not persuade the world of an alternate reality!'

Mitch cringed. Lucifer was right.

'Healing powers will become a nuisance; everyone will want something from you, and you will give and give of your healing energy, until it starts eating away at your own vital energy, and because of that you won't keep sharp, it will start to drain you, leave you with little or nothing for yourself, just drained all the time. You'll become bitter because people always want something from you, endlessly, undeservingly; and remember, you can read their thoughts! And all that combined will further alienate you from your own race. And who needs the ability to jump through dimensional gaps when you never want to go anywhere? Do you see?'

They did; they could see it.

But they said nothing.

To speak, just one syllable, would be tantamount to agreement.

And that would be it.

'But I can make it so that your gifts accelerate; so you have complete mastery. You can control anything at will, and with Everett's company at your disposal, that's a hell of a lot of collateral to start with, to work with, to maintain control and achieve domination with. You'll rival the Anunnaki within weeks; because as we know, as we've learned, Earth is your planet, and once you start ascending, truly expanding your consciousness in an accelerated fashion, the universe is designed to give it back to you; for you to claim ownership. And when you absorb Olivera, as no doubt you will, you can live forever, forever young, with an endless army of servants, the entire world population at your command, because there isn't one soul alive who won't want the Olivera treatment eventually; we know this, we've seen it at work. I can do this, I can make it happen. All you have to do is stop. Say the word, and I will turn us back to the Sirian Complex, no shame, no guilt; you did what you could but you discovered a better option. Turn back, and Earth itself is yours; its solar system, its neighboring stars, and eventually your rightful place in the cosmos, as you and your race were before, with an empire that spans from the planetary cores right up to the Source itself, with the benefit of reclaiming your full buried human history so you don't make the same mistakes again. Turn back, let the earthquake happen, let all the quakes and tsunamis and cyclones and floods and droughts occur as they should, then rise like a pair of phoenix birds from the ashes; allow chaos to flow naturally, into exaltation. Then accept its hand so that order might come from it, order that you control. It can happen; it is happening – the universe has already seen and calculated the possibilities and told me it's a valid path; a possible, viable route of evolution for the reclaimed genetic sequence. It's happening now. Just say the word, and you are on the thrones, King and Queen of the New Age of Mankind. Immortal rulers of the galaxy, forever. So what do we say? Do we turn back? Do you want to be Gods?'

CHAPTER NINETY-EIGHT

Mitch felt the words form in his larynx. They rose to his mouth. He could feel Heather; she was the same. He heard her dry lips smack as they parted. They wanted to say no, but they were going to say yes. It was impossible to refuse. At least, something about the way Lucifer had put it, had spoken, had made it seem that way. They were compelled, without reservation, to agree, to see it that way too.

'I'll find my own way home,' Suzie Saturn spoke.

With that, she ran at Lucifer with all her strength and weight, and all her power and accumulated energy. She ran at him low and struck him with her chest and shoulder in his center of gravity, embraced him, and careened backwards with him into the stern rail.

He flipped backwards and together they plunged over the side of the ship and into the void.

Gone.

CHAPTER NINETY-NINE

'Suzie!'

Mitch heard himself cry out, then the void seemed to snap.

The ship was trembling.

He heard Heather cry out.

'It's the earthquake!'

Mitch was suddenly blind, he couldn't feel.

He was disembodied consciousness.

Then he was standing in the middle of a street, and it was daylight, a chilly day with the sun high in the sky and far away, and clouds breezing overhead.

He was there, but not there; the traffic on the street moved through him.

Was this the astral?

He didn't know.

Someone spoke behind him.

'This is the intersection.'

He turned.

'Cricket?'

'Hey Mitch.'

She looked slightly older and was dressed in a neat, crisp black business suit and a plain white shirt with sharp collars.

'Where…? What happened?'

'There's nothing beyond where you went that you would comprehend. They asked me to bring you back.'

'They?'

'The Elohim. The two who spoke to you in the church; that's who they said they were. We sometimes do each other favors.'

'You do?'

'Two sides of the same coin, and all that jazz. After all this time, I'm still processing.' She touched her stomach. There was a slight bump. 'Still growing.'

'It's… only been hours…' Mitch frowned. He looked around.

He recognized the street, the intersection, the crossroads.

It was the street outside of Los Angeles. The street from his dream.

The earthquake was about to hit.

But things were paused again.

'How can the child grow that quickly?' he asked, confused.

'Oh, this child. It's not yours. Yours is…' Cricket laughed. 'Now that would be telling. I've waited years to do this. It's been on my to-do list for so long now. I waited to come back, and see you here.'

He assessed her again. It was true; the way she looked. She was forty now, nearing fifty.

'Waited? How long?'

'I could have done it right away. But I always knew I did. Because, things happened afterwards as though I did. And yet there was the anticipation, the holding; the wondering… *what if I didn't?* I suppose those thoughts come with the wielding of power; the ability to withhold. But I did, eventually. I did come back and meet you here; I am here. I always was here, and I always did this.'

Mitch was becoming anxious.

He was about to watch Heather die in a gas explosion, as he was flattened by a flying subway car, running to rescue her…

'Heather's down there, isn't she? On the intersection at the next block.'

'She is. She's looking for you. But it was you who made the request; you who stormed the Gates of Heaven. They say you have to participate. That is your condition. You are both at the intersection, and yet, different intersections. For those intersections to unite, you must participate. Do you understand?'

'No! Are they going to stop the earthquake or not?'

'Nothing can stop the earthquake Mitch.'

'But why are all the people still here? We destroyed the talisman, Everett went on television, Heather and Saph called everyone they could think of!'

'You saved thousands.'

'*Thousands?*'

'Isn't that enough? All the exit routes out of town are jammed with people who got the message.'

'How many people are in the city right now?'

'Just over three point eight million, give or take. Including tourists.'

'They're all going to die!'

'Earthquakes don't kill that many people, Mitch. Most people survive. It's more the injuries and property damage. So I'm told.'

'This is a major earthquake in a highly populated area – in the middle of the day! I've seen it; those skyscrapers; they *all fall.*'

'Not all of them. They're earthquake proof, most of them.'

'*Why are we arguing this?*'

'Because you are not *listening*. Do you agree? You must participate!'

'Okay!' Mitch cried out. 'I agree!'

'Then it's a deal. Everyone's very impressed Mitch. You've done extremely well. We'll meet again.'

Cricket vanished.

The city came alive.

Cars immediately blasted their horns as Mitch appeared in the middle of the road. Several swerved. Mitch saw a gap and ran to the sidewalk, with drivers shouting obscenities and pedestrians staring at him as though he were mad.

The earthquake struck almost immediately.

It was exactly like the dream.

He was running through bedlam.

The ground was shaking and he could barely keep his footfalls steady. There was a deafening roar all around.

He knew how this ended, but he kept running.

He sprinted as a huge crop of skyscrapers trembled in the distance, their facades crumbling and falling.

Parked car alarms and security sirens were wailing.

Moving cars were skidding to a halt.

Hydrants were spraying water, mains pipes were bursting.

Power lines were sparking and he could smell gas in the air.

There was an all-encompassing crack, something like thunder, but from below ground, and the intersection ahead split and rose up; water burst from beneath it like a city square fountain. Vehicles were tipped, thrown over. The gigantic rumble drowned all other sound and Mitch was terrified; primal fear rose up and claimed him, and a building collapsed in on itself just behind him, then another down the way.

He remembered, this time, who he was trying to save.

Heather was the woman he loved.

The first of the skyscrapers fell.

Then another, taking out a third.

Heather was at the *intersection*; he knew the word now, why it had resonated. He'd come from the intersection between physicality and abstract, and now was at the intersection of choice. He'd chosen to participate.

But why?

Why had he and Heather been placed in the thick of it?

Why were they being forced to act out this weird analogy; at different intersections?

There was another underground thunderclap and he knew what was coming. The subway train exploded into daylight with an almighty smash, and then time slowed down. He lay on his stomach and craned his neck up.

There it was, coming down on him.

'Mitch!'

Heather was running toward him.

She had seen that he was about to die, that nothing could prevent it, and then the gas main exploded and claimed her.

And the plume, again, paused.

Like a DVD.

The train above, frozen in mid flight.

Time had stopped.

A voice whispered in his ear.

'The call has been answered.'

He turned sharply to his left and saw a face staring down at him. He still couldn't make her out but she was crouching beside him, smiling serenely.

He rolled to his side and got to his feet beneath the subway train.

The woman was standing beside him now. She was stunningly beautiful, but at the same time plain and asexual.

It was the female Elohim.

'You have participated,' she smiled, again. 'You can't save her, the woman you love. You can't save any of them.'

Then he remembered what happened next and looked to the frozen plume of the explosion. Again, denying the paused reality of the scene around him, he saw someone walking toward him, right out of the orange core of the gas explosion. It was the male Elohim, carrying Heather in his arms.

PART SIX

BELOW

CHAPTER ONE HUNDRED

Sitting in his hospital bed, it took Mitch only a few hours to figure out how to work his new laptop, even with a borderline severe concussion, then a few days to piece together what had happened.

The Los Angeles earthquake had struck at twenty-three minutes past midday on a Wednesday afternoon. It was an ordinary work day and the streets were crowded with people in the middle of taking their twelve o'clock lunch breaks. The quake had measured eight point three on the Richter Scale, the epicenter being somewhere near Wiltshire Boulevard in the middle of town. Most of the buildings there had survived, a testament to human ingenuity, created to be 'earthquake proof'. Eight other skyscrapers had collapsed, most of them on the edges of the city, older buildings that the major mass of skyscrapers had grown toward and encompassed over time, buildings that had been difficult to retro-fit and make earthquake proof. Remarkably they had fallen on smaller office buildings in sections of the outer city center that had been almost completely vacated for lunch; there had been casualties but remarkably few, considering. There had been an enormous amount of property damage; it was going to bankrupt California, and send the United States economy, and inevitably the world economy, into a tail-spin from which, this time, there would be no pulling up. The stock market was suspended, teetering on collapse.

The quake had rippled through the entire Los Angeles Basin and destroyed or severely damaged an estimated four hundred thousand homes. It soon became clear that loss of life was shocking; news stations began reporting an estimated two million dead, but at the same time began carrying tales of incredible survival. While reporters were doing their usual trick of seeking out the most shocking footage, the most tearful horror stories and most gut-wrenching loss, they appeared to find only a few, and virtually nothing compared to the vast array of stunning, many would say miraculous tales of freak survival.

A man who had been making coffee a second before his kitchen collapsed: 'I don't remember walking out of the kitchen; something must have told me to… but for some reason I was back on the couch when it struck; the rest of the house is fine!'

Three little girls who had been playing in an upstairs bedroom when their entire house had collapsed, found afterwards playing in the rubble, as though it had been some kind of exciting game. An aged woman, wheelchair bound, who had somehow found the strength to walk for the first time in a decade, found bruised but alive under the remains of her back porch.

Stories like these, first dozens, then hundreds, and then so many that the news ceased to carry them in case their audience became weary of them.

Instead they turned to a rescue story; a small three storey office block in which the twenty staff had all gathered in the basement just before the quake hit because one of the foreshocks had revealed a hidden safe in the wall, behind the plaster; somehow they had been sheltered and now they were being dug out and pulled from the wreckage one at a time, like survivors of a mining disaster. This had been the focus of the news for a few hours until a second such story had emerged; a dozen co-workers who had gathered in an underground parking station to assess their co-worker's new Prius, sheltered from a collapsed skyscraper by a concrete beam. Then another story like that, then another, then dozens from all over town.

The news feeds started to amend the death toll; it had been misreported, it was one million, not two million dead. Still, the greatest natural disaster in modern history. And still, the tears they reported were more often tears of joy at a fluke survival than for loss and mourning.

'A house can be rebuilt; my family are all still alive!'

'It's just a wall; most of our stuff is still in one piece but my daughter managed to get under her bed and got away with a broken collar bone; coulda bin much worse!'

'There's some water damage from a burst main but we're all still here and that's what counts!'

Then, as the day went on, the news feeds amended the numbers again; the misreporting had been misreported; two *million* dead should not have been changed to one million dead, it should have been changed to two *hundred thousand* dead. Someone had added a few too many zeroes. Still, an incalculable tragedy of epic proportions.

Overnight: people still being pulled from the rubble, so many that it was almost hard to believe, and yet it was happening.

But still, who knew how many people had been in the skyscrapers?

Then, news on that. One of the buildings had been evacuated just ten minutes before the quake in a fire drill. Another had been evacuated almost an hour before, on the insistence of the building's owner, a financier who, although he would never admit it, regularly consulted an astronomer to play the stock market. He had been called and told by his psychic that the quake was about to hit, and made no bones on the evening news about the fact that he had effectively saved eleven thousand lives. Another of the collapsed skyscrapers was home to a company that was about to break the news of a financial catastrophe similar to the Enron scandal; the company had tried to hold on to solvency but had been called the previous night and told that it would be forced to suspend trading. All the employees, some twenty thousand workers, had been called in the middle of the night and told not to report for work in the morning, and that the building was in lock-down. Another building simply had an extremely effective evacuation plan that went off like clockwork and got everyone out of the building as the earthquake was hitting, in under five minutes, just before the building collapsed. Their drills had never run as fast; people remembered running down steps as though being carried by a strong wind, as though flying. Fear and adrenalin, said the experts. The fifth and oldest collapsed skyscraper had, almost ridiculously, been closed a week before, having been deemed insufficiently earthquake proof.

And so it went.

The next morning, after a long and dreamless sleep, Mitch followed the news again. It consisted almost entirely of miraculous survival tales on an individual level, and more trapped but only minor injured groups being dug out of the rubble. The death toll was dropped to one hundred thousand and, by the afternoon, half that again.

Many who might have died from their injuries were saved when Oliver Hines appeared on the scene, distributing rapid healing agents from his hitherto unannounced Regenera Medical line, traveling personally from hospital to hospital like Mother Teresa, visiting the sick and even personally dispensing his new, miracle medicine at no cost.

By nightfall, the death toll was reduced to thirty thousand, and then by the next morning down to an estimated eighteen or nineteen thousand.

Mitch watched all this with a low and gnawing sense of guilt; he had picked up his new laptop from the street as he'd wandered about, bleeding from the head. It had been new in the box, and he had clung to it in the ambulance on the way to the hospital and wouldn't let go. Someone had helped him with a wi-fi connection and somehow, though the fog of his mind and a help menu, he had taught himself the basic principles of Windows. Now, almost forty-eight hours later, he was beginning to feel a little more clear-headed about it all, and even a little suspicious when he realized that the logo on the laptop was Olivera.

The nurse told Mitch that he could not be discharged unless someone came to get him, and pointed out that if he wanted to call someone, his phone needed recharging. He told the nurse he did not know how to do this, but she found another patient with a compatible phone and connected the recharge cord for him.

He slept a while longer and then watched the news again, while the phone sat recharged by the bed, wondering whom he would call.

The news had picked up on the term Miracle Quake and was running the term in logo form with all its broadcasts. The death toll was now down to two and a half thousand. Many of them had been heart attacks, a few dozen had been looters trying to access collapsed buildings, and more than five hundred were people who were still missing, presumed dead.

One of the missing was billionaire Bo Everett, whose recent string of disappearances, and shocking appearance at his own memorial service, predicting the quake, were still being investigated. Still, it was pointed out, Everett's early warning had probably saved the lives of three thousand would-be mourners who had finished stamping from the cathedral where the service was taking place around twenty seconds before its total collapse.

Slowly, the population of California began to accept the freakish nature of the low death toll, and the realization settled in that by the sheer volume of similar stories, nobody's miracle tale was particularly special. Power was being restored quickly to blacked out areas, and while both the Governor and the President had declared the event a National Disaster, block parties were being reported all over the city and a renewed sense of community had been restored as neighbors and strangers, in turn, helped other neighbors and strangers repair their damaged properties.

Mitch was watching this in his hospital bed when he heard a familiar voice from outside his tiny room; a converted supply cupboard just big enough for a bed that he'd been shoved into when he'd first been admitted and left there ever since.

'I assure you I am well, and ready to depart. Somebody stole the recharge cord for my phone while I was sleeping, otherwise I would call someone to collect me!'

The door to Mitch's cupboard opened and his nurse stared in, assessing Mitch.

'I'm sorry sir, the man whose cord I borrowed needs it back, would you mind?'

'Of course,' Mitch croaked, the first words he'd spoken all day.

Behind her, Derek Nurding poked his head around the corner of the door.

'I rather think you might have asked before – *Mitchell*?'

'Professor Nurding…?'

'Mitchell, what are you doing in here?'

'Concussion. How about you?'

Nurding shrugged. 'Well, the same.'

They stared at each other a moment, then Nurding looked at the nurse.

'Do you think we could have a moment?'

The nurse sighed, shrugged and went away.

Nurding entered the room and stood at the end of Mitch's bed, just far enough from the door to enable it to close.

'Well, this is a coincidence.'

'You did want me in a hospital.'

Nurding smirked. 'Now, I don't think raking up old ground is going to help us get along, do you Mitchell?'

'So you won't have me committed or anything?'

Nurding laughed, dryly. 'Hardly. I would have to have the whole city sectioned. The Miracle Quake, can you believe it? Well, look who I'm asking; I suppose you would.'

Mitch grinned. 'I don't know about miracle. Maybe something intervened. It is pretty extraordinary, even you'd have to admit.'

Nurding nodded. 'Of course. Tell me Mitch; have you heard of the Law of Large Numbers?'

'Maybe. I can't remember.'

'Look at it this way; you flip a coin a thousand times. Its four hundred and fifty heads, five hundred and fifty tails. But probability suggests it should be even. But the more you flip them, the more likely it is that things will even out to fifty- fifty, even though at certain times during the test, the results will be uneven; do you follow?'

'Sure.'

'Okay then, let's say we flip a coin a trillion times. You're going to see all sorts of things; unusually long runs of either heads or tails, maybe thousands of heads at a time. But eventually, there will be the same amount of tails as heads. You simply have to keep flipping the coin, maybe a zillion times, and it will even out.'

'I see.'

'Do you Mitch?'

'Sure. You're saying if heads were life and tails were death, what happened in the quake was a run of heads; that in a universe this size, it's bound to happen somewhere or other, sooner or later, and Los Angeles got the lucky streak. Right?'

Nurding smiled. 'There you go Mitch. You're learning. No need for sectioning just yet.'

Mitch smiled and let out a short snort of laughter.

'May I have my recharge cord back please?'

Mitch handed it to him.

'It wasn't me, it was the nurse. I lost mine.'

'I see. Of course. Thank you Mitchell.'

'Where were you professor? During the quake?'

Nurding smiled. 'Well, there you have it Mitch. I was delivering a new lecture, in a large hall. Two thousand people, in a university of twenty thousand students. As I was starting, the hall was flooded with rats. It was an awful sight, to be sure. I suppose they sensed something and came up from the sewers; who knows? But the hall was evacuated, then the entire campus was sent home. Health and safety, can't risk a trick these days. So when the quake struck, not long after, all the buildings were empty and anyone who remained on campus was standing outside. Unfortunately a colleague and I were standing at the top of the external stairs that led up to the hall and we fell. He broke his arm and I sustained a concussion.'

'I'm glad you're okay.'

'And what about you Mitch? Do you have a miracle story?'

Mitch considered this.

He held up his laptop.

'Just buying a new computer. I don't know what hit me, I think I fell and hit my head on the road. Next thing I knew I was in an ambulance.'

Nurding smiled. 'Well, there you go. Nothing miraculous about that.'

'There is if you know how technophobic I am.'

Nurding laughed.

'Well good luck. I hope you purchased a Mac?'

Mitch smiled. 'I guess we'll just have to agree to differ on some things Professor. Good luck with the tour.'

Nurding nodded. His eyes sparkled.

'And good luck to you, Mitchell.'

CHAPTER ONE HUNDRED & ONE

Mitch was still afraid to use the phone.

Not for any sustained fear, or hatred of technology; it was the fear of who would, or would not answer. After three days in the hospital bed his mind had finally cleared. The concussion, and the drugs he'd been on, had leveled his emotions out to a point where he had become totally even about everything; he'd call them later, they'd be okay. If they weren't he'd deal. But now the painkillers had worn off, he was starting to recall things; things he was sure were real but didn't seem rational.

As he exited the hospital, out of his gown and redressed in his black funeral suit and enormous black coat, with his guilty laptop under his arm, assured by the nurses that his concussion had passed and that he could leave of his own volition, he went down the external stairs and down onto the pavement, wondering if the diagnosis had been correct. He still felt as though in a daze, still shell-shocked, still drugged.

The dual lane road outside had been reduced to one lane while workmen patched up the cracks in the street. Traffic was moving slowly but people still moved about, dodging scaffolding and walking around condemned buildings. The vast forest of the Los Angeles skyscrapers still stood, still a testament to human ingenuity.

Suddenly Mitch didn't feel like being in the city any more.

He walked down the sidewalk a while. The faces that passed him all seemed to reflect his own state of mind: dazed and confused. When he found a ruined store, he went to the doorframe that was still standing and thought *home*.

Then he walked through the gap.

Pan's apartment was not as he'd left it; someone had been through and tidied up. He wandered around the rooms; both the beds were made and the television had been switched off at the socket. The discs he'd been sent to review were gone. He assumed he'd lost his job, given that he had been pronounced dead.

He sat on the couch and stared at the blank screen.

He'd left his daughter on an astral ship, fighting Anunnaki commandos. Left his two best friends and his boss, the man who had restored his life to him, on an abandoned Pleiadean ship in the middle of the Amazon. Left Trudy on a Sirian space station God Knows Where and the last he'd seen of Suzie and Vance…

He cringed.

And where was Heather?

He'd asked the nurse; she wasn't registered on any of the lists. She'd cross-checked online.

Heather Everett, he was then reminded by another, less sympathetic nurse, was three months dead. Everyone knew that.

And so, he'd wandered out of the hospital and back here.

Back where it had all started.

His phone rang.

Mitch stood on the street outside his apartment block and waited, staring down at his scuffed black Docs. The black car pulled up and he opened the rear door, ready to get in.

Instead, a man leaned out and gave Mitch a piece of paper; a photograph.

'You know what to do with this.'

Mitch stared at it.

'Sure.'

The door closed and the car drove away.

The photo Mitch held was of a strange symbol. It was an odd design, like nothing Mitch had ever seen before. There were lines, and waves, and curves; it was complicated yet held together as one symbol, almost ancient yet not quite modern. He liked it.

It looked… human?

He turned back to his apartment door and made sure there was nobody coming up behind him, or coming through. Then, focusing on the symbol in the photograph, he opened a gap and stepped through.

CHAPTER ONE HUNDRED & TWO

Mitch arrived in a plain white room.

The symbol was stark on the wall, the only feature; huge and bold, painted in gray and violet and pale green. It was soothing, beautiful.

'Do you like it?'

Oliver Hines stood behind him, behind him an open door that led out to a white corridor.

'Yes.'

'It's the new logo. Everett and I are starting a new company together; Lever, we're calling it.'

'Lever?'

'Oliver, Everett; it seemed to make sense. The logo has no Anunnaki connotations; it's pure human. That's why it seems so different. We're going to play them at their own game.'

Mitch put his hands into the deep pockets of the coat and shrugged.

'Sounds right.'

'Humans need some leverage, wouldn't you agree?'

'Absolutely.'

'I need you to sign some papers. Will you come with me?'

They walked down the corridor together to a small but well-appointed office, with minimalist chrome and white decor.

'My office.'

'What are the papers?'

'I'll let her tell you.'

Mitch turned to the door.

Heather embraced him with such force she nearly bowled

him over. Mitch returned it with all his might; they kissed, hard and passionate, until Heather broke it off.

'You won't believe it,' Heather gushed. 'Uncle Bo and Oliver have signed a truce. They're pooling their resources; and they want us to run it, Mitch. They want us to run Lever!'

Mitch turned to Oliver without letting her go.

'Really?'

'I owe you my life, Mitch. Perhaps even my soul. Many people do. Bo proposed it and I agreed, on one condition. Regene is privately held; it will be absorbed into Lever but all profits, all of them Mitch, must go into the emergency funds for Los Angeles. We're projecting in the billions, now that we've gone worldwide. Is that agreed?'

'Of course.'

'Then sign when you're ready. Oh, and there's this.'

Oliver picked up a check from the table and handed it to Mitch.

'It's blank. Bo said you could decide what you earned, as per you deal. He said, consider it a wedding gift.'

Mitch turned back to Heather, still tight in his embrace.

'Okay?'

She smiled.

'Okay.'

Oliver nodded and smiled. He seemed happy for them.

'Mitch, there's one more thing.'

'Only one more?'

'The answer, Mitch. The answer nobody would give you. I have it. Down the corridor.'

CHAPTER ONE HUNDRED & THREE

'Everett told me everything,' Oliver stated, as they walked with him down the white walled corridor, their shoes making hardly any sound on the matching carpets.

'Where is Everett? I've missed him.'

'Where else?' Heather guffawed. 'On the ship.'

'He's going to be there a long time,' Oliver told them. 'Maybe the rest of his life. The Pleiadeans were apparently only forthcoming as to how the day-to-day technology of the ship runs, not so much with the energy systems. It may take him decades to reverse engineer it. Your friends are still there; Pan and Sapphire are recovering, but his sister Trudy and the sorcerer Mendoza have yet to determine how to open the caskets. There has been some progress, however, due to your journey.'

Oliver stopped at a door, and ushered them through.

The room was an observation chamber; a wide glass window spread before them, and within sat a young Latina man, writing down what seemed to be a strange mix of mathematical formulas and an unrecognizable text on large sheets of white paper. As they entered, he finished one, placed it face down on a pile next to him, and continued writing.

'This is Arcani. Arcani Fontana.'

'Fontana?' Mitch rubbed his chin. 'Adriana Fontana was the other member of Pan's team; we know what happened to Tim, and…' Mitch stared Oliver in the eyes. 'Pam. But no-one's…'

'I apologize for my former behavior Mitch. I realize now that it was not Satan, although it's as good a name for him as any, and to be honest I'm not entirely convinced it wasn't him. The Nameless One, as I believe he's properly called, made me do things of which I am not proud. But you helped me with that, Mitch, which is why I am going to show you both what only myself and two other people, both scientists who live down here permanently, know.'

'Down here? Where are we?'

'Below, Mitch. Deep below.'

Arcani stopped writing, placed the cap on his pen and sat back in his chair. Oliver seemed astonished, and even gasped a little. Arcani turned to them through the glass.

'I've finished,' he stated.

Oliver quickly opened the door and entered the room. Mitch and Heather followed.

'Finished?' Oliver demanded.

'My penance is over. I can leave now.'

Oliver stared at him, calming himself.

'That's very good Arcani. You've done a great service.'

Mitch stared at the young man. He looked gaunt, tired.

'Arcani, how long have you been writing here?'

'Nine months.'

There was silence.

'Your tee-shirt,' Heather remarked curiously.

Arcani smiled. 'It's my lucky shirt. I love her; she's not really dead you know. She's going to come back. Nobody knows what happened to her.'

It was a Suzie Saturn tee-shirt; her face and the name of an album tour, *Free Dumb*, an image that both Mitch and Heather were shocked to realize they knew very well.

Oliver turned to them. It was only then that Mitch realized he'd dropped the fake middle-American charm. Oliver now spoke calmly and clearly, with barely a trace of an accent at all. Mitch supposed that after a possession like that, one might feel the need to wipe the slate and begin again. Perhaps that's what had happened to Oliver, but regardless of his charismatic lack, Mitch found he liked the new, bland Oliver immeasurably more.

'From what's been described to me, her status, at least, has been restored. Nobody's ever heard of Mistress, whoever she was, but Suzie Saturn vanished under mysterious circumstances around four months ago. She has not been declared dead, but she is officially missing. Search the web if you want the details; it's not difficult to find.'

'I will,' Mitch stated.

'You will?' Heather was stunned.

'I stole a laptop.'

'*Really?*'

'And your friend, Vance; he's in Los Angeles. If you search the web again, you'll find a considerable resume as to his film career. Two Oscar nominations, no wins. He's lost twice to Geoffrey Rush. Apparently there's something of a rivalry there.'

Mitch guffawed. 'Does he remember anything?'

'I don't think anyone's asked him yet. I would assume not.'

'Good for Vance,' Heather shrugged.

'And you'll be pleased to know that Mister Harding will remain Head of Security at Lever. Mister Harding remembers everything, very clearly. I don't think anything gets past him. I've given him my house. My *tree* house. He intends to restore it in his spare time.'

Mitch couldn't help but laugh. Quite the retirement shack, especially with Eissley frozen in the middle of it. Maybe Harding would make a feature of that?

'But that's not what I have brought you here to tell you; the rest of the news is not so good.'

Arcani stood. 'Can I go now?'

'Go to my office Arcani. Wait there.'

Arcani nodded. 'It's good that it's done. You were right; it should be written.'

'Thank you, Arcani.'

Arcani nodded and departed.

Oliver shut the door behind him.

'You just met the man who shot Pan.'

'*What?*'

Mitch froze; his body just jammed.

What was he supposed to do with *that*?

'Arcani is – was – a devout Catholic who believed that his sister's research was the work of the Devil. Apparently Pan and Adriana Fontana had been lovers for some time; Pan had gone down there with Pam Winters as a couple but, upon hiring Adriana off her resume and subsequently meeting her, he fell immediately in love.'

Mitch sighed. 'It really never ends with him.'

'Theirs was a secret affair, but once revealed… let's just say that it was the resulting jealousy that allowed my people to bribe Pam Winters with a fortune, so she would betray Pan and provide us with his information. As I explained before Mitch, we had already discovered the code to unlock the hidden, materially based DNA sequences, but what we hadn't discovered was the consciousness-based sequence. The Pandora Sequence, as we came to call it. Pan, Pandora, you see?'

Mitch nodded. 'What are you going to do with him? Why did he shoot Pan?'

'Pan was leading his sister astray. He was going to bring her back to Australia with him. We suspect that he gave her the full six doses of the sequence, but we're fairly sure she didn't take them. And of course, we know that she didn't return with Pan.'

'How do you know she didn't take them?'

'Because Arcani did. And these papers are the result.'

Heather reached over and assessed one.

'It's incomprehensible.'

'No. It's Anunnaki. An ancient form of the Draco language.'

'But – why? What does it say?'

'Please, come with me. This is the last step of the tour. Then you have one last choice.'

Oliver led them to another room, this one filled with three workstations and several large metal boxes, sleek and silver, that came up to Mitch's shoulder, running across the back of the room.

Heather whistled.

'That's serious hardware.'

'Supercomputers?' Mitch asked.

'The best,' Oliver nodded. 'We had already crunched much of the human DNA, and Regene was ready to go. But we sent our own people into Peru, to what remained of Pan's workstation, and we found Arcani, wandering the empty office, almost at total bliss with the Pandora Sequence. We're fairly sure he took the dose intended for Adriana. We're not sure if she had a change of heart, or responded to Pan's death, or perhaps she fled from what happened to her brother. But there's a small, secluded convent about ten miles from where she and Arcani grew up. A woman matching her description is living there as a novice. It's not surprising you couldn't find her, Heather; the convent is a secret order, built into a mountainside. I think our people were the first western men to set foot there in more than three decades.'

Heather shrugged. 'Whatever works.'

'We discovered that the Pandora Sequence had done something unusual to Arcani. Maybe because he'd grown up in a village with little western influence, and even lesser Anunnaki influence. He'd been writing on the walls of Pan's workstation, and on a whim, we had it checked out. He was writing genetic code in a way we'd never seen, in a way we could barely understand, until we processed it through these computers. We brought him back here and he wrote. For months and months. More and more. I made him write it by hand, on paper, as is my eccentricity. But finally I was persuaded that it be digitized. These computers are not connected to anything but each other. And they analyzed the data. That was how Regene expanded so quickly; we sent out messages, we made an exhibit of our new power, but Arcani just kept coming up with new combinations, formulas and applications we'd never dreamed possible. We can give people functioning wings. Functioning gills. Chameleon skin. Chimeras of all kinds, all combinations. But that, still, is not all.'

'Go on.'

'I began to suspect that Arcani was hiding something from us. He was muttering to himself, responding to things that were not there. He seemed to read the genetic formulas as though viewing a hologram only he could see, but we knew it made no sense to him. Eventually we got it out of him, what was beneath the formula, what was stored below the science.'

'And what was that?'

'It was a story. A diary, if you will. Of an Anunnaki scientist named Miris, who lived six thousand years ago, at what you and I would now call the dawn of the present age of mankind on Earth.'

'Six million years ago? That's what...'

'The Miris Diary briefly details the pre-history of humanity, up to Atlantis, the last great pre-historical civilization. How humanity expanded to the stars, but eventually fell back, until we fell completely. When human DNA re-emerged on Earth, the Anunnaki were rising in the galaxy. They claimed Earth as their own, and began to alter our DNA. This is what I was trying to tell you Mitch. Our people, when they tried to create new life, and apply their own signature in the DNA, found something else. They found *another* signature.'

'What do you mean, another?'

'Another, Mitch. A signature that was there from almost, what we would call, the beginning. A pre-existing mark that stated without reservation that human DNA had been fundamentally changed. An alien signature, in the human DNA.'

Heather gasped. 'Jesus.'

'The Miris Diary explains how over thousands of years, the Anunnaki manipulated the evolution of mankind. They intended for us to be a slave race, and for a time we were. Then, as we evolved, they realized that we were coming to higher consciousness faster than before, much faster. Their slaves were beginning to grow and revolt; to access the fourth density and manipulate the astral. By the time we evolved to become humans, in the earliest form as we are today, there were already signs of fourth density access.

So, the Anunnaki gelded us. They enhanced the amygdala, the fear center of the brain, and interbred with us so that some of their own DNA, their own reptilian nature, would be present and better manipulated, better understood by them. Miris lived thousands of years, and his work lives on in us.'

'They changed us?'

'They created us – at least, humanity in its present form. But our manipulation through our fear centers is not the least of it. As humanity progressed and evolved, locked into third density with only a sliver of hope to ascend, with our fourth density reality hijacked and pillaged by the Anunnaki, the Earth began to change. As we co-created our reality, we created it based on fear, which led to warfare, and attempts to control and dominate. Our history is a sorry tale of almost nothing but that. As a fear-based race, we created a prison for ourselves, within which there was no escape from the cycle of karma, or even the possibility of ascension to a new cycle of karma in a higher density, such as the races you have encountered. Other races, from higher realms, began to become aware of this; a world of third density where karmic energies burned short and bright, where our imprisoned human race had created a kind of karmic forge. These other peoples, other species, realized that if they so chose, they could incarnate here and gain great self-knowledge very quickly, learn great lessons and acquire great wisdom, then depart, back to their own, higher karmic cycles.'

'Like a karmic detox…' Mitch uttered. 'A health retreat in a third world country, a third world planet…'

'It's as good an analogy as any. The harshest and most difficult of trials, but without the burden of being trapped here on the karmic wheel, reincarnating here again and again, thousands of times. We, the members of the human race, have the honor of doing that. Do you see? We have become cogs in a machine of pain, a torture wheel for the higher-ups to hone their own consciousness while we slave away, confined to one planet, blind to our true nature, the nature that the Anunnaki forced upon us.'

'That's what we are?' Heather gasped. 'Just… pain generators?'

'That's what we are. Spiritually neutered gods, imprisoned by the enforced generation of fear, self-doubt, and masochism, all inspired and supported by the Anunnaki's continued manipulation of our fourth density space, a conquered race, mutated and pitied, but good enough for the whole of the cosmos to exploit.'

'They could have stopped it, couldn't they?' Mitch asked. 'Any of them, at any time? The Pleiadeans, the Sirians, even the Elohim or the Orions? But they kept it going, for their own ends.'

'Cosmic Law apparently forbids direct interference; but there seems to be some kind of acceptance in this matter, that the collective consciousness, that the Source must want it this way, or it never would have allowed the Anunnaki to invade in the first place.'

Mitch scoffed. 'I don't believe that. God's Will? God's Will didn't destroy Los Angeles. The end result of the long Anunnaki occupation did that! And God's Will didn't save all those people. My will did, and Heather's, and Everett's, and Saph and Pan and Trudy and Amy and even Vance! Ancient beings did it, because we implored them to!'

Heather shook her head. 'The Source is conscious Mitch. And it led us here. It wanted you to prove we were worth… not saving; *encouraging*. Remember, Vance is older than all this. Misha too, and Obsidian. They all nudged us; the Elohim *invited* us. They want it to stop; but they know that only we can stop it. Only us, Mitch. Only *us*.'

Oliver nodded. 'So now, you must choose.'

He reached down and grasped something from behind one of the supercomputers. As he raised it, they recognized it. It was Saph's bag, the one she'd given Yelina.

'Your uncle, your friends and your daughter have taken their own paths. They may never return to third density. We have been monitoring Arcani and he will be dead in three days; now his mission is over, his guilt at his own actions is destroying him from within. There is nothing we can do. You two are all that remains of the original mission to save humanity. Pan's research is lost. We can reverse-engineer his gifts, but we barely know where to begin, it might take ten years, it might take five hundred. This bag contains all that remains of his work. You have Lever, you have the gifts; now, the choice remains, Mitchell Pyne, Heather Everett, what do you do with them? Do you destroy them and remain secret super-humans amongst your race? Or do you take on the cosmic order, and risk bringing down the fire of the heavens, and the potential enmity of all the older races? How strong are these alliances? How close are your friends? How strong are *you*?'

Mitch looked at Heather.

They both looked at the bag.

'*What do you do?*'

EPILOGUE

Mitch sat on the couch in Pan's apartment.

It was almost empty now, just a few boxes and the couch to go.

He was trying to write on a small white pad, without much success.

There was a white flash in the room before him and he spoke without looking up.

'Been wondering when you'd turn up.'

'Hi, Dad.'

'Too late to help with the moving.'

'You have telekinesis and gaps. What more help do you want?'

'Just teasing, sweetheart.'

'What are you writing?'

Mitch shrugged. 'Nothing.'

He extended the pad to Amethyst.

She shrugged. 'What do you want me to do with this? It's been so long I've probably forgotten how!'

She accepted the pad and pen nevertheless.

'I want you to make a list for me.'

'A list?'

'Just a short one. I want you to write down the names of the six people you trust most in the world.' Mitch smiled. 'Okay?'

For further exciting titles in this series visit...

www.GalexyTales.com

...where

THE PANDORANS

continues

(or search for "GALEXY TALES" at Amazon!)

COSMIC FORCES

THE PANDORANS

Book One: The Pandora Sequence
Book Two: The Pandora Inheritance
Book Three: The Omega Sequence
Book Four: The Pandora Arcana
Book Five: The Sirens Sequence
Book Six: The Daughters of Pandora
Book Seven: The Lucifer Sequence

AMAZON SEVEN

Book One: Mission Queen
Book Two: Queen Renegade
Book Three: Intergalactic Ingenue
Book Four: Princess Executor

THE CHRONICLES OF THE TERRAGUARD

Book One: Maker of Rules

SAGA OF THE URBAN SORCERERS

Book One: The Summoning of Barker Moon
Book Two: The Reckoning of Emerald Tarragon
Book Three: The Shaping of Cheryl Equinox

DARK STREETS

Book One: Agents of Fear
Book Two: Avatars of Wrath

Also:
Venus IA

www.GalexyTales.com

(or search "GALEXY TALES" at Amazon!)

ACKNOWLEDGEMENTS
(2013 E-BOOK EDITION, REVISED)

The Pandora Sequence was written between September 2010 and February 2011, with test readings, feedback and edits continuing throughout 2011 and into 2013. It was written mostly at night, generally in twelve-hour bursts, interspersed with huge sleeps and strange days of pacing the back yard, where at times the veil was extremely thin. It was fueled with coffee and cigarettes, but also powered by organic meat and vegetables. Go figure.

The original intent was for the e-book version of this novel to contain many footnotes and links in the text to various points of reference, but in the end it was decided that this was too distracting. I hope such a version may appear later.

I would like to thank my employer and publisher Gary Turner. He suggested the basic idea and the conclusion of the novel, although I have taken huge liberties with the subject matter well beyond the short story he first suggested. Without that suggestion, however, and his subsequent support, this book would not exist, and I am very grateful that it does.

I would also like to thank Melissa Sheldrick for her tireless support, encouragement, advice, faith and love.

I am also very grateful for the support of many others; Patrick McNamara for listening to, and putting up with my endless rants and doubts; his late father, the legendary Australian publisher Peter McNamara, who was my first champion; a big thanks to Dave Williams for providing the brilliant cover art and feedback; Simon McGill for a difficult edit; Greg C. Grace for years of patient meta-advice; Jane Intini for her initial guidance along the mystical path; and Greg Moss, Dan Foley, Vicki Healion, Maggie Fiddian and Joe Velikovsky for valuable feedback. Huge thanks also to my uncle Ron Saunders, who gave me an amazing burst of encouragement in my young days, exactly when I needed it; to my early teachers, Margaret Field, Trevor Thomas and Susan Mitchell, who granted me permission; to Jane Cormack, Kerry Wakefield and Paul Hamra for the self-esteem that paid employment and an audience bring, and to all the people back down the line who have read my work and encouraged me as a writer – every little bit helped.

I would also like to acknowledge the huge body of reference material that is available online, with special reference to the nightly American radio show Coast To Coast AM, which has introduced me to a wide body of knowledge, both mainstream and alternative, and everything outside and in between those very malleable categories. The various hosts and guests have provided me with more inspiration than I could ever hope for.

Thanks also to whatever aliens, entities, or beings that might truly exist out there; I genuinely believe that something was helping me along with this story, and I sincerely hope that I have not done a disservice in the telling.

Finally, I would like to acknowledge my family; especially Chris and Jon, my Uncle John, who once offered to be my agent, and my parents, Gennie and Stan, who must have wondered many times what dimension I came from. Go you Tigers.

Much love to you all,
Alex James, 2013

ACKNOWLEDGEMENTS
(2018 PAPERBACK EDITION)

It's hard not to just add thanks every time to the last lot of thanks, and just carry it through every book; but if you have been thanked before, please assume it is a boundless thanks.

Still, enormous thanks again, and all my love as always to Melissa Sheldrick.

Thanks to Michal Dutkiewicz for helping out with the cover layout at the last minute.

Thanks and gratitude to Adam Dutkiewicz for the formatting, and for being so generous in helping me learn.

Thanks to Gretel Newman-Sugrue, for reading and feedback, and so much great advice along the way.

Thanks again to my parents, Stan and Gennie, who have been absolutely amazing.

I would like to thank again, and make a special note of gratitude toward Gary Turner of AngelPhoenix Media for his permission to publish 'The Pandora Sequence' as a paperback. It means a lot - thankyou.

You too, Pat!

On a stranger note… in the seven or so years since I started writing this book, the darkness has made a huge play. It is being met, and that will likely be addressed in subsequent books. However, some icons from the light have fallen, and none confounded nor saddened (and it must be said, sickened) me more than the radical philosophical shift within a certain website that I recommended in the previous ebook edition. I have whole-heartedly removed that recommendation in this edition.

Finally… thanks for all the very passionate support this book has received.

There is more to come.

Alex James, May 2018

About the Author

Alex James is a writer who lives in and is inspired by Adelaide, South Australia.

Alex studied European History, Classical Mythology, Film Studies and Screenwriting under the Communications and Liberal Studies banners at the University of South Australia.

Between 1992 and 2005 he wrote many, many, many outlines, treatments, concept documents, bibles, pilots and screenplays, for just about every active Australian production company there was.

From 2008-2014 he was an in-house writer for Angel-Phoenix Media, who published his first two e-book novels, *The Pandora Sequence* and *Venus AI*, both of which were launched at the 2013 San Diego Comic-Con.

Alex's most recent works are epic novel sagas which include *The Saga of The Urban Sorcerers*, *Amazon Seven*, *Dark Streets*, *The Chronicles of The Terraguard*, and *The Ascension Sequence*.

He publishes via his own independent imprint, Galexy Tales.

'Amy's plan!'

www.GalexyTales.com

(OR SEARCH "GALEXY TALES"
AT AMAZON!)